PENGUIN BOOKS

HOPE

D0190589

Hope

LESLEY PEARSE

PENGUIN BOOKS

PENGUIN BOOKS

Published by the Penguin Group
Penguin Books Ltd, 80 Strand, London WC2R ORL, England
Penguin Group (USA) Inc., 375 Hudson Street, New York, New York 10014, USA
Penguin Group (Canada), 90 Eglinton Avenue East, Suite 700, Toronto, Ontario, Canada M4P 2Y3
(a division of Pearson Penguin Canada Inc.)
Penguin Ireland, 25 St Stephen's Green, Dublin 2, Ireland (a division of Penguin Books Ltd)
Penguin Group (Australia), 250 Camberwell Road, Camberwell, Victoria 3124, Australia
(a division of Pearson Australia Group Pty Ltd)
Penguin Books India Pvt Ltd, 11 Community Centre,
Panchsheel Park, New Delhi – 110 017, India
Penguin Group (NZ), 67 Apollo Drive, Mairangi Bay, Auckland 1310, New Zealand
(a division of Pearson New Zealand Ltd)
Penguin Books (South Africa) (Pty) Ltd, 24 Sturdee Avenue,
Rosebank, Johannesburg 2196, South Africa

Penguin Books Ltd, Registered Offices: 80 Strand, London WC2R ORL, England

www.penguin.com

First published by Michael Joseph 2006
Published in Penguin Books 2007

7

Copyright © Lesley Pearse, 2006
All rights reserved

The moral right of the author has been asserted

Printed in England by Clays Ltd, St Ives plc

ISBN: 978-0-141-01699-3

www.greenpenguin.co.uk

Mixed Sources
Product group from well-managed
forests and other controlled sources
www.fsc.org Cert no. SA-COC-1592
© 1996 Forest Stewardship Council
FSC

Penguin Books is committed to a sustainable future
for our business, our readers and our planet.
The book in your hands is made from paper
certified by the Forest Stewardship Council.

To all my friends and neighbours in Compton Dando for
making me feel so welcome and happy here.
I hope you will enjoy this entirely fictitious story, and
forgive me for taking liberties with our real village history,
and for any mistakes or omissions.

Chapter One

'Screaming don't help babbies into this world!' Bridie snapped irritably, and forced the rope knotted to the bed-head into her mistress's hands. 'Jest pull on this and bear down.'

At the sound of the door opening behind her, she glanced over her shoulder to see Nell, the parlourmaid, coming in with a basin of hot water. 'About time too! I thought you'd skedaddled,' she barked.

Nell was not offended by old Bridie's sharpness; she understood it was only because she was frightened. Bridie was not a midwife and it was only the horror of Lady Harvey being put to public shame that had induced her to deliver this baby herself. She looked all of her sixty years now, with her iron-grey hair escaping from her starched cap, her plump face drawn and yellowy in the candlelight, and her blue eyes, which normally twinkled with merriment, dull with exhaustion and anxiety.

'Maybe we should get the doctor?' Nell blurted out as she saw the angry distended veins which had popped up all over Lady Harvey's face and neck. 'It's surely taking too long and she's in such pain.'

Bridie glared, and Nell took that to mean she was not to offer any further opinions or suggestions. So she took the rag from the cold-water basin, wrung it out and wiped her

1

mistress's forehead. She just hoped Bridie knew what she was doing, for if her ladyship were to die, they'd both be in deep trouble.

The room was fetid and airless, hot as an oven even though the fire was almost out now. The heavy tapestry curtains around the bed and the highly polished dark furniture added to the claustrophobic atmosphere. Nell had seen the first rays of dawn coming into the sky as she fetched the hot water from the kitchen, and she was so tired she felt she might fall down where she stood.

Last year she'd helped at her baby brother's birth, but it had been nothing like this. Mother had been walking around until minutes before, and then she lay down, gave a bit of a shout, and out came the baby as smooth as a greasy piglet. Until tonight Nell had thought that all babies arrived that way.

But Lady Harvey had started her yelling and carrying on at six yesterday evening and it had just got worse and worse through the night. Her lovely white nightgown was sodden with sweat, and beneath it her distended belly looked obscene in the flickering candlelight.

If this was what you got for going with a man, Nell thought, she'd sooner die a virgin.

'Let me die and the baby with me!' Lady Harvey yelled out. 'God, haven't you punished me enough for my wickedness?'

'Push the baby out or you will die,' Bridie yelled back, and gave her mistress a sharp slap on her naked thigh. 'Come on, push the little bugger out, damn you!'

Whether it was the slap or the threat of death that did it, Lady Harvey's screams turned to a kind of bellow, not unlike a cow in labour, and all at once she was pushing with real determination.

Some twenty minutes later Nell's eyes grew wide as she finally saw the baby's head coming. The hair on it was gypsy-black, in stark contrast to her mistress's lily-white thighs.

'That's it! He's coming now.' Bridie's voice was suddenly softer with relief. 'Let him come, don't push no more.'

Nell watched entranced, her exhaustion forgotten as the baby slid out into Bridie's knurled old hands. The belly which had seconds ago looked as taut and swollen as a ripe pumpkin suddenly sagged, and her ladyship let out a gentle sigh of relief that her ordeal was finally over.

Bridie pointedly placed the new baby well away from its mother, not even proclaiming that she'd had a girl. Nell caught the older woman's eyes, saw the fear in them, and all at once the joy and wonder she'd felt at the miracle of new life was extinguished.

This baby wasn't intended to live. Bridie was not going to slap its little back, or breathe into its tiny mouth to help it survive. It was meant to die.

'Is it really over now?' Lady Harvey asked, her voice just a hoarse whisper.

'Aye, it's over now, m'lady,' Bridie said as she quickly tied the cord and cut it. 'Just the afterbirth to come and you'll be able to go to sleep and forget it all.'

Nell looked down at the motionless, silent baby lying on the bed. Her younger brothers and sisters had all been ugly and purple with bald heads at their birth. They'd squalled with anger at their speedy arrival into a harsh new world. But this one was pretty, with dark hair and a mouth like a little rosebud. Nell thought that was perhaps because it was ordained to go straight to heaven.

'Did it die?' Lady Harvey asked sleepily. The angry red veins on her face and neck had already faded, but she looked gaunt and pale. Her long golden hair, Bridie's pride and joy, was matted and dull. Nell could hardly believe this was the same young woman she'd always admired for her serene elegance and beauty.

Bridie merely glanced sideways at the infant as she massaged her mistress's belly. 'Aye, m'lady, I'm afraid so,' she replied with a break in her voice. 'But perhaps that's just as well.'

'Just let me see it?' Lady Harvey asked.

Bridie nodded at Nell, who took up a piece of flannel, wrapped it around the baby and lifted it up. Lady Harvey reached out one finger to run it down the infant's cheek, and then turned her head away as the tears came. 'God's will,' she whispered. 'But I'm grateful for his mercy.'

Bridie nudged Nell towards the door. 'Take it to the still room, then you go to your bed,' she whispered. 'I'll deal with it later when I've finished here.'

Holding the tiny lifeless baby in her arms, Nell walked quickly down the corridor towards the backstairs. Briargate Hall was as silent as a crypt. All the other servants had been sent to the London house three weeks ago to prepare it for Sir William Harvey's return from America. He had been there for almost two years, and this of course was the reason why Bridie hadn't attempted to save the baby. If she knew who its father was, she wouldn't say. She had guarded her mistress's secret pregnancy as if it were her own. Even when she was compelled to include Nell in the conspiracy because she couldn't handle the birth alone, she told her nothing more than that her ladyship was carrying an unwanted child.

It was the end of April, and it was only yesterday that they'd finally seen signs of spring after a long, bitterly cold winter. It was going to be another fine, warm day today too, because the sun was already streaming in through the east window by the backstairs.

In the huge mirror beside the window, Nell could see herself reflected. The image shocked her, not so much because she looked so untidy, her apron stained and her cap all askew with strands of hair hanging down, but because the night's events had suddenly aged her. Just twenty-four hours ago she'd looked like any other sixteen-year-old housemaid: neat and demure in her starched uniform, her cheeks pink from running up and down the stairs, and a sparkle in her dark eyes because Baines, the butler, wasn't here to keep reprimanding her. Her mind had been on Ned Travers, who had said he'd meet her in Lord's Wood that afternoon. He was about to enlist in the army and all the village girls wanted to be his sweetheart. Nell wasn't exactly sure that was what she wanted, but it was good to think he wanted her.

Nell knew she wasn't blessed with beauty. She took after her father's side of the family, as all her brothers and sisters did. They were short and sturdy with black straight hair and dark brown eyes. Ned had said she had a complexion like cream, but that was probably only sweet talk. Her mouth was too small, her nose a little too big, and her eyebrows too bushy.

She didn't get to meet Ned, so she'd never know whether he liked her for herself or because he thought a plain girl like her might be easy. Bridie dropped her bombshell mid-morning and made it quite clear Nell was not to leave the house for any reason.

Up till then Nell had believed, as all the servants did, that her mistress's lengthy stay in her room was because she'd been hurt falling from her horse. Rose, one of the other maids, had said it was a 'queer do', as the previous time Lady Harvey had had a fall from her horse she was hobbling around with a walking stick within two days.

But Nell saw nothing suspicious in this extended period of bed rest. She had noted in her four years of service that ladies of quality tended to suffer from curious ailments which didn't strike common folk.

It was her view that the mistress's problem was melancholia: a combination of the long, bitter winter and her husband's extended absence. Whenever Nell was sent upstairs with a tray, Lady Harvey was either still in bed or sitting by the window with her feet up, covered in a quilt. She looked as beautiful as ever, her golden hair loose on her shoulders, but she was subdued and very pale. Nell often felt Bridie ought to be firmer with her and make her take a short walk outside every day.

Just before Baines left in the carriage bound for London with the rest of the household, he had given Nell her orders. She was to cook, fetch and carry until Lady Harvey felt able to travel to London with Bridie. Then she was to stay on here alone to look after the house, and the gardener and groom would take care of everything outside.

Nell wasn't disappointed at not going to London too. Bridie said that there was always far more work there because it was a much larger house and the Harveys entertained a great deal. She also said the London staff looked down on country yokels, and it was like working in a madhouse.

In fact Nell viewed staying at Briargate as a holiday, for she'd have virtually nothing to do. She would be able to slip home every afternoon to see her mother and younger brothers and sisters, and to wander around the grounds as much as she liked.

When Bridie told her yesterday what really ailed the mistress it was a huge shock. '*She slipped up*,' was how Bridie put it, as if she imagined Nell didn't know how babies were made.

Nell had been promised a sovereign just as long as she never breathed a word of what she would see and hear in the next few hours. Bridie bluntly stated that it was her hope the baby wouldn't survive.

Yesterday that hope didn't seem so terrible. Bridie was

only being practical, just as the groom was when he drowned kittens born in the barn. Everyone knew that ladies got a wetnurse in for their babies anyway, and had very little time for their offspring until they were almost fully grown.

But once Lady Harvey went into hard labour, she wasn't any different to any other woman Nell knew. She sweated, she cried, she even shouted crude oaths like the slatternly barmaid down at the inn. All the fine linen and lace, silver hairbrushes and jewellery didn't stop her having to push that baby out just like a tinker woman in the fields. And just as the commonest beggarwoman would still grieve for a dead baby, Nell knew Lady Harvey would too.

She looked down at the wrapped parcel in her arms and tears welled up in her eyes. Her folks had nothing, ten children brought up in a tiny cottage with a leaking roof, yet each new baby had been greeted with joy. This one had never been kissed, and it wouldn't even be given a name or get a proper funeral.

The burden of being witness to the birth was a heavy one too. Nell didn't know how she was going to be able to talk to Lady Harvey normally after this, or if she could ever forget. She and Bridie might even be cursed for their part in it!

Everyone knew how a curse was put on Sir John Popham. He was an ancestor of the Pophams who still lived at Hunstrete House, the mansion closest to Briargate on the other side of Lord's Wood. Sir John was the judge at the trial of William Darrell of Littlecote who was charged with murdering a newborn baby by throwing it on the fire. Darrell put the curse on the Pophams because the judge took Littlecote, and with it Hunstrete, which was part of the Littlecote estate, in exchange for his acquittal. The curse was that the Popham family would never have a male heir. They hadn't had one either, only girls.

Nell had to suppose Darrell murdered the baby because he hadn't fathered it. She and Bridie hadn't murdered this one, but perhaps not attempting to make a newborn baby take its first breath amounted to the same thing?

If anyone found out they could be hanged!

Nell's heart began to race and her stomach churned. Was Bridie intending to bury the baby's body out in the garden? How did she think they could do that without old Jacob the gardener seeing?

As she began walking down the backstairs, a faint stirring against her chest surprised her. She stumbled and nearly dropped the little bundle before steadying herself. With trepidation she drew the covering flannel back a little, and to her utter astonishment she saw one tiny hand move, and the baby opened its mouth in a yawn.

For a moment she could only stare, convinced she was imagining it, but the hand moved again, more vigorously this time. 'It's a miracle!' she exclaimed aloud, her voice echoing in the stairwell. Everyone knew newborn babies cried to proclaim they were alive and well. She had never ever heard of one remaining silent unless it was too weak to survive.

Unless it was a fairy child.

Nell's education amounted to little more than being taught her letters and a few sums by the Reverend Gosling between the ages of six and eight. But she'd learned super-stitions from birth, from her own parents and many of the old folk in the village.

The story went that fairy children came into this world to bestow good fortune. They could be recognized by their unexpected arrival, their exceptional looks and gentle nature. Joan Stott in the village was barren, and then at well over forty she finally gave birth to a little girl who looked like an angel. Joan and Amos Stott had scratched less than a bare living from their land, and no one expected their baby to survive, but she did. And she was hardly put into her cradle before the Stotts' hens began to lay, their crops increased, and even their old sow produced a litter of twelve fine piglets. That child was over six now, still as pretty as a May morning, and the Stotts were becoming almost prosperous.

But whether Lady Harvey's baby was a miracle or a fairy child, Nell knew Bridie wasn't going to rejoice that it was alive. She had been in service to the Dorvilles, Lady Harvey's family, since she was fourteen. She had risen from scullery maid to nursemaid to the Dorville children, and eight years ago when Anne, the youngest, was to marry Sir William Harvey, Bridie came here to Briargate with her as her personal maid.

Bridie's whole life pivoted around the mistress she'd helped bring into this world, and she wouldn't allow anything or anyone to bring disgrace and shame to her.

But the possibility that this was a fairy child prevented Nell from considering Bridie's feelings or wishes; she had to act on her own instincts. She hastened on down the stairs to the warm kitchen and picked up the shawl she'd left on a chair to wrap the baby more warmly. Ousting the cat from Cook's chair in the corner, she laid the infant down on the cushion, then rushed outside to fill the kettle from the pump.

By the time Nell heard Bridie's heavy, slow step on the stairs almost an hour later, it was broad daylight, with warm sunshine coming in through the lattice window by the sink. The baby was now washed, rewrapped in clean flannel and fast asleep in a linen basket by the stove.

She had opened her eyes as if in astonishment when Nell peeled off the soiled flannel, and she'd wailed indignantly as she washed her. But the moment she was rewrapped she went back to sleep.

9

'I thought I told you to go to bed?' Bridie said grumpily as she came into the kitchen, weighed down with a pail of dirty water in one hand, a covered basin in the other and bundles of bloodstained linen under each arm.

She looked all in. Her apron was bloodstained, her shoulders were stooped and she was wheezing with the effort of walking.

'The baby, it's alive,' Nell said, pointing to the basket.

Bridie blanched and dropped her burdens, splashing water on to the floor. 'Oh Jesus, Mary, Mother of God!' she exclaimed, crossing herself and glancing fearfully at the basket.

'She's very bonny,' Nell ventured fearfully. While she felt some sympathy for Bridie and her mistress because she knew how much trouble a living baby was going to cause for them both, she couldn't help but feel delight she'd helped it to survive. Yet at the same time she also knew girls like her could be dismissed for getting above their station, and Bridie was quite likely to feel that was just what she'd done.

Bridie let out a sob of pain, and put both hands to her face in consternation. 'Oh, my lawd!' she exclaimed. 'What am I to do?'

Nell instinctively moved towards the older woman and put her arms around her, just as she would do to her own mother if she was in distress. Bridie had been kind to her right from her first day at Briargate, when she was a frightened twelve-year-old who had no real idea of what leaving her own family and going into service meant. It was Bridie who had suggested Nell was wasted in the kitchen, and that she should be trained as a parlourmaid; she'd fought the protests from Cook and Mrs Cole, the housekeeper, covered up for Nell when she broke an ornament, and smuggled home leftover food when her father was laid up with a bad chest and couldn't work.

During her four years at Briargate this woman had been Nell's comforter, teacher and confidante. Thanks to her, she could help her family; she had good food, decent clothes, and prospects. She didn't know if there was any way she could help Bridie out of this tight spot, but if there was one, she'd find it.

'Don't take on, Bridie,' Nell said comfortingly. 'We're both tired now, but if we put our heads together we'll think of something. I'll make you some tea, and then you go to bed. I'll put the linen in to soak and listen out for the mistress.'

Bridie drew back from Nell's arms and wiped her eyes on the hem of her apron. Her blue eyes were still swimming but Nell could see she was struggling to regain her composure. 'You're a good girl,' she said, her voice shaking. 'But it's you who must go to bed. I'll sit here with my tea for a bit, and then go back upstairs. I can doze in the chair in the mistress's room.'

'Shall I take the baby in with me?' Nell asked.

Bridie shook her head. 'She'll be warmer here. Go to bed now.'

Nell found she couldn't sleep for thinking about the baby. It would need feeding soon and if Bridie was up in Lady Harvey's bedroom she wouldn't hear it cry. There was so much else which needed to be done too – coal brought in for the stove, linen to be washed and something nourishing cooked for Lady Harvey. She couldn't just lie here wide awake and leave everything to Bridie.

She got up, washed herself and put on the old grey dress she had been given to wear when there were dirty jobs to do, then, carrying her boots, she stole quietly down the stairs from her attic room so she wouldn't disturb the mistress.

Hardly a day passed without her feeling blessed to be able to live at Briargate Hall. It was a light, bright house built just forty years ago by Sir Roland Harvey, William's father, and situated half-way between the cities of Bath and Bristol. Nell had never been to either of these cities; all she knew was the village of Compton Dando where she was born and the surrounding villages. The farthest she'd ever been was to Keynsham, some three and a half miles away.

People did say that Bristol's port was a marvel and you could see wondrous great sailing ships there that sailed to the far ends of the earth. But Nell had no yearnings to go there; a year ago hundreds of people had died from cholera, and only five months ago, in October, there had been three days of terrible riots. Scores of people were killed, many more seriously injured, and dozens of buildings destroyed and burned. Four people were hanged for their part in it and dozens more put in prison or transported. To Nell it sounded a very dangerous place.

Mr Baines, who knew just about everything, said that the riots happened because the system of government was corrupt. He said the Tories bribed and intimidated people at elections so that the reform parties couldn't get in. He took some pride in the fact that the people of Bristol were brave enough to make their voice heard, and he claimed that if he had been a young man he would have joined them.

Nell had heard that Bath, the other city nearby, was very different to Bristol, for it was where the gentry went to take its special waters and have a high old time. Baines said it was beautiful, with wide streets, splendid houses and shops so full of luxury items that your eyes would pop out looking at them all.

Cook claimed that it was a hive of wickedness, the streets full of pickpockets, and the special waters tasted so vile it was a wonder they didn't kill people. So if these were the two nearest cities, Nell didn't think there was much in either of them for a girl like her.

Baines said that old Sir Roland Harvey had been a great traveller, and the design of Briargate was influenced by houses he'd seen in Italy and plantation houses in the West Indies. He had brought the black and white marble for the floor in the hall back from Italy, along with the marble statues in the garden, and instead of building it in the local stone, he'd used brick with a kind of pinkish-cream plaster over it. There was a very grand portico at the front held up by big pillars, and the tiles on the roof were green instead of red.

Long narrow windows almost reached the floor and let sunshine stream in all day; the graceful shutters had been specially designed for Sir Roland, as were the marble fire-places. Nell particularly liked the carved grapes and birds on the staircase newel posts; it didn't seem possible a man could make something so delicate with just a chisel. With the sparkling chandeliers and thick rugs and furniture so highly polished she could see her own face reflected, Nell felt as if she were living in a palace.

When she first came to work at Briargate she could scarcely clear a fireplace for looking at the paintings on the walls. Everywhere she looked there were objects of wonder. Bridie didn't share her enthusiasm. She said with only eight bedrooms, it wasn't anywhere near as large or magnificent as the London house. She did concede that old Sir Roland had his head screwed on right, for he'd designed it to be labour-saving. She usually added somewhat tartly that he must have known that slave trading would be abolished, and that he wouldn't be able to get servants to work for nothing here.

To Nell, a butler, housekeeper and cook, four maids, plus gardeners and grooms, along with various other people who came in as they were needed, seemed to be an awful lot of servants to look after just one house and two people. But Bridie said it wasn't a big staff, and pointed out that they only managed it so easily because of the design.

The main rooms were spacious, but not so big that they couldn't be heated adequately. The dining room was close to the kitchen, so food arrived at the table hot. There was even a contraption in the kitchen where large pails of hot water could be sent upstairs for baths and washing just by pulling on a rope. Bridie laughingly called it 'The Maid's Saviour' and pulled up her sleeve to show a burn on her forearm which she'd got as a young girl from hauling a pail of boiling water up the stairs.

Hearing the baby cry out as she neared the kitchen, Nell didn't stop to put her boots on, but as she turned the corner of the hallway which led to the kitchen, she was horrified to see Bridie leaning over the baby's basket with a cushion in her hands.

There was no doubt as to what she was intending to do for she was crying and muttering something through her tears that sounded to Nell like an apology or even a prayer.

'No, Bridie!' Nell called out, dropping her boots with a clatter and running towards the older woman. 'You mustn't – it's wicked, and she's a fairy child.'

Bridie wheeled round, her old face stricken with guilt. 'But it's the only way, Nell. If she lives it'll be ruin for m'lady, she'll be cast out of Briargate.'

Later that day it was to strike Nell that Bridie had watched indifferently as a maid was ordered out of the house because she was with child. If Lady Harvey was cast out she could go back to her own family, but that poor girl had nowhere to go but the workhouse.

But Nell didn't think of that then – all she had on her

mind was the prevention of murder. 'You can't kill a baby,' she insisted, getting between Bridie and the makeshift cradle. 'It ain't right and you know it.'

For a second or two Nell thought Bridie would strike her and carry on with her plan, for she could see the desperation on her face. But instead she suddenly sagged, sank down on to a chair and covered her face with her hands. 'Heaven knows I don't want to hurt the babby, but what else is there to do?' she asked imploringly.

'I don't know,' Nell said, and put her hand on the older woman's shoulder. 'But it ain't never right to kill her. It ain't her fault she were born, and like I said she's a fairy child. Just look at her!'

The baby had her eyes open now, and had stopped crying, almost as if she knew the danger had passed. Her eyes were not the usual blue of a new baby's, but dark as night, looking up at Nell as if thanking her for the reprieve.

'Maybe we could take her to the church and leave her there then?' Bridie said in desperation. 'Reverend Gosling would find a place for her.'

Nell shook her head. She knew infants left in the church went to the workhouse, and few of them survived beyond a few weeks. She snatched up the baby and cradled her protectively in her arms. 'You know what that means,' she reminded Bridie, and as the sweet smell of the newborn baby wafted up to her it triggered her own tears.

For some minutes neither woman spoke. Bridie remained with her head in her hands, sobbing, and Nell paced up and down the kitchen with the baby in her arms.

Nell felt a surge of anger that Lady Harvey should be sleeping peacefully now, while she and Bridie had somehow to find a solution for a problem which was none of their making. Lady Harvey had been born into wealth, she'd been pampered, dressed in the finest clothes, schooled by governesses, and then married at eighteen to a man who everyone had said was the finest catch in the West Country.

Nell could remember how as a little girl she'd stood with the other village children in St Mary the Virgin's churchyard to throw rose petals at the couple. No queen could have looked more beautiful than Lady Harvey did that day, her golden hair tumbling around her shoulders. Her white silk dress with its twelve-foot train must have cost more than Nell's father had earned in his whole life. And Sir William wasn't just wealthy, he was handsome too, slender and tall with curly fair hair and bright blue eyes. Everyone said it was a love match, and a few years later when Nell came to work at Briargate, she'd seen the couple laughing and running around the grounds like two lovebirds, and that confirmed it for her.

So why did Lady Harvey lie with another man? Why shouldn't she take the responsibility for her own sin, just as Nell and even Bridie would be expected to if they'd gone astray?

Yet even as these thoughts came to her, she knew she couldn't bear to see Lady Harvey disgraced any more than Bridie could. She might be spoilt but she was mostly sweet-natured and generous. Nell couldn't count the times she'd pressed a shilling into her hands to take home to her mother. She'd given her old clothes; let her sew little dresses and shirts for her brothers and sisters while she was supposed to be working. She had never struck her, never even grumbled when she was clumsy; just yesterday morning she'd thanked both Nell and Bridie for their loyalty and promised them that she'd always look after them.

The truth of the matter was that Lady Harvey was like a child in many ways. She had so much life and fun in her, but she was innocent too. This man, whoever he was, must have sweet-talked her when she was lonely. None of her family had visited since the master went away; she had no real friends of her own here in Somerset, only his friends. Nell could remember her crying when Sir William left for America; she'd wanted to go with him, but he wouldn't let her. As Nell's own mother so often said, 'You have to walk a mile in someone else's boots to know how it is for them.'

Thinking of her mother gave Nell an idea.

'I could take baby home to my mother,' she blurted out. 'She'll have milk to spare enough for this little one.'

'She's got too many of her own,' Bridie said, tears rolling down her cheeks. 'Besides, it's too close to here. How would she explain where she got another?'

Nell got a mental picture of the overcrowded cottage and her mother already so tired with too many children, yet she knew the moment this one was in her arms she wouldn't refuse. 'People don't count how many she's got,' she said truthfully. 'They've got so used to her always having a new one in her arms they wouldn't notice.'

'But your father?'

Nell half-smiled. Her father's only real fault was that he was over-generous in every way: with his labour, time and affection. When he had money he was generous with that too. Her mother often said that if he worked only the hours he was paid for, didn't love her so much and saved the little money he had, they wouldn't be in a tumbledown cottage with so many children. But Nell didn't think Mother would have him any different.

'Father likes babies,' she said. 'He'll say one more won't make no difference.'

Bridie dried her tears on her apron, but her eyes were still full of anxiety.

'You can trust them not to talk,' Nell said firmly, knowing that was what was on Bridie's mind. 'Even the bigger ones won't know the truth. If I take her to Mother tonight after they've gone to bed, they'll believe it was born while they were asleep.'

Bridie looked doubtful about that.

'Mother has 'em quick,' Nell insisted. 'When our Henry was born last year they knew nothing till they heard him cry. I was with her, I know, and her belly's so big from so many babbies they half-expects another to pop out any day.'

'But it's a secret that's got to be kept for ever,' Bridie reminded her.

Nell nodded; she understood that well enough.

'The mistress did say a while ago that if it lived she wanted it to be farmed out,' Bridie said softly. 'She asked me to make enquiries, and I did go to see a woman in Brislington village about it. I didn't like the woman, she were hard-faced and the children she had there were sickly-looking and dirty. At least we know your mother would take proper care.'

Bridie lapsed into silence, clearly weighing up all she knew of Meg and Silas Renton, and whether they were trustworthy. Nell said nothing more because she knew her family was held in high esteem around here. She wouldn't have got her position at Briargate if it wasn't for that.

'What shall we call her?' the older woman said eventually, taking the baby from Nell's arms and this time looking at her almost fondly. 'It wouldn't be right not to give her a name.'

Joan Stott's fairy child was called Faith, and it came to Nell immediately that another fairy child born so close should have a similar name.

'Hope,' she said without any hesitation.

Bridie pursed her lips as if she didn't like it, but then as she looked down at the sleeping infant in her arms she began to smile. 'Aye, Nell, that's a good name. I hope your mother will come to love the poor little mite, I hope too that I can forget the wicked thing I was going to do earlier. She don't look at all like our mistress, so maybe you're right and she is a fairy child.'

That evening Nell paused at the edge of Lord's Wood which marked the boundary between Briargate House and the Hunstrete land. She had the baby beneath her cloak, secured by a shawl to her chest. Putting down her basket, she turned to look back at the house, for there was a full moon and she could see as plain as if it were day.

Briargate was best viewed from its long tree-lined drive which came up from the road at Chelwood. It stood proudly on slightly higher ground and you could see the magnificent front porch, the elegant long windows and the large marble statues which stood in the circular rosebed before the house. In summer it was a picture with roses and wisteria scrambling right up to the bedroom windows.

But Nell was on the east side of the house, down at the bottom end of the paddock, for the quickest way to reach the village of Compton Dando was through the woods. Seen from this angle, in moonlight, the fir trees which had been planted around the boundaries of the grounds looked for all the world as if they were guarding Briargate. The moonlight glinted too on the marble statues at the front, and a tear trickled down Nell's cheek as she realized that the sleeping baby in her arms was in fact losing its birthright along with its mother.

'I'll say goodbye to it for you,' she whispered. 'I'm sorry you can't grow up in the fine nursery, that you won't get silk gowns and servants to wait on you. But I reckons you'll get more love in our cottage.'

The feeling she'd aged ten years when she'd looked in the mirror this morning had stayed with her. She was exhausted, but she felt even sleep wouldn't bring her back to the carefree girl she'd been a couple of days ago. She had heard Lady Harvey crying pitifully this afternoon, and suddenly to Nell she wasn't a beautiful, wealthy woman who had the world at her feet, but just another poor soul grieving over the child she had lost.

Hope had begun to cry around the same time, and all Nell could do was spoon sugar water into her tiny mouth to keep her going until later. Bridie had spent most of the afternoon going through the chest in Sir William's old nursery to find baby nightgowns, bonnets and jackets. She had said how bleak it made her feel to have to put back the finer, beautifully embroidered ones and only take the plain ones, for it would raise eyebrows in the village if little Hope was dressed in finery.

Yet the napkins, blanket and other things packed in the basket were still far beyond anything Nell and her brothers and sisters had known. Hope would suck from the same breast all of them knew, know days of hunger just like them, and find out that working began for village folk at an early age. But wouldn't she retain something of both her real parents too? Not just her looks, shape and size, but an inbred knowledge that she wasn't truly one of the servant class?

Nell sighed and picked up her basket. She knew it was no good thinking on these things, and she had to pick her way carefully through the wood, taking care not to stumble in the dark.

Compton Dando lay in a wooded vale with the river Chew running through it. For a small village, the population being a little less than four hundred, it was a busy place, with an inn, a bakery, the church, a blacksmith's, a carpenter's and a mill. By day there was an infernal racket from the copper mills at Publow and Woolard, the two closest villages along the river, and there were several small coal mines dotted all around the area. Although some of the local men worked at the mills or in the mines, most were farm workers like her father, and like him they supplemented their low wages by cultivating their own strips of land, keeping chickens and often pigs or a cow too.

Once through the woods, Nell made her way across the common. Fortunately the Rentons' cottage was this side of the village; had it been right down by the church she might have been spotted by someone going into the Crown Inn.

An owl hooted from the big oak tree by the cottage, but that and the gurgling of the river down below were the only sounds.

'Nell!' Meg Renton exclaimed as she came through the door. 'What brings you here so late?'

The tiny cottage was lit only by a single candle and the fire was just a dull red glow. A stranger coming in would assume Meg was all alone, but in fact it was full of sleeping bodies. Nell's father was in the bed at the back of the room with Henry, the youngest child, in beside him. The other eight children were in the loft room above, reached by steep steps with a length of rope for a banister.

One of the things Nell had found hardest to adjust to when she first went to work at Briargate was that she couldn't go to bed at sundown as she'd always done at home. Gentry stayed up late, but then they could afford dozens of candles and oil lamps, and they didn't have to rise at dawn.

Yet her mother had never gone to bed with the rest of the family, even though she worked harder than anyone else. She would sit by the fire for an hour or two, with one candle. She said it was the only time she had a bit of peace.

Seeing her mother's worn face in the candlelight, Nell felt

a stab of remorse at burdening her with still more work. Meg was thirty-four, and ten children along with one stillbirth too had robbed her of the vitality and strength Nell remembered when she was small. Her hair was still thick and dark, but her once slender body had thickened and her face was becoming lined and saggy. The nightgown she wore was one of Bridie's hand-me-downs, darned and patched flannel, so thin in places it looked as though with one more wash it would fall apart.

'I've brought you a baby,' Nell said simply, unable to think of a less blunt way of introducing Hope, and she took off her cloak and untied the shawl the baby was cradled in. 'I knew you wouldn't like to see her left at the church or the workhouse, and they were the only other choices.'

Hope stirred as she lifted her out and began sucking on her fist. As briefly as possible Nell explained how she came by the infant and that she needed feeding or she would die.

Meg silently unbuttoned her nightgown, held out her arms for Hope and put her to her breast without saying a word. It took a few seconds for the baby to latch on to her nipple; and it was only once she'd begun sucking in earnest that Meg spoke.

'Your mistress should be ashamed of herself,' she said in a low voice. 'It is never right for her to expect that her maid should take responsibility for her wickedness.'

Afraid her father would wake, Nell pulled up a stool close to her mother and whispered the fuller explanation, including the fact that Lady Harvey thought her child had died. 'She's a good woman, you know that, Mother,' she finished up. 'Bridie and I couldn't let her be disgraced, could we?'

'Would she have spared a thought for you if you'd been in the same way?' Meg asked, her lips quivering with emotion. 'No, she'd have turned you out on to the parish!'

Nell shrugged her shoulders. 'After what I've seen today I won't let a man do that to me,' she said.

A ghost of a smile played at Meg's lips. 'Just mind you remember that when you find a sweetheart!' she said tartly. 'But she's a married woman! And she's had learning too – what was she thinking of?'

'Maybe he forced her,' Nell suggested.

Meg tossed her head. 'Who would dare force her?'

Nell had no answer to that. She didn't want to think of Lady Harvey behaving wantonly with a man, but then she didn't want to think this tiny baby was a result of force either.

'Will you take her, Mother?' she asked, and pulled the sovereign Bridie had given her out of her pocket.

'I've got too many children already,' Meg said, but she was already looking down at Hope with the same tender expression that Nell had seen her give her own babies. 'We've got no room; it gets harder to feed them all each week. If I take her, a week or two from now Lady Harvey will be off to her parties and balls without a thought for anyone but herself and I'll be left struggling.'

Nell nodded, for she knew her mother was right. Until Nell went to Briargate she knew nothing of how the gentry lived. They were just the folk in the fine clothes who sat in the front pews at church, or those her father doffed his cap to as they rode by on their sleek horses. She was so excited when the Reverend Gosling arranged for her to have a position at the big house that she didn't think for one minute she would miss living here with her family, or that her work as a servant would be a hundred times harder than the chores she'd done at home.

In fact for the first year she was at Briargate, she cried herself to sleep every night, for it was do this, do that, every waking moment of the day. As scullery maid she did the very roughest work, scouring pots, scrubbing floors and laying fires, at everyone's beck and call. At home there was love, laughter and chatter along with the work; her mother cared if she had an aching back or a cut finger or was just tired. Her father would take her on his lap in the evenings and say she was pretty and clever. She got none of that at Briargate.

She learned to cope with it all eventually. Slowly she climbed the ladder to parlourmaid. Now there were only Baines, Mrs Cole, Bridie and Cook above her, she didn't do rough work, and even had free time to sit with a cup of tea and chat to Cook or Bridie.

But the best time of all was her weekly afternoon off, and the one Sunday in four when she came home after the morning service at church. Her family might be poor but they had pride, dignity and big hearts.

'I'll do my best to see you don't have to struggle.' Nell held out the sovereign again. 'This is what I got for helping and Bridie will see you get more. I'll make sure she gets James and Ruth taken on at Briargate too. That will help.'

Silas, Nell's father, believed himself to be a fortunate man. When he'd had a couple of pints of cider he was prone to boasting that he had the best wife a man could have, ten happy, healthy children, and that this cottage was in the prettiest spot in the whole of Somerset.

Yet the fact remained that however hard Silas worked they lived from hand to mouth, and in periods when he had no work, they were often hungry. Matthew, who at fifteen was the oldest of Nell's brothers, was also a farm labourer, so he brought in a regular wage. But James and Ruth, who were fourteen and thirteen respectively, still hadn't yet managed to find permanent work. After them came Alice, Toby, Prudence, Violet and Joe, from nine down to two and a half, and finally baby Henry, who had just recently had his first birthday.

'I counted on keeping Ruth home to help me with the little ones, but Alice is good with them too,' Meg said wearily. 'Oh, Nell, you've been such a good girl. It's never right you should have this thrust on you.'

Nell thought how selfless her mother was. If she agreed to take the baby, she would love it and care for it just as she had all of them, and Nell had no doubt that in a week or two she would probably have almost forgotten that she hadn't given birth to this one. But that didn't make it right to take advantage of her kindness.

'It isn't me who is getting this thrust on them,' she said. 'It's you, Mother. You can ask me to take her away if you want. It's a big thing I'm asking of you. But if you agree I'll do everything I can to make it easier for you. I promise you that.'

Meg reached out her hand and caressed her daughter's cheek wordlessly. It appeared little Hope had had her fill, for she gave a contented little sigh and let go of the swollen nipple. Meg put her down on her knee and ran one finger affectionately around her chin as she studied her. 'She's a pretty little thing,' she said at length, looking back at Nell. 'I doubt she'll be much trouble to me and your father. So you go off to bed, Nell, you look fair worn out. She's mine now.'

Chapter Two

'Just because I'm a girl and smaller than you don't mean I can't climb trees just as good as you!'

Nell smiled to herself at the loud and indignant claim coming from the far side of the wood. At six years old, Hope had a reputation in the village of being an angel, but in fact she could be a little devil, especially when it came to proving to boys she was as daring as they were.

Nell was on her way home for her afternoon off, and guessed her youngest brothers Joe and Henry were getting the rough side of Hope's tongue.

'It ain't because we don't think you can't climb the tree. It's cos of your dress. You get it torn and there'll be hell to pay.'

Nell chuckled at Joe's diplomacy; he almost always found some way to divert his fiery sister.

'Then I'll take it off,' Hope shouted back at him. 'Henry! Undo the buttons!'

'Hope!' Nell yelled out, aware that hen-pecked Henry would do exactly as Hope ordered.

Nell imagined Hope's dismayed expression on hearing her older sister's voice coming from the wood, and it made her laugh aloud. She knew that by the time she got through the wood to the children, Hope would be sitting down as daintily as a duchess, eyes wide with pretend innocence.

She was the prettiest little girl Nell had ever seen. Hair as dark and shiny as black marble, with a curl to it too. Her eyes were like dark pools fringed by impossibly long lashes, and her skin was perfectly smooth and clear.

Everyone in the family had dark hair and eyes: folk in the village often described a person as 'dark as a Renton'. Their looks were commonplace, though, their skin sallow and their hair coarse. Nothing fancy about any of them.

But Hope made folk turn their heads to look at her. She had a dazzling smile, a gaiety and enthusiasm that would make even the most sober of people laugh. She wanted to talk to everyone; when she was as young as four she'd stand at the gate greeting anyone that passed by. Even the Reverend Gosling, who was normally so aloof, always stopped to speak to her.

Meg and Silas had never once even momentarily regretted taking her on. She had been an easy, placid baby who would smile and gurgle all day long, and almost from her first week with them, the family's fortunes did seem to improve.

Just as Nell had believed she was a fairy child, so did many others. They saw soon after her birth that the Rentons' cottage roof was miraculously rethatched, and that Ruth got taken on as a laundry maid at Briargate, and James as the undergroom. Meg and Silas couldn't tell anyone, not even their older children, that this change of fortune was the result of Bridie's influence, and so, in the absence of any other explanation, people liked to think it was some kind of magic.

Nell was no longer so inclined to believe in fairies or magic. But then, the last six years had been eventful ones, and her horizons were no longer limited to the village. She had visited Bath, Bristol and London now, been to mansions four times the size of Briargate, and, prompted by Mr Baines, she read the newspaper most days.

She now understood why most working men felt aggrieved with the government. All the laws seemed to be made to protect the wealthy – only men of property could vote. The Corn Laws and the enclosing of common land squeezed the poor and forced many to leave the rural areas to go to the cities and try to find work. But the hardships these people had endured in their own villages were mild compared to the ones they found in cities. Overcrowding, filth, disease and desperate poverty forced men, women and children into crime, and the punishments if they were caught were incredibly harsh.

Nell was also less inclined to put such implicit trust in her master and mistress since Bridie's death from pneumonia just two years after Hope's birth. She caught a chill through sitting up in the rain beside the coachman on the long ride home from London to Somerset. No one dared remark openly that it was less than gallant for both Sir William and one of his young male friends to be inside the coach with their ladies, while an elderly maid had to brave the elements outside. But Nell was deeply shocked by such callousness, and it made her realize that the gentry held no real affection for their servants; they saw them as mere packhorses who would be worked till they dropped and then replaced.

Since Hope's birth, Nell and Bridie had become very close, and Bridie had taught her many accomplishments to enable her to rise beyond being just a parlourmaid. Thanks to her, Nell knew how to dress hair in the latest fashions and to sew daintily, and had learned the skills needed to be a housekeeper. Bridie had also taught her how to deal with a mistress who relied on servants for everything, yet rarely acknowledged their value.

Bridie's death hit Nell very hard, and she wept when Lady Harvey told her that she'd left Nell her savings, almost twenty pounds, saying that Bridie had confided in her that she'd come to think of Nell as her daughter.

Nell guessed that Bridie had used the word 'daughter' to convey the hidden message that the money was for Hope's continuing care, and to charge Nell with keeping their secret for ever.

Lady Harvey had never once spoken of the birth, at least not to Nell, but it was clear by a heavy sadness in her during the first two years that she thought about it often. She would rally herself when her husband was home, but as soon as he left again to attend to his business interests in London she would sink back down into grief.

Nell expected that Bridie's death would bring her low again − after all, the older woman had been with Lady Harvey throughout her life. But somewhat surprisingly it didn't, and just after the funeral she asked Nell if she would like to be her personal maid.

That was the one and only time Lady Harvey ever gave any indication that she remembered Nell's part in the events of that night two years earlier. Even then she didn't speak of it outright.

'You are the only person who could take my dear Bridie's place,' she said, taking Nell's hand in hers and squeezing it. 'You have proved yourself to be as loyal as she was, and this is my only way of showing my appreciation.'

As Bridie's death had made Nell look at her mistress with some cynicism, her first thought was that this was mere self-interest rather than a reward. But it was a step up the ladder, and in her first year as a lady's maid she travelled widely.

On her first trip to London, as the coach trundled through the city, Nell saw for herself how much worse it was to be poor there than back in Somerset. Hordes of ragged, barefoot children, their faces pinched with hunger and cold, thronged the filthy streets. She saw cold-eyed hussies with most of their breasts exposed standing around on street corners, and guessed at their occupation. Many people the worse for drink, both men and women, lay slumped in doorways of dilapidated hovels.

Then in 1835 Lady Harvey gave birth to Rufus, the long-awaited son and heir.

Nell was not present at the birth, this time an experienced midwife and a doctor from Bath were in attendance. Rufus was small but robust with a fine pair of lungs, and as blond, blue-eyed and fair-skinned as both his parents.

No wetnurse was brought in – Lady Harvey fed him herself, and her joy and Sir William's affected the entire household. Nell was happy for them too, but at the same time she couldn't help but consider the differences between the life Hope would have and that of her younger half-brother. But when Lady Harvey asked Ruth, Nell's younger sister, to be Rufus's nursemaid, she felt a kind of smug satisfaction that at least both children were being brought up by the Renton family.

For the first four years of Hope's life, fortune had smiled on Nell's family. With mild winters, good harvests, and the older children and their father in regular work, it was a time of relative plenty. There were no more babies and Meg often said she thought she was now too old for childbearing. Although the cottage seemed even more cramped when everyone was home for a visit, it rang with laughter and joy.

But the happy times ended abruptly when Prudence and Violet, aged only nine and eight, died of scarlet fever. The Reverend Gosling said they should get down on their knees and thank the Lord that Joe, Henry and Hope were spared, for it usually took the youngest. But Nell at least was convinced that the other children had been saved by her mother isolating the two sick ones in the outhouse before the younger ones could become infected.

Child deaths were all too common – one in three babies died before their first birthday – but that didn't make it any easier for her family to come to terms with losing Prudence and Violet. That was two years ago now, but they still mourned the girls, and often when Nell went home unexpectedly she'd find her mother crying. Yet Hope, with her loving and affectionate nature, helped. Meg often said that if it wasn't for her she couldn't have borne it.

As Nell had predicted, no one had ever suspected that Hope was not a true Renton. Even the older children, on coming down the morning after her arrival to find a new baby in their mother's arms, had just accepted that she was their sister, for all the other babies had arrived without any fanfare or fuss. Silas would sometimes wink at Nell when an effusive neighbour remarked how much Hope looked like him, but neither he nor her mother ever spoke of how she had come to them, not even when they were alone.

Yet Nell still worried that as Hope got older, people would note her grace, the clearness of her skin, her slender limbs and delicate features, and see her as the thoroughbred she really was.

'We came to meet you,' Hope said sweetly as her older sister emerged from the wood. Just as Nell had expected, she was sitting down, demurely making a daisy chain, as if she'd never contemplated removing her clothes to climb a tree.

'Give us a kiss then!' Nell said with a smile, putting down her basket and opening her arms for all three children to come to her for a hug.

Joe and Henry looked like a pair of scrawny ragamuffins with their wild black hair, dirty faces, bare feet and the seats out of their breeches. Aside from Joe being a couple of inches taller than Henry they were as alike as twins, and they had inherited the standard male Renton features of slightly sticking-out ears and over-large noses. But even if neither of them grew up to be considered handsome they had warm, affectionate natures, and responded with enthusiasm to Nell's hugs and kisses.

With the children whooping and shouting, Nell walked on across the common. It was a beautiful day, unusually warm for May, the cow parsley towering over Hope's head, and the air was full of the scent of hawthorn blossom. Nell was looking forward to being with her mother for a couple of hours and to finding out how Alice and Toby were faring.

Alice had gone into service at a big house in Bath a short while after Prudence and Violet died. The Reverend Gosling had arranged it, and six months later Toby joined the household too, as a junior footman. The little cottage seemed almost spacious with only three children left, and although her mother claimed to like it that way, Nell sensed that wasn't strictly true.

Meg was hoeing the vegetable patch when Nell arrived, but she dropped the hoe and ran to hug her daughter.

'The weeds can wait,' she laughed when Nell offered to help. 'They come up every day, but you don't.'

Her hair had turned grey after Prudence and Violet died, and her face was becoming very lined, yet in many ways she looked younger and healthier than she did when Henry was born. Meg said it was because her body had at last recovered from childbearing, and it was true she was shapely again. But Nell thought it was more likely to be because she ate and slept better, and that she had time to herself at last. She was happy tending her vegetables, feeding the chickens and milking the cow that Nell had bought with some of the money from Bridie.

They sat down on the rough bench Silas had made by the back door, and Nell took from her basket the currant buns Cook had given her to take home, and passed them round.

The three children sat on the ground in front of Nell and Meg, their dark eyes lighting up at the sight of the large iced buns. Matt and James had been very different in character as small boys, but they had been inseparable, and Joe and Henry were the same.

Joe had paid attention during his lessons with the Reverend Gosling and he could read and write very well, but Henry was a dreamer. If he was sent out to chase the chickens into their coop, he was quite likely to forget what he'd been asked to do and wander off watching rabbits or foxes. He would rather draw an animal on his slate than write words or do sums. Joe was more reliable and conscientious, very much the brains of the duo, but he wasn't as physically strong or daring as Henry.

'Don't the vale look grand today?' Nell exclaimed. May was her favourite month, neither too hot nor too cold, and she loved the spring flowers and blossom. It was also the time when the view from the cottage garden was at its best.

The Rentons' land sloped sharply down to the river. Here and there a hawthorn was in full flower, and so many buttercups grew amongst the grass that it was more yellow than green. The blossom on the apple and pear trees was fading now and the primroses were all but done, but down under the trees by the river bank, and in the woods on the opposite side, there was a rich haze of bluebells. Beyond the wood the ground rose sharply again, bright green with young shoots of wheat and barley, and the birds did their best to drown the sound of the thudding from the copper mill at Woolard with their singing.

Nell loved the gardens at Briargate, but she loved this more. Here she could believe life had something good in store for her, while at Briargate she was always reminded she was only a servant.

'I caught a trout the day afore yesterday,' Joe boasted. 'It were as big as this.' He held his two hands some fifteen inches apart.

'It were me who tickled it. You only got it in the sack,' Henry exclaimed indignantly.

Meg looked at Nell with a raised eyebrow. 'More like six inches. And they came home late for supper covered in mud.'

At this lack of appreciation the boys ran off down towards the river to see if they could catch another one. But Hope remained, wanting to hear all Nell's gossip from Briargate.

Hope had never been to the big house, but she'd seen Sir William and Lady Harvey at church on Sundays, and with two sisters and a brother working there, she'd heard enough about the place to be intensely interested in everything that went on.

As Nell had spent her first few weeks at Briargate feeling overwhelmed by how the gentry lived, she wanted Hope to have some preparation for when the time came for her to go into service. So she related how Ruby, the upstairs maid, had slipped on the backstairs with a full slop bucket in her hand, and that Cook had forgotten to put sugar in a rhubarb tart on a day when Lady Harvey had guests for luncheon.

Nell went on then to describe Lady Harvey's new rose-pink silk ballgown which had been sent down from the dressmakers in London the previous day.

'It's got hundreds of tiny seed pearls on the bodice and along the train,' she enthused.

'When I'm a lady I'll have lovely gowns,' Hope said, getting to her feet and holding out the skirt of her worn cotton dress as if she were about to sweep into a ballroom.

'Then we'll have to find you a rich husband,' Nell said

affectionately. When her other sisters wished for things she knew they could never attain she'd always been quick to put a dampener on them. But for some reason she could never do that to Hope. There was something about her, the boldness in her eyes, the tilt of her head, that suggested she might find her way back to where she belonged.

'Maybe I could marry Master Rufus,' Hope giggled. 'Then I could live at Briargate.'

'Don't be foolish, child,' Meg said sharply. 'The only way you'd get to live at Briargate is by working there like Nell does.'

Although Nell understood why Meg had to squash that particular idea, she felt sorry for Hope when she saw her face fall. She hadn't been brought up in ignorance about the world beyond this village as her brothers and sisters had. She not only knew about Briargate, she had been to Bristol once on the cart with her father. For weeks she talked of nothing but the ships, the crowded streets, fancy carriages and shops full of things she'd never seen before. Was it surprising she had fanciful notions?

'Why don't you, Joe and Henry walk back with me to Briargate later?' Nell suggested impulsively. 'I'm always telling Cook about you, and she'd love to meet you. You could see Ruth and James too.'

Hope clapped her hands gleefully. Meg shot Nell a disapproving look.

'Better for her to learn her place is only in the kitchen there,' Nell said as Hope rushed headlong down the field to tell the boys.

Meg sighed but made no comment. That was her way.

Mrs Cole had left Briargate soon after Rufus was born, and Lady Harvey decided she didn't need another housekeeper. As Nell had moved into Bridie's old position as Lady

Harvey's personal maid, she had become third in line after Baines and Cook in the household hierarchy. There weren't so many staff now – when someone left they weren't necessarily replaced – which meant they all had a few more duties. Rose, who had been the upstairs maid, was now the parlourmaid, and Ruby the kitchenmaid had taken Rose's old position. Cook had a new kitchenmaid called Ginny, and all the roughest work was now done by Ada, who came in daily from Woolard. Ruth as nursemaid and James, now the only groom since John Biggins retired, plus the new gardener, Albert Scott, and his assistant Willy, made up the full complement of staff.

Nell took some pleasure in knowing she had the easiest and most pleasant job of all. Lady Harvey wasn't demanding, and Nell had only to dress her and look after her hair and clothes. If the mistress went visiting, shopping in Bath, or even just for a ride in the carriage, Nell went too. When there were visitors at Briargate, Nell filled her time with mending or pressing clothes but if she had no chores to do, the time was her own. Mostly she felt she was very fortunate.

Yet on the way back to Briargate later in the afternoon, with the children trotting along beside her, she was thoughtful. That feeling she'd had of aging ten years the night Hope was born had never really gone away. It was as though it had robbed her of her girlhood, made her too cautious and fearful.

She was twenty-two now, and nearly all the girls in the village she'd grown up with were married with children. Would that ever come to her?

It was what she wanted more than anything. Most nights she fell asleep imagining her wedding, the cottage she'd live in and even naming her children. Yet maybe she was already past her prime?

That frightened her for she didn't want to end up like Bridie, an old woman who lived entirely for the family she served.

Nell wasn't without admirers. She knew Baines had a soft spot for her. But he was in his early fifties and he could never make her heart race. There was Seth O'Reilly too, who brought groceries from the shop in Pensford; he got so flustered whenever he saw her that he could hardly string a sentence together. But he seemed a bit weak, she couldn't imagine him being able to chop wood or milk a cow, and besides, he walked with a limp. She wanted a man like her father, a happy, easygoing man who wouldn't complain after a long day's work out in the cold or wet. The kind of man who could turn his hand to anything, wasn't feckless with money, didn't drink too much, but also had some passion in his soul.

Nell thought Albert Scott, the new gardener, might be that way. He'd come to work at Briargate back in March soon after Jacob, the old gardener who had been here since the house was built, died.

Since Albert's arrival Nell had spent far more time watching for him out of the windows than she should have. He was very handsome, over six feet tall, with black curly hair, a thick dark beard and strong very brown hands, and she believed him to be about twenty-five.

Sadly, as Lady Harvey's maid she didn't get any opportunity to mix with gardeners or grooms as they had rooms over the stable and took their meals after the other servants. That was another reason for suggesting the children came back with her today, for if they asked to see the horses in the stables, she might get the opportunity to speak to Albert.

The children ran ahead of her through the woods, the boys balancing on fallen trees like little mountain goats, shrieking loudly to each other as Hope picked bluebells for

Cook. Nell watched them fondly, reminding herself how lucky she was to have her family so near to her. Cook had left her family when she was twelve, and she'd had no contact with any of them for over twenty years.

The late-afternoon sun was still very warm as they came out of the woods and made their way across the paddock to the stile by the stables.

'Will Cook like the bluebells?' Hope asked excitedly. She looked as if she might burst because she was finally going to the house she'd heard so much about. 'Will she put them in a jam jar?'

'I'm sure she will,' Nell said, amused at her excitement. 'But you won't be able to stay long because they'll be preparing tonight's dinner. And I have to go up and see to Lady Harvey's bath; they've got guests tonight.'

'Will James let us see Merlin?' Henry asked.

Merlin was the master's new stallion and James talked about him all the time.

'I'm sure he will,' Nell said. 'You can see Duchess and Buttercup, her foal, and there's the carriage horses too.'

Cook was delighted to see the children, for she'd heard as much about them as they had about her. She poured each of them a glass of her special lemonade and gave them a slice of apple tart.

Ruth came into the kitchen, neat in her striped blue and white nursemaid's uniform. She was nineteen now, and a slightly thinner and taller replica of Nell. She let out a cry of delight to see her brothers and sister, embarrassing the boys by hugging and kissing them in front of Cook.

'I'll be home tomorrow on my afternoon off,' she told them. 'But I've got to go now because it's nearly time for Master Rufus's tea. But mind you go and see James before you leave.'

Sir William was out riding Merlin, but James showed them Duchess and Buttercup in their paddock, and let them feed the carriage horses with some carrots. To Nell's disappointment she couldn't see Albert anywhere. 'Is he still working in the garden?' she asked James. 'I thought he might show Hope around.'

James grinned. He was twenty now, and since coming here to work he'd grown several inches and developed muscle with all the hard work. He was quite a hit with the other maids, for although a plain lad, with his floppy dark hair and the Renton big nose, he had a nice way with him, funny and warm. 'You mean you hoped you could meet him!' he said pointedly.

Nell blushed. She didn't try to deny it for James knew her too well.

'He's round the front of the house, weeding the rosebed. Take Hope round there!' He grinned knowingly. 'The boys can stay here with me.'

'I can't go there,' Nell said in horror. There was a kind of unwritten rule that the servants didn't go round to the front of the house. She would have felt quite comfortable showing Hope the gardens at the back, but the front was different because she could be seen by anyone glancing out of the windows.

'Don't be daft, of course you can go round there,' James laughed. 'Hope will like seeing the statues. And Albert will like seeing you.'

Emboldened, Nell took Hope's hand and walked back through the arch of the stable yard to the front of the house. Aside from the big circular rosebed, set into the gravel drive, there were more roses along the front of the house, some of which climbed right up the walls in high summer, and that was where Albert was weeding.

He had removed the brown smock he usually wore and

rolled up his shirtsleeves, and the sight of his muscular bare forearms and moleskin breeches tight over his buttocks made Nell feel suddenly shy.

She knew from previous years that in a couple of weeks the roses would be spectacular, but as yet there were none flowering. Had they been in bloom she could have let Hope sniff them, but without any real excuse for being there, she felt vulnerable and rather foolish.

But Hope ran straight up to Albert before Nell could prevent her.

'Why aren't there any flowers here?' she asked him.

'There will be next month,' Albert replied, glancing round at Nell and smiling. 'Roses like the whole bed to themselves, you see. They don't much care for companions.'

Nell took her courage in both hands and walked over to him. By the time she got there Hope was asking why they didn't like companions and that she liked gardens that had flowers everywhere, all different kinds.

'I like that too,' Albert said. 'But this ain't my garden, so I has to do what the master likes.'

Nell blushingly apologized for her sister. 'She's no trouble,' Albert said cheerfully. 'You bring her again once all the roses is in bloom. I bet she'll like that.'

Hope was very taken with the marble statues in the big circular rosebed, making Nell blush yet again when she asked why the ladies had no clothes on. Albert chuckled and said it was his opinion that it was harder to carve clothes than nakedness.

They were a distance of some fourteen feet from the porch and the front door, when Nell heard the door open and Lady Harvey saying goodbye to someone.

Not wanting to be seen talking to the gardener, Nell told Hope it was time they went back. But Hope ignored her, and went skipping away in the direction of the front door, reaching it just as a gentleman stepped out of the porch.

'Hope!' Nell called out. But to her dismay the child just stood there, hands behind her back, smiling sweetly up at the man.

He was perhaps thirty, tall and slender, wearing a dark green riding jacket, brown breeches and long riding boots, with a rakish yellow and green cravat around his neck. He looked down at Hope and smiled. 'Hello! Who are you?'

'Hope Renton,' she replied without any hesitation. 'I came to see the roses, but there aren't any.'

Nell rushed over and grabbed Hope's hand. Lady Harvey had gone in and closed the door behind her. 'I'm sorry, sir,' she said.

'No need to apologize for a polite child.' His voice was deep but it held a hint of laughter at her embarrassment.

Nell looked into his handsome smiling face and blanched. His almost black eyes and hair were identical to Hope's and she was so shocked that she could only stare at him open-mouthed.

'You must be a sister of the young groom who took my horse,' he said with an easy smile. 'You are very alike.'

Nell pulled herself together rapidly. 'Yes, sir, that's James. I'm Nell, Lady Harvey's maid,' she managed to get out. 'I'll tell James to bring your horse round for you.'

Nell ran off then, holding Hope securely by the hand.

After telling James to take the gentleman's horse round to him, Nell said goodbye to the children and warned them to go straight home. She stayed at the stile by the paddock waving to them for some little while because she didn't dare go back into the house while she was so shaken.

She hadn't ever allowed herself to wonder about Hope's father, just as she didn't look for similarities between her mistress and the child. She had decided long ago that it was better never to think about such things.

There were many male visitors at Briargate; some came with wives, sisters or even mothers, and some alone if they were friends of Sir William. But Nell had never seen anyone that looked remotely like Hope, and she'd never expected to. After all, a man who had done that to her mistress wasn't likely to be welcome here.

Yet the underhand way Lady Harvey showed this gentleman out was almost proof of intrigue, for why hadn't she called Rose? And what was she doing having gentlemen callers anyway when her husband was out?

What if the man had recognized himself in Hope? If Nell could see the similarity, surely anyone could?

Nell went up to the nursery a little later to see Ruth, so befuddled that she forgot her ladyship was often in the nursery at this time of day.

'Ruth was just telling me that your young brothers and sister came back with you this afternoon,' she said pleasantly.

'I'm sorry, m'lady,' Nell replied. 'I should have asked if it was all right for me to bring them here.'

'Nonsense, you don't need my permission for them to see their brother and sister.' Lady Harvey lifted Rufus on to her lap and began bouncing him up and down. 'I wish I'd seen them too, and I'm sure Rufus would have enjoyed a visit. He could do with some little playmates.'

The nursery was the place where Lady Harvey was always at her most relaxed, and she welcomed Nell coming in there too, saying she had never liked the idea of small children being cloistered away from people. Nell wished she hadn't come in now, but she could hardly leave immediately without it looking suspicious, so she bent down to pick up some building blocks off the floor.

Nell felt relieved that her mistress looked perfectly normal. She wasn't flushed or excited, and she was wearing a plain, dove-grey gown which was entirely suitable for a mother, but hardly the kind of dress a woman would choose to wear to meet a lover. Her hair was still as neatly pinned up as it had been this morning when Nell fixed it for her. So maybe she was wrong about the man?

'We wouldn't dare bring our brothers up here to meet Rufus,' Nell ventured, trying very hard to act and speak normally. 'They are too rough for a little gentleman like him.'

Rufus looked like a little girl with his long blond curls, blue eyes and the customary long baby dress. Only a few days ago Nell had heard Sir William saying he thought that at three it was time his son was put in breeches, but so far Lady Harvey hadn't instructed Ruth to do so.

'But your sister could come and play,' Lady Harvey said with a smile. 'How old is she now?'

'Hope's six, mam,' Nell said nervously, afraid that her mistress might mull that over later and think it was a strange coincidence that the Renton child was the same age as the one she lost. 'But going on eighteen, she never stops asking questions,' she added quickly.

'Get down now, Mama,' Rufus said, and climbed off his mother's lap and toddled off to Ruth.

Both Nell and Ruth adored Rufus; he was a sweet-natured little boy with a great sense of fun, and as affectionate to them as he was to his mother.

'Bring Hope up for tea on Monday,' Lady Harvey said, getting up off the couch and smoothing her dress down. 'You can pop off to fetch her after luncheon. By the time you get back Rufus will have had his nap. I want him to learn to share his toys and mix well.'

As their mistress swept out of the nursery, Ruth looked

at Nell and giggled. 'Our Hope in here! She don't know what she's letting herself in for.'

Nell was brushing Lady Harvey's hair that night when Sir William came into the bedroom.

'You make a pretty picture,' he said as he leaned against the doorpost. 'Who brushes your hair, Nell?'

Nell giggled. She could tell the master had drunk too much for his face was red and his shirt was hanging loose over his breeches. He was undeniably the most handsome man she'd ever seen, his features as perfect as the marble statues' in the rosebed, hair the colour of ripe corn and eyes of an intense blue. Cook had often said he was pretty like a girl, but Nell didn't agree; his lips might be just a bit too full, but he had a strong chin, and very shapely thighs and buttocks from riding so much.

She knew he was in a good mood, drunk or not, for she'd heard him laughing with his wife as they came up the stairs after their dinner guests had left. 'No one but me, sir,' she replied.

He just stood there silently watching her and his wife, and Nell thought this was because he wanted to come into his wife's bed tonight. She thought it was a good job she'd already got her mistress's corsets off and helped her into her nightgown. Nell didn't think it was quite seemly for a husband to see all that.

'Have you got a sweetheart, Nell?' Sir William asked suddenly.

'No, sir,' she said, blushing furiously.

'But would you like one?' he said, moving right into the room and sitting down on the bed. 'Do you hope to get married one day?'

'William!' Lady Harvey laughingly reproved him. 'Stop quizzing poor Nell!'

'I do hope to get married one day, sir, when the right man comes along,' Nell said.

'Then I think I must look around for a suitable husband for you,' he said with a bright smile which showed perfect small white teeth.

'Well, just don't look too far away from Briargate, William,' Lady Harvey said with laughter in her voice. 'I don't want her running off and leaving me. But you can get off to bed now, Nell. I can manage everything else alone.'

Nell put the hairbrush down on the dressing table, bobbed a little curtsey and said goodnight. As she was leaving the room she turned her head just enough to see that her master had got up off the bed and was kissing his wife's neck. That pleased her, and went some way towards allaying her fears about the visitor this afternoon.

She had discovered who the gentleman caller was from James. He was Captain Angus Pettigrew of the Royal Hussars, a cousin of the Pettigrews who lived in Chelwood House about two miles away.

She couldn't of course tell her brother why she wanted to know about him, or indeed ask any further questions for fear of alerting him to her anxiety. She wasn't even sure what she wanted any information for. All she knew was that she felt threatened.

But by what? She had asked herself that question dozens of times tonight, and had found no answers. But now she'd left her master and mistress together, clearly happy, she thought maybe the Captain might only have called here while he was visiting his relatives because it would have been impolite not to.

Yet Nell was still troubled about her mistress's request for Hope to come and play with Rufus. If Bridie was here now she'd have thrown up her hands in horror. But Nell couldn't refuse, or make an excuse. She'd just have to hope that the visit wouldn't go well, that Lady Harvey would decide Hope wasn't a fit companion for her son, and that would be the end of it.

Nell's hopes that the visit would be a failure were dashed. It was raining on Monday, so the children had to stay in the day nursery. Hope was so thrilled by Rufus's toys, the like of which she'd never seen before, that she was only too happy to play with whatever he wanted. She built him castles with his building blocks and laughed when he knocked them down. They rode on his rocking-horse together, and Hope looked at Rufus's picture books with him.

Lady Harvey joined them for tea, and Hope turned on her charm shamelessly, admiring the delicate china, eating and drinking far more daintily than she usually did, even reprimanding Rufus for not eating the crusts on his bread and jam.

It was clear Rufus thought she was the best thing ever to come into his young life, and when it was time for Nell to take Hope home, he clung to her tearfully, making his mother promise she could come again the following week. As Nell walked across the paddock with Hope she could imagine Bridie shaking her fist at her and asking why she had been so stupid as to take the child there in the first place.

On Sundays as many of the Briargate staff who could be spared from chores and preparing luncheon were expected to go to church in Compton Dando. All those who came from the surrounding villages were also allowed one Sunday in a month to go home after church to visit their families. James and Ruth often got the same Sunday off, but because Nell had to stand in as nursemaid for Rufus when Ruth was not there, she always went home alone.

It was three weeks since Hope's first afternoon at Briargate when Nell got her next Sunday off. She was happy as she walked to church with the other servants through Lord's Wood. The ground was dry, so there would be no mud on her well-polished boots or on her best blue dress, and Lady Harvey had given her a spray of small artificial roses and a blue ribbon to trim her bonnet. Nell was looking forward to seeing her father, for on her regular afternoon off he was always working, and she was lucky if she saw him for more than a few minutes before she had to return to the house. But most of all she was delighted that Albert had joined the other servants today.

As a gardener he didn't work at all on Sundays, and up till now he'd always gone to the church in Chelwood. Nell felt he could only have decided to change churches because he wanted to get to know her. It couldn't be Rose he liked; she was a real old maid of over thirty. Ruby was only fourteen and as skinny as a rake and plain as a pikestaff. That only left Ruth, but to Nell's knowledge they'd never spoken to each other. Nell wondered if she was brave enough to invite him back to the cottage after the service. Would that seem too forward?

As if hearing her thoughts, Albert stopped, looked back at her with a smile and waited for her to catch up with him. 'How many of your family will be at home today?' he asked.

Nell thought he could pass for a country gentleman in his tweed jacket, dark green breeches and neat stockings. 'Just Hope, the two younger boys, and Matt, my oldest brother – he works on the same farm as my father,' Nell replied. 'Where are your family?'

'In Penshurst, that's in Kent,' Albert said. 'Only a brother and two sisters and they are married. Our parents died a few years back.'

'James told me you used to work for the Bishop of Wells.

47

What made you come so far from home to work?' she asked.

Albert shrugged. 'I knew I'd never get a better opportunity than working in a palace gardens.'

'So why did you leave there?'

He gave her a rather odd sideways look, and she thought perhaps she was asking too many questions.

'Because I'd be old before I got to be head gardener. I heard Sir William needed someone, and I walked all the way here on my day off to see him. Soon as I saw the grounds I knew it was the place for me, Sir William liked my suggestions for changes too.'

All the servants had noticed that the master seemed much more enthusiastic about the grounds since Albert arrived. He would go out there in all weathers, often helping with laying out new flowerbeds. Lady Harvey had said she was glad he'd found another interest apart from riding.

'Don't you get a bit lonely here though?' Nell asked. 'I mean, Willy's a bit simple and James is always off to the village in the evenings. You must have had lots of friends in Wells?'

Albert shrugged again. 'I'm not much of a one for company,' he said. 'If I want some I go down to the ale house in Chelwood. It weren't so different in Wells; the other men were either very old or simple like Willy. I like this place better.'

James had told Nell that Albert wasn't much of a conversationalist, but he was wrong. He chatted all the way to the church, and asked Nell dozens of questions about her family. He was a bit serious, he frowned more than he smiled, but Nell didn't mind, she was just happy he wanted to talk to her.

After the service Albert walked back up the hill with Nell and the rest of her family, and it was her father who invited him in for a glass of beer. Albert stayed for about half an hour admiring the vegetable garden, before excusing himself. But as he was leaving he rather pointedly asked Nell what time she would be coming back to Briargate, leaving her with the distinct impression that he intended to meet her to walk her through the wood.

Nell could see that her parents approved of Albert, though they made no comment other than that he was 'a sober young man'. Yet although she was excited that Albert appeared to be as taken with her as she was with him, a Sunday at home with her family was for now more important.

Meg had made a rabbit stew with dumplings, followed by bottled raspberries from the garden, and it was a joyful meal with a great deal of chatter and laughter. Matt had recently begun walking out with Amy Merchant, a farmer's daughter from Woolard, who had been Nell's friend when they were small and attended the Reverend Gosling's lessons in the parsonage. Meg and Silas were clearly very hopeful that this would lead to marriage, for they not only liked Amy, but her tenant farmer father was relatively prosperous, and he had only daughters. Meg teased Matt about polishing up his best boots before he walked over to her place in the evenings. That brought Silas around to telling them all how he used to walk over ten miles to court Meg, and he joked that he only asked her to marry him because he couldn't stand it in bad weather.

Matt said goodbye at four because he was going to meet Amy, and the three young children went off to play by the river, leaving Nell, Meg and Silas half-dozing under the apple tree at the back of the cottage.

It was only when Meg mentioned Hope's weekly visit to Briargate that Silas sat up.

'I dunno that we ought to let this be a regular thing,' he said. 'It can only end in trouble.'

'He's right,' Meg agreed, nodding her head. 'I know Hope loves to go, but it's turning her head. She'll be thinking she's too grand for us soon. Only the other day she asked why we didn't have pretty china cups and plates. It's Briargate this, Briargate that. Lady Harvey's got a pink dress, or Rufus is getting a pony. Where's it all going to end, Nell?'

'I'm sure I don't know.' Nell frowned. 'I told you I weren't happy about it in the first place. But how can we put a stop to it without upsetting Master Rufus?'

'How does Lady Harvey treat 'er?' Silas asked, an anxious look in his dark eyes.

'Very kindly, she really likes her. Everyone does at Briargate.'

'She's bound to like her, she's her own flesh and blood after all, and that's where the danger lies,' Silas sighed.

Nell was just about to say she couldn't see any danger in someone liking a child, but then she had a sudden picture of the way Lady Harvey laughed with Hope, smoothed her hair and touched her cheeks.

'You think she may get to like Hope too much?'

Once again she saw her parents looking at each other. 'Are you afraid she'll take Hope from you?' Nell asked incredulously. 'She wouldn't do that! She couldn't.'

'There's more than one way to take your child from you,' Meg said darkly. 'There's putting notions in her little head that she's different, there's making her want more than she'll ever get. And we can't be sure Bridie didn't tell Lady Harvey her babby lived.'

'No!' Nell shook her head. 'Bridie would never have done that.'

'Everything Bridie did was for her mistress,' Meg retorted. 'She let you bring the babby here because she thought that was best for Lady Harvey, but maybe later when the woman was still grievin' she told her the truth because she thought that was best too.'

'I don't believe that,' Nell said stoutly. 'If she had, Lady Harvey would have been asking me questions about us all, and she's never done that.'

'Gentry ain't like us,' Silas said contemptuously. 'They's born cunning. Anyways, she don't have to ask you nothing, Ruth tells her plenty.'

Nell was about to deny that, but all at once she realized her father was probably right, at least about Ruth. She had been with Rufus daily since he was born, her knowledge of caring for babies all based on watching and helping her mother with her younger brothers and sisters. What could be more natural than saying, 'Mother did this with our Henry', or 'Mother did that with our Hope'? And Ruth had no reason to be suspicious of any questions that followed.

'There in't any way this can end happy,' Silas said sadly. 'Even if Lady Harvey knows the truth, she ain't going to risk her secret getting out by giving our Hope a leg up in life. An' if she don't know, but she grows to care for our girl, she'll jest turn her little head more by makin' a fuss o' her. Either way, Hope's going to be the loser, cos she'll be neither fish nor fowl.'

Nell sighed in agreement. She and all her brothers and sisters had been brought up knowing exactly what their position was in life, just as her mother and father had before them. They were all here to serve someone, whether that was her father ploughing, haymaking or milking cows for one of the rich farmers, or twelve-year-old Nell going into service at Briargate. Even as small children they were toughened up for what lay ahead, collecting wood, hauling up water from the well, even scooping up the horse droppings out in the lane to help the vegetables grow. At harvest time the whole family had to help their father in the fields; from the age of three Nell had been pressed into picking potatoes.

Before Nell went into service she had often been hungry and cold. The darned and patched clothes she'd worn were passed down to Ruth and then Alice; no one ever got anything new. Poor people like them could only scrape along, for if there was a good harvest one year, the following year it could fail. Labourers like her father could get laid off at any time, and they were never able to accumulate savings to help them through the bad times.

In the first month Nell worked at Briargate, her hands bled from continually scrubbing pots and pans, and she was so exhausted by the end of the day that she had a job to climb the stairs. But when she took her first wages home and handed them over to her mother, Meg's smile of gratitude and pride in her daughter made it all worthwhile.

Nell couldn't imagine Hope accepting that. She'd never once gone to bed hungry, she'd never been expected to mind babies, mend clothes or draw water from the well. She hadn't been hardened up as the rest of them were. But if she wasn't servant material, what else was there for her?

'What do we do?' Nell asked in a small voice.

'I dunno,' Silas said with a sigh. All three of them knew that it wasn't wise to offend Lady Harvey by telling her they didn't want Hope to go up to the big house any more.

'Maybe we'd best just carry on then for now,' Meg said despondently. 'See how things go.'

It had been Nell's intention to tell them today about Captain Pettigrew. But she couldn't give them anything more to worry about now. She didn't know for absolute certainty he was Hope's father, and whether he was or wasn't, it was probably something she ought to keep to herself.

Chapter Three

1840

'If we got married, the master would let us have the gatehouse,' Albert said, twisting his cap in his hands, his expression almost as tortured as the cap.

Nell looked at him in astonishment, hardly able to believe what Albert had said. For two years now they'd been keeping company, walking to church, chatting in the stable yard in the evenings, and, as today, Albert often waited for her by Lord's Wood to escort her back to Briargate after her afternoon off. But in all this time there had been no real courtship. He hadn't so much as held her hand, let alone kissed her. She'd begun to think he saw her only as a friend.

'Married, Albert? You're asking me to marry you?'

'That's about the size of it,' he mumbled, eyes downcast. 'Are you willing?'

It was a warm evening in June, rays of late sunshine slanting in through the canopy of leaves overhead. The cooing of wood pigeons and the sound of a stream trickling over stones in the undergrowth nearby should have made it a romantic spot for a proposal, but the lack of passion, or even warmth, from Albert spoiled it.

'I don't know,' she said. 'I mean, you've said nothing to make me think you felt like that about me. It's so sudden.'

'It's been two years,' he retorted, as if that made it

completely understandable. 'I earn enough to keep a wife now, and we're suited.'

Nell would agree they were suited, in as much as they were both devoted to Briargate and the Harveys. Albert was passionate about the gardens; in the last two years he'd built rockeries, made many new flowerbeds and planted such a profusion of new shrubs and trees that it looked stunning. Nell approved of that passion, but she'd always expected that the man she would marry would show some passion for her too, and tell her he loved her before asking for her hand in marriage.

'Is being "suited" enough?' she asked, looking up at him in bewilderment.

Never a day passed without her thinking he was handsome, strong and clever. She liked his manly beard, the wide bridge on his nose, and the way his hair curled into little corkscrews when it got wet. He knew far more than she did about what went on in the world; only a couple of weeks ago he'd told her transportation to Australia was going to end, and explained a great deal about that far-off country to her. Was it possible that a man who knew so much wouldn't know a woman needed to be told she was loved?

'I reckon so,' he said woodenly. 'A canary don't mate with a thrush, does it? Like goes with like, and you and me, we're the same.'

'What about love?' she asked archly. 'There's hundreds of people out there much like me, same as there is like you. But it's love between two people that makes them special to each other.'

'You're special to me,' he said. 'So I guess that's what folk call love.'

'I want a husband who knows he loves me,' she retorted indignantly, and began walking away from him.

Nell was very aware that the vast majority of people

married for exactly the reasons Albert had stated. This was something often discussed by the staff at Briargate as they sat around the table in the servants' hall after supper. Gentry mostly married to strengthen links between two families, or to bring wealth to an illustrious family that was struggling financially. Baines, who had worked at or visited dozens of big estates, had said once that Sir William and Lady Harvey were the only titled people he'd ever met that he would call a 'love match'. It was Baines's belief that servants would do better by selecting a husband or wife for practical reasons rather than through what he called 'love sickness'.

But Nell had been born to parents who were a love match. Meg and Silas had been married now for twenty-five years and despite all the hardships, they still billed and cooed like lovebirds. Her father had once told her he felt no need to drink ale with other men; his favourite place was home beside the fire with his Meg. And that was what Nell wanted from her marriage too.

'Don't run off, Nell,' Albert called after her. 'I'm sorry if I put it badly. Will you marry me?'

Nell stopped and turned to look at him. 'Not until you can tell me you want me as your wife because you can't live without me, and mean it.'

Hope stood watching as her mother fiddled with Nell's hair yet again. She wasn't used to someone else in the family getting all the attention, and she didn't like it much.

The church bells began to ring. 'That means it's time we left,' Silas said. 'That is, if Nell's sure Albert is the one for her.'

It was September, and Nell had finally agreed to marry Albert when, a week after his proposal in the woods, he insisted he did love her, and explained that his slowness in admitting it was only down to shyness.

'I'm sure,' Nell said resolutely.

'You look as pretty as a cherry tree in blossom,' Meg said, placing a crown of white flowers on her daughter's head. Albert had brought them down from Briargate early that morning while Nell was still asleep up in the loft. Meg had fashioned the crown with a little wire, moss and greenery, and fixed the smallest of the flowers on to it. The rest she'd made into a posy for Nell to carry.

Nell had made her pink and white dress herself with some help from Rose, the parlourmaid. It had a low neckline and puffed sleeves, and the skirt had ruffles around the hem and a bustle like a real lady would wear. With a starched lace-trimmed petticoat beneath it and dainty shoes with silver buckles passed on to her by her ladyship, Hope thought her sister looked beautiful.

'Why haven't I got a crown?' Hope asked.

'Because Nell is the bride, and anyway, you've got a bonnet with new ribbons,' Meg said, handing the posy to Nell. 'Now, take that look off your face, Hope, and behave in church.'

Hope knew that Albert was already at the church as she'd seen him come past a little while ago with Ruth and James, who would be his best man. Joe and Henry had left then too. Hope thought Albert looked funny in a wing-collar, but then so did everyone in their best clothes.

Old Gertie Ford was waiting in the lane as they came out of the house. She lived in the cottage across the way and her legs were too bad to make it to the church.

'Good luck,' she called out, tottering on her stick. 'You make a pretty bride, Nell; make sure that handsome man of yours treats you right.'

Hope wondered why people kept saying that to Nell. Did it mean some husbands were bad to their wives?

The whole thing about getting married was a bit mysterious to Hope. She had asked her mother and she said it was because women wanted babies and they needed a man to give them one. But Hope knew babies grew in women's bellies, so that didn't quite make sense.

The clanging of the church bell became louder and louder as they walked down the hill into the village. Nell was holding her father's arm; Hope and her mother were behind them. There was no one else to wave to the little party because almost everyone in the village would already be at the church.

'Stop dawdling, Hope,' Meg called out, 'you'll make us late!'

Hope ran to her mother and took her hand. 'How long will it be before Nell has a baby?' she asked.

'That's for the Lord to decide,' Meg replied, but she looked down at Hope and smiled. 'Don't ask any more questions like that today either.'

Hope peeped through her fingers while she was supposed to be praying. The church looked very pretty as that morning some of the women in the village had fixed garlands of flowers around the pulpit and on the end of each pew. But it was strange to see all the neighbours and friends from the village sitting in the front pews where the gentry usually sat. Mr and Mrs Calway were there, and the whole of the Nichols family, the Carpenters from Nutgrove Farm, Mr Humphreys, the Pearces, Boxes, Webbs, Wilkinses, even Maria Jeffries, the barmy old lady who walked her goat on a lead around the village. Hope had asked her mother where Sir William and Lady Harvey and Rufus were going to sit when they came, but all she said was that they didn't go to servants' weddings. Hope didn't understand that. Nell looked after Lady Harvey, and Albert made the garden nice for her. So surely they should come here today to make things nice for Nell and Albert?

'I'll be nasty to Rufus next time I go to Briargate,' she promised herself.

She still went to play with him on Monday afternoons, unless the weather was bad. Sometimes she got fed up with him because although he was five now, he was still such a baby. She understood that was because he hadn't got brothers and sisters like her, and he'd never done anything or gone anywhere on his own the way she had when she was five, but it was still annoying. Yet she liked looking at all his books, and took pleasure in being able to read them to him. She also liked drawing and painting with him and playing hide-and-seek in the garden.

But above all she loved going to Briargate. Just walking up the big staircase to the nursery made her feel she was a special guest. It was so good to see all those beautiful pictures, to touch polished wood and velvet curtains and enter into a world that was so different to the one she came from.

She didn't think Nell, James and Ruth felt that way, but perhaps that was because they were servants. They were always quick to take her into the kitchen, as though they were reminding her that was where she belonged. But then she liked the kitchen just as much as the rest of the house. It was good to see food they never had at home, to observe the care Cook took in preparing meals, and she rarely came out of there without something to take home – a pie, a cake or a jar of preserves.

Then there was Lady Harvey. Hope thought she had to be the loveliest lady in the land. Her golden hair, blue eyes, soft voice and wonderful gowns were enough on their own, but she was so nice too, and always made a fuss of her.

Nell and Albert were kneeling in front of the altar now. Nell looked so different with her hair down; Mother had washed it for her last night, and twisted it all up in rags to make it curl. Hope had never seen it look so shiny and bouncy, and the little crown of flowers was very pretty. She decided that when she was grown up she'd have her hair like that every day.

She turned her head slightly to look at Alice and Toby in the pew behind her and grinned at them. She was thrilled they'd managed to come as they didn't get home very often because it was so far from Bath. Alice had whispered at the church door that they'd walked all the way, and would have to walk back tomorrow, but it was worth it. She also added that she had something for Hope.

She hoped it might be a paintbox like the one Rufus had.

'Why are you crying, Mother?' Hope whispered later. She was getting bored now because the Reverend Gosling kept asking Albert and then Nell the same things, and it seemed to be taking for ever.

'Shhh,' Meg hissed, putting one finger to her lips.

'I pronounce you man and wife.'

At the Reverend Gosling's words, said in a loud and important voice, Hope got interested again. She hoped that was the end of it now and they could go home for the party.

Everyone had been very worried that it would rain to-day, because the cottage wasn't big enough for everyone to get inside. But it had been warm and sunny for three days now, and last night Silas and Matt had fixed up a long table made of old doors in the field next to the vegetable patch, and there were planks resting on logs for seats. Nell had borrowed some sheets from Briargate as tablecloths, and there was a whole barrel of ale, enough pies, buns and other food for the scores of people, and Gareth Peregrine was going to play his fiddle so everyone could dance.

'You may kiss the bride.'

Hope put her hands over her eyes at the Reverend Gosling's order to Albert; she couldn't bear seeing men kissing women. Matt was always kissing Amy, especially when he thought no one was watching, and she didn't think she could bear it if Nell and Albert kept doing it all the time too.

But she had to peep through her fingers just to check Albert did it, because she'd never seen him kiss Nell before. She was relieved it was just a peck. Matt and Amy did big sucking ones.

Mabel Scragg, who owned the bakery next door to the Rentons, came waddling up to them as soon as they'd got out of the church. Hope didn't like her, she always called her 'a little madam', and once she'd boxed her ears for calling her Scraggy. 'The first one married off then,' she said to Meg, her fat chins wobbling. 'I reckon it will be your Matt next.'

'Aye.' Meg smiled towards her oldest son who as always was standing so close to Amy they could be stuck with glue. 'But it'll be her folk paying for it, thank heavens.'

'Your Nell's done well for herself with Albert and no mistake,' Mabel went on. 'Fancy them getting the gatehouse and Lady Harvey's keeping Nell on too! Mind you, that won't be for long, not if she takes after you!'

Hope frowned at Mabel's last remark. She wasn't the first to make it. Almost everyone had. She wanted to know what they meant.

By the time it grew dark, Hope had her answer. All the grown-ups still at the party were tipsy, including her mother and father. The food was all gone, they had to tip the barrel up now to get the last dregs, and Gareth Peregrine had stopped playing his fiddle and was sleeping off the drink

60

down by the chicken coop. Even Joe and Henry had helped themselves to some ale. Hope had tried it too, but she didn't like it.

She had noticed that ale made people say things they wouldn't normally say. Matt had said he loved Amy in front of everyone, and she'd giggled as if she thought he was wonderful.

There had been a great many gardening jokes all evening about beds, planting and seeds as they were leaving, none of which Hope understood. But as the couple went off over the common hand in hand, someone said they wondered if they'd be wetting a baby's head next June.

'Silas only had to sneeze and I was in the family way,' Meg said, laughing her head off. 'I just hope Nell doesn't take after me, or she ties a knot in Albert's John Thomas.'

There was more talk along these lines later among the women, and Hope listened to it all carefully. One said she thought Albert was a cold fish, and there were several voices raised in agreement, including her mother's. Even Ruth said she'd seen more passion in a rice pudding than in him, and she pointed out Matt who was dreamily dancing cheek to cheek with Amy and said that was more normal.

So putting it all together with bits Hope had learned about breeding from farm animals, she realized that this was what humans got married for, and the result was babies.

Later, when she danced with her father, who was already staggering with drink, he'd said he hoped he wouldn't be too old to dance at her wedding.

'I won't get married,' she said firmly. 'No one is going to do that to me.'

Three months after Nell's wedding, Matt married Amy. It was the week before Christmas, in the church at Publow, the next village. Fred Merchant, Amy's father, had welcomed

Matt into his family with open arms for he'd always wanted a son to pass the farm on to. Everyone in the village believed Matt was made for life.

Once again Hope saw her mother cry at the service and her parents get tipsy, but she had the feeling that they were far happier about Matt marrying Amy than they had been about Nell and Albert. She had never once heard her father ask Matt if he was sure about it, the way he had with Nell. And she'd seen her mother embrace Amy dozens of times, exactly the way she did all her own children.

Hope didn't like Albert. He had a way of looking at people as if they had a bad smell about them, and he hardly ever spoke. Nell had said in his defence that he was just shy and he was talkative to her. That might be so, but Hope couldn't understand why that would make Nell change. She never came home on her afternoon off now; the family only ever saw her at church on Sundays with Albert. Every time Hope came back from Briargate after playing with Rufus, her mother always questioned her about Nell.

'Is she looking well? Did she say anything about Albert? When is she coming home next?'

Hope could only ever tell the truth, that her sister looked just the same as she'd always done; that no, she didn't say anything about Albert, and that Nell said she couldn't come on her afternoons off now she had a home of her own to take care of.

Ruth and James always came home when they had the afternoon off. They said they thought Nell should have more time now she was married because Lady Harvey let her go earlier in the day, and when she went out without Nell, she sent her home.

Hope once heard Ruth say Albert was a tyrant, but her mother had put a warning finger to her lips to stop her from saying any more.

Hope had asked the Reverend Gosling what a tyrant was, and he said it was a man who forced his will on to others.

In the spring of '41, Hope was up in the day nursery at Briargate playing chequers in front of the fire with Rufus when Lady Harvey came in with another lady.

Rufus was good at chequers, so Hope didn't have to let him win sometimes to appease him. He'd won the last two games and at the point when Lady Harvey came in, Hope was concentrating hard on the new game so she could beat him.

Ruth leapt to her feet as she always did when anyone came into the nursery and began tidying away a puzzle they'd been doing earlier. 'Rufus!' Lady Harvey said. 'I want you to meet Miss Bird, she's going to be your governess and teach you to read and write.'

Rufus remained kneeling on the hearthrug and looked up at the tall, stern-faced lady in a grey dress and bonnet. 'Hope is teaching me to read and write,' he said dismissively.

Hope's favourite game was 'school' and she had already managed to teach Rufus all the letters of the alphabet, and to read some simple three-letter words.

'Don't be so rude, Rufus, and how many times have I told you a gentleman always stands up when a lady enters the room?'

'I'm sorry, Mama,' he said, and reluctantly got up.

Hope thought she'd better get up too, and she followed Ruth's example by helping to pick up the puzzle pieces.

Lady Harvey explained to the visitor that Hope was her maid's younger sister, and she came to play with her son once a week. She then went on to tell Rufus that Miss Bird would be giving him lessons in the schoolroom every day.

'I'd rather go to Reverend Gosling like Hope does,' Rufus replied.

'Reverend Gosling only teaches the village children,' Lady Harvey said sharply, looking cross that her son was being so uncooperative. 'And Miss Bird will be teaching you some history, geography and music too. She plays the piano.'

Hope wanted to laugh at Rufus because he looked funny with his lower lip stuck out petulantly. She thought he was a bit of a sissy mostly, though that was partly because he was always dressed in a sailor suit and his white stockings never had a speck of dirt on them. She could see why he didn't like the look of his new teacher. She looked mean with her straight back and her thin, unsmiling lips. She had no chin cither; the bottom of her face disappeared into her neck.

'Will she teach Hope too?' Rufus asked.

'No, she won't,' Lady Harvey said, and moved closer to him to ruffle his blond curls. 'Your father thinks it's time you mixed with some boys, so two afternoons a week Benjamin and Michael Chapel will be coming over here.'

Hope knew from Nell that the Chapels lived in a big house at Chelwood because they came to dine here sometimes. She'd never seen the boys herself but Nell had described them as little prigs.

'I think you'd better run along home now, Hope,' Lady Harvey said. 'I'd like Miss Bird to talk to Rufus alone.'

While Rufus began to complain that they were in the middle of a game, Ruth fetched Hope's shawl and bonnet and nudged her towards the door. It was quite clear to Hope that she was supposed to disappear permanently without a word, but that seemed unfair to her.

'Won't I be able to come to see Rufus any more?' she asked at the door.

Lady Harvey frowned. 'You'll still see him at church,' she said.

As Rufus let out a wail of protest, Hope slipped out of

the room because she was afraid she might cry too. While it was true she was often bored with Rufus, she was fond of him and they'd been playing together for a long time. Yet what hurt most was that James had warned her just a couple of weeks ago that she would be dropped like a hot brick when Sir William decided it was no longer seemly for his son to be playing with a village child.

Hope hadn't believed James; in fact she'd kicked him for being so nasty. But he was right after all.

She ran straight down to the kitchen. Cook looked up from rolling out some pastry. She was an odd-looking woman with crossed eyes and a small hump on her back, but Hope liked her. 'Hello, my little dumpling,' Cook said in her usual affectionate manner. 'You're early today. Or have you been sent down with a message for me?'

Hope blurted out the gist of what had happened. 'So I'm to go,' she finished up. 'I'm not wanted any more.'

Saying it outright like that made her cry and Cook drew her to her bosom for a cuddle. 'There, there,' she said comfortingly. 'They've got to make Master Rufus into a little man for when he goes away to school. But don't take on, he's going to miss you, and I don't doubt he'll play this new governess up because of it. Maybe Lady Harvey will call you back again then.'

'I shan't come back even if she does,' Hope said proudly, sniffing back her tears. 'Where's Nell?'

'Off home,' Cook said, taking a newly baked biscuit off the cooling tray and handing it to Hope. 'She's had her afternoon off changed to Mondays now.'

Hope wanted to cry again at that news, but she bit back her tears, said goodbye to Cook and left.

The way home was over the stile behind the stables and across the paddock to the woods, but she changed her mind as she reached the stile and turned back to march round the side of the house and down the drive. Part of it was because she wanted to see Nell and her cottage was down that way, but the major part was an act of defiance as she knew she could be seen clearly from the house. She wasn't going to skulk off through the woods. If she never set foot in Briargate again, at least the last time she left would be through the main entrance.

The drive was much longer than she'd expected, for she'd never walked down it before. Only a couple of weeks ago she'd overheard her parents talking when she was in bed up in the loft. Father had remarked that it was high time Nell and Albert invited them to their home. He said he understood they wanted to get it all straight before asking anyone there, but he thought six months was quite long enough for that.

The gatehouse, a rather severe-looking stone cottage with leaded window panes and a neat white picket fence around it, had been built long before Briargate. In Sir Roland Harvey's time there had been someone there all day to open and shut gates when visitors came and went, but this had been abandoned some twenty years ago and the gates removed. Until Nell and Albert moved in, it had lain empty for many years.

Nell opened the door only a second after Hope knocked and looked stunned to see her sister standing there. 'Why, Hope,' she gasped, 'whatever brings you here?'

'M'lady doesn't want me at Briargate any more,' Hope blurted out and promptly burst into tears.

'There now,' Nell said, putting her arms around her and drawing her into the cottage. 'Come and tell me all about it.'

Between hiccuping sobs Hope explained. 'Now I'm pushed out, like I was a bit of rubbish,' she finished up.

She was surprised to see Nell had tears in her eyes, and it helped to know her sister felt the injustice too.

'I was afraid this might happen,' Nell admitted. She went on to say that she and their parents had never been sure it was a good idea from the very start, then added that now Hope was nine she was too big to play with Rufus anyway.

She made a cup of tea, and it was only then that Hope began to look around.

It was the cleanest, tidiest cottage she had ever been in. The table was scrubbed almost white; the flagstone floor the same. The stove was like new, as though Nell had only just blackleaded it. Nothing was out of place or askew. The two chairs by the stove had cushions carefully placed; the rag rug in front of it hadn't even been stepped on. The shelves that held dishes, pots and pans had a scalloped trimming of blue and white paper. Even the dishrag was folded neatly. There was a smell of something cooking in the oven, but no sign of any preparation. Even the tin knives, forks and spoons were laid out like a row of soldiers in a box. Every one of them gleaming.

'You've got it looking very nice,' Hope said, but in fact she found such neatness a bit chilling. 'We thought you might still be in a muddle as you hadn't invited us round.'

'I don't get any time,' Nell replied, a little too quickly. 'Besides, it's too small for everyone to come.'

As far as Hope could see it was bigger than home, and Nell had a proper stove and a real sink. But she was eager to see the rest of the cottage and rushed off up the narrow stairs in the corner.

The upstairs wasn't just a loft like at home; Nell's room was a proper one with a door and windows. An iron bed, a washstand with a basin and ewer, and a wooden chest were the only furniture, and the walls were whitewashed the same as downstairs. But again, everything was so neat. The quilt on the bed didn't have one pucker in it. The curtains hung in precise folds. The bare wooden floorboards had a faint sheen on them as if they had been polished. The second room upstairs had nothing at all in it, just curtains at the window.

'Is that for your baby?' Hope asked. 'When you get one?'

'If I get one,' Nell said. 'So what do you think of my new home?'

'It's very tidy,' Hope replied for want of a real compliment.

'Albert likes things just so,' Nell replied, smoothing the already smooth quilt as if she was nervous. 'But you must go home, Hope. It's a long walk from here and Mother will get worried if you're late.'

A few minutes later Hope was making her way home, cutting through the grounds of Hunstrete House rather than walking right up to Briargate again. Young as she was, she knew Nell wasn't concerned about her being back late. She just didn't want her there when Albert got home.

A few months after Hope's last day at Briargate, she found herself counting that day as the one when everything changed for her. It wasn't just that she couldn't play with Rufus any more, or that she didn't see Nell, Ruth and James so often, but because she had to work.

She had of course always had to pitch in and help her father on the farm when there were crops to be picked, seeds to be sown, or at haymaking time. Her older brothers and sisters had done it too; that was the way for the families of farm workers. But in the past Hope's help had only been needed for the lightest of tasks; she went to lessons every day with the Reverend Gosling, and the rest of the time was her own.

But her lessons had ended suddenly, with no explanation as to why. Now she was expected to work as hard as Joe and Henry did, going off with them in the morning even

68

when it was wet and cold. Then on days she was kept at home she had to do washing, clean the cottage and help with the cooking.

'If you don't work, you can't eat,' her mother said sharply when she complained. 'That's just the way it is, Hope, and the sooner you understand that, the happier you'll be.'

Hope was well aware that money was tighter since Nell and Matt had got married and they didn't tip up their wages any more. James and Ruth still gave Mother theirs, and Alice and Toby contributed what they could. But none of them earned very much, and Alice and Toby came home so infrequently that Meg had to wait weeks just for a couple of shillings.

Hope could also see for herself that her parents were getting old and tired. Neither of them had the strength they'd once had. The Reverend Gosling had pointed out to her that her mother was forty-five now, her father a couple of years older, and a lifetime of heavy work and hardship had taken its toll. He said rather sternly that many girls of nine and even far younger had to work as hard as adults, and she should thank God that she had been allowed a real childhood and been able to attend his little school for four years.

So she had to bear it without complaint, even when her back felt as though it was breaking from being bent over all day picking strawberries, or her arms felt as if they were being torn from the sockets as she hauled full sacks of potatoes the length of a field, just muttering a few oaths under her breath. Yet it wasn't just the new hard labour that bothered her. It was her loss of position that really hurt.

'Our baby' was an expression she'd heard to describe her for as long as she could remember. Everyone in the family except Joe and Henry used it, a loving way of acknowledging that she had a special place in the family. They all took care that she was warm enough, had enough to eat, that she wasn't tired. Her mother and Nell had made sure she had decent clothes and boots that fitted, her father and Matt had whittled her dolls out of wood, hung a swing for her on the apple tree. She had been quicker than any of the others to learn to read and write, and while none of them had more than two years with the Reverend Gosling, she'd had four. They asked her to read notices, or any newspapers that came their way, because she was far better than anyone else at it. Even being sent to play with Rufus made her feel that she'd been singled out, for Henry was only a year older.

For the whole two years she was visiting Briargate she was the focus of everyone's attention. She had to be neatly dressed to go there, in the early days she had to be taken and collected, and everyone in the family wanted to know about what she did there and what Lady Harvey had said to her.

Now she was nothing. She had to wear her old frock to work, and no one had any need to ask about what she'd been doing because they knew. She hadn't much liked going to the Reverend Gosling for lessons, but she'd learned things she could tell her parents about when she got home.

But the worst of it was that she knew this was how it would be until she went into service. And that would be even worse.

'Come and sit beside me, Meg,' Silas called out as he saw his wife looking out of the door to see where he was.

It was September, a beautiful evening with the sun just starting to set. Silas was sitting on the seat under the apple tree smoking his pipe, watching the sky turning pink. Down at the bottom of the field by the river bank he could see rabbits feeding. An owl was perched up on a fence post waiting to spot its supper. Everything was just as it should be, the chickens in their coop for the night, Hope, Joe and

Henry already asleep up in the loft, and they'd had a good dinner tonight of chicken and apple dumplings. But Silas was unable to enjoy the peace or the view because he was worried.

Meg came over the grass towards him, a tankard of cider in her hand. She passed it to him and sat down beside him. 'It'll be a year tomorrow that our Nell got wed. Are you thinking we've lost her for good?'

Silas didn't reply immediately, mainly because that wasn't what he was thinking about. He had concerns that Nell never came home to visit any more, but a wife had to obey her husband's wishes, and if Albert wanted Nell at their home in her spare time, then Silas supposed he had to accept that. But he knew Meg couldn't see it that way.

'I know you miss her,' he said eventually. 'But she chose Albert and they've got a life of their own to make now. At least we see her at church every Sunday.'

'Maybe it will be different when she has a baby,' Meg said hopefully.

'Maybe.' Silas sighed because he didn't really believe that. 'But it was Hope I was fretting about. She don't seem herself.'

'She'll be fine, she'll get used to work, we all had to,' Meg said. 'We should've broken her in more gently perhaps, stopped her going up to the big house a year ago. But what's done is done. We do have to teach her that for folk like us there is no easy road.'

Silas turned to look at his wife and wondered, as he had so many times before, how she managed to be so accepting. When they fell in love they believed that one day they'd have a little farm of their own, but here they were twenty-six years on and they were still breaking their backs for a pittance. When he was too old to work and they couldn't pay the rent, they'd be thrown on the parish.

But they were blessed, he knew that. They had each other, their children were healthy and strong, the five older ones were all in good positions, and two of them married off. He hoped he could get Joe and Henry apprenticed in good trades.

Hope was the only one he worried about for she was neither a Renton by blood nor by nature.

'She ain't never going to be right for service, nor for farm work,' Silas burst out. 'She's got too much brain for either. I see her sometimes questioning everything; that spark in her will never let her obey blindly like we've always done. And she's too pretty for her own good.'

'Maybe with her reading, writing and the sums she can do, she'll find work in Bristol or Bath in a shop,' Meg said hopefully.

'But there's dangers in the city.'

'There's dangers everywhere.' Meg took his hand in hers and stroked it lovingly. 'But we've taught her right from wrong, loved her just as much as our own. We can't do more.'

Silas drank the last of his cider as the sun slipped down behind the hill.

'Maybe we could go to Lady Harvey,' he burst out suddenly. 'Tell her Hope is her own and get a pledge from her that she'll help the girl when the time comes.'

Meg looked shocked. 'Whatever are you thinking of, Silas?' she exclaimed. 'We can't do that! She'd think we were trying to blackmail her. Nell, Albert, James and Ruth, they'd all lose their positions. You'd probably lose yours too.'

'She wouldn't do that! Not after all the good service our family has given her.'

'Don't count on it.' Meg grimaced. 'A woman with a guilty secret is a dangerous animal.'

Chapter Four

1843

'Surely Father should be back by now!' Hope remarked. She was looking out of the window at the pelting rain. Her father had left on a cart for Bristol to collect some goods from a ship at the docks three days ago and he had been expected to return the same night.

Her mother sighed, for it wasn't the first time today that Hope had asked the same question. 'Ships can't be relied on if the weather's bad,' she explained. 'But he won't have liked staying in Bristol; he always says it's a noisy, filthy place.'

'And what can Joe and Henry be doing?' Hope said peevishly. 'Surely they can't work in this rain?'

Hope's brothers were thirteen and twelve now. Silas's hope of getting them apprenticed to a trade had been dashed because he hadn't been able to find the money for their indentures. The Reverend Gosling had done his best to find them positions as gardeners, grooms or footmen but without any luck. So until something better turned up they were doing casual work on farms, at present for Mr Francis of Woolard, who had sent Silas to Bristol.

'Cows have to be milked whatever the weather,' Meg replied a little sharply. 'But maybe they've lost a few and had to go out looking for them.'

Autumn had come early this year with high winds, storms and such heavy and prolonged rain that the river Chew burst its banks. The mill in their village was flooded out, and much of the recently harvested grain was lost. At Woolard and Publow several cottages had five feet of water rushing through them. They had heard that a child fell into the floodwater at Pensford and drowned. Everyone had rallied round to move cattle and sheep to higher ground, but many perished before they could be reached.

At night, Hope could hear the river rushing through the valley below their cottage, and although she knew they were too high up to be flooded, it was still frightening. Bad weather made all the daily chores so much harder. They got soaked going out to feed the chickens, they brought thick mud back into the cottage which meant more work, and when the wood they brought in was wet it wouldn't burn.

The vegetable garden had been laid to waste, apples and pears were knocked down before they were ripe and quickly rotted. Only a little hay had been cut before the rains came, and the rest was ruined. Down at the inn, old men sucked on their pipes and prophesied that a bitterly cold winter would follow and everyone would have to tighten their belts.

Hope knew what belt-tightening meant, for the last two years had been bleak for everyone. She no longer resented having to work so hard, especially on the farm with her father, because she understood the necessity of it now. It had always been expected that a farm worker's wife and children would help him at crucial periods, and though there was no extra pay for this, there was often some kind of reward like a couple of laying hens, a sack of potatoes or a bag of flour. But the reward, however welcome, wasn't as important as keeping the farmer's goodwill.

Life was precarious for all farm workers: if they had no work they couldn't pay their rent, and that could mean eviction, and ultimately the workhouse. The only way they could ensure they got work was to make themselves more valuable than any other man. A wife and several children ready to pitch in too helped to achieved this.

Hope had heard the chill in the word 'workhouse' or 'Union' even when she was too small to know what it was, or even where it was. But now she had seen the grim grey stone building in nearby Keynsham, and observed the misery etched into the faces of the destitute who finally had to resort to banging on its doors for shelter.

It was a very real threat for her family now. Last year's harvest had been a poor one, and now this spell of terrible weather was a potential disaster.

It wasn't only the Rentons' winter vegetables that had been destroyed; most of the farmers had lost theirs too. With nothing to sell at the market, and no hay stored for their animals during the winter, they'd be forced to sell them or watch them die of starvation. They wouldn't need farm workers then.

Last winter, when the snow lay on the ground for weeks, the family lived on turnips and potatoes because there was no money to buy meat. The boys set traps for rabbits without any success, and night after night they all went to bed hungry. But if there was more snow again this winter, they wouldn't even have vegetables to fall back on.

'Will we go down to the Merchants' farm tomorrow to see if the baby has been born?' Hope asked, hoping to cheer her mother as she seemed rather glum.

Matt and Amy's first child, Reuben, had been born the previous year. A second child was due any day now, but there was flooding around their farm.

'I think we must wait for dry weather,' Meg replied, but sighed because she was as anxious as Hope for news. 'Amy's got her mother with her, so she'll be fine, and Matt would ride up here if he needed us.'

'Why hasn't Nell had a baby?' Hope asked.

'Questions, questions, questions, that's all I get from you,' Meg snapped. 'The good Lord decides who is to have babies and those to leave without.'

Hope retreated into silence. She had sensed for some time that her parents were unhappy about Nell and Albert, for whenever Hope asked anything about them the reply was invariably a curt one. The family had only been invited to the gatehouse once, and that was some eighteen months ago on a Sunday. Nell had gone to a great deal of trouble, cooking roast lamb, several different vegetables and apple tart to follow, but the meal was overshadowed by Albert's critical remarks about her cooking, and Nell's nervousness.

Yet there had been suspicions that Albert was something of a bully even before that. Nell rarely came home to visit, and when she did, she never stayed longer than half an hour. On Sundays at church with Albert beside her she often looked drawn and anxious. Albert was polite enough, but standoffish, as if he thought his wife's family were beneath him. Ruth reported that Nell never lingered in the servants' hall after work for a chat any more, and even when the sisters were alone together Ruth claimed that Nell seemed unable to hold a real conversation, for she preceded every statement with '*Albert says*', suggesting that she'd lost the ability to express any view of her own.

Just a couple of months ago Hope had called on Nell at her cottage and asked her outright if she was happy with Albert. '*He's a good husband*,' had been her sister's reply, which wasn't exactly an answer to the question.

Daylight was fading when Silas finally returned home. Hope was just lighting the candles when the click of the door latch made her turn to see her father in the doorway, rain cascading off him on to the floor.

Meg gasped, for it was clear by his strained expression

that he was exhausted and chilled to the bone. 'Thank heaven you're back,' she said, rushing to peel the sodden sack from his shoulders. 'You must get out of those wet things this minute! Stir up the fire and make him some tea!' she ordered Hope, stripping off her husband's clothes as if he were a small child.

Once she had him in a chair by the fire with a blanket around him, a hot drink in his hand and his feet soaking in a mustard bath, she questioned him about his trip to Bristol.

'The ship wasn't unloaded so I had to stay in a lodging house. It were terrible.'

Meg got him into bed because he was shivering so violently, but he caught hold of her hand and tried to tell her how it had been for him. He wasn't entirely coherent, he couldn't even put whole sentences together, but the words he did use and the disgust in his voice painted a very vivid picture for both Meg and Hope about where he had stayed.

'Twelve or more men in one filthy room. Dirty straw. Low, brutish types, stupid with drink. Habits that turned my stomach. Animals behave better.'

Meg washed his face and hands tenderly, wrapping the blankets tightly around him and soothing him with the reminder he was safely home at last. But although his voice was becoming little more than a croak he seemed desperate for her to understand what he had been through.

Hope had been to Bristol twice, both times by day and in good weather, but however thrilling she'd found it, she hadn't forgotten the hordes of beggars, the noise, evil smells and the daunting hurly-burly of the place. It wasn't difficult to imagine how she would feel if she were alone, cold and soaked to the skin, compelled to hang around the docks for three days without anyone to turn to for help.

Her father spoke of ruffians who lay in wait for gullible

country folk, of the ragged half-starved child beggars who plagued him after seeing him give a couple of pennies to one of their number. He said there were painted floozies on every corner who loudly belittled him when he ignored them. And all the time there was the fear that any one of the many brutalized drunken men would attack a simple countryman like him just for the few shillings in his pocket, and even for his cart and horse.

Someone at the rooming house picked his pockets during the night. In the morning another man attempted to run off with his boots, and he'd had to run after him on bare feet and fight to get them back. He said he would have turned tail and come home right then, but he knew that Mr Francis would stop giving him and the boys work if he did. So he waited to collect the goods from the ship, cold, wet, hungry and frightened almost out of his wits. He said he would never go there again.

Yet although he said how hungry he had been, he only managed half a bowl of stew before sinking back on to the pillow. He was still shivering, and he said his head and back ached, so Meg got other blankets to cover him and put a hot brick by his feet.

Joe and Henry came back a little later, equally wet and downhearted because Mr Francis had not paid them, or even given them anything to eat. 'We've done a man's work, so we should get paid a man's wages,' Joe said heatedly. 'Mr Francis was grumbling all day because Father hadn't come back. I reckon me and Henry will have to go to London to find work. There ain't nothing fer us around here.'

The boys went to bed straight after their supper, but Hope stayed up with her mother, sensing that she was worried about her husband. Even by candlelight, Hope could see for herself he wasn't right. He appeared to be asleep but he was shivering still, while beads of sweat glistened on his forehead.

'He's a strong man, he'll be fine after a good night's sleep,' Meg said, but there was a hollow ring to her voice.

Hope woke in the night to the sound of her mother poking the fire and the smell of drying clothes. It was pitch dark and still raining hard.

'Is Father any better?' she whispered as she climbed down the loft ladder.

Meg shook her head. 'He won't be able to work for a day or two. He's really poorly.'

Hope went over to the bed in the corner, and although the light of the candle didn't reach that far, she fancied her father's face was unusually gaunt. 'Have you slept at all, Mother?' she asked.

'I lay down beside him for a while, but it was too hot in there for me.' Meg sighed. 'I couldn't take off any covers for he was still shivering, so I sat in the chair.'

'You go up and get into my bed,' Hope said. 'I'll watch over him.'

'Wake me at first light, and keep turning the boys' clothes till they're dry. I don't want them catching a chill too,' Meg said wearily. 'If your father wakes, give him some water. I'll go down to see Lizzie Brierley first thing and see if she can make me one of her mixtures.'

To Hope, that was confirmation of how frightened her mother really was, for she usually pooh-poohed the concoctions Lizzie made.

Over the next four days Hope watched her father grow sicker and sicker. He was feverish, holding his head in his hands because it hurt, and he could barely get up to relieve himself. Meg plied him with both the mixture she'd got from Lizzie and one of her own herbal infusions, good for fevers. She sponged him down when he was too hot, and put a hot brick in beside him when he shivered. Yet by the fourth morning he was muttering deliriously.

'Shall I go and get Nell?' Hope asked.

'No, of course not,' her mother snapped. 'It ain't right to ask anyone's help when there's sickness in the house.'

'But Nell should know how ill Father is,' Hope argued.

'What she don't know can't hurt her. She'd only come rushing round here and make more trouble for herself with Albert.'

Only a few weeks back Ruth had claimed she thought Albert hit Nell, and Father had said if this proved to be right he'd go round and wring the man's neck.

'Well, shall I go and get the doctor then?' Hope asked. She was frightened because Father didn't seem to know her or her mother.

'We've got no money for the doctor,' Meg replied, her eyes bleak with anxiety. 'You go into the bakery and see if they've got some work for you there, meanwhile I'll build up the fire and try to get him to sweat out the fever.'

Hope knew that her mother must be desperate for money to send her in to beg for work at the bakery, for she disliked Mrs Scragg, the baker's wife, as much as Hope did.

Mrs Scragg questioned Hope closely about Silas's sickness, clearly afraid it was something infectious, then set her to work outside, scouring out bread tins. By late afternoon Hope was more exhausted than if she'd been working all day in the fields. After the scouring of the bread tins she was made to clean out two storerooms, scrubbing the walls and floors. She'd drawn bucket after bucket of water from the well, mucked out the stable and washed a huge pile of aprons. For all this she was given a shilling and a loaf of bread.

Her mother stopped Hope at the door when she went home. 'Don't come in,' she said. 'Your father has a rash now; you and the boys must sleep in the outhouse until he improves.'

'Is it scarlet fever like with Violet and Prudence?' Hope asked, tears springing to her eyes because she sensed her mother was afraid he was going to die.

'I wish that's all it was, grown men get over that,' Meg said wearily. 'Go to the doctor, Hope. Tell him how your father was when he came back from Bristol, but that he's delirious now and the rash is a "mulberry" one. He'll know what that means. I don't expect he will call to see your father, but he might be able to give you some medicine for him if you give him that shilling.'

Dr Langford lived in Chewton, a hamlet on the way to Keynsham, a distance of two miles. Hope was too young when Violet and Prudence died to remember the doctor calling then, but she often saw the short, rotund man in a stove-pipe hat driving through the village in his gig, and at church. Her mother had said that years ago he set her father's arm when he broke it, and as they had no money to pay him they gave him a chicken instead. That gave Hope the idea he must be a kindly man, and as she hurried down through the village and up Fairy Hill, she wondered if he'd be kindly enough to give her a drink and maybe a bite to eat, and bring her home in his gig.

That hope was dashed when the lady who answered the door asked her to wait outside when she said her father was sick.

The doctor came out to see her immediately. He was wearing a fancy red waistcoat, and looked much smaller without his usual tall hat. Almost as soon as she began to launch into a description of her father's illness, she was aware he was backing away from her into the porch of his house.

'So he was sick when he came back from Bristol? And this was four days ago?'

Hope nodded. 'He'd had an awful time because he had to sleep in a dirty room at the docks with several other men. He was shivering really badly even after Mother made him get into bed. Now he doesn't even seem to know us!'

The doctor looked alarmed. 'Tell your mother she must keep the room well aired and the windows open,' he said. 'She must try and make him drink water and broth, and to boil any fouled linen. I will make up some medicine for him, but you children must keep well away from him.'

'Mother already told me we'll have to stay in the outhouse,' Hope said. 'Is it something very serious then?'

The doctor looked as if he didn't know how to reply. 'Your father's a strong man, so we can be optimistic. But wait there, Hope, I'll get you some medicine for him.'

'She's the younger sister of the two girls who died of scarlet fever, isn't she?' Dr Langford's wife asked as he came back into the house. 'Do you know what ails her father?'

'I hope I'm wrong, but it sounds like typhus,' the doctor replied with a grimace, going to his cabinet which held various kinds of medicines, ointments and salves. 'There was an outbreak of it at the workhouse recently, and of course Bristol gaol is never without it.'

Mrs Langford was very fastidious and she shuddered. 'But the Rentons aren't low people,' she said. 'I'm told their cottage is a model of cleanliness!'

The doctor sighed. 'He'll have caught it in the foul lodging house he had the misfortune to seek shelter in. Someone there had probably brought it in from a ship or a gaol. And by now his wife may be infected as well, perhaps even the children too.'

'Oh dear me,' Mrs Langford gasped. 'You didn't touch her, did you?'

The doctor gave her a withering glance, somewhat shocked that her first thought would be for herself. But he didn't feel able to reprimand her for lack of compassion, not when he had no intention of putting himself at risk by calling at the Rentons' cottage.

'Of course not. But I'd appreciate it if you'd put a few things in a basket for the child to take home. Brandy, perhaps, a few nourishing things that might stimulate their appetites. I shall send along some belladonna to slow Silas's pulse and help the headache, but sadly that's all I can do.'

'I won't go away,' Hope said firmly, pushing her way into the cottage. 'You're sick too, Mother, and I'm going to take care of you.'

It was ten days now since her father had come back from Bristol, and up till now she'd done exactly as her mother asked. She'd looked after the animals, chopped wood, drawn water, and slept in the outhouse alone every night.

Joe had been to Briargate and to the Merchants' farm to tell the rest of the family that their father was ill and they must all stay away. Mother had even insisted that Joe and Henry sleep in the barn down at the farm in Woolard rather than come home.

Hope couldn't understand why Nell hadn't come regardless of their mother's instructions. She knew Lady Harvey must have insisted Nell obeyed because she was afraid of her taking the disease back to Briargate and Rufus, but it was unlike Nell not at least to come to the gate with a parcel of food and check if there was anything further she could do.

Matt had come to give them the news that Amy had given birth to a little girl and to bring some milk and cheese. He'd shouted out from the lane to ask them to open the window. Mother acted cross with him and ordered him away, making him promise he wouldn't come back until she sent word that Silas was well again. But really she was glad he'd come, and Hope guessed that she hoped Nell would do likewise and secretly held Albert responsible for her failure to.

Hope hated sleeping alone in the outhouse. It was cold and the straw she'd stuffed into a sack for a bed felt damp. She was afraid, too, for she'd heard her father's incoherent ramblings and her mother crying.

But yesterday evening, when she went to the door to collect some supper, she'd seen her mother was ill too. She was swaying on her feet, beads of sweat on her forehead, and there was a hollow look to her eyes. Hope had done what she asked and fetched one more pail of water and another basket of wood before returning to the outhouse, but she'd spent most of the night awake with anxiety. This morning she'd decided she was going to disobey her mother.

'You are only eleven, much too young to take care of us, and I'm afraid you'll catch it too,' Meg said, trying to shut the door and stop her daughter coming in.

'I'm not too young to know you need to be in bed,' Hope argued, slipping in through the door before Meg managed to get it closed. 'I'll keep my distance from you if you like. But I'm not going to leave you two alone in here without anyone to help you.'

Meg was too weak to argue. Hope went up to the loft and dragged down one of the straw-filled sacks to make a bed for her mother by the fire, and the way she flopped down on it without another word proved to Hope she had caught whatever sickness it was that her father had.

Hope approached her father's bed purposefully, but recoiled in horror at his appearance. The rash her mother had spoken of six days ago had given his face and body a mottled look, with small eruptions that looked like measles. His teeth and gums were covered in a brown substance, he was breathing too fast, almost like a dog panting, and he was picking at the bedcover like a madman.

There was an evil smell coming from him and Hope guessed he'd lost control of his bowels. For a moment she almost ran back out through the door, but she glanced at her mother on the mattress by the fire and realized that if she did run away, her mother would force herself to get up and deal with it. She couldn't let her do that.

Washing her father and getting him back on to a clean sheet was the hardest thing she'd ever done. The smell made her retch, and he was so heavy to move. Yet somehow she managed it, and once he was covered up again she propped him up and made him drink some water.

She turned her attentions to her mother then, stripping off her clothes and washing her carefully. She was burning up, yet shivering the way Father had been in the early stages. Hope made her drink some water, then tucked the blankets around her tightly.

'I'm taking care of Father now, you just go to sleep,' she whispered.

There wasn't just the one dirty sheet to wash but several piled in the corner, along with a couple of nightshirts and undergarments. Remembering what the doctor had said about soiled linen, she went to the outhouse to light a fire under the copper.

Some of her earliest recollections were of her mother kneeling on the ground, blowing the flames and poking sticks in until she got a good blaze going. Hope had always helped her on washing day, rinsing the clothes in clean cold water, and then hanging the washing on the line. The one thing she'd always wanted to do, but was never allowed to, was stir the boiling washing. Mother always did that with the big copper stick, and once she was sure the clothes were clean, she fished the steaming garments out one by one into a big bowl.

It took eight buckets of water to fill the copper before she could start the fire, but that didn't prove as easy as it had looked when Mother did it. Hope twisted up some paper and lit that, then added small dry sticks one by one, but the flame flickered and then died. She tried again and again, for over an hour, each time with a little more paper, but still it went out, however much she blew on it.

Hope felt like crying. The sheets had to be boiled up, and if she couldn't do it there would be no clean ones if her father made another mess. The doctor had made a point about boiling them, so it stood to reason that dirty sheets were dangerous, perhaps carrying the sickness.

In her frustration she banged the copper with the poker, and it was only then that she noticed a little lever at the side of the fireplace. She pushed it, and to her surprise she saw it opened a small trap at the back, clearly to let in air, for she could feel a slight draught.

She tried to light it again, and to her delight at last the sticks began to burn. She added more and more, and only when she was absolutely certain she'd got it roaring did she turn her attention to grating up the soap.

That wasn't so easy either. She sliced her fingers twice before she got the hang of it. But finally the soap was in the water, and she could put the washing in.

By late afternoon Hope was exhausted. Between running in and out of the cottage giving her parents water, washing their faces, feeding the chickens, collecting the eggs and milking the cow, she'd had constantly to feed the copper fire with more wood. It took some two hours before the water began to boil, and it was an awful lot harder to stir it with the copper stick than she'd expected.

Hooking the washing out of the copper was harder still, and she splashed herself with the hot water several times. More water for rinsing had to be drawn, and by the time she was through her hands were red and raw.

At least it was a fine day, with a stiff enough wind to dry everything. Once it was all hanging up, she got instructions from her mother to make some beef tea with a small piece of beef a neighbour had left by the gate. She was folding up the clean dry sheets when she smelled the foul smell again from her father, and once again she had to clean him up and change his bed before trying to spoon some of the beef tea into him.

'You're such a good girl,' her mother said weakly as Hope helped her to sit up and drink some of the beef tea too. 'Is your father any better?'

Young as she was, without any first-hand experience of sickness, Hope sensed he was dying. He hadn't had one lucid moment today, and she'd only managed to make him swallow a few spoons of beef tea. It was as if the strong, hearty man she loved had already gone from the cottage.

'He's a bit better,' she lied, knowing that if she said otherwise her mother would try to get up to see him. 'He took some beef tea. He asked how you were.'

It was almost dark when Hope heard someone banging on the gate with a stick. She thought perhaps it was a neighbour, for there had been the piece of beef and other little offerings of pies, vegetables and jars of soup left on the doorstep in the last few days.

She ran out and to her relief it was Nell standing in the lane with a basket in her hand.

'I daren't come in,' she called out. 'Lady Harvey would never let me back into Briargate, and Albert will play merry hell. But I had to see you. How is Father?'

Hope wanted to run to her sister's arms, but she knew she couldn't. 'He's bad, and Mother's got it now,' she called out. 'I'm scared, Nell, I don't know what to do.'

Even in the dim light she could see her sister's anguished expression and knew she wanted to come in and take over. Yet as much as she needed Nell, she couldn't let that happen.

'Just tell me what else I can do,' Hope called out, quickly explaining how their parents were.

'You are doing all there is to do,' Nell said, her voice shaking. 'But you shouldn't have to be doing it, you are only a child. I should have disobeyed Albert right from the start and come here days ago.'

In that moment, Hope saw that Nell was afraid of Albert, and though it was too gloomy to see clearly she thought her sister's cheek looked bruised.

'We wouldn't have let you in,' Hope insisted. 'But Mother will be glad you came tonight. Just leave the basket there. I can manage.'

Hope watched Nell walk away, constantly turning her head back as if torn between love for her parents and duty to her mistress and husband.

Tears ran down Hope's face as Nell disappeared from sight for she understood her sister's dilemma. Only yesterday her mother had said that if five years ago she'd known there was scarlet fever in the village she would have kept Violet and Prudence at home. She also said that if she'd known her husband had brought this sickness back from Bristol, she would immediately have sent Hope away too.

Meg called it 'Ship Fever'; she said she'd seen it before when she was a girl. Her uncle, who was a sailor, caught it, and her mother had nursed him. But Meg didn't say whether he got over it or died.

Later that night Hope got down on her knees and prayed. 'Don't let them die, please!' she begged. 'I'll do anything,

I'll never complain about anything again. Just let them get better.'

As soon as she opened her eyes in the morning, Hope sensed something was wrong. She could hear the birds singing outside, and the sound of wind in the trees, but there was a strange stillness inside the cottage.

She had slept up in the loft to keep an eye on both her parents, and she was out of her bed and down the ladder as fast as her legs would carry her.

Going straight over to her father's bed, she stopped suddenly, clamping her hand over her mouth in horror. She didn't have to touch him to know he was dead. His fingers were not picking at the blankets as they had been all day yesterday. They were still, and his face had grown pale and calm.

Instinctively she turned to her mother for comfort, tears running down her cheeks, but saw immediately that she would get no comfort there. She had the mulberry rash now too, and although she appeared to be awake, her eyes open, there was the identical blankness her father had had.

Hope wanted to scream and stamp her feet, but instead all she did was stand there crying. For her entire eleven years she had been surrounded by older people who'd instructed her, admonished her, cared for her, but now she was alone, and it struck her that her childhood had come to an abrupt end.

She had to behave like an adult now. There was no one she could run screaming to as she'd so often done in the past over the most trivial of things. To call anyone in to help was to ask them to risk catching the disease and spreading it further. But she couldn't leave her mother to seek help anyway.

Forcing herself to go through the usual early-morning chores seemed to be the only thing to do. She raked out the fire and took the ash outside, then relaid the fire and lit it. The kettle went on, and she got a basin of water to wash her mother's face.

'Is it morning?' Meg murmured. 'I must get the boys up!'

'The boys aren't here, Mother,' Hope said, tears flowing again as she saw her mother was delirious just as her father had been. 'They're at work on the farm. It's just me here.'

She managed to feed her mother some milk with an egg beaten into it, and then she tore a sheet of paper from a notebook.

'Please help me,' she wrote in large letters. 'My father has died and my mother is very sick. I don't want anyone to come in and risk catching it too. But can you get the doctor? Call out and I'll speak to you from the door.'

She signed the note 'Hope Renton'. Then, taking it outside, she nailed it to the gatepost so it could be seen by anyone passing by.

The Reverend Gosling called out to Hope later in the morning as she was once again sponging her mother down with cool water.

She put the basin down and raced outside. She had always been a little intimidated by the tall, stern parson who had taught her to read and write, but she was glad it was he who called for he knew everything.

'My dear Hope,' he said, taking off his broad-brimmed black hat and holding it to his chest. The top of his head was bald, but the white hair left lower down was long, lank and rather greasy-looking. 'I am so sorry to hear your father has passed away. Are you alone with your mother?' His pale blue eyes looked far more kindly than usual, and even his thin lips, which always seemed to sneer instead of smile, had a softer look.

'Yes, Reverend.' She explained the circumstances as best

she could. 'Mother insisted the others were to stay away until Father was better. She said it was Ship Fever. She made me stay in the outhouse too, but I saw she was sick yesterday so I came in. Father was dead this morning and Mother is very bad now too. I've been washing her and giving her drinks and broth, but I don't know what to do about Father or how to make Mother well again.'

Hope was determined not to cry, but when she saw the Reverend Gosling move towards her, arms outstretched to embrace her, she couldn't help herself. 'You mustn't touch me,' she said weakly. But all at once his arms were round her anyway, and she leaned against his bony chest and sobbed.

'You poor child,' he said, his voice soft with sympathy. 'If you are brave enough to nurse your mother, then I can be brave enough to hold you. Are you well?' He took her two arms in his hands and holding her a little back from himself, studied her.

'Yes, Reverend,' she sobbed. 'There's nothing wrong with me. And I washed my hands after touching Father as Mother said I must do. But the disease is in the air, isn't it? We breathe it in.'

'I cannot believe that, for if it were the case it would spread all across the country and no one would be spared. This disease flourishes only in crowded, unsanitary places, like ships and gaols. Did your mother sleep in the bed with your father when he got home from Bristol?'

Hope nodded.

'That would be how she caught it,' the Reverend Gosling said sadly. 'But of course she wouldn't have known what it was then. Now, let me come in and see her.'

Despite all the Reverend Gosling's prayers, and getting Mrs Calway to come in and help nurse Meg, she died two days after Silas. She seemed to rally a little, enough perhaps to realize her husband was gone, but then she seemed to give up fighting the sickness and died during the night. When he called the following morning, the Reverend Gosling said that it was perhaps a blessing that she died quickly without the indignity Silas had suffered. Hope had to agree with that, for she knew her mother would have hated to have anyone clearing up her bodily wastes. But that didn't soothe the pain of losing her.

Mrs Calway washed both Meg and Silas and laid them out. Her husband Geoffrey, the village carpenter, brought up the coffins, and Matt and James lifted them in.

The coffins stood on trestles, and Hope scoured the fields and woodland around the cottage for wild flowers to decorate them. However much everyone praised her for looking after their parents, she couldn't help but feel there must have been something she could have done to prevent their deaths.

The morning of the funeral was a beautiful sunny day. There had been mist first thing, but it cleared quickly. Hope stood looking down at the river for a long time before her brothers and sisters arrived, remembering how much her father had always liked this time of year.

'When the harvest is in, and the fields ploughed, I get the feeling the Lord likes to reward us all with a display of His greatness,' he used to say. He would wave a hand at the trees in their autumn colouring, and his eyes would become damp with emotion.

Many of the trees had come down in the recent storms, and others had lost their leaves prematurely, yet the valley was still a patchwork of orange, yellow, russet, scarlet, green and brown. The river, half hidden all summer, was revealed in all its sparkling glory, squirrels scampered up and down trees searching for hazelnuts, and fluffy Old Man's Beard scrambled over hedges. Hope remembered all the times she'd picked blackberries and elderberries with her mother, the way she used to laugh and hold Hope up in her arms to reach the high ones. It was unbearable to think she would never hear that laugh again and never see her parents sitting together on the bench under the apple tree on summer evenings, their hands entwined.

Later that morning as Matt screwed down the coffin lids, Hope looked around at her gathered family and wished she was in a third coffin.

Nell was sobbing, her face against Albert's chest. Amy looked pale and anxious, as if afraid the disease was still lurking in the cottage and she might carry it home to her new baby and Reuben. Matt was grim-faced, struggling to control his emotions, and Ruth and Alice were clinging to each other while James and Toby stood by shuffling awkwardly, not knowing what to do or say.

Joe and Henry were stiff and white-faced. Though not yet men at thirteen and twelve, they were too old to cry, and perhaps they were remembering that one of the last things they said to their parents was that they would go to London for there was nothing for them here.

Hope felt like the odd one out. The other ten all had a close bond with someone else in the family; Matt had Amy and Nell had Albert. It was true that every one of them had put their arms around her and indeed promised she would be taken care of, but she still felt very alone.

The mattress on her parents' bed had been burned, as had all the straw-filled sacks from the loft. She and Jane Calway had scrubbed the whole cottage from top to bottom with vinegar and water. Every piece of linen had been boiled, blankets washed, the chairs and table scrubbed. They had burned sweet-smelling herbs on the fire to rid the cottage of any lingering pestilence, but it would never be a home again.

As yet no one had dared talk about tomorrow, next week or next month. They must surely all realize that the cottage would go, and once it had there would be no place they would gather as a family. Hope could see by Albert's coldness that he wasn't likely to suggest the gatehouse became the Renton meeting place. Matt and Amy only had one room in her parents' farmhouse, so how could they extend an invitation?

James and Ruth would go back to Briargate, Toby and Alice to Bath. Joe and Henry would possibly stay at Mr Francis's place. All in twos, except for her.

Almost everyone in the village, and many from the neighbouring ones too, turned out for the funeral, a mark of their respect for Silas and Meg Renton. Mr Francis, Mr Warren, Mr Carpenter and Mr Miles, all farmers Silas had worked for many, many times, were there with their wives. Frank and Dorothy Nichols were there with their two daughters, Gareth Peregrine, the Boxes, big Nigel with the red hair from the blacksmith's, and Fred Humphreys. Bunches of Michaelmas daisies and chrysanthemums had been brought by everyone who grew flowers in their gardens, and Hope thought they were far more beautiful and meaningful than the hothouse roses and carnations sent by Sir William and Lady Harvey.

Nell, Ruth and Alice cried throughout the service. Even when Hope didn't hear them, she sensed their shuddering shoulders and fingers clenched round sodden handkerchiefs. Her eyes prickled when Reverend Gosling spoke of how devoted Silas and Meg had been to each other, and that their children were a credit to their love and care. But she didn't cry properly until her father's coffin was lowered into the ground, beside Violet and Prudence's small grave, and then her mother's was put on top.

It wasn't, as people said later, that she suddenly realized they were gone for good. She'd known that the minute her mother died. What made her sob was the knowledge that Meg gave up when she knew Silas was dead. She couldn't live without him, not even for her children's sake. She would rather be in the churchyard with him than back in the cottage watching her children grow up, marry and have children of their own. That seemed so selfish to Hope when she'd tried so hard to keep her alive; didn't she realize that her youngest daughter still needed her?

'You will come home with Albert and me,' Nell murmured into Hope's hair as she rocked her younger sister in her arms to comfort her.

They were all in the cottage garden, the family and a few neighbours. It was lucky the sun was so warm, for no one seemed to want to go inside. Toby and Alice would be leaving soon for the long walk back to Bath, and Mr Francis had offered Joe and Henry a room above his stables and a wage each if they would take over the work their father had always done.

'Albert won't want me there,' Hope sobbed. She had seen him looking at her grimly several times since the funeral. He wouldn't want anyone, not even a dog, cluttering up his extraordinarily tidy gatehouse.

'Don't be foolish,' Nell said, stroking her hair. 'Albert knows as well as anyone that you can't stay here alone. I spoke to Lady Harvey yesterday and she said it would be fine, and she thought maybe you could help Cook out in the kitchen.'

Hope dried her eyes, not because she was satisfied she

was really wanted, but because she knew there was no alternative. No one else had offered to take her in, and she loved Nell and liked the idea of helping Cook at Briargate. She would just have to put up with Albert.

Nell washed up the last of the cups and plates, wiped over the table and then sat down for a moment to rest. Albert was talking to Mr Merchant, Matt's father-in-law, and he seemed to have forgotten he was anxious to get home just fifteen minutes ago.

Albert had no real idea how she felt. He seemed to be missing the part which enabled most people to understand another's grief. She'd had more sympathy from Lady Harvey, Baines and Cook than she'd had from Albert. Only this morning he'd said, 'You'll feel better after the funeral.' As if she could just forget twenty-seven years of memories the moment the earth was shovelled over the coffins!

She was utterly devastated at losing her parents, and she wished to God she'd defied both Albert and Lady Harvey and come to the cottage before it was too late. Maybe she couldn't have done anything to save them, but at least she wouldn't have this terrible guilt that she had done nothing.

Yet she was even more ashamed that she hadn't been brave enough to put her foot down with Albert right from the first day they were married, and insisted on spending her afternoons off with her family. What right did he have to say her place was in their home and her parents weren't important? In three years of marriage she'd only spent a total of perhaps five or six hours with them, and that was mostly on the way home from church with Albert. She got the family news second-hand through Ruth, and she hadn't once been able to sit down and really talk to her mother and father and explain things.

But she supposed that if she had had that opportunity

she might have revealed to her mother that she regretted marrying Albert and admitted that he often hit her.

She glanced out through the door, almost as if she believed he was capable of reading her thoughts. But she'd got so used to him ordering everything in her life, from what she cooked to how the furniture was arranged, how she swept the floor or did the washing, that she didn't even feel her mind belonged to her any longer.

He was still deep in conversation with Mr Merchant. That was another thing about Albert; he would only talk to people who were successful or well-bred, and the Merchants qualified because they owned their own farm. He once remarked 'how wise' Matt had been to marry Amy! As if wisdom had come into it! Matt had acted on his heart, nothing else.

Sadly, Nell realized that Albert had only married her because she was so close to Lady Harvey. He didn't want to live above the stables with the grooms, he wanted a house of his own and someone he could lord it over. He knew the mistress wouldn't want to lose Nell, and the gatehouse cottage was empty.

How well it had worked out for him! A wife who obeyed him implicitly, a cottage furnished with castoffs from Briargate, and he could act the big man in the ale house in Chelwood because he was favoured by Sir William.

Nell often wondered what those same men would think of the 'big man' if they knew he had a marriage in name only. There was no married love: he slept in the bed with her, but nothing else ever took place. She felt he despised women, for when she'd tried to tempt him into it when they first got married, he'd slapped her and said she was a dirty whore. She'd never tried it again.

She could almost resign herself to a life without love, and to being less than his maid of all work, but she couldn't accept that she would never have children of her own. That was too cruel.

Glancing out of the door, she saw Hope sitting alone under the apple tree, staring at the view as if trying to hold on to all the good memories it evoked. Nell's tears began to flow again, for she loved Hope so much and couldn't bear to see her so unhappy. She wanted and needed to take her home with her, but she was afraid to. Albert didn't want her there.

He hadn't said it in so many words. He couldn't because everyone at Briargate, including Lady Harvey, expected him to welcome Hope. No one who knew the child would consider her a burden, and Albert would be thought at best uncharitable, at worst a brute, if he refused to take her in. Today, talking to Matt and James, he'd acted as if he welcomed the idea of a child about the house.

But Nell knew the truth. Albert thought only about Albert. He had no tenderness, no compassion. He wanted his life to be like one of his wretched flowerbeds. He dictated what was to go into it. He would whisk anything out that wasn't exactly as he planned, cut back anything that threatened to dominate.

Hope wouldn't fit in at all.

Chapter Five

'Hurry up, Hope,' Nell whispered. 'He's getting cross.'

Hope said nothing, and continued to tie her bootlaces at the same leisurely pace. Albert liked to ape the gentry, insisting Nell should lay the breakfast table properly every morning and wait on him. He also expected Hope to be completely ready for work before joining him at the table.

She thought it was ridiculous laying the table when there was nothing more to eat than a slice of bread. Her father used to swig his tea down as he got dressed, then grab the bread and eat it on the way to his work. But then, he preferred to spend an extra ten minutes cuddling her mother in bed, and he wouldn't have dreamt of giving her the extra work of laying the table at five in the morning.

Hope couldn't voice her opinion because Albert would take it out on Nell, so the only form of protest open to her was to be so slow getting ready that she didn't have to sit there with him.

Albert got up, his chair scraping on the stone floor. 'Right! Nothing for you,' he snapped at her. 'Nell, clear the table. She's got to learn the hard way.'

Hope stifled a giggle. She didn't want any bread anyway; when she got to the big house Cook would give her porridge with honey on it.

Nell had put his coat in front of the fire to warm it,

another thing Albert insisted on. He snatched it up, then turned to his wife. 'Don't you dare give her anything,' he said, pointing a finger at Hope. 'I shall check the bread when I come back later.'

He left without a goodbye, and slammed the door behind him. Hope giggled.

Nell half-smiled, for she knew about the porridge – she always had some herself too. 'I wish you wouldn't tease him that way. Can't you do what he wants, just for me?'

'I would if it made him nicer,' Hope said wistfully, and she went to her sister and hugged her. 'I'm never going to get married if that's what men are like.'

'They aren't all like it,' Nell reminded her. 'Remember Father, and look at the way Matt is. But you'd better go, or you'll be late.'

'Not me,' Hope grinned. 'I'll be there before Albert.'

Once outside the cottage door, Hope broke into a run. Albert was half-way up the drive, but she knew she could beat him to the house easily. She liked running, especially on a frosty February morning like this one, even if it wasn't considered ladylike. She would arrive at Briargate with rosy cheeks, warm inside and out, and it would even make her forget how much she hated her brother-in-law.

She ran past him at full pelt, and once she was well out of his reach turned round to face him and waved cheekily. With luck he would be freezing cold all day working outside. If he'd only learn to be nice to people, Cook would let him into the kitchen to get warmed up and give him porridge too.

It was only four months since her parents had died, but it seemed like years. Some days the ache for them was so acute she thought she could die of it. Their faces were imprinted on her mind, she heard their voices inside her head, and curiously, it was the things that she'd hardly noticed when they were alive that she missed most. The way Father would cluck her under the chin when he came in from work or Mother would always kiss her forehead when she'd finished brushing her hair. This was tangible evidence of their love for her, for neither of her parents was the type to put their feelings into words.

Yet they had been so big on communication in the family. They wanted to know everything everyone had done each day; no one ever escaped being questioned about who they'd seen or talked to.

Nell had been just the same before she married Albert. Every time she came to the cottage she wanted to know every single thing that had happened since her last visit. Hope's earliest memories were of vying with Joe and Henry to get to her lap first and Nell sitting on the floor so all three of them could have a bit of her. She was so gay and fun-loving, always ready to play with them, but so tender and caring too.

Hope thought she wouldn't miss her parents so much if Nell had still been that person, but she was tense and watchful now, rarely laughing when Albert was there, and for ever cleaning and tidying. There was no conversation at all between Nell and Albert. Nell might ask what he'd done during the day, but his curt replies implied he resented her even speaking. It wasn't even possible for Hope and Nell to talk together, either, for he would glare at them, and that made Nell more nervous.

Albert was a tyrant, just as Hope had suspected. He showed no love for Nell; in truth he treated her as though she was his servant. He never lit the fire for her or brought in a pail of water. He would watch as she struggled to empty the tin bath or chop wood. He looked for things out of place – mud on the floor, the rug not straight in front of the fire, dust on the mantelpiece – and then he'd drag Nell over to it, pointing at it as if she were a dog who had pissed in the house.

Once she'd forgotten to make their bed, and when she got back from Briargate late in the evening, he pounced on her and, holding her by the ear, dragged her upstairs to point out her mistake. He seemed to forget she had a job too, and that sometimes she worked far longer days than him. It was always 'What's this?' 'Why have you done that?' or 'How many times do I have to tell you?' He seemed incapable of praise, gratitude or even plain kindness.

The only good times were when he went to the ale house at Chelwood. Hope and Nell would get right up close to the fire and chat about the past, and things that went on in Briargate. But even then Nell couldn't relax completely for she always had one ear cocked for Albert returning, and if he was tipsy he could be even nastier than usual.

Sundays were simply interminable. Nell went off to the big house very early, and Hope had to make the long walk to church alone with Albert. He never spoke, and although once they got to the village the sight of all her old friends and neighbours made her feel the loss of her parents even more keenly, he would not allow her more than the briefest of greetings. If Lady Harvey had guests, Nell had to return to Briargate after church, and Hope had to cook Albert's dinner. Nothing she ever did was right, even though she'd become quite good at cooking since helping in the kitchens.

Later, he would sit right in front of the fire, blocking any heat from her, and he wouldn't allow her to read anything other than the Bible. Those hours alone with him were the ones she dreaded most, for he was a violent man when crossed. He had hit her on several occasions and she knew he often beat Nell, even if she refused to admit it. So, alone with him, Hope had to be extra careful she gave him no excuse to round on her.

Working at Briargate was the only thing that made her life tolerable. She could forget about Albert there because she saw Ruth and James every day, and Cook, Mr Baines and the other servants made her feel she was part of a big family again. Like any family, they were sometimes grumpy and short with her, but she knew in her heart that they liked her, and that went some way to compensate for Albert.

During the time she'd come to Briargate to play with Rufus she had never imagined that one day she'd be expected to scrub pots and pans in the scullery, or spend hours cutting up vegetables, and sometimes she resented that she had to. She so much wanted to go beyond the kitchen, to walk up that beautiful staircase the way she used to and go into the nursery to see Rufus.

But that wasn't allowed. She had to refer to him as Master Rufus now, just like everyone else. The closest she got to him was when she helped with the laundry and had to wash one of his shirts or undergarments. Occasionally he came down to the kitchen to see Cook, and from her position in the scullery she marvelled at his clear, rather high, commanding voice, for she remembered him with a babyish lisp. If she peeped round the door it was hard to believe that the little gentleman in a stiff collar, dark jacket and breeches was the same boy who used to roll around the nursery floor with her, dressed in a sailor suit.

She did, of course, see him at church almost every Sunday. But as the Harveys' pew was right at the front of the church, and her family sat at the back, she only got a glimpse of his blond hair. Before her parents died, Hope had often tried to speak to him in the churchyard, but though his little face would light up when he saw her, Miss Bird, his governess, prevented him from coming to speak to her.

Her mother had always said she'd better learn quickly that gentry didn't want their children mixing with common folk, but Hope didn't see herself as that. She had, after all, been brought up with the story that she was a fairy child, and to her that meant she was destined for better things. While for now she knew she had to keep her place and do whatever she was ordered to do, she comforted herself with the thought that one day she'd be her own mistress.

Baines was very fond of saying that there were few opportunities for girls other than going into service, but then he'd been a servant since he was twelve, so what did he know of the real world? Cook would smile knowingly whenever Hope spoke of wanting to do some other kind of work; she seemed to think marriage was a far better option. But any romantic notions Hope might once have held about marriage had been killed off by observing Nell and Albert. To her, being in service or marriage amounted to much the same thing, a lifetime of drudgery. She wanted something better for herself.

Hope was cleaning some silver in the scullery in the early afternoon when she heard Rose come into the kitchen.

'Captain Pettigrew's come a-calling again,' she said importantly to Cook. 'Funny he always comes when the master is away!'

'Rose!' Cook exclaimed. 'You shouldn't say such things. If Mr Baines was to hear you!'

Hope was out of sight of the two older women but well within hearing distance. She had to hope Baines wasn't too, because Cook was right. Hardly a week passed without him reminding them all that they should not repeat anything they heard or saw their master and mistress doing.

Baines was tall and whip-thin, and in his grey striped trousers, tailed coat and stiff wing-collar, with spectacles perched precariously on the end of his overlong nose, he put Hope in mind of a heron.

He had the sharp eyes, grace and patience of the heron too. He missed nothing, not a smear on a knife or a napkin not properly ironed, and he expected all the servants to maintain the high standards he set so much store by. But for all that he was a kindly, fair man, and he seemed to have the answer to any question and the solution to any problem. Cook always said he was the first butler she'd ever worked under who wasn't an arse-wipe.

Cook also said that when Rose first came to Briargate, she had set her cap at Baines and been very disappointed when he didn't respond. Now in her late thirties, a plain, angular woman who knew she was destined to remain a spinster, she was over-fond of poking her nose into other people's affairs, be that her master and mistress's or the other servants'.

'The Captain's charming, I grant him that,' Rose went on, seemingly not put off by Cook's warning. 'Devilish handsome too! Nell got all in a fluster when she saw him.'

Hope's antennae became finely tuned at Nell's name, and although she continued polishing the candlestick in her hand, she slowed down so she wouldn't miss anything.

'I'd get in a fluster over a charming man too if I was married to Albert,' Cook retorted and chuckled.

Hope smiled; she was always glad when one of the servants admitted they didn't like Albert. They were discreet in front of Nell, but away from her they agreed he was pompous, self-righteous and entirely lacking a sense of humour. Hope could easily have added half a dozen more bad traits, but for Nell's sake she kept those to herself. She had never admitted to anyone, not even James and Ruth, how bad it was living with him.

'I don't mean that I think Nell's sweet on him,' Rose said quickly. 'It's more like she saw Old Nick come through the door. Is she afraid for the mistress? Or has the Captain done something to her?'

'If you know what's good for you, you'll keep such thoughts to yourself,' Cook retorted sharply.

Hope was brimming over with curiosity now; she had to take a look at this man who flustered Nell.

Unfortunately she had no excuse to go anywhere in the house. She was a kitchenmaid, and the kitchen was where she had to stay.

Cook always had a little rest between three and four in the afternoon. Mostly she just sat in her chair by the stove and dozed a little, but that afternoon her legs, which often troubled her, were very swollen and she said she was going to have a lie-down in her room.

'If I'm not back here by four, put the kettle on for tea and come and get me,' she said to Hope.

Baines was in his parlour busy with his accounts, Rose was in the dining room laying the table for supper, and Ruby had the afternoon off and had gone down to the village. With everyone gone, Hope got on with scrubbing the kitchen and scullery floor. When she came back in from tipping the dirty water away out in the yard, she was surprised to see it was almost four, and Cook wasn't back.

This had never happened before. Cook always asked to be called, but it was never needed. While it was the excuse Hope had wanted to go beyond the kitchen, she was suddenly nervous. She put the kettle on, changed her apron, straightened her cap, and after a few minutes' hesitation went out into the hall.

The backstairs on the east side of the house that led from beyond the servants' hall right up to the attic rooms were the ones she was supposed to use, but she wouldn't catch even a glimpse of the Captain that way. But if she took a chance on crossing the hall, going up the main staircase and then nipping along the landing past the master and mistress's rooms, if anyone saw her before she reached the backstairs, she'd be in trouble.

Hearing Lady Harvey's voice coming from the drawing room, which meant the door was open, she turned back. Maybe it would be better to watch for the Captain going round to the stables to get his horse – no one could tell her off for going out into the yard.

As she made her way up the backstairs, Hope reflected on their meanness. They were narrow and steep, and the plain whitewashed walls were marked and gouged from the passage of so many servants carrying heavy loads up and down them. It always seemed absurd to her that while servants had intimate knowledge of their master and mistress's bodies, personal habits and every other aspect of their lives, they had to use a separate staircase.

Hope rapped on Cook's door and called out that it was after four. When there was no reply she opened the door and peeped in.

But instead of finding Cook still fast asleep as she expected, she was lying face down on the floor.

'Cook!' she exclaimed in dismay, rushing to her and rolling her over.

To her horror the older woman's face was chalky-white, with an angry red mark on the forehead, clearly the result of banging her head on the bed as she fell. Her skin was ice-cold, and when she didn't respond in any way to Hope chafing her hands, the girl thought she was dead.

Hope rushed out of the room and clattered down the backstairs two at a time, then, because she was so panicked about Cook, she ran straight for Lady Harvey in the drawing room.

'It's Cook, m'lady,' she blurted out as she charged in. 'She's fallen down in her room and I think she's dead.'

'You didn't knock!' Lady Harvey reproved her. 'Whatever

are you thinking of, Hope? It's Baines who deals with the servants.'

Hope had not only forgotten her manners and Baines, but in her haste she'd forgotten about the Captain. He had jumped out of his chair by the fire as she rushed in, and she immediately recognized him as the same tall and slender man she'd seen in the front garden on her first visit to Briargate almost six years earlier.

'She's just a child,' he said, looking askance at Lady Harvey. 'Look how frightened she is!'

'She's all cold and stiff.' Hope directed this at the Captain for he was clearly more sympathetic than her mistress. 'I turned her over because she was on her face, but I couldn't lift her on to the bed on my own.'

'Has she complained of feeling unwell?' Lady Harvey asked, finally getting to her feet. Her face was cold and stiff too, but Hope realized this was through anger at the interruption.

'No, m'lady,' Hope said, tears springing to her eyes with shock. 'She said her legs were bad, that's all, and she'd have a lie-down for an hour. She said I was to call her if she wasn't down again by four.'

'We must get a doctor of course,' the Captain said. 'But I have a little medical knowledge, m'lady, so maybe I could go up to see what I can do until he gets here?'

'Yes, of course, Captain Pettigrew.' Lady Harvey looked flustered now. She turned to Hope. 'You go and tell James to saddle up, and fetch Nell too.'

The Captain strode out of the room, Lady Harvey following him. Hope ran out to the stables and told James what had happened, then tore back up the stairs to find Nell.

She was in the little room next to Lady Harvey's bedroom where she did her sewing. As the door opened her eyes widened in alarm.

Hope ran into her arms and told her what had happened. 'I think she's dead, Nell,' she sobbed out. 'And Lady Harvey didn't even care, she said I should have got Baines.'

'That's just her way,' Nell said. 'She don't really mean it, 'spect it was a shock to her too. You go on downstairs again, I'll go up and see what I can do.'

The house had been as quiet as a church all the time Hope had been scrubbing the kitchen floor but as Nell rushed up to the attic and Hope ran back down the stairs, suddenly there was tumult. Baines appeared in the hall demanding to know what was going on, Rose came out of the dining room and Rufus came haring out of the schoolroom, closely followed by a distracted-looking Miss Bird calling out that his lessons weren't over yet. Ruth was there behind them too, looking startled; later she was to admit to Hope her first thought was that she'd been up to some mischief.

Ruth was still called nursemaid, and saw to Rufus before and after his lessons, but she filled in the time she wasn't with him by standing in wherever she was needed. This meant she did Rose, Ruby and Nell's jobs on their afternoons off, and quite often helped Cook when there was a dinner party. She was closer to Cook than any one, and looked stricken when she was told what had happened.

Everyone forgot their place, even Baines, and they were out in the big hall all talking at once when the Captain came back down the stairs.

'Back into the kitchen with you,' he said, but his tone was gentle and understanding. 'Cook is not dead fortunately, but she is gravely ill. I believe it is her heart.'

He herded them all back into the kitchen and came with them, saying that sick people needed quiet. James was waiting on the saddled horse for instructions and the Captain went out and told him to ride for the doctor. When he returned he made the suggestion that Ruth should go up and stay with Cook until the doctor arrived, and that Nell should go to her mistress as she was in shock.

'And you, little one,' he said, turning to Hope. 'I think you should make tea for everyone. Can you do that?'

Until then, Hope had looked upon Baines as the most admirable man she knew. Yet suddenly the Captain seemed far more impressive for he'd not only taken her part against Lady Harvey, he'd also taken command of the whole house. She could see exactly why he made Nell flustered, for he was so handsome with his large dark eyes and sharp cheekbones. She felt warm inside that he'd called her 'little one', for her father used to call her that. But there was something more; she thought it was wonderful the way he looked directly at each person he spoke to, taking in their name, their position in the house and even their character, as if he considered every one of them of vital importance. She'd never before met anyone quite like him; Sir William wasn't that way at all; he walked past everyone with barely a nod. Hope didn't think he even knew who worked for him, let alone their names.

Once the Captain had gone back into the drawing room, he said he'd wait there until the doctor came in case he was needed. Baines cleared his throat and gave out his instructions.

Hope felt that although he said he was glad the Captain had been here in the emergency, he was a bit annoyed that a visitor had taken over his role.

'It may be weeks before Cook is well enough to work again,' he said, but the sad tone of his voice hinted that he didn't expect to see her in the kitchen ever again. 'Meanwhile we must all keep the house running smoothly by pitching in and doing extra duties.'

He divided up Rose's parlourmaid duties between the

other maids and told Rose she would have to take Cook's place.

'I can't do that, Mr Baines.' Rose looked aghast. 'Nell and Ruth are both much better at it than me.'

Baines shrugged. 'Then it will be useful practice for you. Hope will help you – she may be very young but Cook has trained her well.'

Hope glowed at the words of praise, but a second later she was smarting because Baines said she would also have to help Ruby with the fire-lighting in the mornings. In effect this would mean Hope would have to do almost all of it, for Ruby was slow, and struggled with just the fires in the nursery and schoolroom.

Baines then went on to say he was also going to ask Lady Harvey if she would consider cancelling the big dinner party she had planned for the following week as Rose was not an experienced cook.

Baines had only just left the kitchen when Albert came to the back door. He was very dirty and his face was like thunder.

'Why are you still here?' he snarled at Hope. 'The fire's out and there's no supper for me.'

Because of all the drama, Hope hadn't noticed that it was well after six. She always went home after laying the tray for Master Rufus's tea, and it was her job to stir up the fire, put the kettle on and heat up whatever Nell had made for Albert's supper in readiness for his return home around six.

'I'm sorry,' she said, then launched into an explanation about Cook.

'That's no concern of mine,' he snapped, cutting her off in mid-sentence. 'A man who has been working outside all day needs his victuals. Get home now.'

Rose came into the kitchen just as Hope was getting her

shawl and bonnet. 'Nell won't be home tonight,' she called out to Albert. 'Baines thinks she might be needed here.'

Hope's heart sank as she saw Albert's face darken even further at discovering he would be without his personal lackey for the night, but Rose had now aggravated him still further by speaking so dismissively.

There was a sharp frost again, and Hope shivered as she trotted along behind Albert in the dark. She was scared: to her knowledge Nell hadn't been able to slip home earlier in the day to prepare some food for his supper as she usually did. If the fire had gone out too, it would be ages before Hope would be able to rustle something up. Albert wasn't going to like that.

The cottage was icy cold, the stove out. This was evidence Nell hadn't been back during the day as she always put more fuel on it when she came in. Hope quickly raked it out, laid a few dry twigs over some paper and then set light to it. She was very nervous because Albert was standing over her, glowering, and she offered up a silent prayer that it wouldn't go out. Luck was on her side: the wood caught quickly and as she slowly added larger pieces of wood they blazed merrily.

'Let me take your coat, and you sit down here where it's warmer,' she said, looking up at Albert. She wouldn't normally have spoken so sweetly to him, but she was afraid he was going to explode.

'I want hot tea and something in my belly,' he snarled. 'And quickly.'

Hope put the kettle on and scuttled out to look in the pantry which was situated in the lean-to scullery. There was half a loaf of bread, some cheese and the remains of the lamb stew from the previous night. She breathed a sigh of relief that she wouldn't have to prepare something from scratch.

Within fifteen minutes Hope had the kettle on the boil, the table laid and the potatoes cooking. She had added a few lumps of coal to the stove to keep the blaze more constant, and as she warmed the teapot she tipped some of the hot water from the kettle into a bowl for Albert to wash his hands.

'There you are,' she said, adding a little cold water to it. 'The tea will be made by the time your hands are clean.'

She glanced round as he was washing and saw he was looking at a bad cut on the palm of his hand. 'That looks nasty,' she said in sympathy.

'This is what I get in my line of work,' he hissed at her, as if it was her fault. 'Hands so stiff with cold I sometimes don't know I've cut them. By then the dirt's got in, and one day a cut like this will become poisoned, and then where will I be?'

Hope couldn't understand why he was so angry. It appeared to be more than just the cold cottage and having to wait for his supper. 'Let me put something on it,' she said. 'Nell's got some ointment that's good for cuts.'

'I want my supper,' he roared at her. 'Not fucking ointment.'

She was shocked that he'd use that terrible oath in her hearing. There had been a casual worker last year at the haymaking who had used it in front of her and her mother, and Father had punched him on the jaw for it.

Turning away in disgust, she made the tea and poured him a cup without speaking. She hoped his hand would become infected, then his arm and finally his whole body. He was hateful.

Hope got up when she heard the mantel clock chime five. It was pitch dark outside and very cold. She lit a candle, wrapped her shawl around her nightgown and tiptoed past Albert's room.

He had gone to bed the minute he'd finished his supper, much to her relief as she had fully expected that he would start finding more fault with her. She took herself off to bed as soon as she'd cleared up, but she hadn't been able to sleep for thinking about Cook, and who would replace her if she died.

The stove hadn't quite gone out, thanks to the coal dust she'd put on it before turning in. She managed to stir it into life, and used the warm water in the kettle to wash herself. She thought she would get herself ready, then call Albert just before she left. That way she wouldn't have to face him again until the evening.

'Albert, it's time to get up,' she said gingerly. 'The fire's lit and the kettle's almost boiling. I have to go now.'

She couldn't see him in the darkness, but he grunted at her call and turned over, making the bedsprings squeak.

'Don't go back to sleep again, it's nearly half past five,' she said, louder this time.

He muttered something, enough to know she'd woken him, so she turned and went back downstairs to put her boots on.

She'd got one boot laced when he appeared on the stairs in his long woolly underclothes. 'You haven't laid the table for me,' he said indignantly as he got down to the kitchen.

'I haven't got time for that nonsense,' she said without thinking. 'I've got fires—'

Before she even finished the sentence he slapped her round the face so hard she felt as if her head had come off her shoulders.

'That nonsense!' he roared indignantly. 'I've been trying to teach you Renton pigs some polite behaviour.'

Hurt as she was, Hope wasn't going to snivel to him. 'Is it polite behaviour to hit women?' she yelled back at him.

He pounced on her, both hands going round her neck as if to strangle her. He lifted her right off her feet and then smashed her head back against the wall. He let her drop, and as she fell to the floor he kicked her in the stomach.

'You will never answer me back again,' he snarled at her. 'I could have sent you to the workhouse, but out of the goodness of my heart I let you come here to live. For that I expect gratitude and humility.'

With his lips curled back, bloodshot eyes, matted black hair and a sour smell wafting from him, he was terrifying as he glowered down at her.

She was too hurt even to cry, but when he turned away for a moment she knew she must seize the opportunity. She got up gingerly, then bolted for the door, threw it open and ran out.

After just a few yards the pain in her stomach made her double up. The wind was bitterly cold, cutting through her like a knife, and she'd left her shawl on the chair. She forced herself to stand up and carry on walking, but each step was agony and her head began to throb too.

She was staggering like a drunk by the time she got to the stable yard; so dizzy she couldn't even see straight. But a ray of light spilling on to the yard from the kitchen window stopped her from giving in and collapsing. It was just a few more steps to safety.

Baines was dressing when he heard Rose cry out. Thinking she was having trouble with the stove, he came out of his room beyond the servants' hall in his shirtsleeves, only to find her kneeling on the kitchen floor beside young Hope who appeared to be in a dead faint.

He assumed it was only the result of exertion on an empty

stomach; he'd found young girls were prone to passing out if they did too much before their breakfast. But Rose was lifting the girl's head to put a cushion beneath it, and as she withdrew her hand, he saw it was covered in blood.

Baines had more than enough on his plate already. Cook had died during the night, and along with the sadness he felt at losing a dear friend so suddenly, he also had the worry of how they would manage until the mistress could find a suitable replacement for her. Now this!

He rushed to get the smelling salts and wafted them under Hope's nose. When she began to come round, her first words were a halting apology. He turned her on to her side to examine her head, assuming she'd had a fall on the drive. Then he saw livid red fingermarks on her neck and knew it was no accident.

'Who did this to you, Hope?' he asked.

She didn't reply, just looked at him with fear-filled eyes.

'Come on, tell me,' he insisted. 'Was it a poacher?'

Poachers were a problem. They were usually after pheasant or deer on the Hunstrete estate, and if the gamekeeper was after them they cut through Briargate's grounds. But Baines had never known a poacher attack anyone who wasn't threatening them.

Hope appeared too shocked to answer, so he told Rose to get a bowl of warm water and a cloth so he could bathe her wound. She was in the scullery when Nell came into the kitchen.

'Hope!' she exclaimed, her face blanching as she saw the blood. 'Did Albert do this to you?'

Baines was astounded that Nell would immediately consider her husband a suspect, and was glad Rose was out of earshot. But as Nell dropped to her knees by her younger sister, her expression held such anger, along with horror, that it was clear she had some good reason to blame Albert.

Baines had always held Nell in the highest regard. Had it not been for his position and the fact that he was so much older than her, he might have been tempted to admit he held romantic ideas about her too. Yet he was glad for her when she took up with Albert, for she clearly wanted a home of her own and children. Albert appeared to be a good choice of husband: he was steady and hardworking, even if he was a trifle dour.

In the light of Nell's revelation, Baines now saw a reason for why she wasn't the vibrant, talkative woman she used to be before her marriage. Up till now, he'd thought this to be the result of increased responsibility, or perhaps disappointment that she hadn't found herself with child. It had certainly never crossed his mind that Albert himself might be the cause.

When Rose came back, Nell took the bowl of water from her and began cleaning the head wound, murmuring little endearments to Hope and begging her to tell her how this came about. Baines watched Hope's face, and he could see she was fighting the urge to admit the truth. That was practically proof enough it was Albert, for the child clearly wanted to protect her sister from shame and embarrassment.

Baines felt a little faint himself now, for the law wasn't kind to women; fathers and husbands could inflict tremendous punishments on female relatives with no fear of prosecution. If Albert could do this to a young girl, what might he do to Nell if she took him to task for it?

Sir William was the person who ought to deal with it. A stern warning that he would be watching out for Hope and Nell in future would probably bring Albert to heel. But Sir William was weak. 'Feeble' was how Cook had once described him, and though Baines had reprimanded her for saying it, she was right.

Surrounded by doting women as a child, and over-indulged, Sir William had never learned to be a real man. He might be charming and look gallant and handsome as he galloped around the countryside on Merlin, but in fact he was completely irresponsible.

Baines knew that the business interests in London and America which his master used as an excuse to be away from here so often didn't really exist. He had a circle of friends there, but it was horses, card games, balls and parties he shared with them, not business.

Sadly, he wouldn't give a damn if his gardener was ill-treating his wife and her sister. As long as the grounds continued to be admired by his friends, the man who was responsible could do what he liked.

Hope wriggled away from Nell's ministrations and got to her feet. 'I'm fine now, Nell, I only fell on the frosty drive,' she insisted. 'I must go and light the fires.'

'Let me light the fires, Mr Baines,' Rose begged. 'Hope's not right yet, that's a nasty wound she's got. Couldn't Nell do what's necessary down here and stay with her?'

Baines recognized self-interest; Rose was just scared of being left to do the cooking today.

'Fair enough, Rose,' he said gravely, for it was clear that Hope wasn't fit for heavy work. 'You run along and see to the fires. And make sure Ruby pulls her weight.'

The minute she'd gone, Baines turned to Nell. 'I think it would be best for Ruth to come down here. Cook, God rest her, has no further need of her help and Ruth is a very able cook. You can get Master Rufus up and bathed before your duties for the mistress.'

Nell nodded, but she put her hand on his arm and drew him towards the scullery to talk more privately. 'What am I to do, Mr Baines?' she asked in a whisper. 'I know it were

Albert, even if Hope won't tell me. I'm often afeared for myself with him, but I never thought he'd lay a hand on her.'

'We'll talk about this later,' Baines sighed. 'On top of all the usual daily tasks, I have to make arrangements for Cook's funeral and talk to Lady Harvey about a replacement for her. Hope will be safe here with Ruth.' He put one hand on Nell's shoulder, wanting to reassure her he wasn't dismissing her because he didn't care. 'We have to tread carefully, Nell, and weigh up the consequences.'

Once Baines had gone, Nell turned back to Hope, tenderly smoothing her hair back from her forehead. 'Tell me the truth, my little love. It were Albert, weren't it?'

'No, I told you I fell on the drive,' Hope lied.

Nell closed her eyes with exasperation. 'Is that what you intend to tell Ruth and James?'

Hope nodded.

Nell fastened a piece of wadding over the wound on her sister's head, then placed a mob cap over it. 'I can't hide those fingermarks on your neck so easily,' she said pointedly. 'But I'm sure you'll be able to think of some excuse for those too.'

At five o'clock that evening, Nell walked down the drive to the cottage carrying a basket containing a loaf of bread and a meat and potato pie Ruth had made for her that afternoon. Her heart was thumping with fright, but she had never been more determined in her whole life.

Hope was staying in Ruth's room at Briargate for the night. She had stubbornly stuck to her story that she just fell on the drive, and Nell knew it was her way of protecting her. But this afternoon Hope had vomited, and Baines had insisted she went to bed immediately and stayed there. Even Hope wasn't brave enough to argue with him.

Nell hadn't discussed Albert any further with Baines because he had been far too busy sorting out Cook's funeral. But she had thought through all the possible lines of actions she could take and weighed up the consequences of each.

All of them were likely to bring her and Hope even greater misery. Legally she had no rights; a wife was a man's property and she was expected to obey him. Nell suspected that the same law meant Albert could do anything he liked to his sister-in-law too because he had given her a home.

It had been very tempting to ask Lady Harvey for some help, but she'd quashed that idea for Nell knew if her mistress refused, she might retaliate and blurt out something she would regret.

Captain Pettigrew had called many times in the last three years, always when the master was away. Maybe they didn't get up to anything wrong, but Nell could feel a charge in the air between them and her ladyship was always lost in a dream when he left, sometimes even a little weepy.

Nell could understand, at least to a certain extent. Over the years she had come to see that Sir William wasn't the perfect husband she once took him for. He was careless with his wife, preferring the company of his friends in London to her. Maybe he'd always been that way and that was why her mistress fell for the Captain's charms in the first place.

Without Lady Harvey's help Nell couldn't run away from Albert, and anyway she didn't want to leave the job she loved, or her family. If James and Matt were to find out Albert had beaten Hope, they would take their revenge. But Albert was an intelligent, determined man and he knew the law. He'd get James and Matt arrested, they would end up in prison, and she and Hope would be completely at his mercy.

She couldn't even hope that by now he was feeling

ashamed of himself, as she knew that he didn't love her. He didn't love anyone but himself.

While there was no way she could either be rid of Albert or punish him, she didn't intend just to lie down and let him walk over her. As her father had been very fond of saying, 'There's more than one way to skin a cat.' And Nell felt she had found a way to skin Albert.

Inside, the cottage felt no warmer than outside, and Nell fumbled in the darkness for the candle and matches she always left on the shelf by the door. Once the candle was alight, she carried it over to the table and lit the oil lamp.

The stove was out, just as she had expected, and the breadboard on the table held just a few crumbs and the bread knife. A broken cup lay on the floor, clearly hurled by Albert, and the hearthrug was scuffed up, but there was nothing else out of place. She picked up the pieces of china and looked for further clues as to what had gone on that morning. Her eyes fell on a splattering of blood on the whitewashed wall by the door.

In a strange way she was glad to see it, for it was the confirmation she needed to give her the courage to carry out her plan. She had the stove lit within five minutes. She put the pie in to warm through, laid the table and then ran upstairs to make the bed and collect the slop pail.

Just after six, she heard Albert's boots scrunching on the stones of the drive and her bowels contracted with fear. She was spooning some tea into the warmed pot as he came in. He stood for a second in the doorway, his eyes narrowing in surprise to find Nell there as she usually arrived back much later than him.

Even after all the misery he'd put her through, she could still admire how handsome he was. Six feet two inches of rock-hard muscle, and a face that would make many a woman swoon: large dark blue eyes framed by long lashes, a perfect straight nose and a well-shaped mouth. He had shaved off his beard soon after their wedding, and though there was a dark shadow on his chin now because he hadn't shaved that morning, his slightly cleft chin was attractive. Even his teeth were still good, and he often pointed out that she should be ashamed that she'd lost so many of hers.

'I've got a nice meat and potato pie for your supper,' she said pleasantly. 'And this tea will be brewed in a moment.'

'Where's the girl?' he asked as he hung up his coat by the door.

'Up at the house,' she replied. 'My father always asked how Mother was, and kissed her when he came in.'

He looked hard at her, clearly not really understanding the sarcasm, but he said nothing and went over to the bowl of water she had ready and washed his hands.

She poured his tea in silence, took the pie from the oven and put it on the table, then cut him a slice of bread.

Every sound seemed magnified, the scrape of his chair on the stone floor as he pulled it out to sit down, his first sip of tea and the crackle of the wood in the stove. Albert was mostly silent, and she usually chattered just to break the deadly quiet. But this time she said nothing, just served him up a large portion of the pie.

It was when he picked up a knife to spread butter on his bread that she noticed him wince.

'What's wrong with your hand?' she asked.

'A cut,' he said curtly.

'Let me see,' she said, leaning closer and reaching out for his hand.

'Leave me be, woman,' he spat at her. 'I'm not a child.'

Nell had intended to wait until after he'd eaten, but the

way he spoke to her riled her so much she could not contain herself any longer.

'No, you aren't a child. You're a big and very strong man. Yet you'd half-strangle a young girl and try to dash her brains out.'

He flushed and began to rise from his chair as if to strike her.

She snatched up the bread knife. 'Sit down,' she ordered him, pointing the knife at him. 'For once you are going to listen to me.'

'Now look here, woman,' he began to bluster, 'I expected that the impudent madam would go snivelling to you, but I doubt she told you the truth. She insulted me, so I chastised her. She deserved it.'

'She didn't snivel to anyone. She wouldn't even admit to Baines or me that she were attacked. But we knew! Fingermarks on her neck, the gash on her head. She couldn't get those from falling on the drive.'

He gave a snort of derision and went to get up, but Nell lunged out warningly with the knife and he sat down again. 'I could get you thrown off this estate,' she hissed. 'Thrown out without a character. Where would you be then?'

'They couldn't do that without throwing you out too,' he said with a smirk. 'I'm your husband.'

'Husband!' she sneered. 'How can you be when I'm still a virgin after three long years of marriage?'

He was clearly astounded that she would dare voice such a thing. Suddenly he looked a little unsure of himself.

'That's my trump card,' she said determinedly. 'I haven't played it yet, but I'm prepared to.' She lowered the knife just a fraction, and leaned forward to nudge his plate nearer to him. 'Eat up, dear Albert, you have to keep your strength up. Ruth made that for you, though if she guessed the truth about Hope's injuries she might well have slipped some arsenic in.'

He looked down at his plate, then back at Nell. He was hesitant, wanting to eat it because he was starving, but afraid to.

'Come on, Albert, eat,' she said. 'There are so many of us Rentons.' She laughed lightly as if she were joking. 'James in the stables with a pitchfork! Matt lying in wait somewhere with a scythe! How about Joe and Henry destroying your rosebeds?'

'Now look here, woman!' he said, his face darkening. 'You can't threaten me!'

'Threaten you?' Nell gasped, as if that was the last thing on her mind. 'Surely you don't think I was threatening you? I was only pointing out the things you *might* think could happen. But none of those things are necessary, not with my trump card.'

She paused, feeling a little more confident now. 'It would be easy enough to go to Lady Harvey and tell her that you aren't a real man and you take it out on Hope and me because it shames you. Do you think she'd want you as her gardener knowing that? I believe a marriage can be annulled if it hasn't been consummated.' She smirked at him, proud that she'd remembered the right word. 'I could speak to Reverend Gosling about that!'

'I never meant to hit Hope,' Albert exclaimed, his face suddenly paler. 'Damn it, woman, I'm sorry I did.'

'I'm sorry you did too,' Nell said fiercely. 'Because it's made me face things about you that I didn't want to examine.'

He looked at her blankly.

'You really don't like women at all, do you?' Nell asked. 'When we got married I thought you loved me and that we'd have children. But you cheated me. You knew that you could never give me that.'

'I take care of you,' he said indignantly.

'Care! You call ordering me around, pulling me up for the quilt not being straight or a speck of dirt on the floor, taking care of me?' Nell's voice rose to a shriek. 'You don't talk or laugh. There's no joy in you. Being married to you is like a prison sentence.'

'I don't know what's got into you. I've said I'm sorry, now let that be the end of it,' he said, and began eating his pie.

'The end of it!' she exclaimed. 'I've barely begun, Albert Scott. You are unnatural, a freak of nature that you don't like women, and I swear on all that's holy that I will expose what you really are unless you do as I say.'

At last he looked frightened and Nell felt she now had some real power.

'So what do you want of me?' he asked in little more than a whisper, dropping his eyes from hers.

'First of all, you will never hit Hope or me again.'

He nodded.

'And you'll make no further complaints about how I run this house. You'll get the coal, wood and the water in like any decent husband would do. You will also welcome my family here and behave as if you like them.'

'Is that it?' he asked.

'You think you've got off lightly, don't you?' she laughed mirthlessly. 'But you haven't, because I know that it will wear you down having to be nice to me. You'll always be afraid I might spill the beans about you and make you the laughing stock of the county. Maybe it will wear you down enough so you leave me. That will make me very happy. I've never considered myself a real wife anyway.'

To her amazement he covered his face with his hands. 'I can't help the way I am,' he muttered as if he were crying. 'God knows I wish I was like other men.'

Nell almost softened then. She was tempted to put her arms around him and say maybe they could learn to be friends like the way they were before they married. But she knew that if he saw her weaken he would use it to his advantage.

Instead she took his hands away from his face. There were tears in his eyes. 'There might still be hope for you if you can shed a tear, Albert Scott,' she said crisply. 'Finish your supper, then let me see to that cut on your hand.'

Chapter Six

1845

Hope was walking home through Lord's Wood after spending her afternoon off in Woolard with Matt, Amy and their children when she heard a crack of something stepping on a dry stick behind her.

She turned, but couldn't see or hear anything. Had it been an animal, she'd have been able to hear rustling in the undergrowth, so it stood to reason it was a human who was now hidden.

She wasn't in the least scared; it was only six in the evening and in June it didn't get dark until at least ten o'clock. Besides, she and her brothers used to stalk people all the time when they were younger. In fact, if she hadn't known both Joe and Henry were fishing by the bridge in Woolard, she would have thought it was one of them. But they'd been warned off coming into the wood by Mr Box, the Hunstrete gamekeeper, because he suspected them of poaching. Fortunately that day Box didn't catch them with any fish from the lake, but he said that if he saw them in the woods again he'd turn them over to the magistrates.

Hope waited a while and when there were no further noises she thought she might have been mistaken so she walked on. But when she heard another crack, she turned just in time to see someone dart behind a tree. She knew it wasn't an adult, for their step was too light, and she thought it was a girl for she'd seen a flash of blonde hair.

The Nicholses, who lived on the common near her old home, had two blonde daughters, and one of them, Anna, was daring enough to play this sort of game on someone. So Hope thought she'd turn the tables on her and hide behind a tree too.

She held the skirt of her brown dress in tight so it wouldn't give her away, and waited. After about a minute she heard the sound of creeping feet. They came right up to the tree where she was hiding and then stopped so close that Hope could hear the girl's breathing. She wanted to laugh because she could just imagine Anna's confused expression as she wondered how Hope had managed to disappear.

Stealthily Hope crept around the big tree and then pounced out. 'Gotcha!' she yelled.

But to her astonishment it wasn't Anna Nichols at all, but Master Rufus. And he looked as startled as a rabbit.

'I'm sorry, Master Rufus,' Hope stammered. 'I didn't know it was you.'

'Didn't you? Well, that's good. I mean, that's the whole point of the game, isn't it?' he said with a beaming smile. 'I'd been waiting for ever for someone to come along. I was so pleased when I saw you – I didn't think you'd scream like I was a murderer, the way Miss Bird would.'

Hope didn't like sour-faced Miss Bird one bit, so that made her laugh.

Rufus was ten now, and almost as tall as Hope, but he still looked as sweet and innocent as he had as a five-year-old. His blond hair almost touched his shoulders, and he had wide blue eyes and a soft plump mouth. He had Lady Harvey's slightly upturned nose and her creamy skin, yet overall he looked like a junior replica of his father, who also had a very girlish mouth and curly hair, and Rufus wore his navy-blue sailor suit with as much style as his father wore his riding clothes.

'Should you be out here, Master Rufus?' Hope said archly. 'I didn't think you were allowed beyond the grounds of Briargate.'

'No, I believe I'm not,' he grinned. 'But don't call me Master. Just Rufus will do. Let's have a game of hide-and-seek?'

Hope might have turned thirteen back in April but she often ached to have the kind of fun she used to have with her brothers before their parents died. Her life was all work, up at five, toiling in the kitchen day after day, often until eight in the evening and later still when there was a dinner party. The only respite was her afternoon off when she visited Matt and Amy, but Amy was as staid as Miss Bird most of the time. All she did was gossip about her neighbours, or boast how clever her children were.

Albert wouldn't approve if she was late home; he'd give her one of his black looks and point to the clock. But she doubted he'd take it any further than that. She often wondered what Nell said to him that evening after he whacked her against the wall, because he'd been different ever since.

He wasn't nicer, for he was just as silent and brooding, but he hadn't hit her again, nor did he order her and Nell about the way he used to. It was rather strange really, for Hope sensed he still resented her every bit as much. He certainly wasn't any kinder to Nell either, but he did draw the water from the well and brought in fuel for the stove. Hope remained wary of him though, and did her best not to upset him in any way.

Luckily she was hardly ever alone with Albert any more. Soon after Cook's funeral, Martha Miles, the new cook, arrived, and Baines told Hope she was to be a proper kitchenmaid, at six pounds a year, and that meant she worked till much later in the evening. On her regular afternoon off on Wednesdays she always went to see Matt and Amy, and Baines arranged it so she and Nell could have the same Sunday afternoon off once a month.

Hope played hide-and-seek with Rufus for quite a while, and it was a bit like old times when they'd played in the garden, only a great deal more fun because now Rufus was old enough to hide properly. But eventually Nell said she'd have to go and told Rufus he must too for his mother would be getting worried about him.

He just shrugged. 'Maybe that will make a change from worrying about Papa,' he said.

Hope frowned, assuming Rufus was a little jealous that his father got more of Lady Harvey's attention. 'You should be glad they are happy together,' she reprimanded him. 'It would be much worse for you if they didn't like each other.'

He looked at her strangely. 'Happy together? They are hardly ever together. Even when he's here at Briargate he's out most of the time. He only comes back for meals.'

Hope had not been aware of that, but then the only time she got a glimpse of Sir William was when he went to the stables to get Merlin. She hadn't heard it from the other servants either, for Baines was very strict about them gossiping about what the master and mistress did. Nell was the soul of discretion; she might tell Hope what Lady Harvey was wearing for dinner, or that she'd had a lie-down because she had a headache, but very little else.

She and Ruth did talk a lot about Rufus, but only in the fond way anyone would speak about a child. They took pride in that he was clever, they repeated funny things he said, and because of this Hope felt she knew him just as well now as she did when they used to play together.

'Where does he go then?' Hope asked.

'Out riding, visiting friends. Mama doesn't like it when he doesn't come home at night.'

Hope sniggered. She thought he meant that his father got so drunk he fell down somewhere and slept it off. Her father had done that a few times and woken up in a field all wet with dew. 'I don't suppose he likes how he feels the next morning,' she said.

Rufus looked puzzled and asked what she meant. Hope explained.

'I don't think my papa ends up in a field,' Rufus said, looking shocked that Hope could even suggest that. 'I think he goes to Bath. I once heard Mama ask if he'd been in a whorehouse! Do you know what that is?'

Hope did know what a whore was, she'd heard Albert say the word a couple of times, and asked Nell what it meant. Nell had said the real meaning was a woman who let a man have his way with her, for money. But she had quickly added that Albert used it for any woman who in his opinion was too lively or flirtatious.

'It's a house of happy women,' Hope said, thinking she'd better not give him Nell's definition.

'Well, I don't blame Papa for going to one then,' Rufus pouted, 'because Mama is always unhappy.'

'How can she be unhappy?' Hope asked. To her Lady Harvey had the best life it was possible to have.

'She is,' he said with a touch of indignation that she didn't believe him. 'She cries a lot about Papa because he doesn't seem to care about her.'

Hope found that difficult to believe as everyone had always told her Lady Harvey and Sir William were a love match. But then people had thought Albert and Nell were too, and she knew first-hand how untrue that was, and what misery it could be finding herself between the pair of them.

'My mother used to say that all married couples have tiffs

sometimes,' she said, trying to offer him some comfort because it clearly troubled him. 'So don't you fret about them. You'll be going away to school soon anyway.'

'I don't want to go away,' he said glumly. 'I know I'm going to hate it. Would you meet me here again? I like being with you.'

Hope thought maybe the fear of going away to school was at the bottom of all his worries, and perhaps he was lonely too. 'I could only meet you on Wednesdays,' she said with a smile. 'But you'd better not tell anyone.'

Albert went down to the ale house in Chelwood as soon as Hope got home, not even stopping to tell her off for being late because he'd eaten up at the big house. He did that quite often now as Martha, the new cook, always made a fuss of him.

Nell often laughingly said that Albert was sweet on Martha, even though the cook was well over forty and fat, with rotten teeth. Yet ridiculous as that was, Albert did seem to enjoy Martha's endless admiration for his work in the garden, and the way she kowtowed to him, as well as her cooking.

As Nell wouldn't be back for some time, Hope sat on the backdoor step to eat some bread and cheese. It was a beautiful evening, still warm with just the softest of breezes, and the air full of the smell of newly cut hay. It was her favourite spot, for Lord's Wood was on her right, on the left there were acres of fields, and straight ahead was the big house at the end of the tree-lined drive.

The sun was going down, and the house had turned the colour of ripe apricots. She was too far away to see the roses, but Nell had said this morning that the climbing ones were right up by Lady Harvey's bedroom window, and they filled the rooms with their scent.

The things Rufus had said about his parents were playing on her mind and made her think back to when she used to play with him. She hadn't been aware of the huge divide between her family and his then. While she marvelled at Rufus's toys, the fine furniture and Lady Harvey's lovely clothes, she'd been enveloped in the same kind of warm atmosphere she felt at home. That gave her the idea that Sir William and Lady Harvey were just the same as her parents.

She knew better now. Gentry were a different breed altogether from working people and the warmth she'd felt in Briargate in those days hadn't come from its owners at all. It came from the servants, three of whom were members of her own family. Lady Harvey hadn't brought Rufus up, Ruth had. He only spent an hour a day with his mama. With Nell in and out of the nursery all day, and James taking him out for rides on his pony, Rufus probably felt closer to the Rentons than he did to his parents.

This, she realized, was partly why Rufus wanted to meet her again, even if he didn't know it himself. While the Rentons looked to Briargate for their living, Rufus looked to the Rentons for affection and care. He had never seen Nell or Ruth unhappy, nor were they sour-faced and prim like Miss Bird. James no doubt teased Rufus and played around with him like a big brother. As for Hope, he probably imagined that because she'd been his first playmate, she could now be his friend, confidante and ally.

She sighed, knowing only too well that Nell wouldn't approve of her having secret assignations with Rufus. She was always reminding her of 'her place'. Hope knew that if she was to try to explain that Rufus was lonely and sad, Nell would snort and say she was talking nonsense. She wouldn't believe that a boy with so much could be anything but gloriously happy.

Seeing Nell coming down the drive, Hope got up and ran to meet her. Even from a distance she could see her sister was very tired and hobbling as if her feet hurt.

'Is Albert in?' Nell asked as Hope reached her.

'No, he's gone to the ale house,' Hope replied.

Nell nodded as if she was glad. 'How were Matt and his family?'

Hope passed on as much as she could remember of what Amy had said during the afternoon. 'I think she might be expecting again. She didn't say she was, but she had that look.'

'I thought that too at church on Sunday,' Nell said thoughtfully. 'And what about Joe and Henry, did you see them?'

Hope wasn't going to worry Nell by admitting she'd seen the boys fishing off the bridge, when they should have been working in the copper foundry at Woolard.

'I saw them from a distance,' she said, for that much was true, and if Nell chose to think this was at the foundry that would spare her any further anxiety.

Hope made Nell a cup of tea when they got in, and fetched a bowl of water so she could soak her feet. Then she sat down with her and asked who had been there for dinner that night at Briargate.

'The Warrens from Wick Farm, and the Metcalfes from Bath,' Nell replied. 'Lady Harvey wore her new blue satin gown and she looked lovely.'

'Would you say she was happy?' Hope ventured.

'She seemed to be tonight,' Nell said, wriggling her toes in the warm water and sighing with pleasure at finally getting to sit down. 'But then she always seems to rally round when the master is at home.'

'So does she get unhappy when he's away?' Hope probed.

'What a one you are for questions,' Nell chuckled. 'Yes, she does. Sometimes, when I know she's been crying, I want to tell her that I'd be as happy as a pig in clover if Albert was to go away.'

Hope knew from that comment that her sister had had a trying day, for although she'd made the remark lightly, as if she were joking, it was quite indiscreet by her usual close-lipped standards.

Nell had never openly admitted that she regretted marrying Albert, but Hope saw it in her face daily. He might treat her better now, but he never showed the slightest affection towards her, and Nell didn't even try to engage him in conversation any more. While she still did all the wifely tasks of cleaning, washing and mending, she no longer nipped home during the day to prepare his supper because he'd begun having meals at the big house. It was as if Nell was his servant, for Hope hadn't seen them kiss or hug since the day they married.

A few months ago when Hope's courses had started, Nell had explained what it meant, and that she would soon start hoping for a sweetheart. She had warned Hope against allowing any boy or man to take liberties with her, and that the outcome could be a baby.

'You are so bonny, a great many men will want you,' she said sternly. 'But don't allow yourself to be deceived, Hope, a man who truly loves you will wait for marriage.' She had fallen silent for a while, and then suddenly caught hold of Hope's hand really tightly. 'But before you agree to marry, be sure that it is *you* he wants, your body, your mind, everything about you. For some men cannot truly love, they are just empty shells, wishing to hide their affliction by having a woman at their side.'

Hope knew then that this was how Nell saw Albert, an empty shell incapable of love. She had a strong suspicion too that they didn't do the act that made babies either, or surely Nell would have had one by now.

Miss Bird, Rufus's governess, left Briargate for good at the end of June to take up a position in Bristol. Ruth and Nell were very pleased to see her go as they had never liked her, but they did express some concern about how Rufus would spend his days until he went away to school in September.

He loathed going out visiting with his mother, but he was bored and lonely at home with no one to play with. He liked going riding with his father, but even when Sir William was home, he rarely took Rufus out with him. James tried to find time to ride with him sometimes, but since the undergroom had left, he had too much other work to do.

Hope justified her weekly secret meetings with Rufus by telling herself she was occupying him so he wouldn't be lonely. She would first go to see Matt and Amy, but left early to have longer with Rufus. His face would light up when he saw her, and he always said that Wednesday was his favourite day.

Sometimes he brought presents for her, toffee, fudge or ripe peaches, things Hope rarely got to eat. They would go deep into the woods, often to the big pond which was surrounded by bushes and reeds, and on really hot days they took off their boots and stockings and paddled.

Hope found it was as comfortable being with Rufus as it was with members of her own family, but he was far more gentle and sweet-natured than her brothers. He didn't mind if she just wanted to sit in the sunshine and talk, he didn't goad her into rough games the way they did.

Although Hope had at first thought she was just being kind to a lonely boy, after the second meeting she was as anxious to see him as he was to see her. She came to see that she had been lonely too, but because she was surrounded by people all day she'd never realized it before. Nell, Ruth and all the staff at Briargate were so much older than her; they talked of nothing but their work or village gossip.

Rufus was very bright. He knew about all sorts of things that she knew nothing about; countries like India, Africa and America. He read books about these places, and would tell her about the customs and the wild animals. He said he wanted to be an explorer and find lands that no other white person had been to. He even made her wish she could go with him.

In return Hope would tell him about the people she'd grown up amongst, and relate funny stories about them.

'I wish I met funny people,' he said rather sadly one day after she'd been telling him how Jack Carpenter from Nutgrove Farm couldn't catch his prize boar when it escaped. He had been hollering at it, brandishing a big stick to try to scare it back in the direction of the farm, when it charged at him and knocked him into the pond. 'In fact I just wish I could meet any sort of people. Do you know that this year I've only spoken to three people apart from everyone at Briargate? Two of those were Miss Lacey and Miss Franklin, the two old ladies who come to visit Mama sometimes. They were really dull, they only talked about how tall I'd grown. The other person was the blacksmith when I rode with James to get the horses shoed. And he only spoke in grunts.'

'That's another good reason for going away to school then,' Hope said. 'You'll have so many people to talk to there, and when you come home you can tell me all the funny things about them.'

As the weeks passed, their conversations gradually became more personal. Hope told him about her two sisters dying of scarlet fever, and then how her parents died of typhus. She had never talked about that to anyone since the funeral, not even Nell, but she told Rufus everything: how horrible it all was, how scared she'd been, and that she'd been angry with her mother for giving up and dying once she knew her husband had slipped away.

Rufus was horrified that he'd never been told of how her parents died. 'How could Ruth look after me and not tell me?' he said indignantly. 'Or Nell, or even Mama? Why didn't they tell me? I could at least have said I was sorry and picked some flowers from the garden for their grave.'

'You were only little. People don't tell children things like that,' Hope said, but she was touched that he wished he could have made some sort of gesture.

'Did Mama or Papa do anything?'

'Well, they let me come and help out in the kitchens,' she said.

Rufus's eyes darkened. 'Nothing else? But Ruth's been my nursemaid since I was born. Nell's been with us for some seventeen years – surely Mama could have done something more?'

'What could she do, Rufus?' Hope shrugged. 'They're gentry, we're just working folk. It wasn't as if I was homeless; I went to live with Nell and Albert.'

'But Mama always used to remark on how pretty and clever you were,' he said in bewilderment.

Hope realized then that however knowledgeable Rufus was about the rest of the world, he didn't have any real idea of how poor people lived. She began to explain some of it: the tiny houses with bare floors and very little furniture, how she'd never had a real bed, just a sack filled with hay. She told him how most children were pressed into some kind of work almost as soon as they could walk, even if that was only scaring birds from the crops.

'I was lucky that I went to Reverend Gosling for four years to learn to read and write,' she went on. 'None of my brothers and sisters had that long, and most people in the village can't read and write at all.'

'But it isn't fair,' he burst out. 'Everyone should have the same chances.'

'That's just the way it is,' Hope said, repeating what Nell always told her when she complained about unfairness.

It was time to go home then, and as she left Rufus at the edge of the wood he walked across the paddock looking very sad and thoughtful.

In the middle of August, Lady Harvey received a letter from her younger sister to say their mother was very sick and asking her to come immediately. Lady Harvey wanted Nell to go with her, but thought Rufus should stay at Briargate because he was due to start at school in Wells in September.

They would be going on the Great Western railway from Bristol, and Hope was very envious because she'd seen pictures of the train and it looked like a very fast and exciting way to travel. She was also nervous at the prospect of being alone in the cottage with Albert, but Nell said she would speak to Baines and ask if she could sleep at Briargate as long as she went down to the gatehouse every day to tidy up for Albert.

It had been very hot for several weeks and at five the following morning when Nell and Hope left the cottage, the sun was already very warm.

'Please be a good girl while I'm away,' Nell said anxiously as they hurried up the drive carrying her bag between them. 'I really don't think we'll be back for some time. Even if the old lady dies almost straight away, it will be a few days before the funeral. And we can't leave straight after, that wouldn't be right.'

'I'll be fine,' Hope insisted, knowing very well Nell was

worried about her. 'Ruth and James are here and Matt's just down the road. There won't be so much work anyway with the master away too.'

He had been in London for some little while, but Nell said that Lady Harvey had written to him to ask him to join her at her family's home in Sussex.

'It's going to be miserable travelling all that way in this heat,' Nell grumbled.

Hope laughed. 'The train goes so fast it will be cool with the windows open. You'll enjoy it, you know you will. It's better to just sit there watching the world go by than rushing about at Briargate.'

'You shouldn't talk like that when you know Lady Harvey's mother is dying,' Nell said sharply.

Hope wanted to retort that Lady Harvey hadn't shown much sympathy when their own mother died. But she didn't say it; Nell had a blind spot where their mistress was concerned.

Hope kissed Nell goodbye in the kitchens, and clung to her a little more tightly than she usually did.

'Who's being a bit of a baby?' Nell whispered fondly. 'I thought you'd be glad to see the back of me.'

'I'll miss you,' Hope admitted, and bit back tears. Nell hadn't been away with Lady Harvey once since their parents died, but now she was going, Hope was scared.

Nell smoothed a strand of hair back from Hope's forehead and tucked it under her cap. 'Have I ever told you what you mean to me?' she asked in a whisper, very aware that Martha and Baines were standing nearby.

Hope shook her head.

'Everything!' Nell said. 'You have done since I first held you as a baby. So you just mind you behave yourself. I don't want to get back here and find you in disgrace.'

*

Once Lady Harvey had left for Sussex, Briargate seemed to slip into a kind of torpor.

With no more meals to prepare for the dining room, no fires to be lit, less cleaning, laundry and all the countless other tasks they were relieved of now neither the master nor the mistress was in residence, the servants could relax. Martha mentioned making some jam with the last of the blackcurrants from the garden, but looked as if she was in no hurry to start. Even Baines settled down in the servants' hall to read the newspaper.

Martha sent Hope down to the orchard later in the morning to pick some plums. Hope took her time, stopping at a small terrace just above the orchard to look around her and savour the beauty of the scene. All the fruit trees were laden – voluptuous purple plums, pale green pears and red shiny apples, all so perfect and luscious. Fat bumblebees buzzed lazily in the sunshine, a thrush was singing his heart out, and the air was laden with the smell of fruit and the lavender at her feet on the terrace.

Beyond the orchard down into the valley and up the other side great swathes of golden corn waved seductively in the light breeze. The harvest had begun; Hope could see silver flashes of sunshine on scythes as the men moved methodically across the fields. Matt would be among those men who looked no bigger than specks, maybe Joe and Henry too, and they would toil until the sun went down, praying that the good weather would last until it was all gathered in.

Hope ate a few of the plums as she filled her basket. They were warm and juicy, so sweet they made her almost delirious with pleasure, and she was glad she'd thought to put on the apron she wore for rough work as the juice ran down her chin in streams, staining it a deep, dark red.

She took her time going back to the house, stopping frequently to admire the many majestic old trees that had been planted when Briargate was built, and the new flowerbeds Albert had created in the last few years.

As she turned by a large horse chestnut, she saw him cutting the long grass around some bushes and she paused, suddenly struck by how handsome he looked with his face and forearms as brown and shiny as a conker, his thick black hair, well-proportioned nose and muscular but graceful body. Although she was usually afraid of him, here he didn't look threatening for he was entirely at one with his surroundings, wielding his scythe with effortless precision.

'The garden looks beautiful,' she said nervously, expecting him to order her on her way. 'That bed there is so bonny!' She pointed towards one planted with tall white daisies and a purple starry flower she didn't know the name of, standing behind a mass of marigolds.

Albert stopped his work and gave one of his rare smiles, showing very white teeth. 'Aye, that one has done me proud,' he said with surprising warmth. 'But the rest is getting past its best now.'

Hope moved nearer to him and held out a plum. 'Try one, they're delicious.'

He looked at her stained apron and she expected that he would pass one of his more usual sarcastic comments, but he didn't, just took the plum and bit into it, and smiled as juice spurted out.

'Umm,' he said appreciatively. 'We'd better get them all eaten before the wasps find them.'

Delighted that for once he wasn't being unpleasant, Hope handed him another. 'You've made a fine job of the garden,' she said.

He looked pleased at her compliment but made no comment.

'It takes an artist's eye to pick colours and shapes that blend so well together,' she said shyly.

He smiled at that, and leaned on his scythe to mop the sweat from his brow with a piece of rag.

'You look very hot,' she said. 'Shall I bring you out a drink?'

'I'll come up to the house myself soon,' he said. 'But thank you for asking.'

Hope went on then, but she felt a little glow inside her because she felt they'd at last made some sort of connection. She thought that when she went down to the gatehouse in the afternoon she'd leave a few of the plums in a bowl for him, and perhaps put a few flowers on the table. Nell would like it so much if she came home to find they were getting on better.

Ten days later, Ruth came into the kitchen from the stable yard, looking worried. 'I can't find Rufus,' she said.

Martha and Hope were preparing supper. 'He was with James in the stables,' Martha replied. 'At least, he was a while back because I heard them laughing.'

'He's not there now. James said he thought he'd come back in here. But he's not in the house anywhere. I've looked everywhere in the gardens. I don't know where else to look.'

'He'll turn up, Ruth, he's not a baby any more,' Hope said.

'But he's my responsibility while his mother's away,' Ruth said, her voice cracking with anxiety.

Only the previous day Ruth had claimed she wouldn't mind if the master and mistress never came back, for the weather had remained hot and sunny, and she, like all the servants, had been very relaxed, doing only the bare minimum of work.

Yet for Ruth it had been an almost complete holiday for right from the first day his mother left, Rufus had insisted he wanted to eat with the servants, and now, a week later, the only time he went back into the nursery was to sleep.

In the mornings he was up early helping James with the horses, and later he'd come into the kitchen and offer his help there. His sunny nature and obvious delight at being let into the servants' world affected everyone. All the normal rigid structure of the day had collapsed, work was done in the early mornings or evenings when it was cooler, meals were far simpler. A table and chairs were taken out into the stable yard, and even Albert, who normally only came in for a drink, gulped it down and left, now sat down at the table and joined in the conversations.

Hope could not remember ever hearing so much laughter at Briargate. One afternoon Baines had taught her, Rufus and Ruth a new card game, on another Rose had instructed them all on making corn dollies. But what Hope liked best of all was that she and Rufus could be together.

At first they were careful to behave as though they barely knew each other, but as the days passed no one seemed to notice or care about any over-familiarity. Baines did point out one Sunday morning when they were going to church that Hope should walk sedately and not run with Rufus like a hoyden, but it was only a very gentle reminder of her position, not a real rebuke.

'He'll be hiding somewhere hoping one of you will come past so he can jump out on you,' Hope said. 'I'll go and look for him.'

She left the kitchen quickly, because she was pretty certain of where Rufus might be, although she just couldn't imagine why he'd gone there now when it was nearly suppertime.

Once over the paddock fence, Hope picked up her skirts and ran to the woods. On Wednesday Baines had let her go off at eleven in the morning. Matt and Amy had been busy with the harvest so she'd only stayed with them for a couple of hours and met Rufus in the woods much earlier than she normally did. They'd found an old boat among the reeds around the pond, and they'd spent much of the time trying to get it out. Rufus had talked excitedly about bringing some tools down so they could mend it and use it on the pond.

She guessed that was exactly what Rufus was doing now, hoping to surprise her and not noticing how late it was getting.

It was much cooler in the woods, and the paths that had been so well defined earlier in the year were now overgrown with weeds and brambles. Hope knew every inch of the woods, but in places it was hard to get through, and in her haste the brambles caught at her hair and scratched her cheeks and hands.

She called to him as she hurried along, urging him to come out because she guessed Ruth would soon send James or Albert down this way. But Rufus didn't answer, and when she stood still for a moment to listen, she couldn't hear anything other than birdsong.

By the time she got to the pond she was out of breath and very hot. Once again she called and listened, but she could hear nothing. Almost the entire surface of the pond was covered with weed and water lilies and teeming with midges which bombarded her as she drew nearer the water. She couldn't see the boat as it was tucked up in reeds on the far side of the pond, but if Rufus had been there, she surely would have been able to see or hear him.

She stood there for a few moments, undecided what to do next. The voice of reason told her she was mistaken in thinking he'd be here and she should go back to Briargate, but a cold feeling at the pit of her stomach urged her to go round the pond and make absolutely certain.

They had found the boat when they had approached

the pond from the other side, but it was very difficult to get round there from where she was now. In winter the stream which fed the pond was often a raging torrent; now it was nothing more than a trickle. But reeds, weeds and brambles had covered the still-damp mud, and she had to pick her way carefully through them. She could hear Albert and James shouting out Rufus's name in the distance too, coming down towards the wood, so she had to be quick for if they found her here she'd have a lot of explaining to do.

Finally she reached the boat, and saw it was half-turned on its side, the keel towards her. She knew then that Rufus had been here for it had been lying flat on Wednesday.

Fear clutched at her innards, for she sensed that he'd either got into the water to try to move it, or slipped from the reed bed as he worked the boat loose. He couldn't swim, he'd told her that the first time they'd come here. And even a good swimmer would have difficulty in water choked with reeds.

Hope wrenched off her boots, dress, petticoat and stockings, and wearing just her chemise plunged into the water and went round the prow of the boat.

She saw him then, completely submerged but for his head which appeared to be resting on reeds. There was an angry gash on his forehead.

Panic made her forget she didn't know how deep the water was and that she couldn't swim either. Suddenly there was nothing beneath her feet and she sank under the water. She thrashed her arms and legs and managed to get her head above the surface again just long enough to reach out for the side of the boat. Spluttering and spitting out pond water, she managed to work her way along the boat till she reached Rufus.

The way he looked was all too reminiscent of her father

when she found him dead. 'Rufus!' she pleaded with him, splashing some water on his face. 'You can't be dead! Wake up and speak to me!'

But there was no response, and hearing James and Albert calling somewhere nearby, she put back her head and screamed out to them to come to the pond.

As she heard their footsteps thundering towards her, twigs cracking, birds flying off in alarm, she hooked her free arm under Rufus's head and drew him closer to her.

All the warnings she'd had from her parents and older brothers about playing by water came back to her in those long moments while she waited for James and Albert to reach her. She should have passed those warnings on to Rufus. He was younger than her, and what could he know about dangers when he had spent all his young life in a safe nursery or driving in a carriage with his mama? She'd brought him here. She was responsible for his death.

Sobbing, she still held on to him, kissing his face, begging his forgiveness for not protecting him. She barely felt the cold water or the midges biting her, she was entirely focused on his sweet young face, and all that they had become to each other.

'Hope!' she heard James yell from the far side of the pond. 'Where are you?'

'Over here,' she shrieked back. 'Rufus has fallen in by an old boat in the reeds. I'm holding him up.'

There was a loud splash as James plunged in, and all at once she saw him swimming through the tangle of water lilies, dark hair slicked back from his face and his eyes mirroring her own terror.

'I think he's already dead,' she managed to stammer out. 'His face was out of the water when I found him but he's hit his head.'

James trod water as he looked at Rufus, then he began to

swim away on his back, taking the boy with him, supporting him with a hand on either side of his head. 'Hold on tightly, Hope,' he called out. 'I'll be back for you.'

He disappeared from her view, but she heard Albert's voice and further splashing as the two men got Rufus up on to the bank.

It seemed a very long time that she waited. Both men's voices were muted, and it looked to her as though they were so distraught about Rufus that they'd forgotten her. Fear and the cold water made her teeth chatter. It wouldn't just be her who would be blamed for this, but all the servants. Yet terrible as that was, the thought of Lady Harvey's grief at losing her only child was worse.

She couldn't bring herself to call out to remind James she was there and she was too frightened to try to reach shallow water by herself. But all at once James was back, reaching out for her just as he had for Rufus, telling her to lie still and not struggle or she'd pull him under.

Albert's big hands came under her arms and she was plucked from the water and put down on the bank beside Rufus.

After the cold water, the sunshine felt very hot. 'Is he . . . ?' she asked, but found herself unable to finish the question because James and Albert were looking down at her so intently.

'He's fine, thanks to you,' James said. 'The bang on the head knocked him out. But if he'd been there much longer he'd have sunk right in and drowned.'

Hope could hardly bear to turn her head to look at her friend; she was sure James was trying to spare her feelings. But as her eyes finally fell on Rufus's bare legs and feet, and she saw one move, she felt bold enough to turn completely.

Albert was washing the wound on his forehead and she could hear Rufus whimpering.

'Oh, thank God!' she exclaimed. 'I thought he was dead.'

James went round the pond and found her clothes and boots, but he had to put her dress on for her as she was shaking too much to do it herself. Albert picked Rufus up in his arms and carried him, and she and James followed on silently behind.

James's silence on the way back was all the confirmation she needed to know that she was in serious trouble. She would surely be dismissed now, for she was to blame even if Rufus had survived. She had never needed Nell more, and although Albert had not yet laid into her, she was sure that was only because he was distracted by taking care of Rufus. Once they got back to Briargate he was certain to give her a beating.

Martha, Ruth, Baines and Rose all crowded round Rufus once they were back in the kitchen. They had wrapped him in a blanket and given him a hot drink, and Baines was telling him what a scare he'd given everyone.

'It were Hope who found him,' James declared as Ruth began to praise him. 'She stripped off her clothes and went in to get him. If she hadn't held his head out of the water he would have drowned. What a brave lass she were, she can't swim either.'

Suddenly everyone's attention was turned on Hope, but although this much of the story was true, she couldn't bask in their admiration. She knew it was only a matter of minutes before Rufus spilled out about their secret meetings and how they had found the boat.

Martha put a cup of tea in her shaking hands, and smoothed her wet hair back from her face. 'How did you know where to look for him?' she asked.

'I don't know,' Hope whimpered.

Ruth put some pans of water on the stove to heat for a bath for Rufus, and Hope saw how badly shaken she was for her face was white and her movements jerky. She let Baines dress the wound on Rufus's forehead, but she took his hand in hers and asked in a plaintive voice why he'd gone to the woods.

At that Hope felt really sick because she realized Ruth thought her job was in jeopardy now: she was the nursemaid and she'd let the young master go off on his own. All at once Hope was sobbing; she could bear punishment herself, but not the thought of Ruth or anyone else in the room being blamed for something she'd done.

'Why is Hope crying?' Rufus asked, his clear, high voice ringing out.

'Because she thought you were dead, Master Rufus,' Baines replied. 'You might very well have drowned if it hadn't been for her.'

'Let me see her?' Rufus asked, and nudging Ruth away from him, he came padding over to Hope, still wrapped in his blanket.

'Don't cry, Hope,' he said, using a bit of the blanket to dry her eyes. 'Look, I'm fine. You were very clever to find me, and I'm sorry if I frightened you.'

He looked right into her eyes as he spoke, a faint smile playing at his lips. 'Mama is going to be very grateful that you saved my life, because I'm sure Ruth will have to tell her what I did. But I was so excited because I found an old boat. I wanted to get it out and play in it. I didn't stop to think it might be dangerous.'

A lump came up in Hope's throat for she knew he was trying to tell her that their secret meetings would remain secret.

'That's all very well, Master Rufus,' she said sternly. 'But your mama will blame Ruth for not watching you more closely. She is afraid she will be dismissed.'

'Then maybe we shouldn't tell Mama about it?' He looked round at the other servants. 'I could have got this bump on the head falling over. And anyway, it might be gone by the time she gets back.'

He turned and went over to Ruth, wrapping his arms around her and leaning against her chest. 'I'm sorry I scared you, Ruthie,' he said. 'I won't do it again. Will you forgive me?'

Hope wanted to laugh then for he had the same easy charm as his father.

'You are going to have a bath, get into bed and stay there,' Ruth said, but though she had clearly meant that to sound like punishment, the break in her voice implied only relief and concern. 'And you will not go out of my sight again or I'll lock you in the nursery.'

'Well done, Hope. You averted a tragedy today,' Baines said as Rose cleared away the supper things. Ruth had taken Rufus upstairs, and Albert had gone home, so they were alone in the servants' hall. 'I think it's as well the young master is going away to school soon, he needs the company of other boys and some discipline.'

Hope hung her head. She had a strong feeling that Baines guessed she had more involvement with Rufus than she'd let on, and he was warning her it had to end.

'There's a storm brewing up,' he said, getting to his feet and going over to the window. 'I can feel the thunder in the air. Perhaps it's as well – this heat has made us all somewhat irresponsible.'

Chapter Seven

1847

Hope was whipping egg whites at the kitchen table one morning in November when Martha returned to the kitchen after her usual weekly meeting with Lady Harvey about the meals for the forthcoming week.

'The mistress will be going down to Sussex again tomorrow,' Martha announced importantly.

Hope glanced up at this unexpected news. 'Is her father poorly now?'

'He's never been right since his wife died,' Martha said as if she knew him personally. 'That poor man all alone in that vast mansion!'

Hope bit back a sarcastic remark. Martha was a decent enough woman, but Hope thought she ought to give her sympathy to those who really deserved it. Squire Dorville had a huge staff taking care of him and his estate, while less than a mile from here there were whole families living on a few shillings a week. They had a struggle to feed their children and could never afford to call a doctor when they were sick.

'Did the mistress say if Nell was to go with her?' Hope asked.

'Of course she is, a lady doesn't travel without her maid.' Martha sniffed. 'Not even here where standards are slipping a bit more every day.'

Hope didn't ask any more questions for she found Martha's superior attitude very irritating. Yet she was right with regard to the slipping standards at Briargate.

She hadn't been here in the old days of course, when there were some fifteen servants, but in recent years, when anyone left, the remaining servants divided up that job between them. Martha was the only new member of staff, taken on to replace the old cook when she died.

When Rufus had gone off to school in Wells over a year ago, this situation, which they'd all accepted cheerfully enough because it wasn't particularly onerous, suddenly deteriorated further. Within a month of Rufus leaving, Ruth departed in anger because she had been asked to become a maid of all work. James was dismissed when Sir William sold all but two of his horses, and Ruby left to get married.

Hope and Nell missed Ruth and James dreadfully, but they had to admit it had turned out for the best for their brother and sister. Ruth went to Bath as housekeeper to a widower with two daughters aged seven and nine, and within six months she was married to him.

He was a stonemason called John Pike, and although it seemed very sudden, Nell and Hope had visited Ruth twice since the wedding and found her to be very happy. John Pike was a kind and hard-working man with a very nice home, and his two daughters were thrilled to have a new mother. Just last week Ruth had written to say she was expecting a baby, which had delighted both Nell and Hope.

Sir William had secured James a new position as head groom at Littlecote Manor in Berkshire, perhaps because he felt guilty at being compelled to make cutbacks. Albert could take care of Merlin and Buttercup, the mare who pulled the trap; he had no reason to keep horses for the carriage when he could take the train from Bath to London.

Whatever reason the servants were given for the cutbacks,

everyone knew the truth. Sir William was in serious financial difficulties. The London house had gone a few years earlier, and there had been a gradual decline in parties at Briargate since then. Nell said she could hardly remember what it was like to prepare for a big dinner party or even weekend guests.

Lady Harvey scrutinized the household accounts now. She suggested to Baines that maybe they didn't need a fire in rooms that were seldom used and she shocked Martha by telling her she must cook simpler meals. On several occasions the wine merchant and the butcher had come to Briargate to demand settlement of the account, though Baines passed this off as mere oversight.

Lady Harvey's melancholia wafted around the house, affecting them all. Nell claimed she was still grieving for her mother, and maybe she was, but she didn't go out visiting or shopping any more and often stayed in bed all day.

Sir William didn't seem to care what went on in the house. He was rarely home, and when he was he drank heavily and quarrelled with his wife.

Every one of the servants was too nervous about their own security to complain about the extra jobs they were expected to do now. Albert didn't grumble that he'd lost Willy, his assistant, or that he now had grooming and driving duties too. Nell said nothing about being expected to clean the master's and mistress's bedrooms, and Hope bit her tongue when she was ordered to empty slop pails, carry bath water and do the bulk of the household laundry.

But it was loyal and long-suffering Baines who bore the brunt of the cutbacks. He had always acted as Sir William's valet, lit fires and cleaned shoes. But now he was filling in everywhere – maintenance jobs around the house, even sweeping the stable yard and polishing the brass on the front door when no one else could find time for it.

As a result of all the extra duties, Hope no longer lived

in the gatehouse with Nell and Albert. She had Ruth's old room up in the attic, and though she had to work far harder now, at least when she was done for the day she didn't have to put up with Albert's sullen silence or his disapproving looks.

She missed Ruth and James, but she missed Rufus far more. After his accident in the pond there had been a special kind of bond between them. As the days of his departure for school grew closer and closer, Baines and Ruth had allowed her to spend much of the day with him. They did jigsaw puzzles up in the nursery, played cards and invented dozens of different guessing games. She could tell he was worried about going away to school; he would scowl at the shiny new trunk in the corner of the nursery that Ruth was gradually filling with clothes, and told her he would run away if he didn't like it. But Hope kept telling him that all the new boys would be just the same as him and he'd soon make friends, then she'd distract him with a new game.

Lady Harvey still wasn't back when he had to leave, but his father returned to take him in the trap. Everyone went out to the drive to wave him off, and there were tears in all their eyes as he bravely shouted his goodbyes and pretended he was happy to go.

Hope expected that he'd be influenced by his new friends and that when he came home for the holidays, he wouldn't want a kitchenmaid for a companion. But she was wrong; as soon as he got back to Briargate he always came straight down to the kitchen to find her. Nell and Baines took the line that it was better for Rufus to be in the kitchen or going for a walk with Hope than seeing his father drunk, his mother weeping, or hearing the pair of them squabbling.

Nell would often sigh and recall the happy times when Rufus was still a baby. Sir William might have been away a great deal at that time, but when he was here he and Lady

Harvey played together with their son, and the master never locked himself away in his study to drink.

Often now when he was reeling drunk, he'd go looking for Lady Harvey and pick a fight with her. Rose claimed she must have had to clear up broken china or glasses a score of times after he'd been on the rampage.

'Those egg whites will collapse if you beat them any more!' Martha exclaimed, bringing Hope out of her reverie.

'I'm sorry, I didn't notice,' Hope replied, and handed the bowl over to the cook for the dessert she was making. 'I wonder how long Lady Harvey will be gone this time.'

Martha shrugged. 'Who knows? She'd better be back for Christmas, Master Rufus won't like it if she isn't. And let's hope Albert can get into Bath tomorrow, the roads will be treacherous.'

There had been heavy rain throughout September and October, and now there were hard frosts every night. It had been a poor harvest this year and if it was a very cold winter too, everyone knew there would be great suffering in the surrounding villages. Even Matt was struggling now. His father-in-law had died the previous year, and with a wife, her one still unmarried sister and his mother-in-law to keep, along with three children of his own, he had a job to keep his head above water.

From time to time Hope thought of trying to find a position in Bristol or Bath, for her life here was nothing but work and more work, with no company of her own age. James would write and describe the harvest suppers and the Christmas party the servants had at Littlecote and it sounded so much fun to be in a big household.

But Baines had advised her against leaving until she was a skilled enough cook to apply for a position in that capacity, for most kitchenmaids got treated far more harshly than she was. So she watched Martha very carefully, asked questions about anything she didn't understand, volunteered to make some of the dishes herself and jotted down the trickier recipes Martha used.

Sometimes she wished she was like Martha and Rose, for their minds didn't stretch beyond Briargate and the local gossip. They couldn't read, and everything they knew came from equally limited people. They grumbled a lot, especially now there was such uncertainty around the house, but neither of them seemed to have any desire to move on.

Hope was well aware she had even less experience than them of the world beyond Briargate, but she read the periodicals, newspapers and the occasional book which found their way down to the kitchen. She knew many working people were brave enough to challenge the government about the unfairness of the laws, and up and down the country there was rioting as there had been in Bristol the year before her birth. She could see that it wasn't right that only property owners could vote. They elected men to Parliament who would only look after their interests, and the poor had to shift for themselves.

'So you're going away with Lady Harvey?' Hope said later when Nell came down. Fortunately, Martha was talking to Baines in the servants' hall so they had the kitchen to themselves.

'Don't look so glum about it,' Nell smiled. 'It will only be for a few weeks.'

'I hate it when you aren't here,' Hope sighed. She was often lonely since Ruth and James had left, but with Nell gone too she knew she was going to feel very alone and isolated.

Nell patted her sister's cheek affectionately. 'I think we'll have to find a sweetheart for you. You wouldn't be thinking about your old sister if a young man took your eye.'

'There's about as much chance of me meeting a young man working here as there is of becoming Queen,' Hope said grumpily.

Nell looked anxious then and Hope felt ashamed of herself. 'I'll be fine really,' she said quickly. 'Just be back before Christmas.'

'Will you go down to the gatehouse now and then and tidy up for Albert?' Nell asked. 'And if I can't get back before Master Rufus comes home for the Christmas holiday, will you promise me that you'll keep an eye on him?'

Hope nodded and smiled. She knew what Rufus would make of that request. He said Nell treated him as if he were still five or six, but he was a strapping lad of almost thirteen now, and his school had hardened him up considerably.

'And don't go anywhere near Sir William when he's drinking,' Nell said warningly. 'If he rings the bell, let Rose or Baines go.'

'Will Lady Harvey stand up to losing her father too?' Hope asked. She sensed Nell was worried about something and thought perhaps it was that.

'I think so — she isn't as close to him as she was to her mother,' Nell replied. 'But his death will give her more problems.'

Hope raised one eyebrow questioningly.

'I shouldn't really tell you this, especially as Squire Dorville hasn't even gone yet. But Sir William is assuming that the estate will be divided between the three sisters.'

'It will, won't it?' Hope said.

'Lady Harvey thinks not. Her father doesn't approve of Sir William's spendthrift ways.'

Hope knew exactly what Nell meant by that. A wife's money became her husband's, and possibly Sir William was banking on Lady Harvey's inheritance to get him out of his problems. If that didn't come about, he would be savage.

'So neither you nor Lady Harvey will have a lot to come home for?' Hope said archly. She didn't mean to be sarcastic, but it had struck her over the past year that the mistress and her maid had a great deal in common as far as their husbands were concerned.

'I've got you, and Lady Harvey has Rufus,' Nell retorted. 'And that's all either of us needs.'

Hope felt ashamed then for she knew that Nell thought of her as her own child rather than a much younger sister. She put her arms around Nell and held her tightly. 'I love you, Nell,' she whispered. 'You've always taken care of me and I can't imagine what I'd do without you. I just wish you had the kind of life you deserve.'

'I'm a great deal more fortunate than some,' Nell said stoutly against Hope's shoulder, but the crack in her voice meant she was crying. 'Will you do something for me?'

'Of course,' Hope replied.

'It's for Lady Harvey really,' Nell said, withdrawing from her sister's arms, dabbing at her damp eyes with her apron and sniffing back her tears. 'What I'm going to tell you is a secret; you must promise me that you will never tell anyone?'

'I promise,' Hope said, wondering what on earth this secret could be.

'Cross your heart and hope to die!' Nell said.

Hope dutifully made the sign of the cross on her chest.

'Right,' Nell said. 'I want you to go through the post in the mornings and retrieve any letters that look like this.' She put her hand in her apron pocket and pulled out an envelope addressed to Lady Harvey. The handwriting was a bold script that was quite unlike any other handwriting Nell had ever seen. 'Will you recognize that?' she asked.

Hope nodded. 'What do you want me to do with them?' she asked.

'Just keep them safe until we get back, and don't say a word to anyone about them,' Nell said, her voice lowered conspiratorially.

Hope's mouth dropped open in shock, for such a request could only mean one thing. 'Has she got a lover?'

Nell put a warning finger to her mouth and looked over her shoulder nervously. 'I wouldn't call him that,' she whispered. 'He's just her friend, but if Sir William was to see a letter from him it would cause her a great deal of trouble, and things are bad enough at the moment without that.'

'Then why doesn't she just write to him now and tell him she's going away?' Hope asked.

'He's a soldier,' Nell said impatiently. 'Letters take a long time to arrive.'

Hope knew there was no point in asking further questions because she could see by Nell's tight expression that this was as much as she was prepared to reveal and she was worried sick at involving her younger sister in something she didn't approve of herself.

'Don't worry, I can be as tight-lipped as you,' Hope smiled. 'I just wish it was you who was getting secret letters; that would make me very happy.'

Nell half-smiled, her dark brown eyes softer with relief. 'You're a good girl,' she said, reaching out to stroke Hope's cheek with the same affectionate gesture their mother had always used. 'Don't forget about tidying the gatehouse,' she said, clearly reminded of her duty to her husband. 'Will you do his washing too?'

'Yes, that's if I can beat Martha to it.' Hope felt she had to try to make her sister laugh. 'With you out of the way she'll be fussing over him even more.'

Nell giggled, and for a second or two she looked like

a girl again instead of a rather worn, tubby woman of thirty-one. 'She's welcome to fuss over him as much as she likes. But just remind her you can't squeeze blood out of a stone.'

Hope gave Lady Harvey's mysterious friend a great deal of thought over the next couple of days. As far as she knew, Captain Pettigrew was the only soldier who had ever been to Briargate, and he was certainly the only male visitor who always seemed to arrive when Sir William wasn't there. Then there was that remark Rose had made years ago about Nell being flustered by him. It hadn't made any sense before, but it did now. When Nell disapproved of anything she always wore that tight expression.

So it had to be him.

It was of course shocking that her mistress had a secret beau, but Hope had retained all the good thoughts she'd formed about the Captain on the day she found Cook unconscious. He was charming, handsome and dashing and she could well imagine that any woman, married or not, would like his attention. For him, Hope was quite prepared to intercept the letters and keep them safe.

The weather grew more wet and windy after Lady Harvey and Nell had left for Sussex. One night the wind was so strong an old oak tree in the garden came crashing down, narrowly missing the stables. The following morning Hope and Rose went out with Baines to look at it and it was fearsome to see the vast roots exposed and a huge hole left in the ground where the tree had stood for probably a hundred years.

'My father used to say when an oak came crashing down that it was an omen of something worse to come,' Rose said fearfully.

'I'm sure your father believed in witches too,' Baines retorted sarcastically. 'I would say this is fortuitous as it means we'll have plenty of logs this winter. So get about your work now, and don't be so foolish.'

Hope missed her sister dreadfully. She hadn't realized until Nell went that it was she who had become the glue that held everyone together. Although she was a quiet person, she really cared about her fellow servants and could stimulate chatter and laughter between them. Without her it was very gloomy. Martha talked of nothing but food. Rose would grumble about how much work she still had to do, and Baines hardly said a word.

Sir William's unpredictability didn't help the mood. They'd lay the dining-room table for him and he'd want his meal in his study; he'd tell Baines he wouldn't be back for dinner, then come in roaring drunk late in the evening and demand a meal. Several times he'd told Martha he wanted a special dinner that evening because he was bringing a friend home, and then didn't turn up at all. Rose said he was a selfish swine, but as Baines pointed out, it was Sir William's house and he paid them to dance attendance on him. He also reminded them all that if they thought they could get an easier job, they were free to leave Briargate.

A letter with the same bold script Nell had shown her came after Lady Harvey had been gone over two weeks, coinciding with one for Hope from Nell. She put them both into the pocket of her apron, placed the rest on the silver tray in the hall for Sir William to look at later, finished laying the drawing-room fire, and then returned to the kitchen before reading her own letter.

Nell couldn't write very well so it was brief and to the

point: Squire Dorville had died. She expected it would be about two weeks before they set off for home, and she hoped everything was running smoothly at Briargate.

Hope knew that if Nell was writing to her, Lady Harvey would have written to her husband, and presumably he would leave immediately for Sussex. She wondered in passing whether he'd collect Rufus from school and take him too, or just write to him to pass on the news of his grandfather's death.

It wasn't until after breakfast, when Hope went upstairs with Rose to see to Sir William's bedroom, that she thought about the letter from the Captain again. She had taken it from her apron pocket and slipped it into the bodice of her dress while out in the privy, but it crackled a little when she moved and she knew she must put it in a better place for safe keeping.

She knew she had to be careful. Rose was extremely nosy and Ruth had always warned Hope never to have anything in her room that she didn't want seen because Rose poked into everyone's belongings. Rose couldn't read, so she wouldn't know who the letter was for or from, but she was crafty enough to take it down to Baines, making out she'd found it on the stairs. That also meant it wouldn't be a good idea to hide it somewhere in Lady Harvey's bedroom for no doubt Rose went through that with a fine toothcomb while cleaning it.

The gatehouse seemed the safest place. She could slide it under the mattress of her old bed, for Albert would have no reason even to go into that room, let alone disturb the bed. She had intended to go down there that afternoon to clean up anyway.

Hope was back in the kitchen later on in the morning, when Sir William came in. She knew immediately why he'd come, but Martha and Baines looked astounded to see him as he seldom visited the kitchen.

As always when she saw her master, Hope was struck by his similarity to Rufus. He was in his mid-forties now, but he looked much younger; even the heavy drinking hadn't spoiled his clear skin or dulled his beautiful blue eyes. The slackness of his full lips and the absence of a strong chin hinted at his weak character, but as he was wearing a bright blue waistcoat embroidered with small roses, made by Lady Harvey, and his blond curly hair was tousled, the overall picture was of a rakishly handsome young man.

'I received a letter from Lady Harvey this morning,' he said. 'Sadly her father died in his sleep three days ago. I shall leave early tomorrow morning to be with her for the funeral. I am sure I can leave Briargate in your capable hands.'

Baines offered his condolences, then asked how Sir William would be travelling and what he would like packed.

'Albert will take me into Bath in the trap, and I'll catch the train from there,' Sir William replied. 'I won't need to take much with me as I'll only be gone a few days.'

Albert came into the kitchen for dinner at around twelve, and as always Martha fussed around him, this time because his coat was wet through. Hope was in the scullery cleaning some silver, and she smiled at the cook's efforts to make him talk to her. The woman ought to have realized by now that Albert was a lost cause.

He informed Martha that he'd spent the morning sawing up the fallen oak, remarked that the river Chew was rising dangerously high again, and that it was his prediction the heavy rain would last another couple of days.

'You mustn't stay out in it again this afternoon,' Martha exclaimed. 'You might be a big strong man but that won't stop you catching a chill!'

Albert said he'd hauled some of the big logs into the woodshed and he'd be working in there cutting them into smaller pieces so he'd be in the dry.

Hope thought he sounded less brusque than usual, almost as if he was warming to Martha. She annoyed both Hope and Baines with her constant prattle about nothing, but she did have a kind heart and she loved to feed people.

She had told Hope that when she was a young kitchen-maid, she had been walking out with a footman and they wanted to get married. Their mistress reacted in the same way as most gentry did about servants marrying, and refused permission.

Martha was over forty now, with nothing but swollen ankles, callused hands and the title of Cook to show for a lifetime of hard work. Hope was absolutely determined her life wasn't going to be the same.

At half past three that afternoon, Martha was dozing in a chair in the servants' hall, and Rose had just put some flat irons on the stove to press some shirts for Sir William, when Hope slipped out of the back door. It was tipping down with rain, but she thought she should go down to the gatehouse today to tidy it, for once Sir William left for Sussex she felt it was quite likely Albert would go home in the afternoons.

She hadn't asked Baines for permission to go because she knew he would probably ask her to wait until tomorrow, and she didn't want to admit she was afraid of running into Albert. He was pleasant enough up at the big house, but down in the gatehouse he reverted to behaving the way she remembered when she used to live there. He ordered her about as if she were his slave, and criticized everything she did.

Baines was up in Sir William's dressing room packing for him, and as it was at the back of the house he wouldn't see her going down the drive. With luck she'd be back before he even knew she'd gone.

The driving rain prevented her from seeing anything more than a few feet in front of her and by the time she reached the gatehouse her cloak was soaked right through and her boots were sodden. She went to the back door, found the key left under a stone, took off her cloak and boots and left them under the shelter of the porch to drip, then entered in her stockinged feet.

To her surprise the stove was alight and the cottage very warm. There was the usual mess, the table littered with plates, cups and glasses, a loaf of bread left out to grow stale, and a half-empty bottle of whisky. Albert was a terrible hypocrite: he ranted about untidiness and squalor, yet was quite happy to create it all around him.

The floor was very dirty too. Albert clearly wasn't removing his boots any longer when he came in, for there were lumps of dry mud everywhere. The kettle was full and still quite warm, so Hope put it back on the stove and went up the stairs to hide the letter from the Captain, and to make Albert's bed before she tackled washing the dishes and the floor.

As she got to the top of the stairs she heard a creaking sound. It sounded as if the window in Nell and Albert's room was open and banging in the wind.

As she opened the door and walked in, the sight that met her eyes made her gasp with horror and clap her hands over her mouth. Albert was in bed and the blond, curly-haired person beneath him was not a woman, but unmistakably Sir William. Both men were naked, Albert's muscular chest and arms virtually covering his much paler-skinned and slender master.

Such a sight was beyond Hope's comprehension. She froze; even her heart seemed to stop beating with shock.

'Get out!' Albert roared at her.

Hope fled down the stairs, but the enormity of what she'd witnessed was so terrible she didn't know what to do. She knew that male animals would attempt to mount one another when there was no available female, but she hadn't known men could do the same thing.

The shock robbed her of any power to make a decision, and she just stood there crying. She could hear Albert's deep voice, and the higher, more plaintive tones of Sir William mingling with it. One side of her brain told her Sir William would walk down the stairs any moment and give her an explanation that would make it all right, yet the other side told her that there was no possibility of an innocent explanation for what she'd seen.

It was probably no longer than a minute that she stood there, not knowing whether to flee or even where to flee to. But as soon as she heard Albert's footsteps on the stairs she came to her senses and realized she must get out through the back door. Her bootlaces were tangled and her fingers had become as useless as toes in her panic; she tried to force her feet into her boots but she couldn't get them in.

She heard the front door slam shut and breathed a faint sigh of relief that the men were gone. But as she reached up for her cloak from the peg, the back door opened and Albert reached out and gripped her shoulder.

'Get in here,' he growled at her.

She tried to wriggle out of his grasp, but he was too strong. He hauled her back into the kitchen, slammed and locked the door behind her, then struck her hard across the face.

He was wearing just his undershirt and breeches, his feet bare.

'You've been a thorn in my flesh for too long,' he roared at her. 'How dare you come creeping in here spying on me?'

'I didn't. I came to clear up,' she said. 'I didn't know you had anyone here.'

He hit her again, four or five times in succession, fast, hard slaps round the face, and with each one she was moved back closer and closer to the door.

'Please stop it,' she cried out, trying to cover her face with her hands. 'I promise I won't tell anyone.'

He punched her in the stomach then, hitting her so hard her spine cracked against the door. 'You won't get a chance to spread your lies,' he spat at her. 'I'm getting rid of you for good.'

She knew that meant he was going to kill her. It was the only way of ensuring this never got out. Sir William might even have ordered it; after all, he had far more to lose than Albert.

He caught her around the throat the way he'd done before, squeezing her neck until her eyes were almost popping out of her head. He banged her head back against the door again and again until she was seeing stars, then as she fell to the floor he kicked her.

Even though he had bare feet it was like being kicked by a horse. Hope rolled herself into a ball to avoid the worst of the blows, but he was frenzied, like a savage animal. She felt that all the hate locked inside him was rushing out to be inflicted on her.

Just when she felt she couldn't take one more blow, he grabbed the shoulder of her dress to haul her to her feet, and the bodice just ripped away in his hand, leaving her chemise and part of her breasts exposed. As she instinctively bent over to hide herself, Lady Harvey's letter from the Captain fell out.

'What's that?' he snarled. 'A letter from your sweetheart? You dirty little trollop!'

He snatched it up from the floor, but when he saw who it was addressed to, he grinned wolfishly.

'Stealing her ladyship's letters now, are we?' he asked.

'No,' she declared. 'Lady Harvey asked me to keep it for her.'

Slamming one foot into her belly to hold her against the door and balancing on his other leg, he quickly ripped open the envelope and pulled out the letter to read it.

'So she's a treacherous bitch too,' he said as his eyes scanned down the single page.

Hope could feel her face swelling, every part of her body throbbed with pain, and she wished he would kill her now and get it over with for she couldn't take any more.

In those few moments as he read the letter, she suddenly realized that the act she'd witnessed must be the root cause of Nell's and Lady Harvey's unhappiness. While she was certain they didn't know what Albert and Sir William did, it must have had an effect on their marriages. Had this been going on for weeks, months or years? Had Albert only married Nell to conceal his abnormality?

'When did this come?' he demanded.

'Just this morning,' Hope whimpered.

He lowered his foot to the floor, looking thoughtful. Hope wanted to try to run but she knew she wouldn't make it to the front door before he caught her. So she just stood there waiting, her whole body throbbing with pain.

'So the mistress has ensnared the loyalty of another bloody Renton,' he said derisively. 'How far would you go to keep her safe?'

Hope had no idea what the letter contained, and therefore she was uncertain as to what Albert meant. 'I don't know,' she whispered.

'I could kill you now,' he said, showing his teeth. 'Bury

your body in the woods or even in the gardens of Briargate, and no one would ever know. But I might agree to let you go if you leave this place for good and never return.'

Hope thought he was just playing with her, wanting her to beg for her life so he had even more power over her. She wasn't going to let that happen. 'You'd be too frightened to let me go,' she said. 'I could tell someone about you.'

'You could, but I wouldn't recommend it,' he said, dark eyes glinting with malice. 'You see, both Sir William and I would say it was just spiteful lies. No judge would take a foolish kitchenmaid's word against that of a member of the aristocracy, especially when that maid was trying to hide her mistress's adultery and we could show this letter to prove it.'

Hope might never have liked Albert, but until today she had always thought of him as totally loyal to his master and mistress. She could hardly believe that he would be prepared to drag Lady Harvey's name through the mud when she had always been so good to him.

'And then there's Nell, another reason you wouldn't want to start a scandal,' he smirked. 'I know she was in on this! Just imagine her life with no m'lady, and only me!'

Hope's blood ran cold. She could imagine only too well what kind of living hell he'd put Nell through.

'You don't need to threaten me or hurt me,' she pleaded. 'There is another way. I don't want anyone to be shamed, not you or Nell. Not the master or the mistress. I won't breathe a word of this to anyone.'

'How dare a prissy little no-nothing bitch speak down to me!' he snarled, striking her across the face again. 'I love Billy and he loves me, we don't give a fig what simple-minded people think about that.'

His calling Sir William 'Billy' suggested that this *thing* had been going on for some time. Hope could also see Albert was unbalanced and one wrong word from her might tip him over the edge.

'What do you want me to do then?' she asked hesitantly. She was hurting so much now that she felt faint and would agree to anything to get away from him.

'Go right away, tonight,' he said. 'But don't think you can doublecross me, I mean right away, not holed up with that dimwit farmer brother of yours down the road, or any other member of your family. Remember I'm holding all the cards. I can denounce Lady Harvey as an adulteress, and that will ruin your precious Rufus's chances too. And I can make your plain, dull sister's life the worst in God's creation.'

He grabbed her round the throat again and squeezed it slowly, grinning at her maniacally. 'If you ever dare set foot in Briargate again, if you write a letter or even send a message by someone else, believe me, I'll do what I said I'd do.'

Releasing her neck, he punched her hard in the belly and as she collapsed on the floor, howling in pain, he kicked at her head.

'One last thing,' he said, reaching down and hauling her up like a sack of potatoes, 'you're going to write a letter to Nell.'

It was an hour or more later, pitch dark and still raining hard, when Albert pushed Hope out through the front door. To be sure she didn't run into anyone who knew her, he had ordered her to take the long way round through Chelwood to reach the Bristol road.

Her cloak had still been sodden when she put it back on, but he had allowed her to wear an old dress of Nell's as her own was torn. She had seen herself in a mirror as she put the dress on; her eyes were mere slits in puffy flesh, and her lip was cut in two places. As for the rest of her, she was so bruised and battered that only her feet didn't hurt. She guessed by the time she'd walked the ten miles or more to Bristol, they would hurt just as much too though.

She sobbed as she walked, her head down, but knowing how Nell would react to that letter he had made her write hurt worse than her injuries, grievous though they were.

Albert was smarter than she'd realized. He'd told her exactly what to write. That she'd met a young man, a soldier, and she was running off with him because she was tired of scrubbing pans and lighting fires. He made her apologize for taking Nell's dress and said she could have all her things.

She guessed Albert was already on his way back to Briargate for his supper, and he'd listen to Baines, Rose and Martha asking where she was, and say he hadn't seen her as he'd been in the woodshed all afternoon. Maybe he'd leave to go home, and return later with the letter saying he'd found it at the gatehouse.

Hope could even picture the scene in the servants' hall, Baines sitting up at the top of the table, the two women either side of him. Baines would argue and insist he would have seen warning signs if she'd been slipping out to meet someone. Martha and Rose, like the silly geese they were, would reminisce about young men who'd made their hearts pound, and that they had always known Hope had someone tucked away.

By the time Nell got back from Sussex the story would be right round the village. And Nell would believe it and her heart would break.

Chapter Eight

A pricking sensation woke Hope with a start. For a moment she didn't know where she was. But as she moved and felt a stab of pain, so the events of the previous evening came back, and how she came to be lying on straw in a barn.

Ironically she was less than two miles away from Matt's farm. If she had disobeyed Albert and walked down to Woolard and then up the hill to reach the Bristol road, she might even have reached the city last night.

It had been the kind of evening you wouldn't even put a cat out into, very cold with high wind and driving rain. By the time she reached Pensford she was in such pain and so despairing that she paused on the bridge and thought of throwing herself into the torrential river running beneath it. But she knew that when her body was found covered with bruises, Nell would believe that they had been inflicted by the soldier she'd said she loved and her grief would be twice as bad then.

Hope had looked longingly at the lit windows of the Rising Sun ale house too. She knew there would be friends of Matt in there, and they would want to help her. But she didn't dare enlist their help; Pensford was far too close to Briargate, and by morning the story would have reached there. And Hope knew Albert would carry out his threat.

So she walked on up the steep hill, and on and on to Gibbet Lane outside the village of Whitchurch. She could hardly put one foot in front of the other and her whole

173

body was screaming with pain. She didn't intend to try to find shelter in that spot, for as a small child her father had told her how they used to hang people there and their bodies were left dangling until the birds picked them clean. It was an eerie place even in daylight, but when she saw the barn she knew she must overcome her fear, for she couldn't walk any further.

The straw in the barn smelled sweet and it was a relief to be out of the rain and wind, but she was so wet she was unable to get warm. She lay there for what seemed like hours listening to the wind howling, and the events of the day kept churning over and over in her mind.

The image that remained clearest of all was that of Albert in bed with Sir William. She might only have seen them for a couple of seconds, yet the contrast between Albert's bronzed back and dark hair, and blond Sir William beneath him with such white skin was unforgettable. Their shocked expressions at being discovered would be imprinted on her mind for ever.

Yet the act they were engaged in puzzled her as much as it disgusted her, for why would a man want another? Were they the only two men in England like that? Or was she just an ignorant country girl who knew nothing about anything?

Yet it did make new sense of certain things from the past: how Rufus had said his mother asked Sir William if he'd been at a whorehouse; and Nell's claim that Albert often stayed out till the early hours of the morning. Were they together?

Then there was the way the old cook used to say Sir William was girlish, and how Albert insisted he walked from Wells to Briargate on the off-chance Sir William would take him on as gardener. Was that because he knew Sir William was the same as him?

But above all she wondered if Albert had known he could never love a woman when he married Nell.

Hope struggled to her feet as she heard a cock crow nearby. Her cloak and boots were just as wet as they had been last night, and it was still raining. Her hair was coming down and without a comb she could do nothing about it. Just the feel of her sore, puffy face told her that she must look as desperate as she felt.

She hobbled from the barn to the road, but each step was agony and she felt so weak and dizzy it was tempting to go back to the barn. Then a wave of nausea overtook her and she vomited into the bushes.

As she stood up she could see down into the valley through a gap in the bushes. It was too grey and misty to make out anything more than the steeple of the church at Publow, but that was enough to make her cry for it wasn't far from Woolard and Matt.

She could imagine him in his kitchen, dark hair tousled from sleep, a shadow of bristles on his chin, perhaps with the baby on his knee while Amy made him tea. He would be furious when he heard about the letter. Gentle Amy would probably think it was romantic, and urge Matt and the boys not to be angry. But not one of them would ever consider that Hope might have been forced to write that letter, and that it wasn't true.

She knew she couldn't hope that Sir William would feel guilty and admit what really happened in the gatehouse. In truth he had probably ordered Albert to silence her and didn't care how he achieved it.

Her disappearance would be the talk of the village for a few days, but once that had died down even her own family would put her out of their minds.

People disappeared all the time. They left the village to

look for work in Bath or Bristol and never came back. Hope could remember her father talking about a man whose son had been gone for three years when he got a letter from a priest in America telling him his boy had died of smallpox. There was never any explanation about how or why the lad went there.

Toby and Alice hadn't been back to the village for eighteen months; they had lost the incentive to take the long walk since their mother and father died. James would probably never come back again either, and once Ruth had her baby she'd lose interest in her brothers and sisters too. That was just the way it was, their family was no different to countless others. But Hope knew Nell would grieve for her, she wouldn't forget her youngest sister, not in a few weeks or even a few years. And she hadn't even got a loving husband to comfort and reassure her.

The clock on St Nicholas's church was striking twelve noon as Hope finally reached Bristol Bridge. It had taken some five hours or so to walk a distance that could be completed in two. It was almost miraculous that she'd got there at all, for she was dizzy with pain all the way and she was so weak now that she had to hang on to the bridge parapet to hold herself up.

Yet she felt no pleasure or relief that she'd made it, for the noise of rumbling carts and carriages and the shrill cries from street vendors was deafening and the river stank like a privy. People pushed and shoved past her; if they even noticed her they wouldn't stop to offer any help to a girl who was soaking wet, swaying with exhaustion and clearly in pain. Her father had always said that city folk had no charity, and Hope had never felt so alone and abandoned in her entire life.

She thought if she could just have a drink of water

she'd feel a lot better, but everyone knew you couldn't drink Bristol water. How could she get a drink without money?

She hadn't been to Bristol since her father died, and his description of how it was for him on that last fateful trip was ever present in her mind. She pulled her wet cloak around her more tightly, letting the hood hang over her face to hide her injuries, and shuffled painfully on.

As she stepped into the road to cross over to the church, she heard the driver of a carriage scream some abuse. It seemed to be directed at her, yet she didn't know why. She felt so strange, as though her mind and body had separated. She could hear noise all around her, smell the horse droppings in the street, and even sensed someone's face right up close to hers. But it was dreamlike, as though she were asleep.

'You gotta get up,' she heard a woman say. 'You stay there and they'll cart you off to the Bridewell or the infirmary.'

'Look at her face!' a man exclaimed. 'She's bin given a right good hiding.'

'Who did this to you, love?' the woman asked. 'You nearly got yerself run over by that carriage! Maybe we should call a constable?'

The word 'constable' was almost like having smelling salts held beneath her nose. Hope came round sufficiently to know she was lying on the ground; that the voices she'd heard belonged to a young man and woman, and that there were other people standing around looking down at her. But she couldn't seem to open her eyes wide enough to see them properly.

'Don't call a constable,' she managed to croak out. 'Just help me up!'

She felt them lifting her, but she swayed on her feet and the young woman held on to her. 'Lawdy! You're soaked through,' she exclaimed. 'You ain't bin having a dip in the river, 'ave you?'

Hope knew that the woman was teasing, and that at least suggested she was kindly. 'I like my water drinkable,' she replied, and tried very hard to smile.

'Lord love her,' the woman exclaimed. 'Well, whoever hit you ain't quite dampened yer spirit, I'll say that. Give us a 'and, Gussie, let's get 'er in the church outa the rain.'

The church was very dark, but it was much warmer than out on the street and smelled of candlewax rather than human and animal waste. Once Hope was sitting on a bench near the door, she tried to thank the couple, but she still couldn't open her eyes enough to see them properly.

'I can't see,' she murmured.

'Shouldn't think you could, both yer eyes are swollen over,' the young man said. 'Who done this?'

'My brother-in-law,' Hope said.

'Yer sister let him do that to yer?' the woman asked indignantly.

'She wasn't there,' Hope said. 'He threw me out the house. I walked half the night, and then came on here this morning.'

'Have you got folks in Bristol?' the woman asked.

'No, and I don't have any money either,' Hope said. 'Do you know anywhere I could get work?'

She felt rather than saw them exchange meaningful glances. Assuming they were doubtful about her being taken on by anyone because of how she looked, she pushed back her hood. 'If you could just lend me a comb and show me somewhere I could wash my face, I'll be all right. I've been a kitchenmaid for over three years, and I can cook very well.'

When they remained silent, she took that to be disbelief and she finally broke down in tears. 'I can do all kinds of work,' she sobbed. 'Please believe me!'

'Well, you ain't gonna be able to get any sorta work with yer face that way,' the young woman said, and to Hope's surprise she drew her into her arms and rocked her. 'Now, don't cry, love. You's just weary and hurt. I reckon we'll take you home with us and patch you up. God knows, we can't leave you here like this.'

'You ain't thinking straight, Betsy,' Gussie said in a whisper, glancing over his shoulder at the girl asleep on the pile of sacks which passed for a bed. 'It's hard enough lookin' out fer ourselves. We can't keep her an' all.'

Betsy had bathed the girl's face, given her some small beer to drink, then helped her out of her wet clothes and covered her in a blanket. Now she was asleep.

The room was in Lewins Mead, a rabbit warren of fetid alleys and ancient dilapidated wooden-framed houses close to the docks. It housed what someone in Parliament had recently dubbed 'The Dangerous and Perishing Classes', a stratum of life well below the working classes – thieves, whores, crossing sweepers, street vendors, cripples, deserters, the most desperate of the city's poor.

A hundred years earlier when Bristol had been the second biggest city next to London, and the docks as busy as London's and Liverpool's, Lewins Mead had been a good address. Great fortunes had been made during the slave trade, for it was Bristol ships that sailed to Africa to pick up slaves, then on to the West Indies to sell them, finally returning to England laden with molasses and tobacco. But as the shipping trade boomed, the wealthy merchants, ships' captains and professional men no longer wished to live close to the pestilence of the docks, and they moved to grand new houses up on the hills of Clifton and Kingsdown.

But the docks were no longer as busy as they had been a hundred years earlier. Exorbitant harbour dues, the tardiness of the Corporation in building the new floating harbour, and the fact that new, bigger ships were unable to get up and down the river Avon, meant that Bristol had lost out to Liverpool docks. The new railways meant that it had lost its place as the distribution centre for the whole of the West of England, Wales and the Midlands.

Once, Bristol had been proud of its many industries – sugar refining, glass, iron foundries and soap manufacture – but they were gone now, aside from four glass companies. That and the countrywide failing economy in recent years had created even more hardship in Bristol.

So now the old merchants' houses were let out by the room, and the tenants sublet floor space to anyone who wanted it. Sometimes there were as many as twenty or thirty people sleeping in each room. The houses sagged and creaked with neglect; wind blew in through the cracks, and the upper windows which overhung the narrow alleyways were boarded up as the glass broke or fell out.

But Betsy and Gussie thought themselves fortunate to have this top-floor room in Lamb Lane. They might share it with four other people, but they were friends, not strangers. The roof didn't leak too badly, they had glass in their small window and a fireplace too, and they'd stuffed up the holes in the walls with oiled rags. To them it was a home.

'She'll bring us luck,' Betsy insisted. 'There's something about her.'

'Aye, there's something about her! Something that makes a man smash her face in,' Gussie said gloomily. 'And she's real sick. What if we catch it?'

'You can't catch what ails her,' Betsy said stoutly. She suspected the girl was carrying a child and her brother-in-law had been afraid she'd shame his family.

Betsy Archer was nineteen. She was five feet five and

buxom, with long dark hair which she plaited and wound round her head like a crown, and her lustrous dark eyes and olive skin suggested she had Italian or Spanish blood. Although she was not a real beauty, people described her as 'comely', for she had an exotic, proud look about her and a vibrancy that even the harshness of her life hadn't erased.

Born in Liverpool, Betsy was eight when her father, a cooper by trade, brought the family to Bristol. Three months later, both her parents and Sadie, her younger sister, died when the lodging house they were staying in caught fire. Her father had lifted Betsy through the upstairs window and dropped her into a man's arms. He didn't have time to do the same for Sadie.

Sometimes Betsy wished she'd died in that fire too. She had survived by mingling with the hundreds of other orphaned or abandoned children who hung around the docks and learned begging, stealing and scavenging from them. Home was wherever she could squeeze in for the night, and she was grateful if she was given a blanket, even if it was crawling with lice.

By the time she was ten many of the children she'd got to know when she was first orphaned were in prison. Some had died. Almost all the older girls had become whores. Betsy didn't want to end up in prison or dead, and she didn't intend to become a whore either.

Even at that tender age she had already learned that her only asset was her virginity. Twice she was foolish enough to be taken in by seemingly motherly women who offered her a home, new clothes and all the food she could eat. But she was lucky both times in being helped to escape before she was presented to a 'gentleman' who had a penchant for children.

She never ruled out using that one asset one day, providing she got big money for it. But until then she intended to stay alive and keep out of prison, so she kept her wits about her and didn't take unnecessary risks.

The dank, stinking alleys and narrow lanes around the docks were her domain. She knew almost everyone who lived there and didn't steal from them. She knew all the marine shops where she could get a few pennies for the wood, nails and metal she managed to scavenge. That paid the rent. When there was nothing left over for food, she would go up to the big houses in Clifton and find one where the cook had been foolish enough to leave the back door open while she was baking. It took only a few seconds to slip in and steal a pie or a cake – once she grabbed a whole leg of lamb straight from the oven.

The docks were a source of many free gifts for anyone prepared to watch and wait, patiently armed with a basket and a pot or jar. Betsy would check every morning which ships were being unloaded, and loiter in the hopes that a dropped crate would spill open. She would pounce on the fruit, sugar or tea and be off with it, often even before the dockers became aware that they'd damaged the crate.

There were also the foreign sailors she could charm into giving her a sixpence to buy a new dress so she could meet them later.

She never bought clothes, just as she never kept those appointments with foreign sailors. But up in the High Street there were second-hand clothes shops where she could whip a petticoat, dress or hat while the shopkeeper was distracted.

Betsy met Gussie when she was thirteen and he was twelve, a small, freckle-faced, ginger-haired boy who'd tramped from Devon to Bristol to seek his fortune. He'd come up to her as she was hanging about waiting for a pie man to turn his back so she could snatch one of his wares, and he'd asked her where he could sleep for the night.

Betsy was so hungry that she said if he could distract the pie man's attention she'd help him. He played a blinder by pretending to throw a fit in front of the stall, and she didn't get just one pie, but three.

She was of course obliged to give Gussie one of the pies and to take him back to the flophouse she mostly stayed at.

Within a couple of days Betsy had decided Gussie was the perfect partner for her. He wasn't tough, but he was wily and daring. Apart from the pretend fits, he could shin up a drainpipe and enter a house by an upper window in broad daylight. He could also make a sound which frightened horses. When they began to bolt, he'd grab the reins and calm the horse, for which the stunned owner would then reward him. He said he'd learned it from a man in a circus who had also taught him acrobatics and clowning.

It was the clowning that really won Betsy over. Gussie would do fantastic funny mimes, twisting his rubbery face to portray emotions and different kinds of people. One night he did a little act while people were queuing to get into the theatre in King Street and they roared with laughter, throwing nearly two shillings in pennies and halfpennies to him. Even his name, Augustus Pomfrey, made Betsy laugh; she said it would make an excellent name for a fat alderman, but was ridiculous on a small, skinny boy with hair the colour of carrots. But then, she found she laughed a great deal with Gussie, for despite his small stature she felt sort of protected and comfortable with him. He might not be able to fight off the many men who tried to have their way with her, but his presence deterred them. And in turn she protected him from the thugs and ruffians that she'd grown up with.

Six years on they were inseparable, an indomitable unit, but not lovers. Betsy had eventually traded her virginity to a sea captain for the princely sum of five guineas, but the experience had put her off men. Gussie, with his brotherly affection and total loyalty, was the only male she trusted completely.

'She's quite a little lady,' Betsy said thoughtfully. 'Hurt as she is, she thanked us real nice. When those shiners have gone I bet she'll be real bonny.'

'You ain't thinkin' of taking her down to Dolly's!' Gussie exclaimed.

''Course not, whatcha take me for?' Betsy replied indignantly. Dolly owned a bawdy house in King Street.

'So what are we going to do with her?'

'We don't have to do nothin' with her. I jest feel sorry fer her. It won't kill us to take care of her for a day or two till she's mended, will it?'

Gussie shrugged. He knew once Betsy's mind was made up about something, nothing would change it. 'I'd best light the fire then so we can dry her clothes, then I'll go out and get us something to eat.'

Betsy sat on the floor by the fire after Gussie left, but she kept glancing round at the sleeping girl. Her whole face was purple and black with bruising, swollen flesh completely covering her eyes. But as she'd helped her take off her sodden dress, the girl had clutched at her stomach, and Betsy guessed she'd been punched and kicked there too.

Men beating women was an everyday occurrence around here. It was equally common to see people weak with hunger. Young girls and boys flocked into Bristol every day in the hopes of finding work, and unless they had a character from a previous employer, almost all of them ended up dead, defeated or criminals.

Betsy didn't normally help anyone. The one thing she'd learned right from the age of eight when she saw that house burn down with her mother, father and Sadic inside, was that it was a tough old world. You had to look after yourself, be quicker, more cunning, braver and smarter than anyone else, for if you just dropped your guard for a moment then someone would do you down.

So she couldn't quite understand what it was about *this* girl that had made her want to help her.

Looking at her clothes drying round the fire, she could see they were well made. Plain cloth, but the stitching was as small and neat as some she'd seen on gowns in the market that had once belonged to rich women. Her undergarments had impressed Betsy too, for apart from the mud splattered around the hems of her petticoats, they were very clean and dainty.

The girl's face was too distorted and swollen to tell if it was a pretty one, but her hair was black and glossy, and where she wasn't bruised, her skin was smooth and very white, not mottled and rough like so many women's round here. Her hands were proof she'd spent years in a kitchen, for they were red and callused, but overall she looked as though she'd been cared for.

Was she carrying a child?

Round here no one could afford to get married, so if a girl got in the family way no one thought anything of it. But Betsy had enough recollection of life before her parents died to know that in more genteel circles bastards were frowned on.

Betsy was just going to wriggle over closer to the girl and look to see if she had a swollen belly, when she began to stir. She moved to sit up, winced with pain and flopped down again.

'How'd yer feel now? Any better for a sleep?' Betsy asked.

The girl looked about her as if confused. 'I can see a bit better now. But both my eyes hurt. Are they very swollen?'

'Let's just say you won't be getting no admirers for a bit,' Betsy said with a chuckle.

'It was very kind of you and your husband to help me.'

The sweetness of her voice touched Betsy, but it also reminded her to be careful. For all she knew the girl could be a magistrate's daughter! 'Gussie ain't me husband; only a friend. I'll tell you right now, we don't normally help no one. So if you wants to stay tonight you'd better spill it out!'

'Spill what out?'

'Well, yer name, how old you are, and where you from, fer a start. We couldn't get no sense out of yer while we was helping you 'ere.'

'Hope Renton, fifteen, and I come from a village beyond Bristol to the south. Did you say your name is Betsy?'

'That's right. Betsy Archer and I'm nobody's fool. So I'm gonna make a cup of tea. And then you're gonna tell me how you ended up nearly getting yerself flattened under a carriage wheel. And when the baby's due.'

'I'm not having a baby,' Hope said indignantly. 'What made you think I was?'

'That's the usual reason for girls running away.' Betsy shrugged. 'But if you say you ain't, then that's one problem out the way.'

Hope watched as Betsy filled an old tin teapot with some water from a jug, and then put it on the fire to boil. She wondered why she hadn't got a kettle.

Her memory of coming here was cloudy. She remembered Betsy and Gussie being with her in the church, then them holding her arms to support her and taking her through some very narrow alleys. But that was all she could remember.

She shuddered as she looked about the small, gloomy

room. It was clearly at the top of the house for the ceiling sloped sharply towards the tiny window, and it had no furniture, only a few wooden crates and piles of sacks which clearly served as beds. On one of the crates there were several cracked cups and a large tin box. A bucket stood in the corner by the door, presumably for slops, and on another crate was a tin basin.

Hope knew people who were very much poorer than her own family, but even they had some sort of furniture, a few trinkets and bits of china. Betsy must be desperately poor, but she didn't look it for she had gold hoops in her ears, and her red dress was stylish, even if it was shabby, dirty and a bit vulgar with such a low neck.

'It's quiet here,' Hope said. 'Is that because you are the only people living here?'

Betsy gave a kind of strangled snort. 'Your eyes must've been bad when we brought you in here,' she said. 'It's like a bleedin' ants' nest, so many people coming and going you can't count them all. It's quiet now cos most are out, but come this evening it'll be a different story. Now, that brings me round to your'n. Come on, tell me!'

Hope thought fast. She was very grateful to Betsy, but she wasn't sure it was sensible to tell her the whole truth, not until she knew she could trust her. So she gave her a safer, shortened version, that Albert resented her living with him and her sister, and while Nell was away he'd hit her and told her to get out.

'Why didn't you go up to the big house and tell them what he'd done?' Betsy asked.

'Because he would have taken it out on Nell when she got back,' Hope said. 'I couldn't do anything to Albert without it coming back on Nell.'

Betsy seemed satisfied with that. The water was boiling in the teapot now, and she lifted it off the fire and put it on the crate, then opening the tin she took out a packet of tea and spooned some into the water.

'We gotta keep any food stuff in this tin cos of the mice and rats,' Betsy said, getting out a small bag of sugar. 'There's a bit of bread if you want it. Gussie's gone to get us some pies, but it'll keep you going until then.'

With the cup of sweet black tea in one hand and a lump of bread in the other, Hope felt a little better, though it was hard to eat and drink with her cut lips. 'I'll pay you back for my keep as soon as I get a position,' she said.

'You got a character?' Betsy asked.

'No, I couldn't, could I? Albert threw me out too fast.'

'Then you'll be lucky to get anything,' Betsy said curtly. 'Whatcha want to be a servant for anyways?'

Hope said it was all she knew, but she wouldn't mind working in a shop.

'You has to be able to figure, writing it down and that,' Betsy said.

'I can do that,' Hope replied. 'I know all the stuff about linen and household things too. And I know about farming and animals.'

'You're a bit of a know-all, ain'tcha?' Betsy said sarcastically.

Hope was embarrassed then and hung her head. 'I didn't mean to be, I was only telling you what I could do because I thought it might give you ideas for places I could go to look for work.'

Betsy didn't know anyone who could read and write, and she was in fact impressed. It struck her that if her own parents had lived, she might have learned such skills. But there was something more about this girl, maybe it was her name, God knows, *hope* was the only thing that kept her going sometimes. Or maybe it was because if her sister hadn't died, she'd be the same age. Yet whatever the reason, she felt drawn to the girl, like it was a kind of fate.

'You can't go nowhere till yer face is mended,' she said, more kindly. 'So jest rest up fer now. Tell us about what you done in the big house. I ain't bin in one, leastways not to stop, if yer know what I mean.'

A week later, Hope studied her face in a small mirror Gussie had brought home for her.

'You look pretty now,' he said, his pale brown eyes crinkling up as he smiled at her. 'We didn't want you to see how bad you looked when we found you.'

Hope's eyes prickled with tears of gratitude. Not for the mirror – she would sooner have remained in ignorance about how she looked, for once the swelling had gone down on her face she had imagined she would look normal again. But the bruising was still purple and at no stretch of the imagination did she look pretty. Yet it was another act of kindness, of which Gussie and Betsy had showered so many on her. They'd let her stay, they'd fed her and comforted her, all when they had so little themselves.

'Gus might be sweet-talking when he says you look pretty, but you don't look like a monster no more,' Betsy said with laughter in her voice. 'It'll be a couple more weeks before them bruises fade, but you look good enough for the Grapes tonight.'

Gussie and Betsy went out drinking every night; it seemed that the only thing which made life bearable for everyone in Lewins Mead was cheap gin or rum. Up till now Hope had declined to go with them, using her injuries as an excuse, but it was clear they thought the time had come for her to venture out.

'I can't,' Hope said in alarm. 'I'm not ready for that. I'll be all right here on my own.'

'I didn't take you for a coward,' Betsy retorted, putting

her hands on her hips and glowering at the younger girl. 'No one will take no notice of a few bruises, they's as common as fleas down the Grapes.'

Hope realized by that response she had to go. It wasn't just that they'd be offended if she refused, she had to prove to them she had spirit. But they couldn't possibly know how terrifying their world was to her.

On the day they'd brought her here, she had felt like an ill-treated dog that was just grateful for being brought inside. Her mind had stopped working and she couldn't think about the next day, or the one after. She answered Betsy's questions as best she could, but she couldn't even summon up enough strength to ask her anything. She would have been glad just to lie down and die for she hurt too much to want to live.

She must have fallen asleep again soon after Gussie arrived back with some hot pies for them and she didn't wake till the following morning. To her shock and horror there were four other people aside from Gussie and Betsy asleep all around her, and a stink coming from the bucket in the corner.

She wanted to relieve herself too, but she couldn't bring herself to add to that already nearly full bucket, and as she lay there wondering if there was a privy downstairs, she became aware of a strange noise. It was a kind of animal sound, deep and irregular, and it was some time before she realized it was people snoring all over the house. Soon there were other sounds too, babies crying, children shouting, and a man bellowing for them to shut up.

Even as the noise downstairs got louder and louder it didn't wake her room-mates. She heard a church clock strike eight and it seemed inconceivable that she and all these other people were still in bed so late in the morning. Not that the pile of sacks and a blanket qualified as a real bed, and she was itching all over as if she'd been bitten by something.

Later that morning, she discovered that the slop bucket was emptied out of the window into the alley below. Water had to be drawn from a pump further down, and there was a privy out the back. But as it served the whole house – eight rooms with an average of ten people sleeping in each – it wasn't a place anyone would visit willingly.

The four extra lodgers, introduced to her as Mole, Shanks, Josie and Welsh Lil, were all around the same age as Betsy, much more shabbily dressed, and almost as sinister-looking as their names. But they disappeared almost as soon as they got up. Betsy said her room was a 'padding ken' to them, meaning just a place to flop, and she and Gussie didn't trouble themselves with what they did all day. There was an implication in that explanation that they were criminals.

Hope's clothes and boots were dry again, and as it had stopped raining at last, Gussie and Betsy insisted they took her out to show her around.

Maybe it was because she was in pain and very aware people were staring at her injuries, but the part of Bristol they showed her that day looked nothing like the splendid, exciting place she remembered coming to as a child with her father. It was grey, filthy and noisy: mean, stinking alleys with human effluent running down them, houses that looked as if they were on the verge of collapse. She saw people that were like something from a nightmare; diseased-looking women with hollow eyes sat like statues in doorways, often clutching a wailing baby in their arms. There were brutish-looking men in broken-down stove-pipe hats and ragged coats swigging from bottles, and hundreds of barefoot, ragged children playing in the muck. Cripples hobbled past on crutches ready for a day's begging in the better parts of town, and she even saw a child pulling a cart along with a woman with no legs sitting on it. There were mad people raving and shaking their fists, gin-soaked floozies and even men who were as black as coal.

Betsy and Gussie appeared to be oblivious to Hope's shock as they pointed out the best stall for herrings, their favourite beer shop, and the marine shop where they sold anything they'd managed to scavenge. They pointed out a man carrying a hoe and a net and said he scavenged in the drains that ran into the river, and it was said he could make as much as five pounds on a good day as money dropped in the street often ended up there. Gussie laughingly told her that such men could drown in those drains if they didn't take careful notice of tides.

Betsy showed her a house with boarded-over windows and said a coiner lived and worked there. Hope had no idea what a coiner was, but it seemed it was someone who made counterfeit money. Betsy said he'd once got her to pass some for him, and all had gone well until one shopkeeper got suspicious, and she had to run like the wind to escape him.

Hope felt a little better once they'd got away from Lewins Mead and went down by the docks. That was every bit as dirty, noisy and stinking, but the beautiful ships bobbing up and down on the wide expanse of river which glinted silver in the weak autumn sunshine made up for it. Gleaming brasswork, shiny varnished wood and neatly coiled huge ropes bleached by salt water were good to look at after the filth of Lamb Lane. She looked up at the tall masts and wondered how anyone would dare climb to the top of them. She was entranced by the carved figureheads on the ships' bows, the sight of sailors sitting on decks mending sails, and even the crates of live chickens, sheep and goats she saw being loaded.

The docks were a hive of industry. Huge barrels of French and Spanish wine were being rolled along over the cobblestones, burly men were hauling great nets of goods on and off the ships, carts came and went carrying more goods, and she saw carriages arriving that looked grand enough for royalty.

The hammering from a ship-builder's yard, sails flapping in the wind to dry, sailors scrubbing decks and the squawking sound of seagulls took Hope out of herself. It was thrilling to imagine the foreign countries the ships set sail for, and in their way, the docks were just as ordered as her life had been back at Briargate.

She thought she would like to work there, in some capacity, but when she voiced this thought to Betsy she cackled with laughter.

'Oh, there's work to be had here,' she said, rolling her eyes at a gang of sailors. 'There's lead the drunks up an alley and rob them; there's wait and watch for them to leave some goods unattended. You can even offer to clean the seagull shit off some fine lady's shoes.'

That wasn't what Hope had in mind at all. She was thinking more of sitting in one of the shipping offices writing things down in a big ledger. But she didn't correct Betsy because she didn't want her to get the idea that the girl she'd rescued thought she was too grand for Lewins Mead.

The days after that first one seemed endless for she elected to stay in alone while Gussie and Betsy went about their business. But there was nothing to do in the room, and she felt desolate whenever her mind slipped back to her family or Briargate. She felt white-hot hatred for Albert, and although she busied her mind plotting her revenge, she knew that in reality there was nothing she could do to him, even killing him, that wouldn't adversely affect Nell.

She felt utterly hopeless. She couldn't get a decent job without a character. She couldn't leave here because she had no money. She couldn't even pass the time cleaning, cooking or mending because there was none of the necessary equipment.

She'd worked since she was a child and although she'd often thought it would be nice to sit and do nothing, it wasn't. Not in a squalid, dirty room anyway, when you were eaten up with hatred for someone and dependent on the kindness of strangers just to eat.

In the next couple of days, sometimes, when her boredom grew bigger than her fear, she ventured downstairs and explored Lamb Lane and the neighbouring alleyways. It was on these occasions that she observed that the kind of housekeeping skills she had were unknown here.

The residents bought food ready-cooked and ate it on the move; they didn't wash or mend clothes, but wore them till they fell apart, or in Betsy's case, until she could steal replacements. The family life Hope had known as a child didn't exist either. Children were out on the streets from first light till after dark, and the man of the house who only went in to sleep wasn't necessarily their father.

In a lesson once with the Reverend Gosling he'd said that a huge proportion of babies born in the poorest areas of cities died in their first year, and for the survivors, life would continue to be an obstacle course. If they recovered from measles or scarlet fever, there were dozens more diseases which could easily carry them off.

Gussie had told her that by the time the children were seven or eight, almost all of them would be living on the streets, foraging for their own food. Some of them were like him, escaping a brutal man in the home and a mother in a constant gin-soaked haze, but the rest had been pushed out to fend for themselves as the home was too crowded, often with three or four families sharing one room. All were ragged and barefoot, and some had barely a shirt to cover them.

Hygiene as Hope knew it was unknown. Neither bodies nor clothes were washed, and the latter were worn until they fell apart. The children had matted hair which had never known a comb or a brush, their scalps crawling with lice. She saw poor little mites with festering wounds, impetigo and hideous boils scrabbling after scraps of food thrown into the street. Hope knew that with no care, schooling or even anyone to set them a good example, those that survived to reach adulthood would perpetuate this appalling state of affairs by bringing still more neglected waifs into the world.

On her third day in Lamb Lane Hope could stand the dirt no more, and she picked up each of the sacks used for sleeping and shook them out of the window. Then she made a broom of sorts with some rags left in a corner. She bundled some together, tied a bit of string round it so it was like a mop, and swept the room. The rubbish and dust filled a box, and she took it out and deposited it in the street where everyone else put theirs.

With another rag she washed over the window and polished it up with some old newspaper she found under the sacks. With the sacks back in neat piles, each with a blanket on top, the room looked marginally better, but it got her thinking about her old room at Briargate, with its soft quilt, clean blankets and white cotton sheets, and that made her cry all over again.

Gussie and Betsy viewed the tidied room with a certain amount of admiration, but mostly amusement. 'We can tell folks we's going up in the world cos we've got ourselves a maid,' Betsy chortled. She lay down on one of the piles of sacks and waved her hand at Hope.

'Make me tea now, girl, and quick about it,' she said in a grand voice. 'Use the silver teapot of course, and once you've done that you can press my ballgown for tonight.'

Hope laughed, for it was impossible not to, Betsy was so warm and irreverent, but her laughter turned to consternation when Gussie pulled two candles out of the front of his coat.

'Are they from a church?' she asked in horror, recognizing them as the same thick, long kind they always had in St Mary's back home.

'Indeed they are,' he said with a grin. 'They last a goodly time too. So while her ladyship sups her tea, we can have light.'

Hope bit back her protest. She'd already observed they had no respect for the law, authority or gentry and teased her because she had. But stealing something from a church was so wicked.

'Don't look like that,' Gussie reprimanded her. 'They've got dozens of them, they won't miss two. Besides, the Church is rich, they takes money from the poor and dresses up all those bishops in swanky folderols so they can live in palaces and lie around all day doing nothing.'

Gussie's caustic remark about the Church was just one of many he made on various subjects, which challenged beliefs Hope had held since childhood. She was soon finding herself far less certain of what was right and what was wrong.

The Reverend Gosling had drummed into her 'Blessed are the Meek.' Gussie said that was put about by rich and powerful people to make sure there were always millions of meek people they could exploit. He pointed out that she had meekly laid fires and emptied chamber pots for the idle rich and that she'd been taught to be grateful for the few shillings a year she got. He said it was time she valued herself a bit more.

Betsy was even more controversial. She thought women should have equal rights to men. She said it was wrong that a woman's property and money should become her husband's when she married, that he could beat her whenever he liked, and take their children away from her if she finally got brave enough to try to leave him. She also thought women should be able to do any job, be that as a doctor, judge, priest or carpenter, if they had the ability. She had a yen to be a carpenter herself, and she was fed up with men laughing at her for it.

Hope walked to the Grapes in trepidation later that evening, but to her surprise it wasn't a hideous dark dive as she'd expected, but a veritable palace, with bright gas lights, gilt pillars, huge mirrors and velveteen seats. She had marvelled at the gas lamps out on the streets, but she hadn't expected to see them in a beer house.

'Shut yer mouth, the fleas will jump in,' Betsy said with a grin.

'But it's like a palace,' Hope exclaimed. She wasn't just amazed by the elegance of the place, but the customers weren't like the woebegone folk in Lamb Lane – some of them in fact were quite smartly dressed.

'It's a gin palace,' Gussie said. 'And you've got to try some.'

Hope didn't much like the taste of her first gin and water, but she had to admit the effect was pleasant. By the second one she'd forgotten about her bruised face, Lamb Lane, and that she could see no future for herself.

Gussie introduced her to his and Betsy's friends as his cousin up from the country, and they were a lively, good-natured bunch of people. Hope guessed some of the girls were whores as they had paint on their faces and plunging necklines, but it was so good to see people who didn't look wretched that she didn't care.

One of Gussie's male friends was called Basher Boulton. He had a squashed nose and a cauliflower ear, but Gussie said he was a champion prize fighter. There was another man who was talking about dog fighting; he appeared to be organizing one a few miles out of Bristol. Both these men were very sweet to her, commiserating over her bruises. Basher said he had some special ointment which would make them go double quick and maybe she could meet him at his lodgings tomorrow night so he could give it to her.

'I know what you want to give her!' Betsy chimed in. 'And it'll be over my dead body!'

Hope had never had such a good time. A man began playing a piano accordion, and she danced first with Gussie, then with everyone else who asked her. Watching the men cavorting around exuberantly, she was reminded of the May Day celebrations and harvest suppers back home. Nell, who had seen gentry dancing, had often remarked in a superior tone that country folk danced like carthorses. But Hope liked it, it was fun to be swirled around until she was dizzy. She understood now why Betsy and Gussie came out every night.

It was after midnight when Gussie took Hope's arm and led her towards the door. 'It's time I took you home,' he said.

'But I don't want to go home yet,' she said, pulling back. 'I'm having a lovely time.'

'You're drunk, Hope,' he said.

'No I'm not,' she insisted.

He caught hold of her more tightly and drew her outside. After the sweaty heat and smoke inside, the street felt icy cold. But she also felt very dizzy and the gas light above them seemed to be swaying.

'I'm just dizzy,' she insisted. 'It was the dancing. Let me go back in and I'll sit down.'

Gussie put one hand either side of her face and kissed her nose. 'You ain't dizzy with dancin', it's the gin,' he said. 'You go back in there and you'll pass out.'

His hands felt good on her face and he was looking at her in such a strange way. 'You wouldn't be intending to get me back home just so you can have your wicked way with me, would you?' she giggled.

She had never noticed before how attractive his eyes were, like amber, with specks of a darker colour too, and his eyelashes were very long and thick.

'No, I weren't,' he smiled. 'But if I don't getcha home some cove will try it on. I'm not tough enough to fight them off for you.'

She laughed, more because of the intense way he was looking at her than thinking he'd said something funny. 'A perfect gentleman,' she said, and leaned against his shoulder for suddenly she felt very strange and woozy.

'And you're a little lady,' he said as he led her away. 'Too good for the likes of them in there.'

Chapter Nine

Nell arrived back at Briargate with Lady Harvey on 23 December, several weeks after Squire Dorville's funeral. It was nine at night as the cab turned into the drive. The gatehouse was in darkness so Nell assumed Albert had gone to bed, but up at the big house there were lanterns shining welcomingly in the porch.

'I expect you're very glad to be home, m'lady?' she said to her mistress.

'I certainly am, Nell,' Lady Harvey sighed. 'These past weeks have been such a trial. I feel utterly exhausted.'

There had been a great deal of unpleasantness between Lady Harvey and her sisters after the reading of their father's will. Sir William hadn't helped the situation by becoming drunk and abusive, then rushing off and leaving his wife to smooth ruffled feathers.

'You'll soon recover now,' Nell said comfortingly. 'Master Rufus and everyone at Briargate will be so pleased to have you home again.'

Even before the cab reached the end of the drive, Baines came out with a lantern, quickly followed by Rose. Nell wondered if he had sat by the window waiting, because he surely couldn't have heard the cab from the kitchen.

Baines and Rose took Lady Harvey's luggage and as they all went into the hall Master Rufus came hurtling down the stairs excitedly.

'Mama, I'm so glad you are back,' he said, throwing

himself at her. 'I was so afraid you wouldn't get here for Christmas.'

Nell smiled at the happy reunion. Rufus seemed to have grown another inch or two since he went back to school in September, and he was growing into a very handsome young man.

She wondered fleetingly why Hope wasn't hovering in the background to greet them too. But when Baines said he would bring some supper to the drawing room for Lady Harvey she assumed Hope was helping Martha prepare it.

After Rose had taken Lady Harvey's fur-lined cloak and her hat, mother and son went towards the drawing room with their arms around each other. Nell hurried out to the kitchen; it was so long since she'd had a drink she felt as though her throat had been cut, and she was perished with the cold.

'Oh, it feels so good to be in the warm at last,' she said as she went into the kitchen, making straight for the stove and resting her bottom against it. 'What I wouldn't have given for a fur-lined cloak on the train coming home!'

Martha was just putting some finishing touches to the tray for the mistress, and she looked up and smiled at Nell.

'It's good to have you back,' she said. 'Albert stayed on to wait for you, but it got so late he had to go to his bed. But at least he will have warmed it for you.'

'Where's Hope?' Nell asked as Baines came into the kitchen.

He ignored her question and picked up the tray. 'I'll just take this in to her ladyship,' he said.

'Is something wrong?' Nell asked after he'd left the room. 'Is Hope sick?'

'It ain't my place to say anything,' Martha said. 'Baines will tell you when he comes back.'

Nell knew then that something *was* wrong, and this was confirmed when she saw Rose scuttling towards the servants' hall, presumably because she didn't want to be questioned either. 'Rose! Tell me where Hope is,' she called out.

'Now, calm down, Nell,' Martha said. 'Baines won't be long.'

'She isn't here, is she?' Nell exclaimed. 'Where's she gone? When did she go?'

Martha's wooden expression and Rose's extreme nervousness told her that Hope had most definitely gone, but neither of them was prepared to say why or when.

Nell paced the floor, cold and thirst forgotten in her agitation. The kitchen smelled of cinnamon, cloves and other spices, good smells that reminded her of past Christmases when she'd had family all around her here. Even with all the misery Albert caused her, here at Briargate she'd always been able to put that aside. She hadn't wanted either James or Ruth to leave, but she never voiced this because she knew it was wrong to stand in their way. But without Hope she didn't know what she would do.

Baines came in and ominously shut the door behind him.

'She's gone, hasn't she?' Nell said.

Baines nodded glumly.

'Why so suddenly? Surely she could have waited for me to get back?' Nell asked. 'Is it a good position?'

Baines flopped down on to a chair and put his head in his hands. 'She ran off with her sweetheart.'

'Sweetheart! She didn't have one!'

'That's what we all thought.' Baines looked up at her, his face wreathed with sorrow. 'But she left a note. Albert brought it up and showed me.'

'When was this?' Nell felt as if all the blood had drained from her body and her legs were going to give way.

'Sit down.' Martha pushed her on to a chair. 'I'll make you some tea.'

Baines explained that it happened back in November about two weeks after Nell left with Lady Harvey. He said there were no warnings or farewells; Hope had been here in the kitchen one minute and gone the next.

'She must have been planning it for some time,' he said wearily, pushing back a lock of hair from his face. 'But I never sensed anything, she didn't act suspiciously, didn't even say anything that I might later take for her way of saying goodbye.'

'She went empty-handed too,' Martha said. 'All her things are still up in her old room. We've left it all there for you.'

'But why didn't you write and tell me?' Nell asked, beginning to cry.

'Albert said it was better not to.' Baines shrugged. 'He thought you'd get distressed and as you couldn't leave Lady Harvey that would make it worse.'

'Did he go looking for her?' Nell's voice rose in despair.

'He went and told your brothers, I know that,' Baines said. 'Reverend Gosling came calling and said that they'd been to him and almost everyone in the village to try and find out who the young man was.'

'And did they find out?'

Baines shook his head. 'Everyone says the same, that it's a mystery. There's been no soldier round these parts.'

'A soldier!' Nell exclaimed. 'She ran off with a soldier?'

The bell rang from the drawing room and Baines went to answer it. Lady Harvey was sitting by the fire, Rufus on the rug at her feet, and she turned her head as Baines came in.

'Is this true what Rufus has been telling me? That Hope left without a word?'

'Yes, m'lady,' Baines said. 'I've just been telling Nell, she's very upset.'

'What an ungrateful little minx!' Lady Harvey said indignantly. 'After all Nell has done for her! Clearly you are giving the servants too much free time, Baines, if they have opportunities to meet men.'

Baines bristled. It was bad enough that she should think servants weren't entitled to a private life, but considering every one of them here at Briargate had been doubling up on jobs because Lady Harvey couldn't afford to hire more staff, he didn't know how she had the brass neck to say such a thing.

'With all due respect, m'lady,' he said, gritting his teeth, 'Hope had no free time other than her afternoon off which she always spent with her brother and his family. Neither he nor I can imagine how and when she met this man. It was out of character too, she wasn't a flighty girl, and she is very close to Nell.'

'Nell may as well go home and talk to Albert,' Lady Harvey said dismissively. 'She won't be any good to me if she's upset; Rose can attend to me.'

Baines felt a surge of anger at his mistress's callousness. Nell had worked for her since she was Hope's age, no one could have a more loyal and devoted maid, and she deserved better than to be told to go home without even a few sympathetic words.

'I don't believe Hope left willingly,' Rufus suddenly piped up.

His mother and Baines looked at him in surprise. His overlong fair curls made him look very young, but his expression was adult. 'I'd say Albert forced her to go.'

'Oh, whatever do you mean?' Lady Harvey said sharply. 'You told me she left Nell a letter.'

'She did, Albert showed it to me,' Baines said.

'It is quite possible to force someone to write a letter,' Rufus said stubbornly. 'I've seen boys do it at school. Hope cared too much for Nell to run off when she wasn't here.'

'You are just a child, and you were at school when this happened,' Lady Harvey retorted scornfully. 'That will be all, Baines, please pass my message on to Nell and Rose. I would like a bath tonight before going to bed too.'

As Baines was leaving the room he heard Rufus speak up again. 'Mama, you shouldn't ask Rose to fill a bath for you this late at night. She's been working so hard today and she must be very tired!'

Baines didn't linger long enough to hear his mistress's reply but he was moved by the boy's compassion. He could also guess that it was Hope who had made him see the unfairness of the master and servant system.

Nell sobbed as she walked down the drive to the gatehouse. Baines, Rose and Martha had done their best to comfort her, but there was nothing anyone could say that would make her feel better about Hope running off.

Nell remembered what she was like at sixteen, so naive, so eager to experience everything, especially the mysteries of courtship and kissing. If it hadn't been for Bridie suddenly telling her that Lady Harvey was having a baby, she would have gone off that same afternoon to meet Ned Travers in Lord's Wood.

She didn't know why she'd never considered that Hope might be just the same as she was then, thinking about lads all the time and aching to have a sweetheart. If only she'd told Hope about Ned it might have encouraged her to reveal her own girlish dreams.

Was it because she'd become so bitter and dried-up that unconsciously she didn't want Hope to find love and happiness either?

As she opened the door of the gatehouse, she could hear Albert snoring upstairs and there was an acrid smell which could only be from an unemptied chamber pot. Groping her way blindly in the darkness, she came to the table and found the candlestick and matches. As the match flared she saw the room was chaotic and her heart sank further.

By the time she had three candles lit, she felt like turning round and going back to Briargate for the night, for the mess was appalling. Dozens of empty bottles were strewn around. Great clumps of mud from Albert's boots lay all over the floor, chunks of mouldy bread littered the table and there were unwashed dishes everywhere, many of which she recognized as belonging to the big house.

She hadn't for one moment expected Albert to welcome her home with open arms, but surely to goodness any man knowing what lay in store for her on her return would try to do something to ease the pain of it. But he hadn't even had enough respect for her feelings to tidy up for her.

Remembering all the times he'd berated her for the rug in front of the stove not being straight, or the chairs not being pushed under the table, she was suddenly furious with him.

As she stood there looking at the filth her anger grew stronger than her fear of Albert. Taking the candle, she marched up the stairs and kicked the bedroom door open. 'Wake up, Albert. I want to talk to you,' she screamed at him.

'What is it?' he said sleepily, and Nell wrinkled her nose at the stink of sweaty clothes and the full chamber pot.

'You filthy wretch,' she yelled. 'How could you leave the place like this for me to come back to?'

He sat up and rubbed his eyes. 'Cleaning is women's work,' he said sullenly.

'Then you should have got a woman in to clean it,' Nell

206

snarled at him. 'I saw Martha has been feeding you, so you could have asked her to clean up after you too.'

'Shut yer mouth, woman,' he said, and lay down again as if intending to go back to sleep.

'You pig!' she exploded. 'Wasn't it bad enough for me to get home and find Hope gone, without this too? And where's the letter she left?'

The question seemed to wake him fully. 'How dare you come in here screaming at me?' he said, swinging his legs out of the bed. 'A working man needs his sleep.'

Nell had always backed away before when he made a move towards her, but she didn't intend to now. 'A woman needs her sleep too, but do you expect me to sleep in that rats' nest?' she retorted, pointing to the bed. The candle didn't give much light, but there was enough to see the sheets were dirty. The white counterpane Albert had always insisted must be smooth and crinkle-free was thrown on the floor and had been trampled over with dirty boots. 'Now, get downstairs and tell me about Hope,' she insisted.

'I can't tell you anything. I didn't see her go. I only found her note.'

The faint whine in his voice alerted Nell that he was lying. 'Liar!' she shouted, the candle jiggling in the candlestick because she was shaking with rage. 'There's a lot more to it than that, I know there is.'

His hand came up before she even saw it move and slapped her hard around the face. 'I will not be called a liar, and I'm glad the bitch has gone,' he hissed at her. 'So get out of here. You'll find the sodding letter on the dresser.'

When he moved as if to hit her again, Nell turned tail and ran back downstairs, suddenly all too aware she was on dangerous ground. She heard the bedsprings creak as he got back into bed, and all at once she was crying as if she would never stop.

She found the letter, and held it close to the candle to read it. There was no doubt it was Hope's writing; she had a bold, clear hand, the only handwriting Nell had never had any trouble in reading. She read it four or five times, but with each reading she became more puzzled.

Her own reading and writing were rudimentary, and if she had to write a letter she couldn't manage more than bald statements which never conveyed her feelings or any kind of description. But Hope had always been able to write as if she was speaking. When she wrote to James or Ruth her letters were always vibrant accounts of all the family and village news. This letter could have been written by Nell herself, except there were no spelling mistakes.

'*I am leaving with a soldier.*' Hope wouldn't say just that; even if she were in a hurry she'd have put some kind of reason, a description of him or his name. '*Please don't be angry with me.*' It wouldn't be Nell's anger she'd worry about, only her heartbreak. Where was the sorrow at not saying goodbye, or the knowledge she would be letting everyone down? '*You can have my things and the wages owed to me.*' Hope wouldn't bother to say that, she would take it as understood. Just as her apology at taking one of Nell's dresses was unnecessary.

Later, Nell got into Hope's old bed in the little room. It felt cold and damp with lack of use, but it was far better than sharing a bed with Albert.

She remembered now the words she'd had with Hope the day before she left with Lady Harvey. Hope had said she had as much chance of finding a sweetheart while at Briargate as she did of becoming Queen. She wouldn't have said that or looked so glum if there had been a young man already on her mind.

Nor would she have left a letter here for Albert to read. She would have left it in her room at the big house. In fact, if she had been running away she wouldn't have come here at all in case she ran into Albert.

Like a beam of light in a dark room, suddenly Nell could guess how it all came about. Hope wasn't running away, she'd come here to tidy up, just as Nell had asked her to do. Albert had probably come in while she was here, and perhaps Hope scolded him about the mess. And he hit her.

Nell could almost see the scene playing out in front of her: Albert losing control completely, but then realizing Hope would tell Baines who would then tell Sir William.

That was why Hope's letter was so strange. She'd written it all right, but coerced to do so by Albert. She might have agreed to leave Briargate just so he'd stop hurting her, but how could he let her go? She would have run straight to Matt.

All night Nell lay awake staring into the darkness, terrifying visions of Albert strangling Hope consuming her. She desperately wanted there to be another explanation, but what other one could there be?

Soon after the clock downstairs struck four she heard Albert come creeping out of the room next door. She braced herself, thinking he was coming for her now. But he crept on down the stairs, and just a minute later she heard him go out of the front door. That was further confirmation of his guilt. If he'd had no part in Hope's disappearance he wouldn't creep around, nor would he go out over an hour early just to avoid seeing her.

Nell's cheek throbbed – she could feel it was swollen – and her anger and grief came back tenfold.

It was Christmas Eve, a day of frantic preparation, yet in the past always a joyous one. Up until a couple of years ago there had always been many guests at Briargate, with a lavish celebration supper on Christmas Eve, followed the next day by an even more extravagant dinner. Nell had known years when a quartet of musicians had been hired, and they'd rolled back the rugs in the drawing room for the guests to dance. There were fancy-dress parties too. She recalled Lady Harvey dressed as Nell Gwynn and Sir William as Charles II, laughter and singing resounding throughout the house.

But this Christmas was not going to be a happy one for anyone.

Two hours later, as dawn was breaking, Nell picked up the pillowcase holding her belongings and made for the door.

She had tidied up, not out of any sense of wifely duty, but merely to fill the time until she left for the big house. As she packed her things she found the dress Hope had taken was her oldest, a plain grey workaday one which would have been far too big for her. That was further confirmation of what she believed. If Hope had really been going to run off with her lover she would have cared what she looked like and taken the pretty pink and white one Nell had worn on her wedding day. But that was still folded away in the drawer, yet another symbol of all the dreams Albert had shattered for her.

'Nell!' Baines exclaimed as she swept into the servants' hall where he was cleaning Sir William's riding boots and plonked the full pillowcase of belongings on the floor. 'What's all that?'

'My things,' she said quietly. 'I can't live with Albert any longer.'

Baines looked stunned, but came over to her and lightly touched her inflamed cheek. 'He hit you?' he asked in little more than a whisper, his faded blue eyes grave with concern.

'Yes, but it will be the last time,' Nell said resolutely. 'I'll take up her ladyship's early-morning tea now and talk to her about staying here. Is Sir William going out riding this morning?'

Baines frowned. 'He's already gone out, but Merlin is still in the stable. He had harsh words with Lady Harvey last night. I don't think you are going to find her very receptive to you this morning.'

'That's too bad,' Nell said tartly. 'Just make sure Rose isn't listening at the keyhole while I'm in with her.'

Baines had a heavy heart as he watched Nell walking back into the kitchen. He had never seen her so steely and grim-faced before; whatever came her way, she always carried on smiling. He guessed she thought Albert was in some way responsible for Hope leaving.

Baines didn't like Albert, neither the way he looked down on the other servants nor his dour uncommunicative nature. He'd had even less time for him since the last occasion when he hit Hope, but he couldn't see how Albert could be responsible for her leaving; since she'd moved into the big house, they hardly ever saw each other.

It had been a huge blow to Baines when Hope left, for she was a good girl and worked hard, but if Nell carried out her threat and left Albert, the whole fabric of Briargate would fall apart.

It was already threadbare: a skeleton staff, who with the best will in the world couldn't take proper care of such a big house. With a drunken master, a mistress who seemed unaware of anyone but herself, and their son and heir growing up without any real guidance, disaster was imminent.

Yet the gentry expected their servants to behave with the utmost propriety, to obey the laws of the land and of the Church, even if they flouted the selfsame laws themselves. Nell had a spotless character, and over twenty years' service in this house, but Baines doubted that would mean the master and mistress would support her desire to leave Albert.

Wives who left their husbands were always pilloried, even if that husband was cruel, a womanizer or a drunk. The chances were they would order Nell back to Albert, and if she refused she'd be told to leave Briargate.

Lady Harvey was awake when Nell took her tray of tea in to her. 'I've hardly slept a wink,' she complained as she sat up. 'The cold seemed to have got into my very bones. Then Rose woke me when she came in to light the fire.'

Nell was tempted to snap at her and launch right in and tell her how *her* night had been. But, as always, she murmured sympathy as she put a light wool shawl round her mistress's shoulders and plumped up the pillows behind her back.

'Rose didn't get the bathwater hot enough last night either,' Lady Harvey went on. 'I think she resented me asking for one!'

'She had been working since five in the morning,' Nell said as she put the tray of tea across the woman's lap. 'She has to clean the whole of the house now, do the laundry and help Cook. I expect she was just very tired.'

'But it's her job to clean and fetch and carry!' Lady Harvey said indignantly.

Nell bit back a sharp remark and went over to the windows to pull back the curtains. It was a grey, cold day, and the trees along the drive were skeletal and gaunt without their leaves, making the gatehouse clearly visible. She remembered how thrilled she'd been when Sir William said she and Albert could live there. She had been so excited at the idea of them having a home of their own she couldn't sleep at night. But that was before the wedding. All those daydreams of a baby in her arms, a loving, caring husband, and her family visiting had all come to nothing.

As she turned back from the window, she picked up from

the floor the dress that her mistress had worn to travel in the previous day.

'There's a bloodstain on that,' Lady Harvey said sharply. 'My courses must have begun while we were coming home. See to it, Nell.'

Nell looked at the woman she had adored and served selflessly for so many years, and suddenly saw her for what she really was; spoiled, vain and entirely self-centred. Even at forty-two, she was still beautiful, her blue silk nightgown the exact colour of her eyes, blonde hair cascading over her shoulders, and skin like porcelain. But there was a permanent sulky droop to her mouth and frown lines on her forehead from spending far too much time in a resentful state because her life hadn't turned out as well as she had expected.

'I will see to the dress,' Nell said. 'After I've talked to you about Hope.'

'Oh, I don't want to talk about that silly girl,' Lady Harvey said irritably. 'She's made her bed, Nell, she must lie in it. Now, do you think the black satin dress I wore for the ball in Bath while I was still in mourning for my mother could be altered to make an afternoon dress? It has yards and yards of very fine material.'

Nell gritted her teeth. 'I must talk to you about Hope, mam. You see, I think Albert has killed her.'

'Oh, don't be ridiculous, Nell.' Lady Harvey gave a humourless laugh. 'She ran off with a soldier. Even Baines has seen her letter. How on earth could you think Albert killed her? He's such a sweet, gentle man.'

Nell stood her ground. 'Look at my face,' she insisted.

Lady Harvey lowered her teacup and glanced up at Nell. 'It is exceedingly flushed, what have you done?'

'I haven't done anything. That was a slap from sweet, gentle Albert. He's a brute, Lady Harvey. He's hit me dozens of times, and Hope too. Now I believe he's killed her.'

Lady Harvey tossed her head in total disbelief and plonked her teacup down into the saucer. 'I won't hear any more of this rubbish,' she said dismissively. 'Hope is a stupid little whore who would rather be fucked than work for a living.'

Nell's mouth fell open in shock and horror at the vile and defamatory statement.

It was bad enough that her mistress had no sympathy for Nell, or concern about a young girl who had once played with her son. But to call Hope a stupid whore, to suggest she'd choose a life like that because she was too lazy to work here in the kitchens made Nell's blood boil. She couldn't let that go unchallenged.

'Well, you'd know about being a stupid whore, wouldn't you?' she retorted, wanting to rip the face off the woman. 'But you had Bridie and me to cover up your indiscretion.'

Lady Harvey looked astounded, then her eyes narrowed. 'Enough, Nell!' She held up one hand to silence her. 'If you want to keep your job you will stop right there.'

'Do you think my job means more to me than Hope's life?' Nell snarled, too angry now to hold back. 'Well, I'll tell you now, your bloody ladyship. Hope *is* that baby I helped deliver, here in this very room, in *that* bed, sixteen years ago. She's your child!'

For a moment or two Lady Harvey didn't react. She just stared blankly at Nell, perhaps unable to process what she'd just heard. Nell stared right back at her, hands on hips, daring the woman to insist she was lying. But then her mistress's lower lip began to quiver. 'But my baby died. Bridie said so,' she said in a weak, faltering voice.

The mention of Bridie's name was a reminder to Nell of the promise she'd made all those years ago. But even as she felt a stab of guilt on breaking that promise, she was angry and wanted to punish her mistress still further for the wicked things she'd said about Hope.

'Bridie believed she was dead because she didn't cry,' she said defiantly. 'But as I carried her downstairs I found she was alive. We knew how much trouble you'd be in if it ever got out you'd had a child, so I took her home to my mother.'

Lady Harvey's face crumpled, her hands went up to her hair and she pulled at it like a madwoman. 'No, no! It's not true! I can't believe you!' she shrieked out. 'You are making this up to distress me!'

'I'm distressed because I believe Hope has been murdered,' Nell hissed at her. 'I'm also furious that you could be so unfeeling towards her. But do you really think I would make up such a story?'

'It can't be true. Bridie would have told me. One of the plans we made before the baby was born, was that if it lived we would farm it out. Bridie said that would be expensive, so she would've asked me for money and kept coming back for more.'

'Don't you dare insult Bridie's memory by suggesting she would resort to blackmail; she would have died for you,' Nell spat at her mistress. 'In fact she did. You worked her to death, just like you'd do to me and Rose.' She paused, allowing that to sink in, for now she had the upper hand she was going to get some of her old grievances off her chest.

'All Bridie wanted was to protect your reputation, because she loved you. She also thought it would be easier for you to bear if you believed the baby died. And neither I nor my mother would have stooped to ask for money from you because we came to love Hope as if she were our own. To us she was a treasure.

'But now she's gone and I think she may have been killed, and if you've got any natural feelings, then help me to get justice for her!'

Lady Harvey wept then, but Nell could feel nothing but disdain for the woman, for she knew she wasn't crying for the child she'd lost, or even out of sympathy for Nell. She was crying only for herself.

'What do you want of me?' Lady Harvey sobbed. 'I can't bear this. I don't even know if I can believe what you've told me.'

'You can look on the parish records and you'll see Hope's birthday is 25 April 1832. You can also look at your Captain Pettigrew's face and see her face looking back at you.'

At that Lady Harvey looked really startled. Her eyes widened and she clapped her hands over her mouth.

'Bridie didn't tell me,' Nell said quickly. 'Wild horses wouldn't have dragged it from her. I saw the Captain for the first time the day you suggested Hope come here to play with Rufus. I knew he was her father the moment I set eyes on him.'

'Has anyone else remarked on that?' Lady Harvey asked quickly.

'Why would they? All us Rentons are dark, and no one else knows you had another child. But I'm surprised *you* haven't seen the similarity. Didn't you ever wonder why Hope was so beautiful, when James, Ruth and me are all so plain?'

There was no response to that question.

'You've never really looked at her, have you?' Nell sneered. 'She's worked in this house every day for four whole years or more, yet you've never noticed that beauty. But then you don't see any of us servants as people, do you?' Nell paused just long enough to draw breath.

'We're not supposed to have feelings, or even a private

life of our own. You don't care if we are tired, sick or distressed, you don't even value our loyalty. I comforted you when your mother died, but who comforted me when my parents died? Not you! All you offered was an afternoon off for the funeral. You don't even care that Albert's hit me, even though I've worked for you for twenty years. What does it take to make you care, m'lady?'

Lady Harvey turned on her side and sobbed even louder, beating at her pillow with one hand. Nell stepped forward and rescued the tea tray from the bed, afraid that it would be spilled.

'I do care, Nell,' her mistress said after a few moments, but her words were almost lost in the pillows. 'I do. I do.'

She rolled back over and looked at Nell with tears running down her cheeks. 'I've often said I don't know what I'd do without you. There have been so many times when I wanted to confide in you about how I felt when I was carrying Angus's child, and indeed about the hopelessness of my situation, then and now. But I was afraid to, not because I didn't trust you, but because I felt if I spoke of these things they would overwhelm me. Can you understand that?'

Nell thought back to the time Lady Harvey first admitted the Captain wrote to her. 'Can I ask that you check the post each morning?' she asked so sweetly. 'Of course he is only a friend, but William is being so difficult these days and he might not like Angus writing to me.'

Like a fool, Nell had felt proud that her mistress trusted her so implicitly. She'd even been glad she got some small comfort from the Captain's letters. But maybe it would have been better if she had spoken up then and informed her that the child of her union with *her friend* was down in the kitchen right now, scouring saucepans, and asked if it wasn't time she did something for that child!

'With all due respect, m'lady,' Nell said sharply, 'your

feelings are not that important to me now. I only want to know what Albert has done with Hope.'

Lady Harvey looked at Nell with shocked eyes. She sat up and dried her tears on the sheet. 'It's Christmas Eve, Nell. Rufus is here too,' she bleated. 'And I don't think my husband will believe for one moment that Albert killed Hope. He has a very high opinion of him.'

'Are you trying to tell me Sir William won't allow us to get the police?'

Lady Harvey began twisting her fingers together in agitation. 'I don't know. It's very difficult for me to talk to him these days about anything. He's not the man I married any more.'

Nell assumed she was referring to his heavy drinking. 'Well, catch him when he comes back in for breakfast,' she said. 'He'll be feeling fine then.'

'He's gone out already?'

'Yes, Baines said he went out very early.'

Lady Harvey frowned. 'I don't know him any more. Why does he keep going out at strange times and getting annoyed if I ask where he's been? He used not to be like that, Nell, once we used to do everything together, we talked and laughed so much.'

Nell nodded out of politeness.

'I expect you wondered how I could have become involved with someone else?'

'I thought you were very lonely when Sir William was away.'

'It wasn't just that,' Lady Harvey protested. 'You've been with me every day for sixteen years, Nell. You do everything for me, you know me better than anyone. Surely you've realized why I turned to Angus?'

Nell shrugged.

Lady Harvey sighed. 'You don't see it, do you? You think

like everyone else, and how I thought too on my wedding day, that I was lucky to have a husband who was young, handsome and wealthy. Oh, I adored him, but I was so innocent then, Nell, I'd never even kissed a man. It was years later before I discovered passion, and it was only then that I realized there had been none of that between me and William, no urge, no spark. In truth we were like brother and sister.'

'Are you saying he didn't lie with you?' Nell asked.

Lady Harvey blushed. 'He did what was expected of him, at first. As I had no real idea what the bed side of marriage should be like, I thought it must be my fault he seemed so disinterested. Then Angus came to visit, and all at once I was getting feelings I'd never experienced before.'

She paused, looking off into the distance. 'He called one afternoon when William was out riding, and we walked in the garden together,' she said. 'We sat for a while in the summerhouse and suddenly he was kissing me. It was like a madness, Nell, so sweet and thrilling.'

She went on to say how in the months following she tried to fight against the passion she felt. How she would have Bridie stay in the room if Angus called and William was out.

'It was the same for Angus,' she said sadly. 'I saw everything I felt mirrored in his eyes. He didn't call often because he was off soldiering, a whole year went by once without my seeing him, but he was on my mind constantly. Then William went to America, and sometimes I'd go out riding alone, and it was on one of those days that I ran into Angus.'

'And you slipped up?'

Lady Harvey nodded. 'As God is my witness, I tried very hard to resist the temptation. I did love William; we had some happy times together. But this thing I felt with Angus was very different, so strong, it swept away morality, loyalty and everything else I held dear. It was so beautiful and powerful, Nell, nothing mattered but to possess and to be possessed. If I'd had only just one tiniest bit of that with William everything would have been different. But I saw then that what William and I had in our bed was a duty; a furtive kind of fumbling that gave neither of us any pleasure, only shame. And I realized that William did not and would never desire me.'

Tears sprang into Nell's eyes as she remembered the humiliation of her own wedding night. She had been so willing, so eager for lovemaking, but Albert had pushed her away, making her feel dirty and loathsome. 'Maybe we have been led astray into believing all men are earthy creatures,' she said hesitantly, tempted for a second to admit that her own marriage was even emptier. 'But you had Rufus!'

'The one good thing to come out of all this mess,' Lady Harvey said with a snort. 'When William came home from America I was so very low. I was racked with guilt and convinced that all that I had been through with my first baby was God's judgement for my wickedness. But fortunately William came home with renewed enthusiasm for producing a son and heir, and maybe because I had more knowledge of pleasing a man, it happened.'

'Surely that was enough for you?'

'Our child's birth marked the end of William's physical duty to me.'

'But at least you have a child,' Nell reminded her. She thought she would gladly settle for that.

'That isn't enough when you have known the bliss of being in the arms of a man who does desire you,' Lady Harvey said with a break in her voice. 'For some years Rufus *was* enough for me. Angus was safely abroad, and we had parties and house guests to distract me. But now—' She broke off as she began to cry.

'William goes off alone, he drinks and gambles too much. He speaks to me as if he hates me,' she sobbed. 'Last night I asked him why he'd left me in Sussex so soon after the funeral and he said that the three days he was there with me were more than enough for him. I thought he meant the difficulties with my sisters, but he didn't. He meant being in my company.'

Nell had to grit her teeth to stop herself from interrupting Lady Harvey as she helped her with her toilette. A torrent of words flowed from her mouth – how wonderful Angus was, how despicable she found her husband – yet almost in the same breath she said she had written to Angus while at her family home to say their relationship must cease. It was the outpouring of someone who was entirely self-obsessed. She had also clearly forgotten that Nell had come to her with a serious problem.

She even asked at one point if Nell thought it wicked of her to wish for widowhood to release her from her unhappy marriage.

'My mother used to say, "Be careful what you wish for,"' Nell retorted, tempted to smack that beautiful face, if only to bring her back to reality. 'But m'lady, we must talk about what is to be done about Hope, and indeed the position I find myself in.

'I can't go back to the gatehouse with Albert ever again. So either you let me live here at Briargate, or I must go today and stay with Matt and his family. But either way you have to get Sir William to call in the police about Hope.'

'I can't do that.' Lady Harvey shook her head irritably. 'I know my husband and he won't believe anything bad of Albert. Nor will he approve of you leaving your husband.'

'Hope is your child,' Nell said fiercely. 'Her body may be buried in the woods or even the grounds here, and you expect me to keep quiet and continue to live with the man who killed her?'

Naked fear came into Lady Harvey's eyes. 'A police investigation will cause such trouble for us, Nell. Remember my son, for pity's sake!'

Nell was bewildered by that plea. 'Are you afraid I will betray your confidences? How can you think such a thing?'

Lady Harvey did not reply, and Nell took that as confirmation of her fears. 'I have kept the secret about Hope's birth for sixteen years,' she said quietly. 'Nothing would make me reveal it now, or anything else you have told me today, for it has no bearing on what I fear has been done to Hope.

'I have to know what happened to her, and if Albert has killed her I want to see him hanged for it. My brothers will feel the same, and if you and Sir William won't help me with that, then I must leave here now and go to my family.'

'You can't leave me!' Lady Harvey exclaimed. 'It's Christmas, and I need you.'

An hour later, Nell heaved the pillowcase holding her belongings over the stile and made her way across the paddock to Lord's Wood. Tears ran down her cheeks unchecked, for leaving Briargate was like cutting off one of her limbs, but she knew she had to.

As she reached the wood she turned to take one last look at the house and she was reminded sharply of the evening all those years ago when she took this same path with Hope in her arms.

It had been dark then, Briargate just a shape illuminated by the moon. Today it looked sullen and bleak in the cold, grey morning light, very like the expression on Lady Harvey's face when she finally realized Nell meant what she said.

She had tried to talk Nell out of it. But the more she said, the more obvious it became how shallow and selfish she was. She cried and said that Angus had never known their union had resulted in a baby because he was called away before she even knew she was pregnant. She was terrified that any kind of investigation at Briargate would result in her meetings and correspondence with him being discovered. She also said that her father had left Rufus a sizable share of his estate in trust, bypassing her because he was afraid Sir William would just squander it. William was already very angry with her about this because he was convinced she'd engineered it, and any further trouble would push him over the edge into madness. She even accused Nell of treachery.

Baines had taken Nell into his arms when she told him she was leaving, and when he let her go his eyes were damp. She'd asked him to say goodbye to Martha and Rose for her, because she couldn't bear to do so herself.

Now she had to face her brothers and tell them that she suspected her own husband of murder, and in truth she didn't know if she could bear that either. She had always been the placid, sensible one in the family to whom everyone turned for advice and comfort. But that wasn't true; if she'd been sensible she'd have made sure Hope had no contact at all with Albert after he attacked her that time before. She should never have asked her to go down to the gatehouse to tidy up; it was like leaving a pet rabbit with a fox.

Chapter Ten

1848

'Just wait until he goes into the room out the back where the oven is, then run in and grab it,' Betsy suggested. 'There's nothing to it, you'll be long gone by the time he gets back and finds one's missing.'

'I don't think I can do it,' Hope whimpered as she looked across Wine Street to Salter's Pies. 'Mother always said it was a sin to steal.'

When she woke that morning she had been absolutely determined to provide a meal for the three of them, but now she was here in Bristol's most prestigious street, within sniffing distance of Slater's Pies, her nerve had gone.

Normally at eleven in the morning this street was full of cabs, carts and carriages with hundreds of people thronging the pavements. But the bitterly cold weather had made the town quiet for over a fortnight, and now snow was expected later today only a few people had ventured out. Betsy said that made it an ideal opportunity for Hope to try her hand at a snatch and run.

'It's sinful that the rich stuff their bellies while people like us starve,' Gussie pointed out. 'As for Slater, he ain't even gonna miss one when he's got that many!'

They hadn't eaten for three whole days and all Gussie and Betsy's usual avenues of opportunity to get food or money seemed to be closed to them. The extremely cold weather had delayed ships, and windows and doors normally left open were now shut. All the owners of food shops and stalls around the quayside were being extra vigilant. Daily they woke to find icicles hanging inside the window of their room, and there wasn't a scrap of wood lying around anywhere that they could burn on the fire. They couldn't even go into an ale house to get warm without money.

Hope felt obliged to do something to help out. Her friends had provided her with food and a roof over her head for two months now, and although she'd paid her way to a certain extent by helping them with scavenging, it didn't seem right to take a share of food they had stolen without ever taking the risk herself.

Both Gussie and Betsy were far too bedraggled to attempt entering Slater's, which catered for the gentry, but Hope still looked tidy enough to pass for a servant out getting her mistress's order.

'You don't have to do it if you don't want to,' Betsy said. She looked worried now, along with being pinched with cold. 'We'll think of something else.'

If either of them had insisted she do it, or belittled her for being such a prude, Hope might well have backed away. But they'd become her new family and they were the kindest and most generous people she'd ever known. Betsy's teeth were chattering, the thin shawl around her shoulders was no protection against the icy north wind, and Gussie had a bad chest. Last night Hope had heard him coughing his very lungs up. He didn't look at all well, his face was chalky-white and his chest rattled, yet these two who had grown up without any of the advantages she'd had were prepared to share anything they had with her.

'All right, I'll do it,' she agreed reluctantly. 'Go away; wait for me at the top of St Nicholas's steps.'

For a moment they just looked at her in silence, their expressions reminding Hope sharply of how Nell used to look at her when she wasn't convinced she could really manage something on her own. But then Betsy slapped her on the shoulder and smiled. 'Be brave and quick. Don't run when you get it; that just draws attention to you. But if someone chases you, go like stink and dodge in and out of the alleys.'

Gussie just grinned weakly, but the way he fiddled nervously with his muffler suggested he wasn't entirely happy to see Hope joining the ranks of criminals.

Once her friends had walked off up Wine Street in the direction of Corn Street, Hope crossed the street and went down towards the pie shop.

Slater's Pies was unique, not only for the dark green and gold frontage or the splendid mahogany counters, but because it had a reputation for making the best pies in the West of England. Just looking in the window was enough to make your mouth water: game, chicken, beef or pork pies arranged on green and white checked cloths, the shiny golden-brown pastry glinting under the gas lights.

Hope always stopped to look at them when she passed. She loved the cleanliness of the shop and the delectable smells, and she admired burly Mr Slater in his sparkling white overall and tall starched hat. His face was as shiny as his pastry, his hands as big as hams, yet he wrapped his pies in white paper and placed them in his customers' baskets as delicately as a woman.

The pies she and her friends normally ate were small with only a scraping of meat in them, and the pastry was dull and soggy and as far removed from Slater's as Lamb Lane was from Briargate. Slater's pies, four or five inches high, stuffed with high-quality meat and brushed all over with beaten egg, were intended for a big household of ten or twelve people.

Hope had seen the old cook at Briargate make similar ones for harvest suppers and parties and they were usually served cold with chutney.

But what Hope wanted today was one of the hot pork pies. She had lain awake last night imagining eating one, till she could almost taste the buttery pastry, feel her teeth sinking into that rich, delectable pork. When she told her friends this morning what she intended to do, Gussie had warned her that few people he knew dared steal in Wine Street because it was so smart. But Hope's view was that this gave her an advantage because Mr Slater probably wasn't used to keeping an eye out for opportunists. But what if she was wrong?

It seemed a very good omen that an organ-grinder was playing just along from the pie shop. The man had a little monkey wearing a red jacket and little cap, which jumped up and down to the music. Everyone was stopping to look at him, so Hope didn't seem out of place lingering by the window of the shop as she kept an eye on Mr Slater.

The wonderful smell of the cooking pies made her drool and her hunger pains came back stronger than ever. Mr Slater was packing four very big game pies into a box and tying it up with string. As she watched, he handed the box to a young lad who was clearly going to deliver it to a customer. He appeared to be cross with the boy as he was wagging a finger at him, perhaps telling him not to dawdle on the way.

The lad came out carrying the box and rushed off down Wine Street, not even pausing to look at the organ-grinder's monkey. Mr Slater was alone in the shop now, and he was looking at a notebook, as if he had orders to fill.

There were five big pork pies at the end of the display, still steaming from the oven. Mr Slater came to the door and looked out, frowning; Hope thought he was irritated that the organ-grinder was spoiling his trade.

He stood in his doorway for a minute or two, checked his pocket watch, then turned and went straight out of the door at the back of the shop.

Hope's heart began to race for she knew this was the moment and she had to seize it before any customers came in. Pulling a piece of cloth from around her waist, she took a deep breath and walked in. She deftly put the cloth over the pie nearest to her and scooped it up. But just as she was turning to leave the shop she heard the sound of returning footsteps and rushed out of the door.

She wasn't quite quick enough, for just as she crossed the threshold she heard Mr Slater cry out, 'Stop thief!'

Her bowels contracted with fear. She'd seen people running after thieves before and they usually caught them. But though Mr Slater's cry was loud, the organ outside was louder, and she darted through the crowd clutching the pie closer to her. It was very hot, and she had to use her cloak to keep hold of it. She could smell it, and she was sure everyone she passed by could too.

'Thief!' she heard him yell again, louder this time. 'That girl in the grey cloak, stop her!'

Hope hitched the hot pie into her arms and ran up Wine Street, not even turning her head to see if she was being pursued. She turned into the Pithay, a very narrow lane which ran down to the river Frome. It was the area where most of the second-hand clothes and furniture shops were and the kind of customers they had were far less likely to want to help catch a thief.

But from behind her she could hear hobnailed boots striking out on the cobblestones. She ran like the wind then, her heart thumping so hard and fast with terror she thought it might burst. She knew she was dangerously close to the

Bridewell and there could well be several constables out on their beat, but remembering what she'd been told she darted into alleys and kept running.

In the two months she'd been with Gussie and Betsy they'd been to the public gallery of the magistrates' court three times to watch someone they knew being tried. One friend got five years' hard labour just for stealing a couple of candles.

Almost every time they went to the Grapes they'd hear about someone being publicly flogged for minor theft – even children as young as eight or nine could be sent to prison. Hope hadn't expected that she would ever get used to the filth, squalor and brutality of life in Lamb Lane, but somehow she had. But many people had told her prison would make Lamb Lane seem like paradise, and she'd rather drown herself in the river than go there and find out.

She had a stitch in her side from running up one alley and down the next, but the man chased her relentlessly. She didn't think it was Mr Slater, he'd probably offered this man a reward to catch her, and anyone doing it for money would be very determined.

But Hope was determined too. The pie was heavy, but she had no intention of dropping it, and even less intention of being caught. She continued to run, trying hard to go faster so she could throw the man off, but the heavy pie was slowing her down, hunger had made her weak and the man was gaining on her.

As she came down Tower Lane, which was close to where she started from the Pithay, she glanced back and saw her pursuer was a tall, thickset, bald-headed man who looked like a prize fighter. He was less than fifteen yards from her now, and she knew she must find a way to outwit him.

As she turned the next corner she looked frantically around her for somewhere to hide, and like a gift from heaven there was an open street door. She darted in and shut the door behind her, then stood behind it quaking as she heard his feet go thundering by. Her breath was rasping now and she felt faint and shaky, expecting that any moment the man would guess what she'd done and come banging at the door.

'Is that you, Tilda?' a feeble old voice called out from down the dark passage, startling her still further.

Hope couldn't see anything with the door shut, but the clean smell of the place told her it was home to someone of the middling sort, and the name the old lady called out was probably that of her maid. But a maid would only leave the door open if she was close by.

She felt sick with fright now, her heart thumping like a steam engine, and she didn't know what to do. For all she knew, the man who was chasing her might be standing out in the lane and might even enlist the help of the maid. She was trapped.

As her eyes got used to the gloom of the hall, she saw a staircase in front of her, and several other doors. One of these was open just a crack and she thought the old lady might be in that room. It seemed logical that the door directly ahead of her might lead to a backyard and another way out, so she tiptoed towards it.

It was bolted, and the bolt creaked as she drew it back. She waited a second, fully expecting the old lady to call out again. When there was no frantic cry or movement, she opened the door, and there to her delight was a tiny backyard with a gate in the eight-foot wall. She slipped out, closing the door quietly behind her, and slunk across the yard. But the gate was locked and there was no key.

For a second or two she thought the game was up. She wasn't just trapped but she'd lost her bearings too and had no idea what might lie beyond the wall. Like most of Bristol, this area was a rabbit warren of narrow lanes and alleys, the upper part of the houses jutting out over the lanes, almost touching the houses on the other side. But she'd never been behind the houses before, and there was nothing familiar in sight to tell her exactly where she was.

After a few seconds she decided that climbing up the wall was the only option open to her. She tied the pie up in the cloth and tied that to the strings of her cloak hood, then, getting a grip on a brick sticking out on the wall, she hauled herself up it.

If she hadn't been desperate, one look at what lay behind the wall might have deterred her. It was an alley no wider than three feet which appeared to act as a drain, but she was beyond caring about jumping into human waste now.

When she finally got to St Nicholas's steps she could see by the stiffness of Gussie and Betsy's stance that they were sure she'd been caught.

'Lookin' for someone?' she called out in an imitation of the foul-mouthed woman who lived in the room below them.

It was a treat to see their faces light up, and an even bigger one to wave her bundle under their noses so they could smell it.

'We thought you was done for,' Betsy said breathlessly. 'We was that worried about you! I jist said to Gus we shouldn't have let you do it.'

They slunk into St Nicholas's church, and there on the same bench they'd led Hope to when they'd helped her on her arrival in Bristol, Gussie cut up the pie with a pocket knife.

Nothing had ever tasted that good as they gorged themselves, not even attempting to speak. The pie was still warm, the juices ran down their cheeks, and the rich pastry stuck to their teeth and gums.

'I'm gonna eat one of those every day when I've made my pile,' Gussie sighed when he'd eventually had enough. 'It was the best thing I've ever eaten.'

Hope wrapped up what was left for them to eat next day. 'Did it give you any ideas of how to make a pile?' she asked teasingly. She felt faintly sick, she'd eaten so much, but she wasn't going to voice that.

'Not yet, but it'll come,' he laughed. 'Now, tell us what happened.'

It felt so good to be the one that had provided for them, and as she told her tale she laughed merrily. 'I was real lucky the ground was frozen in that alley,' she finished up. 'It don't bear thinking about what was under the ice.'

During the afternoon, at Hope's suggestion, the three of them set out towards Stapleton village to find some wood to burn. The pie had satisfied their hunger but they were all very aware they couldn't spend another bitterly cold night without a fire.

All three of them were in high spirits when they set off with sacks to carry the wood home, but once the narrow streets of Bristol gave way to open countryside, Gussie and Betsy suddenly became oddly jittery.

'The wind's too strong and cold,' Betsy complained, hugging her arms around her body. 'And it smells funny!'

'That smell is clean air,' Hope said teasingly, aware her friends never normally ventured out of the town and suspecting that they were intimidated by the barren winter fields and skeletal trees. 'Walk faster, you'll soon get warm.'

'They put me to work on a farm when I was eight,' Gussie blurted out as they walked through a field of cows. 'It were bad enough in the workhouse in Plymouth but it was a darn sight worse on the farm. I was so hungry I used to eat the pig swill.'

'We aren't going to stay out here,' Hope reminded him. 'Just think how good it will be to fill these sacks and go home and light a roaring fire. We might be able to find some potatoes too, and we can bake them on the fire.'

Betsy kept grumbling as if she was being taken to a place of execution and squealed with fright each time a cow walked towards them. Gussie was just silent, and Hope guessed that he was brooding on painful boyhood memories.

In an attempt to cheer her friends up, Hope told them about how she used to collect wood with Joe and Henry. She described the little cart their father had made them and how the boys used to let her ride in it when the ground was hard with frost like today.

'I wonder what they are doing now,' she mused, going on to explain that they'd been working in the foundry when she last saw them, but that they'd often boasted they were going off to London.

Hope rarely talked about her family; normally she avoided even thinking about them for fear of getting upset. But she was still glowing with pride at having got away with stealing the pie and was buoyed up with such new confidence that she felt she was past being pulled down by memories.

'Mole and Shanks went to London but they was only there a couple of days and they was beaten up and robbed of their coats and boots,' Gussie retorted, referring to his two male friends who shared the room in Lamb Lane at night. 'They're as 'ard as nails an' all; so I don't reckon your brothers would stand a chance up there!'

Gussie's suggestion that a couple of farm boys couldn't look after themselves in London didn't bother Hope, but it did trigger the memory of her father staggering in soaking wet and sick, trying to explain the horror he'd experienced in Bristol. All at once she realized that the rooming house where he'd caught the disease which killed him and her mother had probably been in Lewins Mead.

Suddenly she was afraid. Not so much of sickness, though she knew there was plenty of that around, especially among the Irish people who arrived hollow-eyed and starving on every ship out of famine-ridden Ireland. But she had been infected by the other evil her father was so shocked by – theft.

Her parents had always been scrupulously honest. Her father wouldn't even have helped himself to a cabbage or a few potatoes while working on a farm. She knew they would spin in their graves if they were aware of where she was living and what she'd done today.

In her first week or two in Lewins Mead she had been every bit as horrified by the place as her father had been. She used to cry herself to sleep at night, hating Albert because of what he'd done to her. But in front of Gussie and Betsy she had to put a brave face on it; after all, if it hadn't been for them she would have no roof over her head.

Nell always used to say, 'You can get used to anything,' and she was right. The conditions she lived under, wearing the same clothes day in, day out, and never knowing where the next meal was coming from – she'd got used to all of it.

Before long Betsy and Gussie became her new family, and she'd embraced their views and standards, putting aside those she'd been brought up with.

But now, as images of her parents and her brothers and sisters kept coming to her thick and fast, she was ashamed of losing her old values. While it was right and good to show affection and loyalty to people who had helped her when she most needed it, she should never have lost sight of who *she* was, or stopped listening to her conscience.

Tears pricked at her eyelids as she remembered how

cherished she'd been as a child. As the baby of the family she'd been better fed, dressed and educated than her siblings. Every one of them had been proud that she could read and write so well, and Nell had often said that their parents had purposely kept her at her lessons longer in the hope that it would give her chances they'd never had.

Yet she'd become a common thief!

The frozen fields they were walking through, the woods in the distance, even the astringent cold wind were further reminders of home. She could smell wood smoke and cow pats, and hear crows cawing in the bare trees. Up on the hill before her she could see a church spire, and that evoked an image of the Reverend Gosling and his fiery sermons on sin.

Betsy stopped grumbling about the cold as they reached the woods. Gussie became excited at the abundance of fuel for their fire littering the ground. But Hope was so choked up with feelings of shame she couldn't even feel any triumph that it had been her idea to come out here. She began filling her sack quickly and silently, all the while reproaching herself.

It wasn't her fault she had to leave Briargate, or that she ended up in Lewins Mead, but she knew in her heart that she hadn't tried very hard to get herself out of it.

Back in early January when her bruises had begun to fade, she had tried to find respectable work. She'd asked in shops, at inns, even a couple of laundries. But the refusals got her down, and it was far less daunting to go scavenging with Gussie and Betsy. It was a lark doing the rounds of warehouses, factories and workshops to search amongst their rubbish for stuff they could sell to the marine shops.

She liked picking up the money people threw to Gussie when he did his mimes outside the theatre. She even enjoyed distracting shopkeepers while Betsy and Gussie stole things. Only a couple of days ago Gussie had been talking about the rich pickings that could be found in the mud at low tide along the river Avon. Scavengers who worked there were called 'mud larks', and Hope could barely wait for the warmer weather to become one of them. A year ago, if anyone had suggested that she might seriously intend to make a living wading in filthy mud she would have been appalled.

But the unpalatable truth was that she'd allowed herself to become as apathetic as everyone else in Lewins Mead. She slept till late in the morning, roamed the streets rather than looking for real work, and even worse, she had begun to rely on having a few glasses of gin each day because it blocked out the sordid reality of her new life.

Ignorance and apathy were the true evils of Lewins Mead. While it might be said the residents lived under conditions which made it almost impossible to keep themselves clean and healthy, few of them ever attempted it, or even saw that it was desirable. Thieving and prostitution were the main occupations, and the money earned went on drink. Children were pushed out on to the streets to steal or beg almost as soon as they could walk and no one saw anything wrong in it.

But Hope couldn't claim ignorance as an excuse for anything. She knew the difference between right and wrong, she had been educated and had a great many skills that none of her neighbours had. She might have fallen into this pit through no fault of her own, but now she'd got to find a way out of it. If she didn't she'd end up in prison, or selling her body until it was too diseased for anyone to want it.

Daylight was fading and the wind was growing keener as the three friends made their way home with heavy sacks of wood over their shoulders. Hope had found some potatoes missed by a farmer in his field, and miraculously they hadn't become blackened by frost.

'We could sell one of the bags of wood and get enough for a couple of gins each,' Betsy said as they reached the town.

'It's going to snow, so we'll need the wood,' Hope said sharply. 'Gin won't keep us warm.'

'Hark at you!' Betsy jeered. 'So you think you're in charge now you've cracked thieving?'

Hope hesitated before replying. She knew if she voiced all the thoughts she'd had this afternoon her friends would take it as a condemnation of their way of life. 'I haven't cracked it,' she said carefully. 'And I know I daren't try it again. I'm going to get some real work.'

'There ain't no work for people like us,' Betsy replied. 'You should've seen that by now.'

Hope had half-expected that reaction. 'Then I'll collect wood and sell it,' she retorted.

'You'll never be able to collect enough to sell without a barrow,' Gussie said, though he looked at her with sympathy, not scorn. 'But I never thought you was cut out fer thievin' anyways.'

A couple of hours later, back in the room with the fire blazing and the potatoes baking around the edges, Hope attempted tactfully to explain more fully how she felt. As she had expected, Betsy bridled a bit, but Gussie came down on Hope's side.

'I'd hate it if you ended up a dollymop,' he agreed, using the name used by the locals for a prostitute. 'So would Betsy, she wouldn't do that even if she were starving.'

'I might,' Betsy said airily. 'If the cove was young, rich and good to me.'

Hope laughed, for Betsy always liked to have the last

word, and more often than not she argued just for the sport of it. 'If a man like that came along I'd want to marry him, not just lie with him,' Hope said. 'But that isn't going to happen, not when I look like this!'

Gussie looked at her appraisingly. 'You're beautiful, Hope,' he said, clearly not seeing the tangled hair or how shabby and dirty her grey dress had become. 'So is Betsy. You could both get anyone if you put your mind to it.'

'You charmer,' Hope smiled. 'But it isn't any good wishing for a man to whisk me off to a nice home with good food on the table. I've got to work my way to something better.'

It snowed that night and all the next day. Mole, Shanks and their women, Josie and Lil, stayed in too, all of them huddling around the fire. They played cards, drank the bottle of cheap rum Mole had brought in, argued and told stories.

Hope was glad enough of the shelter from the cold, but she wasn't pleased to be forced to spend so much time with the four night-time lodgers. Mole and Shanks were crude, loud-mouthed thugs who didn't hold conversations, they gave monologues on villainy. She had realized weeks ago that Josie and Lil were dollymops who handed over their earnings to their men. The four of them were everything she was nervous of in Lewins Mead.

Mole, a short, squat fellow with dark eyes set very close together beneath thick black eyebrows, got his nickname because he had been a miner. Shanks was tall and thin, with an ugly scar down his right cheek. He came from Dublin, and the only attractive thing about him was his Irish accent. Josie and Lil reminded Hope of tripe, white, flaccid and with nothing to recommend them. They were dull-eyed and slow-witted, their pale, thin faces registering no emotion. All four had quite decent clothes by the standards of Lamb Lane, but the dirt engrained in their skin, the lack of expression in their eyes and the constant barrage of profanity and gutter cant were repellent.

By five in the afternoon Hope thought that this was a taste of what being in a prison cell must be like, crowded together with six other people, breathing putrid air, assaulted by noxious smells of unwashed bodies and forced to endure the boastings of men who were human parasites. She had spent much of the day gazing out of the tiny window, for at least the snow had made the view of rooftops pretty and clean. But now it was dark she was forced to return to her pile of sacks, and in the light of just two candles and the fire, the four lodgers didn't just look unattractive, but menacing too.

She sensed Gussie and Betsy were not happy either to have this company thrust upon them. Betsy called the lodgers friends but that meant she and Gussie knew them well, not that they liked them. They needed the regular lodging money to pay the three shillings a week rent on the room, and until today the lodgers had always cleared out by ten or eleven in the morning and didn't return until late at night.

The enforced imprisonment at least had the effect of sharpening Hope's conviction that she must find a way of getting out of Lewins Mead permanently. Yet as she looked at Betsy and Gussie's faces softened by the candlelight she felt a pang of sorrow that this would almost certainly mean leaving them behind.

'Whatcha' thinking about?' Gussie asked quietly, almost as if he'd tuned into her thoughts.

'Finding work,' she whispered back, knowing if one of the lodgers was to hear her they'd have plenty to say on the subject, and nothing she would want to hear.

'You could go down to the Ragged School,' Gussie suggested. 'There's a cove called Mr Phelps there what teaches. He might be able to help you. They say he's a decent sort.'

Hope had also heard that a preacher's daughter called Miss Carpenter had taken over an old hall in St James's Back to teach the waifs and strays of Lewins Mead to read and write. She was reputed to be passionate about giving the children of the rookery a chance in life. Yet until today Hope had not been interested enough to find out more about her.

'Sounds like you've put your nose around the door there,' she said teasingly. Gussie was something of an enigma. Outwardly he appeared as cunning, cocksure and hard-headed as Mole and Shanks, but behind that lay a far more sensitive, kindly soul. Hope sensed that something appalling had happened to him at a young age, probably at the farm he was sent to work on, for he always clammed up when she asked him questions about it. He had a tender streak that a life on the streets hadn't killed off, and he also had his own moral code which prevented him from stealing from those he considered 'his own'.

'Yeah, I've bin in there a few times,' he sighed. 'I wanted a bit of book learning, but it ain't fer me. The kids wot goes there are young. I can't be doin' wif goin' every day neither.'

'They give lessons at night, don't they?' Hope asked. 'You could go then.'

Gussie shrugged. 'I thought about that an' all, but it would've meant leavin' Betsy on her own. She ain't safe wivout me, nor you neither.'

That explanation made a lump come up in Hope's throat for she knew what Gussie was afraid of: what people called 'White Slavers', who forced young girls into prostitution.

There were countless men in Lewins Mead, Mole and Shanks included, who lived off their women's earnings as prostitutes. Doubtless many of these women had been pushed or even forced into it by their men too. But they weren't to be feared, Betsy knew them all and would not be taken in by any of them.

The White Slavers were very different. They were seemingly respectable, well-dressed and presumably charming, judging by the number of young girls who had just disappeared after being seen talking to a stranger. There was a woman working in the Drawbridge, an ale house on the quay frequented by sailors, who had been captured like this and taken to a brothel in London. Her story, and it was verified by the police who raided the brothel after she was thrown out because she was pregnant, was that a smart-looking man had bought her a drink which she thought must have been drugged. She came round to find herself gagged and tied up in a carriage.

The brothel she ended up in had a wealthy clientele who wanted unspeakable perversions, not a quick release in an alley. Unwilling girls were beaten or starved if they didn't comply; some were dosed with laudanum. But willing or unwilling, the girls received none of the money they earned, and escape was impossible for they were never allowed out and the doors were kept locked.

The people who ran the brothel were caught and sent to prison, but it was thought there were hundreds of other places just like it in London and almost certainly in other big cities too. Every now and then there would be articles about it in the newspapers, a list of names of girls who had gone missing, but it was generally thought that the police didn't strenuously investigate because the men who used these brothels were rich and powerful.

Betsy had had her fingers burned once already. She had told Hope about the ordeal she'd gone through with a ship's captain who had offered her five pounds for her virginity. She had said with her customary bluntness that he was 'hung like a donkey and he weren't satisfied with taking me cherry, he buggered me an' all'. She said she left the inn he'd taken her to bleeding and hardly able to walk, and vowed that even if someone was to offer her a hundred pounds she couldn't go through that agony again.

Yet Hope felt Gussie was justified in worrying that Betsy might be snatched for she attracted a great deal of male attention. She had an engaging, lively personality that lit up a bar the moment she walked in, and she moved in a sensual manner and would talk to anyone. If Gussie wasn't with her it would be easy enough for anyone to drug her and take her away.

'You could ask Betsy not to go out while you were at lessons,' Hope suggested.

Gussie chuckled. 'I know what her answer to that would be!' he said.

Hope did too. Betsy didn't like to be ordered around and she'd laugh at Gussie's fears for her. 'Well, get her to go with you then,' she said. 'I'm sure she'd like to be able to read too.'

He shook his head ruefully. 'She don't like people like Miss Carpenter.'

Hope hardly slept at all that night. She wasn't tired because she'd been indoors all day, and her mind was churning over and over about where she could go to find work. Without a character and any clean clothes she had no chance of getting back into service or any other respectable kind of work. Wood collecting was the only thing she could do. But as Gussie had pointed out, without a cart she couldn't get enough at one time to sell.

It was still pitch dark when she got up. The room stank and Mole was snoring so loudly she couldn't stand another minute in there. She always slept in her clothes because it was so cold at nights, and picking up her boots and her cape, which she used as a blanket, and one of the sacks she'd been lying on, she crept out, side-stepping all the sleeping bodies.

Lamb Lane was treacherous with snow on the cobbles, and as silent as the grave because it was so early, but thankfully it seemed slightly warmer than the day before. She reckoned she would need to sell five or six loads of wood a day to make a living at it. That was an awful lot of walking and a full sack was very heavy. But she could do it if she put her mind to it.

Chapter Eleven

Matt stumbled sleepily down the stairs. It was five in the morning, still dark and raining very hard. It was days like this when he wished he was anything but a farmer and could stay in bed with Amy for at least another hour.

He heard the kettle boiling even before he opened the kitchen door. Nell was sitting hunched up on a stool by the stove and had clearly been there for some time.

His heart sank as she turned to him and he saw her eyes were swollen with crying. He couldn't cope with her misery first thing in the morning.

'You must stop this, Nell,' he blurted out before he could stop himself. 'There's no call for you to be up so early.'

'I've always risen early,' she retorted in a whining tone. 'Amy will be busy enough with the children all day. The least I can do is get the stove going for her.'

Matt sighed and sat down at the table. When Amy complained that she felt Nell was usurping her position, he always told her that doing chores was Nell's way of showing her appreciation they'd taken her in. Amy retorted that she was sick and tired of appreciation, what she wanted was her kitchen back.

'I wasn't talking about you fixing the stove or making my breakfast,' he said wearily. 'You've got to stop brooding about Hope.'

'How can I when I know she's been murdered and the

man who did it is as free as a bird?' Nell asked sharply. 'And I seem to be the only person who cares.'

'Don't be foolish, you know that's not true.' Matt ran his fingers distractedly through his tousled hair. 'We've all just accepted that she ran off with her lover, and you must too.'

'I'll never accept that,' Nell said indignantly. 'That's what Albert wants us to believe. You agreed with me that her letter didn't sound right.'

Matt groaned; it was too early in the morning for this. He'd told her his views on that letter dozens of times, but once again he repeated that Hope had been in a hurry. And that no amount of explaining herself to Nell was going to make her hurt less.

'But she would have written again later to stop us all worrying.' Nell's eyes filled with tears yet again. 'You know she would, Matt.'

As always when Matt saw the pain in Nell's eyes, he was sorry he'd been sharp and irritated with her. He got up and put his arms around her, holding her to his shoulder and patting her back comfortingly. 'Maybe she's too ashamed? I know if I skipped off the way she did and caused all this trouble I'd just want to stay missing.'

Matt wished his feelings were as clear-cut as that explanation. He lurched from extreme anxiety for Hope to near hatred for what she'd done to Nell and the embarrassment to his family.

It was understandable that people were shocked by Hope running off with a soldier; after all, the Rentons had always been steady, sober and well-respected people who never caused scandals. But it would have been just a nine-day wonder if Nell hadn't reacted so dramatically about it. Leaving her husband and Briargate had created all kinds of suspicions, and the way Nell had acted since then only added more fuel to the fire. Many people thought she had gone mad, others thought Albert or even Sir William must have ravished Hope. Hardly a day passed without Matt or Amy being cornered by someone determined to get to the bottom of what they considered a sinister mystery.

When Nell ran in here on Christmas Eve so distressed, Matt had taken her accusations of murder seriously. He'd gone rampaging up to Briargate straight away and would have killed Albert himself if he'd shown his face. But Sir William had taken him into his study and calmed him down. He pointed out that Albert had been chopping wood in the shed on the afternoon Hope disappeared; he said he'd seen him himself when he came back from a ride on Merlin. He reminded Matt too that Albert had gone straight to Baines when he found Hope's letter at the gatehouse, and it was Baines who talked him out of informing Nell by letter because it would be too great a shock for her.

Sir William couldn't have been more understanding. He even agreed that he would get the police to make an investigation to convince Nell no crime had been committed, in the hopes that it would persuade her to return to Briargate and Albert.

On Boxing Day, Matt helped the police comb the grounds of Briargate, the surrounding woods and even the gatehouse, but they found nothing suspicious. Yet still Nell ranted and sobbed, refusing even to speak to Albert when he came to the farm to try to persuade her to go home with him.

Matt had tried to talk her round, explaining that a woman who left her husband became an outcast, and reminding her of the vows she'd made on her wedding day. But it did no good, she said she didn't care what people thought about her, she knew the truth about what Albert had done.

Matt had talked to Albert a couple of weeks after the police search, and he had been very reasonable. He admitted that he could have been kinder to Nell when she arrived home to find her sister gone, but explained that she had woken him up to blame him, and he could hardly get a word in edgeways. He said bluntly that their marriage hadn't been a happy one for a long time and he thought this was because they hadn't had a child. He said he was willing to try again, but Nell must hate him to believe he'd killed Hope.

Matt had never liked Albert, he found him cold, critical and superior, but the man was honest enough to admit he'd been hard on Hope in the past, and that perhaps he should have been more understanding with Nell. In the light of how Nell had been in the past weeks, Matt even felt a little sympathy for the man, for it had to be galling to be branded a murderer by his own wife.

A few weeks later Lady Harvey wrote to Nell. Nell didn't divulge what was in the letter, but Matt had seen the glowing character which was enclosed with it. Yet Nell wasn't even grateful for that kindness. She claimed, rather mysteriously, that she knew bad things about Lady Harvey and the woman had only sent the character because she was afraid Nell would start revealing them.

Matt thought it was very big of Lady Harvey to overlook that Nell had run out on her on Christmas Eve and that she'd brought the police to Briargate's doors and thereby created gossip all over the county. If she hoped the character would get Nell a position well away from Briargate, Matt could hardly blame her, for he was at the end of his tether with Nell too. She filled the farmhouse with her misery; she upset Amy and often frightened the children.

He cursed Hope for all this, yet despite his anger, he couldn't stop worrying about her too. She was so young and unworldly, and a man who could talk her into turning her back on her family would be able to persuade her into anything. Everyone knew the big cities were dens of iniquity and a pretty little thing like her would soon be ruined.

He watched as Nell filled the teapot with hot water. She had become thin and gaunt, her once rosy plump cheeks were pale hollows now, and the dark blue dress she was wearing hung in folds on her. She was thirty-two, but she had suddenly turned into an old lady: her voice had become shrill and whining, she muttered to herself, her dark hair had lost its shine, and she'd even taken to pulling it back so tightly that it made her face almost skeletal. Nothing distracted her from her distress, not his children, the signs of spring arriving, or even a letter from James or Ruth. She didn't worry about Joe and Henry, who had left to seek their fortune in London. She didn't seem the least interested in Ruth's baby boy either. She was too obsessed with Hope to care about anyone else.

What was he going to do?

Amy wanted him to ask her to leave. She said she'd had more than enough of this. But how could he show his own sister the door, knowing she had nowhere else to go?

Nell put the teapot on the table and then got the cups from the dresser. 'I'll take the eggs into Keynsham today, and while I'm there I'll look for work,' she said suddenly.

Matt nodded; he didn't trust himself to speak. He doubted she'd find any work there, but it would save him the journey to sell the eggs, and while Nell was gone it would at least give Amy some respite.

'If I can't get anything there, I'll go to Bath tomorrow and see Ruth.'

'She'll be pleased to see you,' Matt managed to get out.

He had ridden into Bath shortly after Hope disappeared to tell Ruth and John about it. Although Ruth was surprised and concerned, she had pointed out that any young girl would want more life than there was at Briargate. In the New Year when Matt went back to tell them about Nell's reaction and her conviction that Albert had killed Hope, Ruth was irritated by what she saw as melodrama. 'What would he gain by killing her?' she asked, shaking her head in disbelief. 'Nell will end up in the asylum if she goes on this way.'

James, Toby and Alice had all reacted much the same way too. While none of them approved of Hope running off so recklessly, and were very concerned for her safety, they all felt she had been looking for some excitement, and that Nell should accept that.

Matt was pretty certain Ruth wouldn't have much patience with her older sister, especially now she had a baby of her own. He just hoped she wouldn't be too sharp with Nell and make her even more distraught.

When Nell left the farm around six-thirty with the basket of eggs on her arm, it had stopped raining and the first rays of daylight were creeping into the sky. She took the footpath across the fields to Compton Dando, and came out close to her childhood home.

Gerald Box, the gamekeeper's brother, lived there now with his wife and three children. Nell stubbornly kept her eyes averted from the cottage as she didn't want any reminders of her parents or Hope today.

She was very aware that Matt and Amy were losing patience with her. She knew too that she wasn't holding together very well and everyone was horrified that she'd left Albert. Sometimes it was very tempting to tell them that it had been a marriage in name only, for if nothing else it would make Albert a laughing stock. Likewise, she'd like to shame Lady Harvey by telling the story of Hope's birth. Perhaps then people would see how unquestioningly loyal she'd been to her mistress for all these years, and be shocked that a mother took her daughter's disappearance so lightly.

But to tell these things now when people were already convinced she was going mad would only reinforce that belief. No one would believe her and she might well be put into an asylum to shut her up.

Reluctantly she'd come to see that the only solution to everything was to find work well away from here. She was tormented by memories of Hope everywhere she looked, creating friction at Matt's, even though she tried to make herself useful. Lady Harvey had dressed up her real feelings about her former maid in her letter. She went to great pains to avoid saying anything about Hope, she even sympathized with Nell's difficulties with Albert, and pointed out that she'd used Nell's maiden name on the character to help her get another position. But Nell could sense the ice beneath the honeyed phrases about how hard she would be to replace, her loyalty and caring nature. Lady Harvey's real feelings were clearly that she hoped Nell would go as far away as possible, and that she'd shut the door tightly on the maid she once claimed was her only real friend.

By the time Nell had got to the hamlet of Chewton the sun had come out, and though the wind was cold, she noticed for the first time that there were green buds on the hedges and a few early primroses peeping through beneath them. Only last night Matt had said that lambing would be starting within a week, and she remembered how excited she used to get as a child when she saw the first newborn lamb of the season.

Ducks quacking on the river by the mill made her stop and put her basket down to look over the bridge. She had never seen so many in one place, at least twenty or more all chasing one another around on the water. The willows were coming into leaf, and there were a great many daffodils swaying in the wind on the bank. A lump came into her throat at the beauty of the scene, and she realized it was the first time since Christmas that she'd been aware of anything other than her own unhappiness.

Hearing horses' hooves coming around the bend towards her, she stayed by the bridge railing, but turned her head to see who it was.

To her astonishment it was none other than Captain Pettigrew on his piebald horse, and in her position on the bridge she couldn't hide.

'Why, Nell!' he exclaimed in surprise, reining his horse in and looking down at her. 'How are you? I was told you'd left Briargate and I rather assumed you'd gone right away from the village.'

Despite Nell's initial feelings about this man, he had won her over when Cook was taken ill. While her puritanical streak still told her she ought to be wary of a man who had come between a husband and wife, now she knew far more about the relationship between him and her ladyship, her instinct told her that he had truly loved her, and probably still did. It was also hard not to look into that strong, handsome face, knowing that he was Hope's father, and not be willing to trust him.

'I ought to leave here,' she said, blushing because he was looking at her so keenly. 'I have nothing but sad memories here now my sister has gone.'

'I was told about that,' he said, dismounting and moving closer to her, still holding his horse by the reins. 'Rather a rum do! I understand you don't believe she ran off with a soldier?'

'No, sir, I don't,' Nell looked him square in the face. 'For one thing no one had seen a soldier around here, and just before I left with Lady Harvey when her father was sick, Hope told me quite sadly that she had no chance of ever having a sweetheart because she never had the opportunity to meet anyone.'

'She could have made opportunities while you were gone,' the Captain said with a wry smile.

'She only had a half day off each week and she spent those with our brother at his farm.'

'Forgive me being so blunt, Nell, but as I understand it you believed your husband, the gardener, killed her. Is that so, or just foolish gossip?'

'I did believe it, and I still do,' Nell said defiantly. 'Now I am being scorned because I deserted him, but how could I stay with such an evil man?'

'Strong words, Nell,' he said shaking his head thoughtfully. 'But I think you are very brave to stand by what you believe. Lady Harvey must be missing you a great deal; I know how fond she was of you.'

'Lady Harvey cares for no one but herself,' Nell blurted out before she could stop herself.

The Captain raised one dark eyebrow.

'Apart from you,' Nell added, and blushed furiously because she shouldn't have said that either.

'Oh, Nell,' the Captain sighed. 'I know Lady Harvey had no secrets from you, and therefore I feel I can speak frankly. We are both victims of a very rigid society; Lady Harvey and I could have no future together without disgrace. She probably told you that I asked her a year ago to face that disgrace and come away with me?'

Nell was surprised and shocked to hear that. 'No, she didn't tell me that, sir. Only that she wrote while we were in Sussex and told you it was all over.'

'That sounds like Anne.' He gave a humourless chuckle. 'She's a great one for only telling half a story! But maybe that is why she was so hard on you, because you were brave enough to leave Albert!'

'Lady Harvey's situation and mine were very different,' Nell said. Even after all she'd been through she still could not bring herself to be spiteful about her old mistress. 'Albert left me no alternative but to desert him.'

The Captain put one finger under her chin and lifted her face up. 'You look thin and deeply troubled, Nell. I am told that Lady Harvey looks the same. I think you two fell out about far more than Albert?'

Nell's stomach lurched. 'If she is thin and troubled too, then it will only be because she's finding it hard to cope with all the things I used to do for her,' she said tartly.

He half-smiled. 'Another man might believe that to be the reason, but not me. However, I do admire your loyalty,' he said. 'So where are you off to with those eggs?'

'To sell them to a shop in Keynsham, then I shall look for work.'

'I shouldn't imagine there's much call for a lady's maid there.'

Nell shrugged. 'I'll take anything, I can cook and clean. Beggars can't be choosers. I'll even work in an ale house if they give me a bed and food.'

He looked at her appraisingly for so long it made Nell nervous.

'Would you consider being my housekeeper?' he said eventually.

Nell's eyes widened with surprise. 'But you don't have a house, sir,' she exclaimed.

'I do,' he said. 'I acquired it a year or two back. Nothing grand, you understand, just a place to spend my leave and retire to when I get too old for soldiering. I had been thinking of getting someone for some time, but there is so much that needs doing there before I could expect a stranger to cope with the inconvenience. However, it might suit you just now, and you'd certainly suit me.'

Nell's first thought was that he saw her as a way back towards Lady Harvey. But whether that was his reason or not, it was an offer she was in no position to refuse. 'Well, thank you, sir,' she said. 'I'm very grateful for your kindness.'

After giving her directions to the village of Saltford on the Bath road and suggesting she called after selling her eggs, the Captain rode off. Nell picked up her basket and walked on with a much lighter heart. She didn't really care what his house was like, or that she'd be the only servant. He was a gentleman, he cared enough about her plight to help her, and it felt as though she'd been offered a lamp on a dark night.

Nell stood outside Willow End, the Captain's house, for some little while before she opened the gate and walked up to the front door, a little puzzled as to why he'd chosen it. She would have expected a military gentleman to find a residence in either Bristol or Bath, not half-way between the two cities. While it was bigger than a cottage, with a stable and other outhouses, it was the kind of house a shopkeeper or a schoolmaster would live in.

It was one of a few houses straggling along the road into Bath, outside the village of Saltford, around half a mile before the crossroads of the lanes that led to the villages of Corston and Lewton St Loe. It was a pleasant enough spot, overlooking the fields which ran down to the river Avon, but the Great Western railway to London ran through those too.

Captain Pettigrew was right in saying it needed a lot doing to it. The roof and windows were sagging and the garden hadn't been tended in years. She expected that the inside would be no better. But it would be a good place for her to work, far enough away from Albert and yet close enough to both Matt and Ruth to feel safe. She relished the amount of hard work she'd have to do; she didn't want time on her hands.

'So what do you think, Nell?' the Captain asked as they returned to his drawing room after he'd taken her on a tour of his house. 'Could you live here and look after me?'

Nell smiled; it was difficult not to do so for he had shown her round with boyish enthusiasm, vividly describing what he intended to do with each of the rooms. For a single gentleman he had a great many possessions – hundreds of books, many of them still in packing cases, some fine pieces of furniture, clocks, rugs and china – but most of them were still piled up in the downstairs rooms as the roof leaked.

The parlour was the only room that had a semblance of order. It was cold without the fire lit, but he had armchairs, a rug and a table and chairs arranged, even a couple of pictures on the walls. His bedroom offered less comfort than a prison cell, with no rugs on the floor and just a bed, curtains and his clothes hanging from hooks behind the door.

'I would be happy to live here and look after you,' Nell said with sincerity. 'But you must get the roof mended quickly before the rainwater seeps down here too.'

'I have that in hand,' he said with a wide grin. 'Work starts tomorrow. But could you cook in that terrible kitchen?'

Nell laughed then, and it struck her that it was the first time she'd had anything to laugh about in months. It wasn't a terrible kitchen to her; it was filthy, but it was a good size and there was plenty of light, and after a good scrub it would be just fine. 'I learned to cook on an open fire,' she reminded him. 'The stove will work well enough once I get the chimney swept, and it's got a good cold pantry.'

'I brought some friends here to see it and they shuddered,' he admitted ruefully. 'You see, I was looking at its potential. It has a good bit of land, the stables and outhouses, and I thought it had a good feel to it. But my friends said I'd taken leave of my senses and it made me think they might be right.'

'Then we'll have to show them they were wrong, sir,' she said.

He poured some sherry wine into two glasses and handed one to her. 'To the future, Nell,' he said, raising his glass, his dark eyes twinkling. 'And to you for coming along in my hour of need.'

Nell sipped the sherry cautiously, for she had a long walk back to Matt's and she hadn't eaten anything more than a slice of bread. 'I can be here first thing in the morning,' she said. 'That is, if you want me then?'

'The sooner the better,' he said. 'But I shall come and get you in the gig, and we can pick up whatever provisions and other things you'll need on the way. I won't have you creeping away from your brother's farm like a thief in the night.'

'You are very kind, sir,' she said, dropping her eyes in a moment of embarrassment.

'I can imagine what you've been through in these past weeks,' he said softly. 'People can be very cruel, even those who claim to love you. But tell me, Nell, and I want the truth now. Was Hope your daughter?'

'No, sir,' Nell retorted, her chin coming up in defiance. She could see why he might have made that assumption: many a servant girl who had a child out of wedlock might, with a willing mother, pass their offspring off as a sibling. 'She felt like she was sometimes, me being sixteen when she was born, and then our parents dying so sudden. But she was not born to me.'

It was so tempting to tell him then who Hope's real

parents were, but a small voice inside her head told her that it was too soon to reveal that secret.

He looked at her long and hard and she stared back into his eyes without faltering. 'If it's any consolation at all, I don't believe Albert killed her,' he said. 'But I do suspect he found some way of driving her away.'

'But what would stop her writing to me, or her brother or sister, telling us that?' Nell asked, her voice shaking because she sensed he knew something.

'Maybe he threatened to hurt you,' he said, putting one hand on her shoulder, 'or Lady Harvey, or even Rufus. I command men, Nell; I am used to assessing their characters. I have always seen something in Albert that worried me. Perhaps when we get to know each other better you'll feel able to tell me more about your life with him?'

Tears prickled the back of Nell's eyes, for not one person, not even Matt who had always disliked Albert, had offered her such understanding.

'Perhaps,' she said in a small voice. 'But it is difficult to tell a man personal things.'

'I know,' he said, lightly touching her cheek with the palm of his hand. 'It is a sad state of affairs that both men and women feel the opposite sex is so very different. We are indoctrinated from birth to believe this, we are encouraged to hide our true feelings from one another, and so often pushed into loveless marriages. It is no wonder that we cannot communicate freely.'

'You are a very kind man,' she blurted out. 'It will be my pleasure to housekeep for you.'

'I hope we can become friends too,' he said. 'We have more in common than you realize, Nell, both of us out on a limb, victims of circumstance. But I see our meeting today as fortuitous, and I hope you share that view.'

*

257

As Nell cut across the fields to home she felt like singing. Not just because she'd got work and a new home, but more because she felt her pain had been acknowledged. Whether that was enough to get her to pull herself together she didn't know. But she felt optimistic, for if the Captain didn't believe Hope was dead, maybe she could start to believe it too.

'I'm glad for you,' Matt said as he bent to kiss his older sister goodbye the next morning. 'It's not what I would've chosen for you, mind! Him being a bachelor an' all.'

Nell managed a wry smile. She knew Matt's first thoughts were that she wouldn't be safe alone with any man. But then he didn't know that in the six years she'd slept in the same bed as Albert, he'd never wanted to lay a finger on her. A gentleman was even less likely to want her.

'Half the people round here think I've gone mad, the other half think I'm half-way to hell already,' she laughed. 'A bit more scandal won't bother me. But the Captain will be away a great deal of the time. You can come and check up on me at any time. I like him, he's a good man. Don't fret about me.'

'There's talk about him,' Matt blurted out. 'He's got a way with women.'

'You have a way with women too,' Nell said indignantly. 'I've seen those Nichol girls giving you the glad eye at church. Some men are just born that way; it doesn't mean they can't be trusted. Now let me go, we can't leave the Captain sitting out there any longer.'

As Nell climbed up into the gig beside the Captain, Amy came out of the dairy. She was all smiles, hastily shouting out how much she'd miss her. But Nell wasn't fooled any more than she had been on the previous night when Amy had taken her side against Matt's disapproval. She just wanted Nell out of her house; she wouldn't have concerned herself if it was to work in a bordello.

It was close to midnight when Nell finally undressed and got into bed. The only room upstairs that was dry enough to sleep in was the Captain's, so until the roof was fixed she had a truckle bed in the small store room adjoining the kitchen. But the men had begun work on the roof that morning, and when they'd finished they were going to repair all the ceilings, so then she'd have a bedroom of her own.

Nell was exhausted. She had scoured every inch of the kitchen and pantry, the walls and floor, repapered the shelves and cupboards, and unpacked at least a dozen boxes of china, glass and pots and pans. She was a little mystified that a bachelor soldier should have all these household things, but she hadn't liked to ask him about it.

Tired and aching as she was, she felt more like her old self, and she'd even been hungry enough to eat some of the mutton stew she'd made for the Captain. He said it was the best meal he'd had in weeks, and laughed when she said they'd have to get part of the garden clear to grow some vegetables. She didn't think he really believed she knew all about that too.

Satisfied was how she felt, she decided as she began to drift off to sleep. There were long periods of utter boredom being a lady's maid, and turning a hovel into a home was far more rewarding.

Tomorrow she intended to tackle the dining room. He had a very fine table and chairs, and she'd seen some good velvet curtains in a packing case. The Captain had said he'd be going away for two days; by the time he got back she'd have that room fit for dinner guests.

But her last thought of the evening was of Hope. Nell pictured her running across the meadow to Lord's Wood, as she'd so often seen her do on her afternoon off. Her bonnet would bounce back on to her neck, and her shiny dark hair would break free from its pins. Nell would tut as she watched from an upstairs window, and make a mental note to remind her young sister that only hoydens ran, not young ladies. Yet it had always given her pleasure to see the child's delight in her freedom; she was as graceful as a deer and as beautiful as her surroundings.

'If you are alive, my sweet, write to me,' she murmured.

Chapter Twelve

1849

Hope could see Betsy coming towards her along the crowded quayside, but even at a distance of some 300 yards it was clear something was badly wrong with her. She was staggering, bent over as if in pain, for once not stopping here and there as she usually did for a bit of light-hearted banter with sailors and dock workers.

It was late in the afternoon in midsummer and so hot you could probably fry an egg on the quay. During the bitterly cold winter Hope had longed for the heat of summer, but as the temperature had soared in the past weeks, with no rain to wash away the human and animal effluent, the smells had become so evil that it was hard to breathe.

By day Hope could escape up the hill to Clifton where it was clean and sweet-smelling and a breeze blew. People there had drains which took away their waste, they had water piped into their kitchens, and many of their gardens were beautiful. Lately she'd been very tempted to sleep out on the Downs rather than face another steamy night in Lamb Lane. But Betsy and Gussie would have seen that as a kind of defection.

It was while selling kindling during her first winter in Bristol that she managed to beg some work in Clifton. The housekeeper at number 5 Royal York Crescent paid her to scrub the front-door steps and polish the brass. It wasn't until the next winter that the woman eventually trusted her enough to let her come inside occasionally to scrub floors and help with the laundry, but now eighteen months later Hope helped out there twice a week on a regular basis, for which she was paid three shillings.

Hope had to bite her tongue as she was always watched like a hawk for fear she was going to steal something. The other servants looked down their noses at her, and if she was given anything to eat while she was there, it was only ever scraps. But she had stuck it out, for she needed the three shillings to buy flowers from the market and make them into little posies which she sold on the streets for the rest of the week.

The terrible hardships she endured during her first winter in Bristol were just a distant memory now. Nothing, she felt, could ever be as bad as that again. How she had managed to go out each icy morning at daybreak, walk miles on blistered feet with an empty stomach, her fingers cracking open with the frost, she didn't know. There had been days when every bone in her body screamed agonizingly for rest; the humiliation of people slamming their doors in her face, the torture of hunger and cold, all for just a few pennies a day, made her wish for death.

After that, cleaning and laundry work twice a week seemed like paradise, even if the other servants did treat her like vermin because her dress was ragged and her boots had holes in them.

But today at number 5, Mrs Toms the housekeeper had offered to take her on as maid of all work, living in, for which she would pay her five shillings a week, with a uniform and some new boots.

Hope knew she ought to feel overjoyed; after all, it was the kind of respectable job she'd wanted for so long. It would be bliss to sleep between sheets, never to wake as a rat ran over her, or suffer hunger pains again.

But Hope wasn't joyful, she was torn. For by accepting the advantages of going into service, she knew she would also have to accept the restrictions that came with it, along with her reservations about the Edwards household.

Mr Edwards was a fat, pompous little alderman, and it was said he had made his money by taking bribes to get people contracts from the Corporation. His wife was a nervy wraith who liked to ape real gentry. That aside, they were in Hope's eyes a fairly odious couple who also had no idea of how a household should be run. They relied totally on Mrs Toms, and she was a vicious bully who covered up her own ignorance by blaming the other servants when anything went wrong.

Up until today Hope had watched and listened to what went on at number 5 with some amusement, remembering dignified Baines who ran Briargate like clockwork, yet kept the respect and affection of all his staff. She knew he would throw up his hands in horror at her contemplating taking up a position in a household which was managed in such an inept fashion.

Yet it wasn't just the difficulties she might encounter at number 5 that daunted her; she felt it was disloyal to leave Gussie and Betsy. But for their generosity, protection and the survival skills they'd taught her she would not have survived a month in Lewins Mead. Their room in Lamb Lane might be squalid and rat-ridden, but within it she'd felt safe. The meek little Hope Renton who'd slunk away from the gatehouse on Albert's orders had become strong and resourceful. She wasn't even sure she had the ability to be anyone's servant again.

She had lost her respect for the gentry when she saw Sir William in bed with Albert, and since living in Bristol she'd seen and heard about too many other 'gentlemen' who liked boys, or very young girls, to think Sir William was exceptional. As for their ladies, she despised them even more for their hypocrisy. They flocked to their churches in silks and satins and prayed for the poor and the sick, but they never lifted a finger to help those less fortunate than themselves. Hundreds of destitute men, women and children from famine-ridden Ireland disembarked from ships each week in Bristol, but there was no sympathy for their plight. These poor souls could barely stand, they were so emaciated from starvation, yet the gentry brayed that they should be driven out of the city. As it was, most of them were forced to live like animals in the festering, derelict houses down by the river Frome, and with no food or medical help they were dying like flies.

Hope had heard Mr Edwards remark that if he had his way he would order the military to set fire to these unsanitary places, and that he hoped the people within them would perish too. Could she really work for such a man?

It was Friday today, and on Monday morning she was due back at the Crescent with her decision. Unfortunately she was pretty certain that if she turned down Mrs Toms's offer, the woman was spiteful enough to refuse to give her any further work at all.

But on seeing Betsy so obviously unwell, Hope put aside her own problems and rushed to help her friend. 'What's wrong?' she asked as she caught hold of her arm.

'I feel bad,' Betsy groaned. 'Me belly aches, I've been sick, I never felt this way before, I feel like I'm gonna die.'

Betsy was the toughest person Hope had ever known, she didn't ever complain when she was hurt or sick, so that in itself was enough to make Hope worried. Betsy hadn't been herself last night; she was pale and listless and hadn't wanted anything to eat. She'd insisted it was just the heat. But heat alone wouldn't give someone pain or make them sick, so it had to be something far more serious.

In the last few days there had been talk that there was fever among the Irish, and that if they weren't moved on it would spread throughout the city. Hope had dismissed this as scaremongering, but what if it was true?

She didn't intend to alarm Betsy with such a suggestion, so she put her arm round her to support her. 'I'll get you home,' she said. 'I expect you've eaten something bad. But I'll take care of you.'

'I need a drink of water,' Betsy moaned as they went up the stairs. She was really frightening Hope now for her movements were slow and laboured and she was shivering even though it was so hot.

'I'll make you some cinnamon tea,' Hope said. She had never liked the taste of Bristol water, so she never drank it other than in tea. Putting a stick of cinnamon in boiling water had been her mother's remedy for sickness or bellyache, for she had claimed that giving a sick person cold water upset them even more.

As they went into the room they found Gussie was already there. But he was lying down, and one glance at his white face and heavy eyes was enough for Hope to know he was suffering from the same complaint as Betsy.

'I've been sick,' he said, his voice little more than a whisper. He attempted to sit up but clearly didn't have the strength for it.

A cold chill ran down Hope's spine, for while it was possible that her two friends had shared some food that was bad, their symptoms reminded her of those her parents had with the typhus. Reverend Gosling had told her it was a disease which flourished in dirty, overcrowded conditions and she had always been mindful it could easily strike in Lewins Mead.

It crossed her mind that she should flee at once, but when she looked round and saw Betsy slumped down on the floor, her expression one of agony as she clutched at her stomach, she felt ashamed of such a thought.

She got them both to lie down and covered them with blankets, then lit the fire and put the kettle on it. There was enough water in the pitcher to wash their faces and hands, but she would have to get more from the pump.

It was desperately hot in the room, and it would be hotter still once the fire got going. She stood by the open window for a moment trying to gather her thoughts and remember all the remedies her mother and Nell had always used for sickness.

'I've got to go and get water and some things from the shop,' she told her friends. 'Stay where you are, I won't be long.'

Ten minutes later she staggered back up the stairs, weighed down by two pitchers of water and a flask of vinegar, which her mother had always used to wash things in when there was sickness in the cottage. She had the cinnamon, more candles too, and some mustard to make hot poultices.

Since the winter, when their lodgers left for good, Hope had introduced many items into their room which she considered essential for housekeeping. Some had been bought second-hand, others Gussie had acquired for her, but they now had a broom, a large saucepan, a frying pan, bowls for the stews she made on the fire, some cutlery, and another large bowl for washing up dishes. Recently, Hope had also stuffed the sacks with hay to make mattresses, and she always made sure they had soap too, and plenty of rags for cleaning purposes.

But as she walked back into the room and found Betsy on her hands and knees retching over the slop pail, she knew that trying to nurse two sick people with such sparse equipment was going to be very difficult.

Daylight faded soon after Hope had spread the hot mustard plaster on her friends' bellies. She was pleased to see that it did seem to ease their cramping pains, just as the cinnamon tea had calmed the vomiting. They were still shivering, but she had covered them with everything she could find to help them sweat it out and now they were sleeping.

But she could not sleep herself. The room was like an oven, and there was so much noise coming in through the open window. It was never quiet here, but since the hot weather began the noise had grown even worse, more babies crying, more drunks, more fights, and children running up and down the alleys until well after midnight.

Since settling down here, Hope made a conscious effort never to think about the past, but as she stood at the open window wearing only her chemise, dripping with sweat and desperate for air, the stink of human waste assaulting her nostrils, she couldn't help but remember hot summer nights when she was a child. The whole family would sit outside and watch the sun go down, and the breeze would be fresh and pure, scented with honeysuckle.

Even when she'd lived at the gatehouse, she and Nell had often sat on the backdoor step looking up at the stars. She recalled that she had often wished then that she lived in a big town, longing for the excitement of crowds, shops and markets. That wish seemed so foolish now she knew how harsh and unpleasant town life could be. She would give anything to be encircled by Nell's plump arm again, listening to nothing but the hoot of owls and the rustling of leaves.

Nell had surely hardened her heart to her now. Matt's

children would be the recipients of all the love and devotion she had once showered on her youngest sister.

Hope lapsed into a pretty daydream of imagining going back there, just to look at Nell. She could see herself hiding behind a tree in Lord's Wood on a Sunday morning, waiting for Nell to pass through on her way to church. She'd be wearing that pretty blue bonnet trimmed with white artificial daisies that Lady Harvey had given her. Just one glimpse of her would be enough.

Perhaps she'd see Rufus too, for he'd be home for the school holidays now. Maybe he would go down to the pond because he was remembering the good times they once shared? She could jump out and startle him. She would have to pledge him to secrecy of course. But maybe with his help they could think of a way to let Nell know she was safe?

A shouted oath from a drunken man in the alley below acted as a timely reminder of the reality of her situation. Even if it were possible to go back there without Albert getting to hear she'd been, she couldn't bear the thought of anyone she knew seeing her like this. She was the same as all the residents of the rookery now, dirty, thin and ragged – even Rufus would turn away in disgust. And anyway, she couldn't explain to him how it all came about, not without telling him his parents' part in it too.

'I hate you, Albert Scott,' she muttered to herself. 'One of these days I'll get even with you.'

As the first light of dawn crept into the room, Betsy was sick again and her bowels erupted uncontrollably. She cried pitifully from the pain in her belly, the cramps in her limbs and the embarrassment of fouling her bed, and although Hope tried to reassure her that she would start to feel better once all the poisons in her body had been expelled, it was all too reminiscent of her parents' deaths for her really to believe what she said.

A short while later Gussie was in the same state, and Hope was run ragged building up the fire to boil water for more cinnamon tea and darting down the stairs to fetch more water from the pump and empty the slop pail of dirty water. Flies buzzed frantically around the room as it grew hotter and even more foul, and sweat poured from her as she tried to scour the pail and bowls, wash over the floor and keep her friends clean.

By early afternoon, Hope was truly alarmed by her patients' appearance. Their eyes were sunken, their breathing very shallow, and they were no longer really aware of her ministering to them. She knew she must get help, but she had never heard of any doctor coming into Lewins Mead. Miss Carpenter, the schoolteacher, was the only person she could think of who might have enough influence to persuade someone to come.

Hope had only met Miss Carpenter twice. The first time was when she went to the school in St James's Back with Gussie in an effort to encourage him to go to lessons. The second time she had gone to ask the teacher if she could use any help in teaching the youngest children to read.

She admired Miss Carpenter greatly, as almost everyone in the rookery did. Anyone who could be so dedicated to teaching the poorest, most disadvantaged children in the city deserved admiration. She lavished her care and attention on her small charges, cared passionately about each one of them, yet for all that she wasn't an easy person to like. She was frosty, she rarely smiled, and there was an intensity about her that was frightening.

The teacher had also seemed very suspicious of Hope at their last meeting. Betsy had claimed it was because Hope was every bit as clever as her, and far prettier. Hope didn't believe that was the real reason. It was far more likely the teacher couldn't understand why someone able to read and write should end up in her neighbourhood. Yet whatever the woman's reasons for being chilly with her, Hope knew she had to try to enlist her help, or Betsy and Gussie might die.

Hope stopped by the pump to wash her face and hands before running round to the school. Three women had just filled their buckets and were gossiping before returning home. As Hope washed, she pricked up her ears because one of the women was talking about a whole family who had suddenly been taken ill.

'Two days ago they was all fine,' the woman said, a note of alarm in her voice. 'Old Ada went in there to see what she could do, but she soon come out. Said she didn't reckon anyone could help 'em.'

Old Ada was the closest thing Lewins Mead had to medical help. She was responsible for bringing most of the babies in Lewins Mead into the world, and laying out the dead. She was dirty, foul-mouthed and usually drunk, but those helped by her swore by her.

'They ain't the only ones sick neither,' another of the women said. 'I 'eard they got it in Cask Lane too.'

A cold shudder went down Hope's spine, for Cask Lane was next to Lamb Lane. She rushed off towards the school feeling even more frightened.

'Miss Carpenter! Could I speak to you?' Hope called out as she saw the teacher about to leave the old chapel building.

Despite the hot weather Miss Carpenter was still wearing her customary plain grey dress and bonnet, a shawl around her shoulders. She looked round at Hope and frowned. 'Hope, isn't it?' she said. 'I'm afraid I still don't have any work for you.'

'It isn't that,' Hope said breathlessly. 'My friends Gussie

and Betsy are sick and they need a doctor. I thought you might know someone who would come to them.'

Betsy had always had a down on Miss Carpenter; she claimed she involved herself in good works because she was a cranky old spinster with nothing better to do with her time. She sneered at the teacher's unfashionable plain clothes, and at her strong religious beliefs. She even suggested the woman got some vicarious thrill out of sticking her long nose into the rookery.

Hope had always laughed at Betsy's jaundiced views, unable to make up her mind whether she agreed or disagreed. But when she saw real concern flash into the woman's sharp, dark eyes she felt ashamed that she'd allowed Betsy to influence her.

'What are their symptoms?' she asked. 'Are they feverish?'

Hope explained how they were and what she'd already done to help them. 'I'm scared it's typhus,' she said finally. 'My parents died of that.'

Miss Carpenter looked very surprised and took hold of Hope's hand, pressing it in sympathy. 'I didn't realize you had been orphaned. I'm afraid I assumed because you'd been educated that you'd run away from home hoping for some adventure, and that was why I was a little sharp with you. But that isn't important now. I will ask a doctor I know if he will call on your friends, though I can't promise he'll come today as he may be out on other calls. Go home now, keep them warm and give them more fluids. It sounds as if you've been doing all the right things for them already.'

'I haven't got much money to pay the doctor,' Hope blurted out, having no idea at all what a doctor's visit cost.

Miss Carpenter made a little gesture with her hands, implying Hope wasn't to worry about that. 'The good Lord will provide,' she said. 'Not everyone in this world expects payment for their services.'

After checking exactly where Hope lived in Lamb Lane, the schoolteacher hurried on her way. Hope stood for a second or two watching the careful way she picked her way up the narrow alley, holding her skirt clear of the filth underfoot. She thought she must be about forty, yet she was as slight and slender as a young girl. Hope wondered why she hadn't married, for though she was rather plain with her long, pinched nose and thin lips, there were plenty of much plainer married women. Betsy claimed that men didn't like intelligent women, and Bible bashers even less, and perhaps she was right.

Hope had given up on the doctor coming by the time she heard the church clock striking ten that night. It had been an endless, terrible day for as soon as she cleaned up Betsy, Gussie would need washing too, and they both cried out with the pain of the cramps they were suffering. Hope was swaying with exhaustion, dripping with sweat, and beside herself with anxiety. The fluids coming from them now were like rice water, and the pair of them were scarcely aware of their own condition. It was like nursing two large helpless babies, only she had no napkins, sheets or towels to make them more comfortable.

Even more awful was the way they looked. When she held a candle near, their eyes seemed to have sunk into their faces, and their skin was mottled and dark. She talked to them constantly as she rubbed their limbs to ease the cramps, and even though they seemed unable to reply, she felt sure they knew what she was saying.

Raised voices from below suddenly alerted her that a stranger had come to the house. In the eighteen months she'd lived here, she'd grown used to this early-warning system. Anyone coming into Lewins Mead who wasn't known to the residents was treated with suspicion, and by calling out to the visitor, usually quite rudely, they made the stranger's presence known to the whole lane.

Hope opened the door and peered down the dark, rickety staircase. There was the usual cacophony of noise, and more light than usual for many doors were open, but not enough light to see who was there.

'Up the top of the stairs, mister,' someone called out.

A wave of relief welled up inside her, for it had to be the doctor. She nipped back into the room, grabbed a candle and went back on to the staircase to light his way.

The only doctor Hope had ever met was the one in Chewton that she'd been sent to when her parents were ill, so she expected this one to be of similar age and size. So she was somewhat taken aback when a tall young man with fair hair came into view.

'Are you the doctor?' she called down to him.

'I am. Dr Meadows,' he replied. 'And you must be Hope? I'm sorry to say Miss Carpenter didn't tell me your full name.'

'Thank you for coming, and just Hope will do fine,' she said when he reached her. 'I've been so afraid as my friends have become even sicker since I spoke to Miss Carpenter.'

Dr Bennett Meadows had thought himself fortunate when his uncle, Dr Abel Cunningham, invited him to join him in his Clifton practice when he qualified. He had no money to start up his own practice, and he knew that in all likelihood any other doctor offering to take him on as his junior would expect him to work very long hours for a mere pittance.

As a child he'd spent many holidays with his uncle, and he knew that most of his patients were wealthy people, so he imagined that it would only be a couple of years before he'd be in a position to branch out on his own.

But to his disappointment his uncle was no different from

any other successful doctor; he kept his best patients to himself and only allowed Bennett to treat the poorer ones.

'Ask for the shilling fee as soon as you arrive at a house call,' Uncle Abel had advised him. 'If you wait until you've treated the patient they'll think you're soft and find an excuse not to pay you.'

Perhaps Bennett *was* soft, for he found it impossible to demand his fee before looking at a child in the grip of whooping cough, or a man in agony from a crushed leg. And his uncle was right; he often didn't get paid afterwards. At first this frustrated him, but as time passed he came to learn that the poor never called for a doctor unless it was for something very serious. He found he just wasn't callous enough to take their last shilling if it meant the whole family would go hungry because of it, and if he could save the patient, the satisfaction was his reward.

It was because of his altruistic attitude that Uncle Abel mockingly called Bennett and Mary Carpenter 'Twin Souls'. Abel had been a friend of Lant Carpenter, Mary's late father, but he shook his head in bewilderment that the preacher's well-educated daughter had chosen to devote her life to a Ragged School. When Abel first introduced Mary to Bennett he had smirked and said that they ought to get along famously because they were both champions of lost causes.

Bennett didn't think a free school was a lost cause, and neither was the reformatory Mary had started up in the village of Kingswood. He thought it was marvellous that she'd persuaded the courts to give criminal children into her care, so she could teach them to read and write and learn a trade, and keep them out of adult prisons where they would only be corrupted further. She wanted her scheme to be used everywhere in England, and so far it appeared so successful that it seemed she might eventually get her wish.

Bennett did admire Mary for her compassion, intelligence and drive, but he wasn't so keen on her impervious manner, or the way she would often browbeat friends and acquaintances into doing her bidding. He had escaped this until tonight; she'd often invited him to fundraising events, and sought his opinion on treatment for minor ailments, but this was the first time she'd pressed him into making a house call.

She said there was something intriguing about the girl called Hope who had asked for her help. 'She is not typical of the young girls in Lewins Mead,' she said, shaking her head as if mystified. 'She is intelligent, well-mannered and very clean. I shudder to think about the conditions she is living in, but she cares desperately about her two sick friends and I felt compelled to do something to help her.'

Bennett wanted to refuse. Everyone knew the rookery was home to the most brutal and depraved people in Bristol. Even the police wouldn't go in there for fear of an attack. Mary insisted that his doctor's bag should be enough protection, and if challenged, he was to say she sent him, but from what he'd heard from other sources, the residents in that neighbourhood would rob their own grandmother for a tot of rum.

He had to agree to go though. If a slight, middle-aged woman was brave enough to go in there daily to teach, it would look very bad if a young and fit doctor wouldn't do likewise to attend the sick.

But his heart had been thumping with fear as he made his way through the rabbit warren of narrow, stinking alleys. He was disgusted by the filth, appalled by the number of drunken men and women slumped in doorways, and horrified that even after dark so many almost naked, malnourished and dirty children were abroad.

His nervousness had increased as he climbed the stairs to

the attic room, for although it was too dark there to see the filth, he could sense it, covering his nose to keep out the stench. Raised, angry voices were all around him, and he felt a rat brush past his ankles. This, he thought, was as close to hell as a man could get, and had it not been for the sweet voice calling down to ask if he was the doctor, he might very well have turned tail and run away.

Mary Carpenter's description of Hope had formed a picture in his mind of a very plain but kindly girl. But as he reached the top landing and saw her lit up by her candle, he was astounded to see that she was beautiful.

Her grey dress was ragged and stained, she smelled of sickness and sweat, and her dark hair was plastered to her head. But her face! Huge, limpid dark eyes, plump lips and a perfectly formed nose. It was like discovering a rose growing on a dung heap. He was so staggered that for a moment he could only stare at her in amazement.

'Will you look at them now?' she asked, bringing him sharply back to the purpose of his visit. 'I've tried to make them drink, but they aren't taking it any more. I'm so afraid for them.'

Bennett had been into the homes of hundreds of poor people since he came to Bristol, but he had never seen anywhere as grim as this girl's room. By the light of three or four candles, he could see there was no furniture, just a couple of wooden crates which acted as tables, and sacks filled with straw for beds. Hope's friends were lying on two of these and the air was rank with sickness and excrement, yet he could see by the rags hanging to dry by the window that this young girl had done her best to keep her patients clean.

He went to the sick woman first, kneeling down on the floor to examine her. Her pulse was almost indiscernible, she seemed unaware of him or her surroundings, and worse still, she had a bluish-purple tinge to her face.

Bennett stifled a gasp of horror for her colour told him exactly what she was suffering from. He had never treated anyone with the disease before, but he remembered the effects of an epidemic that had occurred before he began to study medicine. He had, however, studied the disease in theory and knew how serious it was, and his stomach churned with alarm as he recalled how fast it could spread.

The young man's symptoms were identical to the woman's, but his pulse was even slower. Bennett looked up at Hope, saw her exhaustion and the fear in her eyes, and he was afraid to tell her the truth.

'How long is it since they were taken ill?' he asked.

'Only yesterday,' she said. 'Betsy said she felt poorly the night before, and Gussie wasn't quite himself either, but we all thought it was just the heat. Is it typhus, doctor?'

'No, it's not typhus,' he said, wishing it were as the recovery rate from that disease was much higher.

'Then what, doctor?' she exclaimed. 'Tell me, for pity's sake.'

He knew he had to tell her the truth. He must give her the opportunity to decide whether she would flee to save her own life now, or stay and catch it too. She might even have it already, for he knew it was a fickle disease. In some it took days to manifest, in others, like these two, it struck fast and without mercy, death following in less than a day.

'It is cholera, I'm afraid,' he said softly, a lump coming up in his throat at having to name the disease which frightened him above all others.

She gasped and covered her mouth in horror. 'Hundreds died of that the year I was born,' she said, tears springing into her eyes. 'I remember my mother talking about it to my sister. Can you make them better? Can we get them to the hospital?'

'Your friends are too sick to move now,' he said gently.

His mind was whirling, weighing up how quickly the disease would spread to the others in this house. He recalled hearing some wailing as he came down the alley, which might have been another victim. Only this morning Uncle Abel had mentioned that there had been reports of several deaths among the destitute Irish immigrants, and now in the light of what he'd seen here, he thought it very likely that was cholera too.

He feared a mass panic when word got out that the dreaded disease was back in the city, and if people began swarming out into the countryside it could lead to a huge, countrywide epidemic.

But these two patients were his primary concern for now. It would be soon enough when he left here to inform the authorities and let them decide what was to be done.

'I will give you some opium to put in their water which will help their cramps,' he said. He knew he ought to tell the girl that her friends' blue colouring meant they were already in the final stages, but he couldn't. At least the opium would make their deaths gentler.

She might have been told about the cholera epidemic in '32, but Bennett had seen it for himself, for he had been twelve years old then. He often felt it was that epidemic which had prompted him to become a doctor. His childhood home was two miles from Exeter, but in the city people died like flies that summer, often dropping in the streets. His mother had been terrified by the disease, refusing to let him go out for fear of catching it, but he had slipped out and seen the bodies being flung on to an open cart, heard the church bell tolling as the mass graves were filled. He could never forget the bonfires on which victims' clothes and bedding were burned, or the fear in people's eyes as they swarmed from the city trying to escape the disease.

That same fear was in Hope's eyes now; she looked at

him as if knowing he was holding something back, but afraid to question him further. 'I've been giving them cinnamon tea,' she burst out. 'That is, until they stopped drinking. I put mustard poultices on their bellies too. Was that right? Should I go on doing it?'

'All that is excellent,' he said, astounded that a girl so young could be so unselfish and practical. 'You'd make a fine nurse, Hope. But leave the poultices now, just give them water with the opium. You must get some rest too, or you will become ill.'

She looked at him long and hard for a moment. 'Why haven't I caught it?' she asked eventually, her voice shaking. 'I didn't get typhus when my parents died of it, even though I nursed them. Was that just luck?'

'I don't know, I'm afraid,' Bennett said, feeling helpless. 'There are so many different ideas about what causes these diseases. Some doctors think they are carried in the air, others think they are passed by contact, but no one knows for sure. I don't personally believe they are airborne, but then if it is passed on by physical contact, it's strange that some members of a family don't get it.'

He wished he could say that if she hadn't already got it, she was safe, but he couldn't lie to her like that. For all he knew she could collapse with it at any minute, just as he could wake up tomorrow with it too.

'Mother believed in washing everything with vinegar when someone was ill,' she said in a small voice. 'Do you believe in that?'

'I do,' he agreed. 'Wash your hands with soap each time you touch one of them and don't drink from the same cup as them either.'

He got up and took a small bottle of opium from his bag. 'Three or four drops, that's all,' he said. 'I'll come back to see them in the morning.'

Bennett felt strangely reluctant to leave her. He knew he must, he couldn't do any more, and it would be folly to stay a minute longer than he had to. But it seemed wrong to leave someone so young with such a responsibility. He wanted to know why someone so beautiful came to be in this terrible place; in fact he wanted to know everything about her.

Mary Carpenter was right, she was intriguing.

'Hope!'

She started at Gussie's weak call, and was surprised to find it was now daybreak and she must have dropped off to sleep for a couple of hours.

Her heart leapt, for if he could call out her name he might be over the worst. 'What is it?' she whispered as she quickly moved over to him. 'Another drink?'

He nodded weakly and she held the cup to his parched lips, but she saw only too clearly that he wasn't getting better after all, for his blue colour was even worse by daylight than it had been by candlelight.

'I'm dying,' he croaked out. It wasn't a question, just a statement of fact. But she denied it vigorously.

'Don't,' he said, his sunken eyes making him look like a very old man. 'I know the truth. You must get out of here now, it's not safe for you to stay.'

That he should only be thinking of her safety when he was so desperately sick made tears spring to her eyes. She picked up a damp cloth and wiped his brow tenderly. 'I love you, Gussie,' she whispered. 'You and Betsy have been such good friends to me and I can't leave you. So don't tell me to go.'

He just looked at her with those sunken eyes fixed on her for some little while. 'I wanted you to be my girl,' he blurted out. 'So many times I wanted to tell you how I felt about you, but I didn't dare.'

Hope blushed, surprised by his statement. But then she remembered all those times he'd taken her hand, the hugs that were just a fraction more than friendship, the way he'd looked at her sometimes. She might have been frightened by it had she realized what it meant, for she hadn't felt the same way. She'd only loved him like a brother.

'I wish you had told me,' she whispered, unable to let him die thinking his feelings for her were not returned. 'I'd be proud to be your girl.'

He smiled then. It was nothing like the wide, joyful smile she was used to, when his eyes would dance and twinkle, but just the ghost of it. Yet she felt uplifted that a small white lie could bring him some measure of happiness.

'I used to dream that our luck would change, that we'd get married and live somewhere beautiful,' he said, struggling to get the words out. 'Get away from here, Hope, find that good life you deserve. I'll go easier if you give me your promise.'

Her mind slipped back to good memories from the past. The many times they'd sat in front of the fire in winter with him massaging her icy feet to warm them. She thought of the surprised delight on his face when he ate a stew she'd cooked on the fire, or how he laughed up on Brandon Hill one day in early spring when they'd rolled down the grassy slopes together.

Gussie might not have been the man she would want to pledge herself to for life, but he'd taught her some valuable lessons that she would never forget. He was warm and funny, loyal, generous and kind, and she would hold those important assets in her heart and make sure the man she did eventually marry had them too.

'I promise,' she whispered, kissing his forehead. 'I won't ever forget you, Gussie, and I'll miss you so much.'

'How is Betsy?' he asked, trying to raise himself enough to look at her.

It was tempting to tell him she was getting better, but on a moment's reflection she thought that as Gussie and Betsy had been such close friends for so long, maybe they'd feel less frightened dying together.

'I think she wants to go with you,' she said.

He slumped back on to the mattress and closed his eyes. He kept them closed for some time, making Hope think he'd fallen asleep, but then his cramps began again, his legs and arms twitching furiously, and she rubbed them hard with both hands as she'd done before.

'Go now,' he rasped while still in the terrible spasm. 'There's nothing more you can do for us. Save yourself!'

That was the last coherent thing he said to her. He said other words, but nothing that made any sense, and she managed to make him drink a little more cinnamon tea laced with the opium until he was still again.

Betsy got the violent cramps soon after, and Hope rubbed her arms and legs until she had no strength left.

'Let me die now,' she shrieked. 'I'm finished.'

She too became quiet again after more opium, and looked at Hope with pleading eyes. 'Don't you go bad without me,' she croaked out. 'You get yerself a nice gent with some brass.'

Betsy had always been one for dishing out advice and opinions, and Hope had no doubt that her friend felt frustrated by being unable to voice all that she felt. Yet what she had managed to say was in fact a condensed version of her philosophy, and even an acknowledgement that she was glad Hope hadn't turned to thieving or prostitution.

Hope had so much she wanted to say to her friend; but there weren't big enough words to cover her gratitude, her affection or her admiration. She could feel scalding tears running down her cheeks, her heart felt it had swollen up so much it might burst, and her head was full of a hundred vivid pictures. She could see Betsy in the second-hand dress shop, vivaciously chatting away to the shop owner while stuffing a petticoat or shawl under her dress; her cheeky grin as she ran away with a stolen pie or piece of fruit, and the way she could captivate a foreign sailor with those big dark eyes and get him to part with a shilling. She was fiery, funny, daring, and a ray of sunshine on the darkest of days. She might have been a thief, but she had her own moral code she lived by, which was in many ways far more honourable than those of the pious ladies who flocked to church on Sundays. She had taken food and clothing down to the poor Irish, and there was scarcely a family in Lamb Lane she hadn't helped out at some time. Hope felt proud that Betsy had singled her out to be her friend, for the time spent with her had been an education, a joy and a gift of love.

'You are beautiful,' she murmured through her tears as she bathed her friend's face. 'A true sister, and one day when I've got children of my own I'll tell them all about you.'

Gussie died first, just as the church bells were ringing for the morning service. Betsy followed him within minutes.

Hope couldn't cry any more, she'd spent all her tears in the last hours, and now she felt only relief that her friends' suffering was over. Their corpses were hardly recognizable as the people she loved, for the cholera had turned their faces to those of gaunt and terrible ghouls. Only their hair, the dark and the red, was a marker of who they once were. Hope needed to go somewhere where she had good memories of their vibrant characters, where she could hear their laughter, remember their stories, and see them again in her mind when they were beautiful. Then she could mourn them.

She hauled Betsy's mattress closer to Gussie and covered them in a blanket, then, collecting up her few things, she tied them into a bundle and left, quietly closing the door behind her and fastening a note for the doctor on a nail.

Chapter Thirteen

Bennett found Lewins Mead by day nowhere near as frightening or noisy as at night, but then he supposed that at ten on a Sunday morning most of the residents were still sleeping off the drink from the night before.

Yet although it felt safer, daylight revealed the full wretchedness of the place. The wooden-framed houses were tottering with age and rotting away. Few had windows intact, weeds grew out of roofs, and walls bulged alarmingly. An open drain in the centre of the alley was blocked by a putrefied dead dog and the human waste thrown from windows was backing up towards doorways. Bennett gagged at the stench, and hearing a warning shout from above, hastily jumped aside as the contents of a full slop pail came cascading down, narrowly missing him.

Further into the rookery by the water pump, a group of women were gossiping. They turned to look at him with sharp, suspicious eyes, but the youngest of them, a pretty but very dirty girl with half her breasts exposed, whispered some comment which made them all laugh raucously. Bennett felt himself blush furiously, but he raised his hat and wished the women good morning. Their semi-naked children were playing listlessly in the dirt close by, and as he noted their distended bellies and stick-thin limbs, he felt guilty that he'd had two fine plump kippers for his breakfast that morning.

How many of them would survive cholera? He doubted any of them could as they were so malnourished.

He had hardly slept a wink for thinking about the disease, and what he could do to prevent it from spreading far and wide. He remembered that during the last epidemic some parish councils had attempted a system of quarantine to contain it. This amounted to forcing the healthy in a disease-stricken area to be shut up with the sick. That to his mind was barbaric, for whole families died unnecessarily under the worst of conditions.

But he rather suspected that Uncle Abel was likely to approve such a plan, as long as it didn't apply to him. This was why Bennett hadn't yet told him what he'd found here last night. His uncle certainly wouldn't have allowed him to come back here today, and that poor girl would be left alone with her sick friends believing he didn't care about her plight.

After he'd seen her today he intended to notify the authorities that cholera had arrived in the town. If Hope was still healthy, he would recommend she left the area as soon as possible before she found herself trapped here.

He paused as he arrived at her lodging house, shocked by the appalling condition of it. Last night the cloak of darkness had hidden its true horror. He had of course known by the shakiness of the stairs that it was severely dilapidated; he'd also known it must be hideous, but even so he hadn't imagined anything as bad as what he saw now.

There was no front door, and the wood panelling in the hall had been wrenched off, presumably for firewood; likewise, the banister spindles and many of the internal doors were gone. There were huge gaping holes in the plaster, showing the lathes beneath, and when he looked up the staircase to the top of the house he could see the sky through a hole in the roof.

It was not fit for human habitation, yet heaven knows how many unfortunate souls were compelled to live here, and the smell was so atrocious that he had to clap his hand over his nose and mouth or he might very well have vomited.

He saw the note pinned to the door even before he reached the last landing, and his first thought was that Hope had run off and was asking him to find someone to nurse her friends.

He felt an odd sense of disappointment in her, even though it was he who had suggested that she should go. He pulled the note off the nail.

'*Dear Doctor,*' he read.

Sadly Gussie and Betsy died this morning within minutes of one another. I didn't know what I should do about them. I haven't got any money for a funeral and I couldn't stay in there with them, so I thought it better to go. I'm going out into the countryside until I'm sure I haven't caught it too. Thank you for coming to see them, it was very kind of you, and I hope I haven't put you at risk too. Yours truly, Hope Renton

A lump came up in his throat. It was astounding that she could write so well, not one spelling mistake, and such good handwriting. But it was the honesty and kindness in her message that affected him most. He thought most people in her position would just run without any explanation or thanks.

He opened the door, but on seeing that the room was full of flies he hastily shut it again. He'd glimpsed the blanket-covered mound on the floor and didn't need to look beneath it to check Hope wasn't mistaken.

Two hours later Bennett walked wearily back to Clifton. As the council offices were closed on Sundays he'd reported the deaths to the police, leaving them to contact the appropriate people. Sadly, the man he spoke to seemed dull-witted, unable to take in how serious cholera was, or how quickly it could spread. He said deaths had been reported among the Irish squatting by the river Frome, but he chuckled as if that pleased him. Bennett had been tempted to wipe that smug expression off his face by informing him cholera wasn't choosy who it struck down, and it could very well be him or one of his family next.

But of course he didn't say it; to point out the gravity of the situation would only start panic. One thing was certain though: this handful of deaths wouldn't be the end of it. And Bennett knew that as a doctor he would be duty-bound to help. He didn't want to – it would be far safer to stay up in Clifton and pray the disease didn't get that far. At least half the stricken would die, and with or without a doctor that ratio would remain the same. But he'd made his oath to help the sick and that was what he must do.

The young girl Hope worried him too. She might be infected, and without any money, a roof over her head or anyone to turn to, she could be in a desperate situation.

He tried to think where she was likely to have gone. She'd only said 'the countryside', which could mean anywhere around Bristol. It would be like looking for the proverbial needle in a haystack!

As the sun was beginning to set on Sunday evening Hope looked down at the Avon Gorge from a viewpoint in Leigh Woods with tears streaming down her face.

The beauty of the scene in front of her was incomparable: the majesty of the rocky gorge, the orange sinking sun reflected in the water, the deep green of the woods on both sides. The tide was high and a large three-masted sailing ship was being slowly hauled down towards the sea by horses on the river banks. She could hear the sailors calling to one another, and someone unseen was playing an accordion. On the ship's deck there was a lady in a white dress and a feathered hat, holding the hands of two small boys.

Hope had come to this spot many times when she was collecting wood, and whatever the weather, she had never tired of watching the ships, or imagining where they had come from, where they were going or what cargo they were carrying.

But today she didn't care if that lady and her small boys were sailing to America or some other far-off land. She didn't care if the ship was marooned without wind for weeks at the river mouth, or even if it sailed into a tempest. Gussie and Betsy, her dear friends, were dead, and she couldn't even be there to say some prayers for them when they were buried.

Betsy had once laughed at her for feeling sad that a dead neighbour had a pauper's burial. She had said that whether you were taken to the graveyard in a gilded coach with six plumed horses, or trundled there on the parish cart, you still met the same end under six feet of earth. Maybe that was true, but it was so unfair that her friends who had been so vibrant and beautiful in life should meet such a horrible death, and then for them to be tossed into a pit without any ceremony was too much to bear.

Hope was afraid for herself too. Except for that one night when Albert had thrown her out into the rain, she'd always had someone to run to. Gussie and Betsy had rescued her soon after that, so she had never been tested to see if she could cope alone. She might have learned to make a living, to cook meals in one pan, even to keep clean under terrible conditions. But she'd had her friends to praise her efforts, comfort her when she felt like giving up, and they'd been there every night, their bodies keeping her warm and their laughter cheering her.

It was so quiet here in the woods, the only sounds the odd rustling in the undergrowth and the occasional coo of a wood pigeon. That was why she'd always liked it so much here, for down in the town the noise was incessant. But it wasn't good to know there was absolutely no one around, not when at any moment she could begin to shiver and feel stomach cramps. She might very well die up here in the woods. There would be no one to hold a drink to her lips, to rub her limbs or offer any words of consolation. Her corpse would be picked clean by crows and no one would ever know what happened to her.

Just two days ago she'd been torn between her friends and the position in Royal York Crescent. Now both options were gone. Even if she felt well tomorrow morning, she couldn't present herself at number 5 and risk taking the disease with her.

Ironically, she had more money on her today than she'd ever had in her life before. She'd found one pound eight shillings in Gussie's pocket, another four shillings in Betsy's, and she had five and sixpence of her own. She'd felt awkward about taking her friends' money, but whoever came to collect their bodies would take it, and Gussie and Betsy would have wanted her to have it anyway.

If not for the cholera that money would have bought her a good second-hand dress and a pair of boots. There would be enough left over to set herself up in a cheap room, and buy flowers from the market to make a living for herself by selling them.

But she couldn't go back into the town until she knew she was well. And if the cholera was raging there by then, it would be folly to return.

In the past weeks of hot weather she'd often tried to

persuade Gussie and Betsy to come up here with her and sleep under the stars. But they'd been horrified at the idea. They said woods were scary and they liked being around people. Betsy had even laughingly said that too much fresh air was bad for a body used to Lewins Mead. Hope had done her best to tempt them by telling them it would be fun, describing how they'd make a shelter, light a fire and get water from a stream, but they only shuddered at the idea.

She had had the presence of mind to bring the old teapot and a few other essentials from Lamb Lane, but it didn't look like fun now; without Betsy and Gussie it felt like a terrible punishment for not dying with them.

'You're just tired, you'll be fine after a good night's sleep,' she told herself, struggling to get a grip on her emotions. Resolutely she turned and made her way back to where she'd left her things. Maybe tomorrow she'd recover the will to build a shelter, and find the pond she'd discovered some months back so she could bathe herself. But tonight she was too overwhelmed with grief and exhaustion to do anything more than wrap herself in her old cloak and sleep.

A week later, Hope woke to the sound of rain falling. She sat up and rubbed her eyes, then parted the branches she'd concealed her shelter with. It was barely dawn, and the rain on the parched earth smelled good.

She lay down again, smiling smugly to herself because her shelter was still dry, proving she'd chosen the right spot beneath the canopy of a large oak, and built it well. As small children, she and Joe and Henry had often built such shelters in the woods, but she'd never imagined then that one day something which had been so enjoyable would prove so useful. It was thoughts of her brothers and home that had comforted her in the past week; they took her mind off the horror of her friends' deaths, helped her cope with her grief and prevented her from giving in to complete despair.

Every ache or pain terrified her in case it was the onset of cholera. It was so tempting to give in to the exhaustion she felt and just wait for whatever fate had in store for her, be that sickness or starvation. But she'd forced herself to scour the woods for the right kind of supple branches she could weave into a shelter, to collect up dry bracken to make herself a bed and store wood for her fire. The meagre provisions she'd brought with her were gone on the first day, but on the third, hunger drove her to walk back down to Hotwells on the outskirts of the town and buy a few things from a stall there.

Nothing had ever tasted as good as those potatoes she baked in the fire, a lump of cheese melting inside them. She had some apples and a bunch of fresh watercress, and somehow she knew as she munched on those peppery leaves that she must be well or she couldn't possibly enjoy it so much.

Yet bathing in the pond had lifted her spirits even more than the food. She had found the pond back in the spring and on many a hot day in the past couple of months she'd remembered it with longing. It took her some time to find it again for thick bushes hid it from sight. Only a faint gurgling of the spring which fed it had alerted her to where it was.

She had clawed her way through thick undergrowth, half-expecting to find it would have dried up to just a bed of damp mud. She almost shouted aloud with joy when she saw it was even prettier than she remembered: clean, fresh water, shining in the hot sun and completely surrounded by thick bushes. She waded in wearing her clothes, holding on to a thick branch for fear of getting out of her depth, and was thrilled to find it only came up to her waist.

She scrubbed her clothes with soap while still wearing them, then took them off, wrung them out and hung them on a bush to dry. She went back in naked then, washing every bit of herself, soaping her hair and revelling in the knowledge that she would finally be free of the stink and lice of Lewins Mead.

Holding on to a small log as a float, she found she could swim, and nothing in her life had ever felt as good as she floated in the cool, clear water, her limbs caressed and stimulated. She remained in the pond for so long that when she finally got out, her fingers and toes wrinkling from the water, her clothes were almost dry. She felt reborn then, her hair silky, her skin soothed yet glowing, and she vowed to herself that she would always live by water in future so she could bathe herself.

Back in her shelter later, she had studied herself in the small mirror Gussie had given her when she first arrived in Lewins Mead. Her hair shone and curled the way she remembered back at Briargate. Her cheeks were pink again and her eyes were bright. For a couple of hours she had even managed to think purely of her own future, rather than dwelling on the past, and it came to her then that Gussie and Betsy wouldn't see that as a betrayal, but be glad for her.

Since that day she'd had new purpose. There were many times she found herself crying for her friends, and she knew it would be a very long time before memories of them stopped hurting. But she had stopped wishing she'd died with them, and resolved to let herself recover from what she'd been through with rest, fresh air and food. She had the idea that she'd be given a sign when the time had come to start out again.

As she lay there listening to the rain trickling from the leaves, she felt this was the sign. She hadn't spoken to anyone other than the man she'd bought food from, and even then she'd only asked the price of his produce. She had glimpsed other people coming through the woods, but she'd kept well away from them. She couldn't hide here for ever, though; it was the end of August now and today's rain might prove to be the start of the end of the summer.

Something kept telling her to go up to Royal York Crescent and explain why she hadn't come last Monday. She didn't hold out much hope that Mrs Toms had kept the maid's position open for her, but she might have. If not, she could go round a few farms to see if anyone was taking on help with the harvest.

The rain stopped later, and the air was much fresher as Hope packed up her belongings. Before making her way down to the lane that led into Bristol she went over to the edge of the gorge and looked out at the view. The rain had not been heavy but it had left everything glistening. A ship was coming up the Avon with enough wind behind for it to skim along at a fair speed. It was the first time since she'd been here that she'd seen any ships with full sails and it made a pretty and welcome sight.

She needed to know what was happening in Bristol, whether the cholera had claimed other lives, and to thank Miss Carpenter for sending the doctor. She remembered her mother had always put great store in thanking people properly who had helped her at difficult times. She said it proved to people you were truly appreciative of their efforts. Hope also thought she should go into a church and say a prayer of thanks for being saved.

By the time Hope had crossed the bridge and reached Hotwells, the sun had come out again, and the earlier rain was drying fast on the ground. She took the steep lane up the hill to Clifton, admiring the many fine new houses on the way.

She had got to know this area well while selling her kindling, and often when she was cold, tired and hungry she used to take her mind off it by pretending she was a rich lady choosing a house to live in. Her favourite had been quite tiny compared with its grander neighbours, hardly more than a cottage. It had a dark red shiny door with a brass knocker like a lion's head, and lace at the small windows.

Once she had knocked at the door and a girl no older than herself had answered it. She wasn't a servant; she wore a fine blue gown with lace ruffles at the neck and sleeves, and ribbons in her fair hair. She gave Hope sixpence for a bundle of kindling and told her to keep the change. That little kindness had warmed Hope more than a hot dinner, and remembering it again now was a reminder that luck could change at any time. Perhaps today something good would happen.

As Hope turned into Royal York Crescent from Regent Street, she remembered how surprised she'd been the first time she came to Bristol that people lived in houses which were all joined together. Her father had explained they built them that way, because land was very costly in towns. He said they were called terraces.

Royal York Crescent, home to some of the richest people in Bristol, was an extra-special terrace because of its shape: one long, curving sweep of beautiful four- or five-storey houses on the top of the hill overlooking the city. Hope had been thrilled when she finally got to take coal into the drawing room at number 5 and had seen the view from the big windows. She could see the ships down in the harbour, St Mary Redcliffe's spire, then all the way across Bedminster right to the hills of Dundry on the horizon. She thought if she were mistress of that house she'd sit at the window all day looking at it.

A carriage was just pulling up outside the first house and Hope stopped to look purely because it had a coat of arms on its door similar to one that came to Briargate occasionally. As she stood there, the red and gold-liveried footman jumped down and opened the carriage door.

Two young ladies stepped down. One was all in pink, the other in pale yellow; even their dainty shoes matched their beautiful dresses. Hope couldn't bring herself to walk on past them for they were giggling excitedly and she was afraid they would laugh at her, suddenly aware just how woebegone she must look to girls like them. Her grey dress was little better than a rag, her boots had holes in them, and she had no stockings or hat.

All at once the front door of number 1 opened and a much older woman in lavender-coloured silk came out, almost running down the steps to greet the young ladies. It was obvious she was their mother by the joyful expression on her face and the way she held out her arms to embrace them.

Tears prickled in Hope's eyes as she remembered her mother greeting Nell that way when she came home on her afternoon off. But it was rare to see the gentry display such affection in public.

The ladies disappeared into the house and Hope moved on, but the happy little scene triggered memories of Nell's wedding day. She could see her mother and father and each of her brothers and sisters, all dressed in their best clothes, faces wreathed with smiles. She remembered hearing her father making a toast. He said that he believed that his eldest daughter's wedding was the start of a golden era for the family.

Hope was too young then to understand what he meant

by that. But she realized now that he hoped that one by one his sons and daughters would marry well and before long there would be grandchildren for him and Meg to love. But her parents were gone now, the entire family broken up and scattered far and wide. And she, the youngest and the one they had the highest hopes for, was a pauper, reduced to scrubbing floors to eat.

'You were expected last Monday,' Mrs Toms said, looking down her thin nose at Hope as she stood nervously outside the servants' entrance in the basement.

Mary, the kitchenmaid, had fetched the housekeeper at Hope's request, but the moment she saw Mrs Toms bustling down the passageway with that tight expression she remembered only too well, Hope knew she was on a fool's errand.

'The friends I lodge with were sick and I had to nurse them,' Hope explained. 'I didn't feel I could come here until I was sure I hadn't got it too.'

Mrs Toms backed away, eyes wide and her hands fluttering with agitation. 'They had cholera?'

Hope's heart sank right to her boots. She wanted to lie, but found she couldn't. She nodded.

'Get away from here!' Mrs Toms flapped her arms like a startled goose. 'How dare you bring that filthy disease to this door? Out, out and don't come back!'

Hope felt she couldn't be carrying the sickness if she was well, but there was no point in trying to explain further, she knew Mrs Toms wouldn't listen. There was nothing for it but to turn and walk away.

'You dirty minx, you and your sort are spreading this plague everywhere!' Mrs Toms yelled after her in high-pitched hysteria. 'You should be locked up!'

At that insult Hope could not hold back her tears, and

almost blinded by them she ran up Regent Street, her bundle of belongings thumping against her legs. She didn't slow down until she reached the Downs, the vast area of open space where she had so often gone to before when she felt the need for quiet and solitude. Under the shade of a large tree she sank down and covered her face with her hands as she sobbed out her pain.

It was as if all the injustices which had been piled on to her from the day Albert attacked her at the gatehouse until now had finally broken her. Images of all of them rushed through her mind: dragging herself through the rain away from Briargate, arriving in Bristol so weak that she scarcely knew where she was, waking next morning to the squalor and filth of Lamb Lane. She saw too all the many times she was refused work, the terrible hunger which forced her to steal the pork pie. Then there was the collecting and selling of kindling, her feet a mass of blisters, her skin so chapped and raw she cried with the pain. So much humiliation, the curt refusals and doors slammed in her face.

Even when she'd got work up here in Clifton, she'd always been treated with suspicion and scorn: no one was ever really willing to give her a chance to prove herself. Then finally the only good thing in her life was snatched from her, her two dear friends.

Why? What had she ever done to deserve such misery?

Other girls might have gone straight from that room in Lamb Lane to service at number 5 not caring if they took the cholera with them. But she hadn't, she'd stayed alone and frightened in the woods to be sure she was well. She didn't care that Mrs Toms wouldn't let her work for her again, she was a vile woman anyway, but her insults had robbed Hope of the last of her dignity, and now she had nothing.

*

Bennett Meadows was almost home to Harley Place on the Downs, when he saw a young girl sitting hunched up under a tree. He was just returning from St Peter's Hospital, and his mind had been on the cholera victims he'd just attended and how many more deaths could be expected before the epidemic ended.

Over fifty people had died in the past week, not just in Lewins Mead either, but in the Butts and Bedminster, and there had even been two cases in the grand houses of Queen's Square. As yet there were no reported cases of cholera here in Clifton but that was thought to be because of its elevated position well above the miasma of the dock area.

Panic was keeping people in their homes. Bennett had noticed that the streets were quiet; the only shops that had a steady stream of customers were those selling items people believed would protect them. He didn't personally think that drinking copious amounts of brandy, burning herbs or soaking bedsheets in vinegar and hanging them over doors and windows could act as a defence. But then he supposed people had to put their trust in something.

The desolate way the young girl was sitting, her head on her knees, alarmed him. If she was sick he knew he must get her to the hospital before she spread the contagion around this area too.

'Are you sick, miss?' he called out as he got closer. He had become far more cautious since his first two cases in Lamb Lane. While it was not possible to avoid touching patients entirely, he kept it to a minimum and scrubbed his hands vigorously afterwards. 'I am a doctor and I can get help for you if you are.'

Her head jerked up at his voice and to his utmost shock he saw it was Hope, the girl he'd been keeping an eye out for each time he went down into the town.

'Hope?' he asked incredulously. 'It is you, isn't it?'

She had clearly been crying for some time. Her eyes were red and swollen and she stared at him blankly as if she'd never seen him before. 'I'm Dr Meadows,' he said. 'I called to see your friends when they were sick.'

There was a spark of recognition. She hastily wiped her eyes on the hem of her dress, and even tried to smile. 'I didn't know you,' she said in a tear-choked voice. 'I didn't see you clearly that night.'

'No, I suppose you didn't,' he replied, remembering how dark it had been, and that she'd put the candle by the patients, not near him. 'I was very sorry your friends died. I got there about ten that morning after you'd left. Thank you for the note. But tell me, what is wrong now? Are you sick?'

'No.' She shook her head furiously, then leapt to her feet, trying to smooth down her hair with one hand and wipe the remaining tears away with the other. 'I was just upset because of something said to me. I'm very healthy. Do I look sick?'

Bennett moved closer. Her colour was good, her eyes were bright despite the tears, and she was remarkably clean, her dark hair positively gleaming. He was as struck by her beauty as he had been on their first meeting; in fact she looked even lovelier than he remembered.

'No, you don't look sick, only unhappy,' he said. 'Would you consider telling me about it?'

Hope looked at the tall young doctor staring intently at her and wondered how it was she had recalled so little about his appearance that night in Lamb Lane. She recognized him by his soft, deep and kindly voice, but she thought she should have noticed that his eyes were like rich brown velvet, or that his complexion was as clear and glowing as a child's.

He was thin, with an angular, rather stern face, and his

moustache looked as if it didn't quite belong to him for it was dark, while his hair was fair. Not handsome exactly, but he had a good face, and as he had been caring enough to return to Lamb Lane that Sunday, she knew she must talk to him.

'Lawdy, you don't want to hear my troubles,' she exclaimed to hide her discomfort at being caught crying in a public place. 'I'm sure you've got enough sick people to worry about without me taking up your time.'

'I can spare time for a nurse as good as you were,' he said with a smile.

The sternness in his face vanished with the smile. His mouth was wide and full, she noticed, and he had good teeth.

'They were my friends, I had to take care of them.' She blushed and lowered her eyes. 'But tell me, has it spread further? I went away to the woods and I only returned today, so I know nothing of what has been going on.'

'Sadly it is now a full-scale epidemic,' Bennett said gravely. 'There have been many deaths and each day the number grows. But come over there and sit with me for a while?' He pointed to a large felled tree some twenty yards from them. 'I've been on my feet for a long time and they ache.'

Hope had never been more in need of a kindly word and a friendly face, so she did as he asked. He told of the woeful conditions in St Peter's Hospital and his concern that the disease would spread beyond the relatively small pockets it was contained in now.

'But enough of that,' he said. 'I really do wish to know what brought you to Clifton today, and what happened that made you cry.'

Hope explained haltingly what had happened when she called at Royal York Crescent, and how vicious Mrs Toms had been.

'It was just too much for me when she was so insulting. I didn't deserve that, did I?'

'No, you didn't, not after what you've been through,' the doctor said thoughtfully. 'But people are afraid, Hope; it stops them from thinking of anyone but themselves. Cholera is such a mysterious disease, you see; it comes, kills at random and then disappears as suddenly as it came. I've even heard some call it a Devil's Plague because they say it takes the good and the pure and leaves the scoundrels alone.'

'I hope you are a scoundrel then,' Hope said, and gave a hollow laugh.

'My uncle thinks I am,' Bennett replied, smiling at her. 'He is appalled that the nephew he supported throughout medical school is deliberately courting infection by going to St Peter's each day. He thinks I should be using my skills on people who can afford to pay me.'

'I didn't pay you either.' Hope blushed with embarrassment.

'I didn't ask for any money,' he said. 'I could see how it was for you. But tell me, Hope, how did you come to be in Lewins Mead? I can tell by your speech and manner that it isn't where you belong.'

Hope told him the same carefully edited story she'd given Gussie and Betsy when she first arrived in Bristol; that she'd fallen out with her brother-in-law. She had often wished she dared tell them the whole story, but she never had; she was too afraid fiery Betsy might insist on going out to Briargate to avenge her.

'How old are you, Hope?' Bennett asked, strangely making no comment about her story.

'Seventeen, sir,' she said, but afraid that he would question her further, she changed the subject. 'Do you know where my friends' bodies were taken?'

Bennett knew that they'd gone to a mass grave close

to the river just outside the city, along with the other victims who died that day. He knew too that the bodies had quicklime shovelled on top of them and they hadn't been given the dignity of even a prayer. But he couldn't tell her that.

'I believe they were put in St James's churchyard,' he lied. 'But so many more took sick that day I cannot be sure.'

She nodded as if satisfied at that. 'Aren't you afraid you'll catch it too?' she asked, surprised that he could bear to go to St Peter's for it was a hospital in name only, a dreadful place that took in the insane, the very old and orphans.

'Yes, I am afraid,' he admitted. 'But I couldn't call myself a doctor and refuse to treat any patient who is suffering from something infectious, could I?'

'The doctor didn't come to my parents when they had typhus,' she said. 'But Reverend Gosling came in, that meant a great deal to me.'

All at once she found herself telling him about how she nursed them at the end.

'That explains why you were such a good nurse then,' he said. 'If we could get nurses like you at both St Peter's and the General Hospital we might not lose so many patients. There are a few Sisters of Mercy who are fine nurses, but the rest!' He shrugged his shoulders and made a hopeless gesture with his hands.

Hope knew the kind of women he meant. Dirty old crones in the main, who could get no other work and saw it as an alternative to the workhouse. Most of them were drunks; they often stole from the sick. With nurses like that it was hardly surprising few people went to the hospital willingly.

'I must go,' she said, getting up. 'I am going to try to get some work helping with the harvest.'

'You are worth more than farm work,' he said quickly.

'Let me ask about and see if I can get something better for you?'

'Why would you do that?' she said in some surprise. 'Surely you wouldn't want to present someone like me to your fine friends?'

He got up and looking down at her, he took hold of her chin and tilted it up so he could see her face better. 'If by that you mean rich or influential friends, I don't have any,' he said with a little smile. 'But my uncle, who is also a doctor, has many well-to-do patients who could do with a nurse to take care of them. It was people such as these I was thinking of.'

'Me be a nurse?' She cocked her head to one side, looking at him askance. 'I wouldn't know what to do.'

'You did very well with your friends,' he said. 'Most of nursing is keeping a patient clean and comfortable and seeing that they get the right nourishment and take their medicine. I know you could do that, and if there was anything which needed more medical skill, I could instruct you on that.'

'But look at me!' she exclaimed, glancing down at her ragged dress and wincing. 'No one would want someone looking like this caring for them.'

'I don't think they'd notice much more than your pretty face and your soft voice,' Bennett said with a smile. 'But a new dress and a clean apron might make you feel more confident. I'm sure my uncle's housekeeper could sort that out for you. Come with me now to his house and we'll talk to him.'

'Why would you do that for me, sir?' she asked. She felt she could trust him, she liked him too, but Betsy had warned her that men only wanted to use young girls.

'Because I know you'd make a fine nurse,' he said. 'And because I think you and I have more in common than you imagine.'

She looked up at him curiously, unable to believe a gentle-man like him had anything in common with her.

He smiled. 'My mother was widowed when I was still a child. There was no money and she had to work as a dressmaker to feed my younger brother and me. My uncle Abel was her brother-in-law, and it was he who paid for my schooling. Without that I wouldn't be a doctor now. But it hasn't been an easy ride for me. I might not have been hungry like you, or forced to live somewhere like Lamb Lane, but I've had to endure being the poor relation, to appear grateful at all times, and to follow my uncle's wishes at the expense of my own desires or needs.'

'Do you mean you didn't want to be a doctor?'

'No, that I love,' he said. 'But I am a fish out of water in society. I do not like or approve of many of the people my uncle expects me to mix with. There is so much hypocrisy, such meanness of spirit and ignorance. And precious little compassion for those less fortunate than themselves.'

Hope nodded, liking this rather odd doctor more by the minute. 'You sound like a swanky version of Betsy,' she said with a grin. 'I think you would have liked her.'

'Would she have wanted you to become a nurse?' he asked.

'Hell, no,' Hope chuckled. 'She was too much of a free spirit to approve of any work which might involve taking orders. But she would think that any doctor brave enough to come into Lewins Mead must have something special about him. I think that too.'

'So you'll come with me to my uncle's then?' he asked. He turned and pointed out the row of elegant houses facing on to the Downs. 'It's only over there in Harley Place.'

Hope looked at the house, the hope that a visit there might lead to something she could be proud of overriding her natural caution. 'I will,' she replied. 'But if he's rude to me I'll leave. I'm never going to let anyone speak to me again the way Mrs Toms did today.'

'She's a pretty little thing, I'll grant you that,' Abel said begrudgingly. 'But she's proud, and that won't go down well with my patients.'

Bennett was with his uncle in the drawing room on the first floor, a gracious room with long, elegant windows, a sparkling chandelier and fine Persian rugs, but the effect was marred by too much furniture. Large, overstuffed armchairs and couches jostled for space between heavily carved and polished chiffoniers, side tables, bookcases and a vast writing desk.

The room reflected sixty-year-old Abel's appearance, for he was overstuffed too, a short, fat-bellied man with a penchant for floral waistcoats which often vied with his high colour and his checked breeches. Alice, his long-suffering but adoring housekeeper, often tried to persuade him he looked rather more like a circus showman than an eminent doctor, but his explanation for his loud taste was that in nature, the male of the species has the brightest plumage. Bennett privately thought it was a ploy to display his wealth and position.

Harley Place had been built during the Georgian period when the slave trade was booming and wealthy merchants wished to escape the noise and filth of Bristol. Abel had inherited enough money from his ship-owning father to set himself up here with a consulting room on the ground floor, when he was still a young man. Mary, his wife, had been very well connected, so almost as soon as his brass plaque was fixed to the door, her friends flocked to the practice. Sadly, Mary had died in childbirth just five years later, their son stillborn, and Abel had never remarried.

Alice lived in the basement along with the two maids,

and although Abel would never admit they were anything more than servants, they had become his substitute family. Bennett often felt Abel was closer to them than he was to his nephew and junior partner.

'She'll make a first-class nurse, I'd stake everything on that,' Bennett said staunchly. He had been somewhat amused that Hope had refused to kowtow to Abel; he was a man who normally intimidated most people at their first meeting.

But Hope had given a good account of herself. She looked him straight in the eye and told him that she could read and write, and she'd been trained in service and was able to cook and sew. She also related explicitly the deaths of her parents from typhus and made it quite clear she understood the need for strict hygiene in the sickroom.

'If you are such a paragon of virtue, why were you living in a rookery?' Abel barked at her.

Bennett realized that his uncle suspected she was a prostitute, and expected that Hope would flounder at his loaded question.

'Because when you have no money you have to take shelter wherever you can,' she said crisply. 'But that doesn't mean I had to fall into the ways of the neighbourhood.'

Abel rang for Alice at that point and asked her to take Hope downstairs while he spoke to Bennett. To his credit, he didn't embarrass Hope further by giving Alice any orders to see she washed and to find her some clean clothes, but Alice was a very kind-hearted woman and Bennett knew she would do this anyway, even if the girl was asked to leave later.

'You've been bemoaning the absence of good nurses at St Peter's,' Abel said as he turned away to pour himself a brandy. 'So take her there.'

'I can't ask her to take that risk,' Bennett said in horror.

'She survived nursing her friends,' Abel said with a shrug. 'You appear to have avoided being infected too.'

'I don't know whether that is just luck or the stringent care I've taken to avoid close contact with the victims,' Bennett said. 'If it is luck, it could run out.'

He had taken every precaution he could think of to avoid bringing the disease home. He kept a cotton coat at the hospital which he only wore there, he had made a point of keeping his distance from Abel and the servants on his return, and he scrubbed his hands until they were almost raw.

'Test her pluck by asking her!' Abel barked at him. 'If she's prepared to do that, I'll find her a softer billet later.'

Bennett knew how his uncle's mind worked. He wasn't one for charity, and he was suspicious and narrow-minded. He probably thought Bennett was sweet on the girl, and his demand would probably make her run off, which was almost certainly what he hoped for. But Bennett didn't think she would flee; her innate kindness would make her want to help those poor souls.

He half-closed his eyes, visualizing the filthy, over-crowded wards at St Peter's which reeked of the most hideous suffering. She'd had more than her share of misery already, was it fair to give her more? To ask her to risk her young life for the dubious honour of maybe later being promoted to nursing some wealthy old crone who wouldn't value her. Surely it would be better to let her go and find work on a farm? She might find love and happiness there.

But he recalled the proud way she'd stood up to Abel, her face as beautiful as a spring morning, and he knew he wanted some way of holding her in his life.

Chapter Fourteen

Hope stopped on the turn of the stairs, transfixed by her reflected image in the long mirror in front of her.

She couldn't remember ever seeing herself in a full-length mirror since she was a child and used to play with Rufus at Briargate. She had of course looked at her face in a hand mirror daily, and caught sight of herself reflected in shop windows, but the latter images were never clear, and she always averted her eyes as she didn't want to be reminded of her ragged and unkempt state.

But here in front of her now was the girl she had ached to be for so long. Her hair was neatly plaited and wound around her head. The dress Alice the housekeeper had given her was a maid's dress, navy-blue with white collar and cuffs, and she wore polished boots. If she lifted the dress an inch or two above her ankles she saw the lace on the hem of a cotton petticoat and black stockings.

She couldn't thank Alice enough for this transformation which had been achieved in such a kindly, diplomatic manner that Hope hadn't even felt embarrassed. Alice said the clothes and boots belonged to a maid who had left to get married some years earlier and they were too small for anyone else.

It was this small size that surprised Hope most of all. She had never realized she was so slender. But then, her old dress had been Nell's and it was so loose her real shape was hidden. Alice had remarked on her tiny waist, and laughingly said that all the Clifton ladies would be jealous of it. She'd also said Hope had beautiful hair and eyes, and that she understood why Dr Meadows had been so concerned about her when he found she had left Lewins Mead.

It was wonderful to feel respectable again, but to know that she'd made enough of an impression on the doctor for him to worry about her gave her a warm glow inside. She wasn't even scared that she had to go back into the drawing room and see whether Dr Cunningham had decided if he would give her nursing work. The wash in hot water, her nails scrubbed and cut and the new clothes made her feel she could deal with anything he might say to her.

Alice said his bark was worse than his bite, but that was because he'd lost both his wife and his baby son. She added that the best way of dealing with his rudeness was to answer him back. 'He likes a bit of spirit,' was how Alice put it.

Well, Hope felt spirited now. She wasn't entirely sure about becoming a nurse, but washing and feeding old ladies was certainly better than working on a farm, or selling flowers or kindling. She was also indebted to Dr Meadows for giving her a chance. So she didn't intend to let him down.

She moved on up the stairs, but as she approached the drawing-room door, she heard raised voices and wondered if they were arguing about her. But she knocked anyway, and barely a second later Dr Meadows opened it.

'Come on in, Hope. Alice has done you proud,' he said, smiling appreciatively at her appearance. Yet she had the feeling that the flush on his face was from anger at something his uncle had been saying.

Dr Cunningham was standing with his back to the fireplace. He looked at her with a sour expression and didn't comment on her changed appearance.

'So you think you'll be a good nurse, do you?' he said curtly.

That sounded like sarcasm, and she wasn't sure how to respond. 'I'm not sure, sir,' she said, clasping her hands together in front of her. 'But I shall try.'

'To prove yourself, d'you mean?' he growled.

'Yes, sir.' She glanced at the younger doctor, noting that he looked distinctly nervous.

'Then I shall place you somewhere where your character and ability will be tested,' he said. 'This evening my nephew will be returning to St Peter's Hospital, you will accompany him and he will hand you over to the head nurse there. As I am sure Dr Meadows has told you, they are in desperate need of nurses.'

Hope's heart plummeted. If Dr Cunningham had said he was sending her to the general hospital by Bedminster Bridge she would have been scared but not horrified because it was a newly built hospital and a good one by all accounts. But St Peter's was viewed with the same terror as the gallows. It was a well-known fact that most entering its doors came out in a coffin, and rumours abounded about the brutality and the squalor within.

She was just about to retort that she would sooner return to the woods to live, when she saw a wily look in the old doctor's eyes. All at once she realized what he meant by testing her. He hoped she'd refuse; that way he could feel justified in ordering her out of his house and his nephew's life.

'I can't say I'm grateful for such a position,' she said with all the dignity she could muster. 'But as I know you wish to test me, then I'll go and prove I have some ability.'

'You don't have to,' Dr Meadows blurted out, and when she turned to look at him she could see dismay written all over his face. 'St Peter's is a hell-hole; there is no other word for it. And with the cholera raging there you will be in danger yourself.'

'Bennett!' Dr Cunningham said reprovingly. 'I will not have you making such remarks about our hospital; the board of health has spent a great deal of money on improving conditions there in the last few years.'

'You haven't set foot inside it since the riots eighteen years ago,' the younger man spat at him. 'If you had, you would know that the money allocated to it was siphoned off by greedy aldermen for their own pet projects. If I could have one wish it would be that the people of Bristol would riot again and destroy St Peter's in the same way they destroyed the prison last time.'

'You were only a child during the riots. What you've heard is greatly distorted,' Dr Cunningham protested.

'I was staying here,' Bennett reminded him coldly. 'I remember you returning covered in blood from patching up the wounds of those slashed by cavalry sabres. You wept about the carnage and the appalling conditions in the hospital. If what I heard was distorted, I heard it from you!'

'Enough!' The old man held up one hand to silence his nephew. 'None of that is relevant. You brought this young woman here today because you believed she could be a nurse. Those poor souls in the hospital need a good nurse far more than a rich dowager with gout does. I say she should go where she is needed.'

All at once Hope saw how the land lay between the two men. Cunningham had probably once been as compassionate and dedicated as his nephew was, but age and perhaps wealth had changed him. Yet what he said made good sense, even if it was hypocritical to send her to a place he wouldn't set foot in himself.

Hope knew that emptying the chamber pot of some rich and possibly cantankerous old woman would never give her any satisfaction or teach her anything new. But she had an affinity with the poor, and if she could offer a little comfort to them in their last hours, that was at least worthwhile.

'I will nurse at St Peter's,' Hope said, lifting her chin defiantly as she looked straight at Dr Cunningham. 'And I'll become the best nurse there, just you see. But don't think I'm going there because you ordered me to. I'm going because I want to!'

'You're a cheeky little baggage,' he replied, but his tone was softer now, almost amused. 'Now, clear off downstairs, my nephew needs some rest before he goes back tonight, and you look as if you could do with a hot meal inside you.'

That evening Hope viewed St Peter's Hospital with some trepidation from the safety of Dr Cunningham's carriage, while Dr Meadows went inside to speak to the head nurse.

In the darkness she could see little more than the front door which was lit by two lamps, but she had seen the place by daylight many times before and knew that its attractive appearance belied the wretched plight of its inhabitants.

It was a fine old building, one of the most ornate in the whole of Bristol, and Hope had been curious enough about it in the past to discover some of its history.

The Norton family had the timber-framed mansion built to replace their old one in 1600 and had it elaborately decorated with carved brackets, bargeboards and plasterwork. At that time its position facing St Peter's church and backing on to the floating harbour close to Bristol Bridge would have been a very pleasant one, but Hope suspected the Nortons had moved on once the river became nothing but an open sewer.

At the end of the seventeenth century it had been the Mint for a while, but later it was purchased by the Bristol Incorporation of the Poor as a workhouse.

Betsy had always been very wary of going near the place because of the lunatics shut away inside it. She also claimed it was haunted. Hope felt she could well be right about that, for in the cholera epidemic of '32 it had been vastly overcrowded and hundreds died there. From what Bennett had said today she couldn't expect the conditions to be any better now.

One thing just about everyone in Bristol agreed on about St Peter's was that it was the very end of the road for anyone unfortunate enough to be taken there.

It was tempting to run off now, while she still could, but her stubborn streak would not allow her to give Dr Cunningham the satisfaction of hearing she'd slipped off like a thief in the night.

Yet some half an hour later, alone with Sister Martha, the head nurse, Hope involuntarily gasped with horror as the door was opened to the cholera ward where she would begin work at six the following morning. Her first thought was that this was hell come to earth.

Some thirty or so men, women and children were in a dark, dank, stinking room hardly big enough for half that number. There were no beds; they lay on straw fouled by vomit and excrement or sat huddled against the walls. In the dim light of two lanterns, seeing the pain-filled eyes which turned to her was like glimpsing the lost souls Reverend Gosling used to speak of in his fire and damnation sermons. The sound of their sobbing, moaning and plaintive calls for help wrenched Hope's heart.

'There's little we can do to help the poor souls,' Sister Martha said, clutching the large wooden crucifix which hung around the waist of her habit as if it might protect her. 'Since this plague started no one brought here has recovered. Many of these will be dead by the morning.'

She whisked Hope out quickly, shutting and locking the ward door behind her. She explained this was necessary as some of the sick became so demented they tried to escape. She also pointed out that the new general hospital in Guinea Street had refused to take any cholera cases.

Hope had seen two elderly crones shuffling among the patients offering water. But she had the feeling that the moment the door was closed again they would withdraw to the small adjoining room Sister Martha had said housed the stove and sink, and get out their bottle of gin.

Sister Martha was a stout, middle-aged Irish woman with a vivid red birthmark on one side of her face. This disfigurement was possibly responsible for prompting her to join the Sisters of Mercy and why she had compassion for others, but Hope thought she should be firmer with those who were supposed to be caring for the sick, for they were clearly doing very little.

'I despair at the conditions here,' Sister Martha admitted in her soft Irish brogue. 'The nurses are often the worse for drink and they steal the laudanum meant for the sick. The orderlies should of course keep the ward cleaner, but they are either feeble-minded or ex-prisoners, and they are so afraid of being infected themselves.'

'What food do you give the sick?' Hope asked.

Sister Martha sighed wearily. 'Gruel is sent up from the kitchen, but I fear that if they are too weak to feed themselves, they do not always get any nourishment.'

The imposing oak-panelled hallway and the staircase leading off it gave a clear idea of how grand the place must have been when it was a family home. This at least was reasonably clean, even if it smelled bad, and the floors were battered with wear from the thousands of pairs of heavy boots which must have tramped across it over the years.

Sister Martha waved one hand towards large closed doors on the opposite side of the hall and said that the old, destitute and orphans were in that part of the building, along with the kitchen.

It was very gloomy, the only light being one oil lamp suspended on a long chain from the ceiling, but Sister Martha picked up one of several smaller lamps standing on a shelf, lit it, and told Hope to follow her up the stairs so she could show her where she was to sleep.

She kept up a breathless commentary as she went on ahead, but much of what she said about the surgical and lying-in wards went over Hope's head. On the first landing she pointed to a closed door and said that the lunatics were through there. But she added, perhaps sensing Hope's fear, that she must not feel frightened by their presence for they were locked up and male orderlies took care of them.

Considering there had to be scores, if not hundreds, of people in the building, Hope found it surprisingly quiet. There were the sounds of heavy shoes on bare wooden floors, the occasional raised voice, a baby crying and some feeble sobbing, but none of the uproar she had expected. She wondered if this was because laudanum was dispensed to everyone who was troublesome. She also wondered why she hadn't seen any other staff aside from Sister Martha and the two old women in the cholera ward. It was about half past eight now, too early surely for everyone to have retired for the night?

As they got closer to the top floor, the sister spoke about Dr Meadows. 'He's a saintly man, to be sure,' she gushed. 'He feels for everyone, only this morning he said, "Sister Martha, you must get some rest or you'll become one of my patients." But then, as his cousin, you must know this, my dear?'

Hope would have said she was mistaken in this, but Sister Martha didn't give her a chance.

'He said you already have some experience with cholera. He's clearly very proud of your nursing skills. And you must have the heart of a lion to want to help us here.'

Hope understood then why the doctor had seen Sister Martha alone. He must have felt that by saying Hope was a relative she'd have an easier time.

'I've got the heart of a mouse,' she said, and she felt that much was true because she didn't feel brave enough to contradict what the doctor had said when it was so kindly meant. 'I hope I feel braver in the morning.'

Maybe it was because of Dr Meadows, too, that Hope was given a room to herself. It was a tiny, cell-like room under the eaves, scarcely larger than the narrow truckle bed, but as she had been expecting similar conditions to the patients, her spirits lifted considerably. There were sheets on the bed and a door she could lock from the inside. The heat of the day was trapped within it; even by the dim light of the candle she could see the walls were grimy, and maybe there would be bugs in the mattress, but after Lamb Lane and her makeshift camp in the woods it looked palatial to her.

Sister Martha gave her a uniform before saying goodnight, a shapeless, rough brown dress, two linen aprons and two mob caps.

As the sound of Martha's stout boots plonked away back down the stairs, Hope sat on her new bed suddenly feeling very alone and unsure of herself.

The entire hospital was very daunting; the unnatural quiet, the many locked doors, the absence of people, and even the tremendous age of the building. She was only too aware that she was going to be forced to deal with hideous sights and suffering far beyond anything she had ever experienced before. She doubted there would be anyone else here who might become a friend, and the work would be exhausting. But with the bolt in place on her door, and the golden arc of light from the candle making her tiny room feel almost homely, she reminded herself that she had been extraordinarily lucky in meeting up with Dr Meadows today. He had handed her a cotton bag as he left her earlier, saying Alice had asked him to give it to her once they were here.

'It'll be a few comforts,' he said with a smile. 'She told me to tell you she's put your other belongings away safely for you as you won't need them here, and that she wishes you well and hopes to see you again one day soon.'

Hope had wanted to look into the bag right away, but Sister Martha swept her away before she could even say goodbye properly to the doctor, let alone rummage through it. But she was glad she had that pleasure now, for it would help to take her mind off what was coming in the morning.

The first thing she drew out was a blue checked shawl, and her eyes misted over at Alice's thoughtfulness because she had nothing for when the cooler weather arrived. Next was a flannel nightdress, another petticoat and a pair of stockings. There was a hairbrush, a new comb, a towel and a box of hairpins too. Right at the bottom was a tin box full of Alice's homemade biscuits, a couple of candles and an enamel candlestick holder.

Hope couldn't hold back her tears then. She had liked the plump, motherly woman on sight and felt so comfortable with her in the kitchen today, but these lovely and practical gifts suggested Alice had taken her to her heart.

It had been a very long, tiring day, but now she was certain her luck had changed. She had work, a place to live and people who cared about her.

While it might be true she'd be doing a job that no one else wanted, and which might even kill her, at least she had a way now of regaining her self-respect. Tomorrow would be a new beginning for her, and maybe in time she could even think of contacting Nell and the rest of the family again.

By noon the following day Hope no longer thought the job was a new beginning, but represented several steps backwards.

When she reported for work at six, four people had died during the night, one of them a six-year-old boy. She watched in abject horror as two male orderlies stripped the corpses of any clothes they were wearing, and then, manhandling their naked bodies as though they were sides of meat, took them down the corridor into a yard and flung them into an open cart. She was told they were being taken to the Pit.

No one came to give her any instructions. The two old biddies she'd seen the night before left as she arrived, to be replaced by another two women who were equally old and dirty and introduced themselves as Sal and Moll. Sal was very small, with no teeth, which made her appear as if her face was caving in. Moll was a much bigger woman with a bulbous red nose, and the grey hair which showed beneath her cap was so matted it looked like skeins of darning wool.

They were friendly enough, but seemed completely oblivious to the needs of the sick on the ward. When Hope asked if they should clean the area where the dead had been lying they cackled with laughter.

'We don't bother with none of that,' Moll replied. 'The cart'll be back with more within the hour. Ain't no point in cleaning a place someone else will shit on. You come in the back wif us and 'ave a cuppa tea.'

Hope wanted a cup of tea badly, and the room they called 'the back' was a great deal more inviting than the ward, with a stove, sink, table and chairs and a window that opened. But she couldn't possibly sit down and drink tea when she knew that more sick people would be arriving soon.

In a quick reconnoitre of the yard at the end of the corridor where the carter came in, she found there was clean straw in a lean-to shed. There was also a brazier that held the clothes of those who had been taken away earlier, which were obviously going to be burned. Taking a large empty box back in with her, she swept up all the foul straw, took it out and dumped it, then scrubbed the cleared area vigorously.

Once she'd put clean straw down she went into the back room. Despite the hot weather, Sal and Moll were huddled close to the stove, and the smell coming from them was almost as bad as the stink in the ward.

In her time in Lewins Mead she'd met many women like them, lazy, dirty and unscrupulous and lacking any morality. Such women would steal the pennies from a dead man's eyes.

But Hope knew that if she was to challenge them in any way, they would make trouble for her, so she hoped to appeal to their better natures.

'I've cleaned up and put fresh straw down,' she said as she washed her hands. 'Do we give the patients tea now?'

'Tea!' Sal exclaimed. 'They only gets water, and they can wait fer that till we's ready.'

Hope had seen the wooden water pail in the ward, and was appalled that the tin mug hanging on the side of it appeared to be used by everyone.

'Come on now, ducks, 'ave a cuppa tea,' Doll said. 'I knows you wants to look good on yer first day, but them in there ain't going nowhere but the Pit. No sense in wearying yerself out fer nothin'.'

Hope bit back a sharp remark, washed a cup out carefully, then poured herself some tea from the pot they'd made. 'I thought that maybe we could move some of the patients on to the clean straw and then wash the floor where they've been,' she said tentatively.

'Yer what?' Doll retorted. 'We don't touch 'em, well, 'cept for givin' 'em a drink and tryin' to get 'em to take some gruel when they brings it.'

That, Hope discovered, was the entire extent of nursing in the cholera ward. Even Sister Martha when she appeared later only hovered in the doorway clutching her crucifix and could offer no practical advice or instructions. It seemed that no patient was ever washed, there were no comforting hot poultices, no extra blankets put over those shivering with fever, and absolutely no one rubbed limbs when they went into cramps.

While Hope could see by the blue colour of the patients and the torpor they'd fallen into that they were probably too far advanced with the disease to save, nonetheless she felt she had at least to try to make them more comfortable and the ward less foul. So one by one she rolled or pulled the patients on to clean straw, washed their faces and hands, then scrubbed the place they had been before.

'Yer mad,' Doll said as she stood lolling against the doorpost looking on in complete disbelief that Hope was scrubbing the floor. 'You'll catch it an' all, pokin' around 'em like that.'

As expected, the men arrived back with the cart, containing three new female patients. All three were already in the final stages, with blue-tinged faces and struggling to draw breath. Hope tried to get them to drink, but they seemed unable to swallow and the water just dribbled out of their lips. She saw a rat looking balefully at her as she put blankets over them, and thought it was just as well the women were unaware of where they were.

*

Hope was kneeling beside a patient, vigorously rubbing his legs because he had severe cramps, when Dr Meadows arrived. She didn't hear the ward door open as the big, red-headed man was tossing his head from side to side alarmingly while roaring with pain.

The doctor came straight to her to take over the friction. 'Take the laudanum from my bag and put a few drops in hot water,' he ordered her.

Hope did as he asked, rushing back to feed the man with it. He clenched his teeth against the cup at first, but Hope stroked his face and implored him to drink it.

'It will make the pain go,' she told him. 'Just drink it for me.'

He seemed to hear her and did as she asked, then within a few minutes he was still.

'Thank you,' he croaked. 'Will you tell my wife to kiss the babbies for me and say goodbye for me?'

'You'll be able to kiss them yourself soon,' she lied. 'Go to sleep now.'

Dr Meadows asked her to come out in the backyard with him when he'd made his rounds of the other patients.

After the darkness of the ward, the sun was so bright she was blinded. But it felt good to breathe fresh air again.

'I fully expected to find you'd already turned tail and run,' the doctor admitted wryly.

'I have been tempted,' she said and launched into a despondent description of how her first morning had been. 'I can't believe that no one does anything for the sick!'

Dr Meadows sighed in sympathy. 'I know exactly how you must feel, Hope. I do what I can when I call, but it isn't anywhere near enough. The truth of the matter is that the sick are just brought in here to die; we aren't tackling the disease at all.

'But there is no medicine which will save their lives. I

can't even claim that clean beds, bathing them or swaddling the sick in more blankets will make any difference to the outcome. In past epidemics it has been evident that it is in the hands of God if they recover, not through nursing.'

'But it's inhuman not to make their last hours more comfortable and give them some dignity,' Hope said heatedly. She was hot and sweaty, hungry too now that the bowl of porridge she'd been given for breakfast before six this morning was a distant memory. 'Besides, those women are paid to do a job, and if they won't do it they should be told to go.'

Dr Meadows ran his fingers through his hair in a weary gesture. 'Those two live here, in the workhouse part of the hospital. Just as the two last night do,' he said with a tinge of reproach. 'They didn't choose to nurse the sick, they were ordered to do it, and their only reward is an allowance of beer or gin. Can you blame them for being less than enthusiastic?'

Hope felt chastened, for she had been promised four shillings a week and her board and lodging. 'No, I suppose not.'

'What we need is some way of recruiting the right kind of women into nursing, and then training them properly,' he said dejectedly. 'At present we have either those from holy orders, or paupers, nothing in between. But with low wages, appalling conditions and the risk of infection, what is there to attract good women? Look at you! If you hadn't been press-ganged into it, would you be here?'

'You didn't press-gang me,' Hope said. 'You've been very kind to me, sir, especially making out I was your cousin! I think that's why I got a room on my own. And Alice was really kind too. Will you thank her for the things she sent me? It meant a great deal to me.'

'Alice liked you very much, her little gifts were her way

of telling you that,' he said earnestly. 'And I will pass on your message. But my name is Bennett. Cousins can't be formal.'

Hope blushed, for he had a way of looking at her that made her feel very odd.

'Have you had your dinner yet?' he asked.

She shook her head. 'I thought Sister Martha would come and tell me about that.'

'She's been assisting in a leg amputation,' Bennett said.

'You've been taking someone's leg off?' Hope winced.

'Not I, the surgeon, but I administered the chloroform. The poor man should make a full recovery, but I don't know how he'll feed his family. He won't be able to work with only one leg.'

Bennett took her down to the room just off the kitchen where she'd had breakfast earlier in the day. There were six people eating, two rough-looking men who appeared to be orderlies, a very old nun whom Bennett introduced as Sister Clare, and three nurses who looked only marginally cleaner and younger than Sal and Doll, and stared at Hope with hard eyes.

She was given a large bowl of greasy-looking greeny-grey soup and a lump of bread. Bennett declined anything himself but sat with her while she ate it.

'What is it like?' he asked.

'Not quite as bad as it looks,' she grinned.

Bennett smiled. 'Are you always so stoical?'

'I am about food, I know what it's like to be starving,' she shrugged.

'You've seen the very worst of St Peter's today,' Bennett said earnestly. 'But the cholera ward is not representative of the whole hospital. Dr Peebles, the surgeon, is excellent; they have a good record for midwifery here too. But the building is old, and isn't really suitable for a hospital.'

'Why are they still using it then?' she asked. 'Surely it is bad to bring people with infectious diseases to a workhouse where there are orphans, old people and the insane?'

'When the new General Hospital was built it was the intention that all the sick would go there,' he said with a shrug. 'But it just isn't large enough, not when an epidemic like this strikes. And St Peter's is not a workhouse exactly; it's more what you might call a refuge.'

'I thought a refuge meant a place of safety?' Hope said with a touch of sarcasm.

Bennett half-smiled. 'You'd better not start me on that subject,' he said. 'It is something I tend to rant about.'

'Tell me,' she insisted.

'Well, in the old days, until just before you were born, most of our unfortunates, the poor and old, simple or sick, got what they called outside relief. They stayed in their own homes and got money from the parish to support them. St Peter's and places like it were for those who had no home or were too sick or old to look after themselves. In the main they were decent places, and St Peter's was one of the best.

'But the government wanted to get the ratepayers on their side by saving money, so they brought in a new Poor Law. Outside relief was stopped because they believed it encouraged people to be idle and feckless, and instead they built hundreds of workhouses all over the country, forbidding, prison-like places with no comforts whatsoever, which would deter all but the most desperate.'

Hope nodded. 'My parents were always afraid of ending up in one,' she said.

'It is people just like your parents who suffer the most from the new Poor Law,' he said with a deep sigh. 'Imagine your father was laid off work for a few weeks, Hope, or became sick. Under the old law he could fall back on parish relief to tide him over to feed his family until he got well, or went back to work. Old people could stay in their villages, helped in their infirmity by neighbours and family. But suddenly all that was wiped out; not a penny would be handed over.

'Once these unfortunates have used up their savings, sold their belongings and are starving, they are forced to leave their home and go to the workhouse.'

He stopped his impassioned outburst suddenly and grinned sheepishly. 'Oh dear, I didn't mean to go into all the iniquities of that! What I really meant to point out was that the trustees of St Peter's have tried to keep it as it always was; a home for those who have nowhere else. It continues to shelter the aged, the feeble-minded, orphans, mothers who cannot have their babies at home, and the sick. It doesn't have the barbaric regime of the Union work-houses; no one here has ever picked oakum, or broken stones for building work. But like most charities, it is flawed. In emergencies the doors are opened too wide, and right now we have far too many sick. Without the facilities or the staff to nurse them.'

Hope noticed that he was blushing, clearly embarrassed that he had tried to defend St Peter's.

'You are something of a rarity,' Hope said impishly. 'I didn't think the gentry cared about anything or anybody but themselves.'

He looked startled. 'Do you see me as "gentry"?'

'Well, you are,' she said.

'No, I'm not. As I told you yesterday, but for my uncle's support when my father died, I would probably have gone into service too. Anyway, to get back to St Peter's and the crisis we are in here, if it wasn't for the Sisters of Mercy, who fortunately think God has personally instructed them to stay here, I don't know what we should do.'

Hope smiled. 'That sounds as if you don't believe in God.'

'I'll believe in Him if He chooses to end this epidemic,' he chuckled. 'Or taps me on the shoulder and shows me how it starts. I have had many an argument with Mary Carpenter about faith. She tells me I should be ashamed for having none. But what about you, Hope? Are you a believer, or a doubter like me?'

'It depends,' she smiled. 'When I was selling kindling I'd offer up a little prayer each time I approached a front door. I believed if they bought some wood, I doubted if they didn't. Betsy used to say that gin worked better than religion. One glass and your troubles fade away.'

She watched his face, expecting a look of alarm which would quickly be followed by a little sermon on the evils of drink. But he only smiled.

'I should go back to the ward now,' she said. 'And you have patients to see.'

'Yes, I have,' he nodded, 'a great many of them. Look after yourself, Hope. Don't despair, will you?'

Hope often thought of that request from Bennett in the following two weeks, for it was hard not to despair, surrounded as she was by suffering. Every day patients died, and as fast as they were carried away to be buried, new ones were brought in. Often these new victims' names were unknown, and to Hope it seemed the cruellest stroke of all to die without an identity.

Sal and Moll took an almost fiendish delight in reporting the panic in the town, and how people were fleeing in droves, the rich in their carriages and the poor trekking out to sleep in fields rather than risk catching the disease. They said that at night the streets were deserted, and many ships were refusing to come into Bristol docks because of the epidemic.

They sagely said that when the weather turned cold and

wet there would be hundreds of poor and desperate people turning to the workhouses for shelter and food. They would be too frightened to return to the infected rookeries they'd run from, and they'd have no money for anywhere else.

But the hot weather continued relentlessly and the stink from the river behind the hospital was overpowering. Hope found herself daydreaming more and more often of walking in the coolness of Lord's Wood. She would remember the clean smell of damp earth, the way the sunlight filtered down through the canopy of leaves, and the utter peace; she wanted to be there so badly it hurt.

At night when she retreated to her little room she would bury her nose in a sprig of lavender or rosemary bought from a young girl who stood by the hospital entrance, and remember the garden of her childhood home. She wished she could see her brothers and sisters, be a child again and feel the warmth of their love for her. It wasn't right that at only seventeen she was shut away in this death house.

Bennett was what stopped her running away. However hard and disgusting her work often was, he was counting on her and she couldn't let him down. Thanks to him she had a few remedies at her disposal now. When new patients were still in the early stages of the disease she spooned syrup of rhubarb into them every few hours, put mustard poultices on their bellies, gave them ginger or cinnamon tea and put more blankets on them to keep them warm. Six of these patients didn't sink into the second stage, which delighted her, but she had no way of knowing whether it was the result of her nursing or merely God's will. But, determined they should recover and defy the legend that no one ever left the hospital, she fed them arrowroot mixed with boiled milk until they were able to manage soup.

But six recoveries out of seventy or more that had either already died or would die soon wasn't good enough, and she had to battle against the apathy of everyone else involved with the cholera ward.

Sister Martha was so weak that everyone took advantage of her. Moll and Sal did as little as possible, only stirring themselves when someone died to rob them of their trinkets. Even the man in the stores often refused Hope more supplies of soap, soda and vinegar. Once he said it was a waste to lavish such things on a ward where no one got better.

But the single thing which distressed Hope most was that no one but her took any notice of Bennett's instructions on hygiene. It made perfect sense to her that hands must be washed after touching a patient, that aprons and caps had to be washed daily, and that all water for drinking should be boiled. Sal and Moll were too lazy to wash either their hands, or caps and aprons, and they snorted with derision about boiling the drinking water and said the doctor was as mad as some of his patients.

Hope had never lost her conviction that the water in Bristol was full of poison. In the nearly two years she had been in the city she had never once drunk water straight from the pump; even when she was dying of thirst she boiled it and drank it as tea. Gussie and Betsy had drunk it, and they had died, while she remained healthy, so she took this as evidence that Bennett was right.

She tried to convince others of it too, pointing out that Doll and Sal only drank tea or any kind of alcohol and that was why they remained in rude health.

Bennett appreciated her spreading his gospel, but he pointed out that he couldn't be certain that the disease came through water, as all the town's water came from the same source. And as almost all those stricken came from the filthiest, most populous parts of the town, this did tend to support the commonly held medical opinion that the disease was airborne.

Yet no one was able to explain the entirely indiscriminate nature of the disease. Most priests, doctors, nurses and the cart drivers who had handled the sick had remained healthy. Sometimes just one person in a large family caught it, while the rest remained untouched. In some lodging houses all but a handful had died; sometimes it was just the children who were infected. There was no pattern at all.

There were plenty of extraordinary theories too. Some people placed the blame for the epidemics on the Jews in the town, which made no sense whatsoever. Others called doctors 'Burkers' after the infamous Burke and Hare who robbed graveyards for bodies for dissection. Some of the more strident evangelical preachers were insisting it was God's judgement for the wholesale depravity in Bristol, and that it was spread by prostitutes around the busy ale houses.

Hope had many a discussion with Bennett about these strange ideas, and he stoutly insisted that the clergy and their pious, hypocritical followers should consider why women were forced to turn to prostitution in the first place, and do something about that.

Hope realized she was becoming increasingly captivated by Bennett. It wasn't just that he was her only friend, or that he treated her as an equal, but because of his understanding of the real evils of poverty and his ideas on how it could be beaten.

There were plenty of gentry who made benevolent gestures, and Hope was sure that these people had good hearts. But sadly their lives were too different from those who huddled in stinking rookeries to understand that a new set of clothes, a daily hot meal or a few shillings could never solve the problem. All this did was offer temporary comfort.

Bennett likened poverty to a kind of swamp which people either stumbled into or were born in. He understood that once in it, it was hard, often impossible, to get out without help, and that for many, criminality, or selling themselves, was the only way to keep afloat.

Like his friend Mary Carpenter, he saw education as the only real and sure ladder out of the swamp. He insisted with some passion that by giving every slum child the tools of reading and writing they could build a better life for themselves.

In a way, Hope was living proof of this. The education she had received had enabled her to understand concepts and ideas beyond the narrow confines of the way she'd been brought up. She felt stimulated by Bennett's somewhat radical views. He was caustic about the idle rich, and deeply suspicious of many who held prominent positions in the town, claiming they lined their own pockets at the expense of the poor.

The brightest part of any day was when Bennett came to the ward. Hope had only to see that thin, somewhat stern face break into a smile and she forgot how tired she was. When he praised her efforts she felt exulted, and when she watched him examining his patients and saw the tenderness in his hands, the grave concern in his eyes, she felt moved to tears.

Almost always he would stop long enough for a cup of tea with her. They would take their cups out into the backyard, and talk.

For the first two weeks their conversations were mainly about the patients, what was going on in the town and how the epidemic was reported in the newspaper. But as the days went by their chats became more personal, and one hot afternoon when for once the ward was very quiet, Bennett told her a little about his time at medical school in Edinburgh.

He painted a picture of a shy, rather awkward young man who felt intimidated by the students who were richer, smarter and far more sophisticated than he was. 'They thought I was a swot because I didn't go out drinking every night,' he said a little sheepishly. 'I couldn't bring myself to tell them I didn't have the money for drinking, or that I didn't dare fail my exams because of my uncle.'

'I don't suppose they became very good doctors,' Hope said stoutly.

Bennett gave a humourless laugh. 'Most of them have gone a lot further than I,' he said. 'Two or three have practices in London's Harley Street. Oswald Henston, a real bounder, is at St Thomas' Hospital. Some of them have become army and naval doctors. I often think I would have done better in the army.'

Hope guessed he meant that he considered joining his uncle in Bristol a mistake.

'But treating the poor must have given you much more varied experience than you'd ever get treating soldiers?'

'Maybe,' he sighed. 'They do say that as an army doctor dysentery is the only medical condition you'll become an expert in. But I should like to go to India or some such exotic place. My uncle is always pointing out that I'll never find a wife until I have something interesting to talk about.'

'Isn't this place interesting enough?' Hope asked. She hung on every word he uttered and she couldn't imagine any woman finding him dull company.

Bennett raised one eyebrow. 'A gentleman doesn't engage in such coarse subjects with a lady!' he said with mock horror.

Hope laughed. 'I suppose it would make most ladies reach for their smelling salts.'

'It is that feigned delicacy in society ladies I find most irksome,' Bennett said thoughtfully. 'Only a couple of months ago I was late for one of my uncle's friends' parties one evening because I'd been delivering a baby. I apologized to the hostess and her two daughters and explained why, but I received a frosty glare. Apparently it isn't "done" to mention such things as childbirth in front of unmarried women!'

'Why?' Hope asked.

Bennett shrugged his shoulders. 'Such things are supposed to remain a mystery until they are wed, I presume. But I find such conventions very small-minded.'

'My sister Nell was far younger than me when she helped our mother deliver her last few babies,' Hope replied. 'She saw it as a kind of training for when she had a child of her own.'

'And that's the way it should be,' Bennett said. 'But tell me about your sister, Hope. Did she have children?'

Hope hesitated, for she was afraid that one question would lead to another she didn't dare answer. Yet she had an overwhelming desire to talk about her family for they had been on her mind a great deal since Betsy and Gussie died.

'Sadly, Nell wasn't blessed with any children,' she said. 'In a way I was like her child really, her being so much older than me.'

Once started, she told him about all her brothers and sisters, about the cottage they lived in, and how first Nell got married, then Matt, about her parents' death and how she went to live with Nell and Albert.

'You almost spit out Albert's name,' Bennett said quietly. 'You mentioned before, that day on the Downs, that you fell out with him and that was why you ended up in Lewins Mead.'

A piercing yell from the ward interrupted them. They rushed back in to find Sal being held against the wall with a knife at her throat.

It was a second or two before Hope realized that the

burly man wearing nothing but a ragged shirt was in fact a patient who had been brought in early that morning.

Yet to her astonishment Bennett didn't hesitate at all. He leapt over the rows of sick people until he reached the man, caught hold of his shoulders and pulled him away from Sal.

'Whatever are you thinking of?' he exclaimed. 'This is a hospital!'

The man threw Bennett off him and turned to face him brandishing the knife, his face purple with anger. 'A hospital! It's a bloody store room for bodies. You fuckin' Burker!'

Hope knew that this man had been brought in with three other people who were all in the same lodging house. It was clear now that he wasn't a cholera victim at all, but had probably been so insensible with drink or opium when the Corporation cart came for his companions, it was thought he was sick too.

'Calm down,' Bennett commanded. 'If you are well you are free to leave here.'

'Calm fucking down!' the man yelled, his eyes rolling alarmingly as he made stabbing gestures towards Bennett with his knife. 'I wakes up to find that old crone robbing me of me breeches, and see I'm locked in a pest house.'

Hope couldn't believe how calm Bennett was. The man was far heavier and taller than him, and his knife was dangerously close to Bennett's chest, yet he stood there fearlessly.

'Put that knife down,' Bennett said in the kind of gentle tone he used with all the sickest patients. 'It is no one's fault but your own that you were collected by the carter. The nurse was only taking your breeches to make you more comfortable; she wasn't to know you were only sleeping off too much drink.'

'You brought me here to cut up my body,' the man shouted back.

Bennett shook his head despairingly. 'I don't have the time or inclination to cut up bodies,' he said. 'If you look around you'll see all these other people are desperately sick, and my task is to try to save them. Sal, give him his breeches back and let him out.'

Sal scuttled towards the small adjoining room. Hope guessed she *had* been stealing the breeches, perhaps because she thought there was money in the pockets. But just when it looked as if the big man was going to back off, he suddenly lunged forward at Bennett with the knife.

Hope screamed, but to her surprise Bennett side-stepped the lunge and caught hold of the man's forearm, in one swift movement disarming him and knocking him off balance so he fell to the floor.

Bennett picked up the knife and looking down at the man on the ground, he half-smiled.

'I could have you arrested right now,' he said. 'But I'll let you off this time because I've no doubt you were frightened when you awoke to find yourself here. Just count yourself lucky you haven't got cholera. And in future don't get so drunk.'

Sal came back with the breeches, her eyes downcast as if expecting Bennett to order her out too.

'I take it any money in those pockets is still intact?' Bennett asked her, his tone and expression very stern.

'Yes, sir,' she muttered, handing them over.

The man pulled the breeches on — he didn't appear to have any boots — and slunk towards the door. Bennett unlocked it, handed him his knife back and let him out.

Once the door was locked again Bennett turned to Sal. 'If I even suspect you've taken anyone's property again, Sal, I shall have you put in the Bridewell,' he said, his eyes burning into her. 'But for the grace of God we could all go down with this terrible disease, but while we are healthy it is our duty to treat the sick with kindness. To rob them is a terrible sin.'

'I'm sorry, doctor,' she said, eyes downcast, surprisingly not even attempting to deny that was what she intended.

Bennett stepped nearer to the old woman and put one finger under her chin to lift her face up. 'Go and make yourself a cup of tea now,' he said gently. 'I'm sure he frightened you very badly. And in future we must all be vigilant when new patients are brought in, especially when they stink of drink.'

Some of the other patients had become agitated after the frightening episode, and it took some time to calm them down. As Bennett washed his hands before he left, he smiled at Hope. 'I think it's time you got out of this place for a few hours,' he said. 'Alice keeps suggesting I bring you back to Harley Place for some dinner. Why don't you come tomorrow? My uncle has gone to Bath for a few days, so we can be at ease with Alice in the kitchen.'

'I can't leave here. It's Sunday tomorrow,' Hope said.

He shrugged. 'Saturday, Sunday or any day it's much the same here,' he said. 'And it will be the same when you get back. Even Sister Martha said you should be allowed to have a day off, she thought you looked pale and tired.'

'But . . .'

Bennett put a finger to his lips as if to silence her protest. 'Spending a day with your cousin is perfectly acceptable.'

Chapter Fifteen

Hope arrived at Harley Place at noon the following day. The front door was opened by a beaming Alice. 'It's so good to see you again,' she said, 'I've been that worried about you!'

She led Hope down to the kitchen in the basement, explaining that Bennett had popped out to see a patient but would be back soon. Between asking if Hope would like a cool drink and grumbling about the continuing hot weather and lack of rain, she also volunteered that she didn't think St Peter's was any place for a young girl.

Hope smilingly told the housekeeper that she liked working at the hospital and that the work wasn't so hard now she was used to it. Although that wasn't strictly true, hearing Alice's anxiety had given her the same warm feeling inside that she used to get when Nell fussed around her.

Alice was rather like Nell in many ways. She was older, perhaps forty-five or thereabouts, taller, and her hair was grey, but she had a similar neat, well-scrubbed appearance and motherly nature. Bennett had told her his uncle had met Alice when her husband became ill. She was still a young woman then, and when her husband died, Dr Cunningham had offered her the position as his house-keeper. Bennett had said that he used to hope they might marry eventually for they were well suited and fond of each other, but he said they were both too stubborn and stuck in their ways even to consider the idea.

Here in Alice's bright, gleaming kitchen, which smelled

heavenly like roasting meat, all at once the hospital, cholera, dirt and misery seemed like nothing more than a nasty but only half-remembered dream. Hope was wearing the blue dress Alice had given her, with well-polished boots, her newly washed hair gleaming, and she couldn't wait to see Bennett.

Despite all the bad things at St Peter's, there were two bathrooms at the hospital, which she'd discovered on the first floor a few days after she arrived. They were the first she'd ever seen with piped water. Sister Martha told her they had been put in the previous year because a cold bath had a calming effect on the insane. There was only hot water in the winter when the boiler was lit and Sister said it was so erratic she preferred to use the small hip-bath down in the kitchen, but if Hope didn't mind cold water she was welcome to use one of the bathrooms.

Hope had rushed up there eagerly the minute she left the ward yesterday. She was so hot and sticky that the cold water almost took her breath away at first, but within minutes she felt she had been transported back to the pond in Leigh Woods, luxuriating in the bliss of washing the hospital stink and grime from her body and hair.

As she lay back in the water, her hair floating around her, her heart seemed to be pumping faster with the excitement of going to Harley Place the following day. Or maybe it was the anticipation of spending a whole day with Bennett.

The incident of the man with the knife had given her even more respect for him; she hadn't expected that he was capable of standing up to a thug. The way he disarmed the man was marvellous, almost as if he'd spent some time on the streets too. Yet his toughness was tinged with compassion, both for the man and Sal. Hope's mother always used to say that was the mark of a real man.

If Betsy had been alive she would have been able to ask her if this feeling she had for the doctor was something more than mere admiration. Back in her village, people always used the expression that he or she was 'sweet on' someone. Was that what this was?

It felt sweet. A glimpse of Bennett was like the sun coming through clouds, or the perfume of a rose as you passed through a garden. Was that what Matt felt for Amy? Was it love?

'I hope you like roast beef, Hope?'

At Alice's question Hope was startled out of her reverie. 'I love it,' she said hurriedly, wondering if she'd missed something important by drifting away in her own thoughts. 'But I haven't had it for a very long time.'

'I don't think you've had anything much to eat for a very long time,' Alice retorted. 'It's a wonder you look so well.'

'That was just the best dinner ever,' Hope sighed as she scraped up the last morsel of roast beef and vegetables from her plate. She beamed happily at Alice. 'But it's going to put me off the food at St Peter's.'

'I hope you've still got room for pudding,' Alice smiled. 'I've made a syllabub.'

'I'll make room,' Hope said.

'It's good to see you eating so heartily,' Bennett said.

He didn't have to add that it proved she was still healthy, Hope had noticed him studying her when he got back from visiting his patients.

'It looks as if it's going to rain at last,' Hope remarked, for the patch of sky she could see through the kitchen window was darkening. 'Will the cholera disappear when it turns colder?'

'That has been the usual pattern,' Bennett replied. 'I

certainly hope so. None of us can cope with much more of it.'

'What will I do when it does stop?' Hope asked. 'Will I be put on another ward?'

'You certainly will,' he grinned impishly. 'In fact, I think you might almost be able to choose which one yourself because Sister Martha is full of praise for you. Though I would suggest you had a couple of days' rest before that.'

'Perhaps you could go and see your family?' Alice suggested.

Hope blushed. 'I can't do that,' she said in a small voice.

'Albert ordered you to stay away?' Bennett asked gently.

Hope nodded glumly.

Alice began to ask what right he had to stop her coming home, but Bennett interrupted, asking about the pudding.

When the meal was over, Alice wouldn't hear of Hope helping with the washing up and suggested she went into the garden with Bennett. 'It might be the last chance you have in a while for sitting out in the fresh air,' she said, looking up at the dark sky.

The garden was quite small, but walled and very pretty with many Michaelmas daisies coming into flower. Bennett led her down to a bench seat at the bottom, and for a little while made idle chit-chat about the flowers, the dinner and the possibility of rain.

'Come on now, tell me what really happened with Albert,' he said suddenly. 'Until you air it, it's always going to hurt.'

'I told you, I fell out with him, he was a bully, that's all.'

Bennett shook his head. 'I thought we were friends, Hope. So why can't you trust me with this?'

Hope kept her eyes on her hands clasped in her lap. 'I suppose it's because I'm afraid of how you will react,' she said.

'Do you mean I might think less of you?'

'No.' Her head jerked up. 'I didn't do anything wrong.'

'But Albert did?'

She nodded.

'To you?'

Hope sighed, guessing that Bennett suspected Albert had raped her, for Betsy had thought that too. 'No, not to me, but I caught him doing something bad and he hit me and said I was to leave his house and never return. I daren't return, Bennett, Nell will suffer and other people I care about.'

'A mere gardener couldn't be powerful enough for that. Surely if he was the one who had done something wrong, then no one could suffer but him?'

'He found a letter,' she said reluctantly. 'He knows something which he will tell.'

'So he's a blackmailer?'

Betsy and Gussie had quizzed her endlessly about Albert when she first met them, but she had been resolute that she couldn't tell them the whole story because of Rufus. Salacious tales about the nobility spread like wildfire, and even though she didn't care that much about Sir William and Lady Harvey's feelings she did still care very much about their son.

Yet she had always longed to unburden herself to someone, and she liked Bennett so much that she wanted him to understand just why she had to leave Briargate and her family. She also knew he would persist in questioning her anyway, and that he could be trusted to keep a secret to himself.

'If I tell you, will you promise you will never interfere and try to go behind my back and sort it out for me?' she asked. 'And of course never tell anyone else?'

'I promise,' he said. 'I only want to understand. That's all.'

She told him then.

She began quite well, explaining about Nell and Lady Harvey being away and why she had to hide the letter from her Ladyship's lover. But when she got to the point where she'd thought the upstairs window was banging and walked into the bedroom, she faltered.

'Albert was in there? With whom?' Bennett prompted. 'Was it another of your sisters?'

She was embarrassed and shamed. Once again she could see the two men in the bed together and the sight horrified her again as much as it had on that terrible day.

'No, it was Sir William,' she finally blurted out.

'Oh God,' he exclaimed, and put his head in his hands. 'I didn't expect that.'

Having told him the very worst part, the rest was easier. The words tumbled out quickly as she wanted to get it over and done with.

'I fainted by Bristol Bridge and Gussie and Betsy helped me and took me home with them,' she finished up.

Bennett let out a low whistle. 'I understand now why you would be so afraid of Albert,' he sighed. 'As for my promise I wouldn't interfere, I couldn't. I wouldn't even know how to begin dealing with it. But do you think Nell knew what Albert was?'

'I know she didn't,' Hope said. 'He was always cold with her; but how could she ever think something like that of him? I doubt she even knew such a thing existed. She might be sixteen years older than me, but I think I am more worldly now than she will ever be.'

'My heart goes out to you,' Bennett said, his voice deep with real emotion. 'No young girl should have to learn of such things in that way. Albert deserves to be horsewhipped, not for his leanings, I'm sure he can't help those, but for his brutality to you, his deceit to your sister and the wretched blackmail.'

'So do you understand why I can't go back there?' Hope asked.

'Only too well,' Bennett sighed. 'He's got you over a barrel. Only the truth would satisfy your brothers and sisters that you didn't leave willingly. But if you *do* tell them what really happened they'll want to attack Albert, and he'll retaliate and hurt anyone he can.'

While it was good to know that Bennett saw the whole picture as it really was, Hope felt disappointed too. She supposed that at the back of her mind there had been a glimmer of belief that a clever man like him might come up with some kind of scheme where Albert got what he deserved, and everyone else remained safe from harm. But then, if there had been such a scheme, she would have thought of it herself by now.

'So what am I to do?' she asked.

Bennett took her hand and squeezed it. 'I think you have to do what your heart tells you. Weigh up whether the need to see your family is greater than the fear of what Albert can do to Nell and the others you care about.'

Hope thought this over for a moment or two. 'Sir William would claim I'd made the whole thing up, Lady Harvey would back him up to spare herself any disgrace, and Rufus would hate me for saying such things about his parents. As for Nell, she'd still be stuck with Albert, and it would be even worse for her then.'

'It might make her leave him!'

'She isn't the kind to do that; she always believed marriage was for ever. And she'd lose her position at Briargate.'

'You could bring her into Bristol with you. I could find her work somewhere.'

Hope shook her head sadly. 'She'd be like a fish out of water in a city.'

'Then it sounds as if you must leave well alone and make a new life for yourself.'

That was the conclusion Hope had come to months ago, but having talked it through with Bennett and realized that he could see no workable alternative, she suddenly felt desolate and began to cry.

He put his arms around her and drew her to his shoulder, rocking her to and fro. 'I know,' he said. 'It's like the Judgment of Solomon, isn't it? I feel for you, my dear, for Albert is a wicked, wicked man and by all that's right he deserves punishment. But I think he'll get it one day. I also believe you will get your family back in the fullness of time. Perhaps you must keep that as your goal and make sure, when you are finally reunited, they will be proud of you for what you've achieved.'

He kissed her on the forehead, and tenderly wiped her eyes with his handkerchief. 'I'm already very proud of you,' he said softly. 'Without you there at the hospital, kind, willing and so practical, I don't think I could have borne the strain of this terrible epidemic. You've made each day brighter for me. You were well named, *hope* is what you give me, and every patient who is fortunate enough to be nursed by you.'

That night Hope lay in her little bed listening to the rain hammering down on the hospital roof, and she felt so happy sleep was impossible.

At long last the breeze through the window was cool and fresh, driving out the rank odours and stale air that had been trapped in her tiny room. Bennett's words had had the same effect on her too, for now she had a goal to work towards.

She would become a first-class nurse, not because it was the only work on offer to her, but because she truly wanted to help the sick. So maybe she didn't like the way things were at St Peter's, but perhaps she could make them better if she really put her mind to it.

But it was Bennett who had made her heart sing. It wasn't just admiration she felt for him, it was love. When he'd held her in his arms to comfort her, she'd wanted to stay there for ever. His lips on her forehead had made her shiver with delight, she'd wanted to turn her lips to his and kiss him. Even the touch of his hand on hers had sent little tingles down her spine.

They'd taken a little walk on the Downs later, and Bennett had taken her over to the edge of the gorge to show her the abandoned works of a bridge to cross it. 'Isambard Kingdom Brunel won a competition for his bridge design,' he said, touching the huge squat tower which was intended to hold the metal cables of the bridge. 'I've seen sketches of it, a beautiful, delicate wonder, but they got as far as building this tower and the one on the opposite side, then abandoned it in '43. But maybe it will be completed one day.'

Hope couldn't really imagine anyone wanting to walk across a bridge that was so high up. Just peering over the edge of the gorge at the Avon so far below made her feel dizzy. She had pointed out where she had stayed in the woods on the far side, and told him about the pond she found to bathe in and the food she cooked on her fire.

'I'd like to camp out,' Bennett grinned. 'I knew boys in Exeter who used to do it, but my mother would never let me go with them.'

'We could do it together one day,' Hope said without thinking, and suddenly realizing that ladies weren't supposed to make suggestions like that to gentlemen, she blushed with embarrassment.

Bennett just laughed. 'I'll hold you to that,' he said. 'I can't think of anything better than sitting by a campfire with you.'

*

Hope closed her eyes and imagined Bennett lying with his arms around her in the tiny shelter she'd made in the woods. Just thinking about it gave her the strangest twinges inside, and made her all hot. Amy had once told her that was the way she felt about Matt when they first started walking out together. She said she used to count the hours till the next time she saw him, and she knew right away he was the man she wanted to marry.

But a doctor wouldn't marry a girl like her, would he? Even if Bennett wanted to, his uncle wouldn't like it. He'd want him to marry a girl from a good family, someone like one of those girls she'd seen in Royal York Crescent. Cook had always said that gentlemen liked to bed kitchenmaids, but they married their own kind.

She had never been able to understand why some girls let men bed them without being married. But this feeling she had inside her for Bennett explained it now. And he hadn't even kissed her yet!

It rained almost constantly for fifteen days. Dirt paths that had been baked hard became quagmires, weeds deprived of water all summer sprang up in walls, cracks in pavements, anywhere they could. The river level rose alarmingly. It was said that many low-lying areas of Somerset were under water, and just as people had grumbled about the lack of rain, now they complained because it wouldn't stop.

In St Peter's rainwater found its way in through holes in the roof. The lying-in ward was the worst; the ceiling looked like a sieve and many of the new mothers had gone home because however bad their own homes were, they weren't in danger of being drowned there. There was one leak in Hope's ceiling, but fortunately it just missed her bed and she caught the water in a bucket. But the evil smells everywhere in the city lessened as the rain washed the filth away, and gradually the reported cases of cholera dropped.

'S'pose me and Doll will 'ave to go back to t'other side,' Sal remarked gloomily on the first day not one new patient was brought in.

Hope didn't know what to say to that remark. Sal and Doll didn't deserve any sympathy as they certainly hadn't shown the sick any. But just the same Hope felt a bit sorry for them, for she'd seen the old folk over in the other part of the hospital. They spent all their time in a crowded dormitory with no comforts; they couldn't make themselves tea as they could here, they wouldn't get an allowance of drink either.

'You'll be all right though,' Sal continued, a touch of venom in her voice. 'You sucks up to Sister Martha an' the doc. Watch out they don't make you look after the lunatics! You won't like that. They eat their own shit, piss all over the place and the last girl they put in there got strangled.'

Hope decided to ignore Sal. While it was true that some of the mad people did truly disgusting things, and a nurse had indeed been strangled a year ago, Sister Martha had promised she wouldn't make Hope work there. Anyway, they still had fifteen patients to look after in the isolation ward, and at least half of them were going to recover, for they hadn't sunk into the final stage of the disease.

When Hope looked round the ward now, she felt quite proud that it was as clean as a very old building could be. Her rough, reddened hands testified to the amount of scrubbing she'd done and she'd even cleaned the windows so that natural light came in during the day. She fully intended to browbeat Sister Martha to get the walls and floor limewashed once the epidemic was over, and to insist proper beds were put in here.

Her victories so far were tiny ones. No new patient was ever put down on dirty straw now; they were fed tea, soup and more substantial food if they could manage it. They were washed regularly, received what medicine was available, and no one ever died alone when Hope was on duty.

But she was all too aware that this wasn't nearly enough. A hospital should be a place where people came in sick and left well again.

In the middle of November, Hope said her goodbyes to the last patient on the cholera ward.

'Just remember to take good care of yourself, Mrs Hubert,' she said warningly, reaching forward to wrap the small, white-faced woman's shawl more securely around her, for it was very cold outside. 'We don't want you back in here, do we?'

Mrs Hubert was one patient Hope had never expected to survive the disease. She'd had seven children, three of whom had contracted the disease too and died. She had clearly been malnourished and worn out before she became sick, and with an out-of-work husband, who hadn't even bothered to come and collect her from the hospital, she clearly didn't have a great deal to live for. But she had lived, and Sister Martha put it down to the care Hope had given her.

'I'd come back just to see you,' Mrs Hubert said, her eyes glistening with emotional tears. 'It was your doing that I'm well again.'

'Nonsense, you're a fighter,' Hope insisted. 'Now, remember what I said, don't try to do too much straight away. You are still frail.'

Sometimes Hope wished she didn't know what patients like Mrs Hubert were going home to. The poor woman still had the grief of losing three of her children to deal with, and with a husband who only came home when he had no money to buy drink, she'd get little comfort from him.

'I hope you marry the doctor,' Mrs Hubert said.

Hope was so stunned that her mouth gaped open. 'There's nothing between us,' she said quickly.

Mrs Hubert smiled, her thin, pale face softer now. 'There is, my dear. I can see it,' she said. 'Even Sal, before she left, said I was lucky he had eyes for you or he'd never bother to come and see people like me.'

'That's not true,' Hope said indignantly. 'Dr Meadows is probably the most caring doctor in the whole of Bristol. He wouldn't ignore any sick person.'

'Well, now you've proved to me you feel the same about him,' Mrs Hubert chuckled. 'There shouldn't be anything to stop you getting wed then? But I'll be on my way now. If you're ever up round my way, you make sure you come and see me!'

Hope stood alone in the cold, empty ward for some minutes after Mrs Hubert had left, her heart singing because of what she'd said. If a sick woman could pick up that Bennett cared for her, then it must be true.

She had been at the hospital for three months now, and she'd seen him almost every day, but although they talked and laughed together, he hadn't invited her to Harley Place again, and he certainly hadn't given her any reason to think he returned her love.

Not that she had anguished over it; she did love him, but the greater part of her brain had already resigned herself to the fact that his interest in her was nothing more than as his protégée and friend. She was content enough being just that, though she suspected she would be exceedingly jealous if he was to tell her he had a sweetheart.

Footsteps out in the corridor alerted her that someone was coming, and she took the broom from the corner of the room to sweep up the remaining bits of straw from the floor.

The door opened and in came Bennett with Sanders, the burly, red-faced man who did odd jobs around St Peter's.

'I've just brought Sanders to show him what needs doing in here,' Bennett said. He looked flushed, and there were bloodstains on his cloth coat, as if he'd just finished an operation. 'I've already told him about limewashing the whole room. Is there anything else, Nurse Renton?' He winked at her as he used the formal address, and Hope stifled a giggle.

'The mouse and rat holes need blocking up in the wainscoting. And the chimney will need sweeping,' she said. 'We'll need to light a fire when we have patients in here again. Oh, and the sink in the back needs unblocking, it takes an age for the water to drain away.'

Sanders looked around him, sucking in his cheeks as if the job was an exceedingly difficult one. Hope had never liked this officious and crafty man. She realized he was going to ask for a great deal more money than the job was worth.

'I took the liberty of asking someone I know to come and give us a price for the job,' Hope lied. 'He said he'd do it for two pounds ten shillings.'

Bennett looked at her in surprise.

'I knew it had to be done quickly,' she said with a shrug. 'And I know Mr Sanders is usually quite busy.'

'I'll do it for two guineas,' Sanders growled. 'Out of the goodness of my heart.'

'But can you start tomorrow and have it finished in two days?' Hope asked.

Sanders glanced from her to the doctor. He looked deflated; clearly he'd hoped not only to make a big profit on this job, but to do it in his own time. 'Two days ain't long nuff!' he exclaimed.

'The other man said it was,' Hope replied. 'And anyway, that's all the time we have, the new beds are coming then and if it isn't ready there will be nowhere to put them.'

'Then two days it will have to be,' he said, his tone sullen. 'Of course, there's them that wouldn't want to work in here after the cholera. But someone's got to make it usable again.'

'What a brave, good man you are,' Hope said sweetly. 'I'm sure you'll make a lovely job of it.'

Sanders left, and once the door had closed behind him Hope giggled.

'I'll wager he was planning on asking for five or six pounds,' she said.

'How lucky then that you had someone else lined up,' Bennett said. 'But how do you know men who do such work?'

'I don't,' she said. 'I made him up.'

Bennett roared with laughter. 'You little minx! Who taught you such tricks?'

'Gussie and Betsy, I suppose.' Hope grinned. 'They were great bargainers; they said you should never look too keen to buy anything, that way the price always comes down.'

'I'll remember that,' he said, still chuckling. He looked around the bare room, taking in the old splatters of blood, squashed insects, and other stains on the walls. 'How strange it looks now. It's difficult to believe that for the past three months it was the scene of so much pain and misery; it's so quiet and still now.'

'Let us pray we never see another epidemic like it,' she said, suddenly serious. It was appalling to think over two hundred had died in here, and a similar number in their own homes. 'But I didn't expect to see you today. I was just going to sweep up in here, and then go and ask Sister Martha where she wants me next.'

'You will have two days off before doing anything,' he

said. 'And I rather hoped you might spend them with me?'

'With you?' she exclaimed in surprise.

'Is that so terrible a prospect?'

'No, of course not,' Hope laughed. 'But where did you plan to go?'

'Will you promise to come wherever it is?'

'I think I might,' she said. Excitement was bubbling up inside her, and though she wanted to pretend to be offhand, she was giving the game away by grinning from ear to ear. 'Unless of course you were planning sailing a raft down the Avon, or camping in the woods. November isn't a good month for such things.'

Bennett laughed. 'I can promise you it will be less chilly than that. Alice's sister lives in the village of Pill. I often go there with her for it is a peaceful, pretty place by the mouth of the Avon. I usually take long walks and leave her and her sister to chatter. Alice suggested that you should come with us this time.'

Hope's heart leapt. 'I'd love to,' she said.

'Then we'll come by in the carriage tomorrow morning at eight-thirty,' he smiled. 'The cottage is very small, but Alice will sleep with Violet and you will have the little room. I shall sleep on the couch. But be sure to bring warm clothes for there is often a raw wind coming off the Bristol Channel.'

Mrs Violet Charlsworth, Alice's sister, reminded Hope of an apple dumpling, short and fat but with a very sweet nature. Her husband had been the pilot of a tugboat that helped big ships up the river to the docks, but he had died of pneumonia three years earlier. Violet's tiny but cosy cottage reflected her husband's passion for ships. Watercolours of them, ships in bottles, some brass and some carved from bone, a collection of old navigational instruments and a ship's bell decorated the walls. There were other exotic items too, brought from sailors back across the seas: frightening-looking African statues, fans, snuff boxes and daggers. Every one of them was carefully arranged and dusted.

The roaring fire was most welcome as it was very cold outside, and Violet's welcome had been equally warm. She said there was nothing she liked better than a houseful of guests.

Over tea and toasted buns, which she held out to the fire on a long toasting fork, she fired questions at Alice and Bennett, her bright blue eyes sparkling with delight at having company.

'So Hope is your young lady,' she said pointedly to Bennett. 'No wonder you haven't been down to see me in six months!'

Hope blushed furiously, and attempted to explain she was only a friend.

Violet just chuckled. 'He wouldn't bring you here unless he had plans for you, my dear,' she said and laughed so much her many chins wobbled.

'Mrs Charlsworth!' Bennett said reprovingly, but he didn't deny what she said and Hope sank back in the comfortable chair feeling extraordinarily happy.

The chair and the warmth of the room made her feel sleepy, and though she tried to fight it off as her three companions chattered, she lost the battle and must have nodded off for a while. Maybe it was the sound of her name being mentioned that brought her round, for suddenly she became aware they were talking about her.

'She's been carefully brought up, I knew that as soon as I saw her,' Alice said. 'She might have been wearing rags, but she wore them like a duchess. And look at that face, will you! When did you ever see such beauty before?'

Hope knew she ought to show she was awake again, but

as their conversation about her appeared to be so complimentary she couldn't resist hearing more.

'She's exhausted,' Bennett said, and his voice was as soft and tender as a caress. 'If you could see the way she works, no job too tough or dirty. She was born to nurse, and I can only think she dropped out of heaven at our greatest hour of need.'

'But what does Dr Cunningham think about your friendship?' Violet asked.

'He doesn't approve,' Bennett said sadly.

Suddenly Hope didn't want to hear any more. She stirred and made a pretend yawn. 'I'm so sorry, Mrs Charlsworth,' she said. 'How rude of me to fall asleep, it was the warmth of the fire and the comfortable chair.'

'We were glad to see you dozing,' Alice said. 'Bennett was just saying how hard you've been working at the hospital. I should think you're worn out.'

'I'm fine,' Hope said, feeling awkward and wishing she hadn't woken until they'd finished discussing her. 'Perhaps I need a walk to blow the cobwebs away.'

'There's a path beside the river which is always pleasant even on a cold day,' Bennett said. 'Would you like me to show you?'

'That's right, you two take a walk and work up an appetite,' Violet said. 'I've got an oxtail stew simmering on the stove, but it won't be ready for a couple of hours.'

It felt very cold outside after the warm cottage and Hope pulled her cloak tighter. She had left the hospital full of confidence that morning, as she had a new red plaid wool dress that she'd bought in one of the second-hand dress shops in the Pithay, and a jaunty red hat trimmed with feathers. But her grey cloak was the same old one she'd left Briargate with, worn so thin now that the wind went straight through it. As they walked down through the tiny village with its straggle of small stone cottages, the cloak which had been made by Nell was a timely reminder that although Hope's circumstances had improved dramatically since she first met Bennett in Lamb Lane, some things would never change.

No one but Bennett thought much of nurses. Like soldiers and constables, they were considered the dregs of society, only valued in times of trouble.

Bennett talked animatedly as they walked. He had heard the Corporation were calling an emergency meeting to discuss health and sanitation in the city, and he hoped this might mean they would pull down places like Lewins Mead and build new houses with piped water and sewers.

'And I suppose that will mean that they'll throw all my old neighbours out on to the street,' Hope retorted. 'Will they ask anyone along to this meeting who actually knows and cares anything for those who will become homeless? I think not. It will be a meeting of only those who will profit from the new houses.'

Bennett looked surprised by the venom in her voice. 'I'm sure that won't be so,' he replied. 'What's got into you, Hope? I thought you'd be glad to hear that a place that harbours so much disease will be swept away.'

'Not if it means people will have to be swept away too,' she snapped. 'They should build new houses first, at rents those people can afford. If they don't, the problem will just shift to Bedminster, St Philips, Montpelier, or, heaven help your uncle, to Clifton! I bet he won't be overjoyed if tens of thousands of guttersnipes like me end up as his neighbours!'

'Why do you mention my uncle?' Bennett asked, facing her and taking hold of both her arms. He had that stern look he always wore when he was concerned. 'And why do you call yourself a guttersnipe?'

'That's how he sees me, doesn't he?' she said. 'He wouldn't like it if he knew you had brought me here, would he?'

'No, he wouldn't,' Bennett admitted. 'But he is not my keeper. I am my own person, I don't allow him to control me.'

'But you live in his house, and therefore you must be beholden to him.'

'To a certain extent, yes. But only as far as deferring to his greater experience in the practice he built up, and treating his home with respect. I do not allow him to choose my friends.'

'But you have to hide ones like me away. You couldn't invite me to Harley Place if he were there, could you?'

Bennett neither denied nor acknowledged that was true. He continued walking, saying nothing. Hope trotted after him, aware she'd already said too much, and not in a manner that would endear her to him.

When they got to the banks of the river, Bennett stopped, staring out at the water which was just a sluggish strip between vast swathes of greasy-looking mud. With the leaden sky above and the few trees growing along the riverside bare of leaves, looking skeletal and grim, the scene had none of the beauty it would have at high tide in sunshine.

'I haven't hidden you away,' he suddenly burst out. 'The epidemic was so bad there were no opportunities to do anything more than try to fight it. My first thought as the last cases either died or went home was about you, in particular your future and my feelings for you. That's exactly why I asked you to come here with me.'

Hope didn't know how to reply to that, so she said nothing.

'Well?' he said sharply. 'No sarcastic comment?'

'I'm sorry,' she murmured. 'I spoke out of turn.'

His chin was jutting out as if he was angry, and his eyes seemed to be boring right into her.

'I am in a dilemma, Hope,' he said. 'It is the circumstances of how we met which make it so very difficult. If I'd met you at a party or a dinner, I'd know exactly how to behave with you. I'd come calling, I might give you a book of poetry, I could even ask my uncle to arrange some function so we could talk and be seen enjoying each other's company. I would then invite you to the theatre or a concert, and provided you had a suitable chaperone, and you and your family didn't take an immediate dislike to me, we could then embark on a courtship.

'But I can't do any of that with you, Hope. You don't live with your family, you have no suitable person as a chaperone.'

'I don't have the right clothes or manners either,' Hope said glumly.

He made a kind of exasperated growl in his throat. 'That isn't it, Hope! Not your manners, background or anything like that. Don't you see it? I love you.'

Hope blinked in astonishment.

'I fell for you almost the first minute I saw your beautiful face,' he went on. 'Every moment with you since then has confirmed that you are the only girl in the whole world for me. All those social niceties mean absolutely nothing to me. But I am trapped in a situation where they are important to everyone else, and if I flout them, you would be the one who would suffer.'

Hope had been sure when he was talking about chaperones, concerts and families that he was just trying to show her why she could never fit into his world. But then he'd said he loved her, and that cancelled out everything else.

'You love me?' she whispered, bubbles of delight running down her spine. 'Truly?'

He looked at her with the mournful eyes of a spaniel. 'Yes, Hope. Truly! Madly and deeply. I spend all day thinking of you, I invent excuses to see you, I can't sleep at night for imagining kissing you.'

'Oh, Bennett.' She flung herself into his arms impulsively. 'I love you too, it's just that way for me too.'

She stood on tiptoe to kiss him, and as her lips touched his, his arms went round her so tightly he almost took her breath away.

Hope had never kissed a man on the lips before. Over the last year or two she had often idly wondered what sort of feeling people got out of pressing their mouths together, for it seemed an unlikely source of pleasure.

But as his warm, soft lips met hers, all those strange yet delightful sensations she had when she lay in bed thinking about him came spurting up in her, twice, three times as strong and sweet.

She didn't care that they were on a river bank, that they could be seen by anyone who chanced along. It didn't matter that he was a doctor and a gentleman, while she was just a kitchenmaid turned nurse. All she could think of was that he loved her, and she loved him. Nothing else was important.

'Hope, my dear, sweet, beautiful girl,' he murmured as they broke for air. 'I have wanted to kiss you for so long.'

There were many more kisses. They would walk a few yards holding hands, then all at once they were kissing again and again, not noticing the cold wind or the mud beneath their feet. His arms went beneath her cloak, drawing her closer still, caressing her in a way that made her feel she was melting. It was only when they realized they had been out for over two hours, and their feet and hands were frozen, that they turned back to Violet's cottage.

'I don't know how I'm going to hide this from Alice and

Violet,' Bennett laughed as they got nearer to the cottage. 'I'm sure it must be written on my face.'

'And I don't know how I'm going to be able to sit making polite conversation for the rest of the day when all I want to do is kiss you more,' Hope replied.

In the months that followed the visit to Mrs Charlsworth's cottage Hope was to think on that last remark to Bennett over and over again. Everything had seemed so simple then; they knew they shared the same feelings for each other, and therefore it followed that before long they would find a way to make them public. But it wasn't that simple.

As Bennett had pointed out that day, the standard route of courtship was closed to them. Hope had no family home for him to call at; Bennett couldn't invite her to Harley Place. Without mutual friends to offer chaperoned opportunities for them to be together, they were left with little more than walks, sitting in coffee shops, and hurried chats at the hospital when Bennett came in to see patients.

Over Christmas Hope didn't see him at all, for his uncle had invited guests and expected him to be there to help entertain them. As church bells rang out for the New Year of 1850, she was helping Sister Martha deliver twins, and it was two days before Bennett came into the hospital to wish her a Happy New Year.

He didn't have to point out to her that it was inadvisable at this stage for anyone to know how they felt about each other. She knew that. Dr Cunningham would almost certainly make sure she was dismissed from the hospital and he might also end his partnership with his nephew. But if they bided their time and let Dr Cunningham find out for himself that Hope had become a very good nurse, with a blameless character, he was likely to become far more receptive to her.

Hope was now nursing in the lying-in ward which she had come to love. Aside from the occasions when there was a very difficult birth, or a mother or her baby died, it was mostly a satisfying, joyous ward to be on. Like all the wards in St Peter's it was overcrowded, and the other nurses were either lazy sluts with a fondness for drink or stern nuns who had little compassion. Yet whatever the faults of these two groups of nurses, Hope soon realized they had a wealth of experience she lacked. As the youngest in her own family she had never witnessed a birth before; her only knowledge of babies had been gleaned from Matt and Amy's brood. The only attribute she brought to the ward on her first day was the knowledge that dirt bred disease, and a conviction that if she made sure the ward was clean, more new babies would survive.

Each time she washed a newborn baby she was humbled by the miracle of birth, and it was pure instinct which guided her. Yet she was also frightened that she had been given responsibility for their well-being, when she knew little or nothing about babies, childbirth, or even anatomy and biology. She borrowed books from Bennett, and although she often worked a fourteen-hour day, she would then spend another two or three hours studying these books, desperate to solve the mysteries of how the human body worked.

Perhaps if she had been on any other ward she'd have found it easier to put Bennett out of her mind, for at least part of the day. But the very nature of the lying-in ward was a constant reminder of physical union. Most of the mothers were bawdy characters who spoke openly and graphically about their sexual experiences. Sometimes she was deeply shocked, at other times she found their stories amusing, but hardly a day passed without her learning something new.

It was at times like this that she felt a wave of grief for

Betsy, for she heard so many things that she would have given anything to talk over with a friend. There were women at the hospital she liked – strangely, mostly the nuns – but she couldn't tell them she couldn't sleep for imagining Bennett caressing her intimately, or ask questions about how big a man's penis was, and if it hurt a woman when it entered her. She couldn't even ask if she was normal to think about such things.

In quiet moments during the day her mind always turned to Bennett, reliving their kisses and the good feeling when he held her tightly and told her that one day they'd be married and have babies of their own. She would spin a little daydream of Bennett being the doctor in a village much like Compton Dando. They would have a pony and trap for him to visit his patients, and their cottage would be a pretty one with roses growing around the porch. She hoped to have at least four children, and that they'd grow up as gentry, never having to go into service.

Her brothers and sisters wafted into this daydream too, bringing their children to visit. She didn't ever try to think how she and Bennett were going to overcome the problem of Albert, for it was a miracle that Bennett loved her, and therefore anything else was possible too.

But she did worry about Dr Cunningham's opinion of her. He very occasionally came to St Peter's, and she was fairly certain he asked about her, for someone always told her when he'd called. But as he never came and sought her out, it was clear that his interest in her was only because he'd been instrumental in sending her here.

On Hope's eighteenth birthday in April Bennett took her on the train to Bath for the day.

She had thought it wonderful at Christmas when he'd bought her a new dark blue wool cloak with a warm hood.

She would have been thrilled if he'd only given her something small, like a handkerchief, a book or scented soap, but for him to have gone out and chosen something so personal and beautiful brought tears to her eyes. Every evening she would sit in her room hugging it round her and thinking of him. He would never know just how touched and delighted she was.

Yet in a different way the trip to Bath meant even more because he'd noted that she was dying to find out what it was like to ride on a train. While they waited to get on it at Temple Meads station she had been so excited she thought she might burst.

The station building was almost enough of an astounding sight with its huge glass-domed roof, but she was so impressed by her fellow travellers that she barely looked at it. Everyone looked so elegant: ladies in fur-trimmed cloaks and fancy hats, gentlemen in top hats and tail coats. There were little children, equally well dressed, in the charge of their nursemaids. Even the people who weren't gentry and who Bennett said would be travelling third class, looked as if they'd polished up their appearance for the trip.

But there was so much going on elsewhere in the station too. Hope had never seen a train up close before, and the engine was so huge and so noisy that when Bennett took her closer to it to show her the furnace, she backed away in fright.

Heavily stuffed Royal Mail sacks, crates of live chickens, trunks and parcels were all on carts waiting to be put on the London train. Hope had looked into the first-class waiting room and seen there was a roaring fire lit in there; there was a tea shop too, and porters in smart uniforms waiting to carry people's luggage.

Yet the sights at the station were nothing compared with the thrill of getting on to the train, settling down in a comfortable seat and then hearing the guard blow his whistle and wave his flag for it to start.

If she lived to be ninety-eight, Hope didn't think she would ever forget the sound of those pistons going round, the chug, chug, chug as the train gradually picked up speed, and suddenly they were racing along at a terrifying speed, the countryside flashing past the windows.

She knew it would take two or more hours to get to Bath with a carriage and four horses, and almost all day by cart. But the journey by train was completed in half an hour.

When they came out of the station, Hope wanted to stand still and just watch, as Bath was astoundingly different to Bristol. While the streets were every bit as crowded with people and horses and carriages, and there were just as many beggars, crossing sweepers and ragged urchins, it had a far more sedate and genteel pace. Exquisitely dressed gentry sauntered arm-in-arm in the spring sunshine, and even the more soberly dressed matrons looked far more well-to-do than their Bristol counterparts. But it was the city itself which impressed Hope most. The main streets were wider and the yellowy stone buildings very elegant, nowhere near as old and ramshackle as those at home. Even the river Avon looked cleaner here, and Hope loved the bridge which had little shops all along it.

'That's because most of it was only built in the last hundred and fifty years,' Bennett said by way of an explanation. 'Can you see how similar some of the houses are to those in Clifton? Many were designed by the same architects. But Bath doesn't have the industry of Bristol to make it so grimy; the Roman Baths are the main attraction. The rich flock here for their health, foolishly imagining a few gulps of the evil-tasting water will cure anything from gout to syphilis.'

Hope smiled to herself. Clearly Bennett didn't believe

there were any magic properties in it at all, and disapproved of those who traded on the gullible.

He seemed to know exactly where he was going, for he pointed out the Pump Rooms where he said the idle rich congregated, then led her into a series of narrow lanes, finally stopping at the door of a small bow-windowed shop.

'This is where I buy your present,' he said, kissing her cheek.

'But coming to Bath was my present,' she said, glancing at the bow-windowed shop and suddenly realizing it was a jeweller's. 'You can't afford to buy anything in there!'

'I can,' he said with a grin. 'But first I have to ask you something.'

Hope looked up at him expectantly. 'Go on.'

'Will you marry me?'

She had expected that he was going to ask if she'd like a brooch to go on her cloak, or maybe even a locket. Not in even her most fanciful of daydreams had she imagined him asking her to marry him, at least not until they had resolved how to tell his uncle how they felt about one another.

'But we can't! Your uncle!'

'I didn't mean immediately.' He laughed at her shocked expression. 'I just wanted you to know my intention, and to buy you a ring as my pledge.'

It took a second or two for her to take in what he'd said. Then she threw her arms around him, giggling with delight. 'I'd love to marry you, this year, next year, anytime. Your word would have been enough for me. I don't need a ring.'

'But I need to show you all you mean to me,' he said, hugging her back. 'Even if that means you can't display it to the world right now.'

'Then I'll wear it on a chain around my neck for the time being. I love you so much, Bennett.'

*

Later, sitting on a bench in the park by the river, Hope held out her hand to Bennett. 'See how it sparkles,' she said.

He had bought her a gold chain to hang the ring on, but for today she was wearing it on her finger. Bennett had apologized that it was such a tiny diamond, but to Hope it was something a queen would wear.

'It doesn't sparkle as brightly as you,' he smiled, and kissed the tips of her fingers. 'You are my love and my life, and I hope you'll remember that when I tell you what I've decided.'

'That we elope tonight?' she suggested.

'No, that wouldn't be wise, not when I don't have any money to keep you. But I've got a plan to sort that out. I've decided to join the army as a doctor.'

Hope's heart plummeted. 'Oh no, Bennett,' she exclaimed. 'You can't do that. I would never see you, you might get killed.'

'Military doctors don't fight,' he said, smiling fondly at her. 'Let me explain it all. Everything is stacked against us while I am under my uncle's thumb. I haven't got the means to start my own practice, and if I was to join someone else's practice as a junior doctor, I'd be worse off than I am at present. But in the army I'd be beholden to no one.'

'But you'd have to go away,' she said, tears prickling in her eyes.

'You could come with me,' he said. 'Wouldn't you find that an adventure? We might get to India!'

'But would I be allowed to go with you?' she asked.

'I'm sure you would. But the reality of it now, while there's no war on, is that we'd be stuck somewhere like Winchester for years and years, with me treating boils and suchlike. What an asset you would be to me! Not many doctors have a wife who is a nurse.'

'Have you made any enquiries about this yet?' She looked

sharply at him, wondering if he'd really thought it through.

'No, I wanted to see how you felt first.'

'I'm not sure,' she said doubtfully.

'Once we are married,' he said, squeezing her hand, 'you could write home. I mean, you *would* be married to a soldier, so apart from apologizing for being out of touch for so long, you wouldn't need to tell them about the real reasons you left.'

Hope smiled because his enthusiasm was infectious. In reality she knew that wouldn't really work, as her whole family would be furious with her for making them so worried. But she wasn't going to spoil his moment by saying so.

'We won't worry about them for the time being,' she said. 'Let's just enjoy today.'

'Right. We'll find somewhere to have some dinner first,' he said, jumping up and pulling her to her feet too. 'Then we can look at the sights of Bath!'

A few hours later in the Pump Rooms, Hope was forcing herself not to laugh. The moment they walked through the doors and Bennett saw the elegantly dressed people congregated there, he pretended to have a terrible affliction. He stuck up one shoulder, hunched his back, grimaced and limped, and made several circuits of the room so everyone would notice him. Some looked offended by his appearance, others whispered together, perhaps in sympathy. Then, when he'd got almost everyone's attention, he hobbled up to the pump for his glass of the medicinal water.

Hope had remained close to the door, guessing what his plan was. If she'd walked round with him she would have laughed aloud and spoiled the whole thing. But he played the part far better than she had expected, and as he gingerly sipped the water she saw everyone was watching him intently.

As he sipped he made little grunts to keep all eyes on

him. His left arm shot up above his head as if it had a life of its own, then he made his left leg shake.

''Tis working,' he shouted out in a broad Somerset accent. 'Aye, 'tis working. I's can feel its powers down deep in me innards!'

Hope had to put her hand over her mouth to stop herself from laughing. He was jerking, twisting, and gulping down the water so fast it was running down his chin. Everyone was transfixed: some looked scared as if they thought he was having a fit, but the rest were wide-eyed with astonishment, and the only sound apart from the groans and sighs Bennett was making were shocked whispers.

Slowly, he straightened up. He looked down at himself as if in disbelief. He held his face in his hands and walked towards a large mirror as if to check he wasn't mistaken.

'Halleluia!' he exclaimed. 'I am cured. I am cured.'

There was nothing for it but for Hope to run and embrace him. 'He's been twisted and bent since the day he was born,' she announced in an equally rustic accent. 'But I must get him home now so our mother can see this miracle too.'

There were tears rolling down her cheeks, but only from suppressing her laughter. As she swept Bennett out through the door she had to bite her lips as the sounds of 'Did you ever see the like?' and 'He was crippled and now he's cured,' and other such remarks resounded behind them.

How they managed to get around the corner without doubling up with laughter, Hope didn't know. But once hidden from view they almost exploded with it, clinging to each other and laughing till their sides ached.

'You are a disgrace to the medical profession,' Hope spluttered. 'They'll all drink gallons of it now and get sick with it.'

Bennett wiped tears from his eyes. 'Their faces!' he exclaimed. ''Tis a miracle. I am cured!'

'You should be ashamed of yourself,' Hope giggled. 'But can you imagine how it will be in a few hours? It will be right round Bath, everyone will be talking about the miracle.'

'There was a real miracle today,' he said, pulling her close to him and kissing her. 'You agreed to marry me.'

'That was before I discovered how silly you could be,' she said. 'Funny thing is, it's made me love you even more.'

Chapter Sixteen

1853

Lady Harvey stood at her bedroom window looking down the drive towards the gatehouse. Thick frost had beautified the bare fields and trees in the kind of stark winter scene she had once liked to capture in water-colours. But she was barely seeing it now, only aware of the small grey stone cottage in the distance, which until Nell left her, she'd barely noticed.

Wisps of smoke were coming out of the chimney, and she wondered what it was like in there now Albert was alone. To her shame she had never called on Nell while she was with him; she hadn't even asked if she was comfortable in the gatehouse, or if there was anything she needed to make it more homely.

Today she knew she must deal with Albert. She couldn't put it off as she might not get such a good opportunity again for months. William was in London, and Rufus had returned to school yesterday morning after the Christmas holiday, so if Albert did make a scene, there was no one to know.

It was six long years now since Nell had left, and Anne's regrets about that day grew with each passing year. At first it was just the breakdown of comfortable order. But then, she had never before been expected to dress herself or arrange her own hair, far less do laundry, tidy rooms or mend anything, but it soon became evident that Nell's departure had caused far wider destruction than was immediately apparent.

It transpired that Nell and Baines had effectively run the house between them; they set the standards for the other servants, and made sure their master and mistress never had to concern themselves with how all the many tasks were completed, or by whom.

Baines was the captain, Nell more of a foot soldier, but it had been her energy, pride in Briargate and the warmth of her personality which had created an environment that kept all the staff happy and willing to work hard. Without Nell, Baines soon floundered, his instructions were ignored, and the remaining servants bickered among themselves, all putting the blame for jobs left undone on someone else.

These days meals were often late, rooms were not always cleaned, and a strained, surly atmosphere had replaced the old cheerful and bustling one. As for Albert, he strutted around the grounds as if he owned the place, and everyone, Lady Harvey and Sir William included, was nervous of him.

Even back in the early days of Nell's departure, Anne knew she ought to stir herself and take control, but she didn't. Too late, she saw Nell had been far more than a mere maid; for along with being friend, sister and mother to her mistress, she'd acted as a buffer between her and the harsh reality of life. Without her maid she felt vulnerable, afraid and very lonely. She was also carrying a heavy burden of guilt at not defending or supporting her when she most needed it.

Six years on, Anne still blushed at the memory of how callous she must have appeared when Nell informed her that Hope was her daughter. Her only defence was that she'd been unable to believe that it could be true. Who would credit that a young maid would take a baby and bring it up as her own sister without any kind of reward, just to protect her mistress? And Nell's insistence that Albert had killed Hope seemed like hysterical melodrama.

In the weeks that followed, Anne remained in a kind of denial that Hope was her child. She veered between rage that her maid had walked out on her, terror that she might spread her ridiculous story far and wide, and a sickening disgust in herself for not foreseeing that a servant who knew too much could be very dangerous.

But as the weeks passed without any scandalous gossip reaching her ears, and with time to reflect on everything Nell had told her, Anne came to see that she'd wronged her. Rumours reached her that Nell had gone mad with grief over her younger sister's disappearance, yet it was clear she still hadn't breathed a word about her former mistress. Even in deep distress Nell had remained loyal.

The Reverend Gosling came up to Briargate, incandescent with rage that Nell had brought shame on her family by breaking her marriage vows. He urged Anne to go and speak to her, to make her see sense and return to her husband, or to leave the village for good.

But Anne knew Nell would never return to Albert, and she couldn't bring herself to suggest the other alternative, or even, if she was honest, face Nell. So she did what she always did when faced with a problem, be that William's heavy drinking or their rapidly depleting wealth, and tried to pretend that it didn't exist.

It was a relief when she heard Nell had left her brother's farm for a new position near Bath. If anyone knew her new master's name it didn't reach Anne's ears, and she did her best to forget Nell.

But Rufus wouldn't let her forget Hope. Every time he came home on holiday from school his first question was always about her. He claimed that Hope had been his only real friend, admitting how they used to meet in the woods and play together. He took an almost fiendish delight in telling the story of how he was saved from drowning in the pond by her, and took his mother to task for her indifference when Meg and Silas Renton died, leaving the girl an orphan. Anne often wondered how he would react if he found out the girl was his half-sister. Just the thought of it made her tremble with fear.

But worse still was that Rufus seemed to have a much stronger attachment to the Rentons than he had to his own mother. Almost the moment he arrived home for the holidays, he'd rush off eagerly to Matt's farm. Sometimes he was gone from sunup to sundown, returning filthy dirty with tales of milking cows, collecting eggs, ploughing and seeding.

Anne felt the tragic irony in the fact that the Rentons had taken in her firstborn and brought her up as their own and now Rufus wanted to join their family too.

Perhaps she should have forbidden him to go there, or at least insisted he went less often, but until quite recently his father's behaviour had been so appalling that she felt her son was better off out of the way.

Shortly after Nell left, William's drinking had grown much worse, to the point where he was rarely sober when at home. He would shut himself away in his study with a bottle, only to come lurching out later to abuse her and anyone else who tried to remonstrate with him.

Then, without any warning, he would disappear without a word about where he was going, and stay away for days. To her shame, Anne often found herself wishing he'd have a fatal accident so that she'd be set free to go home to her sisters. She knew it was wicked to think such things, but she was at the end of her tether and she had no one to turn to. Even Angus had deserted her entirely. She might have been the one who ended it, but she thought he might have retained enough affection for her to drop in now and then to see how she was.

But then, just when she thought she would never see him again, she ran into him.

It was less than a month ago, three days before Christmas. She had gone into Bath to get some presents. Milsom Street was crowded with shoppers, a barrel-organ was playing gaily, the shop windows all looked so bright and festive, and the roast chestnut-sellers were loudly exhorting the crowds to buy their wares. The festive sight cheered her greatly and she reminded herself that Rufus was due home the following day, and only the previous night William had admitted he'd been behaving abominably, and vowed he was going to change.

She wasn't very optimistic about the latter. It wasn't the first time he'd made such promises, only to break them a few days later, but this time he had buried his head in her lap and sobbed his heart out. He said that drinking was his way of shutting out the anxiety about losing his fortune. He added that he'd let her and Rufus down very badly, that the house was falling into disrepair, and it was all too much for him.

Anne felt she had to try to believe in him again. She'd made the suggestion that in the New Year, he should go to his advisers and check exactly how much money they had left; then they could make plans to deal with it, however bad it was.

For now, all she wanted was for them to have a happy Christmas and draw closer to one another.

She had just bought William a blue silk cravat, and was making her way down the street to buy Rufus some new paints when she saw Angus striding towards her. It was such a shock that she almost stumbled.

He was in his uniform, his blue coat with its gold braid

373

and cherry-red breeches making him look taller and even more handsome than she remembered. He didn't appear to be equally shocked to see her, for his expression didn't change.

'Good morning, Lady Harvey,' he said, making a formal little bow. 'I trust you are well?'

She pulled herself together, feeling very glad she'd worn her blue sable-trimmed cape and the matching bonnet, for although it was out of fashion, she knew it flattered her. But she was flustered, for although it was six years since she'd written to him in the aftermath of her father's funeral, it was eight years since they'd last met face to face, and she knew those years showed on her face.

'I'm very well, thank you,' she managed to stammer out, noting that he had a sprinkling of grey hair at his temples and that he'd shaved off his moustache. 'Are you home on leave?'

She remembered he'd made some kind of sardonic remark about there being no good wars just now, and that soldiers were becoming fat and lazy. She asked if he was staying with his relatives in Chelwood.

'No, I have had a house of my own for some years,' he said rather curtly.

'I am sorry that my last letter was so cold and final,' she blurted out. 'I had been having such a difficult time with William, and what with Mother dying, and then Father so soon after, and Rufus going off to school, I was quite beside myself.'

'I assume that is also your excuse for treating Nell so shabbily too?' he said.

'Nell?' she repeated, dumbfounded not only by his accusation but that he'd even come to hear of her maid leaving Briargate. 'I don't know how you came to hear that – Nell left of her own accord!'

'Damn it, Anne, you left her no choice but to go.' He raised his voice in his anger, dropping his earlier formal greeting. 'How could she stay with that blackguard of a husband? I hear he's still with you too!'

Anne looked around her nervously, afraid someone she knew might see them. She wanted to ask if they could talk somewhere where they would be less conspicuous, but she didn't know how to. 'I would have dismissed Albert, but William wouldn't have it,' she managed to say. 'It was Christmas too,' she ended lamely.

Angus raised one eyebrow. 'And as a good Christian you thought it best that the woman who had devoted most of her life to you should be banished to keep the peace?'

'It wasn't like that.' Anne was fast losing her composure in the face of his sarcasm. 'You will only have heard a distorted version of how it came about.'

'No. I heard the plain and unvarnished truth,' he said grimly. 'That Nell believed Albert had killed her young sister, and you and William refused to take her seriously. When I met her and took her home as my housekeeper she was a mere shadow of the able young woman I'd met at Briargate.'

'Your housekeeper?' She gasped, astounded that Rufus hadn't told her this, for surely Matt would have mentioned it to him? Her mind was whirling frantically. Had Nell told Angus he was Hope's father?

'Yes, and the best housekeeper any man could find,' he said with a faint smile. 'Only a fool would part with such a treasure.'

Anne felt chastened. 'We are in agreement there,' she admitted. 'I have missed her so much. But Angus, we did get the police to search for Hope, they found nothing suspicious. It looked to everyone as if she had truly run off.'

'Nell cannot believe that, for she feels if Hope were alive

she would have contacted one of her brothers or sisters by now. I'm inclined to believe she ran off, but I'm absolutely certain Albert forced her to go. If I had my way I'd take a horsewhip to him and force the truth out of him, so at least Nell could have some peace of mind. But it isn't my place to do it; it should be done by her family or by William.'

It was clear by that statement that Angus didn't know Hope was his daughter. He was indignant because he didn't think she and William had showed enough concern for two loyal and hardworking servants. But if he had known who Hope really was, he'd have been up to Briargate immediately to thrash Albert, and he'd almost certainly feel murderous towards Anne too.

She was afraid to meet his eyes now, and although she promised she would tackle Albert herself, and asked him to pass on her warmest wishes to Nell, his stony expression made it clear that he had nothing but scorn for her. Excusing herself, she hurried away, blushing to the tips of her toes.

She had always known that Angus hated injustice and cruelty – he had often spoken out about the terrible conditions for enlisted men in the army – and so it shouldn't have come as a surprise to her that he'd given Nell refuge in his own home.

As he strode away from her that morning in Milsom Street, she saw her own faults all too clearly. She was a weak, vain and selfish woman who had used other people's affections and loyalty all her life, without once offering anything in return. No wonder she saw no trace of love left in his eyes.

All over Christmas she could think of nothing but Angus. She was no stranger to immersing herself in thoughts of her one-time lover. Over the years she'd spent thousands of hours running the whole gamut of emotion, loving him, hating him, blaming him for ruining her life, and yet tingling with arousal as she dwelt on his lovemaking and always burning for more. But now it was different, no tremors of desire, no hate or blame, all she could see was just how self-centred she had been.

Angus was an honourable man. He had fallen in love with her, but he tried to fight against taking it any further because she was a married woman. It was she who made it happen, flirting, tempting and pushing him. He tried to end it countless times, but she clung to him, even threatening to kill herself.

She only ever saw how it was for her: the lack of future, the disgrace if they were caught, the endless waiting while he was away soldiering. She never once considered his feelings or saw that she was preventing him from marrying someone who would make a home for him and give him children.

Anne knew she couldn't make amends to Angus, not for all those wasted years, or the pain she'd put him through. But the one thing she could do, which she knew both he and Nell would appreciate, was to tackle Albert about Hope. If she could get him to admit what really happened that day and why, it might go some way to make up for the misery Nell had been through.

Regrettably she was frightened of Albert; he had a way of looking at her with those dark, penetrating eyes that made her shiver. Normally she avoided all contact with him, because she felt he believed she'd put Nell up to leaving him. But she had to be brave and face him or remain ashamed of herself for the rest of her life. Besides, Hope was her own daughter – what mother wouldn't want to know what happened to her child?

Hope would be twenty-two in April. She might be married

now, with children of her own. How terrible it was to remember that for so many years she'd never allowed herself to think about her firstborn. She'd never asked Bridie where she was buried, she hadn't even considered how old she would have been had she lived, or wondered what she might have looked like. Yet in the last couple of years, when it was too late, she'd thought about her all the time.

Having put on a cloak and some stouter shoes, Anne went out of the front door. Albert was clearing some bramble bushes that had sprung up over the hedge on the far side of the garden. As she walked towards him she became even more nervous. Albert was a powerfully built man, and if he had killed Hope he might attack her too if she pushed him too hard. He was obstinate as well. Anyone else in his position would have moved on, for it was common knowledge that Matt, Joe and Henry Renton hated him.

'Good morning, Albert,' she said as she got close to him. 'I would like a word with you.'

He didn't turn to her, but carried on pulling out the brambles.

'Stop that,' she said firmly. 'I expect you to look at me when I'm speaking to you.'

He turned then, but his expression was wooden. 'Yes, m'lady?' he responded with unconcealed insolence.

'I want you to tell me the truth about the day Hope left,' she said. 'I am not satisfied with the explanation you gave at the time.'

'Aren't you now!' he said, looking her up and down as if she were a common housemaid. 'But then you'll have had it hard without a maid. No one to pin up your hair or fill the bath.'

That he saw her as a pathetic creature who felt nothing more than resentment that she had to take care of herself now her maid was gone was another source of shame. 'She didn't leave me, she left you,' she retorted, trying to keep her voice from shaking. 'Sadly I was unable to keep her on while you were still here. I know you hit her, and Hope too. Men who hit women are cowards.'

'Is that so?' he said, taking a few steps closer to her, his jaw jutting out threateningly. 'You've had a lot of experience with men, have you?'

Anne's stomach contracted with fear, not just at the way he was looking at her, but at the barbed question.

'It is my intention to go back to the police and ask for a new investigation into her disappearance,' she said more bravely than she felt. 'I'm giving you the chance now to tell me the truth before I go to them.'

'You don't want to go talking about me to the police,' he said, smirking at her. 'You've got too much to hide yourself.'

'I beg your pardon!' she said with some indignation.

'I know who you were carrying on with,' he said. 'You make trouble for me and I'll do the same for you. But let me tell you I've got proof, you ain't.'

Anne's bowels contracted with fear. It was a very long time since Angus had called here, and no one but Baines remained who knew about those visits, so maybe she could just call Albert's bluff.

'I haven't any idea what you are talking about,' she said archly. 'You are mistaken. You'd better show me this so-called proof.'

'I ain't got it on me right now,' he said. 'But I've got it safe right enough. A letter from Captain Angus Pettigrew, Royal Hussars, no less. He's been sniffing around you for years.'

A cold chill ran down her spine, for she suddenly realized how and when he'd got the letter. He must have caught Hope with it while she was away burying her father.

'That's knocked the stuffing out of you,' he said dryly, his eyes glinting with malice. 'Still going to the police?'

Anne turned and fled back to the house.

During the next three or four days she berated herself constantly for showing Albert her guilt by running away from him. What was she to do? Now that she'd threatened him with the police, he might tell William just to spite her.

She couldn't eat, sleep or sit still, her heart seemed to be beating too fast, and when William did come home, she had to make out she had a headache so she could shut herself away in her room.

The following morning she saw William talking to Albert out in the garden, and she waited, expecting that at any moment her husband would come running in angrily because he knew.

But that didn't happen. William was quite jovial when he came in, and all he wanted to talk to her about later that day was the possibility they might have to sell some of their more valuable pieces of furniture to raise some cash. But in the days that followed, each time Albert walked close to the windows, he would look in at her, smirk, and wave a piece of notepaper which could only be Angus's letter.

The strain of it, along with not eating or sleeping, made her shaky and clumsy. She knocked an ornament off the mantelpiece, twice she knocked over a teacup, then finally she caught the heel of her shoe in the hem of her dress while coming down the stairs, tumbling right to the bottom.

She had banged her head and arm, and William called the doctor, assuming she was in terrible pain because she couldn't stop weeping.

The doctor told her that she would be fine, that she was only shaken up. But she knew he'd said something more to

William, for as soon as the doctor had left, William came back to her room and sat on her bed.

'Tell me what's really troubling you,' he said. 'You've been nervy ever since I came back from London. Baines told me you haven't been eating.'

It was ironic that he'd chosen to revert to being the gentle, kind-hearted man she'd married, purely out of anxiety for her, and that made her cry even more. He stroked her hair back from her face and told her he knew he was responsible for her distress.

'We used to be such close friends,' he reminded her. 'Remember how we used to laugh so much together? We told each other everything. Can't we try to be like that again?'

She so much wished for that too, but she couldn't tell him the truth however much she wanted to, for it would hurt him too badly.

Days went past and still she lay in bed, wrapped in misery. But William didn't turn back to drink; he brought her meals to the bedroom and even fed her tenderly. Again and again he apologized for his drinking and losing their money and even admitted that he'd been nasty to her and her sisters when her father died.

He did owe her apologies for all these things, but her own wrongdoing was burning away inside her, and because she still couldn't bring herself to admit that, she attacked him.

'You've never been a real husband to me,' she sobbed. 'We've been married for nearly twenty-seven years but you've laid with me fewer than six times. Do you know how that makes me feel? It makes me feel ugly and undesirable.'

William's face crumpled and he began to cry. She felt sorry then and enfolded him in her arms to comfort him, shocked that he had taken it so hard.

As he continued to sob, Anne felt obliged to tone down her accusation. She said that it was almost certainly her fault, that maybe he thought she didn't welcome his advances. She wasn't even thinking about what she was saying; all she wanted was for him to stop crying.

'Don't make excuses for me,' he blurted out eventually. 'The fault is all mine and I wish more than anything else in the world that I wasn't the way I am. Don't you understand what it is, Anne? I have no desire for any woman. Only other men.'

For a few brief moments she thought she'd misunderstood what he said. But when he looked up at her like a little boy caught with his fingers in the jam, she suddenly realized it was true.

'No!' she exclaimed. 'That can't be right. Not you!'

She was beyond shock, beyond even horror. It was too outrageous to take in. No one could be married to a man for all those years and not find out such a thing.

All she knew about men with this problem had been learned from Bridie. Shortly before Anne was to marry William, Bridie had told her a tale of a butler and groom at her previous position. They were dismissed when they were found in bed together. Bridie called them 'nancy boys', but explained such men were often called sodomists. Anne had often wondered what prompted her old maid to tell her such a thing, but now it looked as if Bridie had sensed William might be one and she wanted to warn her.

'I have been so unfair to you,' William cried. 'I swear to God I didn't know when we got married, but I soon realized I wasn't right. I couldn't speak of it, though, not to you or anyone. I truly loved you; I still do, so I beg you not to doubt that. But after I'd managed to give you Rufus I thought it would be all right to go my own way.'

In an odd way Anne felt a kind of relief. Whether that

was because what William had told her gave her some justification for her own behaviour, or because it finally made sense of all those questions about her marriage for which she could find no answers, she didn't know. But all at once she didn't feel quite so hunted.

She listened in horrified fascination as he poured out that he'd been seduced by another man at a card party in London just a year after their wedding.

'I loathed myself for giving in to it,' he sobbed. 'But I couldn't help myself.'

Maybe if Anne hadn't experienced illicit ecstasy herself she wouldn't have understood that explanation. But William's explanation was exactly how she would have described her own infidelity.

She had often raged to herself about the unfairness of a society which not only accepted a man taking a mistress, but almost applauded it, while an adulterous woman was seen as a harlot, and damned by everyone. It was a man's world. Men could rape servants, go with prostitutes and bring diseases home to their wife; they could even deflower children and not be punished. Yet absurdly, a man could not have a preference for his own sex without being considered a perverted animal, and if he was exposed, he would be an outcast in society.

She didn't want William to be an outcast. She didn't like what he'd told her, yet it seemed to her that it wasn't his fault he'd been made that way. But if he had had normal desires, then maybe she wouldn't have been unfaithful either.

In a way, it was like shining a light in a dark corner, for suddenly she was remembering how he was when they first met and married, and seeing that there had been many pointers to suggest he was different from other young men.

He'd been almost pretty with his blond curls and smooth,

hairless chin. He was always more comfortable with women than with men. On their wedding night he'd admired her beautiful nightgown, yet shown no real enthusiasm for what lay beneath it. In truth they had been more like two girl-friends than husband and wife, lying in bed together giggling or chasing each other up and down the stairs. If she hadn't met Angus and found out what real men did with their women, and William hadn't found someone like himself in America, they might have stayed in that untroubled, passionless friendship for ever.

'Poor William,' she said, hugging him to her breast. She could afford to be magnanimous now for she had discovered the beauty and ecstasy of normal passion.

Encouraged by her sympathy, William bared his soul, telling her how he'd found there were many men like him, forced to search one another out in secret, always in fear that they would be discovered and denounced.

'You accused me once of going to a brothel,' he said brokenly. 'I wish that's where I had been for there is terrible danger in consorting with other men like me. Most are as sad and bewildered as I am; we wish more than anything we had not been cursed with such desires. But there are some who delight in their depravity and prey on the weak, bending us to their will. We cannot escape their clutches for they hold us fast by blackmail and intimidation.'

Anne sensed this was what had happened to him, for she'd often felt that when he verbally abused her when he'd been drinking, the words coming out of his mouth were not his.

That was what made her strong enough to tell him about Angus. It wasn't fair to let him pour out all his hurt and shame believing that he alone had destroyed the happiness they once had together. And, as always, she remained self-centred enough to think that once William knew, Albert would have nothing to hold over her.

She poured out her adultery in a torrent, telling him how she was attracted to Angus right from their first meeting, but that she held her feelings in check right up until William left for America.

'It wouldn't have happened if you'd been here,' she said brokenly. 'But you went away without me and I couldn't stop myself.'

She went on to tell him that she'd had Angus's baby, and how she'd been told by Bridie that the infant was stillborn.

William had remained surprisingly calm throughout her revelation. He looked stunned, bewildered, but not angry. He didn't interrupt her once with recriminations or even questions.

'But the baby didn't die. Nell took her home to her parents. The baby was Hope!' she sobbed out. 'I never knew. She came here and played with Rufus, but I never guessed she was mine. Nell didn't tell me until that awful day she said Albert had killed her.'

William's calm vanished then. He sat up straight on the bed and looked at her with steely eyes. 'Hope was your child?' he asked, his voice suddenly louder and harsh. 'You must have known the baby was alive. How could you let it go to someone so close? Was that so you could still see her?'

'No,' Anne insisted, a little bewildered that he was more upset by the child of her union with Angus than the love affair. 'I believed Bridie when she said she was dead. I was exhausted after the birth, and I didn't know anything about babies then. Bridie showed her to me and she wasn't moving or crying. Besides, you were due home from America any day and I was so scared. It just seemed to me to be God's way of dealing with my problem.'

William put his head in his hands and made a kind of wailing sound.

'I'm so sorry, William,' she sobbed. 'I have no idea what

I would have done if I'd known she was alive. I suppose I would have asked Bridie to find a home for her, I couldn't have done anything else, could I? Imagine the disgrace!'

William remained with his head in his hands.

'How could I tell you about it?' she pleaded. 'It was such a terrible time, all alone here with Bridie, for all the other servants had gone to the London house by then. All I could think about was getting strong enough for the drive to London to join you. I did my best to forget it ever happened, and you made it easier because you were so kind and considerate.'

He looked up then, his face pale and haggard. 'Only because I was burdened with guilt too,' he said in a small voice. 'You seemed distant, preoccupied, but I thought you were angry because I hadn't taken you with me to America. Oh, Anne! If only you'd told me all this before.'

'How could I?' she asked. 'And what point would there have been in telling you when I thought the baby was dead?'

William nodded as if seeing her point. 'But did you tell Angus about it?'

Anne shook her head. 'His regiment left before I even knew I was with child,' she said. 'I didn't see him again until some time after Rufus was born. You were here when he called. Don't you remember he came upstairs to the nursery with us to see Rufus? He brought him a little wooden horse. You made us all laugh by galloping it along the edge of the crib.'

William half-smiled ruefully. 'Yes, I remember. I told Rufus he'd have a real one to ride on as soon as he could sit in a saddle.'

'We were so happy at that time,' Anne said wistfully. 'I could have put Angus out of my mind if you'd only stayed the way you were then. But you changed, getting drunk all the time, saying nasty things to me. Why did you change like that? Was it because you loved someone else?'

'Not then,' he said, shaking his head. 'But I could feel the need in you for something I couldn't give you. Every day I awoke knowing I was a fraud,' he said, reaching over and taking her hand. 'At first going riding each day took my mind off it, but soon I had to go looking for what I really wanted. I despised myself so much that I had to get drunk whenever I was at home.'

Anne remembered odd little scenes around that time, her in her nightgown urging him to come to bed with her, and William turning his back on her, protesting he was tired.

'If only you'd told me what was wrong,' she said, wiping a tear away from her cheek. 'I think I would have let you do whatever you wanted just as long as at home you were the William I married.'

'The real problems began at home, when I took Albert on,' he said.

Anne's eyes shot wide open. 'Albert! Did he find out? Was he blackmailing you?'

William pursed his lips, as though he'd just sucked a lemon. 'No, not that. He's like me.'

'You mean . . . ?'

William nodded.

'God in heaven!' Anne exclaimed. She didn't think she could take any more shocks.

'Yes, he's a sodomist, or whatever people like to call us,' William spat out. 'And I, poor fool that I am, fell for him. If not for me he wouldn't have married Nell; that was my suggestion.'

'Oh no, William!' Anne gasped. 'Why did you do that?'

William shrugged. 'Without a wife people might have guessed about him. Nell struck me as a plain, no-nonsense girl who would make a calm, steady wife. I didn't know how cruel Albert could be then, or that he hated women.

I thought he'd be able to give her a child, take care of her, and you'd keep the maid you relied on. I'd still have Albert in a place where we could be together.'

'The gatehouse,' Anne whispered. 'You used to go there?'

William nodded glumly. 'It was bad, I can see that now, but he bewitched me, Anne. I couldn't think of anything else, nothing mattered to me but him. Can you understand?'

She couldn't understand, not with a man as loathsome as Albert. The thought of them doing something so depraved and bestial right under her nose, so close to their son, made her want to shout at him, pummel him with her fists, say he was disgusting.

Yet at the same time she could remember only too well how bewitched by Angus she had been, how she had let him take her in a field or woods, without any thought of her husband or child.

She took a deep breath. 'Do you still feel that way about him?' she asked.

'No, I fear him,' he admitted ruefully. 'It has been over between us for a long time, but he refuses to leave here, and threatens to tell you, Rufus and everyone else what I am if I force him out. I thought it was love he felt for me, but now I know he is incapable of such an emotion.'

'Oh, William,' she sighed, reaching out to hold him, for now they had a common enemy. 'He knows about me and Angus too. He has a letter to me from Angus. Nell asked Hope to hold on to any that came while I was away at my father's funeral, and he must have found her with it. Did he kill her?'

'No, at least not as far as I know,' William said quickly, then fell silent, chewing on his lip.

Anne waited. She knew her husband only ever did this when he was uncertain and very afraid. But she was certain he would eventually tell her what he knew; lying didn't come easily to him.

'She came into the gatehouse and caught us,' he finally blurted out, his face contorted with shame. 'Albert told me to get out through the front door and he'd deal with her. I went down there later in the evening and she was gone. Albert showed me the note he'd got her to write; he said he'd told her never to come back or he'd hurt Nell.'

Anne exploded with rage then, calling him all the terrible names she could think of. 'You coward!' she raged. 'You stood by, letting Nell think she was dead, and all the time you knew what had happened! How could you do that? It was inhuman!'

'What else could I do?' William whined. 'I was terrified that Albert and I would be discovered. Albert even convinced me Hope had wanted to leave Briargate. I didn't know how cruel he was then, and even now I can't see what else I could have done but go along with it.'

Anne felt sick then. She sank back on her pillows, stunned at Albert's capacity for evil. Rufus had told her the man used to hit both Hope and Nell, he said he made their lives a misery. In fact, Anne could remember that Nell often winced with pain, passing it off as a fall on the drive or some such thing. The brute had clearly been terrorizing them both for a very long time, but she'd been too wrapped up in herself to notice.

Maybe Hope did leave as instructed to keep Nell safe, but somehow Anne knew she also went to prevent her and Rufus from being shamed too. Hope was only fifteen then, and she'd seen something not even a grown woman could deal with, banished from her home, family and livelihood and told never to return.

Did Albert beat her before she left? Did she have any money? Where would she go?

William stayed in her bed that night, holding her tightly and telling her that he still loved her, even if he wasn't worthy of love in return. Anne was grateful for the comfort of his arms, but the images of her daughter cast out, terrified and with no one to turn to, prevented her from sleeping. She understood then why Nell had gone mad with grief.

Chapter Seventeen

1854

A sudden hissing from the fire made Lady Harvey jump involuntarily.

'The coal's wet,' William explained, breaking the silence they'd been locked in for some little while. 'I daresay Albert pissed on it again.'

Anne heard the bleakness in her husband's voice and when she turned to look at him she saw his eyes were glistening with tears.

'What are we going to do?' she asked fearfully. 'He'll only get worse, won't he?'

They were in William's study. They no longer used the drawing room in winter because it was too costly to heat. The study was also the only room at Briargate which didn't yet show signs of the neglect so apparent elsewhere. But then the sheer masculinity of the book-lined walls and the leather armchairs suggested the room was designed to look ageless and worn.

Outside it was a raw, grey February afternoon, a keen wind bending the bare branches of the trees along the drive. The light was fading fast, but Anne was reluctant to move away from the fire to light the oil lamp, for her joints were stiff with rheumatism.

The dim light concealed the ravages time and trouble had brought to the once handsome couple. Anne's hair was thin and white now, her face lined and her body thicker. At forty-eight she perhaps still looked younger than many women of a similar age in the village, but this was more to do with a retained elegance in her dress and posture rather than glowing health or nature's kindness.

William was less lined than his wife, despite being three years older, but he was portly and balding. The years of heavy drinking had given his face a bloated look and there was an elderly stiffness in his movements.

Yet aside from the ever-present irritation of Albert's presence at Briargate, they had found new happiness following their revelations a year earlier. William said he'd become too old and disillusioned for desire; Anne was content with his friendship and company. In fact they could count the last year as being the time they'd been closest since they were newly-weds.

They often discussed how they should have dismissed Albert years ago. But setting aside their separate reasons for avoiding confrontation with him, they had also been concerned about the grounds of Briargate. Whatever else Albert was, no one could deny that he was an astounding gardener. He had the energy of three other men, he took a pride in his work, and he would be impossible to replace.

Briargate might be crumbling on the inside, but while the grounds remained immaculate and beautiful, they could convince themselves and others that everything was fine. Not that anyone much came to Briargate any longer. The Warrens from Wick Farm occasionally visited for tea in the garden in summer, likewise the Metcalfes from Bath, but there hadn't been a dinner party here for years. Yet a year ago the Harveys had believed, or rather hoped, that once they were united, they could control Albert and anything else life might throw at them. They'd even convinced themselves they could begin entertaining again.

But they were wrong. First Martha the cook left, giving no explanation other than that she wanted a change. Soon afterwards Rose went too, saying she had found a position in a more lively household. Both Sir William and Lady Harvey had no doubt that Albert had a hand in persuading Cook to leave, and he doubtless knew that Rose would soon follow because she would be lonely without another female servant for company.

Loyal, dependable Baines had stayed; nothing Albert could have said, or offered him, would have induced him to leave. But it would have been difficult for him to obtain another position as he was in his seventies and becoming very frail.

Lady Harvey had taken on Mrs Crabbe, a widow from the village, and Polly, her fifteen-year-old daughter, but both were slovenly and insolent. Sadly, Lady Harvey had to accept that gentry who had fallen on hard times couldn't expect to find good servants, and as there was no one else available, she had to live with lowered standards.

But Albert remained like a malevolent spirit, spoiling all that was good. While he still took great care of the grounds, he did it in a way that implied ownership. And he had many ways of showing the Harveys he considered himself to be the new master of Briargate.

Pissing on the coal for the study was just one of his many nasty tricks to intimidate them. In the past they'd been subjected to a grass snake and a dead rat in the coal bucket too.

He would disappear for days on end, especially in the winter, and each time they hoped he was gone for good. But he always came back, tearing into cutting down a tree or making a new flowerbed without ever consulting them first. And he had demanded higher wages too, testing them to the limit.

*

'I thought I could ask him to come shooting with me,' William said, breaking into Anne's dejected reverie. 'I could shoot him and say it was an accident.'

Anne doubted very much that he could really shoot Albert, however much he'd grown to hate and fear him. But it was touching that he was looking for a way to end this horrible situation.

'He's too clever to be caught like that, he'd sense what you were intending,' she said more sharply than she meant to. 'The only real way out is to stand together and call his bluff.'

'I don't think I'm strong enough for that,' William said, hanging his head. 'He's evil, Anne, you know that.'

'But he can't say anything about you without incriminating himself,' Anne retorted. 'We could just deny my affair with Angus. No one likes Albert, they wouldn't believe a word he said. Nell would never stand with Albert against me, and neither would Angus.'

'Nell may have told him the truth about Hope by now,' William reminded her. 'That might well change his view.'

'If he did know Hope was his daughter he'd be even more likely to support us against Albert,' Anne said wistfully. 'I just wish that I'd told him myself that day I met him in Bath. He would have come round here and dealt with that fiend straight away.'

'How strange it is how things turn out,' William said thoughtfully. 'I met Angus when he was just a small boy staying with his relatives in Chelwood. He used to look up to me, and mostly I was unkind to him because he was a few years younger than I was. He was always pestering me to let him come out riding with me. Maybe if I hadn't given in and lent him a mount, he would never have bothered to come back and look me up after he got his commission in the army. Then he would never have met you.'

'If you asked for his help in getting rid of Albert, I'm sure he still retains enough affection for you to give it willingly,' Anne said.

'I couldn't bear him of all men to find out what I am,' William said in a small voice. 'And you know Albert would delight in telling him.'

Anne realized he was probably right about that. 'What I can't understand is *why* Albert wants to stay here,' she said, feeling it would only hurt William further if she kept on about Angus. 'He knows you don't care for him any longer. He has no friends, no family, what is it that binds him here?'

'Because he's well paid, likes living in the gatehouse, and because he wouldn't have the freedom he gets here anywhere else,' William said plaintively. 'He has a completely free hand with the grounds, and you have to admit he's far more than a gardener, he's an artist! Do you remember how glorious the flowerbeds were last summer, such wonderful colour combinations, the clever way he has of always having something new coming up to hide the fading plants? I've never seen his like before.'

Anne did remember; in fact, the only time she'd ever seen the man looking really happy was when he was admiring his plants. But at the same time he made sure she and William couldn't enjoy them.

If they sat out in the garden for tea, Albert would start scything the grass near them. If they just walked around, he followed them pushing a wheelbarrow; he glowered at them if they picked some flowers, and made them feel they were intruders.

It was as if he wished to imprison them in the house, and even on a winter's day he made sure they were aware of his presence in little ways like the wet coal. Raking the gravel on the drive outside the study window was a favourite too, and in summer he would often disturb a wasps' nest so that the insects flew in through the windows.

Sometimes when he saw Anne looking out of the window he would urinate in front of her. Late at night he would walk around the house, his feet scrunching on the gravel, just a reminder that he was still there, watching and biding his time.

Again and again William had tried to take him to task, but it always ended the same way. Albert would threaten to expose them.

'Damn it,' William exclaimed, jumping up as a definite smell of urine wafted out from either the fire or the coal box. 'Enough is enough!'

'What, dearest?' Anne asked.

'Albert! He's got to go. Tomorrow, first thing, I'll insist he leaves. I'll give him till the end of the week and if he isn't gone by then I'll get a couple of men to empty his belongings from the gatehouse and change the locks on the doors.'

'But what if he attacks you?' Anne said nervously.

William went over to the window and looked out. 'I almost hope he does,' he said. 'Then I can get the police and have him arrested.'

Anne had heard William talk like this before but each time he'd backed down later, often having to give Albert more money to appease him. But she was pleased to hear that this time William really did sound determined and she guessed it was because of Rufus.

He was in his second year at Oxford University now, but he'd declined to come home at Christmas. Albert had sneeringly claimed it was because he'd grown too grand for the shabby house, and the lack of parties and dances, but both Anne and William knew that wasn't the case. Rufus had grown into a tall, strong and handsome young man, but he had no airs and graces. He still liked to go to Matt's farm when he was home; last summer he was there every day helping with the harvest.

They both knew he hadn't come home this Christmas because of Albert. The convictions he'd had as a young lad about the man had remained, and he'd become increasingly outraged as he saw Albert strutting around as if he were the master, and his parents kowtowing to him. Staying away was his way of showing his disapproval, and the message was simple: Albert should be dismissed or Rufus would not be home for any future holidays with his parents.

It had been the most cheerless Christmas they had ever known, and Anne knew that it had made William feel even more aggrieved with Albert.

'Are you prepared for the gossip if he does make good his threats?' Anne asked. She felt she was prepared now, but she didn't want William suddenly caving in at the first whiff of scandal.

'I am, never more so. Come on, old girl, don't fail me now! We've got to do this or stay under his yoke for the rest of our lives.'

William knew by Anne's expression over breakfast that she thought he was going to excuse himself from dealing with Albert today as he'd promised.

She wasn't entirely wrong about that; he had lain awake half the night thinking up excuses. But it struck him that his whole life had been a series of excuses. He'd made a good marriage but failed Anne because of his sexual deficiencies. He'd been born to a fortune and he'd gambled and frittered it away. He had only one thing he could be proud of and that was Rufus, for despite both his parents' weaknesses he'd grown into a fine young man, intelligent, strong, loving and hardworking.

His grandfather had built Briargate intending it to be passed down to William and then to his grandson, but thanks to William's stupidity it was now more of a liability than an asset. Yet he knew that Rufus would sooner inherit a worthless, crumbling estate surrounded by a wilderness, than have a father who was too cowardly to stand up to blackmail.

Fortunately Rufus's security was not under threat, owing to the legacy from his maternal grandfather, but even if it had been, Rufus had the intelligence, enthusiasm and knowledge to change Briargate into a profitable farm. He'd often said he found it immoral to have so many decadent flowerbeds when that land could be turned over to chickens, pigs or vegetables.

So even though William was shaking in his shoes at the prospect of what might happen as a result of dismissing Albert, he knew he had to do the right thing, for Rufus.

'Where are you going?' Anne asked as he got up from the breakfast table. They had barely spoken as they ate. He had looked at his newspaper; she had been reading a letter from her sister. They were usually silent at breakfast, but it was a comfortable silence; today it had been tense with unsettled business.

'To put on my garden shoes,' he said. 'You stay in here and watch in case I need you.'

'You're going to talk to Albert?' she asked. She sounded very surprised.

'I won't be doing much talking,' he said with a weak, boyish grin. 'I shall be giving him his marching orders.'

'Don't you want me to come too?'

William had thought long and hard whether it would be better or worse with Anne beside him. But he'd come to the conclusion he must do it alone. He couldn't subject

Anne to Albert's foul language; he was sure to fire a volley of his favourite expletives.

William let himself out through the back door by the boot room, pulling on his coat as he went. It was very cold, and as he looked down the garden to see where Albert was, he noticed there was fog in the valley down by the river.

The sound of the saw told him Albert was in the wood-shed at the back of the stables. It was the one place he really didn't want to be alone with the man. It was there that he had kissed Albert the first time and said that he loved him.

William couldn't bear to think what a prize fool he'd been. He'd given the man his heart and his money, and risked everything for him. But his biggest mistake was to romanticize him.

William had thought of him as a beautiful, gentle and creative archangel in a working man's smock, who out of gratitude transformed the garden into the kind of Eden he felt William deserved. He even believed that Albert was an innocent; that he succumbed to William because he was the only person who had ever shown him any affection, or valued him.

Much later, when William began to realize the giving was all one-sided, he made excuses for his lover: he'd had a vicious mother; he'd been influenced by brutish men from an early age. Yet William still believed that if he showed him enough love, understanding and kindness, Albert would reciprocate.

Now he was well aware that Albert had never had the capacity to feel love. He might have a heart pumping his blood round like anyone else, but whatever it was in most humans that gave them emotional feelings towards others, this was missing in Albert.

He could play-act emotions superbly; in the past he had shown such tenderness, adoration and sympathy that

William had stopped listening to his conscience and would have run off to live in the woods with the man if he'd asked. But in the end William had seen it was all a sham. The only emotion Albert was capable of was hate, for his humble origins and for anyone he considered more fortunate than himself.

As William reached the open-fronted woodshed, Albert stopped sawing logs. Despite the cold he was glistening with perspiration, and he had stripped off to his smock and breeches. He looked dirty and unkempt, his hair tangled and almost reaching his shoulders, his beard studded with traces of past meals, and the smell of stale sweat was overpowering.

'Come to help me, Billie?' he asked with a sly smirk. 'The old girl's company got too dull for you?'

William felt nauseous that he'd ever lain with this man, for he could see so clearly now that he was just a cold-blooded whore.

'Lady Harvey is very good company,' William said. 'And I have come to tell you that you are dismissed. You will vacate the gatehouse and leave Briargate for good by Friday.'

Albert sat himself down on a log, reaching in his pocket for his pipe and tobacco as if he hadn't heard. 'You can't dismiss me,' he grinned as he packed the tobacco into his pipe. 'We're bound together for ever, Billy boy!'

William was every bit as intimidated as Albert intended him to be. He tried not to look at the man's rippling muscles that strained the sleeves of his shirt, or his powerful hands. He made himself picture Rufus's face, and the smile he knew he'd see when he told him Albert was gone for good.

'We are not bound together. You'll go by Friday or I will have you thrown out.'

'Now, come on.' Albert forgot his pipe and rose from the log, his lips drawing back in a snarl. 'You want me to go telling tales to Lady Harvey?'

'You can if you wish, but she already knows everything.'

Albert made a snort of derision, clearly not believing this. 'Don't fucking well try to bluff me,' he said, and he turned in the direction of the house.

William let him go on ahead a little way; then he walked just far enough across the lawn so Anne could see him from the dining-room window and beckoned her to come out.

Albert was almost at the back door when it opened and Anne stood there.

'Come on out, Anne,' William called. 'I'm having trouble convincing Albert that we have no secrets from each other.'

For the first time in all the years he'd known Albert, William saw him look uncertain. His eyes narrowed and darted between William and Anne, like a cornered rat's.

William felt proud of Anne. She had flung a purple shawl around her shoulders and its regal colour, with her eyes like flint and her poised stance, gave her a queenly and composed appearance.

'I take it Sir William has given you the order to leave?' she said, her voice as crisp and cold as the morning. 'We are willing to give you a character; you have after all tended the garden very well.'

'Captain Pettigrew tended your garden well too,' Albert replied.

William sucked in his breath at that sly retort, knowing it was intended to make his wife scuttle inside in fright. But she just smiled, and walked straight over to William and took his arm.

'My husband is very well aware of my past relationship with Captain Pettigrew,' she said. 'You cannot hurt us, Albert.'

Albert's face grew dark with anger and he started to bluster and swear, threatening to go down to the village and tell everyone all he knew about both of them.

'How can you do that without incriminating yourself?' Anne retorted. 'Country folk don't like "nancy boys". We have only to tell the Renton men that you are trying to slander us and they'll willingly tear you limb from limb. You have no friends in the village, but we have many.'

'Master Rufus won't like what I have to say,' he said, and William could sense he was desperate now, completely thrown by the news that they had admitted their past sins to each other.

Anne laughed humourlessly. 'Really, Albert! What a silly goose you are! Do you really think he'd believe a word you'd say? He loathes you, and has always blamed you for Hope's disappearance. I wouldn't be surprised if he didn't demand a new police investigation into that too. Pack your bags and be gone, Albert, your time here is up. You have nothing left now to blackmail us with.'

'You are forgetting I've got the letter from Captain Pettigrew,' he snarled. 'That's evidence.'

William moved closer to Albert. 'At times like this gentlemen stick together,' he said, putting a snarl into his voice. 'I grew up with the Captain, and he'll say that letter is a forgery. What's more, he'll come over here and give you a good hiding for your trouble.'

'I'll go to law,' Albert said wildly.

William laughed at him contemptuously. 'Do you really think a gardener could challenge a member of the aristocracy and win? You'd be shipped off to Botany Bay. Now, away with you! Leave the gatehouse before Friday morning and you shall have a character. But if you are still there, I'll have you thrown out without one.'

Anne's hand slipped into William's as they watched Albert slink off round the side of the house. 'Will he go?' she whispered.

'I think so,' William replied. He felt good about himself now, for he'd protected Anne, Rufus and Briargate. 'He really has no choice. Even if he does slink down to the ale house and tell a few tales, no one will believe them. Now, we must go in before you catch cold. I think we'll have a glass of sherry to celebrate.'

That night, in the dim light of a flickering candle, Albert sat at his table in the gatehouse with a large heap of money before him. As he counted it into piles, he took long swigs from a bottle of rum. Normally counting his money gave him immense pleasure, for he had enjoyed bleeding William dry for all these years. But tonight he was too full of rage to concentrate.

He had thought he was set up for life here; that he had William and Anne in the palm of his hand. His long-term plan was to wait until they were forced to sell Briargate, and he'd be waiting ready to buy it. He hadn't anticipated that the worms would turn.

He had more than enough money to go anywhere; he had his health, strength and a keen enough mind to do anything he chose, but it was the garden at Briargate that he wanted. He had created it: every tree, shrub and flower was his. He'd toiled over it for sixteen years, nurtured it, dreamed and planned, and now they were snatching it from him.

He had always thought himself as sturdy as an oak, that nothing could shock or dismay him. When weak, pathetic William turned up at the woodshed this morning, his first thought had been that the man wanted him again, even if he was glowering.

When he told him to pack up and leave, Albert wanted to laugh. William had said that before, and he'd always backed down after a brief reminder of how things stood.

He would have bet all the money on the table that William

would never tell his wife what he was. Yet he had, and she'd told him about the Captain. They'd stood there together, smug as you like, and the final body blow was that remark of William's: 'Do you really think a gardener could challenge a member of the aristocracy and win?'

That made him savage. He didn't like reminders that he was a working man.

When he was a small boy he had hated his rough clothes, having to go barefoot and all that went with being born into a poor family. His mother used to say with scorn that he belonged in a palace.

At ten he was packed off to Hever Castle to work in the gardens there. Within just a few months he'd caught the eye of the head groom, and night after night he had to submit to the man using him like a woman.

He was fourteen when the head groom died suddenly of a heart attack, and Albert couldn't have been happier. He wasn't interested in girls, but he thought in the fullness of time the right one would come along and he would forget those acts which had shamed him for so long.

By the time he was sixteen, he was a strapping six feet tall, with glowing olive skin, black curly hair and smouldering dark eyes, and it wasn't only the female servants who looked at him longingly, but many of the grand ladies who visited Hever. Albert found he couldn't respond to them in any way, however. It wasn't shyness, he just didn't like them. Yet he could look at certain men and his pulse raced and his cock twitched.

It was as if the groom had put a curse on him, and in his anger he vowed to himself that he would never let another man use him again. In future he would do the using and make it pay. Fortunately there were many distinguished men who came to Hever and who preferred boys to girls, and Albert found he could recognize them immediately.

He remained at Hever until he was twenty-one, and in between a series of lovers who gave him money and expensive presents, he was happy working in the gardens. He never thought of it as a menial job, to him a beautiful garden was a temple, and he worshipped in it. In his spare time he learned everything he could from the old experienced gardeners and from studying plant books. His vision for the future was to design and build a garden from scratch. He imagined a lake, woodland, formal flower gardens, sweeping lawns, rockeries with tumbling water and secluded bowers.

But the wealthy man who would provide the land for such a project eluded him, and when the whispers about his sexual exploits began to circulate around the estate, Albert found himself banished to the gardens of the Bishop's Palace in Wells.

He never liked to dwell on the humiliations he met there, prayed over by pious men he knew were the same as him, worked to exhaustion by sadistic brutes and ignored by the rest. Then one evening in the neighbouring ale house he met William.

The ale house was mostly frequented by farm labourers; the gentry used the coaching house across the main street. William stood out like a thoroughbred stallion in a field of donkeys, for he wore a blue checked riding jacket which fitted his slender body like a glove, and his ripe corn curls were tousled and shiny. He was drinking with an older man who looked like a farmer, but his eyes locked with Albert's across the crowded bar, and suddenly it was as if they were the only two people in the room.

It wasn't difficult to find out who he was, where he lived, or to be outside when William finally left, the worse for drink. Albert was there to hold his horse steady and help him into the saddle. He asked him if he needed a gardener, and William told him to come out to Briargate the following day.

Albert knew he was taking a big chance leaving the Bishop's Palace for good the following morning. Sir William might not remember asking him to come; he might not even need a gardener, especially one without a character. But Albert thought only of the man's wide sensual mouth, periwinkle-blue eyes and firm, small buttocks as he walked the seventeen miles.

As he turned into the drive past the gatehouse and saw Briargate ahead, Albert felt he'd fallen into his dream. The setting of the house was perfect; someone had already planted many lovely trees, but he could make it much more beautiful. This was the place he'd been looking for.

Luck, or fate, smiled on him that day. William was home, and he not only remembered Albert from the night before, but was delighted to see him again as he did really need a gardener. By nightfall Albert was tucked up in a comfortable bed above the stables, already head gardener of Briargate at the age of only twenty-five, and Willy, the under-gardener, who was half-witted, would do exactly as he told him.

It wasn't hard to make William love him. He was a man so riddled with guilt that he only needed to be shown friendship and understanding. He was keen to work with Albert on the garden, and the hard physical labour of digging and clearing ground gave him new purpose. Albert let William make all the overtures, playing the innocent lad slowly falling for his master.

But Albert's only true love was the grounds of Briargate; to him William was no more important than a resident dog whose company he enjoyed. He was happy to romp with him, he showed him as much affection as he was capable of, but Albert saw himself as master.

The only time William ever got the upper hand was when he insisted Albert was to court and marry Nell. Albert could see why William thought it necessary. But William never understood just how much Albert loathed women. William didn't share that repugnance, he liked their company, and young Rufus was evidence that he could, if necessary, even roger them. William's plan was that Albert should emulate him, impregnate Nell once or twice, and then no one could ever point the finger of suspicion at his master.

Right from the first time Albert met the whole Renton family he knew he could never carry it off. They were typical peasants — strong, virile males and plain but earthy women, built for childbearing. Up against such men he felt inadequate, and even though he knew little of women, he sensed a female Renton would be like a bitch on heat.

The wedding and the party afterwards were torturous. His own family were cold and brooding, his mother a vicious, spiteful woman who had always belittled any displays of tenderness or affection. In contrast, the Rentons hugged and kissed, danced and sang, and he felt like a fish out of water. He shuddered as he overheard many innuendos about the wedding night and the baby they hoped would soon follow. For two pins he would have run away then, anything rather than face what he knew was supposed to come next.

He was aware he'd handled the wedding night all wrong; maybe he should have asked William how he'd managed it. He could bet William never told Anne she was a whore for wanting him, or pushed her away as he did Nell.

But marriage was for ever, and as mere servants they didn't have the luxury of separate rooms either. Sharing a bed with Nell turned his stomach, her soft flesh pressed against him, her repulsive female smell, and that desperate need wafting out of her.

The reproach in her eyes and her silent tears were unbearable and drove him mad with hatred. He knew she was a good woman, but that just made the situation worse, and he had to pick on her constantly to justify the rage inside him.

Then Hope came to live with them, and every time he looked at her pretty, innocent face he felt threatened. She wasn't like Nell, she was smart, sparky and brave and very likely to work out for herself that he wasn't a real man.

His first thought was to kill her that day she caught him with Sir William. He could have wrung her neck like a chicken and buried her in the woods and he would have had no qualms about it. But then he saw the letter and knew there was a better way to get rid of her. He wanted her to suffer degradation and isolation just the way he had at the same age, and with no money or character there was only one route open to her. There was the bonus that he retained the letter from the Captain too, a little insurance in case he ever needed it.

It worked out even better than he'd expected. He got rid of the girl and Nell. He had the gatehouse to himself at last. He wasn't in the least concerned when William wanted to end their affair as he had already become very tired of his heavy drinking and his dependence on him. He was fast becoming a liability.

For six years now he'd been supremely content. He took great pleasure in watching the standards at the big house falling and Anne and William clinging together like shipwrecks as their friends, neighbours and servants abandoned them. Their looks were fading, and it was only a matter of time before their money would run out too. And through it all Albert kept the garden at the peak of perfection, knowing the whole estate would be his one day.

But his plans were shattered now.

He picked up the bottle of rum from the table and took a long, hard swig.

'I won't leave here,' he muttered. 'It's mine. I worked for it.'

Getting up, he lurched drunkenly across the kitchen, pulled open the door and looked up the drive towards the big house. He could only see the dark shape of it for the moon was behind cloud and there were no lights in any window.

There'd been a time when every window was lit, just as there were horses in the stables, wine in the cellars and a dozen servants scuttling around. Now just William and Anne were there, with only old Baines tottering around still trying to pretend he was running the place. Mrs Crabbe and her daughter who helped out by day would be back in their hovel in the village.

He had spent so many evenings, summer and winter, gazing up at the house and dreaming of the day when it would be his. He had never once considered that anything could change them from the weak, fearful and guiltridden people he knew so well, not before their money ran out and they were forced to sell up.

But he hadn't known them today. They were proud, confident and determined, and they had an answer for everything. He had no idea what it was that had given them this sudden strength, but he did know they meant what they said.

'I'd sooner burn the place down than let you two beat me,' he muttered, taking another swig from his bottle.

The cloud obscuring the moon swept away, and all at once Briargate was illuminated. He could even see the ghostly white of the marble statues in his rosebeds, and that taunted him still further. Even though his mind was befuddled with drink, the thought of a fire stayed with him.

The estate would have little value to anyone without the house. Master bloody Rufus was too busy lording it up with his flashy friends in Oxford to want to rebuild it. But it would have value to him, and he'd get it even cheaper then. No one would suspect him; they'd think it was just a burning coal that fell out of a fire. And he'd make sure he was up at the house doing his best to put the fire out when people on the neighbouring farms saw the flames and came running to help.

The study! A few books and newspapers left on the hearthrug would soon catch everything else alight. Leave the study door open and the flames would be across the hall and up the stairs in no time and they'd be trapped.

Of course old Baines was up there too, but he was so frail now that he was no more use to anyone.

Just a few minutes later, Albert was making his way through the field outside the railings of the drive as he didn't want William or Anne to be woken by a scrunching noise on the gravel. He had it all planned now. There was a spare key to the kitchen door kept under a box in the yard. In the past, Baines or one of the other servants had always locked and bolted the door from the inside at night, but for a year now Albert had seen Mrs Crabbe fishing a key out in the morning to unlock it. He'd go in that way, set the fire, and then relock the back door and go back to the gatehouse. He could watch the fire from there, and only run to attempt putting it out once it had really got going.

'A stiff wind tonight too,' he said aloud gleefully, turning his coat collar up. 'That will help spread it.'

Chapter Eighteen

Matt Renton hesitated by the gatehouse of Briargate. He had spent the evening with a farmer friend at Chelwood, and as it was now well after midnight, and very cold and windy, he was anxious to get home quickly. Going up Briargate drive and skirting around the back of the big house was a shortcut, while the other way through Lord's Wood was much longer and treacherous in the dark; he'd come that way earlier and got plastered in mud.

His indecision was because of Albert. If he spotted Matt, he was likely to take a pot shot at him, using the excuse that he thought he was an intruder. But as the gatehouse was in darkness he surmised Albert was fast asleep and therefore he'd be safe enough.

Matt was thirty-seven now. His hair was growing thin and grey, his face very weatherbeaten, but he was still as strong and lithe as he had been fourteen years ago when he married Amy. Life had treated him pretty well. He'd managed to hold his head above water through several bad harvests, and over the last three years he'd done well enough to put a bit of money away. He counted himself blessed that he had four healthy children and the best wife a man could wish for.

His younger brothers, Joe and Henry, had slunk back to the farm three years ago with their tails between their legs. London had not been good to them. They were thin, hungry and filthy, without a penny to their name. Matt acted cool with them, reading them the riot act before agreeing to let them stay, but in his heart he was overjoyed to have them home. And the boys had kept their promise to him, working hard and keeping out of mischief, and they both had sweethearts now, steady girls who would make good wives.

But Joe and Henry always reminded Matt of Hope for they'd been inseparable when they were all small. It seemed incredible to him that she'd kept her silence about where she was for six whole years. Sometimes he thought Albert must have killed her after all, or that she'd been carrying a child when she ran away and perhaps even died having it. But mostly he was concerned she'd got herself into such bad trouble she was afraid to come back.

Nell still believed Albert had killed her, but that didn't stop her hoping for a miracle. Each time she came back to the farm the first thing she asked was if there was any news. Rufus was the same. Going off to that school for young gentlemen and then going away to university hadn't stopped him caring about her. The minute he got back to Briargate he rushed down to the farm. Matt wished more than anything that one day he'd have something good to tell them both.

Matt was about ten feet from the stable yard, just about to go behind the wall to the stile and the footpath to the village, when he heard something.

It wasn't a loud noise, just a clicking sound which might have been the wind moving something, but it could have been a key turning in a lock, so he dived out of sight behind the stable wall.

Straining his ears, he waited. The wind had become quite fierce and he could hear nothing above it, but a sixth sense told him someone was there. He was right; he heard a muffled cough, and then suddenly there was Albert.

Matt knew little about the routine at Briargate, but he couldn't imagine any reason why a gardener would be in the house this late at night, unless of course he was bedding Lady Harvey.

That was improbable. Rufus claimed his mother hated the man, and in any case Sir William was always there these days – rumour had it he only rarely went out. But even stranger was how Albert was behaving. Instead of just walking down the drive he was climbing over the railings.

Matt pressed himself further against the wall and watched, wondering where on earth the man was going. But stranger still, Albert remained close to the railings, going back in the direction of the gatehouse. What's more, he kept turning to look back over his shoulder at the big house.

'He's creeping on the grass so he won't be heard!' Matt muttered to himself. 'I bet he's been up to no good.'

Aware that if he was seen lurking around the house, he might be blamed for whatever Albert had done, Matt slunk away himself, over the stile and down the paddock that flanked the hedged garden of the house, towards the footpath that led across fields to Woolard.

As he got right to the bottom of the paddock and went to climb the stile, he turned slightly. To his surprise there was a faint orange glow in one of the ground-floor windows at Briargate.

His first thought was that someone might have heard something and lit a lamp to go down and investigate. But lamplight was yellow, and surely one lamp wouldn't be that bright.

All at once he realized what it was. 'Fire!' he gasped. 'So that's what he was doing there!'

For a second he was undecided what to do. The first rule in the case of a fire was to raise the alarm, but Lady Harvey, Sir William and Mr Baines were in there, and by the time he raised men in Woolard, then got back to the house, all three of them could be burned to death.

Throwing off his heavy coat, Matt raced back up the paddock. He could smell the fire now, so he didn't bother with the stile by the stables, but forced his way through the hedge into the garden.

He had only been inside Briargate once, the day he came to see Sir William after Nell left, but he remembered the drawing room he'd been shown into ran from the front to the back of the house, with glass doors at the back opening on to the garden.

A piercing scream from upstairs made him run faster. Once at the glass doors he could see inside the room plain as day for it was lit up by the glow of flames at the front of the house. Picking up some kind of heavy flowerpot on the terrace, he smashed the glass doors in, ran across the room and cautiously opened the door into the hall.

It was like opening an oven door. He was blasted by heat and the smoke made his eyes sting. The fire had clearly started in the room next to the front door, and that was an inferno; flames were already licking across the rug on the hall floor towards the stairs.

Cracking, popping and hissing sounds accompanied the roaring of the fire as it devoured everything in its path. Shutting the drawing-room door behind him, Matt took a deep breath and dodging the flames on the floor, ran for the stairs.

Lady Harvey was still screaming as he turned on to the landing. She was wearing a long white nightgown and wringing her hands, clearly too terrified by the flames below to attempt going down.

'It's me, Matt Renton, m'lady,' he said firmly, aware that she was so deeply shocked she wouldn't know him. 'I'll get you out. But first show me where Sir William and Mr Baines are.'

'I can't wake William,' she sobbed. 'I tried just now. He takes drops at night to sleep and he's too heavy to move.'

'Is there any water up here?' Matt asked, wishing he knew his way around.

'Only jugs on the washstands,' she cried. 'We're all going to die, aren't we?'

'Not if I can help it. Now, calm down and show me where Sir William is.'

The room she led him to was right above the seat of the fire below, and full of smoke. Coughing and spluttering, Matt groped his way to the bed, grabbed Sir William like a sack of potatoes, threw the cold water from the jug over his face and then hauled him out on to the landing floor.

'Wake up, sir!' he yelled, slapping at his face. 'There's a fire, you must wake up and get out!'

There was no immediate response, but the roaring sound of the fire below was growing louder by the second. 'Wake him up,' he ordered Lady Harvey, who was bent over her husband, coughing hard. 'I'll get Baines. Where is he?'

'Upstairs,' she said.

Matt ran back to the staircase, only to find it didn't go up a further floor. The flames were at the bottom of it now; they couldn't get down that way.

By the time he'd got back to Lady Harvey and learned from her that there was another staircase and where it was, she was so distraught at not being able to wake her husband that Matt had to lift her bodily out through the door to the back staircase, and leave her there while he ran up to find Baines.

The old man was already trying to put his breeches on, coughing and spluttering in the smoke. Matt heaved him over his shoulder and staggered down the stairs to where he'd left Lady Harvey. But she had disappeared, and assuming she'd gone down the stairs he continued too. He found himself beyond the kitchen in what looked like the servants' hall Nell used to speak of, but there was no sign of Lady Harvey. He kicked open the door on to the stable yard and dumped Baines outside, telling him to get right away from the house.

As he came back through the backstairs door to the bedrooms, the other end of the landing was ablaze, and Lady Harvey was there, collapsed on top of her husband's prone body. Matt didn't know if she'd been overcome by the smoke, or was so frightened that she had fainted.

Matt scooped her up in his arms and carried her down to safety, depositing her on the far side of the stable yard where Baines was slumped, coughing his lungs up.

Smoke was billowing out all over the house now, even under the door Matt had just come through. He could hear crashing sounds inside and the roaring of the flames. Taking the kerchief from his neck, he dipped it in a butt of water by the stables, and tying it over his nose and mouth, went back in to get Sir William.

He could feel the heat from the flames even through the door to the landing, and he opened it carefully just an inch or two to look. He only kept it open for a second, but it was long enough to see he was too late to save Sir William. He was already engulfed by the flames.

The smell of burning flesh and hair made Matt retch. He knew Sir William must be dead already and he'd be killed too if he didn't get out right now. So he shut the door and fled back downstairs.

'Joe, ride into Keynsham and get the constable!' Matt yelled as he came staggering into his farmhouse, supporting Lady Harvey with one arm and Baines with the other. 'Henry, you ride for the doctor!'

The two brothers came tumbling out of the room beside

the kitchen bleary-eyed, pulling on their clothes. 'What's happened?' Henry asked, looking at Lady Harvey in her mud-splattered nightgown as if she were a ghost.

'Albert set fire to Briargate,' Matt said tersely. 'Sir William is dead and these two are lucky to be alive. I must go and round up some men to try to save the house.'

Amy appeared on the stairs in her nightgown. 'Be careful, Matt,' she said, and then coming on down the stairs she went straight into the boys' room, returning with two blankets.

'You are safe now,' she said, wrapping the blankets around Baines and Lady Harvey and nudging them on to chairs. They were silent and motionless as statues and looked too deeply shocked even to know where they were. 'Just give me a minute to stir up the stove and I'll see to you.'

Anne lay in the hard, narrow bed staring at the low, stained ceiling, thinking that this was like one of the terrible nightmares she used to have as a child. She remembered how she used to force herself to wake up, sometimes even to walk around the bedroom, but the moment she got back into bed and closed her eyes again, it would come back.

This nightmare didn't relent for even a moment though. She could still hear the crackling of the flames, feel the heat, smell the burning, and picture William lying there on the landing in his nightshirt.

It was her fault he had died. If only she'd got a grip on herself when Matt arrived to save them! She could have shown him where the backstairs were straight away, and the pair of them could easily have dragged William to safety.

But then, if she hadn't goaded William into getting tough, Albert would have had no need to resort to burning Briargate down. What kind of fool was she that it never occurred to her he would take some form of revenge?

She had been here three days now, lying in this hard little

bed with its scratchy sheets, so full of remorse and sorrow that she was barely aware whether it was night or day. Just the other side of the door Amy and her four children were carrying on with their normal life. From time to time she heard ordinary family sounds, laughter, chatter and arguing. She could smell food being cooked, heard dishes being washed, the stove being raked, chairs scraping on the stone floor. They were familiar enough sounds and smells, yet they seemed alien, as though she'd been transported to a foreign land where everything, language, customs and behaviour, was strange and frightening.

She had never met Amy, Matt's wife, before the night Matt had brought her here, and she couldn't fault the kindness the woman had shown her. She'd washed her as though she was one of her own children, bandaged up her feet because they'd been torn to ribbons walking through the woods to get here, even lent her one of her own nightdresses, yet Anne hadn't even been able to thank her, much less explain how she felt, or even ask why she could still smell smoke.

It was so strange. The soap Amy had used on her was strong enough to banish any lingering smells on her skin and her nightgown was clean. If she felt no pain from her cut feet, why should she still smell smoke?

Yet even in her almost trancelike state she was very aware of how remarkable Matt had been. He'd rescued her and Baines from Briargate, and got them both back here to safety, no mean feat when they were hardly able to walk. He'd then summoned men from the village and gone back to Briargate to try to save it.

Sadly, that was a lost cause. Amy had explained that with only buckets of water and the strong wind whipping the flames, their efforts were wasted. She said the house was razed to the ground, that by morning even the walls had caved in.

Constables were out searching for Albert. It was thought

he might have seen Matt coming out of the burning house with Baines and Lady Harvey and run off in a panic. Matt said that the whole county had been alerted now and he didn't think it would be long before he was caught.

Anne wasn't sure she even wanted him caught. It wouldn't bring back William or rebuild Briargate, but it would give Albert an opportunity to expose both her and William at his trial. It was bad enough to deal with widowhood, the loss of her home and all her worldly goods – she didn't need scandal too.

She smarted with shame as she remembered how she'd often wished for William's death in the past, just so she could be with Angus! How could she have been so wicked?

But she'd got her punishment now. In truth, she would rather have died in the fire with William than have to face Rufus. Amy and Matt might believe there was nothing more to this than Albert taking revenge because he'd been dismissed. But Rufus was sharp-witted and perceptive, he'd know something else lay behind it, and he'd probe, poke and ask questions until he got the right answers.

A tap on the door made Anne look round. 'Come in,' she said wearily, expecting that it was Amy again with yet more food she couldn't eat.

The door opened, and out of politeness Anne tried to force a grateful smile. But it wasn't Amy in the doorway, it was Nell.

Anne gasped involuntarily, not only because she hadn't expected Nell to call, not after six years of estrangement, but because she looked like a well-to-do housewife, not a servant. She was thinner than Anne remembered and far more attractive; her midnight-blue dress and matching bonnet gave her somewhat sallow face a real glow, and the hair visible beneath her bonnet was still raven-black.

'I'm sorry if I startled you, m'lady, but I had to come.'
Nell's voice quivered with nervousness. 'I know I've always
said how wicked Albert is, but I didn't think he'd ever hurt
you and Sir William. I'm so very sorry, m'lady.'

Anne began to cry, not so much because of her former
maid's words but for all the memories her face brought
back. 'You don't need to apologize for Albert,' she sobbed.
'If we'd taken more notice of what you'd said about him
years ago, this wouldn't have happened.'

'There, there.' Nell was by her side immediately, stroking
Anne's forehead comfortingly, just the way she always used
to. 'Don't you blame yourself now, we've got to get you
well again.'

'I'm not sick, Nell,' Anne said, clutching her hand in both
of hers and pressing it to her lips. 'At least, not in body,
only in the heart. I'm so glad you came.'

Anne knew Nell to be ten years younger than herself,
which would make her thirty-eight now, but it was something of a shock to see her looking far younger than she
ever had while she was at Briargate. An uncharitable thought
sprang into her mind that this could be because she'd
become Angus's mistress.

'You've had a terrible shock,' Nell said, sitting beside her
on the narrow bed. 'I know what that does to a body. But
we must get you somewhere more fitting for a lady of
quality. You'll recover quicker where you feel more at home.'

Anne felt shamed that she'd allowed herself to jump to
the wrong conclusion. Sweet, loyal Nell had in fact come to
take her to Angus's house!

'Dear Nell,' she sighed. 'You always did have the ability
to instinctively know what I wanted or needed. But I really
don't deserve your understanding.'

'I slept in this very room myself for a time and I know
how noisy it can be,' Nell said with a fond smile. 'You'll get

some peace at Wick Farm. Mrs Warren is getting a room prepared for you. She sent some clothes for you too; she said to tell you that you are more than welcome.'

Anne felt as though a rug had been pulled from beneath her feet. 'How kind of her,' she managed to say, stifling her disappointment. The Warrens had been good neighbours for her entire married life, but they weren't close friends, and Anne had been quite curt with Mrs Warren when she last visited some months ago. 'I wonder that she can be bothered with me when I haven't seen her for so long.'

'Real friends always rally round in emergencies. Besides, as I'm sure you already know, Mrs Warren has been nursing Mr Baines too, and has made him very comfortable. But sadly I don't think he'll be with us for much longer, he's sinking fast.'

All at once Anne realized that Nell had been to Wick Farm to see Baines. Undoubtedly she felt it was inappropriate that the mistress of Briargate should be nursed in spartan conditions at her brother's farm while her butler lay in luxury. Anne guessed she had raised this matter and given Mrs Warren no option but to extend an invitation to her too.

Anne didn't want to go anywhere on sufferance, and the suspicion that Nell might be more than a housekeeper to Angus was back in the forefront of her mind.

'Poor Baines,' she said, aware she had a position to maintain at all costs, and in any case she was genuinely fond of the old man. 'He shouldn't have had to end his days this way.'

'He'll pass on happily if he can see you first,' Nell said crisply, going over to the doorway to a bag she'd left there, and drawing out a black dress and some crisp white petticoats. 'Mrs Warren sent these for you. Now, up you get and I'll help you dress.'

Anne shuddered at wearing clothes that weren't her own, yet at the same time there was something very soothing about having Nell dressing her again. She'd thought of everything: a chemise, stays, petticoats, even a pair of padded slippers large enough to go over the bandages on her feet. Once she was dressed, Nell turned her attention to her hair, brushing it carefully and fixing it in a neat chignon at the nape of her neck.

'That's better,' she said, tweaking the ruffle around the neckline of the dress. 'You look like my lady again.'

Anne felt that remark held real affection, and although it didn't exactly allay her niggling suspicions, she felt it would be expedient to give Nell a long overdue apology. 'I'm so sorry, Nell,' she blurted out. 'You deserved so much better than the way I treated you. Tell me, is the Captain a good master?'

Nell half-smiled. 'The very best! But I fear he'll be off again soon with his soldiering, there seems to be trouble brewing with Russia.'

'Surely our troops won't have to go to that?' Anne said. William had mentioned something about the Turks and Russians having a dispute just a few days ago, but it hadn't sounded serious.

'It seems to me that any trouble anywhere in the world calls for our army,' Nell said. 'But come now, the Warrens' coachman is waiting. Amy and Matt will come along to visit you in a day or two.'

'How was she?' Angus asked the moment Nell came through the door late that same afternoon. Nell got the impression he'd been pacing up and down the hall waiting for her return.

The passing years had been kind to Angus. At forty-seven he was still as lean, straightbacked and handsome as he had been when Nell first met him. Even a touch of grey hair at his temples only served to make him look more distinguished.

'She looks fragile and deeply shocked,' Nell replied as she took off her bonnet. 'But she's unhurt apart from the sore feet she got walking to Matt's without any shoes.'

'Come in by the fire and have a glass of wine with me,' Angus said, taking her cape and hanging it up with her bonnet. 'Did you persuade Mrs Warren to take her in?'

Nell nodded. 'She sorted out some clothes for her too. She was very kind, but then she is a good woman.'

'And Baines? How is he?'

Nell shrugged. 'Poorly. But he was very pleased to see me. Maybe he will get better with complete rest and good food. I don't think he has had either in the last few years. But I can't help but hope he'll just slip away quietly in his sleep – all that lies ahead for old servants is the workhouse.'

Angus took her arm, drew her over to a chair by the fire and poured her a glass of wine. 'You are not going to end your days in the workhouse,' he said reprovingly.

Nell pursed her lips. 'I hope not, but then I expect Baines imagined he'd see his days out in Briargate. It doesn't seem possible that it's gone. I looked across the fields from Woolard – you used to be able to see the house from there – and it looked right eerie with it gone.'

'And how was Lady Harvey with you?' he asked.

'Uppity as always,' Nell said, pulling a face. 'She did apologize to me for the past, but I don't think she liked to see me so . . .' She broke off, not knowing how to explain what she meant.

'Well cared for?' Angus prompted.

Nell nodded. 'She looked at me with great suspicion. But perhaps I should have worn something older and more suitable for my station.'

Angus chuckled. 'You are my housekeeper, Nell, your clothes reflect your position. I hope you told her I have a maid now too, and that thanks to you I have a home I am proud to entertain in.'

Nell blushed. The Captain was always so appreciative of all she did for him, and it made him a joy to work for. In her first two years here she had undertaken everything that needed doing to turn a ramshackle place into a home suitable for a gentleman. She had whitewashed walls, scrubbed floors, made curtains, dug and planted out the garden, and found tradesmen to do the tasks which were beyond her. She hadn't expected praise, it was reward enough to have a position again, and the hard work prevented her from brooding too long on Hope.

But when the Captain came home from his soldiering he missed nothing. He would smile and pat her cheek when he saw the rows of her preserves in the pantry; he would chuckle as he got into bed on a cold night to find a hot brick already in there warming it. He claimed meals she cooked were as good as banquets he'd attended in the officers' mess, and that no one had ever washed, pressed and mended his clothes so well. He said that all his friends envied him for having such an accomplished housekeeper and that they would poach her from him if they could.

Nell pretended she believed this to be empty flattery, but she knew he was sincere, and that knowledge had helped her confidence enormously. She'd never had a chance before to show what she could do as her whole life had been spent taking orders, and it was a thrill to be trusted to make decisions, to plan menus, to buy any equipment or ingredients she needed. Even in her own home, Albert wouldn't so much as allow her to rearrange the furniture without his permission. She'd got into the way of thinking that she was dull-witted, and that her opinions were of no value to anyone.

*

'Now, tell me all you learned about the fire,' the Captain asked earnestly, clearly desperate for information. 'Was it all as we'd been told?'

They had got the news of the tragedy at third hand. Nell had been in the shop at Keynsham when she overheard two women gossiping about a fire. It was only when she heard one of them mention a farmer from Woolard that she really took notice, and interrupted them to ask which farm had caught fire.

It transpired that the older of the two women was the doctor's cook, and she explained that one of the Renton lads had called early that morning to fetch the doctor. She said that the fire was at Briargate and that Sir William Harvey had died in it, but that was the extent of her knowledge.

Nell had been so horrified she ran straight home without buying the groceries she'd gone for. She sobbed out the story to the Captain and he immediately rode down to Compton Dando to find out more. It was a terrible shock to hear that Albert had set the fire and the police were searching for him, but Nell took some little pride in hearing that Matt had bravely rescued Baines and Lady Harvey.

Nell was dead set on going straight to the farm, but Angus wouldn't let her. He said she must wait and let Lady Harvey recover a little. He pointed out that some people might take a too speedy arrival as evidence she was pleased to be proved right about Albert.

'If Matt hadn't seen Albert leaving Briargate just before it went up, it would have looked like an accident,' Nell explained, for Amy had related everything she knew. 'In the study where it started they found the remains of an oil lamp on the floor. Lady Harvey might have forgotten to put it out when she went to bed, and it could have toppled over in a draught. But the policeman who was investigating it thinks Albert put a burning ember on the hearthrug, then put the lamp on the floor so the oil would run out and catch fire. Maybe he even scattered the oil around too so it would catch books and papers.'

Angus tutted. 'But what on earth made him do such a thing? The men in the village said it didn't make sense to burn the place down as he'd lose his job.'

'It seems Sir William and Lady Harvey had told him that morning that he'd got to leave,' Nell said. 'He would have been very angry about that; he loved the garden and thought of it as his.'

Even after everything Albert had done to her and however much she hated him, she could still put herself in his shoes. He *had* laboured on that garden, turned it into a thing of beauty, and no doubt he had expected he would end his days taking care of it.

'What reason did she give for dismissing him?' Angus frowned. 'He ran the place by all accounts.'

'She said they couldn't bear him around any more,' Nell said with a shrug. 'She said Albert had been intimidating them both for years and they'd had enough.'

Nell hadn't had the heart to question Lady Harvey further for she'd started sobbing her heart out and saying all kinds of foolishness, like it was God's vengeance for her adultery. She kept apologizing to Nell too, and saying that she hadn't really taken it in about Hope being her child until it was too late.

'Maybe they could no longer afford to keep him on,' Angus said thoughtfully. 'It's no secret they were in strained circumstances. But what of Rufus? Has he been sent for?'

'Amy said that Reverend Gosling wrote to him to break the news,' Nell said. 'He also sent word to Lady Harvey's sisters. I expect they will come within a day or two.'

'How old is Rufus now?'

'Only nineteen.' Nell's eyes filled with tears. 'The poor boy! What will become of him?'

'As I understood it, he has money in trust for him from his maternal grandfather,' Angus said evenly. 'And by all accounts he is a level headed, intelligent young man, so he'll be all right, though it will be a terrible blow losing his father. Did your brother say when the funeral will be?'

Nell shook her head.

'I suppose that will be arranged when Rufus gets here,' Angus said. 'Meanwhile, let's hope they catch Albert. He'll be hanged for this, Nell, and that will at least set you free to marry again.'

'Sir!' Nell gasped in horrified surprise.

Angus half-smiled. 'Is that such a terrible thought? You are a comely woman, Nell, with the kinds of skills any man would wish for in a wife. You are still young enough to bear a child too.'

'I couldn't marry again,' she answered indignantly. 'I wouldn't want to be under any man's thumb.'

'Ah, Nell,' he sighed. 'You and I have both been bruised by love, but maybe we should both put it behind us and try again?'

'You should,' she said stoutly. 'Remember Lady Harvey is now free!'

Even as she made that remark she regretted it, for to speak of such a thing before Sir William was even in his grave was very disrespectful.

But to her surprise Angus did not pull her up for it, all he did was look at her with sad eyes. 'I do not feel that way any longer,' he said. 'My love faded when she treated you so badly. All I feel for her now is sympathy, as you would for any old friend.'

So many times over the years, Nell had been sorely tempted to tell him that Hope was his child. It would have soothed her grief if she could share the secret; he might even have been persuaded to order an investigation into what happened to her. But she'd refrained from the temptation purely because of the promise she'd given Lady Harvey.

She was tempted again now for she couldn't believe Angus had stopped loving Lady Harvey. He was a very eligible bachelor; gentry with unmarried female relatives in both Bath and Bristol were always inviting him to parties and dinners. He would often laughingly tell her about ladies who'd made it obvious they hoped he'd become their beau, but though he was gallant, flirtatious and often genuinely liked these ladies, he formed no romantic attachments with any of them.

Once, when he'd had too much to drink, he'd revealed how deeply he'd loved Anne. He said it had torn him apart knowing she was another man's wife. Before Rufus was born he had asked her to run away to America with him. She had turned him down, and he felt it was because she loved her title too much, and that she couldn't face a life without servants, money and fine clothes.

Nell couldn't agree with that entirely. It would take exceptional courage for a woman of quality to face the condemnation of leaving her husband for another man. And Sir William wasn't a cruel man like Albert; Anne had loved him too. Nell had seen the depth of that love today for Anne had sobbed as she related how she tried to wake her husband up while Matt was getting Baines out.

'The fault was all mine,' she had cried. 'If I'd only told Matt about the back staircase straight away, or got him to pull William out while I went to get Baines! I was pathetic, Nell; I just panicked and acted like a frightened child. Now I've lost my dearest friend.'

*

'Have you considered that when Albert is caught, Hope might come back?' Angus said, breaking into Nell's reverie.

Nell's head jerked up; suddenly she was alert again. 'Why would she?'

Angus shrugged. 'As I've always maintained, it's far more likely that he forced her to leave Briargate than that he killed her. Once he is locked up he can't hurt her or you.'

Nell's eyes began to shine with hope. 'I hadn't thought that way. But she might be so far away she won't hear of this!'

'Murder of an aristocrat is newsworthy,' Angus said. 'The story made *The Times* today, even pushing news of the impending war against Russia from the front page. Hope is likely to hear of it, wherever she is.'

Chapter Nineteen

'We'll be frozen solid if we stay out on deck much longer,' Bennett reminded Hope.

'But doctor, it's healthier up here than down below,' she said with a grin. 'Or do you want to have your wicked way with me again?' She didn't really want to go down to their tiny cabin, not yet. The wind and sea spray were so exhilarating and the vastness of the sea astounded her. It was also blissful to be away from people for a while.

Of course she wasn't including Bennett in that, she thought she could spend every hour of every day with him without feeling irritated or bored. But then he had a wonderful talent for sensing when she wanted to be quiet, or if she was in the mood for noise and chatter. Hope thought he was probably the most perfect husband in the whole world.

At times she had despaired of them ever getting married, for it was four years since her eighteenth birthday when he'd bought her the engagement ring. He'd told her that day that he was thinking about becoming a regimental doctor, but she hadn't taken it very seriously. Yet he had been serious – just six months later he joined the illustrious Rifle Brigade as an assistant surgeon, and she thought she might lose him then for his regiment kept moving – Winchester, Canada and finally off to South Africa for the Kaffir war – making it impossible to see him.

Hope moved to Bristol's new General Hospital in Guinea

Street to nurse there. Bennett wrote to her constantly, funny, warm letters which made her love for him grow even stronger. But the post was slow and unreliable, especially once he was in South Africa, so sometimes months went past without one letter, then six or seven might arrive all at once.

There had been some very low points over the last four years. The loneliness was almost crippling at times, particularly when Bennett went to Canada and she moved to the General Hospital where she knew no one.

Back at St Peter's, she'd had the company of the young mothers in her ward, and some of these had become good enough friends for her to visit them in their homes on her day off. But at the General Hospital she was in the male surgical ward, and the ward sister there was a dragon of a woman who belittled Hope constantly, watched her like a hawk for any kind of familiarity with the patients, and made each day seem endless.

It was good to be in a better hospital, but Hope found herself to be an anomaly there. She had far superior nursing skills and medical knowledge to the ladies who worked charitably as volunteer nurses, but she wasn't of their class. And the nurses from her own background appeared to resent her because she wasn't quite one of them either. Missing Bennett, afraid that the day would never come when she'd be his wife, and frustrated that the vast majority of people saw nursing as a lowly profession, there wasn't much to cheer her. Often she felt she was trapped on a kind of treadmill going nowhere.

But in January 1854 Bennett had come back to England, insisting they get married as soon as they could arrange it.

He had changed a great deal during his time in South Africa. Aside from his bronzed face, sun-bleached hair and more muscular body from regular riding, he was also much more assertive, confident and worldly. He'd learned a lot from older regimental doctors and had become used to performing quite complicated surgery under primitive conditions, and to running his own field hospital. Living and working in an all-male environment had toughened him up, and he was no longer concerned what his uncle's opinion might be on how he should live his life.

Hope had seen Dr Cunningham many times while Bennett was away, both at St Peter's and then in the General. He had been very frosty at first as he clearly blamed her for his nephew leaving his practice. But maybe Alice had been working on him, for he gradually began to soften about a year later, and he would stop to talk when he saw her.

Yet it was only last year that he had finally admitted he thought she was a fine nurse, and that Bennett could do a lot worse than marry her. Hope might have been offended by that remark, but she often called to see Alice on her day off, who told her the old doctor spoke about her in glowing terms. Hope sensed that he would still have preferred his nephew to be married to someone who would enhance his career, but if he did think that, he didn't voice it. He even suggested that she should leave the General immediately and come to live at Harley Place until the wedding as there were so many preparations to be made.

They were married just a stone's throw from Harley Place, at Christchurch, in early February, a bitterly cold day with snow threatening. Alice had made Hope a wedding outfit, a deep pink wool dress with a fashionable bustle, and a matching hooded cape trimmed with fur.

There were only a few guests: Alice and her sister Violet, Dr Cunningham and a few old friends of Bennett's, including Mary Carpenter. Hope would have given anything to have had her brothers and sisters there too on such an important day, but as it simply wasn't possible she tried hard not to think of them.

As they set off to Lyme Regis for their honeymoon, Bennett said he thought that as soon as possible they should go and visit Ruth and her husband in Bath. He believed that if Hope explained everything to them, they could decide how to let the rest of the family know so that Albert couldn't take it out on Nell.

Dr Cunningham had lent them his carriage to take them to Lyme Regis, and with a hot brick beneath her feet, a warm rug snuggled round her, and her husband beside her, Hope was so happy that she didn't want to think of anything serious. She'd been away for seven years now, and a few more weeks wouldn't make any difference to her family problems.

Hope knew that whatever great age she lived to, she would never forget her wedding night. Their room in a guest house overlooking the sea had been so warm and inviting. There was a roaring fire, thick brocade curtains shutting out the cold night air, a four-poster bed, and a candle lit and a round table laid ready for their supper.

They had drunk brandy on the way to keep warm, and by the time they'd drunk a bottle of wine with supper Hope was very tipsy. She remembered how Bennett had undressed her, fumbling hopelessly with the laces on her stays, and how she'd been every bit as eager as him to make love.

He kissed the red marks on her body from her tight stays and murmured that they weren't to be put on again for the whole of their honeymoon. He told her too that while he was in South Africa he used to dream about her naked, but that she was a hundred times more beautiful then he'd expected.

She had thought she'd be frightened and embarrassed, and she was convinced it was going to hurt, but from the moment he lifted her up in his arms and laid her on the bed, eagerly jumping in beside her, all those thoughts vanished. He was too tender and gentle to hurt her, and he explored her with such obvious delight that she found it thrilling rather than embarrassing. She was rather surprised at herself for being so wanton, arching herself against him, begging for more, but as this appeared to increase his passion she didn't attempt to curb her own and became completely abandoned.

She recalled how she woke before Bennett in the morning, and for a moment didn't know where she was. Later, she was to tell Bennett it was like dying and waking up in heaven: the soft warm bed, the peace of the house, and the sound of waves crashing on to the shore below the windows.

What she didn't tell him though was how she lay watching him sleep. She had never seen him asleep before, and his features which often looked so stern had become so much softer and boyish.

The hot sun in South Africa had given him little crow's feet around his eyes, which gave the impression he was smiling. He had shaved off his moustache for the wedding, and his lips, which had been partially concealed before, were full, beautifully shaped, and so very kissable.

Until that moment she'd had nothing but hatred for Albert, but it suddenly struck her that but for his cruelty, she would never have met Bennett.

Time had not erased the hideousness of that period of her life. The hunger, squalor and desperation she felt then would never leave her. She could still picture Gussie and Betsy in the throes of that terrible disease, and the relief she'd felt when Bennett had arrived to help her.

She had been so naive then that she hadn't realized just how remarkable it was that a doctor had turned up. It was of course Mary Carpenter's intervention that had brought it about, but even so, once at St Peter's she soon discovered that even that particular benefactor of the poor could not have induced any other doctor to go into Lewins Mead. Later, she'd been told that only a handful of doctors in Bristol had used their skills to help victims of the cholera epidemic. Many were so frightened of catching it themselves that they'd shamelessly left the city with their wives and children, and did not return until it was all over.

Bennett didn't look like a hero, in truth his mild manner and slender build would suggest that he was a clerk or an assistant in a bookshop. But he had hidden depths; his was the quiet kind of courage, doing what he knew to be right, using his medical skills not to advance himself, but for the good of mankind. He was also so loving, kind and fun to be with, and, now she had discovered, such a good lover. She thought that if she was ever to see Albert again she would tell him she was grateful to him for packing her off to meet such a wonderful man.

That morning as she lay there admiring her brand-new husband, she was also excited and curious about the life they would have together. After a week's honeymoon they would be going to live at the barracks in Winchester and she'd be an army wife.

Alice had overseen her wardrobe, and to Hope it seemed ridiculously extravagant. Four new day dresses, two evening gowns, shoes, heaps of petticoats and other underwear, bonnets and a thick winter cloak, all packed into a shiny new trunk. But Alice, aided and abetted by Bennett, insisted it was very important that she project the right image. Not quite so grand as the other officers' wives of course, for although Bennett was technically an officer, being non-combatant he was a lesser being, but she had to be distinct from the other ranks' wives. And as she would have a servant at Winchester, she'd have to learn to behave as if this was something she was used to.

Hope had laughed at that. She couldn't possibly imagine ordering someone to wash her clothes, cook a meal or clean up after her. But Alice had reprimanded her and reminded her that the servant would be a soldier's wife, and if she didn't learn to be firm, the chances were the woman would take advantage of her, and Hope would become a laughing stock.

Hope had already got the idea that most soldiers' wives were like Betsy, colourful, noisy and a bit wild, but then Betsy had always been proud that Hope was educated and more ladylike than she was. Would she and Gussie have been horrified at her becoming a nurse? She could almost see Betsy shaking her head in bewilderment and claiming her friend wasn't right in the head!

But they would certainly be overjoyed that she'd married Bennett. Betsy would give her that knowing look she'd had and tell her she wasn't a girl any more but a real woman.

In the days that followed, Hope felt she really had become a grown woman. She felt confident in her lovely new clothes, and the genteel and demure manner appropriate for a doctor's wife seemed to come easily to her. Yet it was something of a shock to find she could be so lusty. Even as they were eating a meal in a restaurant or braving the high winds along the seafront, she could think of little else but lovemaking. Once out of sight of passers-by she kept making Bennett kiss her, pressing herself up against him wantonly. One day on a walk along the clifftop, she took his hand and put it up her skirt. If Bennett had taken her there and then on the grass, she would have been delighted. As it was, they could hardly wait to get back to their room and devour each other.

*

'Do you think all married couples are like this?' she asked Bennett on the last night of their honeymoon. In the morning they were due to go back to Winchester, and they were reluctant to go to sleep, as if they thought they would never get a chance to make love again.

'I suppose some must be,' he said with a wide grin. 'But I don't think many of the officers I know are so lucky. Their wives look like they'd avoid it at all costs.'

'Well, maybe the officers aren't very good at loving,' she said, sitting astride Bennett and putting his hand on her breasts. 'Maybe they all do it like that ship's captain that Betsy went with. It put her off!'

Bennett laughed. Throughout the week, Hope had taken a great deal of pleasure in relating many bawdy little stories told to her by patients, women she'd known in Lewins Mead and by Betsy. It gave her a thrill being able to share such things with a man. Bennett enjoyed them too, and in turn told her some from men he knew. 'But I don't want you giving out instructions on such things in Winchester,' he said with mock severity. 'A great many of the army wives are very prim, and I don't want them gossiping about you.'

'Then we'd better hope we don't get given a bed with squeaky springs,' she said, leaning forward and covering his face with kisses. 'Because, my darling husband, I intend to have my wicked way with you every night!'

Hope reminded Bennett of that remark as they stood by the ship's rail looking out to sea. She had been appalled to see their bunk beds were so tiny, though she had no intention of sleeping in one alone. 'Do you think we'll even get a bed where we're going?' she asked. 'I heard someone say we'll be sleeping in tents!'

'That might well be true,' he replied. 'I saw a great many being loaded, and I took the precaution of packing two camp beds. But then this whole campaign is a rum do – no one, not even the COs, seem to know exactly where we're bound. I've heard Malta, and Constantinople, but what we'll do when we get there is anyone's guess.'

For months now the newspapers had been getting themselves into a stew about the trouble between the Turks and the Russians. As far as Hope could understand, it had all started in Bethlehem, over a church which had been built on the site where Jesus was born. The Catholics and the Russian Orthodox clerics had both laid claim to it, and then the Turks, who had been rowing with Russia for years, joined in.

Even before Bennett came home in January there was talk of England and France supporting Turkey if there was a war. England didn't want Russia gaining control over the Black Sea as it was an important trade route. But overall there was a general opinion that Russia was overdue for a good thrashing, and no one seemed to know or care what it would be for.

During their honeymoon, Bennett had said the Rifle Brigade might very well be sent out East, and him with it. But he certainly hadn't expected it to happen so quickly. They had barely got back to Winchester when he got his orders that his regiment would be sailing from Portsmouth within a few days.

'Do you think there really will be a war?' Hope asked. She was too excited to be worried. Before her honeymoon all she'd known was Bristol, and the only sea she'd ever seen was the Bristol Channel. It seemed incredible that she was now on the steamship *Vulcan*, along with some 800 men under the command of Lieutenant Colonel Lawrence, going down the coast of France and Spain, and then round into the Mediterranean.

'I sincerely hope it can be averted.' Bennett frowned with anxiety. 'It's forty years since Waterloo, and with the Duke of Wellington dead, I don't think the unblooded officers who'll be running this show will have any idea of strategy, or even what it takes to fight a war. The men of the Rifle Brigade are more than competent, crack shots every one, and they've had the Kaffir war to sharpen them up. But with aristocratic buffoons like Lord Cardigan and Lord Lucan—' He broke off abruptly, perhaps feeling it was bad form to denounce cavalry officers.

Hope knew exactly what he was referring to. Lord Cardigan was never out of the newspapers. He was generally thought to be the most arrogant officer in England, and the most stupid. He'd been taken to task for fighting a duel, flogging his men and victimizing other officers, but because of who he was, he'd managed to escape punishment. Lord Lucan was his brother-in-law, a man with so little feeling for humanity that he'd closed down the workhouse in Castlebar in Ireland during the famine to save feeding the poor wretches who had nowhere else to turn. As the two men hated each other too, it didn't bode well for the men who would be serving under them.

'But the men in Winchester were all so wild for a fight,' Hope said, remembering the excitement in the air at the barracks. She was a complete novice to military life, but she'd been thrilled watching a parade of the Rifles. Their dark green uniforms with black ornamentation had been so smart, their well-polished boots and rifle barrels gleaming in the weak sunshine. All in perfect step, marching proudly to the band, they looked formidable.

'Maybe,' Bennett retorted.

'What is it?' she asked, aware that when he pursed his lips the way he was doing now, he had something more on his mind.

'Their wives and children,' he said tersely. 'Did you know, Hope, that no provision is made for them while their husbands are away on campaign? That raggle-tailed bunch that ran after the battalion in Portsmouth, trying to keep up to have one last word or kiss from their men before they embarked, will be destitute in a day or two.'

'But that's terrible!' Hope exclaimed.

Bennett nodded. 'They will have to turn to the parish for sustenance, but as many of those wives are Canadian, they'll even be denied the small comfort they'd get there, for as you know, you can only receive relief from the parish in which you were born.'

'You mean they'll starve?' Hope exclaimed in horror.

'Yes, unless they have relatives to turn to, or decide to sell their bodies. What else is there when you have small children to feed?'

Bennett stopped short, not wishing to tell Hope the truth about what he'd seen when he was called upon the previous night.

He'd known of course that it was customary for the wives who wished to go with their husbands to be picked by ballot the night before the regiment went on active service. Only six wives per company were allowed to go, and any who were mothers were ruled out.

He and Hope were asleep when Corporal Mears banged on their door and told Bennett his services were required. Expecting that it would be nothing more than a few stitches needed after a drunken brawl, he told Hope to go back to sleep and slipped out with the Corporal.

But the Corporal led him to the back of a shed, and by the light of their lamp he saw Colour Sergeant John Wagner slumped on the ground in a pool of blood, his throat cut and a razor still in his hand. When Bennett touched him he found him icy cold: he had been dead for some time.

'He walked out when the ballot was being drawn,' Mears said. 'We knew he was upset his wife and child couldn't go, but we never expected this.'

'But he was a good soldier with fifteen years' service,' Bennett exclaimed in horror.

'Leaving his wife and child unsupported was just too much for him.' Mears shrugged. 'Though heaven knows how he thought this would help.'

'What is it, dearest?' Hope asked, breaking into his reverie.

'Nothing, apart from thinking that this country doesn't treat its defenders too well,' Bennett replied, feeling unable to dampen Hope's excitement at what she thought was going to be a marvellous adventure by telling her what he'd seen the previous night. 'But you must look around the women on board and approach one to be your servant. All of them will be glad of the extra money, but be sure to pick one who is clean and honest.'

The ship bucked and rolled in the heavy seas all the way down the coast of France and through the Bay of Biscay, and many of the company suffered from sea sickness. But Bennett and Hope stayed remarkably well, and it gave Hope a golden opportunity to mingle with the soldiers and their wives who were sick, taking them first arrowroot and then beef tea to rebuild their strength once the sickness had passed.

Queenie Watson was the woman she picked as her servant, but it wasn't her cleanliness or honesty which singled her out, only her spirit. Queenie and her rifleman husband Robbie had hatched a plan in case Queenie wasn't picked in the ballot. Robbie had trained her in drill and she'd spent the last night in the barracks, hair cut short and in full dress uniform, posing as a soldier. She had carried it off well enough to pass muster the following morning and marched with the troops to the ship undetected. It was only once on board that she had been discovered, but fortunately for her Lady Errol, the wife of the Earl of Errol, a Company Commander of the Rifles, was on board. She was being seen off by her two friends, the Marchioness of Stafford and the Duchess of Sutherland. The three ladies had been sympathetic to Queenie's plight and persuaded the Earl of Errol to let her travel with them.

As soon as Hope had heard about this she'd been sure she would like the woman, and she wasn't disappointed. Queenie had red hair, sharp features and a defiant manner. Along with her courage, Hope found her to have a great sense of humour. If she had to be stuck in the company of another woman for long periods, she wanted someone who would at least be entertaining.

Six weeks after leaving England, they arrived at Scutari in Turkey on 7 April. They had spent some time in Malta, then moved on to Gallipoli where they received the news that England and France had declared war on Russia.

They still didn't know where they were ultimately bound for. A new rumour started nearly every day, which could place the action anywhere between Odessa and the Danube. But Hope had already been initiated in some of the hardships that could befall an army wife on a campaign.

In Malta she and Bennett had a room in the barracks, which was only marginally better than the room in Lamb Lane. In Gallipoli it was a tent, sleeping on the hard ground as the camp beds Bennett had brought could not be found. Water had been in short supply, and wood for cooking fires had to be collected and carried long distances to the camp. It was also very hot, and many of the men collapsed.

On the march to Scutari, they were only allowed a

mule to carry their baggage, yet some of the officers had a couple of mules and a horse too. But Hope didn't mind the march, despite the heat. And she wouldn't have complained about anything anyway for Bennett was now afraid he might be ordered to send her back to Malta in the company of some other officers' wives, for the duration of the war.

Hope believed that she had already proved herself useful by nursing some of the men who had fallen sick in Gallipoli and dressing a bad cut on Lady Errol's hand. She hoped that an exception would be made for her but she couldn't count on it.

The first sight of the Turkish barracks which was to become the headquarters of the Guards and Light Divisions was a favourable one. It was a magnificent building, three storeys high, standing in a courtyard with a tower at each corner. Its position on high ground above a landing stage, the fir trees that surrounded it and the turquoise sea so close by were all very attractive.

A group of riflemen went in for a cursory inspection, but came running out only seconds later looking as green as their uniforms.

They claimed it was the worst thing they had ever seen, and as Bennett was aware that many of these men came from places every bit as bad as Lewins Mead, he realized it would be truly hideous.

As the regimental surgeon he was expected to join the full inspection, and on his return he told Hope that the men hadn't exaggerated. It was utterly appalling, the courtyard awash with sewage from the blocked sewers beneath the building, a rotting horse's carcass in the water supply, and the whole building full of every kind of putrefying rubbish, alive with vermin and fleas. There was no question of the Rifle Brigade taking up residence in the building, so a camp was set up far enough away from the barracks so that they couldn't smell it.

Bennett was not himself that evening. He declined any food, didn't smile when Hope pointed out that Lord and Lady Errol's tent was completely transparent with a lamp lit inside, and that the men were strolling by in pretended nonchalance while Lady Errol removed her stays. He didn't even look at her when she reminded him of the time early in their acquaintance when he'd said he wished he had a chance to camp out.

'Tell me what is wrong,' she begged him. 'Is it concern that I'll be sent back?'

'Yes, I am concerned about that,' he said. 'But I'd rather you were back in England with my uncle and Alice than stuck in Malta.'

'But that isn't all of it?'

'No,' he sighed. 'That filthy barn of a place is to become the main hospital for the campaign. The men can clean it, but we have no beds, blankets or medicine, and I fear that the sick and injured will be filling the place long before those back in England see fit to send us the equipment and provisions we need.'

'You think there is going to be a battle soon?' Hope asked. She couldn't help but feel excited; many of the soldiers had confided in her that they couldn't wait for the fighting to begin, and they'd infected her with their enthusiasm.

He shrugged. 'I heard today they are hoping to take Sebastopol in the Crimea.' He drew a rough map of the Black Sea in the dirt to show her where Sebastopol was. 'But it's worrying. I'm only a sawbones, but if I was commanding, the first thing I'd do would be to reconnoitre this place. Few among us can even say where it is, and no one knows how well it is defended. Our men's uniforms are not suited to this warm climate, I do not think we have enough provisions, we have only a fraction of the medical equipment needed, and so far I have seen nothing that even approaches being suitable for use as an ambulance.'

'You worry too much,' Hope said, going over to hug him. 'Lady Errol told me that we are moving on to a place called Varna soon, and that more troops will join us there. I'm sure all the other equipment will arrive there too.'

On 25 May, the Queen's birthday, Lord Raglan, the Commander in Chief, arrived at Scutari to review the troops. He seemed very old to Hope, however noble he looked in his plumed hat and gold braid, and he also had only one arm. She'd heard he had been the aide de camp for the Duke of Wellington at Waterloo, so she supposed he was the right man to be in charge.

Just a few days later, on the 29th, Hope and Bennett were once again on the move, this time on the *Golden Fleece* bound for Varna in Bulgaria. More troops would be joining them there, along with the French army.

No one had told Bennett to send his wife home, and Lady Errol, with whom Hope had struck up a tentative friendship, said if there was any difficulty she would speak to Lord Raglan himself about it.

'Doesn't it look pretty!' Hope exclaimed as they sailed into the Bulgarian port. While it was true the houses along the quay were ramshackle wooden ones, she thought it very picturesque. But as the ship drew closer to shore, a foul smell wafted out to them and Bennett heaved a sigh.

'I will never complain about anything in England again,' he said, bending to whisper in her ear. 'Not the filth in the streets, the workhouses, the beggars, or even the hospitals. And when we get back there, I'll find us a cottage by the sea and only treat rich patients.'

The town was fetid and had a slovenly population of

some 15,000 Greeks, Turks and Bulgarians who appeared not to notice blocked drains and open cesspits. But the Rifle Brigade disembarked, and with the band playing 'Cheer, Boys, Cheer', they quickly marched a short distance out of the town, and made camp above a lake.

In the days that followed Hope sat up on a hill behind the camp and watched a constant stream of troop ships sailing into the harbour and marvelled at all the distinctive regiments. She was particularly entranced by the Highlanders in their tartan kilts, marching to the wail of their bagpipes which was like no sound she'd ever heard before. The infantry in their red coats and white breeches were stunning, but then so were the French in their blue coats. She'd heard a rifleman being rude about the Russian uniform earlier in the day: he said they wore grey, and looked like a pack of rats. He reckoned they would see all the vivid colours of our men and run a mile.

Then, just when she thought the soldiers couldn't get any more gorgeous, along came the Hussars. It was hard to decide which were the more magnificent, the beautiful sleek chargers, or their riders with their tight cherry-red breeches and blue coats adorned with gold braid.

So many different bands were playing. There was so much shouting, galloping hooves, and equipment being hauled into place. There were gun carriages, bullock carts laden with ammunition, tents and field equipment, mules weighed down with heavy loads, and still more horses, and they stirred up the dust into a storm.

Hope noted that the French seemed much better organized and equipped than the English. They alone appeared to have a real plan, and their tents were struck quickly and efficiently.

Bennett pointed out both Lord Cardigan and Lord Lucan and told Hope there was already a major row brewing between them because Cardigan had believed he was to be in command, yet Lord Raglan had decided that Lucan was to be. Apparently it had eventually been decided that Lord Lucan would have the Heavy Brigade, and Lord Cardigan the Light Brigade, but as Lucan had overall command, trouble was still expected.

Hope didn't think much of either of these two men she'd heard so much about back home. They were both so old, at least fifty-five or more. Cardigan looked every bit as arrogant as she'd heard, and not half as handsome, for he had thick bushy whiskers down his cheeks, and his teeth were bad. As for Lord Lucan, he looked as if he were sucking a lemon, and she'd heard he was so fussy that he went round with a ruler measuring the space between each of the men's tents, and if they weren't exactly so, he made them take them down and move them.

But for days Hope was too awestruck by the sheer volume of soldiers – someone said there were over 70,000 – and the chaos and intense activity going on all around her, to make any real sense of how they were being organized, if at all. One minute men were in full uniform on parade, their tents and kits under inspection. The next they would be lounging on the ground smoking or drinking, only to be galvanized later by some unseen force into moving tents, unloading equipment or collecting wood.

She heard the laughter of soldiers' wives washing clothes in the river, and when she saw them splashing around like children she was tempted to join them, for it was terribly hot, but she knew such behaviour would be noted, and disapproved of.

Without Queenie she would have been dreadfully lonely, as Bennett was part of a team of both French and English doctors who were supervising the overhaul of the hospital in Varna town. He said it was a far more hopeless case even than Scutari, full of fleas and vermin, with no drainage, more suitable for cattle than the sick. But Queenie had many of Betsy's attributes, and was just as saucy, opinionated and full of life. Her cooking skills were non-existent and she had no idea of hygiene, but she was a very good scavenger, able to get practically anything Hope wanted or needed. She was also great fun to be with.

'The water is getting terribly muddy,' Hope said as she and Queenie approached the river to wash some clothes. They had been in Varna for a month now, and though it had seemed a very pleasant place to camp at first, now, with so many thousands of men living here, it was fast becoming very squalid.

'It would do, wouldn't it, wif all those great horses trampling about in it,' Queenie replied. 'S'pose you expects 'em to line up like gentlemen and drink one by bleedin' one?'

Hope laughed. Queenie's squeaky little voice amused her even when she wasn't trying to be funny. 'No, I don't expect that, but they could all drink further downstream and leave this part clear for us to drink. And what's that floating in there?' She pointed to what looked like animal innards floating by.

'Looks like someone killed a sheep or sommat,' Queenie replied. 'Filthy bastard chucking it in the river!'

Bennett had already pointed out that the camp's position by lakes surrounded by marshland was unhealthy because of the hordes of mosquitoes that drove them all mad at night. Now that the river, which had been crystal-clear when they arrived, was looking so dirty, both he and Hope were afraid the troops might become sick, for in this heat they were drinking the water copiously.

'In future we'll get our water from right up there.' Hope pointed further up, where no one bathed and horses rarely quenched their thirst. 'And we'll boil it for drinking.'

Queenie rolled her eyes with impatience. 'Oh, come on, Mrs Meadows, I can't be doing wif trekking right up there in the hot sun! The water's the same wherever we gets it from.'

'It isn't,' Hope said firmly. 'There's already enough men complaining of diarrhoea, we don't want anything worse appearing.'

But a month later something far worse *had* appeared.

Cholera.

It was only in the French camp so far, and the English troops had already moved camp further away from the marshes as a precaution, but there was unease everywhere.

Hope, who probably knew this disease better than anyone else in her immediate circle, was very frightened. She knew it could decimate a whole regiment, and although every single soldier knew he might die in a battle, that at least was a noble end.

She'd got to know many of the men now; she'd dressed the backs of those who had been flogged for drunkenness, she'd reproved some for stuffing themselves with unripe fruit and giving themselves stomach aches. She'd written letters home for two or three who couldn't read or write, and pleaded and cajoled others to help clean up the hospital for Bennett and the other doctors. They weren't unknown faces like the victims who had died at St Peter's; these were friends and comrades, and most of them were so young.

But as the temperatures rose in July, so the death rate rose too, and the sickness was now in the British camp and among the Turks. A party of men heralded as the Hospital Conveyance Corps arrived in Varna. They were intended to be stretcher-bearers and orderlies, but they turned out to be too old, too feeble and mostly too drunk to be of any use. They soon caught cholera and died.

The men were becoming dispirited even before sickness stole into the camp. The heat, dust storms, endless drills, poor food and the interminable waiting for action were sapping their morale. But now every twinge of stomach pain, a slight fever or a headache could be the onset of cholera and the anxiety showed in every face.

Hope worked tirelessly alongside Bennett and the other doctors. The hospital at Varna was still overrun with fleas, so they used a marquee for the sick instead. But the overpowering heat, the shortage of laudanum and other medicine made it hard even to make the patients comfortable, let alone help them to recover. Nearly 400 men died during July and in August the figure doubled. The 2nd Battalion Rifle Brigade alone had lost thirty men in all. Hope had got to know most of them well on the boat coming over, and losing them had been almost as bad as losing Betsy and Gussie.

'You must rest today,' Bennett said early one morning right at the end of August. He knelt beside her camp bed, putting one hand on her forehead. 'I couldn't bear it if you got sick too. When Queenie comes, go and find somewhere shady to spend the day.'

'But I'm needed,' Hope protested, attempting to get up and prepare his breakfast.

'You know as well as I do that they die with or without our care,' he said more sharply, pushing her back down. 'But I cannot live without you, and you look so peaky I'm going to insist you rest.'

Hope knew when he had that stern look that he was giving her an order, and it was best not to disobey. Besides, the prospect of a day doing nothing was pleasing. She thought maybe she and Queenie could take a picnic into the woods.

*

'So tell me how you met the doctor?' Queenie asked later that morning.

They had left the camp soon after eight, before the sun got too hot, and with a small picnic in a basket, a blanket to sit on and a large flask of water, they'd made for the woods a few miles above the camp.

They could still hear some of the noise from the camp – with all the thousands of men there they would have had to go a great deal further for complete silence – but it was none the less muted and distant, and cooler under the trees.

Lying there beside Queenie on the blanket, Hope could almost pretend she had Betsy back with her, for although Queenie's voice was very different, and she was smaller and far spikier than her old friend, she had a similar easiness about her, wits sharpened by hardship, and very colourful speech. Hope got Queenie to tell her about her family.

'Me mam's a whore,' she said without any embarrassment. 'Dunno who me dad is, some sailor I reckon. She's had so many I don't fink she remembers any more. She done all right fer us anyways, we was fed and that. I'm second to youngest, and me mam lives wif me big brother Michael, cos she's got too old fer all that now. He's a blacksmith, does all right fer himself an' all. The others they all got took on in service. I was working in an ale house when I met Robbie.'

Robbie, it seemed, was from Portsmouth too, like Queenie. They'd known each other by sight from childhood, but it was only when he came home from Canada on leave that he ran into her again, they fell in love and and got married.

'I tried to go with him when he went to the Kaffir war,' Queenie said. 'But I didn't get picked. I weren't going to stay home this time, though, whatever it took. I got him to train me wif the small arms and all for days. You shoulda seen me at muster; I fooled the lot of 'em. Shame I 'ad to cut off me 'air though, don't feel the same without it.'

Hope laughed. She thought Queenie looked very pretty with her short-cropped hair. 'There's times when I'd gladly cut mine off too,' she said. 'It's far too much trouble in this heat.'

'Your hair's beautiful,' Queenie said admiringly. She often brushed and checked Hope's hair for lice. 'But then, every-fing about you is beautiful, the way you talk, your face, and the way you are. Everyone goes on about that Mrs Duberly what's come on the campaign, but you are much prettier than her.'

Hope smiled. Mrs Duberly was the wife of a paymaster with the cavalry, a dainty blonde woman who could ride as well as a man. She was much admired by everyone, except Bennett who pronounced her empty-headed and suspected she was in fact Lord Cardigan's mistress as they always seemed to be together. So it was good to know Queenie liked her better.

Queenie asked her again how she'd met Bennett, and Hope told her an abbreviated version of the truth; that she'd met him while working as a nurse. 'Don't know 'ow you can stick sick people.' Queenie shuddered. 'You wouldn't catch me cleaning 'em up and that.'

They fell asleep after eating their picnic, and Hope was woken suddenly by the sound of a male voice.

She was disoriented for a moment, thinking the voice was Bennett's, and she didn't bother to move. But on hearing a second voice and a twig snapping close by, she opened her eyes and saw two men looking down at them.

They were clearly Turks, judging by their olive skins, drooping moustaches and baggy red breeches, though they weren't wearing the standard fez. She couldn't understand what they were saying, but the excited tone of voice and the lust in their dark eyes were enough.

'Wake up, Queenie,' she said, prodding her companion and sitting up. 'English,' she said. 'My husband officer in army.' She pointed in the direction of the camp.

Queenie woke, caught on immediately to what was happening, and jumped to her feet.

'Sod off,' she yelled. 'Go on, get out.'

One of the men said something, and leered at Hope. She got on to her knees as if to pack up their picnic basket, and deftly slid the sharp fruit knife up her sleeve before rising to her feet.

Queenie, meanwhile, was shouting abuse at the men. They backed off slightly, but maybe they understood some of the riper insults, for suddenly their faces darkened and they leapt forward, one catching hold of Queenie, pinning her arms to her sides, while the other, slower man caught Hope's left arm in a vicelike grip, pushing her back against a tree.

All at once Queenie was down on the ground, her captor on top of her. There was no doubt what he was intending to do to her, and it seemed to Hope that the man holding on to her intended to watch that first, then do the same to her.

Queenie screamed at the top of her lungs, fighting like a hellcat to get from under the man. But although not very tall, he was powerfully built, and she was making no impression on him at all except to make him more excited.

Hope screamed too, but she didn't lash out with her free hand because she was trying to get the knife down from her sleeve. But as the man lunged at her skirt to pull it up, at the same time pushing her back against the tree, she had the knife safely in her hand. She waited only long enough for him to straighten up, then thrust it into his side.

His shocked expression was almost laughable. He staggered back, eyes rolling, trying to pull out the knife with his hand.

For a second or two it was as if everything happened in slow motion. The man with Queenie was trying to force her knees apart, her attacker was trying to get the knife out, and any moment he might succeed and use it on her, while Queenie would be raped.

Until that second Hope had been very afraid, but now her fear turned to fury. She hadn't come all this way from England to be killed or raped by one of the Turks they were supposed to be defending. Letting out a bellow of rage, she rushed at the man, yanked the knife out of his side and kicked him to the ground.

'That's it, mam!' Queenie yelled, her voice somewhat muffled by the man on top of her. 'Now stick this bastard!'

Hope rushed over, grabbed the man by the hair, and put the knife to his throat.

Suddenly she heard the sounds of feet blundering through the wood. Still holding the man, she glanced up to see three cavalrymen in their cherry-red breeches rushing towards her.

They took over then, one punching Queenie's would-be rapist to the ground while another checked on the other man still lying there clutching at his side and moaning. The third cavalryman, tall and dark-haired, helped Queenie to her feet.

'We'll take you back to our camp,' he said to Hope. 'But would you mind putting that knife down first? It's making me a bit nervous.'

The tall man, who introduced himself as Trooper Haynes, asked them a few questions as they walked back to the cavalry camp. The other two men were frogmarching the Turks back too, just behind them.

Queenie did all the explaining. Hope was too shocked to

speak. She couldn't really believe she'd actually stuck a knife into a man and might have cut the other one's throat if she hadn't been interrupted.

'I'd best take you to the Captain,' Haynes said as they approached the first line of tents. 'They'll see to the Turks,' he said, nodding back at the two other men.

Hope was fighting to hold back her tears, wanting to talk to Queenie alone, and the last thing she wanted was to have to explain how it all came about to a complete stranger. But she knew enough about army life now to understand an incident like this had to be reported properly.

Haynes led her through a row of tents towards an officer writing at a low table. The man had his back to them, but as Haynes spoke, he turned, and as Hope saw his face, her legs gave way beneath her.

She must have lost consciousness for only a second or two as she was still on the ground when she came round. She could hear Haynes just starting to explain what had happened in the woods, and *he* was kneeling beside her putting something soft beneath her head.

'Lie still,' he said, his dark eyes looking right into hers. 'You've had a very bad shock and you fainted. I understand your husband is a surgeon; I'll send someone to go and get him.'

'If you don't mind me saying so, sir, what she could do with is a drop of brandy or rum.' Queenie spoke up out of Hope's line of vision. 'I know I could do with some an' all.'

That was exactly what Hope felt she could do with. The last thing she'd ever expected to come across out here in Varna, so far from home, was a reminder of Briargate. Coming face to face with Captain Angus Pettigrew was an even bigger shock than finding she was capable of sticking a knife into a man's ribs.

She thought of Nell and her home village often, but her

memories of Briargate had long since become indistinct. Yet now as she saw the Captain's face everything came back to her in a rush.

He was still every bit as handsome and dashing, even if his dark hair was growing grey. As a woman she could now understand why Lady Anne had risked so much for him.

Why hadn't she even considered that he might be here? She'd been told he was a cavalry officer after all.

'I'm fine now,' she said, and sat up. She wanted to get away, afraid he might recognize her. But even as she thought that, she almost laughed at herself. Men like him didn't take any notice of servants, certainly not twelve-year-old kitchenmaids.

He reached down and took her hand to help her up, then insisted she sit down in his chair. His servant came forward with a glass of something for both her and Queenie which burned Hope's throat when she took the first sip. She thought it must be brandy, for when she looked round at Queenie, she was smacking her lips with delight.

Queenie explained everything to the Captain, for Hope was too stunned to say anything. 'Weren't she smart gettin' the knife out the basket?' Queenie gushed excitedly. 'I saw her stick it up her sleeve out the corner of me eye, but I never expected her to use it on 'im.'

'It was quick thinking indeed,' the Captain said, smiling at Hope. 'But then I'd heard the surgeon with the Rifle Brigade had a very capable wife. I believe you nursed one of my men, Trooper Jacks, back to health. He's very fond of telling everyone about his brush with cholera.'

'He was one of the lucky ones,' Hope said quietly, keeping her eyes down. 'Not many pull through.'

'She works *too* hard,' Queenie interrupted. 'Every day she's there, early morning till late at night. That's why Dr Meadows said she had to have a rest today. But if you asks me, the sooner we get going out of this place the better it will be for everyone. It ain't an 'ealthy place.'

Glancing at Queenie's animated face, Hope could see that she'd already got over the shock of her close shave in the woods. But just as Betsy always managed to use any incident to her advantage, Queenie did too. Even if it only meant getting a second glass of brandy, to her this was an opportunity.

The Captain chuckled at Queenie's outburst, and Hope remembered then why she had liked him all those years ago. He hadn't been stuffy then, he'd spoken to all the servants at Briargate as if they were his equals. She thought most officers, especially those in the cavalry, would be quick to silence someone like Queenie.

'I think we should go now.' Hope got to her feet. 'Would you thank the men who helped us for me? I shudder to think what might have happened if they hadn't come along when they did.'

'No, you must wait for your husband,' he said, getting up and nudging her back to her chair. 'Haynes will be on his way back with him now. I know he won't want his wife walking all that way after such an ordeal.'

Hope expected it would be an age before Bennett arrived. She asked for some water to wash the Turk's blood from her hands, and tidied her hair, but she had only just sat down again with a cup of coffee when Bennett came bowling along with Trooper Haynes in a light trap.

The Captain had gone away, leaving the two women with his servant Mead, but as Bennett leapt down from the trap, his face a study of deep concern, Captain Pettigrew returned.

'Mrs Meadows was very courageous,' he said, introducing himself and shaking hands with Bennett. 'I think the Turks underestimated Englishwomen. But I shall make certain they are punished. I don't think they are soldiers, it's more likely they are men from the town out on a thieving mission.'

'I'm fine now,' Hope said as Bennett felt her pulse and fussed round her. 'It was Queenie who got the worst of it. But I'd like to go back now.'

Queenie insisted she'd never felt better, and her face brightened still further when the Captain asked Bennett if he'd like a glass of something.

'I would normally,' Bennett replied, glancing at Hope. 'But I've had an exhausting day at the hospital, and I must get Hope back to our camp before it gets dark.'

'Hope!' the Captain said reflectively, looking at her quizzically. 'Now, there's a good name for a nurse! You didn't tell me where you were from, Mrs Meadows. Do I detect a Somerset accent?'

'You do indeed, sir,' Bennett answered for her. 'Thank you for taking care of the ladies, we must go now.'

The following morning Bennett was at the dilapidated town hospital checking to see what improvements had been made, when Captain Pettigrew rode up on his chestnut horse.

'How are Mrs Meadows and her maid?' he asked as he dismounted.

'They both seem fine,' Bennett said, flattered that a lordly Hussar had the good manners to come and check on her. 'My wife was a little withdrawn last night, but that's to be expected after such a shock. Has the man she stabbed received any medical care?'

'As much as he deserves! Sadly it wasn't a mortal wound,' the Captain said with a broad grin. 'I'm on my way to find someone in authority in the town. The general view is that he should be flogged within an inch of his life, but as he's a civilian we'll almost certainly have to hand him over.'

'It's a poor thing when a couple of women can't leave the

camp without being molested,' Bennett said indignantly. 'Thankfully they were unhurt. But I very much appreciated your concern for them.'

'This may seem an odd and impertinent question,' the Captain said. 'But tell me, was Mrs Meadows ever in service at Briargate Hall in Somerset?'

Bennett looked hard at the man, the cogs in his brain whizzing round at the unexpected question. 'Why do you ask?' he said carefully.

'Because I have a housekeeper called Nell Renton who has a sister she lost track of. Her name is Hope.'

Bennett was staggered and felt he needed to sit down and think this through before replying.

'I have disturbed you,' Captain Pettigrew remarked, looking at him curiously when he didn't answer. 'I have no wish to pry or to make mischief. But I have grown fond of my housekeeper; she has been with me for seven years since leaving Briargate Hall. Her greatest sadness is losing her sister, which undoubtedly was the work of the man Nell was then married to.'

'Nell is no longer with him?' Bennett's heart leapt, but realized too late that he had admitted who Hope was.

'So your wife is Nell's sister!' The Captain's grin was one of delight. 'Nell left Albert Scott the moment she discovered Hope had disappeared from Briargate. She was convinced he had killed her sister. Personally I was never of the same opinion; I thought it far more likely he forced young Hope to leave. But when he burned down Briargate and killed Sir William—'

'He burned down Briargate?' Bennett interrupted.

'You didn't read about it in the newspapers?' Captain Pettigrew looked astonished. 'It was early this year. There has been a manhunt for him since.'

Bennett asked a few more questions and discovered that

the fire had taken place while he and Hope had been on their honeymoon, during which time he hadn't looked at the newspaper. Then coming out here so quickly afterwards he had taken little notice of anything other than war news. 'I am in a quandary now,' he said finally, his head spinning with so much dramatic news which he knew was going to shock Hope. 'I do know everything that occurred between my wife and her brother-in-law, and there were compelling reasons why Hope was afraid to make contact with her sister. But I cannot divulge any of this to you, not without her agreeing to it.'

Captain Pettigrew nodded in understanding. 'This is hardly the right place or time for any of us,' he said as he prepared to remount his horse. 'You have so many sick men to deal with; I'm awaiting orders to move my company on. Talk to your wife, and if she is agreeable, send a message to me and we can arrange a meeting.'

Bennett stood for some time watching the Captain riding off. He had a natural distrust of all cavalry officers, for it was well known that they were to a man arrogant, interbred aristocrats, and the ones he'd met had only confirmed that this was true.

Yet Pettigrew didn't appear that way, and he wouldn't know or care about his housekeeper's family problems unless he was a kindly man.

But there was something more in Bennett's heart, a fear that once Hope knew her sister was no longer with Albert, she would want to go home. He felt ashamed of such selfishness, but in truth it was Hope's spirit that was keeping him going.

He had had bad feelings about this campaign from the start, but he had expected to be posted to one base hospital where he would stay. Instead, they'd just get settled in one place when they'd have to move again, and even now he had no idea where they would end up. He had anticipated grimness, that went with the job, but he hadn't imagined there would be so little equipment or medicine. How could any doctor help the sick and injured without basic necessities?

Even the camp beds he'd brought out from England for himself and Hope hadn't turned up until a month ago. It seemed that like other equipment and stores, they had gone back to England, only to be sent out yet again. Hundreds of horses had perished on the ships coming over here, but now it seemed there wasn't enough forage for the remainder.

None of the troops were in good health; along with cholera there was dysentery and malaria. Unless they were moved quickly to a healthier place, they soon wouldn't have enough fit men to fight a war. It was a complete mess!

Hope didn't seem to mind the lack of comforts, the dust, dirt, hot sun or poor food. She said cheerfully that she'd known worse. While she was here with him he felt he could bear it too, but once she was gone it would be a very different picture.

Chapter Twenty

'Please say something!' Bennett pleaded. 'I could only tell you it the way Captain Pettigrew told me, but maybe I've been too blunt.'

All day the news of Nell had been burning inside him. He'd expected Hope to whoop with delight and ask a hundred questions he wouldn't be able to answer. But he'd forced himself to hold it in until they'd got back to their tent this evening because he hadn't wanted anyone to interrupt them. It hadn't gone the way he expected at all; she had just sat there on the camp bed, her dark eyes fixed on his face, not saying a word.

Was it the shock of hearing her brother-in-law was a murderer?

She reached out for his hand and at last there was a glimmer of a smile. 'It is I who should apologize, not you,' she said. 'I could not speak for shock; it's almost too much to take in. I never thought Nell would leave Albert, not even in my wildest flights of fancy.'

'You find Nell leaving him more extraordinary than him burning down Briargate and killing Sir William?' Bennett was incredulous.

Hope giggled then, her face at last becoming animated. 'Well, that is truly shocking, but then I always knew Albert was an evil man. But Nell! She was always so proper; she believed that marriage vows were unbreakable. I just can't imagine her doing something so extreme.'

'Pettigrew did say she believed he'd killed you!'

Hope's face clouded over. 'Poor Nell, I never imagined she'd think that, or that she'd leave Briargate. You can't imagine what that place meant to her! She worshipped Lady Harvey, and if she walked away from her, and Albert, it must have caused so much gossip in the village.'

Bennett frowned, still puzzled as to why broken marriage vows and gossip appeared to have had so much more impact than murder and a mansion being burnt down.

Hope took his hand and kissed the tips of his fingers, looking at him with a wicked glint in her eyes. 'I shouldn't think anyone in the village can sleep with all this scandal going on. Just imagine what they'd be like if they knew what Albert and Sir William were to each other too? But tell me more of what Captain Pettigrew said about Nell. How on earth did she come to be his housekeeper? Is she well? Was there any other news of the rest of my family?'

Bennett smiled; this was more how he'd expected Hope to react, questions and more questions. 'No, he didn't tell me anything else, but he spoke with such warmth about Nell that I'm certain he'll be very happy to talk to you about her. I too would like to hear more about all my in-laws!'

At that, Hope realized that Bennett not only fully appreciated what this news of Nell meant to her, but was also delighted to embrace her family as his own, and that touched her to the core.

But with that knowledge came guilt too. Why hadn't she felt able to tell Bennett yesterday that she'd met Captain Pettigrew previously, and that he was the author of the letter to Lady Harvey?

'There is another reason why I am so stunned by all this,' she blurted out. 'You see, I'd met Captain Pettigrew back at Briargate.'

463

'Really?' Bennett raised one eyebrow questioningly. 'And why didn't you tell me this yesterday?'

'I don't know. Maybe it's because Nell always drummed into me that I should never divulge anything that I might hear or see there. You see, Captain Pettigrew was Lady Harvey's lover. That was what made me come over all faint when I recognized him.'

'Good God!' Bennett exclaimed. 'And to think I believed it was the shock of those men attacking you and Queenie that made you so anxious to leave the cavalry camp!'

'He made me recall things I wanted to forget,' Hope said in her defence.

Bennett looked at her thoughtfully. 'So how do you feel about the man now that your sister is his housekeeper and Briargate is gone?'

'I really don't know, Bennett,' Hope sighed.

'But Captain Pettigrew spoke of Nell with such affection – she must have a better life with him than with Albert.'

'That's very true. But if it hadn't been for the letter he sent, I wouldn't have gone to the gatehouse that day and seen Sir William with Albert. The Captain began that chain of events which ended in such misery for me.'

Bennett lapsed into silence for a little while.

'If only we'd heard about the fire before we left England,' he said eventually.

'I can write to Matt,' Hope said eagerly. 'I can enclose a letter for Nell too.'

As she jumped up to get some writing paper, Bennett put out a restraining hand to stop her. 'You need to think this through first, my darling,' he said gently. 'There's still the business of what you saw at the gatehouse. Sir William may be dead and Albert a wanted man, but Rufus and his mother are still very much alive. Before you begin a letter you must be clear on what it is right to divulge.'

Chastened, Hope slumped back down on to the camp bed.

'Damn it!' she exploded. 'If I can't tell Matt about the Captain's letter, or about Albert and Sir William, what reason can I give for leaving?'

Bennett pulled her to him and hugged her tightly. 'I think you must wait until you've spoken to Captain Pettigrew,' he said. 'You will need to feel your way carefully and try to find out how the land lies back home.

'Pettigrew struck me as a good man – he wouldn't have come to see me unless he cared about Nell, and therefore you too. But we have to remember that it wasn't very honourable to be making love to another man's wife.'

'Maybe he always knew what Sir William was?' Hope suggested. 'He is a man of the world after all. He might even be intending to marry Lady Harvey now she is free.'

Bennett nodded. 'True. But you can't assume anything, and you must remember that the knowledge you have about Sir William is, in the wrong hands, as potentially dangerous as a keg of gunpowder. Therefore you must be careful you don't accidentally light the fuse.'

Hope went to bed that night with so much on her mind that sleep was impossible. However shocking and sad it was that Sir William was dead and Briargate gone, she was delighted that Nell was no longer with Albert. She would have been happier still if she'd known exactly where her sister was, how Rufus had taken his father's death, and what he was doing now. But at least she could ask the Captain these questions without having to divulge anything else.

Unfortunately, as Nell had always believed Albert had killed her, Pettigrew was bound to question her about what happened the day she disappeared from Briargate. Should she admit she knew he was Lady Harvey's lover? Would he believe the intercepted letter was the sole reason Albert had been able to force her to leave?

The following day Hope felt calmer and had new resolve. She wasn't going to worry herself about questions Captain Pettigrew might ask her. The most important thing was to find out where Nell was, and then write to her. A complete explanation wasn't necessary immediately; Nell would be happy just to know she was alive and well.

Later that same day the order came that all the troops would be departing from Varna to the Crimea by the end of the week, and this temporarily put Captain Pettigrew and Nell out of Hope's mind.

The news was received with universal delight, giving a much-needed lift to everyone. The soldiers took the view that they'd come out here to fight a war, and they wanted finally to get to it, beat the Russians and be home for Christmas. Bennett and the other doctors felt the troops' health would improve with a sea voyage.

The cholera death rate had risen even more sharply during August. Proper funerals had been abandoned long ago, for there were too many, and it was too depressing for the living. Now corpses were just carted away to a communal pit without any ceremony.

But there were thousands more suffering from fevers, bowel complaints and other problems which were attributed to the unhealthy marshy parts of Varna and a poor diet. In truth, in both the French and the English camps there were not many men who could be described as fighting fit.

What with packing and organizing the closure of the hospital, there was no opportunity for Hope to make the journey to the cavalry camp. She had to assume that Captain Pettigrew was in similar straits for he did not come down to the hospital again.

All at once the harbour was full of ships, and the demarcation began. But just as she had got all her and Bennett's personal belongings ready to be taken aboard, she heard that Lord Raglan had given the order that none of the officers' wives would be allowed to go with their men.

Hope was horrified, for it seemed no alternative provision had been made for them either.

In fact very few officers' wives had come on to Varna, and most of those who had were so dispirited they would be glad to get a ship back to Constantinople or Malta. Lady Errol and Mrs Duberly, the paymaster's wife, did want to go on with their husbands, but they had friends in high places and would almost certainly find a way around the order. But Hope had no such influence.

Bennett turned to his commanding officer, Lieutenant Colonel Lawrence, for advice and his suggestion was that Hope should be smuggled immediately into Bennett's cabin on the *Pride of the Ocean*, the ship their company was due to take, and stay there until the ship sailed. Lawrence thought that as long as Lord Raglan didn't see her, they would be in the clear.

So Hope had to endure several days shut up alone in a stuffy cabin, without even Queenie for company, for she and the other ranks' wives wouldn't join the ship until the date set for departure. Hope passed the time writing down all that had happened to her since leaving Briargate, in the hope that before long she could relate it all to Nell.

At dawn on 7 September, the *Pride of the Ocean* finally left Varna, and Hope was at last able to go up on deck and breathe some fresh air. It was good to see Queenie again and to hear her funny stories about the chaos during the last days in Varna, yet even better to see that men who had looked sickly as she watched them waiting on the quayside, already appeared to be regaining their vitality in the sea breezes.

Bennett, however, was more concerned with the ambulance carts. It seemed they had been left behind at Varna.

After a day's sailing they found themselves part of a vast armada. There were hundreds of steamers and sailing ships which made an awe-inspiring and beautiful sight. Anchors were dropped, the officers went to and fro visiting other ships in rowing boats, and although no one seemed to know what they were all waiting there for, it was generally supposed that the commanding officers were still planning their tactics.

Finally, on the 14th, the anchors were hauled up and they set sail again. The first sight of the Crimea was not cheering. It looked a very inhospitable, bleak and barren place, with no sign of any people or even animals.

At Eupatoria two officers went ashore to receive the surrender of the port, but apparently it proved unsuitable as a base. It was decided that the following day all troops were to be landed further along the coast at Calamita Bay. From there they would march to Sebastopol to take it.

Bennett was closeted with Lieutenant Colonel Lawrence for some time that evening, and when he returned to Hope he looked troubled.

'You've got to stay on the ship while I go with the regiment,' he sighed. 'It seems we've got a long march and the Colonel believes we may run into Cossacks.'

Hope realized that although he was worried about her, he was even more concerned about the health and welfare of the men in his regiment.

Bennett liked order, and it was plain to him that his superiors had given very little thought to what would happen to any casualties if the army was attacked on the march. He and the other surgeons would of course be there to dress the wounds, but with no ambulance carts and no hospital set up to take the wounded, they were likely to die.

'Don't worry about me,' Hope said quickly. 'I expect I'll be taken to wherever the base camp will be, and I'm sure they'll have a hospital set up by the time you get there.'

The following morning Bennett stood by the ship's rail watching as the French disembarked from their ships with customary efficiency. A group of them were already raising their flag in the sand. When their ships had moved on, the English would go ashore too.

Calamita Bay was a long sweep of coast with a narrow sandy beach, and a large lake beyond. Fine rain was falling, so visibility was poor, but Bennett believed Sebastopol to be some twenty-five to thirty miles further down the coast. It looked a Godforsaken place, just windswept scrubby grass for miles. He wondered idly how long he'd have to wait to see his first Russian. He supposed that in their grey uniforms they'd be quite hard to spot.

His thoughts turned to Hope. She had stayed in the cabin to mend a shirt with a ripped seam. He hadn't the heart to tell her that he couldn't take a change of clothing, it would only worry her.

He had been blessed in finding her. He couldn't think of even one other man who had a wife to equal her. She was brave, adaptable and uncomplaining, all the virtues an army wife needed. But there was so much more to her than that; she was funny, passionate, kind, fiery when pushed too far, and so beautiful too. Those dark smouldering eyes, full lips and smooth flawless skin had captivated him right from the start; he didn't think he'd ever tire of looking at her.

It was a new experience to be envied by other men. He could almost hear them thinking, 'How did he manage to get a woman like her?' At school and at university he'd mostly been ridiculed by his peers. He wasn't handsome, not good at games or riding, he studied too hard, and he had never managed to acquire sophistication or a way with the ladies. Somewhat fortunately, an army surgeon wasn't expected to have these singular talents, but it felt rather good to see other men supposing he had them because of Hope.

She was exceptional: her natural poise, charm and nursing skills had won her respect from even the biggest snobs among the officer class. Yet her real beauty lay in that she was unaware of her own worth. She didn't have any idea that half the regiment called into the hospital at Varna with trivial complaints, wanting only to bask in her attention for a minute or two.

Bennett smiled to himself remembering how she had clambered up into the top bunk with him before daybreak today without a stitch of clothing on. At least that memory would keep him going for a few days!

It was late afternoon before Bennett disembarked from the ship, one of the last to leave. He stood on the beach, waving and blowing kisses to Hope as the ship sailed away.

All day he'd forced himself to pretend enthusiasm for the march, making jokes about how bored he'd been on the ship and that he needed some exercise. But in reality his heart was in his boots. And now she was gone it was going to be so hard to pretend to be confident and optimistic.

It was still raining, many of the men were suffering from diarrhoea, and Bennett didn't think any of them were fit enough for a long march.

An hour later, when all the ships were just specks on the horizon, it was discovered the tents hadn't been unloaded.

The lake had turned out to be salt water too, and there was no fresh water anywhere.

Then the fine rain became a fearful storm, and because the men had been made to leave their packs on board, they had nothing but their greatcoats and a blanket to cover themselves with.

There was no shelter anywhere. The men huddled together miserably in torrential rain, unable to sleep because they were so wet and cold.

Bennett was relieved when dawn came, for it had been the most miserable night of his life. It defied belief that something as basic as shelter had been forgotten. He thought the officers responsible should be court-martialled.

The sun came up as they began the march, quickly drying out the men's clothes, but there was still no water and they were forced to drink from rainwater puddles.

Worse still, Bennett could see that cholera had come with them. He saw men doubled up in pain, but still trying to keep on marching. He could do nothing for them, for there was no transport to get them back to a ship, nor even a field hospital where they could be left. He and his medical assistants were providing the only medical help for the entire regiment. Their equipment consisted of a couple of straw baskets of dressings, bandages and a variety of operating tools slung into one of the panniers on the packhorse.

Bennett hoped the Russians weren't lying in wait ready to attack. He didn't doubt the courage of the men, nor their ability to put up a strong fight, even if they were sick and tired. But he did doubt his own ability to treat serious wounds with such limited supplies.

Hope was awakened on the morning of 22 September by Queenie banging on the door of her cabin, demanding to be let in.

After the men disembarked at Calamita Bay the ship had sailed back to Eupatoria with the rest of the fleet and weighed anchor just outside the harbour. If Hope hadn't been so worried about Bennett, and frustrated that she couldn't talk to Captain Pettigrew about Nell, it would have been idyllic, for the weather was perfect – warm, with a very calm sea. It was peaceful too, for there was only a handful of people left on board, mostly staff on the administration side of the army and a few civilians involved with provisions. Hope had spent most of the time dozing on deck, or playing cards with Queenie.

Queenie ought to have gone on the march with the other soldiers' wives, for they were needed to do the cooking and washing for all the men, but Robbie had asked Bennett if she could stay on the ship with Hope because he was afraid she wouldn't be able to keep up. Bennett had been only too glad to agree as he hadn't liked the idea of his wife being left alone without a female companion.

'Whatever's wrong, Queenie?' Hope grumbled as she got out of her bunk to open the door.

Queenie burst in, her face damp with tears and her eyes brimming with more. 'There's been a terrible battle and thousands killed,' she burst out. 'Do you think my Robbie's safe?'

For a moment or two Hope was more shocked by Queenie's tears than by the news she'd brought, for the girl was always so bright and bouncy, regardless of what was going on all around her.

'I'm quite sure he's safe,' Hope said, enfolding Queenie in her arms. 'Now, where did you get this information?'

They had heard guns a couple of days earlier, but Captain Kyle had claimed it was the Russians along at Sebastopol, and they were probably firing at a Turkish ship that had come too close.

Queenie was crying too hard to make any sense, so after Hope had dressed she went to see the Captain.

'There has been a battle,' he agreed. 'I don't know about the casualties yet. But I don't think they can be as high as you've been told.'

There were several more days of terrible tension before the *Pride of the Ocean* sailed into the harbour at Balaclava, which had been designated as the British base camp. In Eupatoria, rumours had been rife. At one point it was said that the whole cavalry had been wiped out, and Lord Errol of the Rifles killed. Queenie remained tearful, pacing up and down the deck wringing her hands, and all Hope could think was how on earth would the surgeons cope if there were so many casualties.

It transpired that the cavalry had not been wiped out, and Lord Errol had only been wounded in the hand, needing a finger amputated. But there had been a battle. It was at the river Alma, some twenty-five miles from Calamita Bay, and the 1st, 2nd and Light Divisions had all been engaged. Though it was a victory in as much as the British had attacked and seized the Russians' redoubts and defences, there were serious losses, with over two thousand British killed and wounded. And the French casualties were reported to be higher still.

The port of Balaclava was little more than a single street nestling in the cleft of two formidable steep hills. But it was a good, safe, albeit small harbour, the inlet leading to it almost concealed from passing shipping by high cliffs. Apparently, a few pot shots had been fired at the advance party of soldiers who'd arrived to take it, but there was no further resistance, and the town's baker had come out with a roast turkey and some bread for the soldiers.

As the *Pride of the Ocean* pulled into the small harbour,

easing its way between dozens of other ships, Hope was at the bows, frantically scanning the soldiers on the quayside for Bennett.

She could see dozens of green Rifle Brigade uniforms among the scarlet coats, but not him, and she was appalled to see how many walking wounded there were. Some had bandages around their heads, others were hobbling along with their breeches cut open and fearsome-looking wounds that hadn't even been dressed.

By the time the ship had squeezed into a space on the quay, Hope had observed some stretchers being carried up to a building set back from the main street. It had the appearance of a school and would therefore make a good hospital.

She hopped from one foot to the other, waiting impatiently for the sailors to put a gangplank into place so she could run off and find Bennett.

'Mrs Meadows!' Captain Kyle called out, just as she was about to leave the ship. 'It's mayhem out there. I doubt your husband will be able to find any accommodation for you both immediately.'

Hope realized the Captain was concerned for her, and desperate as she was to find Bennett, she felt obliged to stop and speak to him.

'I'll find something,' she said edging towards the gangplank.

'You won't, not today,' he insisted. 'Both you and your husband will need proper rest after dealing with so many wounded, so come back here to sleep until you can make other arrangements.'

'That is so kind of you,' she said gratefully. 'I know my husband will appreciate the offer too.' She saw Queenie running off at full tilt to find Robbie and couldn't delay a moment longer. 'I must go now, but I'll be back.'

The view of the quay and little town had been picturesque from the ship. The water had sparkled in the sunshine, and the low stone buildings, the church and the steep rocky hills had implied a sleepy but secure and healthy place for a base camp.

However, once Hope and Queenie had joined the mêlée of soldiers, carts, and goods being unloaded from the ships, it took on a nightmarish quality. Even men who had appeared unhurt had a stunned, haunted look about them. They were dirty, their uniforms dusty and stained, and all of them were unshaven.

But if the street was frightening, the scene which met Hope's eyes as she squeezed past stretchers to gain entrance to the hospital was terrifying.

Despite the bright sunshine outside, it was dark within, and the first thing which assaulted her was the sound of men in fearful agony, calling for help, moaning deliriously and some even screaming.

There were no beds, and the men were lying or sitting so close to one another that there was no room to get in between them. Many had only recently suffered a limb amputation and the dressings were bright with fresh blood. Others had gaping exposed wounds in their chests, legs and bellies, so frightful that Hope's first thought was to flee, for she didn't have even the first idea where to start.

Queenie did flee, her hand over her mouth, but Hope had spotted Bennett in the far corner of that dark and terrible place. He was kneeling to dress an amputated leg, the linen jacket he always wore over his uniform soaked in blood. Even in the dim light she could see he was grey-faced and exhausted.

All at once she was appalled that she'd lain in her bunk early this morning contemplating whether to wear her pink dress with the ruffles around the neck, or the blue one with lace to meet Bennett. She had only been concerned which dress was the more flattering, and had decided it had to be the pink one.

She was dressed as if going for a picnic with her sweetheart. She'd even put pink ribbons in her hair! But Bennett didn't need a sweetheart now, or a silly, vain woman whose thoughts didn't stretch beyond a night of lovemaking. What he needed was someone to help him patch up those heroes who had been torn apart by bullets, so that maybe they might live to return to their own wives and sweethearts one day.

Turning sharply, she ran back down the hill, side-stepping the stretcher-bearers and pushing through the crowds on the quay. Back in her cabin, she pulled out her old grey dress and white apron.

Within five minutes she was running back up the hill. Her hair was tied back, her petticoats were gone, the sober dress and apron replacing the frivolous pink one. And as she ran she offered up a silent prayer that some kind of instinct would take over and show her how to dress gunshot wounds, for she knew that nothing she'd ever done previously had been appropriate training for this horror.

Bennett had moved on to another soldier by the time she got back to the hospital, and he had his back to the door so he didn't see her come in.

'Nurse Meadows reporting for duty, sir,' she said softly as she got closer.

He turned at her voice and smiled wanly. 'It's good to see you, but I don't think you can cope with this.'

'I can,' she said firmly. 'Just tell me what to do.'

It was dark when Bennett finally insisted they'd done all they could for one day. Their clothes were stiff with dried blood, backs aching from continually bending over, even their eyes were sore from peering in poor light.

All the doctors had worked like demons; there had been no breaks for meals or even drinks. Bandsmen who had been pressed into service as orderlies would bring whichever man was next in line to an area where there was some light, and there on a rough table, bullets would be removed, the wound stitched and dressed. Often amputation was required.

Hope didn't think she'd ever forget the horror of the first leg amputation she helped with. The infantryman was no more than eighteen, with wide, childlike blue eyes full of fear. There was no chloroform to anaesthetize him, yet he'd found the courage to smile at her and kept his eyes on her, unwavering, as his limb was sawn off, never once giving way to screaming.

The sound of the saw on bone was so horrible, with so much blood, and all the time his poor young body was twitching uncontrollably in agony. All she could do was bathe his face, tell him how brave he was, and silently pray for him.

She knew that he and most of his comrades would have come from places like Lewins Mead. To men like him, joining the army was a way out of poverty, a smart uniform being better than rags. Yet sadly, they were defending a country that felt nothing for its poor and needy. If he survived the amputation, he would be shipped home to nothing. Maybe he'd get a medal, but what good was a medal when he couldn't work? It wouldn't buy bread or meat.

She heard that some of the wounded had lain on the battlefield among the dead all night, without receiving even a drop of water. They said they'd seen the surgeons drenched in blood cutting off limbs and tossing them to one side.

The Rifle Brigade's casualties were light compared with other regiments. Two sergeants, one corporal and seven riflemen were killed. Twenty-five more were wounded. But Robbie had been seen by Bennett that very morning in Balaclava, and Queenie had clearly found him as she hadn't returned to the ship.

'Tell me what it was like at the river Alma,' Hope asked Bennett after they had eaten and retired to their cabin.

'The men were incredibly brave, even formidable,' he said weakly, his face etched with weariness. 'That's all you need to know.'

'I meant, what was it like for you?'

Bennett slumped back on the bunk and closed his eyes. 'Much like you saw today,' he said. 'Except we had no table to operate on, in fact we didn't even have a field hospital. I had to examine men on the ground with only a candle for light. There weren't enough stretchers and during the night I could hear men calling out for help, but it was too dark to find them. We had to use peasants' carts as ambulances. It was a shambles.'

She felt his sense of guilt that he hadn't been able to save more men, and his anxiety that this was surely the first of many more bloody battles.

'It won't be like that again,' she assured him. 'They'll get things right by the time of the next battle.'

He opened his eyes and looked at her sadly. 'I doubt it, Hope. There are too many obstacles. Now we are to lay siege before Sebastopol. But as yet there are no tents, and precious little in the way of provisions or medicine. You sailed past Sebastopol this morning. It isn't a tiny place like Balaclava, it's big and it's fortified, bristling with cannons and Russians who will fight to the death to keep it.

'Furthermore, all the supplies for the army will come in here, and the only way to get them to our boys at the siege is up that steep track on to the Heights. Easy enough now while the ground is dry, providing we've got horses or mules. But what about when the autumn rains come? Or in winter when it's freezing? How will they get the wounded back here?'

'It will be over by then,' she said hopefully.

'I doubt that,' he said gloomily. 'Not when the generals can't even agree how and when to attack.'

On the morning of 27 October, Hope woke to find Bennett had slipped out without waking her. The *Pride of the Ocean*, which had been their home, had left for Scutari two weeks earlier, taking many of the wounded to the hospital. Now, until such time as they could find better accommodation, they had a tent.

It was pitched a few hundred yards from the hospital, behind the main street, and just far enough up the hill to be away from the filth and commotion of the quayside.

The small port now had more in common with Lewins Mead than the picturesque sparkling harbour that Hope had seen when she first arrived. The hundreds of wounded men might be gone, sent back by ship to Scutari, where rumour had it they would die faster than if they were left here on the quay. But a different, less understandable squalor had taken its place. Piles of unloaded goods littered the quayside because no one knew where to take them. Some of them were foodstuffs, and after a few days of the sun burning down, or rain soaking them, they rotted. Livestock brought in on ships were slaughtered and their entrails thrown into the water. Corpses often floated back into the harbour, bobbing up to the surface because the weights tied to them weren't heavy enough to keep them down. Along with the gallons of slops created by the now vast number of residents, and the waste from horses, mules and oxen, the stench was overpowering and the water murky.

It seemed strange to Hope, who knew so little about army campaigns, that all those tens of thousands of troops which she had seen in Varna were now here in the Crimea, somewhere, but she didn't know where or how close to the port. The cavalry were reported to be camping up on the plain above Balaclava. She'd seen a few of their men in the town, but she hadn't seen Captain Pettigrew. She was terribly frustrated by being unable to speak to him about Nell. Nursing filled every minute of the day, but her thoughts kept turning to her sister, and she'd have given anything to have some sort of positive picture of Nell to help her overcome the endless horror she was subjected to daily in the hospital.

She knew that thousands of men had been marched around Sebastopol to lay siege before the town. She'd seen picks and shovels being carted up the track to dig the entrenchments, just as she'd noted the incredible amount of ammunition and cannons being hauled up that way. The French army were based in a place called Kamiesch Bay, which she understood to be along the coast nearer Sebastopol. She had no idea where the Turks had camped.

But even though there were far fewer wounded men, the hospital was almost as full as it had been on her first day at the port, only now most of the patients were cholera cases.

If the port of Balaclava was to have a motto, Hope thought it should be 'Not Enough'. For they finally had beds at the hospital now, and bed pans, bowls and some medicine too, but not enough. They had already enlarged the hospital, using outhouses, sheds and marquees, but there still wasn't enough room. Every day ships arrived laden with goods, but all too often these goods were not what they needed. Not enough wood for fires or building work. Not enough medicine, not enough doctors, not enough nutritious food.

A large consignment of boots had arrived, but they

were too small for most of the men who needed them. There were still precious few tents, and the goods which were desperately needed up at the trenches on the Heights mostly couldn't be got up there.

Autumn had come, bringing very changeable weather. It could be pouring with rain and very cold for several days in succession, then suddenly the sun would come out again as warm as a summer's day. As Bennett had predicted, the track up to the Heights, which was the only way to reach the troops, became a mudslide after rain.

Lord Cardigan's yacht, the *Dryad*, was moored out in the harbour, and he slept on it in luxury while his men huddled in greatcoats in the open. Dr Mackay, a man Bennett had much admired, had died of exhaustion after his heroic efforts to save lives at the battle of Alma.

Bennett and Hope's knowledge of the progress of the war was all received at second or third hand, for they rarely had a chance to venture out of Balaclava. From the commencement of the troops digging their trenches before Sebastopol, the Russians were firing on them. But it was only on 17 October that the allied army were finally ready to answer the fire. From six in the morning until darkness fell they kept up the barrage of shot and shell on the batteries and forts. The following day a steady stream of wounded were brought down, but many bled to death on the bumpy ride down the track.

They had heard a huge explosion and everyone in Balaclava had rejoiced imagining it was the town walls being breached. But sadly it was a French powder magazine that had been hit, killing forty men, and fifteen guns were lost.

Hope got up and dressed hurriedly, for she knew why Bennett had left for the hospital so early. The previous evening it had been said that 25,000 Russians under the command of the formidable General Liprandi were gathering a few miles from Balaclava, with the intention of seizing back the port.

Balaclava was the sole lifeline of the British army; the food, the ammunition and every item of equipment came through it. But because Lord Raglan could not spare troops to guard it, it was garrisoned only by the 93rd, the Argyll and Sutherland Highlanders, 100 men from the Invalid Battalion and 1,200 Turks. The cavalry camp was a couple of miles outside the town. But there were nowhere near enough men to defend it.

It was a misty, cold morning as Hope made her way down to the hospital. When she reached the hospital, as she had expected she found Bennett doing the rounds of patients, checking which ones could be sent on to Scutari.

She could sense his anxiety, even though he turned and smiled at the sight of her. A week ago, in an unguarded moment, he had likened this task to the Judgment of Solomon. He knew that the sea trip and then the appalling conditions at Scutari were likely to kill his patients. But he had no choice, for unless he freed up beds, there would be no room for fresh casualties. If there was a battle today, there would be a huge influx of wounded. If the Russians seized the port, they were all likely to be killed or left to die anyway.

'I want you to go with this lot,' he said, waving the list in his hand.

'No, Bennett,' she said. 'I'm staying here.'

'Do as I say,' he said curtly. 'It's an order.'

'You are not my commanding officer,' Hope said with a defiant toss of her head. 'You're just my husband, and I'm staying here with you.'

'Please, Hope.' His tone was pleading now. 'I doubt those Cossacks have any respect for women. And I can't bear to think what they'd do to a pretty one like you.'

'Then don't think about it,' she snapped. 'Now, which ship will be taking the patients to Scutari?'

Up on the plain above the town the British had built six redoubts in a semicircle to house naval twelve-pounder guns. These were to defend the Woronzoff road which ran from the port up to the Heights, the sole line of communication with the troops up there. The redoubts were manned by Turkish soldiers, and shortly after the first volleys of gunfire were heard down in the port that morning, some of these men, desperate and terrified, came fleeing into the town yelling, 'Ship, ship!'

Bennett had just finished overseeing the last of the patients on to the ship to Scutari as the Turks appeared, and guessing that the casualties would be enormous as there were only 550 men of the 93rd and 100 Invalids standing between Balaclava and the Russians, he decided that he would borrow a horse and ride up to the plain to get a better idea of how things stood.

The early mist had vanished and by mid-morning the sun had come out hot and strong, giving a clear view for miles. As Bennett reined his borrowed horse into a high vantage point to one side of the road into Balaclava, he was staggered by the scene that met his eyes.

Wheeling cavalry, the artillery, Highlanders in their kilts and red coats, all made a glorious and somewhat unreal spectacle. The air was so still that he could hear the clink of sabres, the champing of bits, and shouted orders as clearly as if he were down there with them.

To anyone looking down on the plain, which was some three miles long and two miles wide, surrounded by hills, it looked flat, but in fact there was what they called back in England a 'hog's back' running down the centre. This created two valleys, and it was clear to Bennett that the troops in one valley couldn't see or hear those in the other.

In the north valley a huge square of Russian cavalry was slowly advancing, while the British cavalry were motionless in their saddles in the south valley, and the two sides were oblivious to the other's presence.

Lord Raglan and his entourage of commanding officers up on the high ground had a perfect view of the whole plain, but Bennett quickly realized that they were not aware the troops couldn't see one another, and in fact they had selected a dangerous command post.

Bennett glanced over towards the small group of Highlanders who held a defensive position to prevent the Russians taking Balaclava and a tremor of fear ran down his spine. Five hundred and fifty men were just not enough, even if they were commanded by Sir Colin Campbell who, it was said, was one of the finest officers in the entire British army. He had ordered his men to lie in a line two deep, a difficult position for anyone to maintain, especially when they came under fire.

As Bennett watched, all at once a body of some four squadrons of the Russian force broke away from the main group and began galloping over the central hillocks towards the Highlanders.

Bennett watched unbelievingly as Sir Colin Campbell calmly rode along that thin line of men and his order made Bennett's blood run cold.

'Men, remember there is no retreat from here,' he told them. 'You must die where you stand.'

Bennett's heart was in his mouth, not just because those pitifully few men were being urged to give their lives for their country, but because they were all that stood between the formidable Russian force and Balaclava. If the base camp was taken by the Russians, the war would be lost too, and tens of thousands would be killed – civilians, the sick and his precious Hope too.

He knew that if he were in the Highlanders' boots, he would run just as fast as the Turks had earlier, for it seemed impossible that they could summon the nerve to hold their ground, much less vanquish the enemy.

But as Bennett watched the Russians come on, all at once he realized they were not aware that the hillock they were approaching was occupied by British soldiers. Suddenly the Highlanders sprang up like Jack-in-the-boxes. Having been told they were to die, it was clear they were not going to sell their lives cheaply, for they faced the enemy steadfastly and aimed their guns to kill.

Bennett held his reins ready to flee, for it looked inevitable that this was going to become a massacre. He could scarcely bear to look, yet he was entranced and staggered by the sight of the stalwart Highlanders firing calmly and accurately without any apparent fear for their own safety.

Maybe it was that cool courage, coupled with their fear-some appearance in kilts and red coats, that made the Russians waver at the second volley of fire; but they were wavering, and the Highlanders sensed it, moving forward, clearly eager to engage in hand-to-hand fighting.

Sir Colin Campbell's voice rose up loud and stern. 'Ninety-third, ninety-third! Damn all that eagerness!'

The Highlanders steadied, another volley was fired, and then to Bennett's awe and surprise the Russians wheeled and withdrew back in the direction of the main cavalry.

The Scotsmen cheered and whooped, the victorious sound bringing a lump to Bennett's throat. Goose-pimples came up over his whole body and he had to wipe away tears of emotion, for he could not imagine anything more courageous than what he'd just seen. This was heroics on the grandest of scales, something he hoped he'd live to tell his children and grandchildren about.

Bennett couldn't stay to see any further heroics, for he could see the ambulance carts being loaded and he would be needed to tend the casualties. But for the time being Balaclava was safe.

It was to be a day of incredible valour. General Scarlett of the Heavy Brigade, with 500 of his troopers, was on his way to support Sir Colin Campbell's men, but his route took him straight across the front of the advancing Russian cavalry coming down the hill towards him.

The Russians were 3,000 or more strong, yet despite the odds against him, Scarlett sounded the charge and tore like hell into the enemy with the Irish Inniskillings yelling like banshees.

Those who were watching from the safety of the Heights reported back later that the British had disappeared into the vast mass of Russians, and they expected them all to be annihilated. Yet among the seething grey-uniformed hordes brilliant red coats were observed, swords slashing, thrusting and hacking in the sunshine.

Then a second line of British came, wild with battle rage, yelling ferociously as they too launched themselves into the fray.

Finally, on fearing all men would be lost, Lord Lucan ordered in the 4th Dragoon Guards. They came crashing into the mêlée on the flank, and all at once the Russians swayed, rocked and suddenly fled.

Bennett was back with Hope in the hospital when they heard the cheers, and they assumed the battle was over for the day, and that any moment the carts of wounded would arrive.

They began to arrive within the hour. Once again it was a revisiting of Hope's first day at Balaclava as stretcher after stretcher was carried in, soon overflowing into the surrounding tents and outhouses and on to the quay. Bennett and the other surgeons moved methodically among them, amputating where necessary, removing pieces of shell and stitching sabre wounds.

Hope, who worked wherever she was needed most, giving water, cleaning wounds, cutting fabric to expose wounds, was astounded how even badly, often mortally, wounded men could be so cheerful and optimistic. When they said the British had the Russians on the run, she believed them.

The triumphs of the morning soon turned to shock and horror that afternoon, however, when the news arrived of the disastrous charge of the Light Brigade.

Further cowardly Turks fleeing to the safety of the port were the first indication something had gone badly wrong. It appeared that Lord Raglan had seen the Russians attempting to seize English guns from the abandoned redoubts and had ordered the Light Brigade to take action.

Why Lord Cardigan led 700 of his men straight into an ambush of the Russians who had earlier fled from the Heavy Brigade, no one understood. Bennett, having noted the two valleys on the plain earlier and how they obscured the vision of the soldiers in the field, thought that was to blame. In the weeks that followed, all kinds of theories were bandied about and the blame was attributed mainly to Lord Lucan. Yet the most logical explanation was that Cardigan couldn't see the Russians waiting in the north valley of the plain from his position, or that he had misinterpreted the order he had been given. But whatever the true reason, the result was absolute carnage, for the Light Brigade rode into a three-sided trap without escape. Russian gunfire rained down on them.

Only 195 men came back, including Lord Cardigan, and some 500 horses were killed.

Back in the hospital, everyone was too busy dealing with the casualties of the morning to take much notice of the gunfire. It was some time after the charge, which had only lasted twenty minutes, that a messenger arrived with the devastating news. By the time the wounded were brought down into the town it was late afternoon, already growing dark and cold.

A handful of the men, swaying in their saddles, rode down on their horses despite pieces of shell embedded in their limbs. A few staggered in on foot, supported by other soldiers, and the most seriously wounded came on carts. Their faces were blackened by smoke and smeared with blood, the once vivid colours of red or blue jackets were dull with dirt and more blood, tattered and singed by bullets.

For the second time since she'd arrived in the Crimea, Hope felt like running away. The little hospital was already full to bursting point, the air was thick with the stench of blood, and the moaning of those in agony was too dreadful to bear. She had already seen over thirty men die from their wounds that day. Most of them were very young, mere boys of eighteen or nineteen, and it was wrong that they should have died for a cause they didn't even fully understand.

But as she stood at the hospital door, watching the lights from the quay glistening in the water of the bay, she knew she would have to find the strength from somewhere, as long as Bennett remained working.

'Leave me here to take my turn. There's a great many worse off than me.'

She started at the familiar voice, and realized it was coming from one of the carts filling the quayside. The darkness had added a new problem. Earlier, in daylight, they had been able to check over the wounded, selecting the most urgent cases first. This was impossible now, and it was too horrible to think that someone might die of blood loss for the want of a simple tourniquet. Taking a lantern down from the wall, she called to two orderlies to come with her. Then, going from cart to cart, she quickly looked the men over, telling her assistants which ones she wanted taken straight in.

It was on the fourth cart back that she found the owner of the voice she had recognized.

Captain Pettigrew.

She hadn't seen him at all since she landed here, much to her frustration when she wanted to know all about Nell, and she hadn't had the time or opportunity to go to search him out.

'Where are you wounded, Captain?' she asked, holding the lantern up so she could see him better.

'Why, if it isn't Mrs Meadows!' he exclaimed in some surprise. 'I thought you'd been left at Varna!'

'Not me,' she smiled. 'I was always disobedient. Where are you hurt?'

'Just a sabre slash,' he said, indicating that it was on his thigh. 'It can wait.'

Even in the darkness she could see a vivid flash of white flesh where his cherry-coloured breeches had been slashed. The sleeve of his blue jacket was cut too, and the surrounding material was dark with blood.

'Take this man,' she said to the two orderlies.

'No, leave me, there's others more urgent,' he said.

'Allow me to be the judge of that,' she said. 'A clean wound if stitched up quickly heals in no time. Stay here and you'll bleed to death. Don't argue with me.'

He grinned at her and made a mock salute. But despite his jovial manner she could see his face was alarmingly pale and there were beads of sweat on his forehead.

By the time she'd checked the other carts and gone back into the hospital, Captain Pettigrew had been laid on a palliasse and she could see he was already weak from loss of blood.

Taking the scissors from her apron pocket, she cut away the sleeve of his jacket and the leg of his breeches, then bathed both the wounds. Once cleaned, she could see they were deep, but she was sure stitching would be sufficient.

She called Bennett over for his opinion. He'd just finished one leg amputation and was about to start on another man's arm.

'You can do this, nurse,' he said, glancing sideways at her, perhaps guessing she was nervous of stitching up an officer. 'They are longer wounds than you've done before, but good clean ones. I expect the Captain could do with a tot of rum before you start.'

Pettigrew tried to smile but it was more of a grimace. 'Will her stitching be as good as her sister's?'

'It's better,' Hope said. 'And I give bigger tots of rum too. Now, just you lie still.'

It took over an hour to stitch the two wounds, and although he grimaced a great deal, he didn't cry out. Hope's knees hurt from kneeling on the stone floor, her eyes felt sore from squinting in the bad light, and she was so tired that there were moments when she thought she wouldn't be able to finish the job. But finally the last stitch was in and she was able to bandage the wounds.

'Can you get someone to take me back to camp?' Pettigrew asked, his voice weak and shaky now.

'Certainly not,' she retorted indignantly. 'Jolting up that rough road will just break the wounds open. You'll stay here and keep still. You aren't out of the woods yet.'

She washed his face and hands, then got another blanket and tucked it round him.

His eyes were fixed on her face and the look was so intense it made her blush. 'What is it?' she asked.

'Your colouring is the same as the rest of your family's,' he said. 'But your features are different.'

'Have you met them all?' she asked in some surprise.

'Of course,' he replied. 'Not James recently though, but I remember him from Briargate.'

A warm glow of delight ran through her. 'There is so much I want to ask you about them,' she said eagerly. 'But I can't now, you need to rest and I've got other men to nurse.'

'Nell will be so proud of you,' he said, putting one hand on her arm to stress his sincerity. 'I did write to tell her I found you. I hope you don't mind?'

'No, I'm glad, but tomorrow you must give me the address so I can write too. We have a great deal of catching up to do.'

'Did Albert force you to write that letter?' he asked.

Hope nodded.

'And how did he ensure you'd never come back?'

'Blackmail,' she said simply. 'But that's enough for one night. Try to sleep.'

Three hours later, Hope was finally leaving the hospital. Although she was close to complete exhaustion, she stopped to look at Captain Pettigrew for a moment. A lantern nearby gave enough light to see him clearly, and in sleep his face looked youthful and handsome.

She could understand why Lady Harvey had fallen for him, not just because he had fine, strong features, or that air of sheer masculinity Sir William lacked, but something more. She couldn't define it, but she felt it inside her. A strange, warm feeling, not unlike the way she'd felt about Bennett when she first met him.

Chapter Twenty-one

'And where do you think you are going?' Hope asked indignantly as she arrived at the hospital early in the morning to find Captain Pettigrew about to dress himself in some new clothes.

It had been two days since he'd been brought to the hospital, and his wounds were already healing, but he wasn't fit enough to be walking around.

'I can't stay here, nurse,' he said, flashing his brilliant grin at her. 'I need to see my men and the horses. Besides, you've got plenty of really sick patients to fuss over.'

A great many of the wounded from that disastrous day had already died from their injuries, but the hospital was still vastly overcrowded, and more men would need amputations today if gangrene had set into their wounds. Looking around her, Hope thought the place had more in common with a squalid 'padding ken' than a hospital. There were men everywhere, shoved up together like sardines in beds, under beds, every inch of space filled.

'You will lie down and let me re-dress those wounds,' she said sharply, snatching the new breeches and jacket from his hands. 'Just stretching to put those clothes on is likely to open you up again. Or do you want an infection, then an amputation, so you can go hopping around with only one leg and one arm?'

'Now there's a cheerful thought,' he responded teasingly. 'You are even bossier than Nell.'

But he did obey her, and didn't even wince as she removed the bandages and washed the wounds.

'There's no sign of an infection,' she said after she'd examined him and begun to re-dress the wounds. 'But that doesn't mean you are able to walk or ride yet. I think you should be moved somewhere to convalesce though, you need a strong stomach to stay here.'

'Don't you dare suggest I go to Scutari,' he said with some indignation. 'I'd sooner lie here and look at you than face that hell-hole.'

Hope had been told that just the previous day a copy of *The Times* had been circulating which had reported on what a terrible place the hospital at Scutari was. As a result, most of the wounded were fearful about being sent there.

'Ask Lord Cardigan if you can stay on his yacht then,' she retorted. It was something of a miracle that Cardigan had survived the charge. Apart from a minor sabre slash he was unhurt. He had retreated to his yacht and ordered his company surgeon to treat him there. It was said he was drinking heavily, as well he might, for many here held him responsible for the carnage.

'He doesn't like "Indian Officers",' Pettigrew said cheerfully. 'He probably hopes I've croaked.'

Hope smiled. It was hard not to be amused by Pettigrew; he was brave, outspoken, charming and like a naughty boy at times. Apparently Lord Cardigan had slighted many officers who had served in India, which was ridiculous, as they were the only officers who had recent battle experience.

'We could put you in a tent out the back,' she suggested. 'I daresay if your servant couldn't come down to wait on you, I could bring you the odd bowl of gruel to keep your strength up.'

He laughed heartily but then winced at the pain in his arm.

'No laughing, no walking, no anything,' she said with

mock severity. 'You've already used up all your luck, so if you've got any sense you'll just lie low.'

'Can you spare some time to come and talk to me today?' he said. 'There are so many questions I want to ask you.'

'There's plenty I want to ask you too,' she said tartly. 'But meanwhile I've got more important things to do.'

It was noon before Hope had finished changing dressings. Most of these wounded would be cleared out of the hospital shortly, but they would soon be replaced by others brought down from the Heights. The shelling was going on right now, though she hardly noticed it over the moans. She just hoped Robbie would stay safe up there. He'd been ordered there with his company the day after she and Queenie arrived. Queenie had gone with him, and she really missed her friend for there were so few women down here, and none that she felt as comfortable with as Queenie.

Hope was terrified that Bennett might be ordered on to the Heights. By rights he should be there with his regiment, but maybe his superiors realized that they had few doctors as experienced in surgery as him and felt he was more valuable here.

The army certainly didn't value their rank and file. The men had no shelter, hardly any food, and when it rained the trenches were knee-deep in mud. Everyone was concerned about what would happen when winter set in.

Hope found time to go and see Captain Pettigrew that evening. The surgeon who had treated Lord Cardigan's wound had moved him to a small house along the quay being used by officers from the 93rd Regiment.

She was ushered towards a room at the back of the house by the same servant she'd met at the cavalry camp in Varna. He was a wiry man of about thirty with very bad teeth and a completely bald head.

'You done a good job with the Captain,' he said cheerfully. 'Didn't think I was going to see him again!'

Hope smiled at the rather blunt remark. 'You take good care of him and don't let him exert himself,' she said.

Pettigrew looked remarkably comfortable in his new surroundings. The bed wasn't quite long enough for him, but he had a pillow and a colourful quilt tucked round him. The damaged jacket was gone and had been replaced by a loose white linen shirt.

'I hope you had help getting your clothes off?' she said tartly.

'Mead stripped me as tenderly as if I were a baby,' he grinned. Then, looking up at Mead who was still in the doorway, he asked him to bring in some coffee.

'Have you eaten?' Pettigrew asked. 'Mead will make something for you if you haven't. He's a good cook. He'd put most women to shame.'

'I had something with my husband,' she said. 'I just called to see how you were. I can't stay long.'

'Surgeon Lewis said it was the best bit of stitching he'd seen in a long time,' Pettigrew said. 'I suspect he wished he'd got you to stitch up "the noble Yachtsman's" wounds too.'

Hope laughed. 'I think I would have let my scissors slip,' she said.

'Are scissors your weapon of choice?' he asked.

Hope sat down in a chair beside his bed. A fire was burning in the hearth, the oil light gave a honey-coloured glow to the bare, rough walls, and after the hospital and the tent, it felt very luxurious and almost homely.

'They could become so,' she said airily. 'But without further ado, I want to know about Nell and how she came to be your housekeeper.'

Hope hung on his every word as he explained how he'd

met Nell while out riding in the early spring of '48 and offered her the position as his housekeeper. When he said he met her on the bridge at Chewton she could visualize the millpond, the willows coming into leaf, and the sound of running water.

He was neither sentimental nor brusque, and while providing only a modicum of detail, he still managed to give Hope a very clear picture of how it all came about. He touched lightly on Nell's state of mind following her discovery that Hope had vanished, but lessened any anxiety Hope might have had by enthusing about how she'd taken him and his house in hand, and explaining that she was secure and contented now.

It was the account of a man who fully understood heartbreak; a compassionate man who was more than aware how hard and unfair life could be for women in Nell's position. In that respect he was very like Bennett, and Hope found herself warming more to the man as each minute passed.

Pettigrew went on to explain how he and Nell had heard about the fire, how Nell had taken Lady Harvey from Matt's to the Warrens' house, and he also spoke of Sir William's funeral which he had attended.

'It was quite the most disturbing funeral I have ever been to,' he sighed. 'Usually there is just deep sadness, especially when the death has been unexpected. But this was bafflement; the ordinary people from the village could not accept that a man they knew, who had prayed with them in church, could be evil enough to set fire to a house knowing there were people in it.

'Poor Nell was distraught, even though it had been years since she'd left Albert, and indeed had spoken out against him to anyone who would listen. I think she felt partially responsible.'

'She would,' Hope agreed. 'She always felt it was her fault

when any of us did something wrong. But how did Rufus stand up to the funeral?'

'His rage was palpable. He gave a reading from the Bible during the service and his voice was firm, but he was quivering, and his eyes were like ice. He had by all accounts been of the opinion for years that Albert was dangerous – he told me he had refused to come home that Christmas because he didn't like the liberties the man was taking with his parents. He's a fine young man now, Hope. Tall, athletic and very handsome. He is so like William at the same age, it took me right back to when I used to pester him to take me riding.'

Hope hadn't realized that Pettigrew had known Sir William since childhood and she encouraged him to talk about it.

'I was six and he was ten when we first met. My father was a soldier too. I was staying with my aunt and uncle in Chelwood when the news came that both he and my mother had died of fever. I suspect William's parents had told him he had to be kind to me because of it. And he was very kind, like an older brother.'

He stopped abruptly, half-closing his eyes, and Hope guessed he was feeling guilty about Lady Harvey.

'Enough of me,' he said suddenly. 'Tell me about the day you left Briargate.'

'It was your letter to Lady Harvey,' she began.

She cut the story right to the bone and merely said that she'd gone into the gatehouse to hide the letter and Albert had caught her.

Yet even as she told him how Albert had hit her and forced her to write a goodbye letter, she could feel the weakness of her story and kept hesitating.

'He said if I didn't go he'd take the letter to Sir William and that Lady Harvey would be disgraced, and Nell would be dismissed too for covering up,' she said, blushing because

Pettigrew was looking at her so intently. 'He told me that if I left and never came back he would keep quiet.'

'But if Nell had been dismissed, surely he would have had to go too?'

'That would have been even worse,' Hope said quietly. 'Nell would have been alone and friendless with him.'

'Why didn't you go to Matt?' he asked, his face very stern. 'Or Ruth in Bath?'

She didn't know why she suddenly started crying. It might have been because he knew these people she had missed for so long, or perhaps she was upset that once again Albert was forcing her to keep quiet about what she knew.

'He told me I wasn't to go to them, and if I did he would make Nell's life a misery,' she sobbed out. 'He hit me, shoved me out in the rain without a penny, you can't imagine what I went through.'

'I think I can,' he said softly. 'Bristol is not a good place for anyone young and friendless. I talked about you to Rufus after the funeral; he said that he always knew Albert was responsible for you leaving and he hated him for it. He also felt the man had something over his father.'

'Of course he did, he knew about you and Lady Harvey.'

'At first I thought it was that. But Rufus was quite specific about his father and Albert. You see, he had discovered that Albert had been given a great deal of money by William over the years. Now, I have my own opinion as to what this hold might have been, but I have no proof. Although I think you do.'

Hope lifted her head, and she saw he knew the truth.

'I would never have voiced what I suspected, ever,' he said quietly. 'And now he is dead, it should die with him for Rufus's sake. He's a fine young man, Hope, with none of his parents' weaknesses. I know from Nell how close you were as children. That, of course, was the most compelling reason for you to obey Albert, wasn't it? For you couldn't go to anyone for help without revealing what you knew.'

There was no point in denying it, so she nodded. 'I walked in on them together,' she whispered, tears running down her cheeks. 'But it wasn't just Rufus; it was Lady Harvey and Nell too. They would all have been shamed.'

His hand reached out and took hers. 'Your loyalty is a credit to you, Hope,' he said with a break in his voice. 'I think most people would only have thought of themselves. But don't be afraid, I will never divulge what you've told me.'

'I must go,' she said, getting to her feet and wiping her eyes. 'I've stayed too long and Bennett will be worried. But what do I tell Nell?'

'Just about the letter, that will do fine, she's not as suspicious or as worldly as I am. Don't feel badly towards William for he couldn't help the way he was made. I've met many men like him since I've been in the army, good, brave men who try so hard to suppress it. Sometimes they just can't any more. I did my best to fight off loving Anne, but I couldn't. In many ways that's the same.'

'I never felt hatred for Sir William,' she said, her eyes swimming with tears. 'Only for Albert, and not because of that either. But for his cruelty to Nell and for forcing us apart.'

He looked at her long and hard, then smiled. 'You know, you are everything Nell said you were, and more. Write to her at my home, Willow End, Bath Road. You see, there is a God, even in this place where it seems He has deserted us. She will have had my letter by now, but it will be you she wants to hear from.'

On an impulse Hope bent and kissed his forehead, then rushed for the door and left without another word.

*

On the day after the battle of Balaclava there had been another small battle near a deserted village called Inkerman. Shortly afterwards, Russian troops were observed massing up on the Fedioukine Hills, and it was clear they were planning another far more powerful attack soon. But worrying as that was, while the guns were firing constantly up at Sebastopol, sending a daily stream of wounded and sick soldiers down to the hospital, there was too much to be done to consider how they would cope with yet more casualties.

On 4 November it rained hard and the men on picket duty keeping an eye on the Russian troops reported a quiet night, but, as they were coming off duty at dawn on the 5th, the attack came.

There was thick fog, and the allied troops were heavily outnumbered and short of ammunition, but what they lacked in numbers, they made up for in courage and initiative, and by mid-afternoon the Russians were in full retreat.

Word of the victory came quickly to the hospital, but it was hard for anyone to feel a celebration was in order, not with 2,500 of their men killed and wounded, and another 1,700 French soldiers likewise. They had no doubt either that some of the 12,000 Russian casualties would end up here too. But they did what they had to, rolled up their sleeves and prepared for the onslaught as best they could.

That night, and for the following three nights, Hope had only a couple of hours' sleep. She knew the surgeons were justified in saying they would do more harm than good attempting to operate in poor light, and understood why they took themselves off to their beds at night, but she could not walk away with the cries of the suffering ringing in her ears.

It was so cold, and many of the wounded lay shivering on the carts that had brought them there, for there was no space to bring them inside. All she could do was tuck a blanket around them, help them sip some brandy or merely wash their faces. But at least asking their names, telling them they'd be seen as soon as possible, and showing that she cared, helped them to get through the night.

Captain Pettigrew came to the hospital at dawn on the fourth day when she was alone in the room with the most seriously injured. He was walking with the aid of an improvised crutch, and when she saw him, she flew at him to reprimand him.

'Are you stupid?' she hissed at him. 'You'll break that wound open!'

'It's fine,' he said. 'Nothing compared to some of these injuries. I came to see if there was anything I could do.'

He was clearly serious, and Hope saw the horror in his eyes as he noticed a box of amputated limbs which hadn't yet been taken away for disposal by one of the orderlies.

Hope quickly covered it with a blanket. But she couldn't conceal the number of men with blood-soaked dressings, or the wailing from one soldier in the corner. Everywhere the Captain looked there was horror, and even to someone with no medical knowledge it was clear most of them would die.

'It was good of you to offer help,' she said. 'But you shouldn't be in here. Maybe in a day or two you could talk to some of the less seriously injured — a lot of them can't manage to write a letter home and they'd appreciate you doing it for them. But go now, before you fall and burst your stitches.'

He held on tightly to the crutch, but reached out and tucked a stray curl back under her cap. 'With the best will in the world, you can't make everyone better,' he said with the tenderness of understanding. 'I know you've been here for at least twenty hours a day and you'll become ill if you continue to do that. You need some rest, food, and probably a bath. Come to my house later and you'll get all that.'

'A bath?' she said in astonishment. He had hit on the one thing she would sell her soul for. 'You have a bath?'

'We do,' he chuckled. 'And Mead will fill it for you. Bring Bennett with you, for I know he's worked as many hours as you.'

'But . . .' she started to protest.

'No buts,' he said firmly. 'Nell would want me to bully you into seeing sense. And I've had a letter from her. If you don't come, I won't let you see it.'

'What does she say?' Hope was suddenly like a young girl again, excitement bubbling up inside her, for this letter had to be in reply to the Captain's news that he'd met her in Varna.

'You'll find out after you've had a meal and a bath. Not a word till then.'

Bennett smiled as Angus nudged him and pointed at Hope. She had been sitting on the bed, running her fingers through her hair to dry it, but now she'd slumped back on the pillow and was sound asleep.

'I'd better get her back to the tent,' Bennett said, rising to his feet.

'You'll do nothing of the sort, she can stay there,' Angus said firmly. 'And you can get in there with her, you look close to collapse too.'

Bennett took the quilt from the bottom of the bed and covered Hope, standing by her and looking down at her for a moment. She had been so happy to have a bath, even though it had only been six inches of hot water in a tub barely big enough for a child. Now, sound asleep with her damp hair loose around her face, she looked no older than she had the first time Bennett saw her.

'She is a very beautiful woman,' Angus said softly.

'Isn't she?' Bennett agreed. 'But there is so much more

to her than a lovely face. I met her, you know, when she was nursing her two friends with cholera. Just seventeen, yet so strong, capable and compassionate.'

'Today has been a good one for her,' Angus said thoughtfully. 'Those few words from Nell meant so much, didn't they?'

Bennett nodded and returned to his chair. They had come to Pettigrew's house at noon, and his servant had made them a wonderful robust stew with herb dumplings. Then they'd had their baths, and put on clean clothes. It was only then that Pettigrew, or Angus as he insisted they should call him, had got out Nell's letter.

Bennett had been rather surprised that Nell wasn't as literate as Hope. She had written only a few lines, and clearly she'd laboured long and hard over them. But not even the greatest writer in England, neither Thomas Hardy nor Charles Dickens, could have got so much feeling and delight into such a few words.

'*You have given me the Crown jewels,*' was how it started.

I haven't stopped crying for joy yet. Imagine my Hope married to a doctor! And there where you can keep an eye on her for me. This is the happiest day of my life. But how much more I will cry and laugh when she comes home. Kiss her for me. Tell her to keep out of danger. And make her write soon.

'Fate moves in mysterious ways,' Bennett chuckled. 'Fancy us having to come right across Europe for this.'

'You could have just gone to the village back home and had a short cut to it,' Angus said with a wry smile. 'Tell me, Bennett, why didn't you?'

'When was I supposed to? You aren't the only one in the army! I got home in January, got married, had a short honeymoon and then we came out here.'

'Yes, I can see you had little time. But when you first wanted to marry Hope, knowing what you had learned of her circumstances, I would have thought that might have been an appropriate time to do some investigation on her behalf. You could have gone into the local ale house and asked a couple of questions and you'd have discovered for yourself that Nell was with me.'

'That's easy for you to say now, after the event. But Hope wouldn't hear of me going there to ask questions.'

'I don't think you ever suggested it,' Angus retorted. 'You wanted to keep her all to yourself, didn't you?'

'Now, look here!' Bennett exclaimed.

'No, you look here,' Angus interrupted him. 'I saw your face when Hope read out that letter. You were touched, but a little afraid too, afraid that Nell and the rest of the family would steal her from you.'

'Of course I'm not afraid.' Bennett snorted with derision.

'Yes you are. It's hardly surprising, she's a great prize, and when you are the only person in her life, you can have all of her. But take some advice from me, don't cage her. Let her fly!'

'And am I supposed to believe that you understand anything about married love?' Bennett said with icy sarcasm.

'Sometimes those on the outside can see it clearer than from the inside. But Bennett, I've said enough for one day, and you are as exhausted as your wife. Go to bed now before you keel over.'

Bennett was sorely tempted to lift Hope from the bed and take her home, just to show Captain Pettigrew that he cared nothing for his advice or opinions. But he was too tired for protests and Hope looked far too comfortable to disturb.

'But where will you sleep?' he asked.

Angus gave a wry smile. 'Don't worry about me, I'll find another bed.'

In the cold, wet days that followed, the general euphoria in Balaclava which had come with the Russian retreat at Inkerman faded quickly. The almost constant gunfire up at Sebastopol, and the received reports that little or no damage had been done to the town defences, made it increasingly clear that it could not be taken quickly. The harsh reality was that the troops would almost certainly be in the trenches all winter.

Anxiety grew daily in the hospital. Forty or fifty men reported sick every day and were sent down there. Another twenty or thirty would be wounded – in fact there were only 16,500 men fit for service when initially there had been 35,000. Cholera was still with them, along with typhus, typhoid and malaria, although the last three were usually just classed as general fever. With few medicines, and not enough nutritious, easily digestible food available for the sick, their chances of recovery were poor.

Bennett was often filled with white-hot rage, for the urgently needed goods and provisions would come into the port, but bureaucratic bungling made it impossible to get them to the appropriate destination. Men were building a railway for a siege train which when it was finished would make transportation to the Heights much easier. But this monstrously hard work was enough to kill men already weakened by sickness and hunger.

Had it not been for a black Jamaican woman called Mother Seacole by the men, the wounded lying for hours on the icy quay in stretchers waiting to be taken aboard a ship bound for Scutari would have perished. She was one of the army of sutlers who had turned up to sell their goods to the men. But although she was in the Crimea for business, and had a store outside the town where she sold everything from hot meals to new boots, she was a genuinely kindly woman who had good nursing skills, and she was there on the quay most days, doling out cups of tea and other little comforts.

Up at the siege, warm clothing and blankets were desperately needed, the food was scarce, monotonous and barely edible, and it was hard to find fuel for fires. The sick sent down from there spoke of sitting in a water-filled trench all night, then going back to their leaking tents without a change of clothes to put on.

Hope and Bennett might not have to sit in the rain all night, but they too had found how miserable a home a tent could be in bad weather. With no chairs, table or other comforts, they had to make do with medicine crates, and when it rained they couldn't even light a fire to cook something to eat.

On the night of 14 November, Bennett had managed to get hold of some chicken from the butcher, and they'd fried it and baked some potatoes in the fire. Washing this down with rum and water, they felt they'd had a banquet. For once, instead of falling asleep immediately from exhaustion, they'd chatted, about Captain Pettigrew's good recovery, of how long it would be before Hope got a letter from Nell, and whether Alice would send out the foodstuffs and warm clothes Bennett had asked her for.

They woke with a start to the sound of wind hauling at the tent, threatening to rip it to shreds, and when they looked cautiously out they saw what could only be called a hurricane.

It was six in the morning and not yet light, but even so they could see tents, planks of wood, buckets, camp kettles and items of clothing flying around in the wind.

'Heaven help us!' Bennett exclaimed. 'Are we to be swept away by wind now?'

'But what of the wounded in the tents behind the hospital?' Hope gasped. 'It's more exposed there! They might be lying in the rain!'

Bennett was hanging on to the tent pole, afraid it would snap in two. 'Get dressed while I hold this,' he said hurriedly. 'Pack all our loose stuff into boxes and then we'll go.'

'What is that cracking sound?' Hope asked as she struggled into her dress and put on her boots.

'It will be the ships in the harbour banging against one another,' he replied. 'They will break up, I shouldn't wonder.'

Leaving their tent as secure as they could make it, they headed for the hospital. The wind was so strong that Hope would have been blown over if Bennett hadn't kept hold of her hand. But once they came away from the protection of the buildings, the wind blowing straight from the sea caught them, knocking them back against a wall.

Others arrived to help them get the sick out of the most exposed tents and in through the back door of the hospital, but it was a long, hard job, with refuse blowing into their faces as they worked.

It was after nine before they were able to go to the windows at the front of the building and see the damage in the harbour. The sight that met their eyes was truly appalling. The waves outside the harbour wall were so huge that spray was going over the clifftops and bucketing down into the harbour like a flood. The tightly packed ships were grinding into one another and the sides were slowly being torn apart. The *Star of the Sea* had already lost most of her stern and many ships had lost their masts, causing damage to others as they came down. And the sea was boiling and heaving as if it intended to devour every last vessel in the harbour.

'But what of the ships outside?' Hope asked Bennett.

Only a few days earlier in a high wind, several ship's masters had asked permission to enter the inner harbour, and been refused. They were still out there at anchor, and in real peril.

It was the blackest of days. At ten in the morning the word went round that the *Prince* had sunk with all hands outside the harbour. Other ships suffered terrible damage too and many lives were lost. When the wind dropped later it began to snow.

The following day was very cold, but fine, and only then could the full extent of the hurricane be counted. Up at the siege, far more exposed than Balaclava, tents, clothing and equipment had been blown away, never to be seen again, including the tents that were being used as field hospitals, and the sick and wounded within them had been left exposed to the wind and rain.

The harbour was full of wreckage, roofs and windows had been torn off buildings, and there was hardly a ship bobbing on the now calm water that hadn't received extensive damage.

But it was the loss of the *Prince* that left grown men weeping. For she was laden with all the goods they so desperately needed: warm clothing for the troops, supplies of medicine, brandy, blankets, palliasses, tea and sugar. Ironically, one of the passengers to lose his life when the ship went down was Dr Spence, the Deputy General of Hospitals, who had come out to make an inspection following libellous reports about the medical conditions in the Crimea.

'Dr Meadows!'

Bennett looked up on hearing his name shouted and saw Angus Pettigrew waving to him from behind some heavily laden bullock carts. The quay was as crowded and chaotic as usual – even a recent order for the filth to be cleared away, a new site built for slaughtering animals, and the decomposing bodies in the water to be towed out to sea, hadn't made much difference. It was still a disgrace.

Bennett wasn't anxious to talk to Angus. Although it had been three weeks since he'd shown Hope his letter from Nell, Bennett was still smarting at what had been said to him. He knew Angus had a point. If he had been a real man he would have gone out to Compton Dando long ago and discovered that Nell had left Albert.

But he wasn't a real man then, he had still been in essence the lad who had been the butt of every joke at medical school. It still made him smart that he'd allowed Uncle Abel to bully him, and that he hadn't put his foot down to stop Hope being sent to work at St Peter's.

He'd joined the army purely because it was a way of getting out from under his uncle, not because he was brave. He hadn't thought then that he'd be pushed into active service, and if he had, he would have run a mile. He'd had a rosy little picture in his mind of being the medical officer attached to a barracks, and that in a couple of years he'd be able to marry Hope and raise a few children.

Yet what he hadn't expected was that he would find his niche in the army. Sick men didn't need another tough Sergeant Major yelling at them, they wanted someone who listened to them and had the knowledge to make them well again. And neither officers nor rank and file cared about his background or financial or social standing. To them he was a first-class doctor and they felt fortunate to have him with their regiment.

Feeling appreciated, having his opinions valued and his medical skills admired, had made him lose his timidity. He found he was able to stand against injustice and former bad medical practices. The harshness of army life out in South Africa had toughened him up too and the Regimental Surgeon Meadows who had come back to marry Hope Renton was a very different man to the one who had been scared to death that first time he walked through Lewins Mead.

He had said as they set off on their honeymoon that he thought it was time Hope contacted her family, and he had meant it. But of course he hadn't known then that just a couple of weeks later they'd be bound for the Black Sea.

Had he known what hell was in store for them, he wouldn't have let Hope come. But what was done, was done, and she had proved invaluable. All they could do now was slog on in the hope that things might improve. He supposed he'd also have to get used to the idea that Captain Angus Pettigrew was going to continue to be as irritating as a louse.

'How are the wounds?' Bennett asked as he got within speaking distance of Angus.

'Pretty well healed now, thank you, though the leg is still a bit stiff,' Angus grinned. He was in full uniform, and it was clearly almost new for the gold braid wasn't tarnished, and the blue jacket and cherry breeches had no stains or patches. Only his worn boots gave an indication that he'd been through action.

'You're the smartest man on the quay,' Bennett said with more sarcasm than admiration. 'Lucky for you that you had a second uniform.'

'I feel overdressed,' Angus said, his smile fading as he glanced at a couple of infantry men walking past, their uniforms literally mud-covered rags. 'But I'm going up to the camp and, you know . . .' He broke off, perhaps embarrassed to say aloud that his superior officers would take him to task if he wasn't correctly dressed.

'It was a terrible blow, the *Prince* going down,' Bennett

said. 'The sick coming down from the Heights tell me the men up there have the soles coming off their boots and that they wear their blankets under their greatcoats to try to keep warm. But I'm sure you know that. Are you intending to ride up to the camp?'

'Yes. Mead brought my horse down this morning, though he's in a sorry state. I gave him a handful of oats, but what he needs is a bucketful. There's damn-all forage left for the horses now. I heard Lord Raglan is pushing for more. If it doesn't come soon we'll have to shoot some of the horses.'

'I daresay some of the men who are cold and hungry would like to be put out of their misery too,' Bennett sighed. 'There won't be much cheer this Christmas.'

'I hoped to give you some cheer today by asking if you and Hope would like my room,' Angus said, thumbing towards the building behind them. 'I'm going to stay up at the camp, and you two can't live in a tent now it's getting so cold.'

'That's very decent of you.' Bennett suddenly felt more light-hearted. During the previous two or three nights the temperature had dropped below freezing. 'Hope has never complained but there's a limit to anyone's endurance.'

'She's made of stern stuff,' Angus smiled. 'Has she had a letter from Nell yet?'

Bennett shook his head. 'She's on the lookout for the mailboat every day. And she must have written a dozen letters home. But no one has had any for two weeks now, so they must come soon.'

'You can move in today,' Angus said. 'My stuff's all packed, ready to be taken away. I got a Tartar woman to clean it for you and light a fire. Her name is Rosa, at least that's what I've been calling her.'

'That is really very good of you.' Bennett suddenly felt a little ashamed of his thoughts about the man.

'You should have been given a decent billet from the start,' Angus said. 'All you doctors deserve a medal for what you've done here under the most appalling conditions. It makes my blood boil to read in the papers from home that the general public is being encouraged to believe some of you are being derelict in your duty. I'd like to string up those who really are responsible for the chaos out here. And some of the bloody dimwit officers who can hardly wipe their own arses, much less lead their men.'

Bennett smirked. 'Calm down, Angus, you'll burst your stitches,' he said.

Angus chuckled. 'Hope did too good a job for that,' he said. 'But I must be off now. I hope I'll be welcome to call on you both next time I'm down here?'

'We'd be disappointed if you didn't,' Bennett said.

'Are you sure I'm not in your way, Nell?' Rufus asked. 'Just say the word and I'll clear off.'

It was a few days before Christmas and they were in the kitchen at Willow End. Rufus had turned up just as Nell was making some marzipan to cover the rich fruit cake she'd made to send out to Hope.

'Bless you, Master Rufus.' Nell beamed at him. 'Of course you aren't in my way, it's a pleasure to have you here with me. Just let me get this on the cake and then I'll fetch Hope's letters for you to read.'

In Nell's opinion Rufus was the finest gentleman she'd ever met, and the most handsome. He had the best of his parents' looks, the pure blond hair, bright blue eyes, and the elegance. She liked to think, though, that it was the Rentons who had influenced his character, for he was stalwart, capable and kind-hearted. As for his determination and strong backbone, that must have come from his paternal grandfather, for legend had it that he'd been a force to reckon with.

Rufus had gone back to Oxford after his father's funeral, leaving his mother with the Warrens at Wick Farm. But at Easter he had returned home and informed Lady Harvey he wasn't going back to Oxford, and that he intended to farm the Briargate estate, not sell off the land as everyone expected.

'So tell me, sir, how is Lady Harvey coping now?' Nell asked. Her former mistress had been horrified when Rufus had told her they would be living in the gatehouse. Her first question had been to ask where the housekeeper would live!

'Don't call me "sir", Nell,' he said with a grin. 'Nor Master Rufus either, it's just plain Rufus now. As for Mother, she's still bemoaning the rough furniture, the smallness of the rooms, and having to do so much for herself, but I think this is just habit. She does seem a little less miserable now, and she's become an able cook.'

He picked up a piece of marzipan left on the table and nibbled it thoughtfully. 'Tell me, Nell, was I cruel to make her live there?'

'As I see it, she was lucky to have somewhere *to* live,' Nell said tartly. The years away from Briargate had made her see her old mistress in a different light. Sympathetic as she was to Lady Harvey in the loss of her husband and home, she didn't think anyone, however highborn, should expect others to support her. Left to her own devices, she would have stayed on with the Warrens indefinitely. Her sisters had made it plain they didn't want her in their homes. And she had no money to live anywhere else.

'Sometimes I think maybe I should have sold the land, and taken a small house somewhere like Bath. I know Mother would have much preferred that.' Rufus sighed. 'But I would have had to find some kind of employment, and what could I do except become a clerk or some such thing? I had to use most of the money left by my grandfather to pay off Father's debts, and I felt it was wrong to squander the rest staying on at Oxford while mother was living like a poor relation at Wick Farm. At least this way we still own the land, and if I make a go of farming, I might be able to rebuild Briargate and one day my children might have all the advantages I had.'

'You did the right thing,' Nell said stoutly. 'Our Matt reckons you were born to farm, and I don't think Lady Harvey would have been any happier in Bath, not without fine clothes, a carriage and servants. At least she's got friends in the village, people who care for her. If you were my son I'd be right proud of you.'

'Funny how things turn out,' he said with a wry grin. 'When I was small I was so envious of the village children. It seemed to me they had so much more fun and freedom than I did. Now I've got to work for a living it looks very different.'

Nell finished her work on the cake and took it to the pantry. 'All our lives have been turned upside down,' she said as she returned. 'I just wish the police could find Albert and hang him. It's like having a bad tooth. You know that the pain will keep coming back until it's been pulled out.'

'He won't dare come anywhere near here,' Rufus said comfortingly. 'Whatever else he is, he isn't stupid.'

'No, but he was obsessed with the garden at Briargate, and I think he's likely to come back to look at what's happened to it,' Nell said in a small voice.

'Then he'll die of shock when he finds it gone,' Rufus chuckled. 'I ploughed up the bottom lawn back in November, and I've got pigs where the rose garden used to be. You must come up and take a look, Nell. Not just at the farm, but the gatehouse too. The curtains you made for us are lovely.'

Nell shook her head. 'I couldn't, Rufus, too many bad memories for me. Maybe when Hope and the Captain come home I'll feel different, but I doubt it.'

Nell stirred the soup while Rufus read Hope's letters. Now and again he'd chuckle at something amusing, and she'd glance round at him, wondering how he'd react if he was ever to find out that Hope was his half-sister.

Proud and happy as she was that Hope had done well for herself and married a doctor, the secret of her true parentage worried Nell almost as much as the prospect of Albert turning up one day.

Hope mentioned Captain Pettigrew a great deal in her letters. Nell hadn't of course given Rufus the first one in which she explained how Albert had caught her with the letter from the Captain to Lady Harvey and made several references to their love affair. But it was clear from the subsequent letters that she'd formed an attachment to the Captain while nursing him.

Angus's letters showed the attachment was mutual, and though common sense told Nell this was probably because of their respective links with her, it felt like more than that. On the one hand she told herself that maybe she should tell them the truth. Hope had no other father now, the Captain had no other children. They would be a comfort to each other.

But there was Rufus. He might very well be so delighted that his childhood friend was in fact his half-sister that he'd overlook his mother's infidelity. But she doubted he'd appreciate discovering that Captain Pettigrew, a man he'd known all his life and looked up to, was the villain of the piece.

When Nell heard the wonderful news that the Captain had met Hope in Varna, she'd gone straight to Matt to share it with him. He had passed it on to Rufus, who in turn had told Lady Harvey.

Lady Harvey had found a man to bring her here in a trap the very next day and she was all of a twitter. It was difficult to tell what she really felt: whether it was joy that Hope was alive and well, terror that her guilty secret was about to be exposed, or just plain jealousy that Nell received letters from the Captain and she did not. Perhaps it was some of each.

Nell had given her former mistress short shrift that day. She was so full of joy that her seven-year wait was finally over that she wasn't going to allow it to be diluted by anyone. Lady Harvey had gone off in a huff, but not before she'd sobbed about how hard her life was now, and how misunderstood she was.

It was only days later that the whole of England had been shocked by the news of the carnage of the Light Brigade at Balaclava. Nell had been beside herself as she waited for news of Captain Pettigrew, and even when she knew he was one of the wounded, she couldn't stop worrying for he might very well die later from his injuries. But finally his letter had arrived to tell her he had just been moved from the hospital where Hope had stitched up his wounds and he was doing well.

She must have read that letter a hundred times, crying each time. She had stopped going to church after Reverend Gosling had told her she was sinful to leave Albert, and showed no concern for Hope. But she went to the church in Keynsham that day and thanked God. Even now, with two more letters from the Captain and five in all from Hope, she remained totally convinced that it was God's hand that had brought the two of them together, and that it was for a purpose which He would soon reveal.

*

'Imagine Hope stitching up Captain Pettigrew!'

Rufus's remark brought Nell sharply out of her musing. He looked so incredulous, wide-eyed and filled with the romance of war.

'Eh! To think I taught her to sew too,' she laughed. 'But she makes it sound so dirty there. If it's that bad, I don't know how she can stand it.'

'She's just telling us how it really is. She doesn't seem to think Lord Cardigan is the hero we've been led to believe,' Rufus said, looking down thoughtfully at one of the letters. 'Or Lord Raglan such a great general! It is appalling that so many soldiers are dying of disease, that they're hungry with no warm clothes or even proper shelter.'

'She always was soft-hearted,' Nell said.

'But very truthful, Nell,' Rufus reminded her. 'It looks to me as if we're being given a false picture back here. How dare they put the blame for so many deaths on to the doctors, when really it's the fault of the government because they didn't plan this campaign properly from the outset.'

'Well, I daresay you read all the newspapers and under-stand them,' Nell said. 'I can't make head nor tail of it.'

'Well, it does seem to me that they glorify war. They don't tell us, like Hope has, about the men collapsing with the heat on the march to Balaclava because their uniforms were too warm, nor that they had nothing to drink. Imagine them being left there to die because there were no carts to put them on!'

'I don't like the parts of her letters when she goes on about things like that.' Nell wrinkled her nose with distaste.

'Then you are as bad as my mother,' he said scornfully. 'She's only interested in soldiers when they are in full dress for a review, with the band playing.'

Nell turned back to her pot of soup so Rufus wouldn't see her face, for she was afraid it would give her feelings away. She was pretty certain Lady Harvey would be eager to hear every last piece of news of the Captain when he got back to Briargate later. And she would see Captain Pettigrew's injuries as the perfect excuse to write to him and try to win his heart again.

If she did secure it, where would that leave Nell?

Chapter Twenty-two

Hope rubbed away the ice on the inside of the hospital window with the corner of her apron and couldn't help but smile at the sight which met her eyes. Snow had fallen during the night and now at daybreak the harbour looked beautiful.

The ships had been transformed into fantastic fairy vessels, every rope, beam and railing lightly sprinkled with snow. No footprints had yet spoiled the virgin whiteness on the decks; even the planks to shore had a thick carpet of white.

All the terrible ugliness, filth and squalor on the quayside was covered. Crates, carts, barrels and other goods had been transformed into incredible snow sculptures. The steep craggy cliffs across the harbour had the appearance of a gigantic meringue.

The scene evoked memories of snowfalls in her childhood. She could almost see Joe and Henry eagerly dragging the sledge from the shed and arguing over who would have the first ride.

They would take her on it down to the village. She would cling to Henry's waist as he steered in front, Joe pushing them until the sledge went fast enough to jump on too, and they'd whizz down the lane so fast she would scream with a heady mixture of terror and joy.

Hope had been at the hospital all night as there had been

several amputations on her ward yesterday. Two of the patients had been in so much pain when they came round from the chloroform that she had been reluctant to leave them in the less than tender care of the orderlies. But they, like all the other patients, were asleep now, and the ward was filled with the sound of snoring, the breath rising from their mouths like smoke in the cold air.

She turned away from the window at the sound of feet stamping beyond the door, and saw it was Bennett coming in.

'Doesn't it look beautiful out there,' she said as she walked over to him. 'Was it fun being the first to walk on it?'

He gave her a withering look.

'Sorry I dared speak to the eminent surgeon,' she retorted with sarcasm. 'Was it a night without me to warm you? Or just that you've become so used to ugliness you don't recognize beauty any more?'

'If we have this much snow down here, imagine how bad it will be up on the Heights,' he said sharply.

That hadn't occurred to Hope and she felt chastened that his thoughts were for the men in their trenches, while hers were of happy times in her childhood.

Hope wasn't one for apologizing, so she began to tell him how Pitt and Moore had been during the night. 'I gave them both a few drops of opium about two o'clock,' she ended up. 'They settled after that.'

He nodded, and she had to take that as confirmation he approved of her administering the only drug they had which actually had some benefit.

'You're very early,' she said. 'I didn't expect you for at least another hour.'

'I couldn't sleep,' he said. 'And I had some things I needed to do.'

His tone was so chilly that Hope looked at him more

carefully and saw his eyes were heavy, the way they often were when he hadn't had any sleep. But there was something more – his mouth was set in a stiff, straight line, a sure sign he was worried about something.

'What is it?' she asked. 'What's happened?'

He took off his cap and ran his fingers through his hair distractedly. Hope knew he was playing for time. 'Come on, out with it,' she said sharply.

'Colonel Lawrence came to see me last night,' he sighed. 'At Dr Anderson's recommendation I am to rejoin the regiment before Sebastopol.'

Hope felt as if a rug had been pulled from beneath her feet. Dr Anderson was in charge of the hospital and he had always liked and appreciated Bennett. 'Why?' she gasped. 'I don't understand. Why send such an experienced surgeon up there?'

Bennett shrugged. 'He didn't give me a reason, but it's almost certainly because someone feels I've been favoured by staying down here.'

'Favoured!' she exclaimed. 'Working over eighteen hours a day!'

Bennett gave a humourless laugh. 'They do that up on the Heights too. I suppose I'm getting a reputation as a nuisance, always complaining about the lack of medicine and provisions for the sick.'

'Colonel Lawrence said that?'

'Not in so many words, but he hinted at it.'

'I suppose you can't refuse?' Even as she asked she knew the answer. An order had to be obeyed.

She felt almost faint with the shock. The three months since the hurricane had been incredibly grim for the men at the siege. While gunfire had been only sporadic and desultory on both sides during this time, and there had been no actual assaults, it had been bitterly cold, with rain, sleet and snow. The *Prince* going down with all the warm clothing, boots and other supplies they so desperately needed had been a monumental tragedy, which had become even more apparent as the winter set in.

There might have been fewer wounded men during the three-month period, but the numbers of sick men had increased enormously. Both doctors and officers had made endless complaints about the men spending all night getting soaked to the skin in the trenches and having nothing dry to change into. All the men were weakened by lack of food and the fatigue of digging trenches, building fortifications and hauling heavy equipment up to the Heights, which left them exhausted. But then to be expected to sleep on the cold ground, wrapped only in a sodden worn-out greatcoat and blanket, was inhumane.

It hurt everyone working in the hospitals to discover that the newspapers back home were implying that the high mortality rate of the sick and wounded was due to their negligence. The much-publicized arrival of Florence Nightingale and her nurses in Scutari, and their reports of the terrible conditions, appeared to have turned every hack reporter into an expert on hospitals.

Many of the senior doctors in Balaclava were incensed that it had taken a well-connected lady with precious little medical experience to galvanize the government into improving conditions, when their professional advice, reports and requests for supplies had been ignored.

Yet everyone continued to do their best, even though every single day was a battle they could never win. The sick and wounded were shipped off to Scutari too fast in their opinion, just when the patients were at their most vulnerable.

Yet however difficult and in the main unrewarding the conditions in the base hospital were, it was in a different league from the field hospitals up on the Heights.

Hope had twice made the trip up there with Bennett since Christmas to take much-needed dressings and medicine, and what they'd seen had appalled them.

All grass, bushes and trees were gone, leaving only a vast muddy quagmire studded with tents. The hospitals were just marquees, the wounded and sick had to lie on the ground, and the care they received would be of only the most basic kind until some form of transport could be found to take them the six or seven long miles down a steep slope to Balaclava. Sometimes, in the worst weather, this was on the backs of their comrades.

None of the men looked like soldiers now. They were thin, gaunt, lice-ridden creatures with thick, bushy beards, often wearing bizarre hats and other pieces of non-uniform clothing over their mud-daubed, ragged official one. Russian coats and boots had been taken from the dead at Inkerman and some infantrymen wore naval pea jackets bartered from sailors. Many had old newspapers bound to their legs or body with webbing, for warmth. Some didn't even have boots, just sacking wrapped around their feet. Personal hygiene was impossible as water had to be hauled a great distance and they had to contend with snow, ice and heavy rain. The only fuel available was roots, but it could take a whole day to dig up just a small bag for the cooking fires. As a result, the salted meat was often eaten semi-raw and was no doubt responsible for the increase in bowel disorders. Scurvy had appeared, along with pneumonia and various bronchial problems, and there were also many cases of frostbite. Cholera had disappeared for now, but other fevers were still just as prevalent.

Morale was at rock bottom. Many of the men brought into the hospital had said they would rather risk death in an assault on Sebastopol than continue this long-drawn-out, seemingly hopeless siege. They had told Bennett that sometimes their rations didn't turn up, and when they did, the salt pork and biscuit were so unappetizing they could hardly eat them. Hope had felt the desperation in every man she'd spoken to.

'You'll stay here,' Bennett said, his stern tone implying she was not to argue. 'They do at least value *your* help in the hospital.'

'I can't stay in the house without you,' she said. 'Not with all those men.'

'The Crimea is full of men wherever you go,' he said impatiently. 'At least the ones in the house are known to you. I can't have you freezing to death or being shot at.'

'I'm coming with you,' she said stubbornly. She hated the idea of going, but she hated the idea of being apart from him still more.

'No, Hope,' he insisted. 'God knows, I'd like you by my side, but not there. It's no place for a woman.'

'But Queenie's up there, and other soldiers' wives,' she argued.

'No,' he said, his face darkening. 'You do an invaluable job here. I'll be able to ride down from time to time and I'll need the thought of you safe and snug in our room at night to keep me going.'

She knew then why he'd been awake all night. It was her he was concerned for. His own comfort didn't worry him – he probably felt he owed it to the men in his regiment to be with them. He had known she'd insist on going with him, but he wasn't going to let her put herself in danger.

'I've packed my bag,' he said. 'I'm only staying now until I can hand over details of men I've been treating to other doctors. Please don't make it more difficult for me.'

Hope took a deep breath and bit back her tears. She was, after all, a soldier's wife and she must behave like one.

'Who will wash your clothes?' she said.

Bennett half-smiled. 'You. I'll bring them back with me when I visit. I'm sure I can wangle it so I always come down with the wounded. Now, give me a kiss before the men wake up.'

It was a bittersweet kiss, and Hope clung to him, trying to blot out her fear. The firing might have stopped for the winter, but there was still the odd sniper taking pot shots. Several doctors had even died of diseases caught from their patients because hygiene was so bad. And she knew too that Bennett would be outspoken at the callous way the army treated its rank and file. He just wouldn't be able to hold back.

But even above her fear for him, she was angry too that his superior officers had allowed petty jealousy to cloud their judgement. Bennett was one of the most experienced and skilled surgeons down here, and in his absence men would die who could have been saved by him. Any of the hastily recruited young doctors just out of medical school could apply tourniquets, field dressings, or splints to broken limbs, for that was all that was required up on the Heights. But it made her shudder to think that one of those inexperienced young men might be sent down here to take Bennett's place.

In early March, a month after Bennett had been sent up to the Heights, Hope took a walk out of the town to see how the construction of the siege train was progressing. It was vital, for it would put an end to the soldiers hauling heavy guns and ammunition up to the front themselves, and navvies had been brought in to speed up the work.

Hope was glad they'd brought men out from England to do this, and it was good to see big, brawny men in rude health for a change, but she, like many other people, resented their preferential treatment.

It wasn't fair that they should have large quantities of

fresh meat daily, while the soldiers had none. Nor was it right that the soldiers who were already weak and sickly were expected to build huts for the navvies, while they still slept in leaky tents.

But Hope was pleased to see there had been great progress. The track was already past the village of Kadikoi, about a mile and a half out of town and close to the cavalry camp. Soon it would be right up to headquarters.

The past month had been the most miserable time. She missed Bennett so much, worried about him all the time, and felt dreadfully alone.

When Bennett had been with her, people had dropped in for a visit, and they had sometimes visited others too. But now she had to be very careful. She couldn't have male visitors for fear of gossip about her, and the few women here were either so deadly dull that she'd rather stare into her fire than spend time with them, or so uppity she felt like slapping them.

Bennett had only managed to come down twice, and both times he had been so exhausted that he had fallen asleep immediately after a bath.

Letters from home were the only thing that brightened the gloom. Nell wrote every week, and even though her letters had a frustrating lack of detail about her life, just a glimpse of her big, childlike writing made Hope feel loved. Matt had written three times on behalf of Joe and Henry too, and Amy always added a bit of village gossip at the end.

Ruth's two letters had been the most entertaining. She wrote well, in a good hand, about her three children, her husband and two stepchildren, and about her life in Bath. She thought it was very exciting and adventurous that Hope was in the Crimea and said she boasted to her friends about it. She saw Nell quite often and said she was blooming now that she knew where Hope was. But it was the little details

Ruth put into her letter that pleased Hope most – how her hair was growing grey and she was getting matronly, or what she'd cooked for a special dinner, and funny little things her children said. In the second letter she'd ended by saying what a great deal of catching up they'd have to do when she got back, and how there would always be room for her and Bennett in her home.

James had written his one letter in a tearing hurry, but it had been warm, with promises of another as soon as he had more time. He expressed his joy at hearing Hope was safe and well, and he told her that he was now married to Joan, who had been a parlourmaid at Littlecote. Their daughter was now four, they had a small cottage on the estate, and a second baby was due soon. He hoped that she and Bennett would come to visit when they came home.

Alice and Toby had written a joint letter just once, and Hope had got the impression that it was penned out of duty because Nell had ordered it. While this made her feel a little sad, it was understandable. They had gone into service together in Bath when Hope had still been a small child, and they'd made a life for themselves quite separate from the rest of the family.

None of her brothers and sisters had quizzed her about her disappearance. Whether this was because Nell had already explained it, or because they weren't curious, she didn't know. But it was rather odd after spending so many years worrying about their reaction to find they didn't have one.

The siege train did look impressive. The big engine at the top which would haul the train over the steepest part of the route was in place now. She just hoped that those who said this would hasten the end of the siege were right, just as she hoped that the news that Czar Nicholas had died the previous day might bring peace.

The sight of a clump of flowers growing by the roadside made her stop to look closer. They were similar to a crocus, and as they were the first tangible sign of spring, and in fact the first flowers she had seen here, she bent to pick one.

'That's almost as pretty as you, Hope!'

Startled at hearing her name, Hope stood up and turned to see Angus astride his horse, grinning down at her. The last time she'd seen him had been back in January, when he'd been beside himself with anxiety about the cavalry horses which were dying of starvation. She'd seen him limping back up the road to the cavalry camp carrying a heavy sack of oats on his shoulders.

But he was looking fit and devilishly handsome now, even if his red breeches were decidedly faded, worn and mud-splattered. His chestnut horse was very thin and nowhere near as sleek as she remembered in Varna, but it was a relief to see it hadn't died during that terrible period.

'How good to see you,' she said, and stroked the horse's nose. 'And good to see Brandy is getting some food again. How are your wounds?'

'What wounds?' he said, dismounting.

Hope laughed. 'Well, it wouldn't do to make you drop your breeches to check on the scar,' she said. 'But it's clearly not troubling you.'

'Thanks to you, angel fingers,' he said, taking her hand and kissing it. 'Why aren't you down there now stitching up some young soldier who will remember your face till the end of time?'

'No wonder Lady Harvey got led astray,' Hope giggled. 'But you must behave. Bennett's been sent back to his regiment up on the Heights, so it wouldn't do for me to attract gossip.'

Leading his horse, Angus walked back to the harbour beside her, and they talked about Bennett's move, the Czar's death, and the tremendous increase in the number of men reporting sick during January and February.

'Morale is at an all-time low,' he sighed. 'We should have gone on the attack as soon as we got here last year. Lord Raglan is an old woman, can't make his mind up about anything. Delaying only gave the Ruskies time to build better fortifications and get in more supplies. Now we've hardly got a fit man in the whole army. Even the new bunch that arrived in January look as bad as the oldtimers now. But you, Hope, you've got a bloom about you! Why's that?'

'Have I?' she said in surprise.

'You certainly have,' he said, looking at her intently. 'You've filled out. Have you found some source of good food that you are keeping to yourself? Or could it be a happy event is expected?'

Goose-pimples erupted all over her and she looked at the Captain in horror.

'Not a happy event then,' he said, but when she didn't speak his grin faded. 'Oh dear, I've been too presumptuous. I'm so sorry, Hope, but I've come to think of you almost as family. Forgive me?'

He meant, of course, that it wasn't done for men to remark on such things as pregnancy. But her shock wasn't at his comment, but the jolt of realization that she could well be carrying a child.

Bennett had been very careful every time they made love, for clearly it would be a calamity to become pregnant in a place like this. He always withdrew before his seed was spent, often to her disappointment. But on Christmas Eve he hadn't.

It had been such a lovely evening, almost balmy, with a big, bright full moon. Some of the bandsmen from various different regiments had joined together to play their instruments on the quay. The pipers from the Highlanders came down from their camp too. For that evening the siege was forgotten. Music and singing were heard from the Russians inside Sebastopol, the French too were playing instruments up on the Heights, and not a shot was fired on either side.

Some of the Turks had slaughtered and roasted an ox. There were bottles of wine, port, brandy and rum in profusion and Hope had danced with scores of different men as there were so few women. She had bathed and put on the pink dress she'd worn on her honeymoon, and Bennett had looked so handsome in his full-dress uniform. She remembered thinking that the Rifles' tight green jacket gave him a rakish charm and enhanced the colour of his eyes.

They had been very tipsy when they had finally gone to bed, and caution had been forgotten. Bennett had transported her to places she'd never dreamed of that night. Even recalling it now sent a shiver of pleasure down her spine.

But however magical that night had been, they had shot straight back to reality soon afterwards. January had been the very worst month at the hospital, a bleak and desperate time with the sick coming in by the score each day. It was hardly surprising she couldn't remember whether she'd had her courses that month or not.

'Hope? Tell me I'm forgiven?'

Angus's plea brought her back to the present. 'Of course you are,' she said hurriedly. 'A country girl like me doesn't get the vapours at a man mentioning such things.'

'But you have turned a little pale,' he said anxiously.

'Oh, do talk of something else,' she said irritably. 'Tell me what you've been doing, it's been so long since I last saw you. Has Nell sent you any more food parcels?'

He'd had a big fruit cake at Christmas, of which he'd brought her and Bennett half. Nothing had tasted quite as good as that, at least not until another arrived for Hope in mid-January along with jars of mincemeat, several different kinds of preserves and warm mittens and scarves.

'I should think I'm about due for one any day,' he said in his more usual jocular manner. 'But of course now she has you to lavish her treats on, I'm not doing so well.'

They continued their walk, Angus remarking on all the improvements in the town. Conditions had become absolutely disgusting, for apart from all the usual mess hundreds of Turks had made a hideous shanty town behind the main street. All their waste and dead animals had been left lying around, and there was tremendous sickness in their camp. They hadn't buried their dead properly either, and this had posed the most serious health problem.

But now the main thoroughfare had been cleaned up and macadamized. New warehouses had been built and pre-fabricated wooden huts sent out from England had sprung up everywhere in the last few weeks. The hospital had been extended with new huts too, and further ones were being erected up by the old Genoese fort on the clifftop for convalescence.

Angus went on to tell her about his hunting exploits up on the plain with some of the other officers. In the absence of foxes they'd chased the many wild dogs that roamed around the camps. He said too that they'd come across a small band of Cossacks one day and fought them off. The way he spoke gave the impression he was one of the band of officers Bennett despised most; dull-witted, over-privileged, rich and arrogant men who carried on here as if they were still in England. But Hope knew he was none of those things. She'd met some of his troopers in the hospital and knew they'd lay down their lives for him, for he cared more for their welfare than his own. He even shared his parcels from home with his men. It saddened her to think he felt it was expedient to hide his true character behind that of a buffoon.

They parted company and Hope went into the house to change into her old dress for the hospital. But once inside her room she sat down on the bed and tried hard to remember when her last courses had come. She remembered them at the start of December because that was when they had first moved into this room. But she couldn't recall anything about January or February.

More worryingly, now that she was looking for evidence, she was aware that Angus was right in saying she'd filled out, for her clothes weren't as loose as they'd been back at the end of last year. Until now she had put that down to eating more in the cold weather. The baker often gave her a whole loaf, which she'd wolf down with some of Nell's jam. In fact, she was always hungry lately.

Then there was her reaction to certain smells! The officer next door smoked cigars, a smell she'd once liked but now couldn't bear. Horse droppings too – something she'd lived with all her life – had suddenly grown offensive.

Her stomach began to churn with anxiety. If she had fallen pregnant at Christmas that made her well over two months gone now! Once she showed she would be sent home, and Bennett wouldn't be allowed to go with her.

What if he was killed or he became sick and died? What would happen to her then?

She brushed that aside. Nell would help her, and so would Uncle Abel and Alice. But she didn't want to be parted from Bennett. It was bad enough at the moment, but he was after all only a few miles away. Who would take care of him if she was sent home?

Picking up the small looking-glass Gussie had given her all those years ago, she held it down to her side to see how she looked. Her stomach was as flat as it always had been, so maybe she was mistaken. She just wouldn't think about it any more.

As March slowly crept by, Hope found that it wasn't possible to ignore her problem. Each passing day made it clearer that she was indeed pregnant, and she was undecided whether to view this with terror or joy. She had loved the newborn babies while she was in the lying-in ward at St Peter's. Just thinking of holding her own in her arms made her melt inside. But the fact remained that this was the wrong time and the wrong place for a baby.

Other men might not show any interest in their children until they could walk and talk, but Bennett was different. He'd want to deliver his baby, to be with her throughout it all. He would hate to have to send her home alone, but he'd be terrified of it being born here because of all the disease. If she was to tell him about the pregnancy, he'd be so worried it would affect his work.

Hope finally resolved not to tell him yet. News had come in that in early April there was at last to be a massive bombardment of Sebastopol, both from the army and the navy. She had seen more big guns being brought in, and vast quantities of ammunition. With luck, that might end the siege and they could all go home.

Hope daydreamed all the time of home. Not just of seeing her family, or even England in the spring. She wanted natural order again, of knowing what to expect with each day, for everything here was disorganized and baffling.

At the end of March, just as the weather was growing warm again, all the winter clothing for the troops which had been lying in warehouses for weeks was finally distributed to the men, and wooden huts at last replaced the field hospital marquees. Bennett reported that the men had been delighted finally to get new boots, shirts, socks and flannel drawers, but were somewhat bemused by the heavy warm coats they no longer really needed. New bedsteads had arrived for the hospital too, and mattresses and even some sheets for the beds.

Hope would have taken great pleasure in these improvements if she hadn't suddenly been ordered to move to one of the new huts at the back of the hospital. Almost all the patients there were foreigners, Turks, Poles, Armenians, Croatians and a few Russians, and she felt she had been sent there for a similar reason to the one which had seen Bennett sent back to his regiment.

Almost as soon as he'd gone, she'd noticed that some of the doctors became rather disagreeable with her in little ways – not answering when she asked a question, turning away when she came into the ward, calling an orderly to help them when once they would have called for her. It was, of course, possible that they had always resented her; after all, she wasn't a lady like Miss Nightingale, or an ordinary soldier's wife who could be ordered to do the roughest work. But if that had been the case, they had hidden it well all the while Bennett was here.

It seemed to her that by sending her into a ward where she couldn't communicate with anyone, and where she might be frightened, they were hoping she might leave the hospital.

Daunting was the only word for the new ward, for the patients were the very roughest of men, in the main muleteers or labourers. Most had either suffered some kind of accident in their work or were sick, and because they were civilians they couldn't be sent on to Scutari. As they didn't speak any English the duty doctor had to have an interpreter with him when he did his rounds.

But if petty jealousy or prejudice against women was behind it, Hope had no intention of letting them win their pathetic crusade. While she was offended by some of the men's filthy habits, and practically all of them were swarming with parasites, they were no worse than some of the patients at St Peter's. She could manage very well with sign language, and often she was glad that she didn't have to make conversation as she had so much else on her mind. She was a nurse, and she'd carry on until such time as she decided to leave. The patients were more important than a few bigots.

Bennett wasn't too pleased when he saw where she had been moved to, but as he only came down once a week with patients for shipping to Scutari, and had to return to the Heights the same day, he didn't have time to investigate anything.

He was happier now he had his patients in a hut, and optimistic he could deal with the outbreaks of scurvy because he'd managed to get supplies of lime juice. Cholera had raised its ugly head again, but he believed that now the weather and the rations had improved, so too would general health in the camp.

One evening, as he was leaving early on a borrowed horse, Hope asked Bennett if she could go with him. They had seen scaling ladders and grappling hooks being unloaded from a ship that afternoon, so it was clear that along with the planned bombardment there would also be an assault on the fortifications of Sebastopol.

She didn't plead with him, she only pointed out that she could be far more useful to him at the field hospital than she was here.

'I can't agree,' he said, reaching out for one of her curls and twisting it around his finger. 'It will be too dangerous once it starts.'

The gentleness of his tone and the way he looked longingly at her was evidence he was wavering. Maybe he wasn't so sure that she was entirely safe here either, not in a ward full of rough foreigners.

For a moment or two she wanted to beg him, tempted to blurt out how isolated she felt, how the two orderlies on her ward were surly, that she couldn't talk to the patients and that she felt she was being victimized just like him.

But she stopped herself in time. If she began to tell him some of it, the rest would surely follow, and once he knew about the baby, he'd never have any peace of mind. The bombardment would mean many wounded, and he needed to be single-minded in dealing with that. It wasn't fair to add to his burdens.

'You are right, of course,' she said, more bravely than she felt. 'I must stay here; it's just that I miss you so much.'

He enfolded her in his arms, holding her so tightly she could scarcely breathe. 'I miss you too, my darling, but it won't be for much longer. With all the firepower we have this time, Sebastopol doesn't stand a chance.'

On 8 April, Hope was cleaning a Croatian labourer's wound. He had injured his hand while unloading a ship and hadn't sought any treatment until it was so severely infected it had to be amputated. She felt her patient stiffen and his eyes go to the door, and when she turned to see who was there, she realized it was Angus.

'Give me a moment,' she called out.

He ignored the request and came over to her. 'Are you all alone in here?' he said, a look of extreme concern in his dark eyes.

'Yes, for the time being,' she said. 'The orderlies are collecting the rations.'

He watched her cleaning the wound in silence; then, as she began to dress it, he moved closer and said something to the patient, presumably in the man's own language, making him look afraid.

'What on earth have you said?' she asked. 'And why would you know any Croatian?'

'I know a few useful phrases in many different languages,' he smirked. 'That one was a warning that if anyone in here upsets you he'll have me to answer to.'

'That isn't necessary,' she said indignantly.

'It's always necessary to warn men off when a pretty woman appears to be quite alone. Whose idea was it to send you to this ward, Hope? And why?'

Hope shrugged.

His face darkened. 'No wonder the newspapers back home are full of reports of chaos and mismanagement out here! Any orderly could take care of these men. You should be where it counts.'

'These men count too,' Hope said indignantly.

'In my opinion they should be at the back of the queue for treatment, behind our men,' he said gruffly. 'But you weren't sent here for their good, anyway. Whatever fool made that decision, made it out of spite.'

'That's as maybe,' she said tartly. She was very aware of twenty-five pairs of eyes watching them intently and sincerely hoped they didn't have any idea what they were talking about. 'But I'm here now and I'll make the best of it until Bennett lets me go up with him on the Heights.'

'You must never go there,' he said, looking alarmed. 'The ball will open tomorrow.'

Hope chuckled at his pretty way of describing the bombardment. 'I wasn't planning on going to the ball. I thought more of helping with the clearing up afterwards.'

'You stay here in Balaclava,' he said fiercely, punctuating his order with a pointed finger. 'Nell would have me hung, drawn and quartered if you got hurt.'

*

The bombardment did start as planned early the following morning. It was a wet, miserable day, made even more depressing by the knowledge that before long the wounded would begin to arrive. Hope, stuck out at the back of the hospital, could only listen to the booms, cracks and whistling sounds with dread, wishing she had someone with whom to share her anxiety for Bennett.

Day and night, day after day, the bombardment went on ceaselessly. Every few days there was a truce for a couple of hours so that the dead could be collected for burial, but according to the stream of casualties coming down to the hospital, Sebastopol was still undamaged.

A rumour came that Menshikoff, the Russian General, was dead, confirmed a day or two later, and there was jubilation that this would end the war. But the Russians kept firing their guns, the wounded kept coming, and now the talk changed to an all-out assault on the town. The general belief was that if gunfire alone couldn't make Sebastopol crumble, then it would have to be done with bayonets.

Hope shuddered at the thought, for hand-to-hand fighting would mean even more carnage. Meanwhile, newspapers sent from home told her that Lord Cardigan had arrived back in England to a hero's welcome. She could hardly believe what she read – that his picture was in every shop window, his biography in every newspaper. They'd even copied his woolly jacket and called it a cardigan.

This was the man who had lived on his yacht while his men were shivering in tents up on the plain and their horses had no shelter at all. When the horses were dying of starvation and the Commissariat had said there was no transport to get forage to them and he must either collect it himself or bring the horses down to feed, Cardigan had refused to do either. He stubbornly insisted on keeping his men and their horses ready for a Russian attack. Troopers had to watch the horses trying to eat bridle straps and each other's tails as they stood knee-deep in mud, the bitter wind whipping their emaciated bodies. The troopers couldn't even shoot them to put them out of their misery as Cardigan had given an order that shooting was only for broken bones.

Sometimes the horses took three days to die, lying in the mud in agony, for no one dared defy Cardigan and shoot them and run the risk of a flogging. Yet the people back in England thought this pompous, cruel and self-serving ass was a hero.

Hope knew the real heroes of this war were still here, lice-ridden, thin and weary, battling it out in the trenches, or lying in a vast hospital ward in Scutari with missing limbs.

As each day passed, Hope saw that the doctors in the main reception ward were becoming stretched to breaking point with the sheer volume of wounded, and her frustration grew. As Angus had pointed out, the orderlies could easily take care of the men on her ward, but try as she might, she couldn't gain permission to leave them to it and go and help with the recently wounded.

The baffling thing was that she couldn't find out who was so intent on keeping her out. She could see in the weary faces of all the doctors that they wanted her help, but to a man they stubbornly said they'd had orders that only recognized army personnel were to work in acute wards.

In early May, Hope had arrived on her ward at six in the morning and by eight she had finished all her duties. Regular doctors' rounds were a thing of the past now that the hospital was so frantically busy, but having found one patient, a Pole, with an infected wound, she went looking for a doctor, leaving the orderlies doling out the porridge for breakfast.

Once through into the main hospital she found a scene very reminiscent of her first day here. It was chaos – there had clearly been a huge influx of men at the same time. Men brought in on stretchers had been placed on the floor because there were no more free beds to put them in, every field dressing she glanced at was bloody, men were vomiting on the floor, others were writhing and screaming with pain. Almost all of them had blackened faces from gunpowder.

Four surgeons were hard at work in the smaller room off the main ward, removing bullets and shells and amputating limbs, and assistants were giving chloroform. But most of the orderlies clearly had no idea what they were supposed to do.

Hope hesitated for a second or two. She knew that obeying orders counted for everything in the army, even to the point of insanity like the fateful Charge of the Light Brigade. But remembering that she was in fact a volunteer, it seemed to her that no one had a right to tell her what she could or couldn't do.

Taking a deep breath, she took charge.

First, she got the orderlies to move men who had been admitted a few days earlier and had already received surgery into one of the less crowded wards. After that, she got the newly wounded settled into the free beds, clearing most of the space on the floor. While one orderly was told to mop up the mess on the floor, she instructed the others to give the wounded water, to get them out of filthy uniforms and wash them.

'Maybe we can't take away their pain,' she explained. 'But by cleaning them up and trying to make them more comfortable, we are reassuring them that they are going to be seen by a doctor soon and that we care.'

Doctors came past her all morning, most acknowledging her presence with a nod or a brief greeting, but often there was a warm, grateful smile. She continued to wash men, get them drinks, or help them if they were vomiting. As patients were brought back from operations, she checked on them regularly, offering bed pans and bottles.

By two in the afternoon everything was under control again, and after leaving a few instructions with the orderlies she went back to her own ward.

As she opened the door her heart sank, for Surgeon Truscott was examining the man she had been going to get help for that morning. He looked round at her and glowered.

'And where have you been?'

Truscott had arrived in Balaclava some weeks after the base hospital had been established and so he hadn't got used to her helping with the sick in Varna as many of the other doctors had. Hope had always known that he didn't approve of women in regimental hospitals; he had often made barbed comments about her in the past.

He was a big, bumptious man with a swirling moustache, close to sixty, who believed that the scope of medical assistance given in the days of the Peninsular War was quite adequate for this one. Bennett thought him an able surgeon, but very out of date with his techniques. In the past few months he'd barely been seen in the hospital; according to gossip he went out riding a great deal.

'I went to find a doctor to look at this man's wound,' she said truthfully. 'But they were so much in need of help with the recently wounded that I stayed.'

'So this man's life wasn't important to you?'

Hope was fairly certain that the Polish man's infection was only a mild one, and that a delay of a few hours would have done no harm at all.

'Of course it was, sir,' she said. 'But there were men in much more grievous danger in the main hospital.'

'So you decide who needs medical assistance now, do

you?' he bellowed at her. 'Deserting your post while on duty is a very serious offence!'

'I hadn't deserted. I was just giving assistance elsewhere,' she said, her anger rising. She wished she had told a doctor about this Pole's wound first, but even if she had, she knew none of the doctors would have broken off from what they were doing to treat something they would have considered trivial. 'Besides, I can hardly be accused of desertion when I am only a volunteer.'

'I will not stand for insubordination,' he roared, making every man in the ward look round. 'Do you know who I am?'

She was tempted to retort, 'A jackass,' but she held that back. 'Yes, sir, you are Surgeon Truscott.'

'With over thirty years' experience in surgery,' he shouted. 'There is no place for women in regimental hospitals. What sort of a milksop is your husband to bring you out here with him? And then to inflict you on us!'

Suddenly, and without any warning, the surgeon was struggling, for a man had crept up behind him and was holding a knife to his throat.

Hope gasped in shock. She had not seen Asiz, the little Croatian man, get out of his bed and steal across the floor. He was only slightly taller than her, while Truscott was six feet tall, but the knife he was holding looked very sharp. He wasn't the man Angus had given his warning to, but clearly all the Croatians had taken it as an order to protect their nurse from any man threatening her.

'Asiz, no!' she called out.

But Asiz did not put the knife down and every other man was either getting out of bed, if he was capable, or sitting up and shouting in his own tongue.

'You've done this,' Truscott said, turning very red in the face. 'Get him off me.'

Hope went behind him and made signs to Asiz that she was fine, and taking his arm she led him back to his bed. She put her finger up to her lips to tell the others to be quiet.

'I want you out of this hospital this minute,' Truscott said, rubbing his neck as if convinced it was cut. 'You are clearly not to be trusted.'

Hope glanced round the ward. The men were quiet now but they were watching and waiting. All at once she realized that it must have been Truscott who was responsible for her fate, and no doubt one of the orderlies had been persuaded to act as a stool pigeon.

It was tempting to tell him how childish he was. To ask why, if he was such a great surgeon, he wasn't out there dealing with the seriously wounded. But that was likely to cause trouble for Bennett, and if she riled Truscott any further, it just might lead to the men attacking him.

'Very well, sir,' she said, and, biting her lip so she wouldn't call him any of the foul names Betsy had taught her, she marched out of the ward with her head held high.

Chapter Twenty-three

Hope was dripping with perspiration by the time she reached the top of the steep path leading to the Heights. It was just six in the morning and would remain chilly until the sun rose further in the sky, but it was a hard climb and her bag was heavy.

For two whole days she'd stayed in her room, angry, frustrated and often tearful, yet quite certain someone would come and ask her to go back to the hospital.

But no one came, not even the few young doctors and orderlies she had counted as friends. Eventually she decided this wasn't just because they were afraid of Surgeon Truscott, but far more likely because they had never really approved of her.

Disapproval of women nurses in military hospitals was widespread. When it was heard that Florence Nightingale was going to Scutari, Bennett had said that most of the older doctors were outraged. Probably the only reason Hope had been tolerated all this time was because she'd already proved herself useful in Varna, and because she was Bennett's wife.

Yet whatever Truscott and the others who were backing him felt about her, it was an act of monumental stupidity to get rid of her just when the hospital was so overstretched.

So today she was setting off to join Bennett at the Rifle Brigade field hospital.

She was scared; about Bennett's reaction, how his fellow officers would view her turning up, and what it would be like to live in a camp again. Back in Varna it had been very different – everyone was just waiting to be moved on, and when people fell sick they were grateful she could help, regardless of who she was.

No one had anticipated that within a year half their number would be dead or wounded. She recalled the excitement when they'd finally sailed away from Bulgaria, everyone so certain they'd left all the sickness behind and that they'd be home in time for Christmas.

Would they even be home for next Christmas?

She sat down on a rock to get her breath, looking down at the harbour, anxious tears filling her eyes. She was over four months pregnant now, and although her clothes hid her ever-increasing belly, they wouldn't for much longer. Bennett would realize the truth very soon, and he'd be angry that she hadn't told him before.

She turned at the sound of men's voices and hastily wiped away her tears. A couple of soldiers were coming towards her, carrying gabions, the curious funnel-shaped baskets which were filled with earth and used in building defences. She thought they were probably out searching for roots and wood for their fires.

It wasn't possible to make out which regiment they were from, for neither was wearing anything that approached a uniform, just dark breeches and filthy loose shirts, both with thick dark beards and straggly long hair.

One called out, asking if she'd lost her way.

'No, just resting after the climb,' she called back. She got up and walked towards them to explain she was going to find her husband.

'Keep over that way,' the taller of the two men said, pointing in the direction of the sea, where she could see tents and huts in the distance. 'If you stay on this path you'll come to the trenches and that could be dangerous.'

Hope set off in the direction they'd advised, but as she drew nearer to the camp she became confused. Nothing looked the way it had when she'd last come up here with Bennett.

It had of course been a grey day in winter then, and there had been only a sea of mud and tents. She couldn't get her bearings now for the sun made everything look different, and with all the new huts, and even some patchy grass growing back, she didn't recognize anything. As she recalled it, the hospital marquee had stood out from everything else, and it had not been far from the trenches. Surely when they replaced it with a hut, they would have put it in the same spot or very nearby?

She wished she'd told those soldiers who her husband was, and which regiment he was with, then maybe they'd have been able to direct her straight to him. Her feet were throbbing from the long walk, her arm was aching from her heavy bag, and she didn't want to walk right down to the end of camp, only to have to turn and go back again.

Standing for a moment and shielding her eyes from the sun, she studied the layout of the camp. To her far left were the Russian defences – every now and then a volley of gunfire came from there, and the wisps of smoke hung in the early morning air. Much nearer, still on her left, were the British trenches, not that she could see much more than mounds of earth from where she stood. She wasn't even sure if they were manned because she couldn't see anyone and no one was answering the Russian fire.

Nearer still there were tents, huts and a great many men, carts, horses and mules. One of the huts was larger than all the others, and she thought that maybe the carts were being loaded with wounded to take down to the base hospital.

To her right was the rest of the camp, extending right

over to the French camp, where heavy gunfire was taking place.

But straight ahead of her was a large open area with a flagpole which she had no memory of seeing before. She was sure that if Bennett had taken her across that to the field hospital, she would recall it.

So she turned to her left, making straight for the biggest hut. It wasn't until she was near the first row of tents that she saw how close they were together, guy ropes and pegs making an obstacle course she couldn't get through. She managed to find a way through in one place, then found herself in another row just the same, and then another. There were no men here, nothing but tents and more tents, and she couldn't see the hut she wanted to reach any more for she was lower down.

Just as she was beginning to despair of ever leaving this maze, she slipped between two tents and found herself on a path with nothing ahead but the trenches. Some soldiers moving a gun on its carriage were 300 yards further down and she began to walk towards them.

Suddenly she heard someone yell, 'Mrs Meadows!' from behind her. Wheeling around, she saw Robbie, Queenie's husband, with a group of other riflemen she recognized.

It was good to see friendly faces, and she stood still, waiting for them to reach her. Suddenly a burst of gunfire came from the Russian lines. The men dived for cover, but to her shock she saw Robbie reel back, dropping his rifle and clutching at his thigh.

She had never seen anyone shot before, and for a second didn't realize that was what had happened, not until he fell to the ground.

The other riflemen immediately began firing back at the Russians. But Hope could see to her horror that Robbie was right in the line of enemy fire. She could see blood spurting out on to the ground beside him as he tried to scrabble along the ground to get out of range, but he wasn't going to make it on his own.

Without stopping to think, Hope dropped her bag and darted towards him.

'Get away,' Robbie yelled at her when he saw her coming. But she ignored his order, reached him and rolled him over on to his back.

A bullet whizzed past her ear, so close that she felt the heat of it, but she put her two hands under his arms and hauled him backwards towards the row of tents.

He was a big, heavy man and her arms felt as though they were being pulled right out of their sockets, but still she yanked and tugged, ignoring yet another bullet which came dangerously close.

'Are we out of range now?' she asked breathlessly once they were through the first row of tents.

'I thought we were out of range back there,' he said weakly. 'They must have moved closer, but we should be all right here.'

Hope laid him down. His thigh was a gory mess, but with his breeches on it was impossible to tell how bad the wound really was. She tore off the sash from around her dress to make a tourniquet and fastened it above the wound, then stood up to pull off her petticoat to use it to staunch the bleeding.

Still the firing continued, and as she held the cloth over Robbie's injured thigh she looked around frantically for help. Seeing a soldier further down the line of tents, she jumped up and shouted at him, waving her arms.

Something hot and stinging hit her left arm. She sank down beside Robbie, supporting her arm with her right hand. 'Bugger me, I've been shot too,' she said.

The wound was between her elbow and wrist, a patch of

crimson bloody flesh some two inches wide beneath a hole in the sleeve of her blue dress. She had seen hundreds of far worse wounds and barely turned a hair. It didn't even hurt much, but the sight of it made her feel faint.

'I hope that soldier gets someone,' she said weakly. 'I don't think I'm going to be much more use to you, Robbie. Loosen that tourniquet in a minute, then tighten it again in a little while.'

'Hope! Wake up!'

Bennett splashed cold water on her face, then tore what remained of her sleeve away from the wound on her arm.

'Is that you, Bennett?' she asked feebly, her eyes still closed.

'Yes, it's me,' he said. 'You are in the hospital now. You fainted.'

'Is Robbie here too?'

'Yes, he's here too. Right beside you. Open your eyes and you'll see him.'

Bennett felt faint himself. He'd heard the gunfire, but there was nothing unusual about it, so he'd hardly looked up from what he was doing. Then someone had yelled out to him that there were two down and one was a woman. For some unaccountable reason he'd known it was Hope.

Rifleman Tomlinson was already carrying her towards the hospital as Bennett ran to get her.

She lay so lifeless in the man's arms, her dark curls cascading down and her face like chalk, that for one terrible moment he'd thought she was dead.

'I think she's only fainted, sir,' Tomlinson said. 'She's been shot in the arm. She dragged Robbie away from the firing. Bravest thing I ever saw.'

In the second or two before he pulled himself together

to take Hope from Tomlinson's arms and saw that her wound was a fairly minor one, Bennett felt a stab of white-hot agony run through his entire body.

As a doctor he knew that anyone, even his beloved wife, could fall prey to disease, but he'd never for one moment imagined she'd be shot at. He had had many close shaves himself, but then, he and his assistant often ran to collect the wounded under fire.

'Come on, dearest, open your eyes,' he said tenderly, smoothing back her hair from her face.

Her lovely dark eyes opened and she half-smiled at him, then turned her head to look at Robbie lying beside her. 'Will he be all right?' she whispered.

'I think so, thanks to you,' he said. 'You got that tourniquet on quickly and covered the wound. I'm going to take the bullet out now. You haven't got one in you, it skimmed past.'

Bennett dressed Hope's wound and gave her a few sips of brandy, then took over from the orderly who was cleaning Robbie up in readiness for the bullet to be removed. Compared with most gunshot wounds it was a relatively simple job for the bullet hadn't gone in very far. Robbie was also in better health than most of the men because Queenie took good care of him. With good nursing he would survive.

But even as Bennett was carefully removing the bullet, his mind was on Hope. One of the men had brought along the bag she'd dropped, and just a quick glance into it told him that she'd come up here to stay. He knew she wouldn't have come unless there had been some kind of trouble down at the hospital.

She had fallen asleep and her colour had reverted to its normal peachy tone; in fact, she looked more beautiful than usual, her dark lashes like tiny fans on her cheeks.

It was several hours before Bennett had a chance to talk to Hope properly, for there had already been five wounded men and two sick with fever in the hospital before she and Robbie had been brought in.

Bennett had his own hut now, and once Queenie had been persuaded that Robbie could be left for a while, he asked her to take Hope over to the hut and make her something to eat.

By the time he got over there himself, Hope had made herself at home. Despite her injured arm, she had rearranged most of his things, and was sitting on the camp bed sewing a button on his shirt. The domesticity of the scene brought a lump to his throat.

'You should be resting,' he said, sitting down beside her and taking the shirt from her hands.

'I *am* resting,' she insisted. 'My arm's fine. It hardly hurts at all now.'

Bennett didn't believe that. He knew it would hurt for some time. 'Well, just tell me what made you come up here then.'

She explained, and it was only then that she began to cry.

Bennett was livid. In fact, it was all he could do not to storm out, borrow a horse, ride down to the hospital and attack Truscott. But he forced himself to wait until he'd had time to think it through. Hope needed a husband and a doctor now, not a hothead.

It was her sadness that no one had come to see her after Truscott dismissed her that affected Bennett the most. He guessed that the two days she'd spent alone in their room, imagining that no one liked or cared about her, must have been akin to the distress she'd felt when Albert threw her out of the gatehouse at Briargate.

'You are very wrong to think no one liked you,' he said, holding her tightly. 'It's true some of the older surgeons are prejudiced against women in hospitals, but almost all of them have remarked what an excellent nurse you are. Truscott is a dodo. He ought to be stuffed and put in a glass case as an example of an extinct species.'

'Why didn't anyone come to see me then?' she sobbed.

'I'll wager they didn't know about it,' Bennett said. 'That ward is quite separate from the rest of the hospital. Remember, you don't even go through the other wards to get in and out of it. Unless one of the orderlies told someone what had happened, how would they know? And they weren't likely to talk about it if one or both of them were bribed with extra rations by Truscott.'

Hope dried her eyes. 'It doesn't matter any more anyway,' she said. 'Not now I'm with you.'

Bennett smiled at her resilience. 'You won't be saying that when we get some more rain. It's the most cheerless place in God's creation then.'

'Not to me,' she smiled. 'It can't be when you're here.'

It was two weeks before Bennett really noticed that Hope had changed slightly since they'd been apart. He was delighted that her arm was healing very well, and that she had a good appetite, and although he had observed that she seemed to tire easily, he put that down to the arduous nature of the work she'd been doing for so long. As she looked a picture of health, with pink cheeks, bright eyes and shining hair, the fact that she was quieter, maybe sometimes even a little withdrawn, wasn't in the least worrying. She had been through a great deal in the last year and he couldn't expect her to remain impish and over-excited, the way she'd been on their honeymoon.

Bennett had accompanied Robbie to the base hospital, and after making his recommendations for Robbie's future care, he discovered he was correct in thinking that the majority of the doctors, including the Chief of Staff, had not known that Hope had been dismissed.

Everyone he spoke to was appalled; many said they'd never understood why she'd been moved away from the reception ward where she was so valuable. Dr Anderson said he would look into the matter and showed deep concern for Hope. To his great disappointment Bennett couldn't find Truscott; it seemed he'd ridden over to the French base camp the day before, and it was not known when he would return.

But by then Robbie had spread the story of how Hope had dragged him to safety under fire, and been wounded herself. As Bennett left the hospital that day, he had the supreme satisfaction of seeing Mr Russell, the war correspondent for *The Times*, at Robbie's bedside. He was listening intently to Robbie's story, which Bennett had no doubt would include Hope's merits as a nurse, and how she came to be up at the trenches that day.

It was a very hot night in early May when Bennett's suspicions were finally aroused that Hope was holding something back from him. There had been heavy fire from the French trenches all night, and Bennett woke to find her sitting at the open door gazing out into the darkness.

He joined her at the door, and in silence they watched the sky lighting up with cannonfire for some time.

'You would think that with so much firing Sebastopol would be razed to the ground by now. Will we ever be able to go home?' Hope said suddenly, and her words sounded so bleak.

'We ought to have made the assault on the town as was planned,' Bennett said, putting his arm around her. 'But Lord Raglan seems to have bowed to the wishes of the

French, and I suppose as they have so many more men than us, maybe that's wise.'

'I don't care what it's all about,' she said brokenly. 'Too many have died, and for what? Will the outcome of this war do anything for anyone?'

Bennett couldn't answer that. At the back of his mind was the spectre of the streets of Portsmouth, Plymouth and other ports all full of limbless men begging. It would be the same in Moscow, Paris and Constantinople. Hope was right, what good was it doing anyone?

He looked at her and saw she was crying, and it struck him to the heart because she was so beautiful, even in tears. Her dark hair was tumbling on to bare shoulders, for she wore only a flimsy white petticoat, but as one hand wiped the tears away, the other rested on her stomach, almost protectively, and he saw for the first time that it was no longer flat.

He had been glad when he'd noticed she'd gained some weight while they were apart, for that meant she had been getting enough to eat. It had never occurred to him there might be another reason.

Bennett knew all the theory about pregnancy, but in practice his personal experience merely encompassed the end result, when the baby came into the world. And usually a doctor was only called when there were complications.

Immediately he wanted to round on Hope and ask why she hadn't told him, but somehow her dejected stance gave him that answer. She didn't want to be sent home without him, but neither did she want to stay here in this cruel madness.

He did what his heart told him to do. He stood up, then reached down, picked her up bodily and carried her to the narrow camp-bed. Then he made love to her.

Bennett hadn't attempted this since she'd come up to the

camp, however much he'd wanted her, for her arm was sore and she'd seemed so tired. Now he put all thoughts of his own desire to one side and thought only of giving her pleasure, and their baby inside her.

Kneeling beside her, he kissed her again and again, delicately pulling her petticoat down to expose her breasts, which he saw and felt were much fuller and heavier. As he kissed and suckled at them she began to respond and slowly he drew the petticoat from her until she was naked.

Stroking and kissing every inch of her, from her feet right up to her neck, delighting in the scent and silkiness of her skin, he lingered on her belly, licking it until she squirmed and writhed under him. Then he parted her legs and used both tongue and fingers on her.

He could feel her fingers gripping at his hair, her nails raking his neck and shoulders, but she suppressed any cries for fear of being heard. He half-smiled to himself for at Christmas she'd had no such delicacy, but then she'd had a great deal to drink that night. It pleased him to give her so much pleasure, to hear her gasps and low moans, and he loved the dark, hot and wet depths of her.

The cries she'd tried so hard to suppress erupted as she came, and she grabbed at him, pulling him on to her, kissing him with fiery passion. As he slid into her, her legs went round his back, her body arching under his, urging him deep inside her. Two thoughts flitted across his mind, first, that he didn't want to hurt the baby, and second, that he wouldn't have to withdraw at the last moment. But thought vanished, to be replaced only by ecstasy and need. Nothing mattered any more, not the war or his duty to the army. All that counted was here, just the two of them, and love.

The camp bed collapsed just as he came, and they lay panting, sticky and sated on the floor, wrapped in each other's arms.

Outside there was more gunfire from the French camp, and they heard someone stumble against a bucket somewhere close by. They heard the man cursing and had a mental picture of him hopping on one leg holding his grazed toe. Then Hope began to laugh, and the sound somehow wiped out the darkness, the ugliness all around them, and the hopelessness.

Bennett laughed too as he knelt back and looked at her lying there. The first light of dawn was just coming into the sky, enough for him to see her clearly, dark hair all tousled and wild, her face rosy with lovemaking and her body full and womanly.

Bennett put his two hands on her naked belly, caressing it. 'We made him in a night of passion, but perhaps after another one, you'll tell me officially?'

Chapter Twenty-four

Hope clung tightly to Bennett's hand as they walked up the gangplank on to the steamship *Marianne* on 1 July. It was blazing hot, her dress was sticking to her swollen body in the most undignified way, and she was glad of the broad-brimmed straw hat Mary Seacole had given her as a leaving gift.

The old Jamaican woman was there on the quay with dozens of other people who had shared such a big part of Hope's time here. But now she was leaving she felt a pang that there had never been time to get to know some of them better. She counted them as true friends, but what did she really know about any of them? Would Sergeant Major Jury, who had always been so gentle with his wounded men and so cheery with her, eventually marry the sweetheart he'd spoken of so often? Did Cobbs the orderly, who had worked beside her right from her first day in the hospital, have any children? Had Assistant Surgeon Francis, the man who had so often made her laugh during some of the most desperate times, really spent some time as a clown in a music hall as he claimed?

She could see Lieutenant Gordon of the Engineers waving at her, and she was reminded that he'd generously given her a tartan rug back in the winter to keep her warm at night, despite desperately needing it himself.

There were dozens of dear and familiar faces, every one of them special in some way, and she'd miss them all. As people waved and smiled, she felt their sympathy that she had to go home alone, but also their joy that she was leaving here in good health and that she and Bennett had created new life in a place of so much death.

In her hands Hope held a bag containing many little presents given to her by everyone from tradespeople to soldiers and doctors. There were books, fruit, cake, soap, and a few sketches from some of the more artistic friends. A few riflemen had come down from the camp to see her off, their boots polished, beards shaved off and uniforms brushed in an attempt to honour her with parade-ground smartness. Tomlinson, known to everyone as Tommy, Robbie's closest friend and the man who had carried her to Bennett after she was shot, had carved her a rattle shaped like a cat from a piece of wood. She hoped fervently that he would stay safe, for he'd done so much for her in the past weeks, bringing her fresh water, lighting her fire and making her drinks. But then, there wasn't one person waving her goodbye she didn't hope would stay safe.

Hope knew that she should have left a month ago, but first there had been the British victory at the Quarries, and when the French took the Mamelon, one of the Russians' main defences, she had felt compelled to stay and help with the casualties.

A week later the fourth bombardment of Sebastopol began, and the English were defeated at the storming of the Redan and the French defeated at Malakoff, so once again she felt she had to stay on for there were so many hundreds of wounded.

Lord Raglan died on 28 June, and although the official cause of death was cholera, everyone believed he died of a broken heart because the allies had failed to seize the two most important defences. Even after so many bitter words had been said about him, there was real grief that the General who had lost his arm beside Lord Wellington in the Peninsular War had not survived to see victory here. He might not have been a bold leader, but he had been honourable, kind and loved his men, and Hope didn't feel it was right to leave until after his funeral.

Even a king could not have had a more magnificent send-off. Troops lined the entire five-mile route to the barge that would carry his remains to the *Caradoc*, the ship waiting to take his body home. The cavalry escorted his coffin, borne on a gun-carriage, and the vivid colours of their uniforms in the bright sunshine, and the music from all the many military bands, belied the sadness of the occasion.

'Just ten minutes till you sail,' Bennett said, but his bright smile did not reach his eyes. 'Make sure you rest on the voyage. Uncle Abel will be waiting for you at Portsmouth to take you to Nell.'

'Do stop worrying about me, dearest,' she said, squeezing his hand. 'I will be fine, just you make sure you come back to me soon.'

Bennett was denying that he was worried about her, when at last Hope spotted Angus riding along the quay. She pointed him out with delight for he had been a constant visitor up on the Heights, and he had been the first person in whom she and Bennett had confided about the baby. She knew he would be very relieved to see she was actually leaving today, for she had seen him briefly on the day of Raglan's funeral and he had given her a stern warning that she mustn't delay any longer.

He leapt off his horse, handed the reins to a soldier, and was up the gangplank in a few quick strides.

'I was afraid I was going to miss saying goodbye,' he said breathlessly, bending to kiss Hope's cheek.

'It's only au revoir as I'll be there in your home when you get back.'

'So, two women to order me about,' he said, his dark eyes twinkling. 'Maybe that will be too much for me, especially with a screaming baby too?'

Hope knew he didn't mean this, for as soon as he'd heard about the baby he'd insisted she could stay at his house for as long as she wished. He didn't fool her any longer with his sarcasm and buffoonery; she knew that he was soft-hearted, generous and noble.

'Look out for Bennett for me,' she said, her eyes filling up with tears. 'And mind you both come home in one piece.'

'You patched me up too well for me to fall apart now,' he grinned. 'And I shall be whisking Bennett off to some races once you're out of sight. That's the trouble with wives, they spoil all the fun.'

Hope laughed. Most of the time Angus acted as if life was just one riotous fun-packed adventure. He would be good for Bennett; there were times when her husband was a little too serious.

'We have to go now,' Bennett said, looking anxious as he heard the ship's bell. 'Write to me every day, I want to know every detail. And I promise I'm going to try to talk Lawrence into letting me go by the end of the month.'

Angus kissed Hope, said goodbye and diplomatically went off down the gangplank. Hope took Bennett's face in both hands and kissed him. 'Don't fret about me; I've got Nell and Uncle Abel to take care of me. But it would be wonderful if you were back for the birth, or soon after.'

'I love you, Hope,' he said, his eyes brimming with tears, and as he turned to leave her he was almost stumbling with sorrow.

*

Hope waved until the ship was right out of the harbour, tears rolling down her cheeks unchecked as she caught her last glimpse of Bennett waving a red handkerchief and Angus beside him, resplendent in his blue and gold jacket. The Crimea had been the worst of times, yet this soiled little harbour, the grim hospital, the cliffs and the Heights would stay in her heart, as would all the people she'd met there.

Her wish was that one day hospitals would be better places, that rank-and-file soldiers would be treated humanely, and nursing become an honoured profession. Maybe when she was old and grey with her children all grown-up, with children of their own, she'd tell her stories about this war, and they'd smile to humour her, thinking she was exaggerating the horror of it.

Would future generations ever be able to believe that the vast number of men who died here, died for a cause they never really understood? Or that even more died of disease or infected wounds?

Hope thought her grandchildren were more likely to want to hear about the Christmas when the bands had played on the quay, and she had danced with more men than was good for any girl, for that was a far prettier picture. If she kept her arm covered they would never see her scar, just as they would never see the hideous images printed indelibly on her mind.

She pulled up her sleeve and looked at the ugly red puckered wound. To her it was a permanent reminder of how blessed she was to escape so lightly when so many others were disfigured or dead. She didn't want it to fade.

The sea breeze felt and smelled good and her spirits lifted, knowing that the sadness of goodbyes was finally over. The *Marianne* was reported to be a fast ship; she would only be putting in at Malta, and then sail straight back to Portsmouth. A great many of the other passengers were officers and staff sent home on sick reports but there was also a fair proportion of those who back in Balaclava had been called 'tourists': gentlemen and their ladies who had travelled out here to view the war.

Her heart quickened a little at the prospect of teasing some of these ghoulish rich people who got their excitement from watching others die. It would be enjoyable to wait until they were eating their dinner and then relate a few choice tales about gangrene and cholera.

She hoped she had let her pink dress out enough to look presentable at dinner.

As the ship steamed into Portsmouth harbour in late August, Hope was beside herself with excitement. She had loved every minute of the voyage, and although she was so huge and slow now, she had never felt better. The food on the ship had been wonderful, her cabin comfortable and the weather in the main glorious, and she'd enjoyed having nothing more pressing to do than make herself a new dress, read a book, write a letter or chat to someone.

Coming up the coast of Spain, some of the passengers had suffered from sea sickness, but Hope had resisted the urge to go and take care of them. It was such a joy to be entirely selfish, and to revel in her quite unexpected new status.

She had never imagined back in the days of Lewins Mead and St Peter's that the day would ever come when she'd be considered a lady, let alone a heroine. But one of the officers on the ship knew all about her, including her rescue of Robbie and how she'd been wounded herself, and had clearly passed it on. Each time she went into the dining room someone always begged her to sit next to them. The men were attentive and curious, telling her she must write her memoirs and get them published when she got home. And the women cooed over her courage at travelling so late in her pregnancy, and asked how she managed to keep her hair so beautifully shiny and her complexion so clear.

She was completely bored with all that now, but it had been good to bask in a little limelight for a while. Bennett would have been very amused to see her hold court with the kind of people she had always been intimidated by in the past.

All she wanted now was to go home. To sit with Nell and talk through all the things that had happened to them in the last seven years. She couldn't wait to see Matt's and Ruth's children. To walk in fields and woods, to sit by streams and smell flowers. And wait for her baby to arrive.

If the strength of his kicks was anything to go by, he would be a real Renton, tough and strong. But she hoped he'd also inherit his father's sensitivity and intelligence.

As the ship came in closer to berth, Hope scanned the waiting crowd for Uncle Abel. Excited as she was, she was also nervous because she realized that he was, to all intents and purposes, a stranger. In his letters to Bennett he always asked after her with warmth and interest, but she couldn't quite forget that for a very long time he'd disapproved of her.

All at once she spotted him, looking the picture of a tubby English gentleman in a grey top hat, tail coat and a high wing collar. But as she waved, she saw him incline his head to a woman beside him and point towards the ship.

Hope's heart leapt, for it was not Alice beside him but Nell, wearing a white bonnet trimmed with blue flowers.

She forgot the ladylike demeanour she'd taken such pains to preserve on the voyage and jumped up and down, waving with both hands.

A band on the quay struck up a lively welcoming tune, and now she could only see the waiting crowd through a mist of emotional tears.

Hope was one of the first to go down the gangplank. She had pushed and elbowed her way to the front of the queue in a way that would have appalled Bennett. But it thrilled her to see Nell was every bit as eager, dodging through the crowd like a street urchin.

Hope was almost blinded by her tears now, and Nell's round, sweet face was just a blur, but she saw the out-stretched arms and ran full tilt to them. She was home at last!

'Are you two going to stop that caterwauling and come and get in the carriage?' Abel said gruffly.

Hope and Nell released each other from their tight embrace and dabbed at their eyes. 'I'm so sorry, Dr Cunningham,' Hope said. 'It's just been so long.'

'I understand that,' he said with a smile. 'But I'd like to embrace you too, you know! And I think it's high time you addressed me as Uncle Abel.'

As the carriage bowled along through the countryside towards Bristol, Hope tried to remember to keep to topics which would not exclude Uncle Abel, but her excitement at being with Nell again made it almost impossible. She was very aware that they sounded like a pair of chattering monkeys, leaping from one subject to another, gasping, giggling, and often crying too.

Nell had changed a great deal from how she'd been when Hope last saw her. Even though Angus had reported she was far more confident, in both her dress and her manner, Hope had still expected to find her greying, slower and stouter. She did have a peppering of grey hair, but she moved as fast as she ever did, she was shapely, not fat, and her face was as unlined as when she was a bride. But it wasn't the physical changes that were so notable.

Nell had been so biddable before, a sweet and pliant person who never stepped out of what she considered to be 'her place'. Hope couldn't imagine her allowing anyone to order her around now. She had an air of authority, and she seemed far sharper and more worldly. Some of her remarks about people had been quite caustic. Her clothes, too, illustrated her knowledge of self-worth. She wore an elegant blue and white striped dress which enhanced her curvy body rather than concealing it. Her white bonnet with its blue trimming was youthful, not matronly. In all, Hope thought her sister had steered exactly the right path. She wasn't aping gentry, but nor was she defining herself as a servant.

When they stopped to water the horses, Hope felt she must apologize to Uncle Abel for her and Nell's constant prattle. She explained that they were overexcited and that it must be very dull and wearing for him.

'Not a bit of it, my dear,' he chuckled, and patted her hand. 'But maybe I'll take my revenge when Bennett comes home!'

It wasn't until the evening of the following day, when Hope and Nell were finally alone at Willow End, that calm settled. They had stayed overnight at a coaching inn, and as they had to share a bed, which Nell was convinced was full of bugs, they had talked nearly all night.

Hope had dozed off for the last few miles of the journey and it was a surprise to have Nell wake her and tell her they were there.

The sun was setting, turning the grey stone walls of the cottage pink as they walked to the front door. Hope brushed against the lavender bushes, and the sweet, pungent smell took her straight back to her childhood, when she used to pick lavender from the garden and tie it into bunches for her mother to hang from the cottage beams.

It was something of a surprise to find Angus lived so simply. The picture she'd had of Willow End in her head while out in the Crimea was of something grander. Yet she was pleased rather than disappointed, for it was yet more evidence that Angus had a soul.

She loved the low-beamed ceilings and the comfortable, slightly battered old furniture. It was a real home, and she could see Nell's hand everywhere, from the smell of polish and the sparkling windows to a large vase of Michaelmas daisies on the hall table.

'I often think that a woman who had the Captain's love and this house to live in would be the happiest woman in the world,' Nell said as Hope darted around, inspecting everything with exclamations of glee.

Hope looked at her sharply, suspecting her sister of wishing for his love. But Nell laughed at her expression. 'You misunderstand me. I only meant that this is what most women hope for. I count my blessings every day, Hope. I have his respect, and this house to live in. And now you back too! That's more than enough for me.'

As Nell got cold meat, pickles and bread from the pantry for their supper she explained that she had a maid who came in each day. 'I really couldn't imagine what I'd give her to do each day when the Captain first said I must have help,' she said. 'But Dora is a good girl, and I'm glad of her company and the hard work she does. She is looking forward to meeting you tomorrow because I've told her so much about you.'

After supper, they sat in the two chairs by the stove and it was only then that Hope asked what news there was of Albert.

'None,' Nell said, and a flicker of anxiety crossed her face. 'I'm sure he'll return to Briargate one day, but Matt says I'm foolish to think such things.'

Hope privately thought that neither of them would have complete peace of mind until he was caught and tried for his crimes. But she didn't voice this and asked about Lady Harvey and Rufus instead.

'Rufus is doing well with the farm, he had a real good harvest this year,' Nell said with some pride. 'But Lady Harvey!'

Nell had mentioned her several times in the last two days, but always with a kind of exclamation mark, as people did when mentioning a wayward child.

'She hasn't settled at the gatehouse then?'

'I don't think she'll ever settle anywhere,' Nell sighed. 'And she's so full of regrets.'

'I suppose she would be bitter at losing her home,' Hope said, a little surprised that Nell seemed so impatient with the woman she'd once adored.

'She's not bitter,' Nell frowned. 'Oh, but you must go and see it for yourself. I can't explain. But both she and Rufus were so happy to hear you were coming home and so impressed by that piece about you in *The Times*. Did I tell you that Matt said Reverend Gosling read it out in church?'

Hope suppressed a giggle, for Nell had not only told her this several times already, but carried the newspaper cutting around with her. It was mainly about her getting shot at while rescuing Robbie, but also about her work at the hospital in Balaclava. The crumpled state of the cutting suggested Nell had been showing it to everyone for several weeks.

'I'd better go and see Rufus soon,' Hope replied, looking down at her large belly. 'While I still can.'

'On Sunday everyone's coming here,' Nell said excitedly. 'Alice and Toby are coming over from Bath with Ruth, John and their family. Matt and Amy with their little ones, and Joe and Henry will be here too. We'll have a full house then and no mistake. It's a pity it's too far for James to come as well.'

'So we'll be busy cooking for the next few days?'

'That we will,' Nell chuckled. 'I just hope the weather holds; it's easier when the children can be outside for there's so many of them now.'

For the first two days at Willow End, Hope felt she was wrapped in a beautiful dream from which she didn't ever want to wake. Apart from her honeymoon, she'd never had the kind of comfort and ease she was experiencing now. A spacious, pretty bedroom with a soft bed, leisurely meals, and her clothes washed and pressed for her. She could watch carriages going past the cottage, or amble down to the river at Saltford and revel in the tranquillity and beauty of the countryside.

All the anxiety about her family during the long years of separation had been wiped out the moment Nell had embraced her at Portsmouth harbour, and as a result of their talks together Hope had a clear picture of everything that had happened to all of them during these years.

It wasn't until Sunday, when the rest of the family arrived to see her, that Hope experienced an awakening from the blissful cocoon she felt she'd been wrapped in since her arrival.

Everything began so well. It was a warm, sunny day, Nell and Dora had produced a veritable feast, and the family arrived with what seemed a flock of children. It was glorious to be enveloped by their excitement and love. She marvelled how Joe and Henry had grown into men while she'd been away; that Matt was now a replica of her father, and there was a sense of comradeship in sharing Amy's and Ruth's childbirth stories. Yet even as they all milled around her, faces glowing with delight at having her back in their midst, Hope found herself feeling strangely isolated and different.

She couldn't work out why this was, for apart from Matt, Joe and Henry who still led a very similar life to the one she'd grown up in, they'd all changed. Ruth and her family were relatively well-off and living in Bath. Alice and Toby were still in service and could talk of little else but the goings-on in their household. And Nell, too, had gone up in the world. Yet changed or not, they all reacted with one another just the same as they always had. Only she was different, as if she didn't belong.

Later, when everyone had gone home, Hope tried to talk about how she felt to Nell, but she'd just got cross and impatient. 'Of course you belong,' she snapped. 'I don't want to hear any more of this foolishness.'

Two weeks after her arrival home, Hope set off in the morning with Mr Tremble, the local carter, to see Rufus and Lady Harvey at the gatehouse. It had been something she'd wanted to do since she'd first returned, but although Nell had seemed keen for her to go at first, today she appeared to have had second thoughts about it.

Hope could quite understand Nell's sudden change of heart. The gatehouse had bad memories for both of them, and it was terrible to think of Albert burning Briargate down and killing Sir William. But Hope knew she had to go back there; she had ghosts to put to rest.

Matt had told her how worried Rufus had been after she left, how he'd helped on the farm during his holidays, and what a fine young man he'd turned into. Hope felt she owed it to him to show she valued their childhood friendship still.

But perhaps Nell's fears about this visit were because she was afraid her younger sister would forget her place and say something disrespectful to Lady Harvey?

That riled Hope, for she didn't have 'a place' any longer. She was neither a servant nor gentry. She was just an army surgeon's wife who knew far more about Sir William and Lady Harvey's personal lives than she felt comfortable with, and far more about Albert than Nell knew. Sometimes she wished she could tell Nell it all, then perhaps she'd stop treating her as if she were a child.

'So you'll be the Renton what ran off?'

Hope looked askance at Mr Tremble. He hadn't said a word since she climbed on the cart beside him, and then had suddenly come out with this very pointed question. With his small head, long nose and no neck to speak of, just a thick muffler where it should have been, the man made her think of a mole.

'Yes, I am,' she admitted. 'But I'd rather not talk about that.'

'They said that Albert killed you,' he said, totally ignoring her reply. 'But my missus reckoned he done sommat else to you.'

Hope gulped. She could guess what that was!

'Mr Tremble,' she said in the stern voice she had always used with patients, 'it was all a long time ago and I wish to forget I ever met Albert Scott. Now, that is all I'm going to say on the subject.'

The carter was quiet for some little while. 'Rum do that they can't find him though,' he suddenly burst out. ''E could've joined the army, 'e might have been out where you was.'

'Possibly,' Hope agreed. Several people had put forward

that same suggestion already, and she wondered what she would have done if he'd been brought into the hospital wounded. She quite liked the idea of strapping him down to have a limb amputated without chloroform.

'When's the little 'un due?'

Hope smiled, relieved to be asked something she didn't mind talking about. 'Two weeks or so,' she said. 'So don't go hitting any ruts in the road or I might have it today.'

Strangely, that shut him up, and Hope was able to sit back and enjoy the ride.

She had almost forgotten how beautiful England was in September. The sun was no longer too hot, the harvest was in, and the leaves on the trees were just beginning to change colour. She loved the undulating quality of the landscape and the small fields surrounded by hedging, which from her viewpoint high up on the cart looked like a plump patchwork quilt. How good it was to see cows and sheep grazing, and the neat rows of vegetables in gardens! She would have given a king's ransom last winter for a carrot or a cabbage.

'What's the Crimea like then?' Mr Tremble asked, almost as if he'd read her thoughts.

'Barren and bleak,' she said. 'Nothing like this.'

He nodded, seemingly satisfied with that sparse description. 'D'you want me to pick you up on me way back?' he asked.

'No, that won't be necessary, but thank you for offering. I'll walk down to my brother's farm in Woolard and get him to take me home,' she said.

Mr Tremble had barely helped her down from the cart before Rufus came haring down the drive to meet her. 'Hope! How good to see you!' he exclaimed, arms outstretched to hug her as he always did as a small boy. But he stopped short just a few feet from her, looking faintly embarrassed.

Hope understood. The last time she'd seen him he had been just a small boy several inches shorter than her. Now he towered over her, a grown man with a deep voice and broad shoulders.

'I know there's an awful lot of me to hug,' she laughed. 'Or are you shy because we're all grown-up?'

He laughed and hugged her anyway, but the mere size of her belly made it difficult.

Hope took both his hands. 'Let me look at you, Sir Rufus Harvey. My, but you've grown into a handsome chap.'

He still had the best of his parents' blond, blue-eyed looks, but there was strength in his features that had been lacking in theirs. In plain workingmen's clothes, he looked more like a farmer than a knight.

'And you've grown from the prettiest girl in the village to the most beautiful woman in the county,' he said.

'You've spent too long on the farm,' she joked. 'Have you ever seen anyone other than a sow quite so huge?'

'I think I have spent too long on a farm,' he laughed. 'Mother would be appalled that a gentleman even noticed such a "condition".'

'We'd better go in and see her,' Hope said, glancing nervously at the small cottage that held so many bad memories. It looked less stark now, for Virginia creeper had grown all over it, and its leaves were just starting to turn red.

'A word of warning,' Rufus said, his face tensing. 'Mother isn't the way she used to be. At times she's distinctly odd. If you feel uncomfortable with her, just make the excuse that you've got to go and I'll walk you down to Matt's. I saw him last night; he told me he would be taking you home.'

'Does that mean we can play hide-and-seek in the woods?' she grinned.

'You couldn't hide from me now,' he laughed. 'Remember what good times we had?'

'Some of the very best,' she sighed. 'I haven't forgotten any of them.' She could feel that time hadn't weakened the old bond between them, and even if Lady Harvey should prove difficult, she was very glad she'd come today.

Yet everything else was different. The drive was full of weeds now, and rutted by farm carts. At the end, where the big house once stood, was nothing but a flat ploughed field. Almost all trace of the beautiful garden was gone, apart from a few lovely old trees.

The stables were still intact, but as the arch which connected them to the house was gone, they looked like farm buildings.

'Does it shock you?' Rufus said.

Hope nodded, remembering how often she'd sat at the back door of the gatehouse looking up at the house and thinking it was the finest in all England.

'Does it hurt you? I mean, that it's gone?'

He smiled wryly. 'No, not really. Of course I still feel savage that Albert could do such a thing, and if he ever came here I think I'd tear him apart with my bare hands. But my sorrow is about not being able to say goodbye to Father, and of course what it's done to Mother, not about the house. In a strange way I often feel that it never belonged there. That this was meant to be farmland. Do you know what I mean?'

Hope looked thoughtfully over the land. It didn't look as if anything was missing at all. 'Yes, I think I do,' she agreed. 'And Nell says you are happier farming than you were studying. Is that true?'

His wide smile came back. 'Yes, Nell's right, I am much

happier. I feel a sense of purpose, a belonging that I never felt before.'

'Then you are lucky.' She reached out and touched his cheek affectionately. 'I felt that way when I was nursing. It's a good feeling.'

'I want to know everything about the Crimea,' he said eagerly. 'But we'd better go and see Mother first.'

It was the strangest sensation to go into the gatehouse again. Hope glanced up the stairs, remembering in a flash what she'd seen there. She could almost feel Albert's blows raining down on her, and her terror that he would kill her.

But it didn't look the same now. The rough old table and chairs were gone; it seemed bigger, softer and warmer, almost gracious, with a carpet on the floor, comfortable armchairs and a polished wood table. It was a minute or two before she realized that part of the reason for this was because another room had been added, presumably a new kitchen, beyond where the back door used to be.

'How good of you to call, Hope.' Lady Harvey rose rather stiffly from a velvet armchair by the fireplace to greet her. 'You look well, and the happy event will be soon, I understand?'

Lady Harvey had aged dramatically. Her hair was white now, her face was almost skeletal, and the flesh appeared so thin that it was as if her sharp cheekbones could pierce through it at any time. Her mouth was sunken too, and Hope guessed she'd lost a good many teeth. Her black dress drained any colour there might have been in her face; even her blue eyes seemed to have faded.

Hope realized this change must have come about gradually over a long period or Nell would have warned her, but coming upon it so unexpectedly, she felt suddenly tongue-tied.

'I am so very sorry about Sir William,' she said in a rush. 'I didn't hear of it because I had just got married.'

'Don't let's dwell on that,' Lady Harvey said, and smiled, which brought back a glimmer of the beautiful woman she'd once been. 'I was so pleased when Nell told me you were found, and that you'd married a doctor. And now a baby!'

'Yes,' Hope said. 'Only a couple more weeks now, but I'm hoping it will wait until Bennett arrives home.'

She'd had a letter soon after she got home saying he thought he would be allowed to go on the next ship. That letter had arrived with nearly a dozen he'd written prior to it, and it was dated 1 August. As no more had come since, she was sure that meant he had got on the ship almost immediately, and that he would be home any day now.

'I do hope you won't have to have the child alone,' Lady Harvey said, and to Hope's astonishment she began to cry.

'I won't be alone, I'll have Nell with me,' Hope said, touched by this extraordinary display of concern. She moved forward and took the older woman's hand. 'Don't cry,' she said. 'I'll be fine.'

'Just make sure she doesn't whisk the baby away,' Lady Harvey said.

Her words were strange enough, but her expression was even stranger, for it was as though she was baring her teeth, except there were only a couple of brown stumps left.

Hope looked round at Rufus for an explanation, but he only shook his head and indicated the door.

It seemed incredibly rude to leave so quickly, but she really couldn't bear to stay. Not just because Lady Harvey was so strange, but the cottage itself was making her feel tense and anxious. 'I'm sorry this was such a brief visit, but I have to go now,' she said. 'I'll come and see you again soon.'

'You haven't even had any tea with me.' The older

woman's voice was shrill and pleading. 'I was just going to ring for some.'

Rufus ushered Hope out.

'I'm sorry,' he said once they were outside, wearing a hangdog expression. 'She says some very odd things sometimes. As for ringing for tea! Perhaps she thinks Baines will pop out of the churchyard and bring her some.'

Hope giggled nervously. 'I shouldn't laugh at that. Poor old Baines. He was such a nice man.'

'One of the best,' Rufus said. 'I saw him before he died, and he told me he wanted to go. He said it had been a privilege working for my folks, but he was tired now. He died the next day, and I was glad, really. I mean, if he had lived on where would he have gone?'

Hope knew as Rufus did that it would have been the workhouse. She was glad to see her childhood friend hadn't lost his social conscience.

'How do you manage with your mother?' she asked as they walked along the old drive.

'You mean when she's mad?' he said with disarming frankness. 'She isn't a danger to herself or anyone else. She only says strange things. She told me one day I had a sister!'

'Really?' Hope giggled. 'And what happened to this sister? Did Nell whisk her away?'

They both laughed, and then moved on to talk about more cheerful things.

They walked down to the lake for old times' sake, and were pleased to see that the old boat was still there. They sat on a log in a patch of sunshine and talked about anything and everything. Hope even told Rufus about Gussie and Betsy and the time she stole the pie when they were starving.

It was what she had needed, without knowing it: to be able to talk truthfully about the past, for she'd only glossed over her time in Lewins Mead to Nell for fear of putting ugly pictures into her sister's mind.

She didn't linger on that part of her life, though; it was enough to give him a brief glimpse of it and move on. Rufus wanted to know about the battles in the Crimea, particularly the Charge of the Light Brigade which had been reported on in great depth in every English newspaper.

Hope gave him her own scathing views on the so-called hero, Cardigan, and told him she felt it was appalling that back here everyone had cast Lord Lucan as the villain of the piece.

'My very favourite battle was the one they dubbed "The Thin Red Line",' Rufus said.

'Bennett watched that one,' Hope responded eagerly. 'He thought the Highlanders were the bravest men in history.'

'Russell of *The Times* wrote about it so passionately, I almost felt I was there,' Rufus said. 'He described them as "The Thin Red Line tipped with steel". Isn't that a marvellous description?'

'I just hope when they come home they are truly rewarded for their valour,' Hope sighed. 'There were so many heroic incidents out there, many of which will never be reported. Angus was badly wounded in the cavalry charge, but he still hauled an unseated trooper on to his horse with him and rode back with him through the blazing guns. As for Bennett, he might not have led charges or killed any Russians, but to the men whose lives he saved, he was, and still is, a hero.'

Rufus hung on her every word as she described the hospital and the endless procession of wounded and sick arriving daily. 'But now they've taken Sebastopol, it must all be over bar the shouting,' he said. 'They'll surely all be home for Christmas?'

'I hope Bennett gets home long before that, and warns

me when it will be,' Hope said with a grin. 'It will be just like him to walk in the one day I'm in a mess. But enough of war and me. What about you, Rufus? Have you got a sweetheart?'

He grinned bashfully. 'I have indeed. Lily Freeman, she's the rector in Chelwood's daughter.'

'I'm very happy for you,' Hope said. 'Is she beautiful?'

'She is to me,' he said looking all dreamy-eyed. 'I love her and want to marry her. But I can't while Mother's this way. I can only just about keep us, let alone a wife, at the moment.'

It seemed incredible to Hope that Rufus's life had changed so dramatically. Whenever she'd imagined him in the past it was always in some kind of grand setting – balls, parties, out hunting on a horse like Merlin. She could never have pictured him in worn rough clothes with dirt beneath his fingernails, ploughing a field or feeding chickens.

'You are still a very young man,' she reminded him. 'Lily will wait if she loves you. I had to wait a long time for Bennett, but it was worth it in the end.'

'It's so good to have you back,' he said, slinging an arm around her shoulder. 'And even better to find that we can still talk about everything, just the way we used to. We'll always be friends, won't we?'

She kissed his cheek then. 'Always. For ever and ever. But now I must go on to Matt's, I've taken up too much of your day already. But come and see me at Nell's very soon?'

On 29 September Hope woke in the early hours with a twinge of pain in her stomach. It disappeared, but some ten minutes later there was another. By the fifth one, now nearly an hour later, she knew the baby was coming and went to wake Nell.

Uncle Abel had arranged for a midwife in Brislington

village, who he considered to be the best, to attend the birth, and he'd already given his instructions that when the time came Nell was to send for her, and notify him.

Nell was very calm. She got dressed, stirred up the stove and made them both tea, then slipped out to see a neighbour who had a pony and trap and had already promised to fetch the midwife when the time came.

Hope had no intention of going back to bed until she absolutely had to. One of the sisters at St Peter's had always claimed that she'd noted babies came easier and quicker when the mother walked around.

Nell had everything ready for the baby; she'd made a whole drawerful of flannel nightgowns, jackets, bonnets and bootees. She'd got a wooden crib from somewhere, and knitted blankets and a shawl. Hope had glanced at them all before, but now that the event was so close she decided to take a better look.

She felt a surge of love for her sister as she saw the care that had gone into making the tiny garments. The little flannel nightgowns had delicate embroidery on the yoke, and she had trimmed the bonnets with lace.

At the bottom of the pile there was an older shawl, and Hope pulled it out to look at it. It was yellowing with age, but as soft and delicate as a cobweb. She wondered where it had come from, for it was clearly handed down, but she couldn't imagine anyone Nell knew having such a fine shawl.

She was holding it to her face when Nell came in, flushed from rushing up the road. 'Where did this come from, Nell?' Hope asked. 'It's so lovely.'

'It was yours,' Nell said.

'Mine! How could our family afford such a thing?'

'Someone gave it to Mother. I don't know who,' Nell said, and her voice was strangely sharp.

'I'm going to be just fine,' Hope said, assuming Nell was worried about her. 'Women have babies all the time, and I've delivered a few too, so I know what it's all about.'

'I shall remind you of that if you start screaming,' Nell said tartly.

The midwife, Mrs Langham, arrived at twelve. She was a big, bossy woman with a large wart on her nose, but Hope was pleased to see she was very clean, and didn't look as if she swigged gin as so many so-called midwives did. Her husband had despatched a boy to inform Dr Cunningham the baby was on its way.

'But we'll have this one ready for him when he gets here,' Mrs Langham said jovially. 'You don't look the kind to hang around for a couple of days.'

She was right. By four in the afternoon the pains were so bad that Hope got into bed, and by six she was bearing down. In less than half an hour Mrs Langham was catching the baby in her hands and announcing it was a girl.

Hope lay back on the pillows and took the baby in her arms. She had expected the birth to be hell, and it had come close. But she had never truly believed that when a baby was put into its mother's arms she would immediately love it. She had been wrong on that count, however, for the feeling which welled up inside her was so strong that tears flowed down her cheeks. Nothing in her life so far had ever felt so good, so utterly moving as the sight of that tiny little face.

'Oh, Nell,' she sighed. 'Can anything be more perfect, more wonderful?'

'She looks just like you when you were born,' Nell said, and she began to cry.

'Screamers I can deal with,' Mrs Langham said. 'But cryers, I need a brandy for those.'

Hope looked up at the big woman and her tears turned

to laughter. 'You shall have a brandy,' she said. 'As big as you like. And Nell had better have one too.'

'So, what are you going to call her?' Uncle Abel said. He had arrived an hour after the delivery and seemed quite shaken that his skills were unnecessary. He had examined the baby, pronounced her strong, healthy and quite the most beautiful he'd ever seen. Then he sat down and cradled her in his arms.

'Betsy,' Hope said without any hesitation. 'Betsy Hannah Meg Meadows.'

He looked pleased that the second name was to be his late sister's and the third that of Hope's mother. 'Why Betsy?' he asked.

'After someone I loved,' she said simply. 'I know Bennett will approve, it was when he came to visit her during the cholera that we met.'

'Have you had a letter lately?' he asked.

'Not since the one he wrote in August,' she replied. 'I think that means he's on his way home.'

'What a devil of a time it takes for letters from abroad!' Abel said reflectively. 'We have the telegraph now and that gives us news of what is happening just a couple of days after the event. But letters still take weeks!'

'There's a letter for you from the Captain!' Nell shouted up the stairs exactly a week after Betsy was born. 'I'll bring it up in a minute.'

Hope would have run down the stairs immediately had she not been feeding Betsy. Feeding was the best part of motherhood. She had a comfortable chair by the bedroom window which looked out on to the garden, and she could gaze dreamily out at the fields beyond the garden wall as Betsy suckled greedily at her breast.

Nothing before had come close to the joy of looking down at her small face, or feeling her tiny fingers clench hers; there was a faint smell on her head that Hope would sniff rapturously, and it was bliss after the feed to lie back in the chair cradling her in her arms.

Nell and Dora complained that she didn't allow them to have much time with her, and sometimes she was aware she was too possessive. But Betsy was *her* baby, and right now while she was so tiny, all she wanted was her mother.

Nell came up with some tea on a tray. 'Can I hold her while you read the letter?' she asked as she put the tray down.

'She needs changing,' Hope said as she moved to hand the baby over and saw her dress had a wet patch. 'I never expected babies to be so leaky.'

'You just wait till she's a bit bigger,' Nell said as she laid Betsy down on a towel and removed the sodden napkin. 'You'll find it hard to deal with the washing. But come on, get that letter read; I want to hear his news.'

Hope sat back down and opened the envelope. It was only one page, and at the second line she blanched.

'Oh no,' she gasped. 'Bennett's sick.'

She continued to read, and when she'd finished she dropped the letter in her lap and covered her face in her hands.

'Tell me?' Nell said, hastily putting Betsy back in her crib and moving to drop on her knees in front of her sister. 'What does the letter say?'

'You read it, I can't. I think he must be dead.'

Nell picked up the letter and took it over to the window for better light.

'*Dear Hope*,' she read.

I hope you are well and that the baby has arrived by now, I also
fervently hope that Bennett is now home with you and recovering his
health. I have just got back from being off with the cavalry for a
while, and of course I went looking for him only to be told he'd been
taken sick with fever. By the time I got down to the hospital he'd
already been sent off to Scutari.

Nell stopped reading when she heard Hope wail. 'It's all
right, my love.' Nell dropped the letter and moved over to
comfort her sister. 'He doesn't say Bennett's dead, only that
he was sent off because he was sick.'

'That letter is dated 20 August,' Hope sobbed. 'Bennett
had already been ill for a while then – if he's alive, why
hasn't he written?'

'You know how erratic the post is from there,' Nell said
soothingly. 'Bad news travels faster than good, we all know
that. If he'd died you would have heard.'

'You don't know what it's like there,' Hope insisted. 'Men
die all the time and sometimes no one knows who they are.'

'But he's an officer,' Nell said firmly. 'They don't lose
them!'

Hope looked up at Nell with fear-filled eyes. 'They took
him to Scutari, Nell. That place is a hell-hole, everyone
knows that. He's dead. He's never coming back to me.'

Chapter Twenty-five

Nell woke with a start, sat up and fumbled for the candle. Betsy was screaming and it was clear that once again Hope wasn't going to move to comfort her.

It had been this way for days now, and Nell was at the end of her tether. She got out of bed, pulled a shawl over her shoulders, and taking the candle, padded barefoot across the landing into Hope's room.

'There, there, my little love,' she said as she scooped the baby up into her arms. 'Nell's got you now.'

Betsy was soaking wet and clearly very hungry, sucking at her little fists.

Nell stripped off the wet nightgown and napkin and replaced them with dry ones, then moved closer to the bed. Hope was just the same way she'd been for days, lying flat on her back, staring into space, seemingly unaware of anything.

'You must feed Betsy,' Nell said.

When Hope didn't reply, or even look at her, Nell called her name, tugged at her arm and repeated her request, louder this time. There was still no response.

'What will Bennett say if he comes back and finds his child half-starved?' Nell said angrily. 'You are her mother, for God's sake!'

'He won't come back. He's dead.'

An icy shudder ran down Nell's spine at the cold and expressionless tone of her sister's voice.

'If he is dead, then all the more reason for you to take care of his baby,' Nell spat at her. 'Sit up this minute and put her to your breast.'

Betsy began to scream again; even in the gloom of one candle Nell could see that her face was almost purple with rage.

'You are inhuman. This little scrap wants nothing more than your milk. You can lie there for as long as you like feeling sorry for yourself, but you'll feed her first.'

Nell put the child down on the bed and wrenched Hope's nightdress open. Her breasts were as big as melons, the veins standing out because they were so engorged with milk. 'You will let her feed. I won't stand by and let you be so selfish.'

She picked up Betsy and put her to Hope's breast. She latched on hungrily, but still Hope didn't attempt to cradle her in her arms, or even look at her.

Nell perched on the bed supporting the baby, so tired she felt she could drop to the floor at any minute, but she knew she couldn't go back to bed until Betsy's hunger was satisfied and she was back in her crib.

She could have understood Hope's reaction better if she'd been informed officially of Bennett's death. But the Captain clearly didn't think he was dead, so why should Hope believe it to be so?

After some twenty minutes of feeding, Betsy fell asleep. Nell took her from Hope's breast and winded her, then put her back into the crib. As she turned back to Hope, she saw she hadn't even covered her breasts.

'Can't you even cover yourself?' Nell said angrily. 'Do you know how tired I am? Can't you think of anyone but yourself?'

There was no reply, and Nell was so incensed that she slapped Hope's face hard. But it had no effect – her sister just lay there as before, as if she couldn't see, hear or feel anything.

'You're wicked,' she shouted. 'Even the most miserable wretches that end up in the workhouse will take care of their own. As soon as it's light I'm going to send for Dr Cunningham, because I don't know what to do with you any more.'

She left the room then, fearing she'd do the girl a mischief if she remained with her.

'I don't know what to do, Master Rufus,' Nell sobbed when he dropped by the next morning. 'I'm all in, I can't do no more.'

Rufus had been in Keynsham collecting some corn for his chickens and on an impulse decided to stop off at Willow End to see Hope and her baby. The moment he saw Nell he knew something was drastically wrong. Her eyes were puffy with crying and she looked completely exhausted.

Then she related how it had been for her in the last ten days since Captain Pettigrew's letter and began crying again, sobbing out that she was afraid Hope would end up in an asylum.

Rufus hadn't seen Hope since the day she came over to the gatehouse, but Matt and Amy had called just a few days after Betsy's birth and they'd reported back to him that both mother and child were doing well, in fact they said they'd never seen a happier new mother.

He hadn't heard about the letter from Angus Pettigrew, however. If he had, he would have called immediately.

Rufus could well imagine that getting such a shock so soon after giving birth would be shattering, but like Nell he couldn't understand why it would make Hope reject her baby.

Nell showed him the letter from Angus, but to him it didn't sound unduly alarming, for there were only three or four lines about Bennett and the rest was taken up with what the Captain had been doing and the plans for yet another bombardment of Sebastopol.

'He wouldn't have written about Bennett's sickness so lightly if he thought there was a possibility he might die,' Rufus said.

'No, he wouldn't,' Nell sobbed. 'But it is suspicious that Bennett hasn't written himself. Even if he was so poorly he couldn't hold a pen, surely he would have asked someone to write for him?'

Rufus agreed on that point, but he had no intention of encouraging Nell to think the worst. 'He probably did, but it just hasn't got here,' he said firmly. 'Now, you go and rest, Nell. I'll go and talk to Hope.'

Rufus walked into Hope's room without knocking and went straight to the window to pull the curtains back. Betsy was asleep in her crib, but as he turned back from the window and saw how much Hope had changed since he last saw her before the birth, his heart sank.

She had been glowing then, her cheeks pink and plump, her eyes sparkling the way they did when she was a young girl. Now her face was thin, white and drawn, and her dark eyes were blank and lifeless.

He sat on the edge of the bed and took one of her hands in his. 'This won't do, Hope,' he said gently. 'I've read the letter from Angus and there is nothing in it to suggest Bennett is dead. You know perfectly well that post can be delayed for weeks coming from the East. And, as Nell says, bad news travels at twice the speed of good. If he had died you would have been informed by now.'

'They've buried him without knowing who he was,' she

replied, her face contorted by grief. 'That happened many times out there.'

'Maybe it did with rank and file, but not officers,' he insisted. 'Nell has written back asking Angus to find out more. But meanwhile you must remember you are a mother and have a duty to take care of Betsy.'

'I can't,' she said wearily.

'You named her after your friend who died. You didn't neglect her in her hour of need. You stitched up the Captain when he was wounded, and nursed countless other men too. Are you telling me they were more important than your own little baby?'

'You don't understand,' she said, turning her head away from him.

Rufus put his hand on her cheek and drew her head round to face him again. 'Just because I'm a man without a child of my own doesn't mean I can't understand the torment you are in. I have taken care of my mother since Briargate was burned down; I've dealt with her endless self-recriminations, the tears and the explosions of rage. There were days she couldn't wash or dress herself, when she wouldn't eat, and paced the floor at night instead of sleeping. I was afraid that I might have to put her in an asylum. Nell is afraid that is where you are heading.'

'They can put me anywhere; it's all the same to me.'

'I don't believe that,' Rufus exclaimed, his voice rising in agitation. 'You might feel like that now, but you can beat it because you are strong. You have to get out of that bed, pick Betsy up and think only of her. In a little while you'll find she will be a comfort to you.'

'What do you know?' she snarled at him. 'You grew up in luxury. While you were still sleeping in your featherbed I was clearing the grates, scrubbing floors, carrying your damned mother's slops, even cleaning up your father's vomit. If it wasn't for Bennett I'd have been forced to live my whole life in a rookery. I might have had to sell myself just to eat. I can't live without him.'

'You can if you have to,' Rufus said, holding her two arms and shaking her a little. 'Remember, you are the girl who ran away from Albert, who had the courage to stay away because you didn't want him to hurt Nell. You bravely worked in St Peter's, nursing those whom no one else would. Angus wrote home and told us that the men over in the Crimea worshipped you for what you did for them. A woman who can do all those things can nurse her own baby, even if her heart is breaking.'

She stared at him with blank eyes. 'Loving Bennett was what made me strong then,' she said. 'He filled up all the empty places inside me. You don't know what that's like.'

Rufus looked at her, and tenderly stroked her face. 'Don't I? You think you are the only one with empty places inside you? I might have slept in a featherbed, Hope, but I never had the kind of love you had from your family. My father was either out somewhere or drunk, and Mother only spent an hour a day with me at most. It was Ruth and Nell who took care of me and I always envied you because you had their love. Have you any idea what hell I went through at school? Beaten by the masters and the older boys, half-starved, always cold during the winter. I felt I was sent away as a punishment, but I didn't understand what I'd done to deserve it.

'As for the years after you disappeared, I had nothing and no one at Briargate, not you, not Nell, no one. Baines was too old to do anything; Mother and Father skulked in the study while Albert strutted around like he was lord and master. It was hell at school, but misery at home.'

He saw a slight softening in her expression and knew he must continue.

'I only went to Oxford to get away,' he said. 'But I never fitted in there either. They called me "Farm Boy", and other crude terms I can't repeat. It was only at Matt's farm that I felt I was worth something.'

Betsy began to cry and Rufus got off the bed and went over to the crib.

'Hello, little one,' he said, bending to pick her up. 'Now, stop screwing your face up like that, it doesn't become you.'

Holding her against his shoulder, he stood by the window with her. 'Your mother saved my life years ago,' he told the baby. 'She once said that she was angry that her mother had given up and died and left her alone. Personally I thought that was a bit strong, after all, the poor woman was very sick. What do you think, Betsy? Should a mother put her husband or her child first? Would you understand if your mother turned her back on you because she was afraid of living without your father?'

He heard a faint sniff from behind him, and knew Hope was crying.

'She was the prettiest, funniest, liveliest girl for miles around,' he went on, kissing Betsy's little head. 'Brave as a lion, kind, caring and as sharp as a box of knives. Not the kind of person you'd expect to end her days in an asylum at all. I hoped too that she was going to come up to Briargate soon and give me her opinion on whether I could turn the stables into a house for Lily and me.'

He turned as the sobbing became louder. Hope was distraught, tears pouring down her face as her head thrashed from side to side on the pillow.

Nell had told him that Hope hadn't cried, apart from briefly when the letter first arrived. She said it was as though her sister's spirit had left her and all that was left was a shell. But as he looked at Hope now he thought maybe these tears were necessary to free that spirit from whatever dark place it had hidden itself in.

It hurt to watch her anguish – he wanted to take her in his arms and comfort her. But he had Betsy in his arms and he knew that his role today must be as her protector.

So he watched and waited patiently until Hope's tears began to subside and she fumbled for a handkerchief to blow her nose and dry her eyes. She looked terrible, her face blotchy and red and her eyes swollen. But it was better than the blank nothingness there had been before.

'You'll feed her now,' he said. It was an order, not a question, and he was relieved when she nodded.

'Good girl,' he said, and laid Betsy on the bed for a moment. He helped Hope sit up, wiped the tears from her cheeks and plumped the pillows up behind her back, then put the infant in her arms.

'I'd like to stay and keep you company while you feed her,' he said with a smile. 'But I don't think Nell would approve of that! I'll be downstairs, though – just call when you've finished.'

He paused at the door, relieved to see she was cradling Betsy tenderly.

'You aren't alone, Hope,' he said softly. 'You've got so many people who love you. Come what may, we'll never desert you.'

Rufus felt as if he'd been wrung out as he walked downstairs and into the kitchen. Nell was still slumped at the table.

'She's feeding Betsy now,' he said, putting his hand on Nell's bowed shoulders. 'I'll stay for the rest of the day, now go and lie down.'

'But there's meals to be got, napkins to wash,' Nell protested.

'Dora can do that,' he said gently, for he could see Nell

was almost as distraught as Hope. 'It won't hurt to let things slide for now. You've worked so hard all your life, Nell, it's high time you took a rest when you need one.'

He helped her to her feet and hugged her to him. It seemed such a short time ago that he had been a little boy running to her and burying his head in her soft breasts for comfort. Now she was the small one, her head only reaching his chest, and he hoped he was comforting her.

'I think she'll be all right now,' he said soothingly. 'You Rentons are made of stern stuff. I'll write to the Captain today too. Now the war over there is drawing to a close, maybe he can go to Scutari and find Bennett for us.'

Three weeks later, Rufus arrived at Willow End again, this time with a pony and buggy, to take Hope and Betsy to see his mother.

He felt a surge of absolute delight when Hope came out eagerly, wearing a becoming red hat with a jaunty feather, and with Betsy tucked beneath her red-checked cloak. Rufus had been in and out several times in the last three weeks, and although Hope still hadn't heard anything more about Bennett she appeared only worried and tense, not melancholic.

Yet today she looked really well again, her smile bright and her colour good. A little thin, perhaps – Nell had reported she wasn't eating very well. But she looked much better.

Nell was just behind them. As always, she wore a snowy-white apron over her dark dress and a lace-trimmed mob cap.

Rufus jumped down from the buggy and took Betsy from Hope's arms, pretending to nearly drop her. 'My goodness, you're getting heavy. I don't know if Flash will want to pull you all that way!'

'She's a greedy girl and no mistake,' Nell said fondly. 'And you take good care of them, Rufus, and get them back before dark.'

'It's so good to see the sun again, even if it is very cold,' Hope said. She sprang up into the buggy and held out her arms for the baby. 'All that rain we've had! I haven't set foot outside for the past four days.'

'This might be the last good day before winter comes upon us,' Rufus said. 'The animals' drinking troughs were iced over this morning, and all the leaves have come down now.'

He got up into the buggy beside Hope, tucked a rug over her knees and pulled her cloak a little closer over the baby. Then, lifting his cap to Nell, he clicked at the horse and they set off down the road.

Hope leaned out beyond the buggy's hood and waved goodbye to Nell. 'She isn't entirely happy about me going to Briargate. There's something between her and your mother; do you know what it is?'

Rufus glanced sideways at her and grinned. 'Reckon it's just that business of Mother not supporting her when you disappeared.'

'I don't think it's that,' Hope said thoughtfully. 'She isn't one to bear a grudge, and besides, she's far happier now as Angus's housekeeper. It's more to do with me. She doesn't seem to like the idea of me seeing your mother.'

'Nell's just stuck in the old ways,' Rufus said lightly as the horse broke into a trot. 'She can't quite deal with the idea of her young sister taking tea with her ladyship.'

'Then I must be very careful not to offend her ladyship with unseemly behaviour, and you must report back that I struck just the right note of gentility and respect,' Hope replied with laughter in her voice. 'Oh, Rufus, it's so good to be out in the fresh air. I am well again, but Nell is not entirely convinced of that.'

Hope's memory of what Nell tactfully referred to as 'when she wasn't quite herself' was very hazy. She had been told bluntly by Dora that she was completely mad, that she refused to feed or even hold Betsy, and that Nell had been in despair. Looking down at Betsy swaddled in shawls in her arms, Hope found it difficult to believe that she could have done such a thing. But she could recall a feeling that she was drowning in some kind of all-enveloping black swamp.

Strangely, she was aware that it was Rufus who pulled her from that swamp with his confidences about his childhood, for she could recall most of what he had said that day. She had always perceived him as being so fortunate that it was something of a shock to discover he had felt unloved and cast off, and that his years at school had been so miserable. Later, when she came to think about how hard he'd had to work to make a new life for himself and his mother since his father's death, she felt very ashamed of herself.

Her fears for Bennett hadn't diminished; if anything, they'd grown stronger each day without word from him or about him. But when she felt most wretched she would think about all the soldiers who were killed in action, buried up by the river Alma and at Balaclava in unmarked graves.

She knew none of their widows would have the comforts she had, but she was quite sure that however desperate their circumstances they would not abandon their children. She could count herself fortunate to have so many friends and family around her to support her, and for Betsy's sake she must keep up a brave front.

Yet even with the best will in the world it wasn't possible to be brave at night when the fear that she might have to live without Bennett washed over her like a scalding flood. Often it was so bad she would stuff the sheet into her mouth to stop herself crying out. She might have the security of knowing Nell and Uncle Abel would never see her and Betsy homeless, but it was Bennett and his love she needed to survive.

Every single day she waited with trepidation for the post. There had been two more letters from Angus, but they were full of the news of Sebastopol falling, of riding into the city and the sights of devastation he'd seen there, for he hadn't yet received any of her or Nell's letters asking about Bennett.

She had written to the Rifle Brigade barracks at Winchester to ask if they could tell her anything, and to Dr Anderson at the Balaclava hospital, asking him if could enlighten her about what had happened. She had also penned several letters to Bennett too at Scutari, hoping they would reach him. They were so difficult to write, for if he was alive but very sick, she couldn't worry him by showing her fears and anxiety. But to be forced to write bright breezy notes about his beautiful daughter and the mundane news of home when in her heart she felt he'd never read them, was almost impossible.

There were times too when she felt like raging at the normality all around her. It didn't seem right that while her mind was tormented with whether he was alive or dead, Nell was asking her what she'd like to eat for dinner, or should they go into Keynsham and buy some material for a new dress?

The newspapers continued to report on the progress of the war. Sebastopol had fallen on 9 September, which indicated peace would soon be declared. Yet it riled Hope that all anyone seemed to be interested in was who would be commended for valour, or promoted. The government didn't appear to be making any plans for the wounded, who might never be able to work again, or for the wives and families of the men who had died out there.

She knew Uncle Abel was lobbying anyone he could for

information about Bennett, but even he had told her quite sharply that he also had patients to attend to.

She silently cursed the time it took post to reach England; the restraints of motherhood had prevented her from going to Winchester and demanding an explanation from the regiment in person. She told herself it was only three months since the date Bennett last wrote, which in reality wasn't so very long, but it seemed like eternity to her.

'I really don't know how Mother will hold up this winter,' Rufus said as they drove through the village of Corston. 'Last year she was crippled with rheumatism and stayed in bed a great deal, and I can only expect that it will be worse this year.'

'It must be a very bleak life for her,' Hope said in sympathy, thinking back to the days when Nell dressed her and arranged her hair, and she went out visiting in her carriage most afternoons. 'Does anyone call to see her?'

'Not really,' he sighed. 'Reverend Gosling does, and the Warrens, but their visits are becoming less frequent. I can't blame them, for she can be so very odd and difficult. I feel I ought to stay in with her more than I do, but how can I when there is so much to do on the farm?'

He turned his head and smiled at Hope. 'But let's not talk about gloomy things. We must make the most of today, and I can hardly wait to show you my plans for the stable block. It will make a good-sized house, and as the roof is good, and the pump right outside the door, it won't cost too much. Matt, Joe and Henry have all offered to help me, and Geoffrey Calway will do the carpentry.'

'He must be getting old now,' Hope said, remembering the man who made her parents' coffins. 'How is his wife? She was very kind to me when Mother and Father died.'

'Still as funny as ever,' Rufus said. 'You were probably too young then to appreciate what a character she is – seeing her is like getting a dose of sunshine. But then, the village is full of good people. When Bennett returns I think you should come back. There is no doctor now, everyone is always complaining about it.'

Hope liked the positive way he said 'when' Bennett returns. 'I'd like that,' she said, imagining living in a little cottage on the common, close enough to walk to Matt and Rufus, and Betsy growing up doing all the things she did as a child.

'Nearly there now,' he said as they went past the signpost to Hunstrete. 'Let's just hope Mother is in one of her better moods today. She seemed very pleased when I left that she was going to see Betsy today, she had even put on her best dress. But her moods are like the weather, I never know when they are going to change.'

Rufus's fears that his mother might be difficult appeared ungrounded when she came out of the gatehouse door and greeted them warmly. Hope could see she'd taken a lot of care with her appearance. Her hair was arranged almost as well as Nell used to do it, and she had a cream lace collar on her mourning dress to enliven it a little.

'You can't imagine how excited I've been at the thought of seeing your baby,' she said, as she ushered them into the warm by the fire. 'May I hold her?'

Perhaps because this time Hope was prepared for how prematurely old and thin her former mistress had become, she felt more comfortable. She was touched too that the woman was so eager to hold Betsy. And she took her in her arms with all the care and delight that Nell and Dora did.

Hope offered to make some tea while Lady Harvey nursed the baby, and they chatted easily while Rufus went off for a while to take Flash up to the stable and attend to some small jobs.

'I am so sorry to hear about your husband,' the older woman said, her lined face showing real sympathy. 'But you mustn't worry, my dear, I'm quite sure you'll hear from him very soon.'

Hope told her about the letters she'd written and everything Uncle Abel had done. She avoided mentioning Angus for fear that might open doors in Lady Harvey's mind that were better kept closed.

On this visit Hope even felt able to put aside the shocking events which had taken place in the gatehouse. Lady Harvey pointed out various bits of furniture, pictures and rugs which had been sent up from Sussex by her sisters.

'Sometimes I find it quite hard to imagine that I ever lived in a big house,' she said quite cheerfully. 'The last few years up there weren't very pleasant. We were often very cold; at least this cottage is warm and cosy.'

She showed Hope the new kitchen with pride, and it seemed absurd that this woman who had rarely set foot in the kitchen up at the big house could be so delighted that the new stove had two ovens, or that she should boast she had a stew cooking in one of them that she'd made completely by herself.

'I'm not a bad cook now,' she laughed merrily. 'Mrs Webb from the village used to come and give me lessons when I first came here. I put a rice pudding in the very hot oven one day and it boiled over and made a terrible mess. But I get better at it every day. I can even make cakes.'

Hope was impressed; she'd imagined that Lady Harvey could do little for herself, but this clearly wasn't so.

She fed Betsy a short while later and was just tucking her into a laundry basket to sleep when Rufus came back. He grinned delightedly to find everything was going well, and

Hope guessed that he'd been convinced it wasn't going to be so.

After they'd had the stew, which was every bit as good as anything Hope could make, Rufus said they must go and look at the stables. It was already half past two and he wanted to get her home before darkness fell.

'You will come again soon?' Lady Harvey asked, lifting Betsy from the laundry basket and tucking her into her mother's arms. She arranged Hope's hat more carefully too, and patted her cheek like a fond aunt.

'Yes, of course I will, m'lady.' Hope kissed the older woman's cheek. 'It was such a lovely dinner, and so good to see you again. Maybe Rufus could bring you to Willow End for the day. I know Nell would love that.'

Lady Harvey beamed happily, for a moment or two looking just the way she had when Hope was a girl. 'Bennett will come home,' she insisted. 'I know he will. Try not to worry, my dear.'

'That was quite remarkable,' Rufus said as they walked up the drive. 'I fully expected that Mother would go on and on about her ailments, or complain about how dreary her life is now. I can hardly believe she could show such concern for you and Betsy. She has never shown much sympathy for anyone before.'

'Did you tell her I went mad for a while?' Hope asked teasingly. 'Maybe that made her feel we have something in common.'

Rufus chuckled. 'No, I didn't, and anyway you weren't mad, just in the doldrums. And it was quite understandable given that you'd so recently given birth.'

Once at the stables, Hope decided to leave Betsy in the buggy while they looked around. Under the hood, bundled up in a rug, she would be warmer and safer than in her arms, and if she woke Hope would be only a few feet away.

So many memories came back for her as she looked at the green-painted stable doors, now blistered and blackened by the fire. When she was scouring pans at the scullery sink she overlooked the stables, and she'd watch James grooming the horses or mucking out. She could recall feeding Merlin and the other horses with Rufus, climbing up to sit astride Sir William's saddle when James had slung it over the wall of one of the stalls, and playing hide-and-seek with Rufus up in the hay loft.

'Remember that hot summer when mother was away in Sussex and just before I went away to school?' Rufus asked. 'We had a table and chairs out here in the yard because it was too hot in the kitchen and Martha made that raspberry cordial for us.'

Hope smiled. That summer was one of her best memories for the days were so long and languid and everyone so good-natured. Some nights they all sat out here in the stable yard till well past ten, and she and Rufus would look up at the stars above and try to count them.

Many of the cobblestones in the yard were broken and dislodged now, and all that remained of the big house was one layer of brick and stone. But the step up to the kitchen door where she'd so often sat that summer shelling peas or peeling potatoes was still there, like a monument to the good times.

'Was nothing saved from the house?' she asked, unable to take in that the drawing room had been where the chicken run was now, or that the magnificent staircase had been burned completely.

'Pots and pans, that was all,' Rufus said ruefully. 'And the statues from the rosebed out the front. I sold those to a man in Bath, and much of the stone from the outside walls of the house I saved. But the furniture, books, paintings and china were all destroyed. But don't let's think on that, come on inside and I'll show you what I've got in mind.'

He was only using the first stable, for Flash and his plough horse. In the other two larger ones Rufus had already stripped out the stalls and made a vast space.

'I'll have the kitchen here,' he said, pacing out an area some fourteen feet square. 'Then a passageway with a staircase up to the bedrooms, and the parlour beyond that. I'll build fireplaces and chimneys on the back wall.'

They had just climbed the old ladder inside the stable which led to the loft above, when they heard a bell ringing.

Rufus groaned. 'That will be Mother. It's the old bell on the gatehouse wall. I wish I'd never suggested she ring it if she needed me; on her bad days she can ring it three or four times a day.'

They went back down the ladder and looked down the drive; Lady Harvey had gone back inside the cottage.

'Sometimes she rings just because she's lost something,' Rufus said, frowning with irritation. 'But I'd better run down there and see what's wrong. You wait here, I really need your opinion about the windows and whether I should have the front door going straight into the kitchen or the hall.'

'I'll give it some thought while you're gone,' Hope said. 'And you'd better hurry, it might be something serious. Ring the bell again if you need me.'

As Rufus raced off down the drive, Hope went back inside the stable and imagined what she'd want if it was to be her house. The first thing that struck her was that there should be windows in the outside wall, to let in the morning sun. She thought too that Rufus should build the chimney and fireplaces up through the middle, with the kitchen stove on one side, the parlour fire on the other, and that way the bedrooms upstairs would be warmer.

She heard the sound of footsteps on the stones outside. 'You were quick!' she called out.

All at once there was a rank smell, and she spun round

to see a man in the doorway. He was a vagrant, with filthy, ragged clothes. He was so big he blocked out the light, so she couldn't see his face clearly.

'Are you looking for someone?' she said nervously for his stance was distinctly threatening and she was afraid he'd come here looking for food. 'Sir Rufus will be back in a moment.'

'I thought I told you never to come back here?' he growled at her.

She knew who he was immediately and her blood turned to iced water.

'Albert!' she gasped. This man didn't look or sound like him. But only Albert would say such a thing, and no other man could ever have such power to frighten her.

In a flash of intuition she realized this was why Lady Harvey had rung the bell. She must have seen him, perhaps crossing the field or coming out of the woods.

'Cat got yer tongue?' he snarled.

'I'm just surprised to see you,' she managed to get out. 'I heard you'd joined the army.'

Her heart was hammering with fright for it was obvious the man wouldn't risk coming back here unless he had some evil purpose. It was more likely he intended to hurt Rufus or Lady Harvey – after all, he couldn't have known she would be here. In fact, unless he'd been hanging around all day watching the gatehouse, he could well be as shocked as she was to come face to face with her again.

'Shut yer mouth,' he snapped at her. 'Get over in that corner.'

He came towards her, and she could see him clearly now. His good looks had gone, his once fine features bloated and ingrained with dirt. His hair, which had always been black and shiny, was now long, matted and grey. A thick greying beard covered all of his lower face, and he had several teeth missing. He looked like many of the brutalized men she'd seen in her time in Lewins Mead.

She backed away, hardly able to breathe for fear. If he'd been on the run constantly since burning Briargate down, he wouldn't be troubled by killing more people, and Betsy was out in the buggy. If she should wake and cry out, Hope knew he wouldn't spare her.

'Go away now, Albert,' she said as calmly as she could, even though her legs were almost giving way. 'There's nothing for you here but further trouble. I have a little money I can give you.'

'I don't want yer blasted money,' he hissed. 'I gave this place the best years of my life, and it's all been destroyed. I want vengeance.'

His dark eyes glowed like hot coals and she instinctively knew he'd lost his mind. He hadn't ever been a man of reason, so she knew that any attempt to cajole or plead would have no effect. She had to either fight him or outwit him – if she didn't, he would kill her and anyone else who got in his way.

'I didn't destroy anything,' she said, desperately trying to play for time while she thought of a plan. 'I was just a child caught up in something I didn't understand. I kept to my word. I never came back here until a few weeks ago. I didn't tell anyone what I saw that day in the gatehouse.'

Out of the corner of her eye she saw a pitchfork leaning against the wall to her right.

'You think I give a tinker's cuss about you or what you said to anyone?' he said with menace. 'I never cared about anything but my garden, and it's all gone now, trees cut down, my flowerbeds laid to waste. But you helped destroy what I had, and for that you'll pay. Now, get back in that corner so I can tie you up, then we'll wait till his bloody lordship comes back.'

She knew then it was Rufus he planned to kill, but now he'd found her here he was going to force her to watch Rufus die before killing her too.

He fumbled beneath his ragged coat, pulling out first a length of twine, then a knife. 'Get back and turn round,' he ordered her.

The sight of the long, shiny blade had her transfixed with horror for in the past she'd often seen him slitting a rabbit open with such a knife.

'It's good and sharp,' he said, running the blade along the back of his hand and shaving the hairs to demonstrate it. 'Now, get back there.'

She did back up further, pleading with him all the time, and with each step she came slightly nearer to the pitchfork. He was heavier and slower than he had been eight years earlier, and she hoped that in his disturbed mental state he wouldn't consider that she would attempt to fight him.

'Where have you been all these years?' she asked, playing for time rather than wishing to know. 'Have you been working on another garden?'

'How could I work anywhere when I was being hunted!' he snarled. 'I'm the best gardener in England but I was forced to live like a vagabond. Ruffians stole my money when I was sleeping. And it's all your fault, and now you're going to pay.'

'Please, Albert,' she whimpered, knowing it was vital to impress on him she was helpless to keep him off his guard. 'Just let me go and I'll never tell anyone I saw you.'

'Turn round to the wall,' he shouted at her. 'And shut yer bloody mouth!'

She turned, but as she did so she grabbed the pitchfork and wheeled right round to face him, pointing the prongs at him.

All she had in her favour was that she was quick and light

604

on her feet. She knew that if he managed to grab the fork she was done for.

'You back off!' she yelled, lunging forward at him, and as he moved back she jumped nimbly to one side. 'Come on, grab it if you can,' she said. 'I'm dying to run you through with it.'

She cursed her heavy cloak weighing her down, and knew she hadn't the strength to hold him off for long, but if she could just manoeuvre him around so his back was to the wall, she might be able to take a run at him and stab him with it, or at least hold him off until Rufus came back.

She danced around him like a butterfly, jabbing then jumping back as he tried to grab the pitchfork from her or slash her with the knife. Her hat fell off, her hair began to tumble down, and several times the blade of his knife came within a whisper of her arm.

He was tiring, his breathing laboured and his movements becoming more sluggish. She thought it likely he was very hungry too. 'Come on,' she taunted him. 'What's happened to you? Too much drink, is it?'

She had one ear out for Rufus, for surely he must by now be wondering why she hadn't come down to the gatehouse. Yet her overriding fear was that Betsy would start crying, for even if Albert had lost his mind he'd surely realize a baby was the perfect hostage to get everyone where he wanted them.

Her dancing and jabbing were growing increasingly feverish, and finally she had him with his back to the wall, and hers to the door. Then Betsy began to cry.

Albert stopped moving and he listened, a sneer twisting his lip grotesquely. 'So you've got a babby!' he said, bringing the knife up threateningly.

He could easily throw the knife at her, but she thought it was more likely he would charge her with it.

'Don't,' she warned him, getting a firmer grip on the pitchfork. A cold sweat broke out all over her, for she knew if she didn't prevent him leaving the stable he would go for Betsy first. All the hatred for this man she'd kept inside her for so many years bubbled up. He wasn't going to lay one finger on her daughter. She would have to kill him to prevent that.

'You can't stop me with that,' he sneered, and took a step forward.

She knew that his weight and strength put all the odds in his favour. He only had to charge her and she'd be brushed aside as easily as a cobweb. But she had to stop him; her daughter's life, her own and possibly Rufus's and Lady Harvey's too were at stake.

The image of the soldiers in the Rifle Brigade up on the Heights before Sebastopol practising attacks with fixed bayonets suddenly came to her. She remembered the Sergeant screaming at them, *Kill or be killed.*

A surge of white-hot fury rushed through her veins. So what if she was smaller and lighter than him? She had right on her side, and her cause was a far greater one than his.

'Die, you bastard!' she screamed, and charged at him just the way she'd seen soldiers do.

She caught him in the stomach and threw all her weight behind the pitchfork to force him back against the wall, yelling like a banshee. His knife clattered to the floor, his eyes opened wide with shock, and only when the stink of him overwhelmed her did she see that she had imbedded the fork so far into him that its prongs had disappeared.

His arms flapped, his hands instinctively moving towards the fork. His mouth gaped open and he made a rattling, rasping sound. Blood spurted out, spraying on to Hope's clothes, and she backed away in horror.

A wounded soldier had once told her that he could shoot

any number of the enemy with his rifle and cheer at every one, but he had nightmares about the ones he'd killed with his bayonet, for he saw their faces, felt their pain.

She knew exactly what that soldier meant now. Albert was sliding slowly down the wall, his hands bloodied as he clutched at the fork, and his expression one of agony. She had sat in the church watching this man marry her sister. She'd cooked him meals, washed his shirts.

She might never have liked him — he was a loathsome creature who had bullied and terrorized both herself and Nell. He had killed Sir William and he should have been hanged for it. But she was aghast that she was capable of killing.

A wave of nausea overtook her and she staggered to the door. Rufus was running up the drive carrying his shotgun, closely followed by Lady Harvey.

'He's in there,' Hope managed to get out before she vomited.

Shaking from head to toe, she somehow managed to get to the buggy and pick Betsy up. She stopped crying immediately, but the sensation of the small warm body pressed against her own made tears spring to Hope's eyes.

She turned with the baby in her arms to see Rufus and Lady Harvey standing at the stable door looking in. 'Is he dead?' she asked.

'Not quite,' Rufus said in a white-cold voice. 'And I hope it takes a long time before he is.'

Chapter Twenty-six

Hope had gone back to the gatehouse without Lady Harvey and Rufus, expecting that they would follow immediately. Although trembling from head to foot, she made a pot of tea and then sat down to feed Betsy, struggling to come to terms with what had just happened.

It was a good half an hour, maybe longer, before the other two returned, by which time she'd just finished feeding the baby and was changing her napkin. Lady Harvey came in without saying a word, sat down by the fire and bowed her head almost to her knees.

Rufus said very little. He asked Hope how she was and insisted she have a glass of brandy before he took her home. He said that he would then go on to inform the police about what had happened. He went over to the window and just stood there silently, looking out.

Hope could understand their silence, she didn't feel able to discuss what had happened either. They were all deeply shocked, but as she sipped her brandy she became aware that it wasn't just silence, it was tension.

She had felt the selfsame thing when she'd lived here with Albert and Nell. In those days she'd always thought she was to blame for the chilling atmosphere, and she did again now. Were they blaming her for bringing more trouble to their door?

Her head was whirling with unwanted images. She could see Albert's surprised expression as the pitchfork went into him, his blood spurting out and the knife dropping from his hand. One side of her brain was telling her it was good that she had killed him, but the other kept reminding her, 'Thou shalt not kill'.

But why wasn't Rufus telling her that it was the only thing she could have done?

She finished changing Betsy, gulped down the last of the brandy and stood up.

'I'm ready to go now, Rufus,' she said.

'Fine,' he said, not even turning to look at her. 'I'll go and get the buggy.'

But he didn't move; he was still staring out of the window.

'We must get someone to come and sit with your mother while you're gone,' she suggested.

He turned to face her then, but there was an expression on his face she couldn't read, for it was more than anger or anxiety. 'I don't know that I can trust Mother not to talk,' he said.

Hope frowned. 'Everyone will talk about this anyway,' she said. 'Surely you aren't thinking of telling the police you killed him, instead of me?' That seemed the logical explanation of his odd statement. Rufus was after all a gentleman and perhaps he believed he must keep her out of this.

He put his hands to his head as if it was hurting.

Concerned, she put Betsy down on the armchair, went over to him and put her hand on his arm. 'None of us will be in any trouble; Albert was a murderer. He came here today to hurt you and possibly your mother too. I'm not afraid of telling anyone I did it. It was horrible, but it's done now and I'm glad he's dead.'

His hands dropped from his head, and he looked at her bleakly. 'He talked before he died.'

Hope's stomach lurched. The one thing she had comforted herself with was that Albert's death would put an end to her nasty memories and save Rufus from ever knowing the whole truth about both his parents. But she might have known Albert wouldn't die quietly.

'What did he say?'

'About Mother and Nell's precious Angus,' Rufus spat out. 'I don't know which is the more hurtful, that my mother was unfaithful, or that you and Nell knew about it and covered it up.'

A strangled sob came from Lady Harvey. Hope felt a slight sense of relief that Albert didn't appear to have revealed his relationship with Sir William, but she felt indignant that Rufus would blame her and Nell for his mother's wrongdoing.

'Have you forgotten we were servants?' she retorted. 'We would've been cast out if we'd uttered a word about it.'

He looked suddenly deflated and despairing. 'Yes, of course, that was unfair of me. I suppose I want to rage at my mother, as this was clearly what Albert held over her for years. But how can I rage at her? Just look at her!'

Hope turned. Lady Harvey looked so old, frail and vulnerable, with no trace left of the vivacious young woman who had captured the Captain's heart.

'Let it go,' Hope pleaded. 'Hasn't that dreadful man done enough damage to both our families? Don't let him do any more. Now, please take me home because I can't bear anything more. But we must get someone to come in with your mother because she shouldn't be alone after such a shock.'

'I'm not just his mother; I'm your mother too.'

Both Hope and Rufus wheeled round at Lady Harvey's strange statement.

She was sitting upright now, and although she was still crying she had a steadfast look about her.

'Don't be silly, Mother,' Rufus said, his tone softer as

though he was speaking to a child. 'How can you be Hope's mother?'

'I am,' she insisted, looking up at them both. 'Hope is the result of my love for Angus. Nell and Bridie told me she was stillborn because of the scandal, and Nell took my baby home to Meg Renton.'

Hope and Rufus stood like statues, staring in silent astonishment at Lady Harvey. The wind was getting up outside, making a roaring sound in the chimney, and Betsy was making little gurgling sounds, but no one spoke or moved for some minutes.

Lady Harvey broke the silence. 'I know my mind wanders sometimes now, that I forget things and get mixed up. But this is the truth and you must believe me,' she said, her voice cracking with emotion. 'Hope is your half-sister, Rufus. If I'd known she had lived and where she was, maybe I could have found a way to bring you up together. But I didn't know who she was until the day Nell left Briargate; that's when she told me.'

Hope and Rufus stared at each other.

'But Nell believed Albert had killed Hope!' Rufus exclaimed. 'If you knew Hope was your daughter, why didn't you do something? Can you really have so little feeling?'

Hope put one hand on Rufus's arm to calm him. 'She was frightened of the scandal, I expect.'

'You know what your father was like back then,' Lady Harvey said defensively. 'I was scared, but I did tell him the truth eventually because Albert was blackmailing me. That's why he burned the place down, because we stood together and told him to leave.'

Rufus put his hands to his head again. 'So why didn't you tell me too?' he asked. 'I kept asking you both why you kept him on. I knew there was something. Surely you knew that I would help you, whatever you'd done?'

'I wish I had now, but we didn't want you upset or embarrassed. I almost told you when we heard that Hope was out in the Crimea,' she said. 'But I couldn't find the words.'

'Does Angus know any of this?' Hope ventured. It was all too much for her. She knew it had to be true, for even a deranged old lady could hardly make up such a story. And clearly this was what lay behind Nell's reluctance for her to see Lady Harvey.

'No. He never knew.' The older woman began to cry again. 'Maybe Nell has told him since she went to work for him, but I doubt it as he would have come to see me and demanded to know why I kept it from him.'

Rufus looked as if he'd seen a ghost. His face was white and his eyes were wide and startled.

Much as Hope wished to give him comfort, his mother needed it more for she was shaking and distraught, so she went to her, drew her head to her chest and patted her back comfortingly. 'I don't know what to say to you,' she said softly. 'I need to think about it all and hear it from Nell too.'

'Do you believe me?' The older woman drew back from Hope's arms and looked up at her.

'Yes,' Hope nodded. 'But right now I can't deal with it. I need to get Betsy home.'

'I don't want you getting anyone to come in here,' Lady Harvey whimpered. 'I couldn't talk to anyone, I'd rather be alone.'

Hope didn't speak as the buggy bowled along the road. The clip-clop of Flash's hooves and the whizzing of the wheels seemed entirely at one with her thoughts as she pinpointed little incidents that gave credence to her real parentage.

Nell's nervousness about Angus when he came to Briar-gate, the feelings she'd so often had of not entirely belonging in her family, even that old tale about her being 'a fairy child' had new meaning now. There was the bond between her and Rufus, and one with Angus too. She certainly couldn't be ashamed or sorry she was related to either of them.

But it was the knowledge that Nell wasn't her true sister that hurt. She'd been everything to her, often more of a mother than an older sister. It was devastating to know there was no blood tie between them and that Nell had kept this secret for all these years.

Where Lady Harvey was concerned she felt nothing, for there was little to admire the woman for. Meg Renton was a far more admirable person, for she'd brought Hope up and loved her as if she were her own.

She glanced at Rufus. It was dark now but she could see his profile well enough to see his mouth was tight, and that he was struggling to come to terms with the shattering events of the day.

'What a day, eh!' she said and slipped one hand over his on the horse's reins.

'At least I gained a sister,' he sighed. 'I always had a special regard for you, but I could never have suspected this. We are so completely different! There isn't one similarity. Me blond, you dark, one with blue eyes, one with brown, how can it be?'

'You had two blond-haired, blue-eyed parents,' Hope said. 'Clearly I inherited everything from Angus. Imagine if I had been like you. Questions would've been asked! In the village they talk about people being "as dark as a Renton".'

'I have to say that if one has to hear one's mother had a secret love child, I'm glad it was you,' he said, but his voice cracked with emotion as if he was struggling not to cry.

'Try not to be angry with your mother,' she said sooth-ingly. 'It must have been terrible for her. None of us know what we'd do in such circumstances.'

'I always knew there was something lurking in the past,' Rufus said thoughtfully. 'But I thought it was to do with my father.'

'She did love him,' Hope ventured.

'But he couldn't love her, could he?' Rufus said.

Hope's heart skipped a beat, for that sounded very much as if Rufus knew about his father's nature too. As she didn't know how to reply she stayed silent.

'He loved other men,' Rufus blurted out. 'That was the problem between them.'

The sound of the wheels and the horse's hooves seemed to grow louder and louder as Hope racked her brain for the right response.

'Your silence tells me you already knew this,' he said. 'And I can guess at what point you found out too. I remained in ignorance until after Briargate was burned down. I went down to Wells because I thought someone at the Bishop's Palace might know something about Albert. Someone did, and he told me what Albert was.'

Rufus held the reins with his right hand and with his left caught hold of Hope's chin and tilted it so he could look at her. 'I'd had little suspicions about Father long before that. You learn about such things at boarding school, you see, and at Oxford I met men who were that way. But when I knew about Albert it all fell into place. My parents' fear of him, the missing money, the way he strutted around Briargate and, of course, your disappearance.'

He let go of her chin and took her hand. 'I'm sorry,' he sighed. 'Maybe I should have kept all that to myself the way you have. On our first meeting after you returned here, I noted how you said nothing about my father, other than the usual polite condolence. That was all the confirmation I needed that my guesswork was correct. But I'll wager you wouldn't ever have told me?'

'No, I wouldn't,' she said in a small voice. 'I wish to God you didn't know.' She leaned her head against his shoulder, feeling such sadness and sympathy for him.

'I'm not going to ask you for any details,' he said in a choked voice. 'I want to put it aside, and start anew.'

Hope nodded against his shoulder.

'I won't come in with you tonight either,' he went on. 'I must get to the police and back to Mother. But in a day or two I'll come and talk to Nell. Did she know about Albert and my father?'

'No, and please don't tell her,' Hope said. 'She's suffered enough at that man's hands.'

'I won't speak of it again to anyone,' he said, glancing round at her. 'It was in the past, it doesn't matter any more.'

As soon as Nell opened the front door to Hope, she sensed the day had not been a good one for her sister's eyes looked heavy and she was very pale and drawn. 'Why didn't Rufus come in?' she asked, taking the sleeping baby from her sister's arms. 'I hope you haven't fallen out?'

'No, Nell. He just needed to get back to Lady Harvey,' Hope said. 'Would you put Betsy up in her crib for me?'

Nell hurriedly did as she was asked, and when she came back downstairs Hope had gone into the kitchen and was standing by the stove warming her hands.

'Let me take your cloak and hat,' Nell said. 'Then I'll make you a hot toddy, you look frozen.'

As Hope removed her cloak Nell saw the stains down her dress. 'What on earth is that?'

'Blood,' Hope blurted out. 'Albert's blood. I killed him.'

Nell clapped her hands over her mouth. 'Albert? He came

to Briargate?' she exclaimed. She thought she'd misunderstood what Hope said.

'Yes, Nell, of course he did,' Hope said somewhat impatiently. 'I just said, I killed him. I was in the stables when he came in. I killed him with a pitchfork.'

Nell felt as if all the blood had suddenly left her body. Over the years she'd often pondered what her reaction would be if Albert was caught and hanged for his crimes. She knew she wouldn't like the renewed gossip it would bring, but she'd always felt that it would be like a weight off her shoulders to know he'd gone for good.

But Hope standing there with his blood on her dress, calmly telling her she'd killed him with a pitchfork, wasn't a situation she could ever have prepared herself for.

'Oh, my Lord,' she exclaimed, and suddenly she was crying as though she would never stop.

'I'm sorry I told you so bluntly,' she heard Hope saying above the sound of her own sobbing. 'I didn't think you'd be so upset.'

'I'm not upset that he's dead,' Nell managed to get out. 'If I'd heard he drowned, died of a disease, or was even shot by a gamekeeper I would have rejoiced. It's the thought that he came near you again. That once again he has hurt those I love.'

Hope made some tea and sat down with Nell, explaining exactly what had happened. But as Nell began to pull herself together she realized that retelling it had brought all the horror back for her sister for she was shaking and crying.

'You're a brave girl and no mistake,' she said, enveloping Hope in her arms. 'You should never have had to see that beast again; he did enough to you in the past. I had a bad feeling this morning about you going up to Briargate; I didn't want you to go. Thank God you and Betsy are safe, I couldn't live without you two.'

She made Hope a hot toddy, and insisted that she must go to bed because she was all in. 'We'll talk some more about it tomorrow,' she said as she helped Hope out of her clothes and slipped a warm nightgown over her head. 'When Betsy wakes I'll change her and bring her to you for her feed, but you must stay in bed.'

After she'd tucked Hope into bed, Nell went back downstairs and sat by the stove. She felt chilled to the marrow and sick at heart.

She should never have agreed to marry Albert; in her heart she'd always known it wasn't right. He was a strange fish, everyone always said that. And here she was at thirty-nine, free of him at last, but too old now for any man to want.

Tears ran down her face. She was crying for the girl inside her who had never experienced real love and been cheated of a family of her own. When she looked back, her life had been nothing but hard work with so little joy.

But her tears were for Hope too. They said she was a fairy child, and yet she'd had the hardest life of all. And Nell loved her so much that Hope's pain was hers too.

Hope pretended to fall asleep again when Nell took Betsy from her arms after her night feed, but she was watching Nell from beneath her eyelashes.

Everything about her was neat. Her hair was always clean, shiny and pinned up with never a stray lock escaping, her collars and cuffs were always crisp and white, she kept an apron on for most of the day but it was never dirty. Her boots were polished, her nails neatly trimmed, even her face looked as if it had just been scrubbed. She moved so neatly too, and was never clumsy or noisy. She often described herself as plain, but in fact there was beauty in her simplicity, or maybe it was her honesty and integrity which shone through, making her so special.

Hope hadn't felt able to tell her what Lady Harvey had revealed – Albert's death was enough for one day. A secret that had been kept for nearly twenty-four years could wait another day.

As she watched Nell tenderly rocking Betsy in her arms she thought how astounding it was that a sixteen-year-old girl could have entered into a pact with an older maid just to protect her mistress from scandal and ruin. What selflessness that had taken, such loyalty and love! And that devotion had never faltered; not to Lady Harvey, nor to her. Hope had felt Nell's love for her right from when she had been a small child. Albert had done his best to snuff it out, but it had been too strong for that.

Yet even more astounding was that when Lady Harvey failed to support her, Nell didn't retaliate in any way, not even telling Angus that he had a child. She was a very remarkable woman in every way.

'I love you, Nell,' she whispered to herself. 'Blood-sister or not, I am the lucky one to have you.'

It wasn't until the evening of the following day that Hope finally managed to get Nell on her own to tell her what she knew.

Dora had been bustling around cleaning in the early part of the morning. Then a police sergeant had called to question Hope about Albert's death. Fortunately he had taken part in the manhunt for Albert following the fire at Briargate, so agreed that Hope must have acted in self-defence and congratulated her on her bravery. He'd no sooner gone than a neighbour called, and after that Betsy kept crying and it just wasn't possible to have a serious conversation while Nell was flapping around making the supper.

But once the supper things were washed up, Betsy bathed and asleep in her crib, and they were finally sitting beside the fire in the parlour, Hope told Nell how Lady Harvey had revealed she was her mother.

Nell turned very pale, and she looked frightened too.

'I'm not angry, I'm not sitting in judgment on either you or Lady Harvey,' Hope assured her. 'I just want to understand how it all came about. So please tell me the whole story, right from the start.'

Nell spilled it out in fits and starts, stammering with nervousness at some points, at others showing indignation that at only sixteen she was forced to be party to something she knew to be very wrong.

'It never crossed my mind that she could be carrying a child,' she said as she explained how Lady Harvey had stayed up in her room for several weeks. 'It was only when the other servants had gone to London, and Bridie and I were alone in the house with her, that Bridie told me.'

It was clear to Hope that Nell had relived that scene up in her mistress's bedroom many, many times over the years for she described it all in great detail once she got going. As she related how she was taking what she thought was a dead baby down the backstairs and it moved, she began to cry.

'I knew Bridie didn't want it to live, but once I looked at you and saw your little hands moving, I was done for,' she said.

Hope winced at the part where Nell caught Bridie about to smother her. 'Don't judge her!' Nell exclaimed. 'She was frightened, she loved Lady Harvey and she couldn't bear what would happen if this got out. That's when I thought of taking you home to Mother.'

'And she took me, just like that?' Hope asked in astonishment as Nell described how Meg took her in her arms and fed her.

'She loved babies,' Nell said. 'And she couldn't bear to think of what would happen to you if she refused. She told me some time later that Father was angry the next morning to find she'd agreed. He went off to work grumbling and complaining about how little they'd already got without another mouth to feed. But that night he came home and picked you up and kissed you. He never said another word about it.'

Hope could remember sitting on her father's knee, how he used to tell her stories and sing to her. She hadn't once felt inferior to the older children, if anything she received more love and affection than any of them.

'Wasn't anyone suspicious?' she asked. 'What about Matt, James and Ruth? Surely they were old enough to know Mother hadn't given birth to me?'

'When there's already ten children and they've grown used to another one arriving every couple of years, they don't think beyond whether that means they'd have to help feed and change it,' Nell said with a wry smile. 'Matt did say once after his first was born that he didn't know how Mother managed to stay so quiet having you, because Amy screamed the place down. But he wasn't suspicious, he didn't remember Mother making any fuss having any of the younger ones.'

'What was Lady Harvey like after the birth?'

'Very sad and weepy she was. But soon after she went up to London to join Sir William, and I stayed at Briargate. She was gone for three months, and I was glad about that because I could go home most afternoons and see you. You were the prettiest baby I've ever seen.'

'Oh, Nell,' Hope sighed. 'That was such a big burden for you!'

'You were never a burden,' Nell said looking fondly at Hope. 'I suppose I was at that age when some girls become mothers themselves. I was scared stiff though that day I took you up to Briargate and you ran into the Captain. Do you remember that?'

Hope nodded. 'You knew he was my father even then?'

'No! That was the day I realized. I just took one look at his face and saw you in it. Bridie was dead by then; there was no one I could ask. But I knew. I wonder you haven't noticed it too.'

'I didn't have any reason to be looking for such things,' Hope said. 'But will we tell him now?'

'Well, of course you can.' Nell smiled then, as if suddenly she had something to feel good about. 'He'll be father and grandfather all at once, won't he?'

'I sort of felt something with Angus almost from the first time I met him,' Hope said pensively. 'But it didn't work that way with Lady Harvey. Why do you think that was?'

Nell shrugged. 'She's not one to think about other folk much. And of course I did my best to keep you in your place. Mother, Father and me, we weren't too pleased when you used to go and play with Rufus. We didn't want you getting ideas above your station, and neither did we want Lady Harvey to grow fond of you. You see, we thought of you as ours. But sometimes I thought the whole world could see that you were born to gentry.'

They talked and talked until the small hours. There were shared memories of Meg and Silas to mull over, Nell's viewpoint of her little sister's childhood scrapes and triumphs, and there were new tales about the other siblings which Hope hadn't heard before.

As one story after another was related, some with hilarity and some with sadness, Hope felt truly part of the Renton tribe, and if in the past, she had had the odd feeling she didn't 'belong', she could see now that it was because of her position as youngest in the family, nothing else. Nell pointed out that being the eldest made her different too.

'I had to help Mother when the little ones could play,' she said. 'I was washing and feeding babies when I was six or seven. I didn't get to run about in the fields the way you all did. Matt had to be a man too, well before his time. That is just the way it is in a big family. But you, Hope, you were the little darling, everyone's pet. We all made big allowances for you.'

Later, Nell went on to tell Hope about each and every time she was reminded of who her little sister's real parents were. 'You were never cowed by gentry. You'd stand out in the lane and talk to anyone who came riding by. You just couldn't seem to understand that folk like us were supposed to be humble. And I was so frightened when you got older and you and Rufus became so close.'

'But why?' Hope asked with some amusement.

'In case you became sweethearts later on,' she admitted. 'I can't tell you how many nights I lay awake worrying about it. But I feel like a load has been taken off my shoulders now. If we hear Bennett is coming home tomorrow that will end all my worries.'

'At least this has distracted me from thinking about him for a while,' Hope sighed.

Nell got up stiffly from her chair, and held out her arms to Hope. 'What will be, will be,' she said as she embraced her. 'I wish I could promise you he will come home, but I can't. But whatever happens I'll be right beside you.'

The autumn days went slowly by, each one a little colder, wetter or windier. It was dark by four in the afternoon, and mostly the weather was too bad to go out. Yet still no letters came from either Angus or Bennett.

Uncle Abel got word that post from both the Crimea and

Turkey had gone astray. He also went to Winchester to the Rifle Brigade barracks, and was told that Bennett had not been reported dead. But by the same token they could offer no proof he was alive either for his name wasn't on any of the lists of sick sent to Scutari. But from talking to a couple of soldiers who had been invalided home, it seemed their families hadn't been informed either, and letters they'd written from hospital hadn't turned up until after they'd got home.

Angus had definitely left the Crimea — there was evidence he'd boarded a steamer bound for Constantinople. Uncle Abel felt sure he had gone there to look for Bennett.

Hope's anxiety had settled into a constant dull ache, but almost every day there was some distraction to take her mind off it. Two weeks after Albert's death there was the inquest in Bristol, in which she and Rufus had to give their evidence. It lasted less than twenty minutes and the coroner pronounced it self-defence and complimented Hope on her courage.

Before they went home that day, Hope took Rufus to Lewins Mead to show him where she had lived. It was shocking to see the appalling conditions there again and Rufus thought it a miracle she'd survived it. But Uncle Abel told them later that plans were afoot for it to be pulled down, the river Frome covered over, roads widened and new houses with piped water and drains built.

Hope put some flowers in St James's graveyard, for although she suspected that neither Gussie, Betsy, nor any of the cholera victims had actually been buried there, it was a place they had often walked through together. She even thought she heard Betsy's laughter on the wind, and knew her friend would be thrilled to think she was accompanied by a titled gentleman and that she had given her name to her child.

The strangest thing about that visit was finding she was a target for beggars. Until then she'd imagined she could walk around there at any time without being troubled. She realized then it wasn't only her neat dress, bonnet and fur-trimmed cloak which identified her as someone who might hand out a few pennies, she remembered how she too had once been able to sniff out sympathy and concern and play on it. She gave what little money she had to some ragged barefoot children, and then walked quickly away.

'When Bennett comes back,' she said thoughtfully on their way home, 'we'll have to find some way of really helping those children. A hot pie now and then does little. But education with a hot dinner thrown in could do such a lot.'

Aside from the day-to-day chores and making clothes for Betsy, who seemed to be growing at an alarming rate, there were many visits from all her brothers and sisters to keep Hope's mind off Bennett. She also visited Matt's farm, Ruth's home in Bath and many of her old neighbours in Compton Dando. Sometimes during the family gatherings Hope felt an overwhelming desire to tell them that she wasn't a true sister, especially when Ruth claimed that her daughter Prudence was just like her. But she refrained from the temptation; she needed to discuss that with both Lady Harvey and Angus first, for they would be the ones to suffer scandal, not her and Rufus.

Rufus kept saying that he would bring Lady Harvey over to see her and Nell just as soon as there was a mild, dry spell. But on 30 November she died in her sleep.

Matt brought the news to them. Leaving Betsy with Dora, Matt drove Hope and Nell over to see Rufus, and they arrived just after the doctor had left, confirming her heart had given out.

'She was a little odd last night,' Rufus explained distractedly. 'She said she thought she saw Father on the drive and that he was waiting for her. But she went to bed as normal, and when I went in there early this morning, she was dead.'

Once Matt had gone home leaving Hope and Nell alone with Rufus, they all cried. 'I should have come over again,' Hope sobbed. 'I might have known that she was too frail to live much longer. Now I can't say any of the things to her that I wanted to.'

'I wish too that I'd been kinder,' Rufus admitted. 'She was on her own so much, I used to get so impatient with her. But you've got nothing to reproach yourself for, Hope, you were kind to her.'

'I could have said I understood how it was for her when she had me,' Hope said. 'I could have told her that none of that mattered any more.'

'I think she knew that was how you felt,' Rufus said, drying Hope's eyes with his handkerchief. 'A few days after you'd been here, she said that she was proud of you, that you had all the best of Angus in you and that the Rentons had made you strong and loving.'

Nell had listened to all this saying nothing. Then she got up from her chair and put an arm round each of them. 'If I'd seen her one more time I would have pointed out how lucky she was to have you two and how fortunate it was that neither of you inherited her selfish nature.'

'Nell!' Hope exclaimed. 'Don't speak ill of the dead.'

'I can say it for I was with her through thick and thin,' Nell said firmly. 'I loved her; I would have done anything for her, and I think I knew her better than anyone. She didn't want to be an old lady, she'd settled everything, and I think she was happy to go. Maybe William did come back for her. There was a lot of love between them despite all the problems they had. So we should be happy for her.'

'Would you like to see her now?' Rufus asked, biting back tears. 'I was going to get Jane Calway in to lay her out later, and then we'll bring her down here.'

'Let me lay her out,' said Nell, her voice as soft as a prayer. 'I know how she liked her hair, how she'd like to be dressed. And I'd like to say my goodbyes that way.'

'Of course, Nell.' Rufus wiped his eyes on his sleeve. 'Shall Hope and I go out while you do it?'

Nell nodded. 'Yes, you go for a walk, I'd like to be alone with her.'

Rufus and Hope walked in silence into the woods. The trees were bare, and the recent heavy rain had swollen all the streams so they gushed over rocks, making a beautiful, peaceful sound.

'All the times we came here as children, we never knew we were brother and sister,' Rufus said sadly as he threw stones into a stream. 'I was miserable because Mother and Father were always arguing; you had Albert to contend with. Now they are all gone, it's just you and me, back here again. I'm a farmer, and you're a mother yourself. And the troubles go on and on.'

'Not for ever,' Hope assured him. 'Bennett will come home, I'm sure, and you can get married now. There's nothing to stop you.'

'Maybe in the spring,' he said lethargically. 'That is, providing Bennett is back, because I'd want you there at my wedding, happy again. Was it a mistake to let Nell lay Mother out? I'll wager she's crying over her!'

Hope nodded. 'She's as good at holding in her feelings as she is at keeping secrets. But now the secrets are out there's no reason not to let the feelings out too.'

*

Nell was indeed crying. She had stripped off Lady Harvey's nightdress, washed her from head to foot, and put on her undergarments through a veil of tears.

It felt so strange to be back in the bedroom which had been a source of such unhappiness, but it was no longer a stark, sterile space, for Lady Harvey had filled it with frippery. She might have lost all her old belongings in the fire, and only worn mourning since then, but Nell had to assume her sisters had sent her some of their old things.

A pink velvet dressing-gown was tossed over a button-back chair by the window; there were pretty hat boxes piled up, and an array of perfumes, necklaces and combs for her hair on the dressing-table.

The bed itself was a beautiful carved mahogany one which matched the dressing-table, and the carpet on the floor was as fine as any Nell remembered in Briargate.

Dressing her mistress now she was dead was like dressing a life-size doll, and it grieved Nell to see how thin she'd become. Her breasts were little more than loose flesh, and her hip-bones jutted out through her petticoats. But Nell put two rolled-up stockings into the top of her camisole to give her more shape, then went to the wardrobe to look for a dress.

They were nearly all black, but right at the back she found a turquoise one. She guessed that Lady Harvey's vanity had got the better of her sense of decorum at some time since her husband died, for it had always been her favourite colour.

An hour later Nell stood back to admire her work. The dress had long sleeves and a high neck, and she'd padded it a little on the hips to give it a good shape. Gauze pads inside her lady's cheeks had filled them out perfectly, and with a little rouge she'd managed to bring youthful radiance back to the once beautiful face. Even her eyelashes had been given a smudging of ink to darken them. Nell thought the hair was her very best achievement, for she'd taken it up over hair pads so it looked fuller, and fastened it becomingly with two artificial rosebuds. With a few tendrils curled around her face to soften the gauntness, and gloves on her hands to hide the cruelty of age, she could pass for thirty again.

'You look beautiful, my lady,' Nell whispered. 'Rest in peace. I'll be watching over both your children.'

She tried to suppress her tears, for it seemed ridiculous that she should still care so much for this foolish, self-centred beauty. But such a large proportion of their two lives had been spent together, and everything Nell knew about society, fashions, love and marriage came from Lady Harvey. She'd been to grand shops in London with her, to concerts in Bath, to country houses ten times larger than Briargate. They'd ridden together on the Great Western train, and even shared a bottle of champagne on many an occasion.

'And I ended up with Angus,' Nell whispered. 'I know he can never love me the way he loved you. But I'm in his house and in his heart. Thank you for that, my lady.'

Hope and Rufus looked down at Lady Harvey and tears rolled down their cheeks. To both of them the clock had been turned back and she looked just how they remembered her from when they were children.

'Sleep peacefully, Mother dearest,' Rufus whispered as he bent to kiss her cheek. 'And thank you for giving me a sister.'

Chapter Twenty-seven

'What are you doing?' Nell yelled from the kitchen as Hope opened the front door and a squall of icy rain blew in. 'You can't go out, it's pitch dark and you'll catch your death of cold.'

But Hope could hear nothing but the voice inside her head telling her to run.

Once out on the road she ran headlong down the hill. The driving rain was so heavy that she was soaked to the skin within seconds and she lost one of her slippers in thick mud, but all she was aware of was her own misery and the need to end it.

The day had begun with torrential rain, and Hope had a sinking feeling that such weather on the day of Lady Harvey's funeral was a portent of worse things to come.

The cab which took her and Nell to Compton Dando had a leaky roof, and by the time they'd got to the church both she and Nell were wet through. Their umbrella blew inside out in the high wind as they got out of the cab and the church was so cold their teeth were soon chattering.

The church was full, the front few pews all taken up by gentry, some of whom Hope recognized as people who had called at Briargate in the past. Nell whispered that the rest were Dorvilles, Lady Harvey's family from Sussex, most of whom she'd met on her trips down there.

But the bulk of the congregation were ordinary people

from the surrounding villages and their wet clothes created a steamy, evil-smelling fug. Hope recognized a great many faces from her childhood. The Nicholses, the Webbs, Boxes, Pearces, and Calways, all so much older now and all looking as cold and uncomfortable as she herself felt.

Rufus, Matt, Joe and Henry carried the coffin in on their shoulders, Rufus's blond hair standing out like a beacon against the Renton darkness. The wreath of holly and Christmas roses on the top of the coffin seemed to Hope to be too stark for Lady Harvey, who had always favoured flamboyant flowers. But she had to suppose that in December it wasn't possible to get anything more colourful.

The Reverend Gosling seemed to have shrunk since Hope last saw him and his voice was quavery and uncertain throughout the service. When he spoke of Lady Harvey it was as if he had no memory of when she was a young and vivacious woman, but had only met her after Briargate was burned down when she was frail and disturbed.

Even the hymns were gloomy, tuneless ones, which Hope knew Rufus would never have chosen.

Hope had not expected to be uplifted by this service, yet she had thought she'd gain some kind of comfort that her true mother's earthly struggles were over, and that she had gone on to a better place. But there was no comfort in this cold, pitiless rite, not even a few well-chosen words spoken with some emotion by a family member.

When they moved outside for the interment, the strong wind, driving rain, and the mud underfoot made most of the village people scurry for the shelter of the Crown Inn without so much as a thought for the final words at the graveside. Hope saw Rufus's desolate expression and she knew he felt his mother had been slighted.

Hope herself was emotionally confused for she wasn't sure which camp she belonged in. She was aware that many of the village people had already lost a day's wages to come and pay their last respects to Lady Harvey; to also expect them to risk their health by standing in pouring rain was perhaps asking too much. Yet she was very disappointed as she had expected, and perhaps needed, to see a huge outpouring of grief from everyone today. But to want that seemed ridiculous; she'd scarcely shed a tear herself, and in fact only the previous night she'd been nasty enough to remark that she saw no good reason why anyone in the village should attend the funeral.

Nell had been outraged at that, but Hope had pointed out that Lady Harvey had never done anything for the villagers, not even back in the days when she and Sir William had been wealthy.

Yet the sight of the yawning grave, already half-full of rainwater, suddenly made her feel utterly bereft. Taking Nell's arm firmly, she drew her through the ranks of women holding black-edged handkerchiefs to their eyes and ignored their sharp, disapproving looks. Maybe they didn't think anyone but gentry should come so close to the grave, but Hope felt she and Nell had the right to be among the chief mourners.

As the Reverend Gosling intoned the last words of the burial service, Hope looked down at the polished oak coffin with its brass handles and plaque bearing the inscription 'Lady Anne Harvey, 1806–1855', and thought of the burials in the Crimea. There were no coffins for those brave men; often their boots and clothing were snatched before they were even cold. They would be shoved unceremoniously into mass graves, the only marking a roughly made cross which would probably be lost in the first storm. Bennett, who had spent his whole life caring for others, might be in such a grave, while Lady Harvey could sleep for eternity next to her husband, marked by a marble headstone.

Hope was reminded too of the day they buried Meg and Silas Renton and how abandoned and angry she had felt then. Their grave was over by the churchyard wall, next to Prudence and Violet, with only the smallest and simplest of headstones. She remembered with a pang of conscience that she always felt jealous when Meg came here to put flowers on the children's grave.

Yet the incident which set off Hope's rage came later. Lady Harvey's two sisters were standing in the shelter of the lychgate waiting for their carriage and Nell went over to them to offer her condolences. To Hope's astonishment and outrage, they brushed her aside as if she were a beggar asking for money.

To Hope it was unbelievable they could be so callous as Nell had met the sisters before on innumerable occasions and had even attended both their parents' funerals. Hope almost ripped into them, telling them that Nell had been far more than a loyal servant, she was also Lady Harvey's one true friend. But angry as she was, she was aware that once she started she might very well follow it up with a loud proclamation that she was in fact their niece. Knowing that such an admission would only distress Rufus, Nell and her other brothers, she forced herself to turn her back on those women and lead Nell away.

The wake was being held at Hunstrete House, and it was very clear that common folk like the Rentons wouldn't be welcome there. Rufus came running after them as they made for their waiting cab to go home, but Hope told him they had to get back for Betsy.

The bleakness in his eyes told her he understood the real reason they were leaving, and she urged him to go back to his relatives for a while, then perhaps join them later at Willow End.

The journey back seemed endless, and when they reached

the mill at Chewton the river had burst its banks, flooding the road. The horse was reluctant to go through the swirling water at first, and Hope had visions of being forced to retreat and take the long way home. But fortunately he moved with a touch of the whip, and eventually they arrived home, very wet and chilled to the bone.

Betsy was screaming fit to burst because she hadn't liked the milk Dora had tried to give her while they were out, and she latched on to her mother's breast like a leech before Hope could even change her wet clothes. And Nell kept going on and on about the funeral and the sisters who had been so hurtful.

'I shouldn't have spoken to them,' she said with a quiver in her voice. 'It was my own fault, they probably blame me for everything as Albert was my husband. Of course they wouldn't have wanted the likes of us up at Hunstrete.'

'What on earth do you mean by "the likes of us"?' Hope snapped indignantly. 'We are all better mannered than that stuck up lot. Sir William took Albert on, it was he who allowed the man to run the place, and therefore his own fault things went badly. I despise those sort of people – who do they think they are? I pity poor Rufus having to suffer an hour or two with them, he'd have been better off in the Crown with our boys who at least care about him.'

'I saw them all looking at Matt, Joe and Henry. They didn't think it was fitting they were carrying her coffin.'

'Are they numbskulls?' Hope exploded. 'Matt rescued Lady Harvey from the burning house, all three of them spent the whole night trying to put out the fire, and they've done countless jobs for her without ever expecting payment. Who could be more fitting? And who else would have done it? Most of that family are too decrepit to wipe their own backsides.'

'You mustn't say things like that,' Nell exclaimed. 'You should show them some respect.'

Hope launched into a bitter tirade about the upper classes, including the fools of officers she'd met out in the Crimea. It was only when Nell began to cry that she stomped off to her bedroom with Betsy. But she had no intention of apologizing to Nell, for why should she? It was all true.

It seemed to her that she had no 'place'. She had got too much spirit and fire to be anyone's lackey, and she couldn't ever pass for gentry because of how she'd been brought up. Even if Rufus was to acknowledge her publicly as his sister, that wouldn't change anything. They would just tag 'bastard' on to her name, 'fly blow', or any of the other ugly words they used for illegitimate children. The Dorvilles wouldn't want to be associated with her, and after seeing them today she wouldn't want to lay claim to being related to them anyway.

If Bennett did come home and set up a practice away from here she would probably be accepted as 'the middling sort', but she doubted her ability to accept the narrow confines of that kind of life either.

She had seen and done things few women could even imagine. How could she settle down in a neat little house with lace at the windows and a maid doing all the chores? She wasn't cut out to spend her days doing embroidery and receiving visits from dull women who could only talk about the price of fish, or the latest fashion.

The walls seemed to close in on her then. She had been glad to leave the Crimea; being reunited with her brothers and sisters was everything she expected, and bringing Betsy into the world in a clean, safe place had been wonderful. But now it all seemed so empty.

She put Betsy down to sleep, and stood at the crib watching her. She wasn't as dark as Hope now, nor yet as fair as Bennett. The slightly uptilted nose came from her, but she had a very solemn look most of the time, just like Bennett.

Icy fear gripped Hope as she contemplated that Betsy might never know her father. That year after year she would have to look at her daughter's face and be reminded of all she'd lost.

This time last year she and Bennett had climbed up the slippery steep path to the Heights with baskets on their backs packed with dressings, bandages and medicines for the field hospital. She could remember how the icy wind had stung her face, that she was hungry and lice-ridden, but Bennett had kept turning to her, holding out his hand to help her over the worst places, telling her that it was imperative they made it up there because men were dying for want of these precious items.

It was the most wretched she'd ever felt in her entire life, but with Bennett leading the way, urging her onwards, she made it to the top. Later, when they'd finally staggered into the field hospital and seen the relief on those gaunt, pain-filled faces, she had felt it had all been worth the struggle.

She couldn't have made it up there without him, and she couldn't bring Betsy up without him either. Without him she was nothing and no use to anyone.

Unable to breathe because the room suddenly seemed so hot and stuffy, she knew she had to get out of the house immediately.

Hope's second slipper disappeared into the mud unnoticed as she ran full tilt down the road in the direction of Bath, and she kept running blindly until she was down on the flat, past the last of the cottages.

Way over to her right and up on the hill was a big house, lamplight in the windows twinkling in the darkness. To her left were the meadows which the train from Bristol to London passed through, and beyond that the river Avon.

By day, in the sunshine, it was beautiful, but seen in darkness it felt threatening.

She was almost at the crossroads by the Globe Inn when a stitch in her side forced her to slow down, and at once total desolation washed over her.

Bennett was never coming home, she had just been fooling herself that he might. The only future ahead of her was that of a lonely widow, dependent on the charity of others. She began to sob, all the images of the life she and Bennett had planned together streaming through her head as if to mock her for ever believing they would come true.

They would never live in a cosy cottage with poorer patients paying Bennett with a chicken or a few eggs; they would never sit outside in the moonlight on warm summer nights, or pull their children on a sledge through the snow. Never again would she know the bliss of lovemaking, or wake to find Bennett holding her in his arms. It was all a foolish fantasy; in real life people didn't get what they wanted.

Lady Harvey loved Angus but she had to live out her life with a man who wanted other men. She'd even died without knowing her daughter didn't hate her for what she'd done. Rufus might marry Lily, but he'd have years when his crops would fail, chickens wouldn't lay and they'd go hungry. Nell would never have a baby of her own. Matt would never be rich. Even dashing, handsome Angus had not got what he wanted. He might come home to find he had a daughter, but that wasn't going to make up for Lady Harvey being dead.

She felt she was back to the night Albert had thrown her out of the gatehouse, the same feeling of despair overwhelming her, the same icy rain mingling with her tears. She'd forced herself to survive then, ever the optimist that things would get better. But she knew better now: life was just one long series of calamities until you died.

She couldn't bear any more. She hadn't the will, the strength or even the curiosity about what might lie ahead to go on. If she just climbed over the wall and went down through the meadow, she'd reach the river. The water would wash over her head, and all this pain would be gone.

But she felt confused when she looked down, for it seemed she was already in the river. It was black and shiny in the darkness, washing over her feet. The wind was pulling at her coat and her hair as if trying to draw her in deeper.

Above the noise of the wind she could hear something else, but she couldn't identify what it was, only that it was coming towards her. She was frightened now, for the sound was filling her head and she didn't know how to get away from it.

'Shit my britches,' the coachman exclaimed as he saw a flash of white up ahead and realized it was someone standing in the road. 'Whoa!' he yelled, pulling on the reins for all he was worth. 'Whoa, boys, whoa.'

'What is it, coachman?' his passenger called from the carriage. 'Is the road flooded?'

The coachman didn't answer for he was intent on stopping his horses. Through the heavy rain he could see now it was a woman by the narrowness of her shoulders and the fullness of the clothes, and she was looking right at him, her eyes glinting in the reflection of his coach lights.

'Move,' he yelled, but she stayed right where she was. He grabbed the brake, and heard the grinding sound of wood against the metal-rimmed wheels, pulled tighter on the reins, and finally, only a few feet from her, his horses came to a halt.

The coachman leapt down from the carriage. 'You crazy mare,' he yelled, reaching her in two strides and catching hold of her arm. 'I could have run you down. Ain't you got nuffin' better to do than stand in the highway?'

She just stared at him, her eyes wide and frightened.

'Can't you hear?' he shouted over the noise of the rain. 'Where you from?'

He heard the clatter of one of his gentlemen getting out of the carriage behind him. 'What shall I do, sir?' he called back over his shoulder. 'She don't seem like she's got her wits about her.'

The coachman heard his gentleman gasp, and suddenly he was standing there beside him. 'Hope!' he exclaimed. 'My God, it is Hope, what are you doing out here?'

'You know her, sir?' the coachman asked incredulously.

'I do, coachman,' he said, lifting the woman up into his arms. 'We'll take her home with us.'

Nell was beside herself with worry, looking at the clock, pulling back the curtains to look out of the window, then looking at the clock again. Hope had been gone for over an hour now, and even a stray dog wouldn't stay out in rain like this.

She went to the front door and opened it, then shut it again when a gust of wind blew out the candle in the hall. She put on her cloak, then, remembering Betsy, took it off again.

'Where can she be?' she asked herself aloud. 'I don't like this one bit.'

Hope had been a little odd after Albert's death; agitated, forgetful and often a bit vacant as if her mind was elsewhere. Yet that was to be expected. She had, after all, killed a man, and that would take some time to get over. But as she was nothing like as bad as she was after hearing about Bennett, Nell had ignored it, and it had passed. It started again after Lady Harvey's death: there were several times when she began a job, then walked away without finishing it. Yesterday she had left Betsy on the floor in her bedroom wearing only a vest while she went downstairs for something, and forgot to go back and dress her.

But all day today she'd been most peculiar. She'd come down the stairs ready to leave for the funeral without her hat, she didn't give Dora any instructions about Betsy, and when they'd reached the church she hadn't kneeled to say a prayer, just stared around her as if she'd never been there before.

On the way back from the funeral she'd hardly said a word, and when she did it was to snap. Later she'd seemed so angry. Nell wished now that she'd taken all these pointers more seriously, for funerals had a way of disturbing folk and bringing back the past.

It was after eight now, but what could she do? She couldn't leave Betsy alone in the house while she went to get help, but she couldn't take her with her in rain like this.

'Please come, Master Rufus,' she prayed aloud. 'I'm scared now.'

She put the kettle on to boil and filled up a large pan from the jug in the scullery.

Hearing a noise, she rushed to the front window, and through the rain she could just make out a carriage, and a man getting out.

'Thank the Lord it'll be Master Rufus,' she sighed with relief, and dabbing her tears with her apron she rushed to the front door and flung it open.

She didn't know the man standing there, but ducking under the big bush by the gate was a figure she knew very well. And he had Hope in his arms.

'Oh, my Lord!' she exclaimed. 'You've come like an answer to my prayers, Captain Pettigrew! I've been that worried. What's wrong with her? Where did you find her?'

*

Nell's wits came back sufficiently to direct the Captain to take Hope in by the parlour fire. She was white-faced, her eyes staring sightlessly, and not knowing what else to do, Nell ran upstairs to find towels, blankets and dry clothes. But she was all of a flutter that the Captain had come home to such a thing, with company too, and she hadn't got anything for their supper.

But as she came back into the parlour the tall, slender, pale-faced man to whom she had opened the door was alone with Hope, kneeling beside her and stripping off her wet clothes.

'I won't have a stranger do that to my sister,' she said sharply. 'I'm surprised at you, sir.'

'I'm her husband, Nell,' he said without even looking round. 'And I'm a doctor. So if you'd be so good as to see where Angus has got to with the brandy, I'll just carry on.'

'You are Bennett?' Nell said stupidly.

'The very same,' he said, glancing round. 'I expected to greet my sister-in-law for the first time under better circumstances, but we can't help that now.'

Nell shot off to get the brandy, too stunned to say anything further.

By the time she came back Hope's sodden clothes were on the floor and Bennett had wrapped her in a blanket and was cradling her in his arms.

'Come on now, my darling,' he was saying to her. 'Speak to me, it's Bennett, your husband. I'm home.'

Nell handed over the brandy and watched with her hands over her mouth, hardly daring to breathe as Bennett held the glass to Hope's lips.

'Good girl,' he said softly as she sipped it. 'You're quite safe now, it's only me, and you'll soon be warm again. Now, drink a little more for me?'

She lifted her head a little, sipped and then coughed.

'That's better,' Bennett said. 'Now, you are going to sit right up and drink the rest. To think I believed I was coming home to be nursed by you!'

It was as if the sound of his voice, the touch of his hands suddenly broke through to her. 'Bennett?' she questioned cautiously. 'Bennett!' she repeated. 'Is it really you?'

A hand on Nell's shoulder drew her back out of the room. 'Come on, Nell,' Angus said. 'Let's leave them to it.'

Bennett wound a towel round Hope's wet hair, then lay down on the rug beside her, propping himself up on one elbow so he could look at her. It was too soon to ask why she'd been in the road on such a night, and he certainly wasn't going to tell her that he'd nearly died of fright when Angus carried her into the carriage and she didn't know either of them.

For now it was just enough to look at her. To see those beautiful dark eyes gazing back at him, her plump lips curved into the sweetest smile, for it was all that he had dreamed of while he was so sick. He knew very well that he'd been a hair'sbreadth from death and he was sure it was only his will to see Hope and their baby that had kept him alive. None of the other men who had gone down with typhoid fever with him survived, and if Angus hadn't come and rescued him from Scutari when he did, the chances were he'd be gone now too.

Bennett was still so weak he couldn't have picked Hope up from the road, but now he was back with her, he felt his recovery would be speedy.

'We have a little girl, I believe?' he said. 'Angus told me he had a letter from you as he was leaving Balaclava. She is well, I hope?' He stopped, suddenly afraid that this wasn't so and that was why Hope had been out in the rain.

'She's beautiful,' Hope said, and suddenly her face lit up

with a radiant smile. 'Oh, Bennett, I was so afraid you'd never see her, that you weren't coming back. So much has happened. Why didn't you write?'

'I asked a nurse to write for me when I first became ill,' he said sadly. 'But she had so many patients, maybe she forgot. I was so ill that for a while I hardly knew who I was, let alone being able to write myself. But I daresay the letters I wrote when I began to recover will turn up one day soon. I didn't get any from you either, so maybe we'll get those eventually too.'

'Kiss me,' she asked, wriggling her bare arms out of the blanket so she could hold him. 'Then I'll really believe it is you.'

This was the moment Bennett had waited for and dreamed of so often on the long voyage home. As they had sailed up the coast of Spain in a tremendous storm and he had been racked with seasickness, he'd clung on to the taste and feel of her to get him through it.

But as their lips met it was even sweeter than he had imagined. Firecrackers exploded in his head, he heard angels singing and bands playing. All of the hideousness of the Crimea and Scutari faded away. He was home, his beautiful Hope was in his arms, and all was right with the world.

Angus and Nell stayed in the kitchen while Hope and Bennett were in the parlour. Nell gave Angus some bread and cheese and of course he asked why Hope had been out in the rain and clearly not rational.

'She was poorly after she got the letter from you about Bennett,' she began to explain, but realizing there was too much to tell all at once she cut it short. 'And I think Lady Harvey's funeral today was finally too much for her.'

Even as the words came out she wished she could retract them. If everything had been as it should be, tonight all four

642

of them should have been celebrating the men's homecoming. Nell had prayed for this day, planned it in her head a hundred times. She'd imagined a big spread on the table, the Captain's bed aired and a fire lit in his room. But instead of feasting, laughing and crying tears of joy, she and the Captain were here in the kitchen with only bread and cheese, and now she'd made his homecoming even sadder by telling him that his love was dead.

'I'm so sorry, sir,' she said hastily. 'So much has happened that it's hardly surprising Hope isn't herself, but I shouldn't have told you about Lady Harvey straight off.'

He had more lines on his face than he'd had before he went away, he was thinner too and he looked tired. But he was still such a handsome man. Those dark eyes, so much like Hope's, had a way of looking at Nell which made her feel he could see right down to her soul.

'Anne's dead? What caused her to die?'

'Her heart, sir.' Nell hung her head. 'But she died peaceful in her sleep.'

She looked up and saw his eyes were damp. 'I'm so sorry, sir,' she whispered.

'All of us wish to die in our sleep,' he said sadly. 'But for most it is a painful process. I am very glad that she escaped that. How is Rufus holding up?'

'Well enough, sir,' Nell said. 'He has been a good friend to us in the past months. But will you tell me how you found Bennett?'

He looked relieved that she'd changed the subject and explained that he'd gone to Scutari to look for him.

'It was the very devil of a time,' he sighed. 'His name was not on the list of patients at the hospital. I had to go through endless ships' reports and eventually found his name on one of those. Three unnamed men died on that voyage, and they were buried at sea, so it seemed that Bennett was one of

643

them. But I searched out other patients taken on that ship, and one rifleman who knew Bennett well assured me he had seen him carried off the ship on a stretcher. So then I had the job of searching for him in the hospital. With over a thousand sick and wounded it was a long job, but I found him in the end. He had been listed under the wrong name.'

'But how could that happen?'

Angus shrugged. 'The place is vast, with so few nursing staff, it's a wonder the records are kept as well as they are, especially when many are brought in too sick even to say their own name. He was still in a bad way when I found him, but once I started cracking the whip and got him moved to a healthier ward with a bit more attention he began to improve.'

At that point in their conversation Betsy had started crying and Nell got up to see to her. But her parents had got there seconds before her.

Nell had never seen anything more beautiful and touching than Bennett's reaction to his daughter. Half-laughing, half-crying, he took her into his arms and told her she was to stop crying because that was no way to greet her papa.

'You go down and take care of Angus,' Hope said to Nell, smiling with the radiance of a new bride. 'We can see to Betsy. I've given you enough trouble for one evening, and Bennett is very tired too. Tell Angus all the news and tomorrow we'll all celebrate the homecoming together.'

Nell paused before leaving the bedroom and looked back. Bennett had Betsy cradled in his arms, Hope, wearing only the nightgown Bennett had put on her, had her arms around him, both their heads bent towards their child. It was a beautiful tableau and some sense deep within Nell told her they would all be fine from now on.

*

When Nell went back downstairs Angus had moved into the parlour and was slouched in his favourite chair by the fire.

'So where were we?' he asked. 'You said so much has happened. Tell me about it.'

'Well, Albert was the main thing,' she began cautiously, unsure that she could even explain it in a way he could understand.

She had forgotten what a good listener he was. Apart from getting her to expand on a couple of points, he didn't interrupt.

'My God,' he exclaimed as she finished. 'I knew Hope had a very tough streak but I wouldn't have thought her capable of taking on that blackguard. But how was she afterwards? That is not a pretty image to be left in anyone's mind.'

Nell agreed. 'But that wasn't all,' she went on. 'Before Albert died he told Rufus about you and his mother.'

Angus winced. 'Can I expect him to come round here like a mad bull?'

Nell smiled faintly. 'No, he was upset at first, but not now. You see, her ladyship chose to tell both him and Hope something else that day too. And you might be the mad bull when I admit my part in that.'

'Go on,' he said, leaning forward in his chair.

'That Hope was her daughter, and you are Hope's father.'

He looked at Nell in puzzlement. 'I don't understand. How can I be? Hope is your sister.'

Nell began to tremble then, afraid he was going to be angry she hadn't told him this when she first came to work for him, or even after Sir William Harvey's death.

It was far harder telling him than it had been to explain it to Hope. She stumbled over the words, she wept, and she felt afraid because his expression was so stern and cold.

'I didn't have any choice but to go along with it then,' she cried when she'd finished. 'I didn't know you then, or who her father was. I was so young myself and I needed my position because my folks depended on my wages. I didn't tell her ladyship that the baby hadn't died until the day I left Briargate.

'I am truly sorry I didn't feel able to tell you before. But you see, I gave her ladyship my promise.'

He sighed deeply, sat back in his chair and closed his eyes.

The rain was still pouring down outside, splattering against the windows, and the wind was howling in the chimney. Nell squirmed in her chair, expecting that at any moment he would make an angry outburst.

'Why didn't Anne write and tell me she was carrying my child?' he asked eventually, his voice shaking with emotion. 'I would have come for her, taken care of her.'

'You know why. She knew her reputation would be lost. You might have lost your commission.'

'I'd have worked as a farm labourer if necessary,' he spat out. 'I'd have overcome every obstacle, fought any battle for her.'

'I know that now,' Nell said softly. 'And I think she always knew it too. But it was a tough time for her; she cared for her husband, and her position. Maybe if Bridie hadn't told her the baby was dead it might have been different.'

He asked her a great many questions, about both Anne and Hope. Nell thought he was never going to get to the end of them. She was so tired, it had seemed an interminable day, and all she wanted was her bed.

'And how did Hope feel when she was told the man she'd always called Father wasn't her real one, or that you aren't even her sister?' he said finally. 'It is no wonder she came close to losing her mind!'

'You will have to ask her that yourself, sir,' Nell said

wearily. 'She hasn't said much about it to me. But I do know she is very fond of you.'

'She saved my life in Balaclava,' he said with feeling. 'I have seen men die from far lesser wounds than I had. She has a healing touch. One of the other officers asked me soon after that if she was a relative of mine as he thought we were very alike.'

'You are alike, sir.' Nell nodded. 'The first time I met you I knew you were her father, just by your looks. I wondered that her ladyship didn't see it.'

'Mostly we only see things we want to see,' he replied, and smiled. 'And I see you are tired, Nell. Go to bed now.'

Angus stared pensively into the fire for over an hour after Nell had gone to bed, his thoughts bittersweet. Anne's death was sad, but not entirely unexpected, for when he'd seen her at William's funeral she had looked old and seemed confused, and he'd heard later that her health had deteriorated still further.

There was no point in being angry that she had kept the birth of their child from him; he had, after all, always known that position and wealth meant more to her than love. But he found it hard to forgive her for not coming to him when she discovered that Hope was that child. Surely she must have known that he would have moved heaven and earth to find her?

Yet clearly it was written in the stars that he was intended to have Hope in his life, even if the path to that end was circuitous. When he met Nell by pure chance that day by the mill, he offered her the position of housekeeper more from sympathy than real need for help in his home. Yet it was one of the best decisions he'd ever made, for Nell had become a valued friend, and she'd created a stable, comfortable home, which was something he'd never had before.

When he discovered that the pretty surgeon's wife who had been attacked in Varna was none other than her missing sister, he saw it as the most remarkable stroke of good fortune, a way of repaying Nell for all she'd done for him. Yet she was his daughter!

Looking back, and setting aside the connection with Nell, there was something about Hope which had drawn him to her right from the start.

He had, of course, thought it was only because of her sultry eyes, dark curly hair and her sweet face. In fact, he'd pulled himself up from thinking about her too often by reminding himself he was old enough to be her father.

Thankfully his feelings for her had never been ones of desire, but admiration at her courage, stoicism and nursing skills. Later, after she had stitched his wounds, there was deep gratitude, and amusement too because she was such a little firebrand.

Yet as time went on and he got to know both her and Bennett very well, he'd been stirred by what he could only call paternal feelings towards her. He felt real affection, he worried about her health when he knew she was carrying a child. When she left Balaclava he had felt emotional and even bereft.

It was that which had made him search for Bennett; and through the difficulties, he had urged himself on, going that extra mile for her. On the voyage home he felt so proud of himself for bringing her husband back to her. He had in fact been as excited at the prospect of seeing her again as Bennett was.

And now he'd been told she was his flesh and blood, that her baby was his grandchild. And that was like being presented with the sun, the moon and the stars.

*

'She's beautiful,' Angus said gruffly, looking down at Betsy in her mother's arms. 'A father and a grandfather in one day! That's enough to make even an old soldier cry.'

It was ten in the morning. Bennett was still in bed, Nell in the kitchen and Hope had come into his study with Betsy in her arms so he could see her.

'Nell told you everything, then?' Hope asked.

Angus nodded, and quickly wiped a tear from his cheek. 'There's so much to say, but I don't know how to say it,' he said. 'I lay awake most of the night thinking on it. I thought I had it all straight in my head, but now I'm looking at Betsy . . .' He stopped, fresh tears filling his eyes as he let the baby grasp one of his fingers.

'We don't need words surely?' Hope said, looking up at him with tears in her eyes too. 'We were friends from the first, weren't we? Through you, Nell and I were reunited, and you made the Crimea a better place for me and Bennett by just being there. Then you rescued Bennett for me. So if it was some kind of apology you were trying to make, don't.'

'It wasn't an apology I wanted to make,' he said, reaching out to touch her cheek with tenderness. 'It was more of a joyful outpouring of my delight. I am of course horrified and ashamed that I had no part in your childhood, for had I known of your birth I would have taken you and brought you up as my daughter, regardless of how others viewed that.'

'Then perhaps it was as well you never knew about me,' Hope said, and took the hand caressing her cheek and kissed it. 'You would have been away soldiering and I would have been left with nursemaids who might not have been as loving as Meg Renton and Nell were.'

'Always so practical and level-headed!' He nodded. 'But my dear girl, you have been through so much since Betsy

649

was born, far too much, and we must be sure there is no repetition of what occurred last night.'

A cloud passed over her face. 'I don't know what possessed me,' she said, dropping her eyes shamefacedly.

'The human mind can only take so much,' he said gently. 'I have seen many men become irrational after battles and hardship, I suspect it is nature's way of demanding that they allow themselves to rest. But Bennett is back safe and sound, and I hope you will let me take care of my family now?'

'Your family?' she repeated, looking up at him in wonder. 'That sounds so lovely.'

Angus put his arms around both mother and child and drew them to his chest.

'It sounds lovely to me too,' he said softly, his voice breaking with emotion. 'I've never had a family, I was always the cuckoo in someone else's nest. But the extraordinary thing is that if I could have handpicked the people I wanted in my family, you are all the very ones I would have selected. And with young Betsy, I will be able to give her the love and attention I never got the chance to give you. I think that makes me the luckiest man alive.'

Christmas, something Nell and Hope had barely thought about until the men came home, was suddenly only a week away and each day was full of frantic preparations. Bennett was still too weak to do more than play with his daughter as the women made pies and puddings and cleaned silver around him. Angus chopped wood, brought in huge bunches of holly and ivy, and went off to the market in Bristol. He brought home not just provisions, but a horse to pull the trap which had languished in one of the sheds since he'd been away.

Willow End was full of chatter and laughter. There were so many stories to share, lengthy discussions on past events, and what they would like for the future, but every now and then all four adults would sit around the kitchen table, just beaming at one another in their delight that they were all together again at last.

How much, or how little, they were going to tell the rest of the family about Hope and Angus when they arrived for Boxing Day was a source of endless debate. It was Angus who finally suggested they should wait until Christmas Day in the company of Rufus, Uncle Abel and Alice and make the decision then, with them.

At five in the afternoon on Christmas Day it was already dark outside, but the dining room at Willow End was ablaze with light from two dozen candles and a roaring fire. The ceiling beams were decorated with garlands of holly, ivy and red ribbon, and the red tablecloth was barely visible beneath the wealth of glasses, plates and silver tureens. The goose was a mere skeleton now, the vegetable tureens empty. Everyone had agreed they'd need a rest before they could possibly manage plum pudding.

'I had dreamed of a Christmas like this for years,' Bennett said reflectively. 'But I never thought it would come true.'

He looked around the table, aglow with wonder that he'd survived to be here today with all the people he loved: Hope in a red dress on his right, her dark curls shining like ebony in the candlelight; Nell wearing pale blue came next, followed by Uncle Abel, Alice and finally Rufus. Not forgetting Betsy, who lay gurgling in her crib by the window.

For Bennett, past Christmases had been mostly rather dismal affairs, usually spent with people he didn't much care for, or barely knew. Even the ones spent with Uncle Abel had not been happy because of their often strained relationship.

But everything had come right at last. Abel had grown very fond of Hope, and he was clearly proud of his nephew now. Alice had always shown Bennett a great deal of affection, but she was positively radiant now that she could do this openly, and lavish attention on Hope and Betsy too.

Nell was just as Hope had described her, placid, kind and motherly, yet she was not dull as Bennett had feared, she laughed a great deal, she could be very funny, and when riled she didn't mince her words. He thought she was perhaps the most ideal of sisters-in-law.

When Bennett looked at Angus, his heart swelled up with gratitude. He'd admired the dashing Captain right from the start because he wasn't one of the usual weak-chinned, aristocratic, brainless oafs who bought their commissions in the cavalry because they wanted to parade around in a flashy uniform. Angus's courage was unquestionable, but it was his humanity that had touched Bennett. Many of his troopers had recounted how he'd given them food, clothing and blankets during the last winter; he'd visited them when they were sick and wounded; he wrote letters home for them.

Yet it was Angus coming to search for him in Scutari that made him love the man. He would never forget the moment when he opened his eyes to see Angus in his blue and gold coat and cherry-red breeches grinning down at him. The fever ward was the grimmest one of all, a dark, stinking room in a basement that was overrun with vermin, but Angus had brought light and fresh air in with him.

'You can't skulk down here,' he'd said. 'Hope needs you at home. So up you come, my lad.'

He had lifted him out of that bed and slung him over his shoulder, and sick as Bennett was at that moment, somehow he knew that Angus's will to get him home was too strong to allow him to die.

Angus would never relate to anyone that he had washed and fed him like a baby for days until Bennett could manage it for himself. Like all true heroes, he didn't find it necessary to talk about his deeds. Yet back in Scutari he'd known just what to talk about to get Bennett to rally round.

He had described this very room in detail, even down to the chintz curtains Nell had made and the rosewood of the table. He'd said they would be round it for Christmas, and that the goose would come from Matt's farm. He'd described Nell's cooking until Bennett's mouth was watering, and reminded him that Hope would be sitting next to him, prettier than a rose in full bloom.

Now that Bennett knew Angus was Hope's father, he wondered why he hadn't suspected it long ago for they were incredibly alike. Not just their identical dark eyes, but the shared courage, loyalty and dogged determination. What could be sweeter than having a father-in-law who had already proved himself to be the best and truest friend?

As for the seventh person at the table, Hope had told him so much about her childhood friend in the past that, coupled with what he knew of the behaviour of both his parents, Bennett had been expecting a real milksop. But here was another surprise, for Rufus wasn't weak in any way. He was as tough and hardworking as Matt Renton, quick-witted, big-hearted, with a fine social conscience and entertaining too. Bennett had never much liked the sound of Lady Harvey, but he had to admit she must have had some good qualities to produce two such outstanding offspring.

'You'll never have a lonely Christmas again, not with our family,' Nell said, interrupting his reverie. 'But in a few years' time you might be wishing for a quieter one.'

'I propose a toast to many more happy occasions like this one,' Angus said, raising his glass of wine.

'To many more!' everyone said as they clinked their glasses.

'Next year Betsy might be walking,' Hope said, glancing

over to the crib in the corner where she was lying awake, waving her hands. 'Then there won't be peace for any of us.'

Bennett squeezed her hand under the table for he was delighted to see her fully recovered. She was too embarrassed to discuss what had ailed her the night he came home; all she would say was that she was afraid she'd never see him again. Clearly it had been a whole raft of things, shock, fear and anxiety, but whatever the cause, she was her old self again now.

'Remember last Christmas?' Hope said, addressing Bennett and Angus.

'I think I had a scrawny bit of chicken with a lump of bread.' Angus laughed. 'How about you?'

'I don't remember eating anything,' Bennett said. 'But the jollifications on the quay on Christmas Eve were memorable, if only because I couldn't get my wife out of other men's arms.'

'I was only dancing with them,' Hope pointed out, looking round at the rest of the company. 'Bennett always likes to make out he was so hard done by that night, but as I recall he drank a whole bottle of rum.'

'You three talk about the war as if it were a jolly picnic,' Rufus remarked. 'I can't pin any of you down to tell me what it was really like. Angus and Bennett haven't even said anything about the nurse Florence Nightingale, yet the newspapers are full of her heroics.'

'Maybe that's just because we are a little weary of the public's adulation being centred on her,' Angus retorted. 'We saw soldiers' wives risking their lives on the battlefields to help the wounded. They, Hope and doctors like Bennett were there from the start of the war, doing what they could without medical supplies or any facilities, hamstrung by governmental bungling. Miss Nightingale is undoubtedly a good woman – she brought about better conditions in the hospital at Scutari, and I'm sure she has turned the tide so that nursing will from here on in be seen as a noble profession. But those of us who were at the sharp end of the action would rather like to see less illustrious people honoured for their courage and self-sacrifice. They gave everything they had for their country and their fellow man. Of those who have survived, many will come back here with missing limbs to find their wives and children in the workhouse. That is where many of those brave men will end their days too. But Miss Nightingale won't share that indignity.'

Hope shared Angus's views and she knew Bennett did too, but this wasn't the appropriate time for airing them.

'Come now, Angus,' she wheedled, giving him an arched look. 'As Nell would say, "That's not a suitable subject for the dinner table."'

'It certainly isn't,' Nell said indignantly. 'Conversation at the table should be light and frothy.'

Rufus snorted with laughter. 'Hark at you, Nell! I bet if you said that down at Matt's they'd fall off their chairs with laughter. They talk about butchering pigs and castrating bullocks at the table.'

Hope smiled. 'What about you, Uncle Abel? What do you talk about?'

'He's been known to discuss the contents of someone's stomach after he's done a post-mortem,' Alice said impishly. 'At one dinner party one of his guests came running out as green as grass!'

Abel looked faintly embarrassed. 'That was unfortunate but I was under the impression he was a doctor too.'

'I count myself rebuked.' Angus smiled at Nell. 'War, medical matters, religion and politics are best avoided at dinner.'

'That's good for me as I know very little about any of those subjects,' Rufus said lightly.

'You'd better brush up on religion if you are going to marry the rector's daughter,' Hope retorted. 'And when is it going to be?'

'Well, that brings us back to the ticklish subject of blood ties,' Rufus said, suddenly looking more serious. 'Before I ask Lily to marry me we have to decide whether I should tell her that Hope's my sister.'

Before dinner they had informed Uncle Abel and Alice about the recent developments. Both had been so astounded they said they needed time to think about it before they could comment. But Hope had sensed Abel much preferred the idea of her being the love child of aristocrats than the legitimate child of peasants.

'If you do tell her, we'll also have to tell Matt and the rest of the family,' Nell said, looking worried.

In the discussions before Christmas they had all felt that the ultimate decision about this had to be made by Rufus, as he was the one most likely to be affected by the scandal.

Angus pointed this out to him. 'Much as I'd like to acknowledge Hope as my daughter,' he said, 'I do not wish to tarnish your mother's name.'

'Does that matter now she's no longer with us?' Rufus shrugged. 'I would gain a sister, a niece and a brother-in-law, all of whom are important to me, and are likely to be important to my future children too. Hope would gain a father.'

'But Hope would lose the whole Renton family she's grown up with,' Uncle Abel said, just a little too eagerly.

'No she wouldn't,' Nell said indignantly. 'They aren't going to feel any different towards her. To us she'll always be our sister.'

'What do you think, Bennett?' Rufus asked.

'Well, it seems to me that we've already seen what misery secrets can inflict,' he said. 'If you were to go ahead and marry Lily without telling her, it could very well erupt later, Rufus. But more importantly than any scandal that might ensue, Lily is going to be hurt you didn't confide in her.'

'No one but us knows the truth, so how can it erupt?' Nell asked.

Angus put his hand over Nell's on the table. 'We are not all as good as you at keeping secrets,' he said. 'There are seven of us here today. Any one of us could let it slip sometime.'

All at once Betsy let out a bellow. Hope laughed. 'I think Betsy wants to remind us that we aren't just seven people to her, but family, mother, father, grandfather, aunts and uncles.'

Rufus moved to take Betsy out of the crib, and as he picked her up she stopped crying and her small face broke into a wide smile.

'Well, Betsy,' he said, looking down at her. 'Far be it from me to deprive you of the dubious distinction of having a titled uncle, when you've already got a brace of war heroes in your family. So I guess I'd better slip round and tell Lily you will be her niece.'

Bennett got up from the table and went over to Rufus. 'Are you absolutely sure about this, Rufus? There will be talk and it may well be hurtful to you.'

Rufus looked down at Betsy in his arms, then across the room at Hope, his blue eyes full of affection.

'Let them talk, I'm proud to tell anyone that Hope is my sister. Maybe a few eyebrows will be raised, but what does that matter?' He turned Betsy in his arms so she was facing everyone. 'This little one and any other children Hope or I have matter. They must be brought up with love and honesty. And I know that Hope, like me, will tell them how we were brought up by Rentons, and that everything we learned that was good and true came from them.'

He kissed Betsy, then passed her to her father.

'I'm absolutely certain,' he said to Bennett. 'Now, let's fill our glasses one more time and drink to our family.'

Acknowledgements

To Glenn Fisher of the Crimean War Research Society, for inspiration, information and encouragement above and beyond the call of duty. Without your help and enthusiasm I would have floundered and probably sunk. My apologies to Jo, William and James for monopolizing so much of their husband's and father's time. Glenn, you will be mentioned in despatches.

To Sue Hardiman of the Bristol branch of the Historical Association, not just for her informative pamphlet on the 1832 cholera epidemic and its impact on the City of Bristol, which is so well written, fascinating and well researched, but also for her keen interest in my project and helping me to get my facts right.

I read dozens of books on Victorian England and the Crimean War in my research, but these ones were particularly notable and informative:

Journal Kept During the Russian War: From the Departure of the Army from England in April 1854, to the Fall of Sebastopol, by Frances Isabella Duberly (Elibron Classics, 2000)

Eyewitness in the Crimea: The Crimean War Letters of Lt Col. George Frederick Dallas, 1854–1856, edited by Michael Hargreave Mawson (Greenhill Books, 2001)

George Lawson: Surgeon in the Crimea, edited, enlarged and explained by Victor Bonham-Carter (Constable and Co., 1968)

Several works on Bristol's history, by Peter MacDonald

Mary Carpenter and Children of the Street, by Jo Manton (Heinemann Educational, 1976)

Wonderful Adventures of Mrs Seacole in Many Lands, by Mary Seacole, edited by Sara Salih (Penguin Books, 2005)

The Crimean Doctors: A History of the British Medical Services in the Crimean War, by John Shepherd (Liverpool University Press, 1991)

The Reason Why, by Cecil Woodham-Smith (Penguin Books, 1991)

Lesley Pearse

Lesley Pearse is one of the UK's best-loved novelists, with fans across the globe and book sales of over 2 million copies to date.

A true storyteller and a master of gripping storylines that keep the reader hooked from beginning to end, Lesley introduces readers to unforgettable characters who it is impossible not to care about. There is no easily defined genre or formula; her books whether crime, as in *Till We Meet Again*, historical adventure like *Never Look Back*, or the passionately emotive *Trust Me*, based on the true-life scandal of British child migrants sent to Australia in the post war period, she engages the reader completely.

Lesley's life has been as packed with drama as her books

Truth is often stranger than fiction and Lesley's life has been as packed with drama as her books. She was three when her mother died under tragic circumstances. Her father was away at sea and it was only when a neighbour saw Lesley and her brother playing outside without coats that suspicion was aroused – their mother had been dead for some time. With her father in the Royal Marines, Lesley and her older brother spent three years in grim orphanages before her father remarried (his new wife was a veritable dragon of an ex-army nurse) and Lesley and her older brother were brought home again, to be joined by two other children who were later adopted by her father and stepmother, and a continuing stream of foster children. The impact of constant change and uncertainty in

Lesley's early years is reflected in one of the recurring themes in her books: what happens to those who are emotionally damaged as children. Hers was an extra-ordinary childhood and, in all her books, Lesley has skilfully married the pain and unhappiness of her early experiences with a unique gift for storytelling.

She was three when her mother died under tragic circumstances

Lesley's desperate need for love and affection as a young girl was almost certainly the reason she kept making bad choices in men in her youth. A party girl during the swinging sixties, Lesley did it all – from nanny to bunny girl to designing clothes. She lived in damp bedsits while burning the candle at both ends as a 'Dolly Bird' with twelve-inch mini-skirts. She was married, fleetingly, to her first husband at twenty and met her second, John Pritchard, a trumpet player in a rock band soon after. Her debut novel, *Georgia,* was inspired by her life with John, the London clubs, crooked managers and the many musicians she met during that time, including David Bowie and Steve Marriott of the Small Faces. Lesley's first child, Lucy, was born in this period, but with John's erratic lifestyle and a small child in the house, the marriage was doomed to failure. They parted when Lucy was four.

This was a real turning point in Lesley's life – she was young and alone with a small child – but in another twist of fate, Lesley met her third husband, Nigel, while on her way to Bristol for an interview. They married a few years later and had two more daughters, Sammy and Jo. The following years were the happiest of her life – she ran a playgroup, started writing short stories and then opened a card and gift shop in Bristol's Clifton area. Writing by night, running the shop by day, and fitting in all the other household chores along with the needs of her husband and children for seven years was tough.

'Some strange compulsion kept me writing, even when it seemed hopeless,' she says. 'I wrote three books before *Georgia*, then along came Darley Anderson, who offered to be my agent. Even so, a further six years of disappointments and massive re-writes followed before we finally found a publisher'.

There was more turmoil to follow, however, when Lesley's shop failed in the '90s recession, leaving her with a mountain of debts and bruised pride. Her eighteen-year marriage broke down, and at fifty years old she hit rock bottom – it seemed she was back where she had started in a grim flat with barely enough money for her youngest daughter's bus fares to school.

Lesley did it all – from nanny to bunny girl to designing clothes

'I wrote my way out of it,' she says. 'My second book, *Tara*, was shortlisted for the Romantic Novel of the Year, and I knew I was on my way.'

Lesley's own life is a rich source of material for her books; whether she is writing about the pain of first love, the experience of being an unwanted abused child, adoption, rejection, fear, poverty or revenge, she knows about it first hand. She's a fighter, and with her long fight for success has come security. She now owns a cottage in a pretty village between Bristol and Bath, which she is renovating, and a creek-side retreat in Cornwall. Her three daughters, grandson, friends, dogs and gardening have brought her great happiness. She is president of the Bath and West Wiltshire branch of the NSPCC – the charity closest to her heart.

GEORGIA
Raped by her foster-father, fifteen-year-old Georgia runs away from home to the seedy backstreets of sixties Soho ...

TARA
Anne changes her name to Tara to forget her shocking past – but can she really be someone else?

CHARITY
Charity Stratton's bleak life is changed forever when her parents die in a fire. Alone and pregnant, she runs away to London ...

ELLIE
Eastender Ellie and spoilt Bonny set off to make a living on the stage. Can their friendship survive sacrifice and ambition?

CAMELLIA
Orphaned Camellia discovers that the past she has always been so sure of has been built on lies. Can she bear to uncover the truth about herself?

ROSIE
Rosie is a girl without a mother, with a past full of trouble. But could the man who ruined her family also save Rosie?

CHARLIE
Charlie helplessly watches her mother being senselessly attacked. What secrets have her parents kept from her?

NEVER LOOK BACK
An act of charity sends flower girl Matilda on a trip to the New World – and a new life ...

TRUST ME
Dulcie Taylor and her sister are sent to an orphanage and then to Australia. Is their love strong enough to keep them together?

FATHER UNKNOWN
Daisy Buchan is left a scrapbook with details about her real mother. But should she go and find her?

TILL WE MEET AGAIN
Susan and Beth were childhood friends. Now Susan is accused of murder, and Beth finds she must defend her ...

REMEMBER ME
Mary Broad is transported to Australia as a convict and encounters both cruelty and passion. Can she make a life for herself so far from home?

SECRETS
Adele Talbot escapes a children's home to find her grandmother – but soon her unhappy mother is on her trail ...

A LESSER EVIL
Bristol, the 1960s, and young Fif Brown defies her parents to marry a man they think is beneath her.

Research for my books can take many forms – reading books on the subject required, talking to people who have specialized knowledge, newspaper archives etc. But I find the most valuable source of inspiration to make all the facts come to life, is visiting the place I am setting the story in.

Before and during the writing of *Hope* I read dozens of books about the Crimean War, but it only really came alive for me when I went to the Crimea for a week in October 2005.

no one spoke English and it was a long way to the battle fields

My heart sank when I arrived in Yalta – it reminded me of shabby seaside places built in the '50s, no one spoke English and it was a long way to the battle fields. What I had really wanted to do was walk alone over these places and kind of soak up the vibes, but I couldn't do that as I had to go on an organised tour with a Russian guide, who explained all the history from the Russian point of view. What's more, she rushed us along at a great pace, with no time to stand and stare, much less wander at will, and she bombarded us with information which was mostly pretty dull.

The little harbour of Balaklava (as it is now spelt) is pretty and full of elegant yachts. The guide insisted the main building had been rebuilt in the original style, but that patently wasn't true, for I've seen old pictures of the port in the 1850s and it was very ramshackle, made a million times worse by the hordes of troops. She also showed us where Florence Nightingale had her hospital, and I was forced to point out that Florence only went to the Crimea once, fleetingly, where she became sick and went straight back to Scutari. She never nursed there at all. But despite the guide's inaccurate information, with a little imagination, old pictures and eye witness reports, it was possible to recreate that little port as it must have been during the war.

The sheer steepness of the cliffs gives you some idea of the terrible struggle the soldiers had to get stores and equipment up to the siege. I've always been quite good at imagining unimaginable squalor and deprivation – I sometimes think in a previous life I must have lived that way!

the Russian navy entertained us one night with their singing

Sevastopol (there again the spelling has changed), is pretty impressive. It was razed to the ground during the Crimean War, rebuilt afterward, and flattened again in the Second World War, but it did give a flavour of how it must have been. It is a jewel in Russia's crown as the Black Sea Fleet is based there. My father, who was in the Royal Marines, would have been horrified by the rusting ships in the harbour, but then the Russian navy entertained us one night with their singing and dancing, which was superb, so I suppose they are too busy practising to paint their ships or swab the decks!

Yet it was there that I saw the most astounding and impressive piece of art I've ever seen – a panoramic painting of the siege. You go up into a circular room and the painting wraps right around it. But it was three-dimensional, with modelled ox carts, trenches, huts and other such things in the foreground, so you felt you were stepping into the siege, not just looking at a painting.

I could have stayed and looked at it all day. Granted, it was painted from the perspective of the Russian troops – seen from inside Sevastopol – and the British and French are in the distance. But you could understand the scale and the atmosphere of the war, and get a sense of the hardships the men on both sides had to endure.

the most stirring part of my trip was to stand where the Highlanders held their ground in the defence of Balaklava

My trip to the battle fields gave me an important understanding of how the battles were fought. The Valley of Death isn't anything like I had envisaged. It is a plain of about three miles long and two miles wide, not some kind of ravine as I imagined when we learned Tennyson's poem at school. When you stand in different parts of it you can see why that fateful blunder, which sent so many men to their deaths, was made.

But for me, the most stirring part of my trip was to stand where the Highlanders held their ground in the defence of Balaklava. Now known as The Thin Red Line, and immortalised in a painting in Edinburgh Castle, Sir Colin Campbell's instruction to his men sends shivers down my spine: 'There is no retreat from here. You must stand until you die.'

What supreme courage that must have taken! A few hundred men facing hordes of Russian Cavalry, galloping towards them. And that indomitable courage, and perhaps the Highlanders' fearsome appearance, were enough to make the Russians retreat. It's no secret I love men in uniforms, but men capable of such nobility and bravery makes me weak at the knees.

But the women who were at the Crimea were a tough, dogged breed too. They were few and far between, but they made their presence felt. When some of the Turkish soldiers ran away from the battle of Balaklava, one soldier's wife battered one of them around the head to try and stop him fleeing. Those soldiers' wives nursed the sick, cooked for the men, washed their clothes and carried ammunition. They lived under the most appalling conditions during the siege, and almost certainly made life just a little more bearable for their men.

I love men in uniforms, but men capable of such nobility and bravery makes me weak at the knees

It is a terrible thing that more men died during the Crimean war from disease than were killed in battle. We have Florence Nightingale to thank for making nursing an honourable profession, and improving the life of the ordinary soldier. But as I have pointed out in *Hope*, there were countless other unsung heroes and heroines, whose courage, determination and sheer stoicism in the face of terrible hardship should be remembered. *Hope* might be a work of fiction but each of the characters has a counterpart in history.

Some of you may remember that Penguin Books ran a competition in 2005 to become a character in *Hope*. It was very hard to pick the winner for many of you sent me so much detail about your lives, all of which was fascinating.

But we finally picked Betsy Molyneux from Liverpool. Her Christian name was suitable for the period and she sounded like the kind of plucky, loveable girl I wanted in my book. After some lengthy consultation with her, I decided to use her maiden name Archer, as Molyneux sounded a little too posh for the character I had in mind. The real Betsy is in fact a welder by trade, a job I couldn't fit into that period, but she was happy to be portrayed as a young woman living on her wits in the slums of Bristol. The real Betsy was quite an inspiration to me; I got to like her very much during our chats and, though her life with her husband and son is a million miles from the fictitious one I've chosen for her, I hope I've succeeded in portraying her pretty face, warmth, irreverent sense of humour and her ability to work in a predominantly masculine world.

Thank you, Betsy, and I hope you'll enjoy your adventures!

'Amongst Friends'

THE LESLEY PEARSE NEWSLETTER

A fantastic new way to keep up-to-date with your favourite author. *Amongst Friends* is a quarterly email with all the latest news and views from Lesley, plus information on her forthcoming titles and a chance to win exclusive prizes.

Just go to **www.penguin.co.uk** and type your email address in the 'Join our newsletter' panel and tick the box marked 'Lesley Pearse'. Then fill in your details and you will be added to Lesley's list.

IS THERE AN AMAZING WOMAN IN YOUR LIFE?

Has someone you know done something special, either for herself or someone else?

If so, we want to know about it. Whether it's your mum, your grandma, your sister, your daughter, a friend or just an acquaintance, if they have shown courage in their life, why not nominate them for an award?

The Lesley Pearse Women of Courage Award is an annual event that was launched by Lesley and Penguin in 2006 to celebrate the achievements of ordinary women.

Following regional heats, five finalists and their families are invited to a sumptuous awards lunch. Here, the winner is announced and presented with her award, plus a cheque for £1000, by Lesley herself.

For more information about prizes and to nominate your woman of courage, please visit:

www.womenofcourageaward.co.uk

Alternatively, you can complete the form opposite and post it to:

The Lesley Pearse Women of Courage Award, Penguin General, 80 Strand, London, WC2R 0RL

The
Lesley
PEARSE
Women of Courage Award

OFFICIAL ENTRY FORM

NAME OF YOUR WOMAN OF COURAGE:

HER ADDRESS:

POSTCODE:

HER CONTACT NUMBER:

YOUR RELATIONSHIP TO HER:

YOUR NAME:

YOUR ADDRESS:

POSTCODE:

YOUR DAYTIME TELEPHONE NUMBER:

YOUR EMAIL :

**ON A SEPARATE SHEET, TELL US IN NO MORE THAN
250 WORDS WHY YOU THINK YOUR NOMINEE DESERVES TO WIN
THE LESLEY PEARSE WOMEN OF COURAGE AWARD**

For Terms and Conditions please visit **www.womenofcourageaward.co.uk**

LESLEY PEARSE

SECRETS

Kent in the 1930s and when her mother is declared insane, sweet-faced Adele is sent to a children's home ...

Yet her new home masks a terrible secret that forces Adele to run away to Sussex and seek out the grandmother she has never known. Unsure at first of a warm welcome, Adele soon makes a life for herself in the beautiful Rye Marshes, where she meets dashing Michael Bailey. Over time their friendship blossoms into love, as he joins the RAF and she becomes a nurse.

But just as Adele thinks her troubled past is behind her, war breaks out and her mother appears – bearing shocking family secrets. Suddenly, all Adele's hopes for the future seem ready to crumble ...

LESLEY PEARSE

FATHER UNKNOWN

West London, 1990, and the death of Daisy's adopted mother reveals a family secret that threatens everything she's ever known …

As Daisy tries to come to terms with her devastating loss, her secure existence is thrown into turmoil after the discovery of a scrapbook full of her mother's memories. Suddenly she is confronted with the knowledge that her real mother was a farmer's daughter from Cornwall – but her biological father's identity remains a mystery. Daisy drops everything to go in search of her roots, but in doing so she risks hurting not only her adored Dad, but also her relationship with her policeman boyfriend, Joel.

As a gripping story of greed, misery and corruption unravels, how will she cope with the truth about her real parents – and the real Daisy?

LESLEY PEARSE

TRUST ME

South London, 1947, and when young Dulcie Taylor loses her parents, she is sent far, far from home …

Deprived by tragedy, little Dulcie and her sister May are sent first to an orphanage and then shipped off to begin new lives in Australia. But the 'better life' the sisters are promised turns out to be a lie. It seems everyone who ever said 'trust me' somehow betrays that trust. But then Dulcie meets Ross, another orphanage survivor, and finds a kindred spirit.

Can Dulcie ever get over the pain of the past and learn to trust again? And does she have the strength to fight not only for herself, but also for her sister?

LESLEY PEARSE

NEVER LOOK BACK

London, 1842, and one good deed takes Matilda Jennings from the dirty backstreets of London to the bright lights of America ...

Matilda was a poor Covent Garden flower girl until the day she saved the life of Tabitha, a minister's daughter. Drawn into the bosom of Tabitha's family, Matilda is given the opportunity of a lifetime.

She is taken from the London slums to the darkest corners of New York, then the plains of the Wild West and San Francisco's gold rush. Streetwise and strong-willed, Matilda forges a new life for herself and Tabitha, and encounters Captain James Russell – a man she knows she can truly love. Yet a war is raging and they must brave not only separation but also the birth pangs of a new nation.

But all Matilda knows is that she must carry on – and never look back.

LESLEY PEARSE

CHARLIE

Devon, 1970, and one glorious summer's day, sixteen-year-old Charlie Welsh sees her mother brutally attacked by two strangers ...

With her father away, Charlie must do all she can to protect her mother from further attacks. And somehow she must find out who would want to hurt her family – and why – without losing faith in her beloved parents. Luckily, Charlie is not alone. She meets kind, funny student Andrew, whose strength she'll desperately need.

Can the couple unravel the mysteries of the past that haunt Charlie's family? Or will facing up to those mysteries destroy their love for each other?

'Characters it is impossible not to care about' *Daily Mail*

LESLEY PEARSE

If you enjoyed this book, there are several ways you can read more by the same author and make sure you get the inside track on all Penguin books.

Order any of the following titles direct:

0141016905	SECRETS	£6.99
0141006498	REMEMBER ME	£6.99
014100648X	TILL WE MEET AGAIN	£6.99
0141006471	FATHER UNKNOWN	£6.99
0140293353	TRUST ME	£6.99
0140282270	NEVER LOOK BACK	£6.99
0140272232	CHARLIE	£6.99
0140272224	ROSIE	£6.99

He just wanted a decent book to read ...

Not too much to ask, is it? It was in 1935 when Allen Lane, Managing Director of Bodley Head Publishers, stood on a platform at Exeter railway station looking for something good to read on his journey back to London. His choice was limited to popular magazines and poor-quality paperbacks – the same choice faced every day by the vast majority of readers, few of whom could afford hardbacks. Lane's disappointment and subsequent anger at the range of books generally available led him to found a company – and change the world.

'We believed in the existence in this country of a vast reading public for intelligent books at a low price, and staked everything on it'
Sir Allen Lane, 1902–1970, founder of Penguin Books

The quality paperback had arrived – and not just in bookshops. Lane was adamant that his Penguins should appear in chain stores and tobacconists, and should cost no more than a packet of cigarettes.

Reading habits (and cigarette prices) have changed since 1935, but Penguin still believes in publishing the best books for everybody to enjoy. We still believe that good design costs no more than bad design, and we still believe that quality books published passionately and responsibly make the world a better place.

So wherever you see the little bird – whether it's on a piece of prize-winning literary fiction or a celebrity autobiography, political tour de force or historical masterpiece, a serial-killer thriller, reference book, world classic or a piece of pure escapism – you can bet that it represents the very best that the genre has to offer.

Whatever you like to read – trust Penguin.